A TEXT BOOK OF

DIGITAL COMMUNICATION

For

T.E. SEMESTER – I

THIRD YEAR DEGREE COURSES IN
ELECTRONICS AND TELECOMMUNICATION ENGINEERING

As Per New Revised Syllabus of UoP, 2014

G. R. PATIL

M. E. (Electronics)
Associate Professor, E & TC Dept.
Army Institute of Technology
Dighi, **Pune.**

NIRALI ®
PRAKASHAN
ADVANCEMENT OF KNOWLEDGE

N 3171

DIGITAL COMMUNICATION

ISBN 978-93-5164-135-3

First Edition : June 2014

© : Author

Published By :
NIRALI PRAKASHAN
Abhyudaya Pragati, 1312, Shivaji Nagar,
Off J.M. Road, PUNE – 411005
Tel - (020) 25512336/37/39, Fax - (020) 25511379
Email : niralipune@pragationline.com

DISTRIBUTION CENTRES
PUNE

Nirali Prakashan
119, Budhwar Peth, Jogeshwari Mandir Lane
Pune 411002, Maharashtra
Tel : (020) 2445 2044, 66022708, Fax : (020) 2445 1538
Email : bookorder@pragationline.com

Nirali Prakashan
S. No. 28/25, Dhyari,
Near Pari Company, Pune 411041
Tel : (022) 24690204 Fax : (020) 24690316
Email : dhyari@pragationline.com
            bookorder@pragationline.com

MUMBAI
Nirali Prakashan
385, S.V.P. Road, Rasdhara Co-op. Hsg. Society Ltd.,
Girgaum, Mumbai 400004, Maharashtra
Tel : (022) 2385 6339 / 2386 9976, Fax : (022) 2386 9976
Email : niralimumbai@pragationline.com

DISTRIBUTION BRANCHES

NAGPUR
Pratibha Book Distributors
Above Maratha Mandir, Shop No. 3, First Floor,
Rani Jhanshi Square, Sitabuldi, Nagpur 440012,
Maharashtra, Tel : (0712) 254 7129

BENGALURU
Pragati Book House
House No. 1, Sanjeevappa Lane, Avenue Road Cross,
Opp. Rice Church, Bengaluru – 560002.
Tel : (080) 64513344, 64513355,
Mob : 9880582331, 9845021552
Email:bharatsavla@yahoo.com

JALGAON
Nirali Prakashan
34, V. V. Golani Market, Navi Peth, Jalgaon 425001,
Maharashtra, Tel : (0257) 222 0395
Mob : 94234 91860

KOLHAPUR
Nirali Prakashan
New Mahadvar Road,
Kedar Plaza, 1st Floor Opp. IDBI Bank
Kolhapur 416 012, Maharashtra. Mob : 9855046155

CHENNAI
Pragati Books
9/1, Montieth Road, Behind Taas Mahal, Egmore,
Chennai 600008 Tamil Nadu, Tel : (044) 6518 3535,
Mob : 94440 01782 / 98450 21552 / 98805 82331, Email : bharatsavla@yahoo.com

RETAIL OUTLETS
PUNE

Pragati Book Centre
157, Budhwar Peth, Opp. Ratan Talkies,
Pune 411002, Maharashtra
Tel : (020) 2445 8887 / 6602 2707, Fax : (020) 2445 8887

Pragati Book Centre
Amber Chamber, 28/A, Budhwar Peth,
Appa Balwant Chowk, Pune : 411002, Maharashtra,
Tel : (020) 20240335 / 66281669
Email : pbcpune@pragationline.com

Pragati Book Centre
676/B, Budhwar Peth, Opp. Jogeshwari Mandir,
Pune 411002, Maharashtra
Tel : (020) 6601 7784 / 6602 0855

PBC Book Sellers & Stationers
152, Budhwar Peth, Pune 411002, Maharashtra
Tel : (020) 2445 2254 / 6609 2463

MUMBAI
Pragati Book Corner
Indira Niwas, 111 - A, Bhavani Shankar Road, Dadar (W), Mumbai 400028, Maharashtra
Tel : (022) 2422 3526 / 6662 5254, Email : pbcmumbai@pragationline.com

www.pragationline.com   info@pragationline.com

Dedicated to ...

My Father
Late Shri. R. B. Patil

...G. R. Patil

PREFACE ......

This book is strictly written as per the New Revised Syllabus of University of Pune for the Third Year Degree Course in Electronics and Telecommunication Engineering for the subject **'Digital Communication'**.

The objective of this book is to provide understanding of the various aspects of digital communication through examples and illustrations. Digital Communication Systems are used almost in every information transmission and are growing at an exponential rate. This book explains the basic concepts of Digital Communication. Various types of Communication Systems are discussed in detail with their performance analysis. The working of these systems is explained with extensive waveforms and mathematical treatment wherever necessary is also given. Number of Solved Problems are also given to strengthen the concepts.

The Earlier version of this book was referred by number of teachers in Pune University and they have provided some useful suggestions which are incorporated in this New Edition.

I hope the readers will find this book most useful for gaining maximum benefit in terms of knowledge and scoring in examinations.

Pune   **Author**

SYLLABUS ......

Unit I : Digital Transmission of Analog Signal   8L

Introduction to Digital Communication System: Why Digital?, Block Diagram and transformations, Basic Digital Communication Nomenclature. Digital Versus Analog Performance Criteria, Sampling Process, PCM Generation and Reconstruction, Quantization Noise,Non-uniform Quantization and Companding, PCM with noise: Decoding noise, Error threshold, Delta Modulation, Adaptive Delta Modulation, Delta Sigma Modulation, Differential Pulse Code Modulation, LPC speech synthesis.

Unit II : Baseband Digital Transmission   7L

Digital Multiplexing: Multiplexers and hierarchies, Data Multiplexers.Data formats and their spectra, synchronization: BitSynchronization, Scramblers, Frame Synchronization.Inter-symbol interference, Equalization.

Unit III : Random Processes   8L

Introduction, Mathematical definition of a random process, Stationary processes, Mean, Correlation &Covariance function, Ergodic processes, Transmission of a random process through a LTI filter, Power spectral density, Gaussian process, noise, Narrow band noise, Representation of narrowband noise in terms of in phase & quadrature components

Unit IV : Baseband Receivers   8L

Detection Theory: MAP, LRT, Minimum Error Test, Error Probability, Signal space representation : Geometric representation of signal, Conversion of continuous AWGN channel to vector channel, Likelihood functions, Coherent Detection of binary signals in presence of noise, Optimum Filter, Matched Filter, Probability of Error of Matched Filter, Correlation receiver.

Unit V : Passband Digital Transmission   8L

Pass band transmission model, Signal space diagram, Generation and detection, Error Probabilityderivationand Power spectra of coherent BPSK, BFSK and QPSK.Geometric representation, Generation and detection of - M-ary PSK, M-ary QAM and their error probability, Generation and detection of -Minimum Shift Keying, Gaussian MSK, Non-coherent BFSK, DPSK and DEPSK, Introduction to OFDM

Unit VI : Spread Spectrum Techniques   7L

Introduction, Pseudo noise sequences, A notion of spread spectrum, Direct sequence spread spectrum with coherent BPSK, Signal space dimensionality & processing gain, Probability of error, Concept of jamming, Frequency hop spread spectrum, Wireless Telephone Systems, Personal Communication System.

◈ ◈ ◈

CONTENTS ......

◈ ◈ ◈

Chapter 1

DIGITAL TRANSMISSION OF ANALOG SIGNAL

1.1   OVERVIEW OF DIGITAL COMMUNICATION SYSTEMS

- A communication system consists of three blocks :

- (i)   Transmitter (ii) Channel (iii) Receiver

- Most of the times the system consists of two way transmission, wherein the transmitter and receiver will be there at both ends.

- A digital communication systems consists of at the transmitter end,

(i) Information source

(ii) Encoder

and at the receiver end,

(i)   Decoder

(ii) Information sink

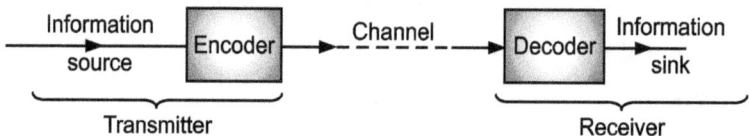

Fig. 1.1 : A Block diagram of digital communication system

- The designer has to understand the channel behaviour and design the encoder and decoder accordingly.

- An errorless transmission of information will be the aim of the designer.

- With this view number of techniques are evolved over last few decades viz.

    (i)   Digital modulation techniques

    (ii)   Error control techniques

    (iii) Optimum receiver design

    (iv)   Modeling of channel etc.

- It is not only less error transmission that matters. The efficient transmission is also a key parameter. Hence, some more blocks are to be added as shown in Fig. 1.2.

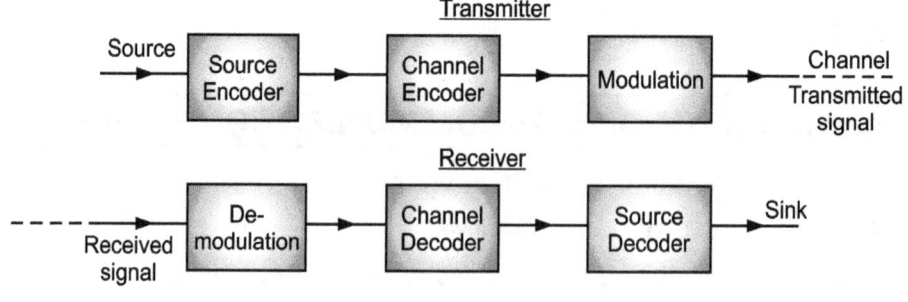

Fig. 1.2

- Information transmission in today's world has major role to play. The communication systems used for transmission and receiving the information can be analog or digital.
- In the second year, you have studied various analog communication systems such as AM, FM, PM etc.
- Digital communication system however have added advantages over analog systems.
- Hence, we find most of the communication systems digital.

1.1.1 Applications of Digital Communication

- There are number of applications of digital communication influencing our day-to-day activities.
- Popularity of internet and television are two most obvious examples.
- Following are some applications of digital communication.

    1. Analog continuous-time signal such as voice, music, video and pictures are transmitted by converting them into digital form.

    2. Storage systems such as magnetic and optical media (CDs) use digital communication techniques.

    3. In computer to computer communication the data transmission involves variety of data. Digital communication techniques are used in such transmissions.

1.1.2 Introduction to Digital Communication System

- Digital communication systems are most prevalent communication systems in today's world of Internet, mobile or any other means of communication. These systems are popular because of number of advantages they offer.

Why Digital?

Almost all the communication systems are going digital because of following reasons.

1. **It is easy to regenerate a digital signal compared to an analog signal :** The signal when transmitted through a channel gets distorted because of non ideal frequency response of the channel. Unwanted electrical noise and other interference also affects the signal. In case of digital signal it is easy to regenerate the signal using simple circuits called as regenerative repeaters. The process is illustrated in Fig. 1.3.

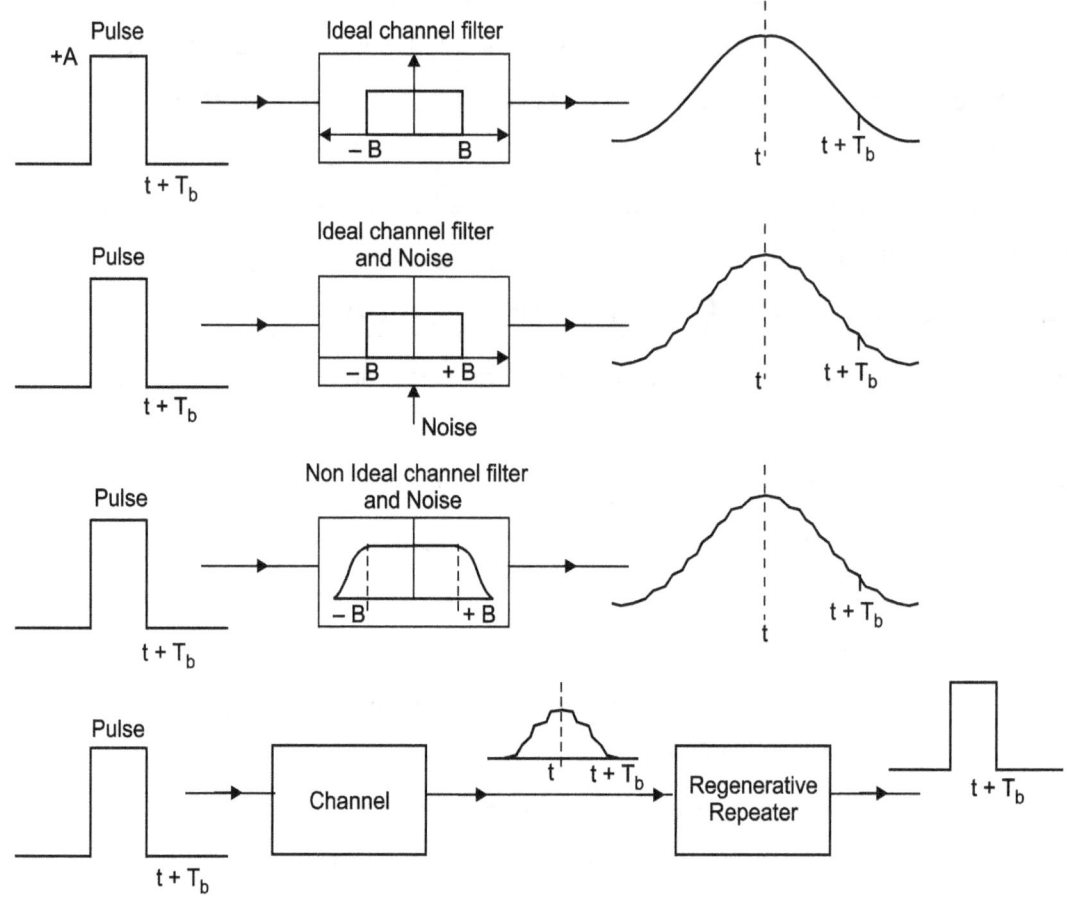

Fig. 1.3 : Distortion of signal in channel and regenerative repeater

2. **Noise Immunity :** Digital circuits operate in finite number of states (e.g. two in case of binary). The disturbance and interference must be large enough to change the state. Thus, the noise and other disturbances are prevented in digital circuits.

   In analog circuits there are infinite states hence a small disturbance can entirely change the shape of waveform. The distorted analog signal cannot be regenerated using amplification as in case of digital signal.

3. **Flexibility :** With the help of digital signal processors it is possible to implement digital communication system. These processors can be programmed to make any change in the system.

4. **Multiplexing :** Using time division multiplexing we can combined digital signals so that different types of messages like data, voice, audio, video etc. can be multiplexed. It is simpler than combining analog signals using frequency division multiplexing.

5. **Cost :** Because of the very large scale integration (VLSI) technology the cost of implementing a digital communicating system has reduced drastically.

6. **Compact :** The digital communication system are most compact due to Increased Scale of Integration (VLSI).

7. **Reliability :** The digital circuits are more robust compare to analog circuits. They are insensitive to variations is temperature, humidity etc. and mechanical vibrations.

8. **Storage and retrieval :** It is easy and inexpensive to store and retrieve the digital information.

9. **Security :** The digital information can be encrypted before transmission and hence can be protected against intruders. They can also be protected against interference and jamming using special signal processing techniques.

8. **Trade-off :** Bandwidth, power and time can be traded-off in order to optimize their use.

9. **Compression :** Data compression is possible using the source coding techniques which reduces the bit rate.

10. **Suitability :** Most of communication now a days is from computer to computer or from a digital equipment to computer, hence a digital communication system will be more suitable for such data communication.

Disadvantages :

1. **Signal Processing Complexity :** The signal processing involved in case of digital communication systems is more complex than analog.

   Intensive signal processing is required is digital communication system compared to analog, hence these systems are more complex.

2. **Need of Synchronization :** Synchronization at various levels is required in digital communication. Digital systems are required to allocate significant share of their resources to this task. Lot of attention needs to be provided for synchronization while designing these systems compared to their analog counter parts.

3. **Non-graceful Degradation :** When the signal to noise ratio drops, the performance of the digital communication systems drops drastically. When the signal to noise ratio drops below a specified level the performance of the system becomes very poor. Analog systems on the other hand degrade steadily.

4. **Bandwidth Requirement :** They require more bandwidth than the analog communication system.

1.1.3 Block Diagram and Transformations

- Block diagram of a typical digital communication system (DCS) is shown in Fig. 1.4.

- Note that all the blocks may not be present in every digital communication system. It depends on type of message to be transmitted, transmission medium, distance of transmission, transmission power, whether multiplexing and multiple access is required or not etc.

(i) Formatting : The information generated by source needs to be converted into binary format. The formatting block converts the source message into bits which are grouped to form a messae symbol. (m_i). e.g. an audio signal is converted into bits using pulse code modulation (PCM).

At the receiver end we require to convert these message symbols into original format. We will study various formatting techniques in Unit I.

(ii) Source Coding : Is applied to the message symbols to take advantage of redundancy in order to compress the message. This is one way of improving transmission efficiency. Source decoding is used at the receiver to decompress this message.

(iii) Encryption and Decryption : In order to protect the transmitted signal from unauthorized users or intruders, a suitable encryption technique can be used at the transmitter so that only authorized user can decrypt the message at the receiver end.

(iv) Channel Coding : There are number of transmission impairments the transmitted signal can undergo when it is transmitted through a noisy channel. The distorted signal gives rise to errors in the detection. Suitable error control coading techniques at the transmitter and decoding technique at the receiver is used to improve the reliability of transmission.

The source coding and channel coding techniques will be studied in the next semester subject information theory and coding techniques.

(v) Multiplexing and Demultiplexing : Digital communication techniques for the advantage of Time Division Multiplexing (TDM) because of discretisation of the signal. Number of similar or dissimilar messages can be combined and transmitted together using TDM at the transmitter end.

Demultiplexing at the receiver end allows there messages to be distributed to the respective destination sink. Because of this proper synchronization between transmitter and receiver is required.

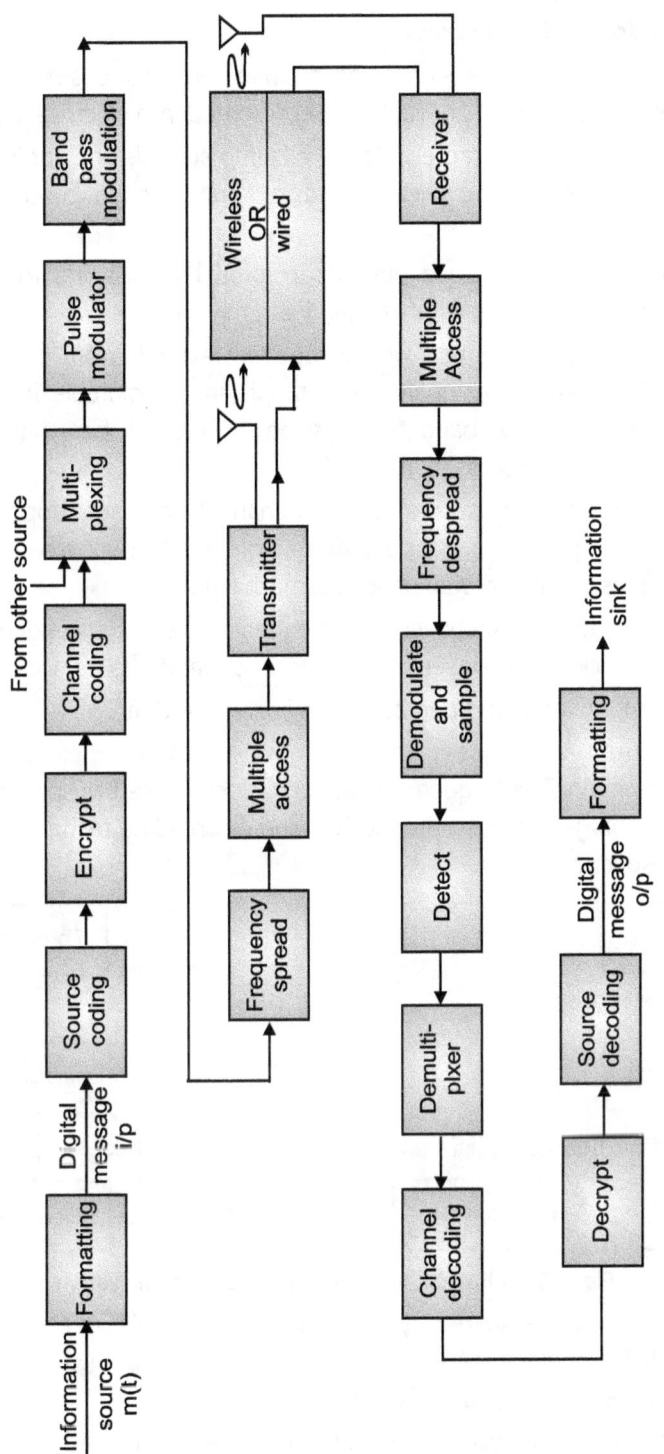

Fig. 1.4 : Block diagram of a typical digital communication system

(vi) Pulse Modulation and Detections

- Till now in previous stages the signal was in binary format and is ready for transmission. If the channel is wired, the bits noise to be represented into electrical pulses.

- The pulse modulation block represents the bits into suitable line coding format (such as polar unipolar, RZ, NRz etc.). This depends on transmission bandwidth transmission power etc.

- At the receiver end the received pulses corrupted by noise are to be reshaped and detected. Naturally we require filters to eliminate the noise.

Note that we are dealing with signals whose spectrum extends from dc to few megahertz. Such signal are called baseband signals. The multiplexing, demultiplexing, line coding and synchrouzation aspects of base band transmission in DCS will be studied in Unit II. The detection techniques will be discussed in Unit III.

(vii) If the transmission medium such as wireless channel does not support transmission of pulse like waveforms we need to translate these signals into high frequency region using carrier. This techniques is called digital bandpass modulation.

- The bandpass modulator up converts the frequency of baseband signal. At the receiver, we have a frequency down converted in the form of bandpass demodulator.

- The bandpass modulation and demodulation is given in Unit V.

(viii) Spread spectrum techniques are used now a days to protect the signal from interference and jamming. The frequency spreading block is used to spread the spectrum of original signal over a larger band. At the receiver end dispreading technique is use to recover the original signal spectra.

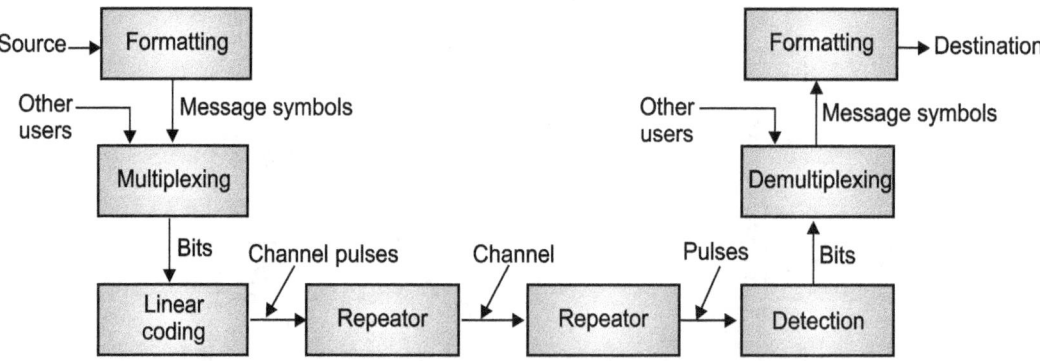

Fig. 1.5 : A Baseband digital communication system

(ix) A single channel can be shared by multiple users. Multiple access techniques such as Time Division Multiple Access (TDMA), Frequency Division Multiple Access, (FDMA) and Code Division Multiple Access (CDMA) can be used.

The spread spectrum and multiple access techniques are discussed in Unit VI. As stated above not all the blocks will be used in every digital communication system. Fig. 1.5. shows a simple baseband DCS and Fig. 1.6. shows a simple bandpass DCS.

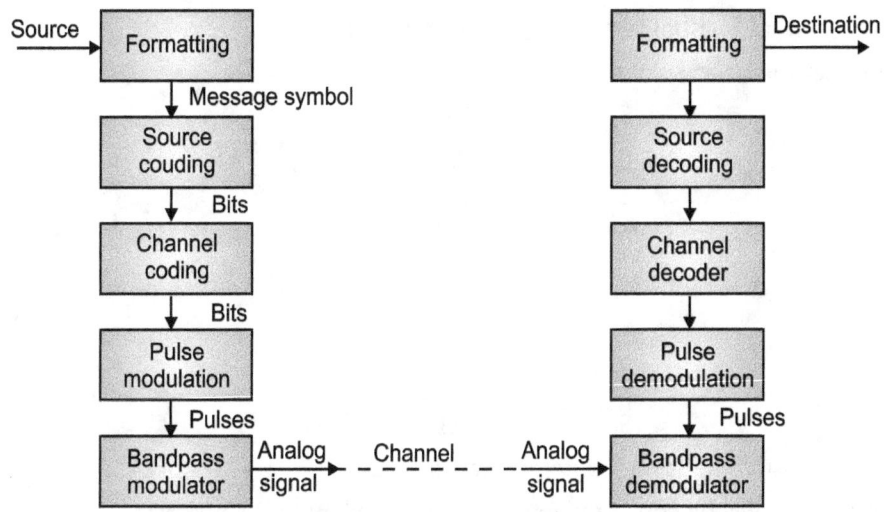

Fig. 1.6 : Bandpass digital communication system

1.1.4 Digital Communication Nomenclature

(i) **Information Source :** The device that generalise the information to be transmitted through communication system is called information source. They can be analog or discrete. Analog source can be transformed into digital by sampling and quantization process.

(ii) **Textual Message :** It is a sequence of characters either digits or symbols from a set of alphabets.

(iii) **Characters :** It is an element in the set of alphabets or symbols. For digital transmission they can be represented in terms of binary codes such as ASCII.

(iv) **Bit (Binary digit) :** It is fundamental unit of information for all digital system.

(v) **Bit Stream :** It is a sequence of bits. It is also called baseband signal.

(vi) **Symbol (Digital message) :** It is a group of a k bits considered as a unit. For example a message with 4 bits will have 16 different symbols.

(vii) **Digital waveform :** A waveform representing digital message is called digital wavefrom.

(viii) **Data rate :** It is number bits transmitted in one second duration expressed as bits/sec.

Example 1.1

1. Consider a message word "ABC". Let us use 7 bit ASCII code to encode this message.

2. The bit stream will be

Message	A	B	C
Bit stream	1000001	1000010	1000011

3. Let us use M = 8 symbol sets with group of n = 3 bits.

The symbol set will be as below.

S_1	000
S_2	001
S_3	010
S_4	011
S_5	100
S_6	101
S_7	110
S_8	111

Symbols are transmitted using 8 different waveforms.

4. The bit stream will be converted into symbols as below.

Bit stream	100	000	110	000	101	000	011
Symbols	S_5	S_1	S_7	S_1	S_5	S_1	S_4

1.1.5 Digital Versus Analog Performance Criteria

- The performance of analog communication system is expressed in terms of fidelity criteria such as signal to noise ratio, expected mean square error between transmitted and received waveforms.

- In digital communication we deal with digital symbols. We can calculate number of errors introduced between transmitted and received symbols. The probability of error (p_e) is the performance criteria used in DCS.

1.2   FORMATTING ANALOG INFORMATION (SAMPLING PROCESS)

- Sampling is a process of selecting or recording the ordinate values of a continuous function (analog) at specific values of its abscissa.

- This process is most often required in communication systems to convert analog signal in discrete or digital form. Thus sampling process is link between analog signal and its sampled version

- When we convert an analog signal into discrete form, we should see to it that the converted signal retains all the information which is there in the original signal.

- In this chapter we will discuss, what are the conditions under which the information is retained in the sampled signal.

- Before we analyze this, we will look into some terminologies involved in the sampling process.

1.2.1 Band Limited and Time Limited Signals

1. A signal g(t) is said to be absolutely band-limited to W Hz if

$$G(f) \;=\; F\,[g(t)] \;=\; 0 \qquad ; \;\; \text{for} \; |f| \geq W$$

2. A signal g (t) is absolutely time limited if,

$$g(t) \;=\; 0 \qquad\qquad ; \;\; \text{for} \; |t| > T$$

- While studying Fourier transforms of various signals, we have seen that an absolutely band-limited waveform cannot be absolutely time limited and an absolutely time limited waveform cannot be absolutely band-limited.
- In practice, we have time limited waveforms and hence they are not band-limited. But most of the waveforms have their amplitude spectrum a negligible level above a certain frequency.

1.2.2 Narrowband Signals and Systems

- A narrowband or bandpass signal is a signal g(t) whose frequency domain representation G(f) is non-zero for frequencies in a usually small neighbourhood of high frequency fo

  i.e. $G(f) = 0 ; \;\; |f - fo| \geq W$ where fo >> W

- A bandpass or narrowbnad system is a system which passes signals with frequency components in neighbourhood of some frequency for

  i.e. $H(f) = 1; \;\; |f - fo| \leq W$

  and highly attenuates frequency components outside this frequency band.

1.2.3 Sampling Theorem in Time Domain

- The sampling theorem can be stated in two parts as below :

1. A band limited signal of finite energy which has no frequency component above W Hz, can be completely described by specifying the values of signal at uniform intervals of

    $$T_S \;\leq\; \frac{1}{2W} \; \text{sec.}$$

    This statement is also known as the uniform sampling theorem.

2. A band limited signal of finite energy, which has no frequency component above W Hz, may be completely recovered from a set of uniformly spaced discrete samples taken at a rate fs ≥ 2W.

- Let us, prove this theorem for different sampling approaches. There are three types of sampling :

    (i) Impulse or Ideal Sampling.

    (ii) Natural Sampling.

    (iii) Flat top Sampling.

1.2.4 Impulse or Ideal Sampling

Consider an arbitrary signal g(t) having finite energy which is specified for all times. Let the fourier transform of this signal be G(f) as shown in Fig. 1.7.

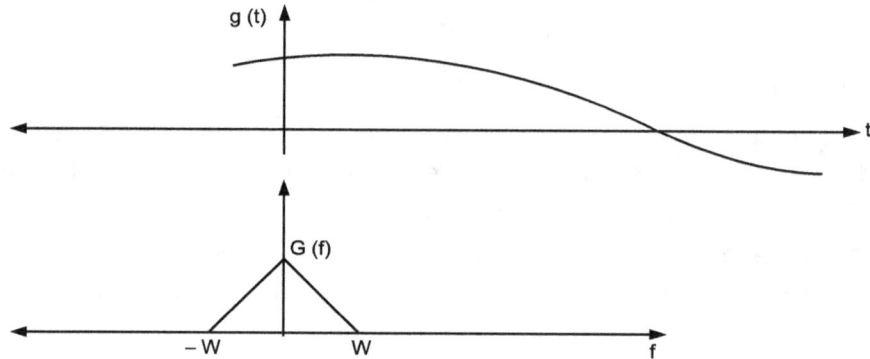

Fig. 1.7 : The Signal g(t) and its fourier transform (Spectrum)

We sample the signal using train of impulses as shown in Fig. 1.8.

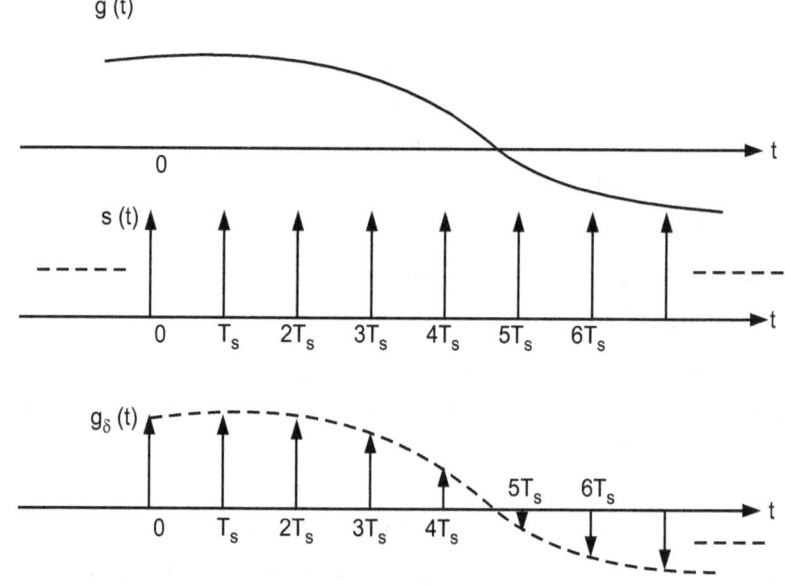

Fig. 1.8 : Impulse sampling in time domain

Let,   g(t) be the signal to be sampled.

          s(t) is train of impulses.

          $g_\delta(t)$ is sampled signal.

The sampled signal is obtained by multiplying g(t) and s(t),

$$\therefore \qquad g_\delta(t) \;=\; g(t) \cdot s(t) \qquad \qquad \ldots (1.1)$$

But,
$$s(t) = \sum_{n=-\infty}^{\infty} \delta(t - nT_s)$$

$\therefore$
$$g_\delta(t) = g(t) \sum_{n=-\infty}^{\infty} \delta(t - nT_s) = \sum_{n=-\infty}^{\infty} g(t) \delta(t - nT_s) \qquad \dots (1.2)$$

But,
$$g(t) \delta(t - nT_s) = g(nT_s) \delta(t - nT_s)$$

$\therefore$
$$g_\delta(t) = \sum_{n=-\infty}^{\infty} g(nT_s) \delta(t - nT_s) \qquad \dots (1.3)$$

Let us, now find out the spectrum of the sampled signal.
$$g_\delta(t) = g(t) \cdot s(t)$$

$\therefore$
$$F[g_\delta(t)] = F[g(t) \cdot s(t)]$$

$\therefore$
$$G_\delta(f) = G(f) * S(f) \qquad \dots (1.4)$$

Now,
$$s(t) = \sum_{n=-\infty}^{\infty} \delta(t - nT_s)$$

$\therefore$
$$S(f) = \frac{1}{T_s} \sum_{n=-\infty}^{\infty} \delta(f - nf_s)$$

[Refer Fourier Transform of Periodic Signal Chapter 1]

$\therefore$
$$G_\delta(f) = G(f) * \frac{1}{T_s} \sum_{n=-\infty}^{\infty} \delta(f - nf_s) \qquad \dots (1.5)$$

But,
$$G(f) * \delta(f - nf_s) = G(f - nf_s)$$

$\therefore$
$$G_\delta(f) = \frac{1}{T_s} \sum_{n=-\infty}^{\infty} G(f - nf_s) \qquad \dots (1.6)$$

It means the spectrum of sampled signal $G_\delta(f)$ consists of $G(f)$ and its shifted versions i.e. $G(f)$, $G(f \pm f_s)$, $G(f \pm 2f_s)$ ... etc. i.e. the spectrum $G_\delta(f)$ repeats periodically in frequency every f_s Hz. Let us, plot the spectrum $G_\delta(f)$ for three different cases.

From these plots, we see that,

1.   If $f_s \geq 2W$ then spectrum of g (t) is retained in g (t).

2.   If $f_s < 2W$ then spectrum of original signal is not retained in the sampled spectrum.

Thus, it is possible to recover original signal only if $f_s \geq 2W$.

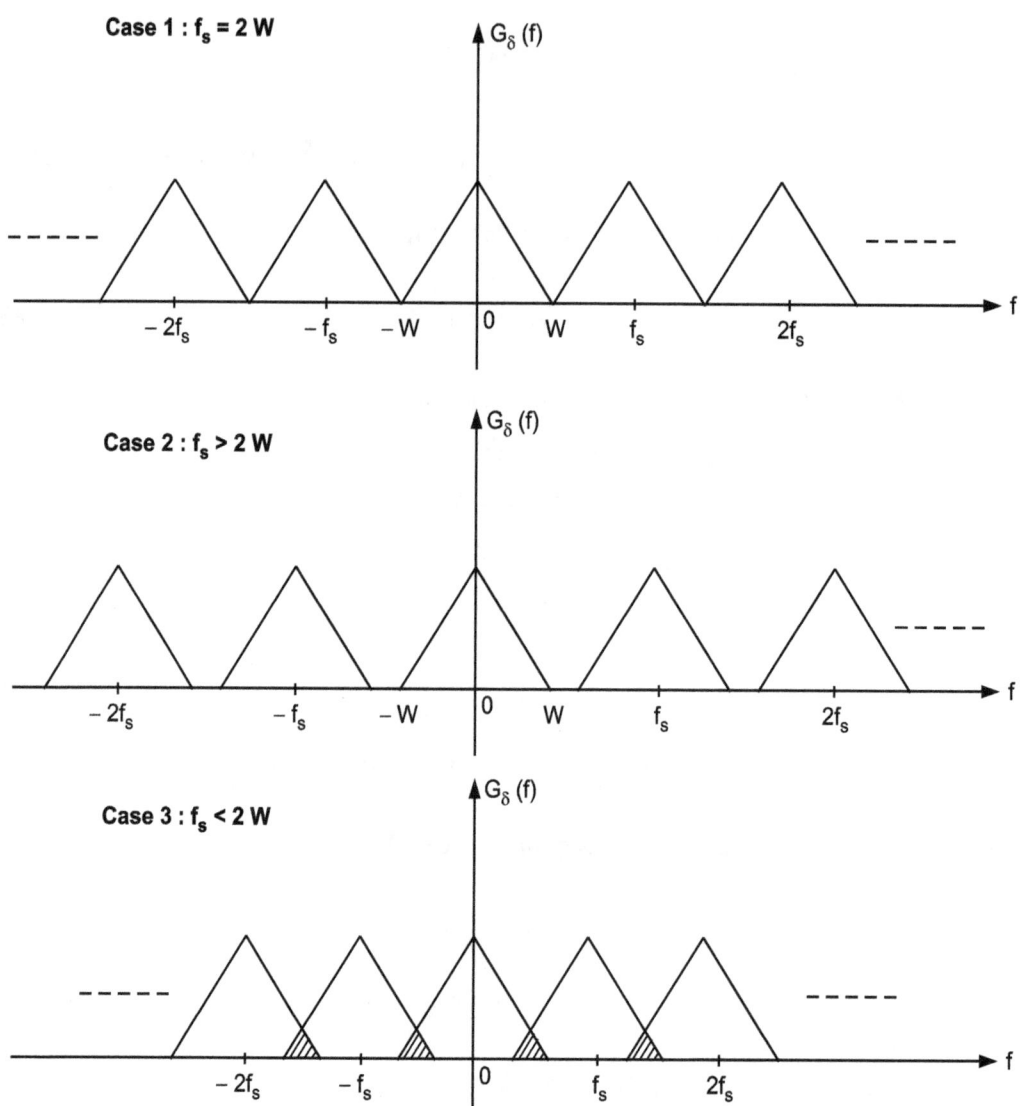

Fig. 1.9 : Spectrum G$_\delta$(f) for three different cases

Hence, we may state sampling theorem as :

If a signal contains no signal component higher than W Hz, then it is completely described by specifying values of the signal at the instants of time separated by $\dfrac{1}{2W}$ sec.

Let us now come to the second part of sampling theorem, the recovery of original signal from sampled spectrum.

We know that the sampled signal $g_\delta(t)$ is expressed in time domain as,

$$g_\delta(t) = \sum_{n=-\infty}^{\infty} g(nT_s)\, \delta(t - nT_s) \qquad \text{... (1.7)}$$

Taking Fourier transform of above we get,

$$G_\delta(f) = \sum_{n=-\infty}^{\infty} g(nT_s)\, e^{-j2\pi nfT_s} \qquad \text{... (1.8)}$$

$$[\because\ \delta(t - nT_s) \Leftrightarrow e^{-j2\pi nfT_s}]$$

Put $\qquad\qquad f_s = 2W \qquad \therefore T_s = \dfrac{1}{2W}$

$$\therefore \qquad G_\delta(f) = \sum_{n=-\infty}^{\infty} g\left(\frac{n}{2W}\right) e^{-j2\pi nf/2w} \qquad \text{... (1.9)}$$

We know $\qquad\qquad G_\delta(f) = f_s \sum_{m=-\infty}^{\infty} G(f - mf_s)$

$$= f_s\, G(f) + f_s \sum_{\substack{m=-\infty \\ m \neq 0}}^{\infty} G(f - mf_s) \qquad \text{... (1.10)}$$

Hence, under following two conditions

1. $\qquad\qquad G(f) = 0 \qquad\qquad \text{for } |f| \geq W$

2. $\qquad\qquad f_s = 2W$

We write equation (1.10) as,

$$G(f) = \frac{1}{2W} G_\delta(f) \qquad -W < f < W \qquad \text{... (1.11)}$$

$$= 0 \qquad\qquad |f| \geq W$$

In other words under above two conditions, the spectrum of original signal is retained in G.

Substituting equation (1.9) in equation (1.11), we get,

$$G(f) = \frac{1}{2W} \sum_{n=-\infty}^{\infty} g\left(\frac{n}{2W}\right) e^{-j2\pi nf/2w} \qquad -W < f < W \qquad \text{... (1.12)}$$

Above expression shows that if sample values $g\left(\dfrac{n}{2W}\right)$ of a signal g(t) are specified for all time, then the Fourier transform of original signal G(f) can be uniquely determined by using above equation. Since G(f) is Fourier transform of g(t). We can say that g(t) can be uniquely determined by the sample values $\left\{g\left(\dfrac{n}{2W}\right)\right\}$ for $-\infty < n < \infty$. To reconstruct g(t) from $\left\{g\left(\dfrac{n}{2W}\right)\right\}$ we write,

$$g(t) \;=\; \int_{-\infty}^{\infty} G(f)\, e^{j2\pi ft}\, df$$

$$=\; \int_{-W}^{W} \frac{1}{2W} \sum_{n=-\infty}^{\infty} g\left(\frac{n}{2W}\right) e^{-j2\pi nf/2W}\, e^{j2\pi ft}\, df$$

Interchanging order of summation and integration,

$$g(t) \;=\; \sum_{n=-\infty}^{\infty} g\left(\frac{n}{2W}\right)\frac{1}{2W} \int_{-W}^{W} e^{j2\pi f\left(t-\frac{n}{2w}\right)}\, df$$

$$=\; \sum_{n=-\infty}^{\infty} g\left(\frac{n}{2W}\right) \times \frac{1}{2W}\left[\frac{e^{j2\pi f\left(t-\frac{n}{2w}\right)}}{j2\pi\left(t-\frac{n}{2W}\right)}\right]_{-w}^{+w}$$

$$=\; \sum_{n=-\infty}^{\infty} g\left(\frac{n}{2W}\right) \times \frac{1}{2W} \times \left[\frac{e^{j2\pi w\left(t-\frac{n}{2W}\right)} - e^{-j2\pi w\left(t-\frac{n}{2W}\right)}}{j2\pi\left(t-\frac{n}{2w}\right)}\right]$$

$$=\; \sum_{n=-\infty}^{\infty} g\left(\frac{n}{2W}\right) \times \frac{\sin(2\pi Wt - n\pi)}{(2\pi Wt - n\pi)}$$

$$\therefore \qquad g(t) \;=\; \sum_{n=-\infty}^{\infty} g\left(\frac{n}{2W}\right)\, \text{sinc}\,(2Wt - n) \qquad\qquad \text{... (1.13)}$$

Equation (1.13) is an interpolation formula for recovering original signal g(t) from the sequence of samples $\left\{g\left(\dfrac{n}{2W}\right)\right\}$. The sinc function is the interpolating function. This reconstruction is shown in Fig. 1.10.

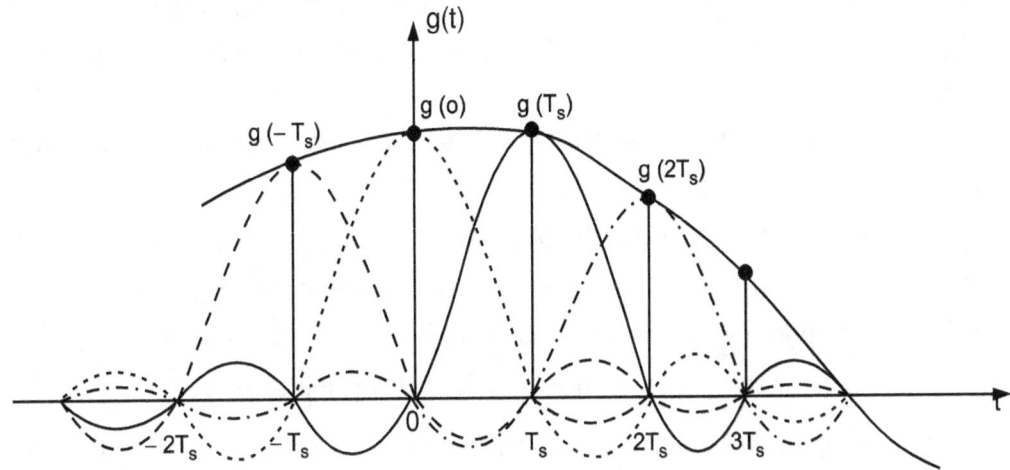

Fig. 1.10 : Reconstruction of waveform from its samples

- The reconstructed waveform is obtained by the weighted sum of time delayed sinc waveforms sinc (2Wt – n); where, the weights are sample values $g\left(\dfrac{n}{2W}\right)$ denoted by dots.

- It can be seen that at sampling instances only one sinc waveform contributes and contribution from other sinc waveforms is zero.

- Hence we can state the second part of sampling theorem as,

  "A band-limited signal of finite energy, which has no frequency components higher than W Hz, may be completely recovered from the knowledge of its samples taken at a rate 2W samples per second.

1.2.5 Nyquist Criteria and Aliasing

- As per the sampling theorem seen above minimum sampling rate required to reconstruct the original signal g (t) is twice the bandwidth of g (t).

- This sampling rate f_s = 2W is called Nyquist rate and the interval $T_s = \dfrac{1}{2W}$ is called Nyquist interval.

- The discussion above regarding sampling process was based on certain assumptions which are ideal conditions. Hence, it is called ideal sampling.

- But practical sampling differs from ideal sampling in three aspects :

  (i) The sampled signal cannot have periodic impulses but will have pulses with finite duration and finite amplitude.

(ii) The practical reconstruction filters are not ideal filters.

(iii) The messages to be sampled are time limited, hence they cannot be strictly band-limited.

- In the next section, when we study natural sampling and flat-top sampling we will see that the pulse shape of sampled waveform does not have much effect on sampling and reconstruction.

- If we have $f_s = 2W$, we require an ideal low pass filter to reconstruct the signal as shown in Fig. 1.11.

- But this filter is not practically realisable. If we take sampling frequency $f_s > 2W$, it is possible to recover the spectrum of original waveform as shown in Fig. 1.12 (a).

- If the filter response is flat over the message band its output will be g (t) plus the spurious frequency component at $|f| > f_s - W$ outside the message band.

- The effect of these components can be minimized by careful filter design and creating adequate guard band by taking $f_s > 2W$.

- The signal reconstruction process using zero-order hold (ZOH) and first order hold (FOH) is shown in Fig. 1.12 (b).

- The error is minimized by using higher sampling rate or using equalizer.

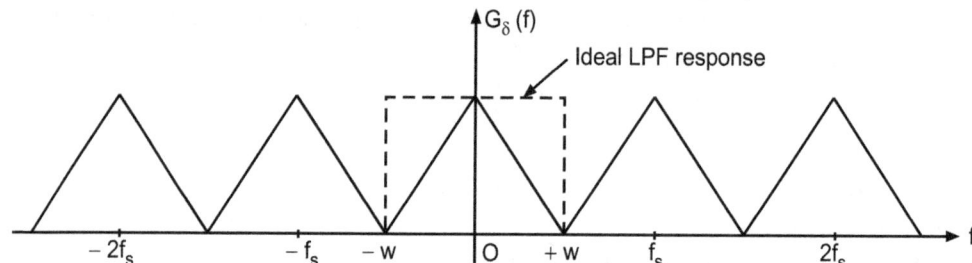

Fig. 1.11 : Ideal LPF reconstruction

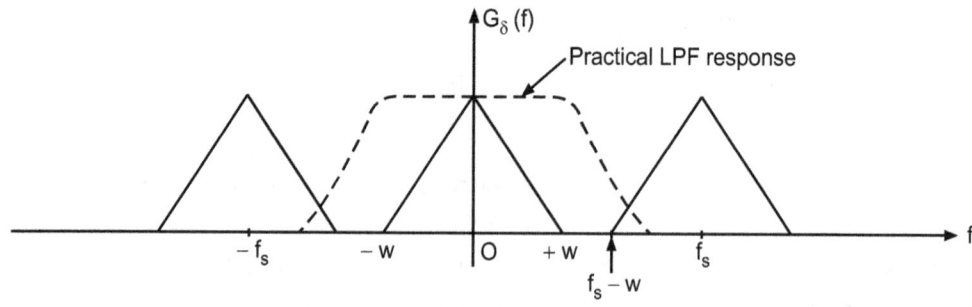

Fig. 1.12 : (a) Practical LPR Reconstruction

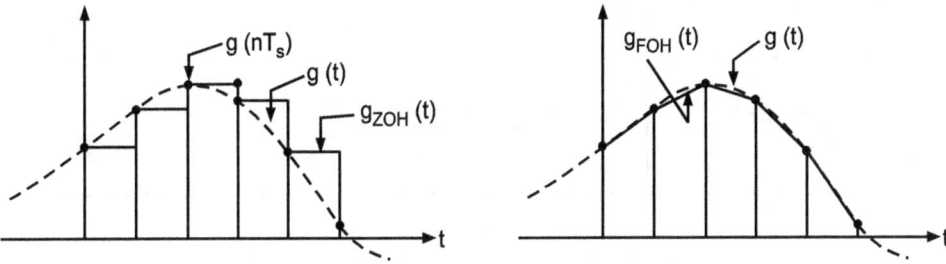

Fig. 1.12 : (b) Practical reconstruction from samples

Aliasing :

- Consider the case of undersampling the signal i.e. $f_s < 2W$.
- Following Fig. 1.13 shows the positive half of baseband spectrum and one of the replicates.
- There is overlapping of spectral components.

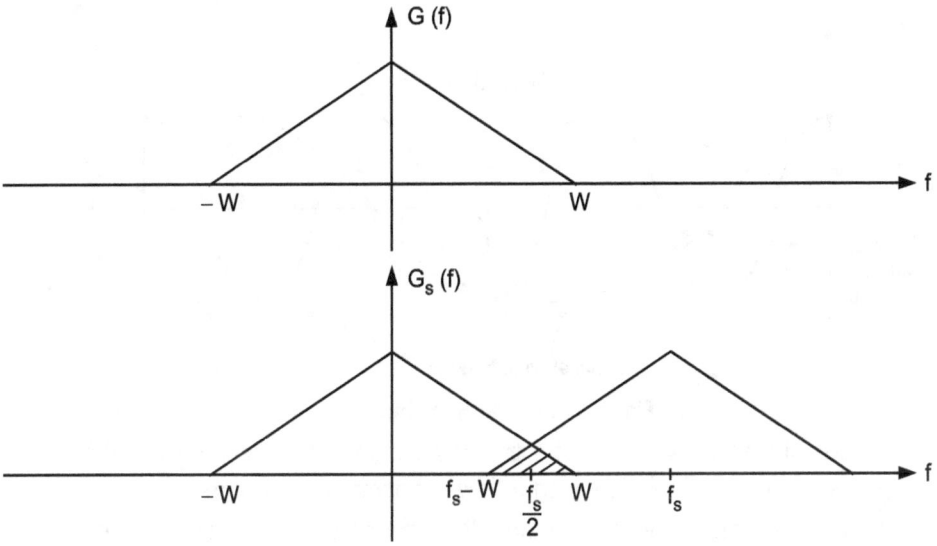

Fig. 1.13

- The overlapped region has that part of spectrum which is aliased due to undersampling.
- The spectrum of original signal g (t) is distorted in the region between $f_s - W$ to W.

Now, consider a practical signal.

- It is going to be time limited signal and hence it will have infinite bandwidth i.e. $W = \infty$.
- For such signal f_s will be ∞, if we select some finite value of f_s, the signal will be under sampled and results into aliasing as discussed earlier. It is shown in Fig. 1.14.

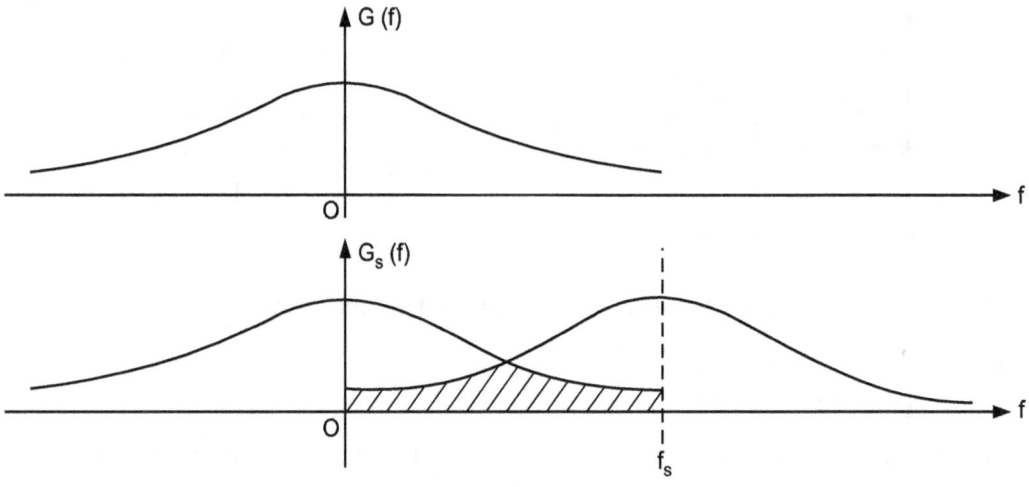

Fig. 1.14

Let us look into the aliasing effect in time domain. Fig. 1.15 shows a sinusoidal signal and its samples.

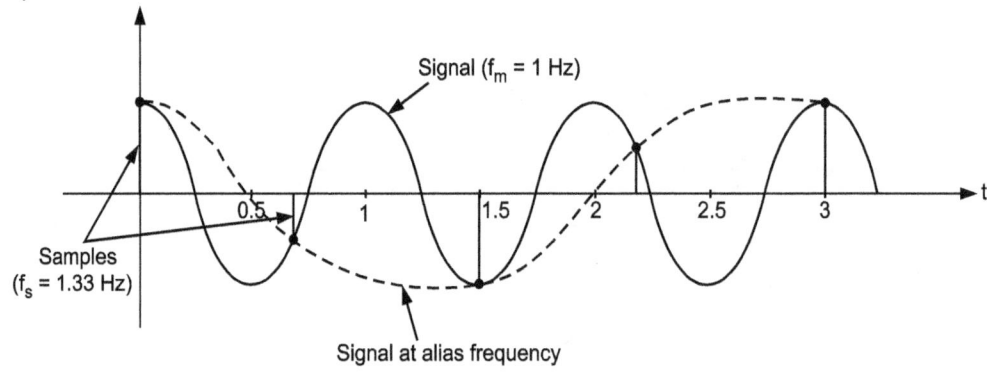

Fig. 1.15 : Aliasing in time domain

- The sinusoidal signal is sampled at a rate lower than 2W. Hence, the signal redrawn from samples is a different sinusoid which follows undersampled points.
- Aliasing can be avoided by using an antialias filter before sampling the signal.
- The antialias filter removes higher frequency components, so that the message becomes strictly band-limited.
- But then we have to make sure that, by doing so we do not lose major spectral information. Another solution to aliasing is to use sampling rate higher than Nyquist rate.
- This is done when antialiasing filter does not have sharp cut-off characteristics (like RC filters).
- It is called oversampling.
- Practically a signal is sampled at a rate 20% more than the Nyquist rate i.e. Practical $f_s \geq$ 2.2 W.

Example 1.2

Find the Nyquist rate and Nyquist interval for following signals.

(i) $g(t) = \dfrac{1}{2\pi} \cos(4000\,\pi t)\cos(1000\,\pi t)$ **[Dec. 2000]**

(ii) $g(t) = \dfrac{\sin(500\,\pi t)}{\pi t}$

Solution : (i) Given :

$$g(t) = \frac{1}{2\pi}\cos(4000\,\pi t)\cdot\cos(1000\,\pi t)$$

$$= \frac{1}{2\pi}\left[\frac{1}{2}\{\cos(4000\,\pi t + 1000\,\pi t) + \cos(4000\,\pi t - 1000\,\pi t)\}\right]$$

$$= \frac{1}{4\pi}[\cos(5000\,\pi t) + \cos(3000\,\pi t)]$$

Thus, the given signal has two frequency components.

$$2\pi f_1 = 5000\,\pi \qquad\qquad 2\pi f_2 = 3000\,\pi$$
$$f_1 = 2500\ \text{Hz} \qquad\qquad f_2 = 1500\ \text{Hz}$$

The highest frequency present in the signal is 2500 Hz (W).

$$\text{The Nyquist rate} = 2\times W = 2\times 2500$$
$$= 5000\ \text{Hz}$$

$$\text{Nyquist interval} = \frac{1}{2W} = \frac{1}{5000\ \text{Hz}} = 0.2\ \text{ms}$$

(ii) Given : $\qquad\qquad g(t) = \dfrac{\sin(500\,\pi t)}{\pi t}$

We have to find Fourier transform of this signal to get the highest frequency component present in it.

$$g(t) = \frac{\sin(500\,\pi t)}{500\times\pi t}\times 500 = 500\ \text{sinc}(500\ t)$$

We know, $\qquad\qquad A\ \text{sinc}(2Wt) \rightleftharpoons \dfrac{A}{2W}\text{rect}\left(\dfrac{f}{2W}\right)$

$\therefore \qquad\qquad 500\ \text{sinc}(500\ t) \rightleftharpoons \dfrac{500}{2\times 250}\text{rect}\left(\dfrac{f}{500}\right)$

$\therefore \qquad\qquad 500\ \text{sinc}(500\ t) \rightleftharpoons \text{rect}\left(\dfrac{f}{500}\right)$

Thus, Fourier transforms of given signal is rectangular function as plotted in Fig. 1.16. Hence, the signal has highest frequency component of 250 Hz in it.

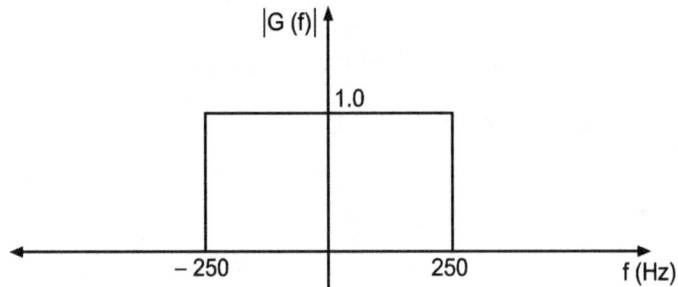

Fig. 1.16 : Spectrum of 500 sinc (500 t)

∴   Nyquist rate $= 2 \times W = 2 \times 250 = 500$ Hz

Nyquist interval $= \dfrac{1}{2W} = \dfrac{1}{500} = 2$ ms

Example 1.3 :

If an RC low-pass filter is used as antialiasing filter with R = 100 kΩ and C = 100 pF then find the sampling frequency to get an aliasing error of 10% below cut-off frequency of LPF.

Solution : Given :

$$R = 100 \text{ k}\Omega$$
$$C = 100 \text{ pF}$$

∴   Cut-off frequency of LPF,

$$B = \frac{1}{2\pi RC} = \frac{1}{2\pi \times 100 \times 10^3 \times 100 \times 10^{-12}}$$

$$= 15.9 \text{ kHz}$$

% aliasing error is given by,

$$\% \text{ error} = \frac{\dfrac{1}{0.707}}{\sqrt{1 + \left(\dfrac{f_a}{B}\right)^2}} \times 100$$

$$10 = \frac{\dfrac{1}{0.707}}{\sqrt{1 + \left(\dfrac{f_a}{15.9 \times 10^3}\right)^2}} \times 100$$

∴ $f_a = 224 \times 10^3$ Hz

$f_a = 224$ kHz

∴ $f_s = f_a + B$

∴ $f_s = 224 + 15.9 = 239.9$ kHz

$\simeq 240$ kHz

Example 1.4 :

A signal $g(t) = A \cos(2\pi f_m t)$ is sampled at a rate $f_s = f_m/5$. Plot the spectrum of the sampled signal. Interpret your result.

Solution : Given :

$$g(t) = A \cos(2\pi f_m t)$$

$$\therefore \qquad G(f) = \frac{A}{2}[\delta(f - f_m) + \delta(f + f_m)] = \frac{A}{2}\delta(f \pm f_m)$$

Now, $\qquad f_s = \dfrac{f_m}{5}$

We know that the spectrum of sampled signal is given by,

$$G_\delta(f) = f_s \sum_{m=-\infty}^{\infty} G(f - mf_s)$$

$$G_\delta(f) = f_s[G(f) + G(f \pm f_s) + G(f \pm 2f_s) + \ldots]$$

$$G_\delta(f) = \frac{Af_s}{2}[\delta(f + f_m) + \delta(f - f_m)$$

$$+ \delta(f + f_m + f_s) + \delta(f - f_m + f_s)$$
$$+ \delta(f + f_m - f_s) + \delta(f - f_m - f_s)$$
$$+ \delta(f + f_m + 2f_s) + \delta(f - f_m + 2f_s)$$
$$+ \delta(f + f_m - 2f_s) + \delta(f - f_m - 2f_s)$$
$$+ \delta(f + f_m + 3f_s) + \delta(f - f_m + 3f_s)$$
$$+ \delta(f + f_m - 3f_s) + \delta(f - f_m - 3f_s)$$
$$+ \ldots\ldots\ldots\ldots\ldots]$$

Put, $\qquad f_s = \dfrac{f_m}{5}$

$$= \frac{Af_m}{10}[\delta(f + f_m) + \delta(f - f_m)$$

$$+ \delta\left(f + \frac{6f_m}{5}\right) + \delta\left(f - \frac{4f_m}{5}\right)$$

$$+ \delta\left(f + \frac{4f_m}{5}\right) + \delta\left(f - \frac{6f_m}{5}\right)$$

$$+ \delta\left(f + \frac{7f_m}{5}\right) + \delta\left(f - \frac{3f_m}{5}\right)$$

$$+ \delta\left(f + \frac{3f_m}{5}\right) + \delta\left(f - \frac{7f_m}{5}\right)$$

$$+ \delta\left(f + \frac{8f_m}{5}\right) + \delta\left(f - \frac{2f_m}{5}\right)$$

$$+ \delta\left(f + \frac{2f_m}{5}\right) + \delta\left(f - \frac{8f_m}{5}\right)$$

$$+ \ldots\ldots\ldots\ldots]$$

The spectrum is plotted in Fig. 1.17,

The spectrum is an under sampled signals spectrum since $f_s \ll 2f_m$. The spectrum also depicts the aliasing effect where the higher frequency components of the signal are translated in the lower frequency range.

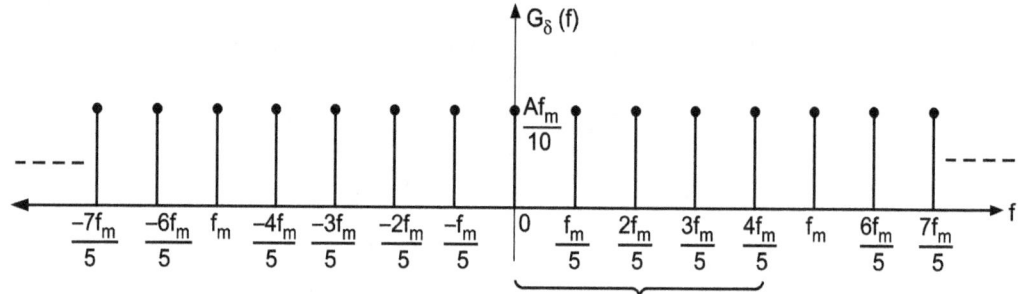

Fig. 1.17 : Spectrum of under sampled signal

1.2.6 Natural Sampling

Practically, a signal is sampled using switching operation shown in Fig. 1.18.

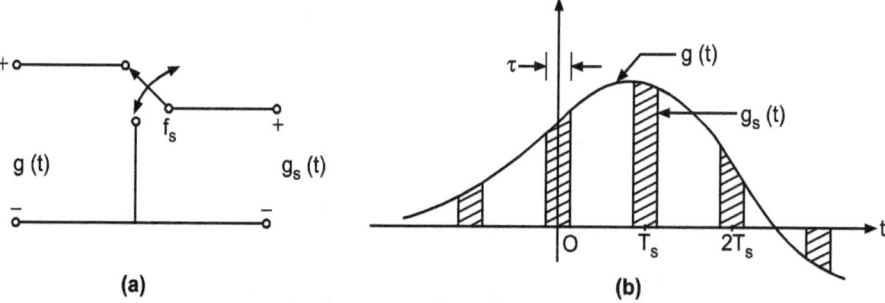

Fig. 1.18 : Natural sampling (switching sampler)

- The switch periodically shifts between two contacts at a rate $f_s = \frac{1}{T_s}$.

- It remains in first contact for T seconds and on the other grounded contact for rest of each period. The operation is called single-ended or unipolar chopping.

- The operation thus is a multiplication of signal g(t) with a signal s(t) which is train of pulses of duration T and amplitude 1 and period T_s.

Hence, the sampled signal can be written as,

$$g_s(t) = g(t) \cdot s(t) \qquad \text{... (1.14)}$$

s(t) is a periodic signal with a rectangular pulse duration T repeating every T_s seconds.

i.e. $\qquad\qquad\qquad s(t) = \sum_{n=-\infty}^{\infty} \text{rect}\left(\frac{t-nT_s}{T}\right)$

A periodic signal is represented in the form of fourier series as below :

If we have periodic signal $g_p(t)$ with period T_0 or frequency $f_o = \dfrac{1}{T_0}$ given as,

$$g_p(t) = \sum_{n=-\infty}^{\infty} g(t - nT_0)$$

and G(f) is fourier transform of g(t) then,

$$g_p(t) = \sum_{n=-\infty}^{\infty} \frac{1}{T_0} G\left(\frac{n}{T_0}\right) e^{j2\pi n f_o t}$$

For our signal s(t), $\qquad\qquad g(t) = \text{rect}\left(\frac{t}{T}\right)$

$\therefore \qquad\qquad\qquad G(f) = T \, \text{sinc} \, (fT)$

$\therefore \qquad\qquad\quad G\left(\frac{n}{T_s}\right) = T \, \text{sinc} \left(\frac{nT}{T_s}\right)$

$$= T \, \text{sinc} \, (nf_sT) \qquad\qquad \left[\because f_s = \frac{1}{T_s}\right]$$

$\therefore \qquad\qquad\quad s(t) = \sum \frac{1}{T_s} T \, \text{sinc} \, (nf_sT) \, e^{j2\pi n f_s t}$

$$= f_s \sum_{n=-\infty}^{\infty} T \, \text{sinc} \, (nf_sT) \, e^{j2\pi n f_s t}$$

$\therefore \qquad\qquad\quad g_s(t) = g(t) \, f_s \sum_{n=-\infty}^{\infty} \text{sinc} \, (nf_sT) \, e^{j2\pi n f_s t}$

$$= f_s \sum_{n=-\infty}^{\infty} \text{sinc} \, (nf_sT) \, g(t) \, e^{j2\pi n f_s t}$$

$\therefore \qquad\quad F\,[g_s(t)] = f_s \sum_{n=-\infty}^{\infty} \text{sinc} \, (nf_sT) \, G(f - nf_s) \qquad \text{... (1.15)}$

Thus, spectrum of sampled signal can be written as,

$$G_s(f) = f_s \, G(f) + f_s \, \text{sinc} \, (f_sT) \, [G(f - f_s) + G(f + f_s)]$$
$$+ f_s \, \text{sinc} \, (2f_sT) \, [G(f - 2f_s) + G(f + 2f_s)] \, \dots\dots$$

- It can be seen that the amplitudes of replicas of G(f) at f_s, $2f_s$, $3f_s$ ...... etc. are governed by f_s sinc (n f_s T).

- Hence, the frequency plot will follow sinc pattern as shown in Fig. 1.19.

- The spectrum is plotted in Fig. 1.19 assuming the spectrum of g(t) to be strictly band-limited to W Hz.

- From the spectrum, we can see that for $f_s \geq 2W$, the spectrum of original signal is retained in sampled signal.

- Hence, it is possible to recover original signal from sampled spectrum if $f_s \geq 2W$.

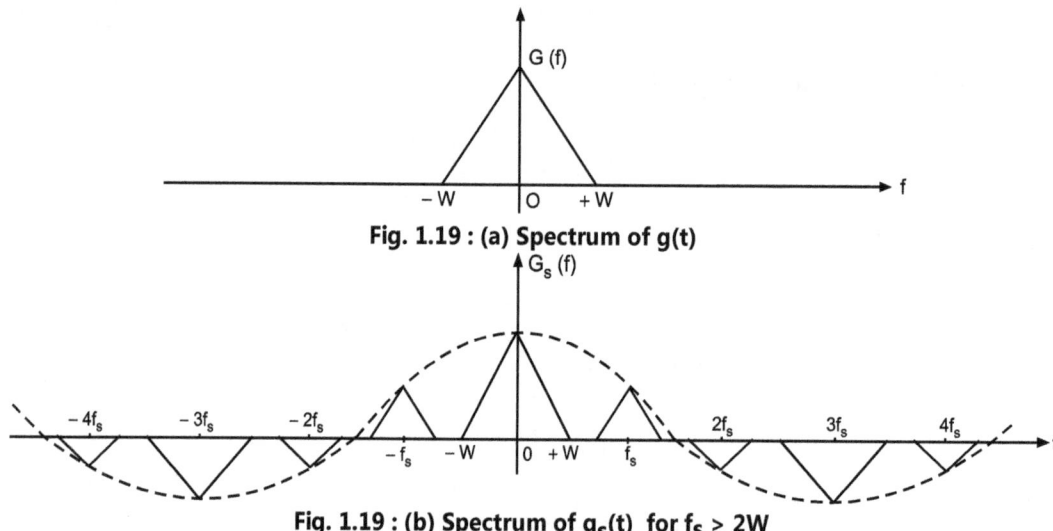

Fig. 1.19 : (a) Spectrum of g(t)

Fig. 1.19 : (b) Spectrum of $g_s(t)$ for $f_s > 2W$

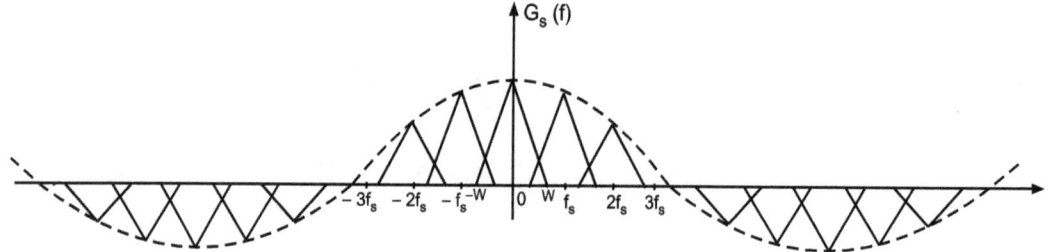

Fig. 1.19 : (c) Spectrum of $g_s(f)$ for $f_s < 2W$

- Sampling at $f_s > 2W$ also creates a guard band into which the transition region of a practical LPF can be fitted. For $f_s < 2W$ there is aliasing.
- Thus, it can be concluded that the pulses of finite duration and amplitude of sampled signal have no major effect in sampling.

1.2.7 Flat-Top Sampling

It is a method of sampling which employs Sample-and-Hold (S/H) technique as shown in Fig. 1.20.

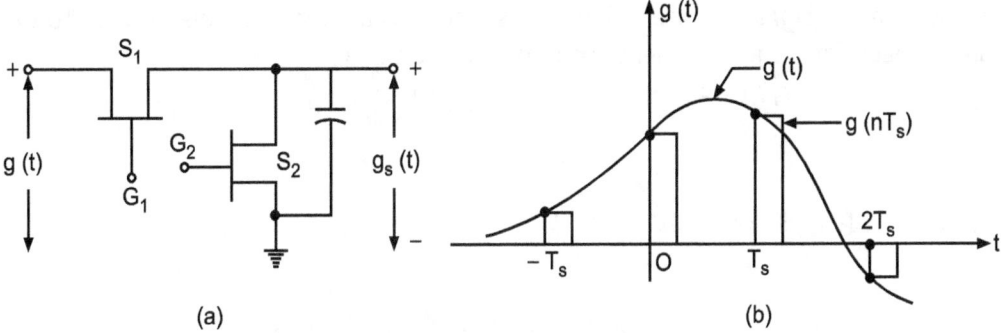

(a)   (b)

Fig. 1.20 : Flat Top sampling circuit and waveforms

- The operation produces flat-top samples. This is a more popular method for generating Pulse Amplitude Modulated (PAM) signal than the chopper sampling seen earlier.
- The circuit for producing flat-top samples consists of two FETs used as switches and capacitor.
- A gate pulse of small duration applied to sampling switch (S_1) allows the capacitor to hold the signal amplitude.
- When discharge switch S_2 is operated by a pulse, the capacitor is discharged.
- This process is done at every T_s interval to produce the sampled wave $g_s(t)$.

The sampled wave can be written as,

$$g_s(t) = \sum_{n=-\infty}^{\infty} g(nT_s)\, p\,(t - nT_s) \qquad \text{... (1.16)}$$

where, p(t) is basic pulse shape of unit amplitude given by,

$$p(t) = 1 \quad ; \quad 0 \le t \le T$$
$$= 0 \quad ; \quad \text{otherwise}$$

We know from the property of delta function,

$$g(t) * \delta(t - t_0) = g(t - t_0)$$
$$\therefore \qquad p(t) * \delta(t - nT_s) = p(t - nT_s)$$

Hence, we can write $g_s(t)$ as,

$$g_s(t) = \sum_{n=-\infty}^{\infty} g\,(nT_s)\,[p(t) * \delta(t - nT_s)] \qquad \text{... (1.17)}$$

$$= p(t) * \sum_{n=-\infty}^{\infty} g(nT_s)\,\delta(t - nT_s) \qquad \text{... (1.18)}$$

Now, $\sum_{n=-\infty}^{\infty} g(nT_s)\,\delta(t - nT_s)$ is an ideally sampled signal denoted as $g_\delta(t)$.

$$\therefore \qquad g_s(t) = p(t) * g_\delta(t) \qquad \text{... (1.19)}$$

Thus, the sampled signal is convolution of basic pulse with ideally sampled signal. To get a nature of spectrum, we find Fourier transform of above signal.

$$\therefore \qquad G_s(f) = F[g_s(t)] \ = \ F[p(t)] \times F[g_\delta(t)]$$

$$= \ P(f) \times G_\delta(f)$$

p(t) is a rectangular pulse shifted by $\dfrac{T}{2}$.

i.e.

$$p(t) \ = \ rect\left(\dfrac{t-\dfrac{T}{2}}{T}\right)$$

$$\therefore \qquad P(f) \ = \ T\ sinc\ (fT)\ e^{-j2\pi f\frac{T}{2}}$$

$$= \ T\ sinc\ (fT)\ e^{-j\pi fT}$$

$$G_\delta(f) \ = \ f_s \sum_{n=-\infty}^{\infty} G(f - mf_s) \qquad\qquad ... (1.20)$$

$$\therefore \qquad G_s(f) \ = \ T\ sinc\ (fT)\ e^{-j\pi fT}\ f_s \sum_{n=-\infty}^{\infty} G(f - mf_s) \qquad\qquad ... (1.21)$$

We can think of $G_s(f) = P(f) \times G_\delta(f)$ as an output of ideally sampled signal passed through a filter with frequency response p(f). [Since it is similar to $Y(f) = H(f) \cdot X(f)$]. This will have an effect as shown in Fig. 1.21. Note that the spectrum of g(t) i.e. G(f) is assumed to be rectangular in shape as opposed to triangular in previous cases. This is done to understand the aperture effect in correct perspective

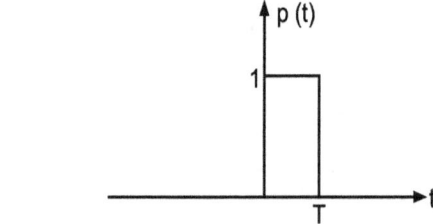

Fig. 1.21 : (a) Single pulse p(t)

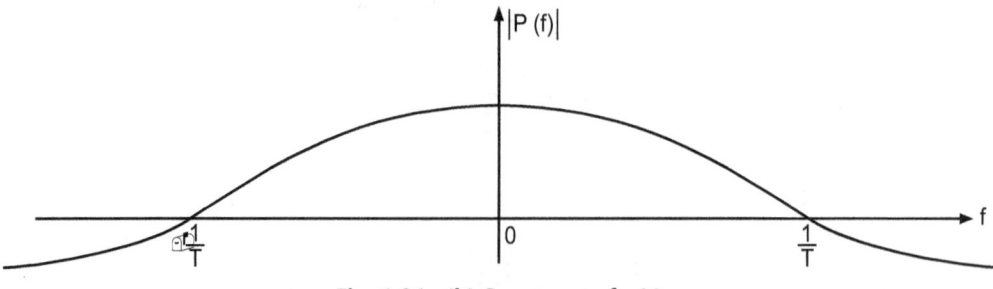

Fig. 1.21 : (b) Spectrum of p(t)

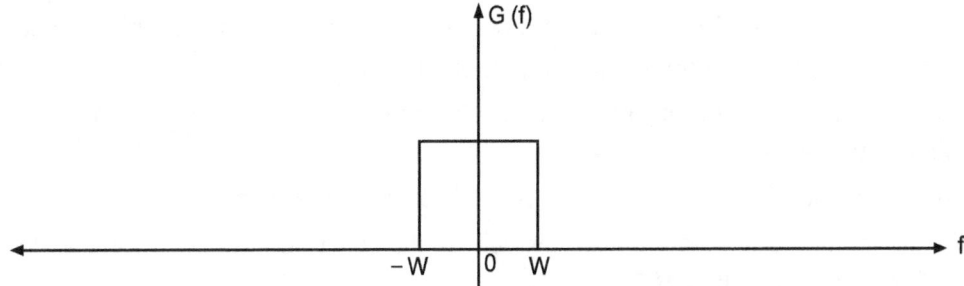

Fig. 1.21 (c) : Assumed spectrum of g(t)

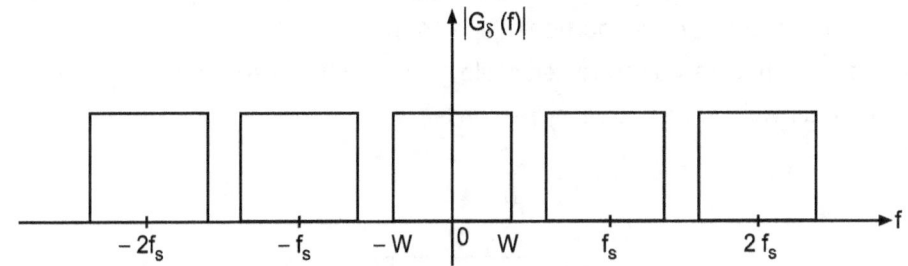

Fig. 1.21 : (d) Spectrum of ideally sampled signal

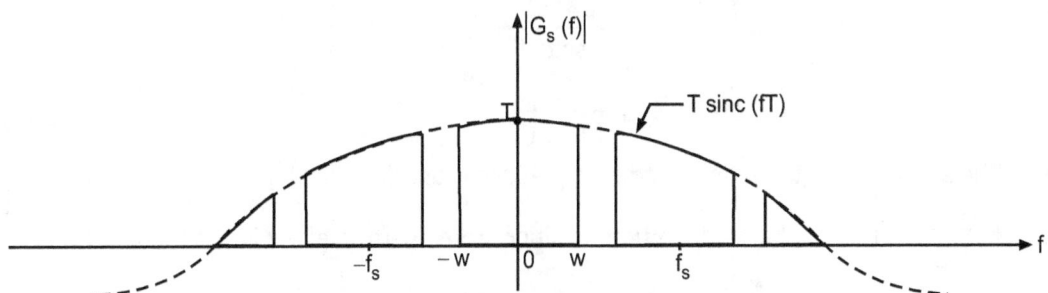

Fig. 1.21 : (e) Spectrum of flat-top sampled signal

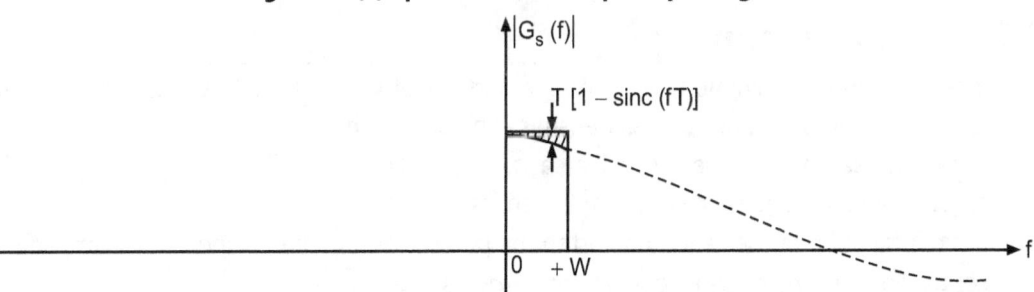

Fig. 1.21 : (f) Aperture distortion shown in shaded area

Aperture Effect :

- The multiplication of $P(f)$ and $G_\delta(f)$ results into a spectrum of sampled signal as shown in Fig. 1.21 (e).

- Thus, we see that P(f) acts like a low pass filter and attenuates high frequency components (upper portion) of message spectrum.
- The original spectrum of g(t) is almost retained except that the high frequency component get attenuated.
- This loss of high frequency components is called **aperture effect.**
- The larger the pulse duration (T), larger will be the effect because the roll-off of P(f) will be larger for large values of T.
- It is also worth noting that as $T \to 0$, it will lead to ideal sampling since there will be no roll-off and no loss of upper portion of spectrum.
- The aperture effect can be corrected while reconstructing the signal using equalizer.
- The equalizer will have a frequency response.

$$H_{eq}(f) = \frac{1}{P(f)} \qquad \dots (1.22)$$

$$= \frac{1}{T \sinc(fT) \, e^{-j\pi fT}}$$

$$= \frac{e^{j2\pi fT}}{T \sinc(fT)}$$

$$\therefore \qquad |H_{eq}(f)| = \frac{1}{T \sinc(f)} \qquad \dots (1.23)$$

- The amount of equalization needed in practice is usually small for small duty cycle.
- If $\dfrac{T}{T_s} \leq 0.1$, the amplitude distortion resulting from aperture effect is less than 0.5%.
- The % error due to aperture distortion $= \left(1 - \dfrac{\sin \pi fT}{\pi fT}\right) \times 100 \qquad \dots (1.24)$

1.2.8 Why Oversampling?

- If sampling rate is minimum, $f_s = 2W$, the number of samples are less (per sec). This will require low storage space or less transmission bandwidth.
- When the sampling is performed at a rate $f_s > 2W$, it is called oversampling. It will require more storage space or more transmission bandwidth.
- But oversampling is better compared to the process of sampling without oversampling.
- Let us look into the steps involved in the processes.

Without Oversampling :

(i)   The signal has to pass through a low pass filter since the practical signal is not bandlimited. The low pass filter has to be high performance analog filter.

(ii) The filtered signal is sampled at fs = 2W (i.e. Nyquist rate).

(iii) The continuous value samples are converted into finite discrete output levels by analog-to-digital converter.

With Oversampling :

(i)   The signal is passed through low pass filter which can be a low performance analog filter hence less costlier.

(ii) The filter signal is sampled at a rate of $f_s > 2W$ (higher than Nyquist rate).

(iii) The continuous value samples are converted into finite discrete output levels by analog-to-digital converter.

(iv) The digital samples are then processed by a high performance digital filter to reduce the bandwidth of discrete signal.

(v)   The reduced bandwidth of discrete signal also reduces the sample rate of output.

Advantages of Oversampling :

•   The practical signal requires prefiltering (i.e. antialias filter).

•   The antialias filter has response shown in Fig. 1.22.

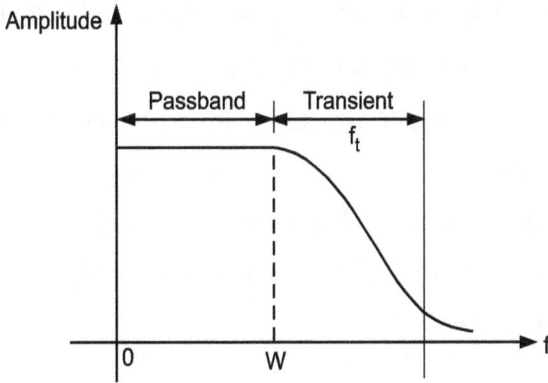

Fig. 1.22

•   The sampling frequency now should be,

$$f_s \quad = \quad 2W + f_t$$

where f_t is the transition bandwidth of the filter and W is the highest frequency in the sampled signal.

•   Hence, the sample rate is increased by almost 10-20% of Nyquist rate.

•   For f_s to be as low as possible the transition bandwidth f_t of the filter has to be narrow.

•   This calls for high order filters which are costly.

•   The narrow transition band also gives rise to distortion due to non-linear phase versus frequency.

•   Hence, if we use transition bandwidth f_t high, we can use low order filters which are less costly and the distortion can be minimised.

Ch. 1 | 1.31

- This will require higher sampling frequency i.e. oversampling.

- For example, we can sample CD signal (20 kHz) at 44.1 kHz with transition bandwidth of 4.1 kHz. This will require 10th order filters (10 capacitors and inductors).

- If the CD signal is sampled at 176.4 kHz we can have transition bandwidth of 136.4 kHz which will require 4th order filters.

- The sampled data is passed through high-performance, low cost, digital filter to perform desired anti-alias filtering.

- Digital filters can have narrow transition bandwidth without distortion.

- The digital filter output can be resampled to reduce sample rate.

- The analog prefilter introduces some amplitude and phase distortion.

- This distortion can also be taken care of by the suitable design of digital filter.

- Thus, it is possible to obtain a signal of high quality at reduced cost.

- The recovery process from digital samples to analog can employ oversampling in digital to analog converter (DAC).

- The DAC output is given to analog filter which may not have narrow transition bandwidth since the output data given to DAC is oversampled.

- The process is shown in Fig. 1.23.

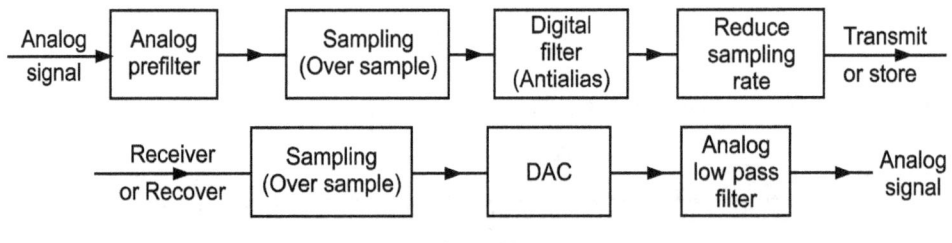

Fig. 1.23

- There are four ways in which analog source information can be described as shown in Fig. 1.24.

(i) Original Analog Waveform.

(ii) Natural Sampled Data (PAM).

(iii) Quantized Samples.

(iv) Sample and Hold Signal.

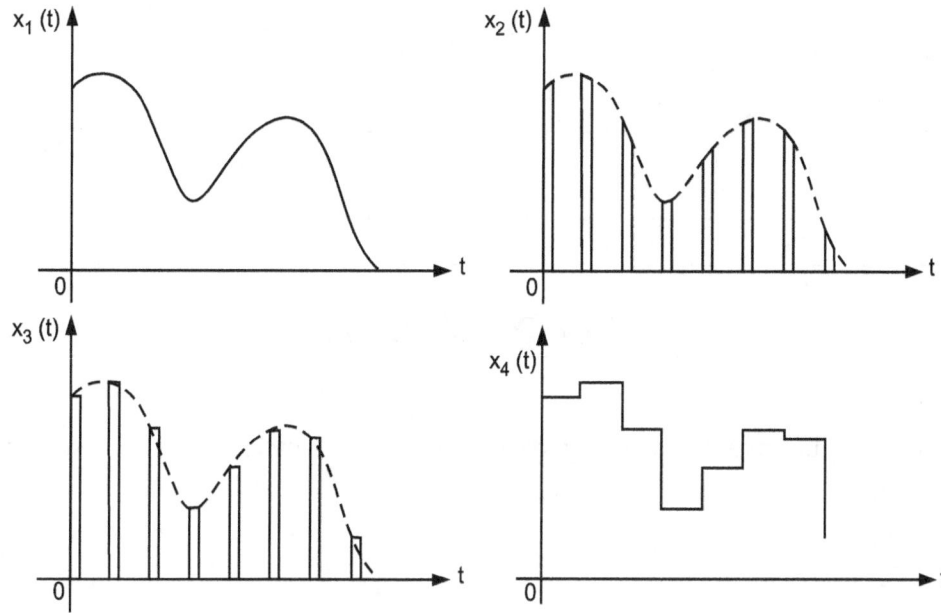

Fig. 1.24

1.3   COMPARISON OF VARIOUS SAMPLING TECHNIQUES

Basis	Ideal Sampling	Natural Sampling	Flat-top Sampling
1. Waveform			
2. Circuit			
3. Method	Train of impulses is used to multiply the signal.	It uses switching operation called chopping. Hence, it is multiplication of train of pulses with the signal.	Sample and hold circuit is used to sample the signal.
4. Practical Implementation	It is not possible to implement the method practically.	This can be implemented practically.	This can be implemented practically.
5. Time domain representation	$g_\delta(t) = \sum\limits_{n=-\infty}^{\infty} g(nT_s) \times \delta(t - nT_s)$	$g_s(t) = \sum\limits_{n=-\infty}^{\infty} f_s \, sinc \, (nf_sT) \, g(t) \, e^{j2\pi nf_s t}$	$g_s(t) = \sum\limits_{n=-\infty}^{\infty} g(nT_s) \times p(t - nT_s)$

6. Frequency domain representation	$G_\delta(f) = f_s \sum\limits_{n=-\infty}^{\infty} G(f - mf_s)$	$G_s(t) = f_s \sum\limits_{n=-\infty}^{\infty} \text{sinc}\,(nf_sT)\; G(f - nf_s)$	$G_s(f) = G_\delta(f) \cdot P(f)$
7. Frequency spectrum			

SOLVED PROBLEMS

Problem 1.1 :

What is Nyquist rate and Nyquist interval to adequately sample the following signals.

(i)   sinc (100 t)

(ii) sinc² (100 t)

(iii) 10 cos³ (2π 10⁵ t)

Solution :

(i)   Given : $g(t) = \text{sinc}\,(100\,t)$

∴ $G(f) = \dfrac{1}{100}\,\text{rect}\left(\dfrac{f}{100}\right)$

$$\left[\because\; A\,\text{sinc}\,(2Wt) \Leftrightarrow \dfrac{A}{2W}\,\text{rect}\left(\dfrac{f}{2W}\right) \right]$$

Hence, the maximum frequency present in the signal is W = 50 Hz.

∴   Nyquist rate $= 2 \times W$

$= 2 \times 50$

$= 100\ \text{Hz}$

Nyquist interval $= \dfrac{1}{2W}$

$= 0.01\ \text{s}$

(ii) Given : $g(t) = \text{sinc}^2\,(100\,t)$

We know that

$$A\,\text{sinc}^2\,(Wt) \;\rightleftharpoons\; \dfrac{A}{W}\,\Delta\left(\dfrac{f}{2W}\right)$$

$\left(\dfrac{f}{2W}\right)$ indicates triangular pulse of width 2W.

∴ $G(f) = \dfrac{1}{100}\,\Delta\left(\dfrac{f}{200}\right)$

Thus, the spectrum of highest frequency component W = 100 Hz

$\therefore$ $\qquad$ Nyquist rate f_s = 2W

$\qquad\qquad\qquad$ = 200 Hz

$\qquad$ Nyquist interval = $\dfrac{1}{2W}$

$\qquad\qquad\qquad$ = $\dfrac{1}{200}$ = 0.05 s

(iii) Given : $\qquad\qquad$ g(t) = $10 \cos^3 (2\pi \times 10^5 \, t)$

$\qquad\qquad\qquad$ = $10 \cos (2\pi \times 10^5) \times \cos^2 (2\pi \times 10^5 \, t)$

$\qquad\qquad\qquad$ = $10 \cos (2\pi \times 10^5) \, [1 + \cos (4\pi \times 10^5 \, t)]$

$\qquad\qquad\qquad$ = $10 \, [\cos (2\pi \times 10^5 \, t) + \cos (2\pi \times 10^5 \, t) \cdot \cos (4\pi \times 10^5 \, t)$

$\qquad\qquad\qquad$ = $10 \, \{\cos (2\pi \times 10^5 \, t) + \cos [2\pi \times (10^5 + 2 \times 10^5 \, t)]$

$\qquad\qquad\qquad$ $+ \cos [2\pi \times 10^5 \, t]\}$

$\qquad\qquad\qquad$ = $10 \cos (2\pi \times 10^5 \, t) + 10 \cos (6\pi \times 10^5 \, t)$

$\qquad\qquad\qquad$ $+ 10 \cos (2\pi \times 10^5 \, t)$

$\qquad\qquad\qquad$ = $20 \cos (2\pi \times 10^5 \, t) + 10 \cos (6\pi \times 10^5 \, t)$

From above, we see that there are two frequency components in the signal.

$\qquad\qquad$ $2\pi f_1$ = $2\pi \times 10^5$ $\qquad$ and $\qquad$ $2\pi f_2$ = $6\pi \times 10^5$

$\therefore$ $\qquad\qquad$ f_1 = 10^5 Hz $\qquad\qquad\qquad$ f_2 = 3×10^5 Hz

Hence, the highest frequency component in the signal is,

$\qquad\qquad\qquad$ W = 3×10^5 Hz

$\therefore$ $\qquad\qquad$ Nyquist rate = $2 \times W$

$\qquad\qquad\qquad$ = $2 \times 3 \times 10^5$ = 600 kHz

$\qquad$ Nyquist interval = $\dfrac{1}{2W} = \dfrac{1}{2 \times 3 \times 10^5}$

$\qquad\qquad\qquad$ = 1.67×10^{-6} s

Problem 1.2 :

Find a signal g(t) that is band-limited to 1 Hz and whose samples are

$\qquad$ g(0) = 1, g($\pm$ 0.5) = g($\pm$ 1) = g($\pm$ 1.5) = ... = 0

Solution :

The signal g(t) can be recovered from its samples using interpolating formula.

$$g(t) = \sum_{n = -\infty}^{\infty} g\left(\frac{n}{2W}\right) \text{sinc} (2Wt - n)$$

We have, $W = 1\ Hz$

Samples are taken at $T_s = 0, \pm 0.5, 0, \pm 1, \ldots$

$$g(t) = g(0)\ \text{sinc}\ (2t) + g\left(\frac{1}{2}\right)\text{sinc}\ (2t-1) + g\left(-\frac{1}{2}\right)\text{sinc}$$

$$(2t-1) + \ldots$$

$$= g(0)\ \text{sinc}\ (2t) + g(0.5)\ \text{sinc}\ (2t-1) + g\ (-0.5)$$

$$\text{sinc}\ (2t-1) + \ldots$$

Given : $g(0) = 1,\ g(0.5) = 0,\ g(-0.5) = \ldots$

It means only first term is retained.

Hence, $g(t) = 1 \cdot \text{sinc}\ (2t)$

$\therefore$ $g(t) = \text{sinc}\ (2t)$

Problem 1.3 :

A flat top sampled signal of maximum frequency 1 Hz with 2.5 Hz sampling frequency has a pulse duration of 0.2 seconds. Find the amplitude distortion due to aperture effect at highest signal frequency. Find the equalizer transfer function.

Solution : Given :

$W = 1\ kHz$ (signal BW)

$f_s = 2.5\ Hz$ (sampling frequency)

$T = 0.2\ seconds$ (pulse duration)

Amplitude distortion due to aperture effect is given by,

$$\% \text{ error} = \left(1 - \frac{\sin\ (\pi fT)}{\pi fT}\right) \times 100$$

This is to be calculated at highest frequency,

$$f = 1\ Hz$$

$\therefore$ $$\% \text{ error} = 1 - \frac{\sin\ (\pi \times 1 \times 0.2)}{\pi \times 1 \times 0.2} \times 100$$

$$= 1 - 0.9355 = 0.0645 \times 100\%$$

$$= 6.45\%$$

The equalizer transfer function is given by,

$$\left|H_{eq}\ (f)\right| = \frac{1}{T\ \text{sinc}\ (fT)} = \frac{1}{0.2\ \text{sinc}\ (0.2\ f)}$$

SOLVED UNIVERSITY QUESTIONS

U.Q. 1 : Explain the term aperture effect and method to minimize, with the help of neat time domain and frequency domain diagrams.   **(8 marks) (Dec. 2005)**

Solution : Refer Section 1.2.7

U.Q. 2 : A cosine wave of 1 Volt and 5 kHz frequency is sampled at sampling frequency f_s = 8 kHz. Sampling is ideal. Output of the sampler are then passed through an ideal low pass filter of 0 Hz to 4 kHz bandwidth. The output of LPF is observed on CRO. Draw this output wave shape on graph paper to the scale comparing it with input wave shape. Interpret the result. Also draw the spectrum at the input, output of sampler and at the output of filter for the given case of cosine 5 kHz wave on the graph paper and to the scale.   **(Dec. 2005)**

Solution : Given, For sampled signal frequency,

$$\text{Frequency, } f_m = 5 \text{ kHz}$$
$$\text{Amplitude, } A = 1 \text{ V}$$

For sampling signal,

$$\text{Frequency, } f_s = 8 \text{ kHz}$$

Low pass filter,

$$\text{Cut-off frequency} = 4 \text{ kHz}$$

For ideal sampling, the spectrum of ideally sampled signal is given by,

$$G_\delta(f) = f_s \sum_{m=-\infty}^{\infty} G(f - mf_s)$$

where, G(f) in our case is a cosine wave,

i.e.
$$g(t) = A \cos(2\pi f_m t)$$
$$\therefore \qquad = \cos(2\pi \times 5 \times 10^3 \, t)$$

$$\therefore \qquad G(f) = \frac{1}{2}[\delta(f - f_m) - \delta(f + f_m)]$$

$$G_\delta(f) = f_s \sum_{m=-\infty}^{\infty} \frac{1}{2}\delta(f - f_m - mf_s) + \frac{1}{2}\delta(f + f_m - mf_s)$$

$$= 8 \times 10^3 \sum_{m=-\infty}^{\infty} \frac{1}{2}\delta(f - 5k - 8k \times m)$$

$$+ \frac{1}{2}\delta(f + 5k - 8k \times m)$$

at   m = 0 $\frac{1}{2}\delta(f - 5k) + \frac{1}{2}\delta(f + 5k)$

          m = 1 $\frac{1}{2}\delta(f - 13k) + \frac{1}{2}\delta(f - 3k)$

$$m = -1 \qquad \frac{1}{2}\,\delta(f + 3k) + \frac{1}{2}\,\delta(f + 13k)$$

$$m = 2 \qquad \frac{1}{2}\,\delta(f - 21k) + \frac{1}{2}\,\delta(f - 11k)$$

$$m = -2 \qquad \frac{1}{2}\,\delta(f + 11k) + \frac{1}{2}\,\delta(f + 21k)$$

$$m = 3 \qquad \frac{1}{2}\,\delta(f - 29k) + \frac{1}{2}\,\delta(f - 19k)$$

$$m = -3 \qquad \frac{1}{2}\,\delta(f + 19k) + \frac{1}{2}\,\delta(f + 29k)$$

The spectrum is plotted in Fig. 1.25 as shown below :

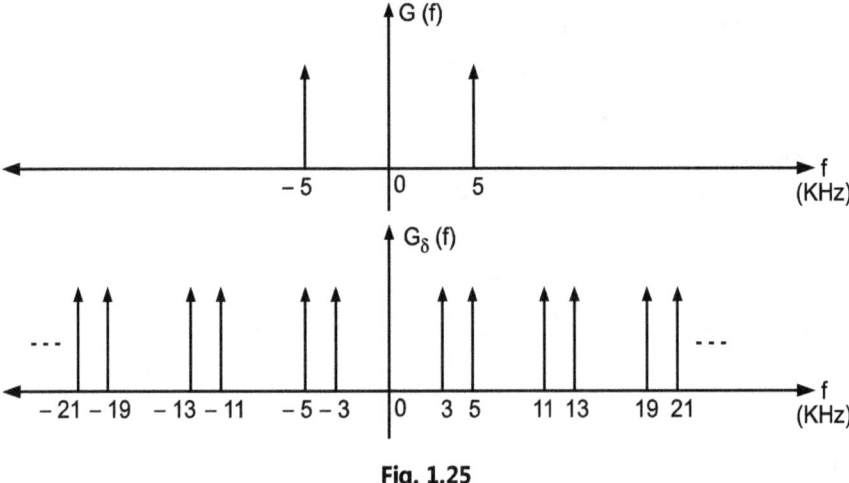

Fig. 1.25

Above spectrum is passed through a filter of 4 kHz cut-off frequency. Hence, only signal of 3 kHz will be passed through it.

Therefore, output signal will be a cosine wave of frequency 3 kHz.

U.Q. 3 : With reference to waveform and spectrum explain flat top sampling. What is aperture effect ? Also explain aliasing effect. **(10 marks) (Dec. 2006)**

Solution : Refer Sections 1.2.5 for aliasing and 1.2.7 for aperture effect.

U.Q. 4 : A signal $x(t) = 10 \cos (1000 \, t + \pi/3) + 20 \cos (2000 \, t + \pi/6)$ is to be uniformly sampled.

    (i) What is the maximum allowable time interval between sample values that will ensure faithful signal reproduction ?

    (ii) If one hours of signal to be reproduced, how many samples needs to be stored.

(8 marks) (Dec. 2006, May 2014)

Solution :

(i) The given signal is

$$x(t) = 10 \cos (1000 t + \pi/3) + 20 \cos (2000 t + \pi/6)$$

$$= x_1(t) + x_2(t)$$

$$x_1(t) = 10 \cos (1000 t + \pi/3)$$

and
$$x_2(t) = 20 \cos (2000 t + \pi/6)$$

Comparing these with standard cosine wave signal $A \cos (2\pi f_1 t + \phi)$,

We find for $x_1(t)$

$$2\pi f_1 t = 1000 t$$

$$\therefore \quad f_1 = \frac{1000}{2\pi} = \frac{500}{\pi} \text{ Hz}$$

For $x_2(t)$
$$2\pi f_2 t = 2000 t$$

$$\therefore \quad f_2 = \frac{2000}{2\pi}$$

$$f_2 = \frac{1000}{\pi} \text{ Hz}$$

Since f_2 is larger the maximum frequency component in x(t) is $1000/\pi$ Hz.

$$\therefore \quad W = \frac{1000}{\pi} \text{ Hz}$$

Since $f_s \geq 2W$.

Minimum sampling frequency $f_s = \dfrac{1000}{\pi} \times 2$

Hence, maximum time interval will be,

$$T_s = \frac{1}{f_s} = \frac{\pi}{2000} s = 1.57 \times 10^{-3} s$$

$$= 1.57 \text{ ms}$$

(ii) The number of samples per second is $\dfrac{2000}{\pi}$.

Hence, in 1 hour i.e. 3600 seconds, the number of samples will be

$$= \frac{2000}{\pi} \times 3600 = 2.292 \times 10^6.$$

U.Q. 5 : Explain sampling theorem for low pass signals in time domain. Also explain reconstruction of signal from samples. **(10 marks) (May 2007)**

Solution : Refer Section 1.2.3

U.Q. 6 :   The signal x(t) = cos 200 πt + 0.25 cos 700 πt is sampled at the rate of 400 samples per second. Sampled waveform is then passed through an ideal low pass filter with 200 Hz bandwidth. Write an expression for filter output. Sketch the frequency spectrum of sampled waveform.   **(May 2007)**

Solution :

Given :

$$x(t) = \cos(200\,\pi f) + 0.25 \cos(700\,\pi t)$$

$$f_s = 400 \text{ Hz}$$

The signal x(t) consists of signal with two cosine waves.

$$x_1(t) = \cos(200\,\pi t)$$

$$x_2(t) = 0.25 \cos(700\,\pi t)$$

∴ $$2\pi f_1 t = 200\,\pi t$$

∴ $$f_1 = 100 \text{ Hz}$$

$$2\pi f_2 t = 700\,\pi t$$

∴ $$f_2 = 350 \text{ Hz}$$

Since f_s = 400 Hz, it is less than Nyquist rate, x(t) will be undersampled.

The spectrum of x(t),

$$X(f) = \frac{1}{2}[\delta(f - 100) + \delta(f + 100)] + \frac{1}{8}[\delta(f - 350) + \delta(f + 350)]$$

The spectrum of sampled signal,

$$X_\delta(f) = \frac{1}{T_s} \sum_{n=-\infty}^{\infty} X(f) + X(f - 400) + X(f + 400) + X(f - 800) + X(f + 800) + X(f - 1200) + X(f + 1200) + \dots\dots]$$

∴ $$X_\delta(f) = 200\,[\delta(f - 100) + \delta(f + 100)]$$

$$+ 50\,[\delta(f - 350) + \delta(f + 350)]$$

$$+ 200\,[\delta(f - 500) + \delta(f - 300)]$$

$$+ 50\,[\delta(f - 750) + \delta(f - 50)]$$

$$+ 200\,[\delta(f + 300) + \delta(f + 500)]$$

$$+ 50\,[\delta(f + 50) + \delta(f + 750)]$$

$$+ 200\,[\delta(f - 900) + \delta(f - 700)]$$

$$+ 50\,[\delta(f - 1150) + \delta(f - 500)]$$

$$+ \dots\dots$$

The plot of above spectrum will be,

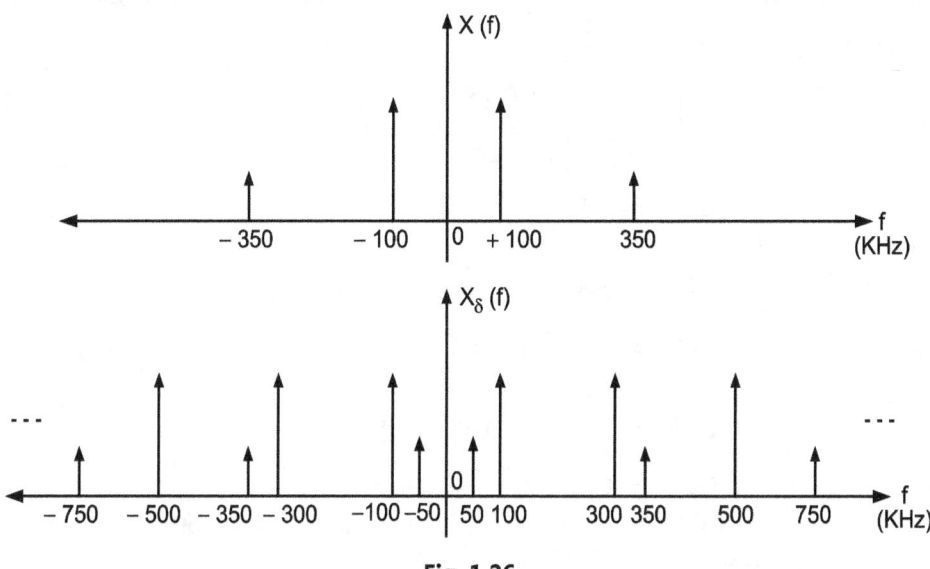

Fig. 1.26

The above signal when passed through a filter of cut-off 200 Hz, it will pass only two components 50 Hz and 100 Hz. Hence, output will be,

$$y(t) = 50 \cos (100 \, \pi t) + 200 \cos (200 \, \pi t)$$

U.Q. 7 : With the help of mathematical expression and spectral diagrams, explain the time domain and frequency domain approach of sampling theorem.

(10 marks) (Dec. 2007)

Solution : Refer Section 1.2.3

U.Q. 8 : A waveform g(t) = 20 + 20 sin (500 πt + 30) is to be sampled periodically and reproduced from the samples.

(i) Find the maximum allowable time intervals between the samples.

(ii) How many sample values are need to be stored in order to produce one second of this waveform, if sampled according to the result in (1).

(6 marks) (Dec. 2007), (8 marks) (May 2014)

Solution :

Frequency Domain Approach :

A time limited signal g(t) given as,

$$g(t) = 0 \text{ for } |t| > T$$

and
$$G(f) = F[g(t)]$$

Then G(f) can be uniquely determined from its values $G\left(\dfrac{n}{T}\right)$ at equidistant point spaced $\dfrac{1}{2T}$ apart and G(f) is given by,

$$G(f) \; = \; \sum_{n=-\infty}^{\infty} G\left(\frac{n}{2T}\right) \frac{\sin(2\pi fT - n\pi)}{(2\pi fT - n\pi)}$$

Let $\qquad\qquad\qquad g(t) \; = \; 0 \text{ for } |t| > T$

and $\qquad\qquad\qquad F[g(t)] \; = \; G(f)$

shown in figure as follows.

The spectrum G(f) is sampled using s(f).

Where, $\qquad\qquad\qquad S(f) \; = \; \sum_{n=-\infty}^{\infty} \delta(f - nf_s)$

$\therefore \qquad\qquad\qquad G_\delta(f) \; = \; \sum_{n=-\infty}^{\infty} G(nf_s) \, \delta(f - nf_s)$

Now, $\qquad\qquad\qquad G_\delta(f) \; = \; G(f) \cdot S(f)$

$\therefore \qquad\qquad\qquad g_\delta(t) \; = \; F^{-1}[G_\delta(f)] \; = \; F^{-1}[G(f) \cdot S(f)] \; = \; g(t) * S(t)$

$\qquad\qquad\text{Now, } S(t) \; = \; F^{-1}[S(f)]$

$$= \; \frac{1}{f_s} \sum \delta(t - n/f_s)$$

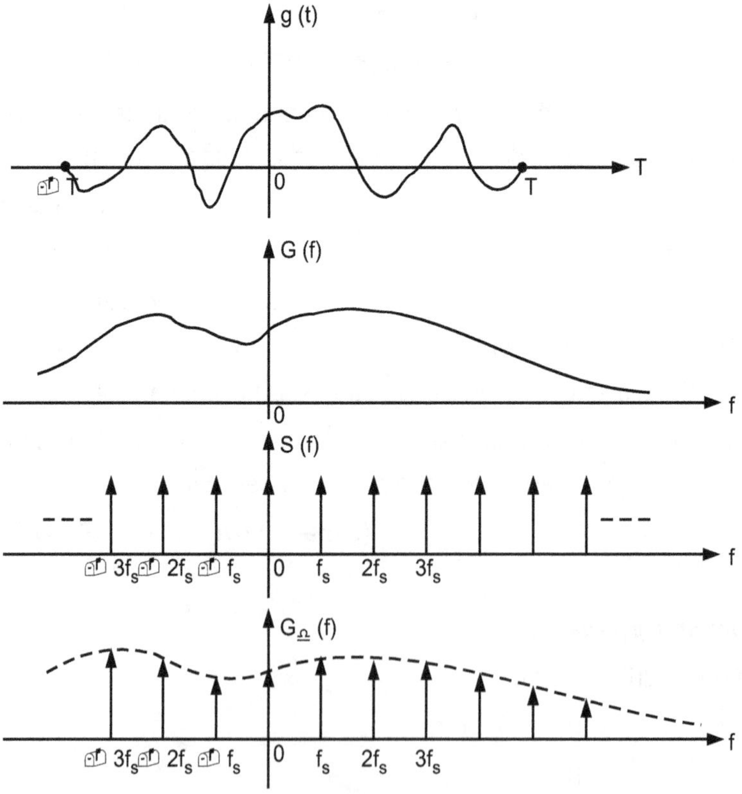

Fig. 1.27

$$\therefore \quad g_\delta(t) = g(t) * \frac{1}{f_s} \Sigma \, \delta\left(t - \frac{n}{f_s}\right) = \frac{1}{f_s} \sum_{n=-\infty}^{\infty} g\left(t - \frac{n}{f_s}\right)$$

Thus, $g_\delta(t)$ consists of $g(t)$ and its shifted version. $g(t)$ can be recovered from $g_\delta(t)$ provided there is no overlap of $g(t)$ and its shifted versions. It is possible if $f_s \leq \frac{1}{2T}$.

$$\text{If } f_s = \frac{1}{2T}$$

$$\therefore \quad g_\delta(t) = 2T \sum_{n=-\infty}^{\infty} g(t - 2nT)$$

Now, let us see how we can recover $G(f)$ from its samples $G_\delta(f)$.

$$G_\delta(f) = \sum_{n=-\infty}^{\infty} G(nf_s) \, \delta(f - nf_s)$$

$$\text{Put } f_s = \frac{1}{2T}$$

$$G_\delta(f) = \sum_{n=-\infty}^{\infty} G\left(\frac{n}{2T}\right) \delta\left(f - \frac{n}{2T}\right)$$

$$\therefore \quad g_\delta(t) = \sum_{n=-\infty}^{\infty} G\left(\frac{n}{2T}\right) e^{\frac{j2\pi nt}{2T}}$$

$$\text{But } g_\delta(t) = 2T \sum_{n=-\infty}^{\infty} g(t - 2nT)$$

$$= 2T \, g(t) + 2T \sum_{\substack{n=-\infty \\ n \neq 0}}^{\infty} g(t - 2nT)$$

$$\therefore \quad g(t) = \frac{1}{2T} g_\delta(t) \qquad\qquad -T < t < T$$

$$= \frac{1}{2T} \sum_{n=-\infty}^{\infty} G\left(\frac{n}{2T}\right) e^{\frac{j2\pi nt}{2T}} \qquad\qquad \ldots T < t < T$$

$$\therefore \quad G(f) = F[g(t)]$$

$$= \int_{-\infty}^{\infty} g(t) \, e^{-j2\pi ft}$$

$$= \int_{-\infty}^{\infty} \frac{1}{2T} \sum_{n=-\infty}^{\infty} G\left(\frac{n}{2T}\right) e^{\frac{j2\pi nt}{2T}} e^{-j2\pi fT} \, dt \qquad\qquad -T < t < T$$

$$= \int_{-\infty}^{\infty} \frac{1}{2T} \sum_{n=-\infty}^{\infty} G\left(\frac{n}{2T}\right) e^{\frac{j2\pi nt}{2T}} \cdot e^{-j2\pi fT} \, dt$$

$$= \sum_{n=-\infty}^{\infty} \frac{1}{2T} G\left(\frac{n}{2T}\right) \int_{-T}^{T} e^{-j2\pi fT \left[f - \frac{n}{2T}\right]} \, dt$$

$$= \sum_{n=-\infty}^{\infty} G\left(\frac{n}{2T}\right) \frac{\sin[2\pi fT - \pi n]}{(2\pi fT - \pi n)}$$

U.Q. 9 : Differentiate between natural, ideal and flat top sampling diagrammatically with application. **(8 marks) (May 2008)**

Solution : Refer Section 1.2.4, 1.2.5 and 1.2.6

U.Q. 10 : Explain Aperture Effect by drawing the spectrum of sampling and sampled signals. Suggest a remedial measure to compensate for aperture effect.

(4 marks) (November 2008)

Solution : Refer Section 1.2.7

U.Q. 11 : An continuous time signal g(t) of finite energy and infinite duration which is strictly band limited to W Hz is ideally sampled $g_\delta(t)$ i.e.

$$g_\delta(t) = \sum_{n=-\infty}^{\infty} g(nT_S) \, \delta(t - nT_S)$$

also

$$g_\delta(t) \rightleftharpoons f_S \sum_{m=-\infty}^{\infty} G(f - mf_S)$$

Determine the expression of $G_\delta(f)$ and $G(f)$. Draw the spectrum of $G_\delta(f)$ and $G(f)$ with and without Aliasing.

Reconstruct the signal g(t) and derive interpolation formula, comment on it.

(6 marks) (November 2008)

Solution : Refer Section 1.2.3

U.Q. 12 : Represent and discuss on the time domain and frequency domain approach of sampling theorem. **(8 marks) (May 2009)**

Solution : Refer U.Q. 8.

Dec. 2010

U.Q. 13 : What is aperture effect? What is the effect of pulse duration on aperture effect? Justify your answer with suitable mathematical analysis. **(10)**

Solution : Refer Section 1.2.7

U.Q. 14 : A signal m(t) bandlimited to 4 KHz is sampled at a rate 50% higher than Nyquist rate, The maximum acceptable error in the sample amplitude is I% of peak amplitude. The quantized samples are binary coded. Find minimum bandwidth of a channel required to transmit the encoded binary signal.   **(8)**

Solution : Given : $W = 4$ kHz

∴   Nyquist rate $= 8$ kHz

∴   Sampling rate $= 8$ kHz $+ 50\%$ of 8 kHz

$= 12$ kHz

Maximum quantization error $= \pm \dfrac{\Delta}{2}$

∴ $\dfrac{\Delta}{2} = 1\%$ of A_{max}

∴ $\dfrac{\Delta}{2} = 0.01\ A_{max}$

∴ $\Delta = 0.02\ A_{max}$

Now, number of quantization levels L,

$$L = \frac{2\ A_{max}}{\Delta} = \frac{2\ A_{max}}{0.02\ A_{max}} = 100$$

∴   Number of bits per quantization level

$$v = \log_2 L = \log_2 100$$
$$= 6.64$$

We select $v = 7$ bits

Minimum transmission bandwidth

$$(B_T)_{min} = v \times W = 7 \times 4\ \text{kHz}$$
$$= 28\ \text{kHz}$$

May 2011

U.Q. 15 : Explain formatting and transmission of different baseband signals with the help of block diagram of digital communication system.   **(6)**

Solution : Refer Sections 1.1.3 and 1.2

U.Q. 16 : Why oversampling is needed ? Draw and explain effect of undersampling in time domain and in frequency domain.   **(6)**

Solution : Refer Sections 1.2.8

U.Q. 17: A signal m (t) = cos 200 πt + 2 cos 320 πt is ideally sampled at fs = 300 Hz. If the sampled signal is passed through an ideal LPF with a cut-off frequency of   250 Hz, what frequency components will appear at the output?   **(4)**

Solution : Given : $m(t) = \cos(200\pi t) + 2\cos(320\pi t)$

∴ $f_1 = 100$ Hz

and $f_2 = 160$ Hz

Now, $f_s = 320$ Hz

The spectrum of signal m(t) is

$$M(f) = \frac{1}{2} [\delta(f - 100) + \delta(f + 100) + 2\delta(f - 160) + 2\delta(f + 160)]$$

The spectrum of sampled signal is,

$$\frac{1}{2} f_s[(\delta(f - 100) + \delta(f + 100) + 2\delta(f - 160) + 2\delta(f + 160)$$

$$+ \delta(f - 420) + \delta(f - 220)$$

$$+ 2\delta(f - 480) + 2\delta(f - 160)$$

$$+ \delta(f - 740) + \delta(f - 540)$$

$$+ 2\delta(f - 800) + 2\delta(f - 480) + \ldots\ldots$$

When above signal is passed through LPF of cut-off frequency 250 Hz, we get

$$M(f)_{LPF} = \frac{1}{2} f_s [\delta(f - 100) + \delta(f + 100) + 2\delta(f - 160) + 2\delta(f + 160)$$

$$+ \delta(f - 220) + 2\delta(f - 160)]$$

Thus, frequency components with frequency 100 Hz, 160 Hz, 220 Hz and 160 Hz will appear at the output.

$$\boxed{\text{Dec. 2011}}$$

U.Q. 18 : Explain with a neat sketch, the block diagram of digital communication system and discuss the various formatting techniques involved in it. **(8)**

Solution : Refer Sections 1.1.3 and 1.2

U.Q. 19 : The signal g(t) = 10 cos (40 πt) cos (400 πt) is sampled at the rate of 500 samples/sec.

(i) Determine the Nyquist rate.

(ii) Calculate the cut-off frequency of ideal reconstruction filter.

(iii) Draw the spectrum of resulting sampled signal.

(iv) If g(t) is considered to be a band pass signal, determine the lowest permissible sampling rate.

Solution : Given :

$$g(t) = 10 \cos (40 \pi t) \cdot \cos (400 \pi t)$$

$$= 5 [\cos (440 \pi t) + \cos (360 \pi t)]$$

$$f_1 = 220 \text{ Hz, } f_2 = 180 \text{ Hz}$$

∴

$$f_m = 220 \text{ Hz}$$

$$G(f) = \frac{5}{2} [\delta(f \pm 220) + \delta(f \pm 180)]$$

(i) Nyquist rate $f_s = 2f_m = 440$ Hz

(ii) Cut-off frequency for ideal reconstruction filter will be 220 Hz.

(iii) To draw spectrum the sampled signal will be

$$G_s(f) = f_s \sum_{m=-\infty}^{\infty} G(f - mf_s)$$

$$= \frac{5f_s}{2} G(f) + \frac{5}{2}f_s \sum_{m=-\infty}^{\infty} \delta(f \pm 220 - mf_s) + \delta(f \pm 180 - mf_s)$$

$$= \frac{5f_s}{2}[\delta(f - 280) + \delta(f - 720) + \delta(f - 320) + \delta(f - 680) + \dots$$

The spectrum will be

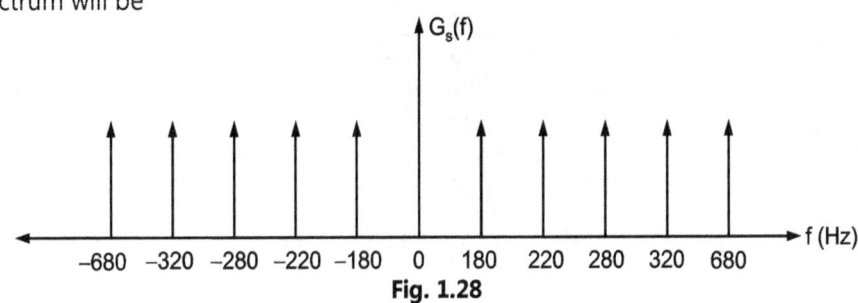

Fig. 1.28

(iv) $f_H = 220$ Hz

$f_L = 180$ Hz

∴ $B = f_H - f_L = 40$ Hz

$$Q = \frac{f_H}{B} = 5.5$$

∴ Applying bandpass sampling criteria

$$2 \times B \left[\frac{Q}{n}\right] \leq f_s \leq 2B \left[\frac{Q-1}{n-1}\right]$$

$$2 \times 40 \times \left[\frac{5.5}{n}\right] \leq f_s \leq 2 \times 40 \left[\frac{5.5-1}{n-1}\right]$$

Q is not an integer

∴ $n = \text{int}(Q) = 5$

∴ $$2 \times 40 \left[\frac{5.5}{5}\right] \leq f_s \leq 2 \times 40 \left[\frac{4.5}{4}\right]$$

$88 \leq f_s \leq 90$

∴ Minimum sampling frequency $f_s = 88$ Hz.

May 2012

U.Q. 20 : What is a digital baseband system? Explain how a textual data is encoded using ASCII and Baudot codes with suitable examples.   (8)

Solution : Refer Sections 1.1.3 and 1.2

U.Q. 21 : The spectrum of the signal g(t) is shown in Fig. 1 below. This signal is naturally sampled with periodic team of rectangular pulses of duration $\dfrac{50}{3}$ m secs. Plot the spectrum of sampled signal for frequencies upto 100 Hz for the following two conditions: **(10)**

(i) f_s = Nyquist Rate, (ii) f_s = 20 samples/sec.

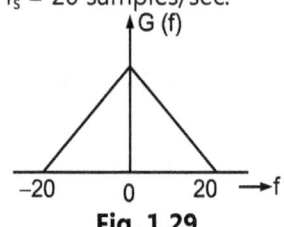

G (f)

-20   0   20 →f

Fig. 1.29

Solution : Given : $\qquad\qquad\qquad\qquad f_m = 20$ Hz

$$\text{Pulse duration, T} = \frac{50}{3}\ \text{ms}$$

(i) $\qquad\qquad f_s$ = Nyquist rate = $2\,f_m$ = 40 Hz

The sampled signal will be $\qquad G_s(f) = T\ \text{sinc}\ (fT)\ e^{-j2\pi fT}\ \displaystyle\sum_{m=\infty}^{\infty} G(f - mf_s)$

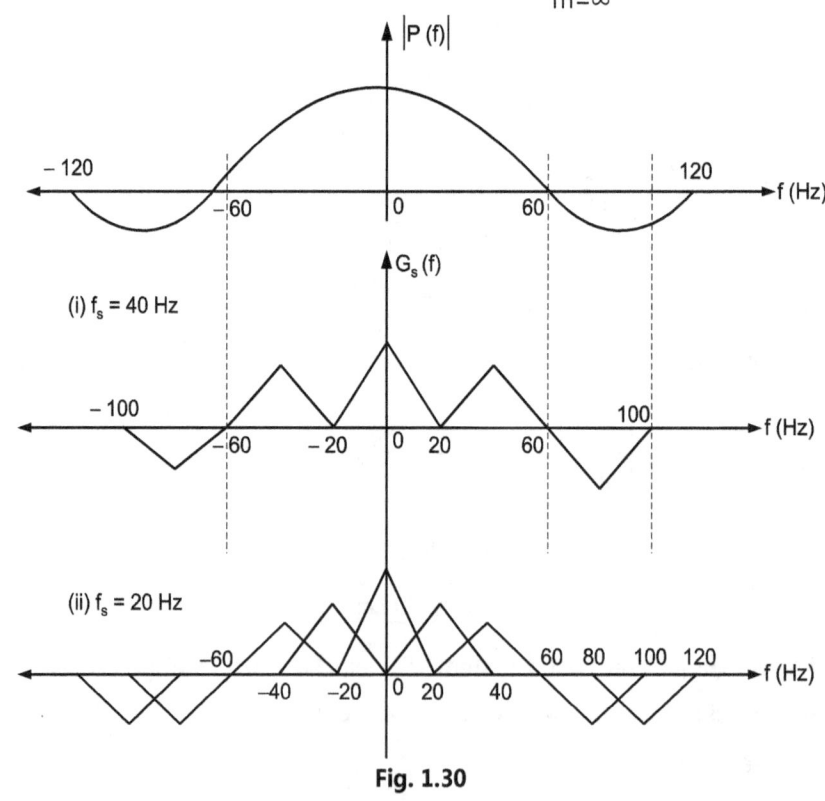

$|P\ (f)|$

- 120   120
   -60   0   60   →f (Hz)

(i) f_s = 40 Hz

$G_s\ (f)$

- 100   100
   -60   - 20   0   20   60   →f (Hz)

(ii) f_s = 20 Hz

-60   60 80   100 120
   -40   -20   0   20   40   →f (Hz)

Fig. 1.30

U.Q. 22 : Explain with help of diagram the formatting steps for textual, analog and digital data with example. **(8)**

Solution : Refer Section 1.2

U.Q. 23 : A voice signal (300 to 3300 Hz) is digitized such that the quantization distortion $<=\pm0.1\%$ of peak to peak signal voltage Assume a sampling rate of 8000 samples/s and a multilevel PAM waveform with 32 levels. Find the theoretical minimum system bandwidth that avoids ISI. **(8)**

Solution : Given : $\dfrac{\Delta}{2} \le \pm 0.1\%$ of A_{max}

$\therefore \quad \dfrac{\Delta}{2} \le 0.001\, A_{max}$

$$f_s = 8000 \text{ samples/s}$$

M-ary waveform with M = 32.

$\therefore$ Number of bits per level = 5.

Number of quantization levels;

$$L = \frac{2A_{max}}{\Delta} = \frac{2A_{max}}{2 \times 0.001\, A_{max}}$$
$$= 1000$$

$\therefore$ Number of bits per sample

$$v = \log_2 1000$$
$$= 10 \text{ bits.}$$

Hence, there will be 2 levels per sample. (Since there are 5 bits/level).

$\therefore \qquad$ Symbol rate (r) = Number of samples/sec × Number of symbols per sample

$$= 8000 \times 2 = 16000 \text{ symbols/sec}$$

$\therefore \qquad$ Bandwidth $= \dfrac{r}{2} = 8000 \text{ Hz}$

Dec. 2012

U.Q. 24 : Explain with help of diagram the formatting steps for textual, analog and digital data with example. **(8)**

Solution : Refer Sections 1.2

May 2013

U.Q. 25 : Explain with a neat sketch, the block diagram of digital communication system and discuss the various formatting techniques involved in it. **(8)**

Solution : Refer Section 1.1.3 and 1.2

Dec. 2014

U.Q. 26 : With the help of detail diagram explain function of each block of digital communication system. **(8)**

Solution : Refer Section 1.1.3 and 1.2

May 2014

U.Q. 27 : Waveform g(t) = 20+20 sin(500t+30), is to be sampled periodically and reproduced from these sample values- **(8)**

(1) Find the maximum allowable time interval between sample values.

(2) How many sample values need to be stored in order to reproduce 1 sec of this waveform if sampled accounting to the results in 1.

(3) Determine and sketch the spectrum of the sampled signal when sampling frequency fs = 750 Hz.

Solution : Given $\qquad$ g(t) = 20 + 20 sin (500 t + 30)

(1) The signal contains dc and sinusoid of frequency

$$2\pi f_1 = 500$$

$$f_1 = \frac{500}{2\pi} \cong 80 \text{ Hz}$$

∴ Maximum frequency component f_m = 80 Hz

∴ Minimum sampling frequency f_s = 2 f_m = 160 Hz

∴ Maximum Allowable time $T_s = \dfrac{1}{f_s} = 6.25$ ms

(2) Sampling frequency $\qquad$ f_s = 160 Hz

∴ Number of samples per second = 160

(3) The sketch of sampled spectrum will be as below when f_s = 750 kHz.

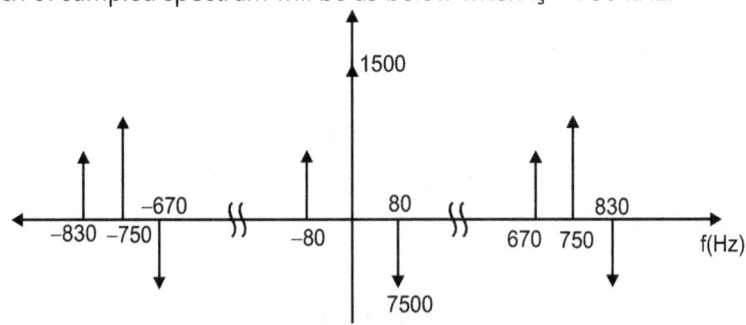

Fig. 1.31

U.Q. 28 : What is aperture effect ? What is the effect of pulse duration on aperture effect ? **(8)**

Solution : Refer Section 1.2.7

SUMMARY

1. Baseband systems transform and transmit baseband signal.

2. The source information can be in digital or analog form.

3. Sampling is used to convert analog signal in digital form.

4. Sampling theorem is the basis of sampling process.

5. According to Sampling theorem, "A bandlimited signal at finite energy having frequency components below W Hz, can be completely described by specifying values of signal at uniform intervals of $T_s \leq \dfrac{1}{2W}$ sec.

6. There are three types of sampling :

   (i)   Impulse or Ideal sampling

   (ii) Natural sampling

   (iii) Flat-top sampling.

7. The sampling rate f_s = 2W is called Nyquist rate and $T_s = \dfrac{1}{2W}$ is Nyquist interval.

8. If f_s < 2W, it results into aliasing i.e. high frequency components are folded back into the low frequency region of the spectrum of original signal.

9. Flat top sampling results into aperture effect where high frequency components of the signal are attenuated.

EXERCISE

1. State and prove sampling theorem in time domain.

2. What is Nyquist rate and Nyquist interval ?

3. What is aliasing ? How it can be reduced ?

4. What is aperture effect ? How it can be reduced ?

5. What is flat-top sampling ? Derive an expression of spectrum of flat-top sampled signal.

6. What is natural sampling ? Derive an expression of spectrum of naturally sampled signal.

7. What is ideal sampling ? Derive and draw the spectrum of ideally sampled signal.

8. Compare the three techniques of sampling.

9. Explain the practical aspects of natural and flat-top sampling with waveforms. Comment on recovery of baseband signal. **(Nov. 2009)**

10. An continuous time signal g (t) of finite energy and infinite duration which is strictly band limited to W Hz is ideally sampled gδ (t) i.e.

$$g\delta(t) \; = \; \sum_{n=-\infty}^{\infty} g(nTs)\, \delta(t-nTs)$$

also,

$$g\delta(t) \; \Leftrightarrow fs \; \sum_{m=-\infty}^{\infty} G(f-mfs)$$

Determine the expression of Gδ(f) and G(f). Draw the spectrum of Gδ(f) and G(f) with and without Aliasing. Reconstruct the signal g(t) and derive interpolation formulae, comment on it. **(Nov. 2008)**

11. Explain the term aperture effect and method to minimize, with the help of neat time domain and frequency domain diagrams. **(Dec. 2005)**

PULSE CODE MODULATION

2.1 INTRODUCTION

- We can transmit analog signal in digital format.

- The different methods of doing this are Pulse Code Modulation (PCM), Differential Pulse Code Modulation (DPCM), Delta Modulation (DM), Adaptive Delta Modulation (ADM), Linear Predictive Coding (LPC), etc.

- Pulse Code Modulation (PCM) is a method of converting an analog signal into digital form.

- The information contained in instantaneous samples of analog signal is represented by digital words in a serial bit stream.

- It is a digital pulse modulation technique.

- It is also a waveform coding technique.

- It is a simple technique in which the same information is sampled and quantized to one of the L levels.

- Each quantized level is digitally encoded into v-bits.

2.2 PCM GENERATION AND RECONSTRUCTION

- When analog signal is converted into digital format, the two basic operations required are :

  (i) Time Discretization   (ii) Amplitude Discretization.

- Sampling operation does time discretization, whereas amplitude discretization can be achieved using quantization.

- The quantized amplitudes are converted into sequence of symbols (usually binary). They are called codewords.

- The general block diagram of a PCM system is shown in Fig. 2.1 (a).

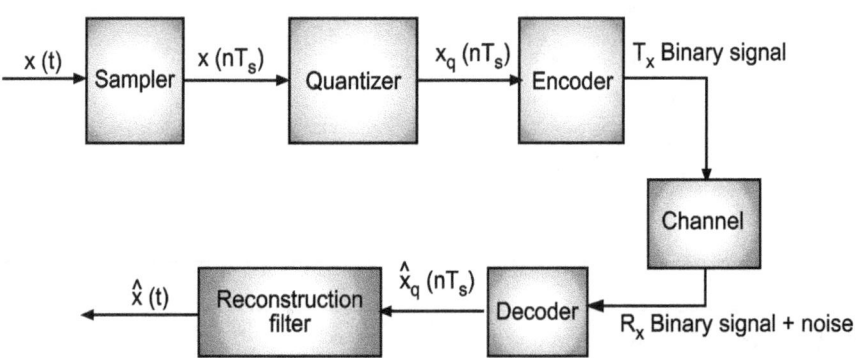

Fig. 2.1 (a) : PCM system

- x(t) is analog information signal to be transmitted.

- It is sampled at intervals t = nTs to given x(nTs) by sampler block.

- The quantizer converts each sample to one of the pre-selected set of finite number of amplitudes.

- The encoder represents the quantized samples by v-bit codeword.

- The bits are transmitted over channel and received by the receiver.

- The decoder converts v-bit codewords into corresponding samples.

- The reconstruction filter interpolates the samples to recover the analog information $\hat{x}(t)$ which will be approximately same version of $x(t)$.

- Now, let us go into more details of the PCM systems and see what additional things are required. More detailed block diagram is shown in Figs. 2.1 (b) and (c).

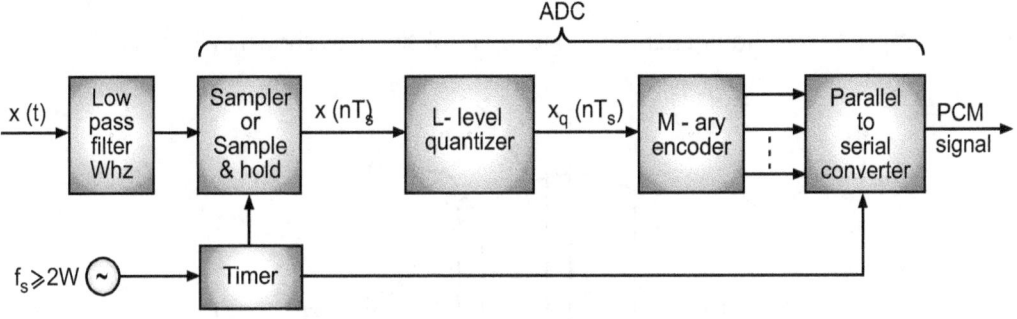

(b) PCM transmitter

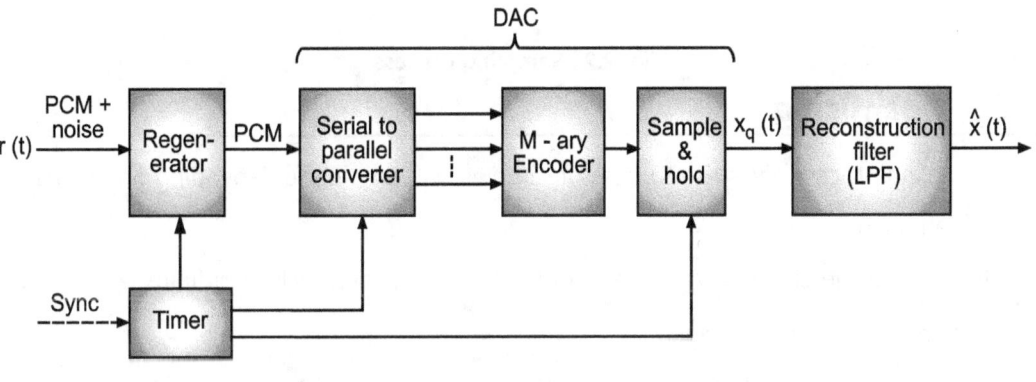

(c) PCM receiver

Fig. 2.1

2.2.1 Low Pass Filter

- In order to convert an analog signal into digital form, we need to first sample the signal.

- The practical signals are time limited. Hence they will have infinite bandwidth. The sampling frequency required to sample such signals will be infinite. Hence we need to limit the bandwidth of the signal to say W Hz.

- Hence, we pass the signal which is time limited and hence having infinite bandwidth through a low pass filter. This filter is also called **antialias filter.** By doing so we will be loging some information from the original signal.

2.2.2 Sampling

- The low pass filtered analog signal is sampled with sampling rate slightly above Nyquist rate (fs > 2W).
- This will create a guard band to facilitate use of practical low pass filter for reconstruction.
- The sampling operation generates a flat-top PAM signal as shown in Fig. 2.2.

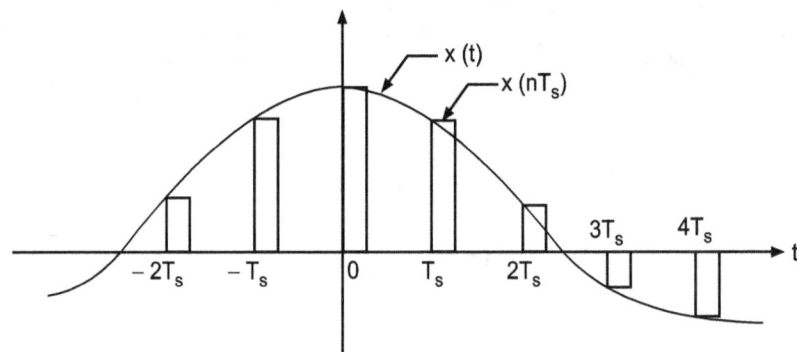

Fig. 2.2 : Sampling process

2.2.3 Quantizing

- Sampling process gives rise to train of samples with amplitude depending on the instant of sampling.
- If the message signal x (t) ranges from + A to − A, there will be infinite levels x (nT$_s$) assumes between this range.
- In order to convert the samples into bit stream, we need to limit the number of levels of sampled signal.
- For this the amplitude range (− A, A), is divided to finite number of levels and the sampled amplitude is approximated to nearest possible level.
- This process is called quantizing. It is shown in Fig. 2.3.
- This means original continuous signal is approximated by a signal having discrete amplitudes from an available set.

- Thus, amplitude quantization is the process of transforming sample amplitude x (nT$_s$) at t = nT$_s$ into a discrete amplitude x$_q$ (nT$_s$) taken from finite set of amplitudes.

- The quantization process is assumed to be memory less and instantaneous.

- Memory less means the quantization of current sample does not depend on its past values.

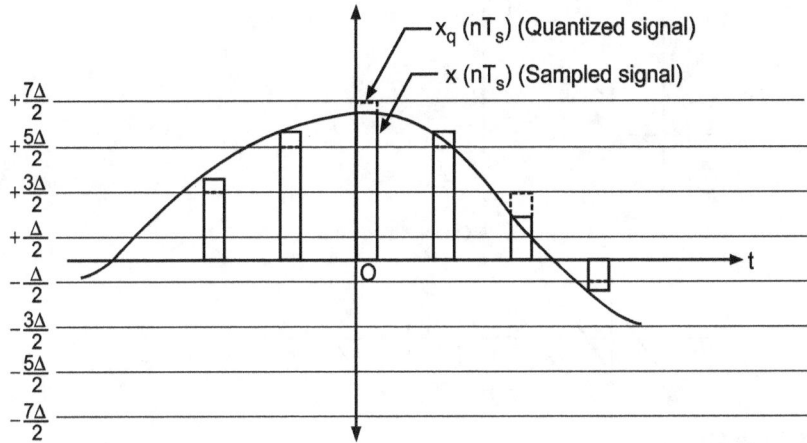

Fig. 2.3 : Quantization process

- Let L be total number of amplitude levels used in a quantizer. There will be L decision level or decision thresholds.

- The input X (nT$_s$) is transformed into X$_q$ (nT$_s$) which is called representation level or reconstruction level. Thus, the output of quantizer will be one of the L representation levels.

- The difference between two adjacent representation levels is called quantum or step size (Δ).

- Quantizer can be of uniform or non-uniform type.

- In uniform quantizer the representation levels are uniformly spaced.

- In non-uniform quantizer the approximated levels are spaced non-uniformly.

- The quantizer characteristics can be midtread or midrise type. The input-output characteristics of these types of quantizers are shown in Fig. 2.4 (a) and (b).

(a) Midtread type :

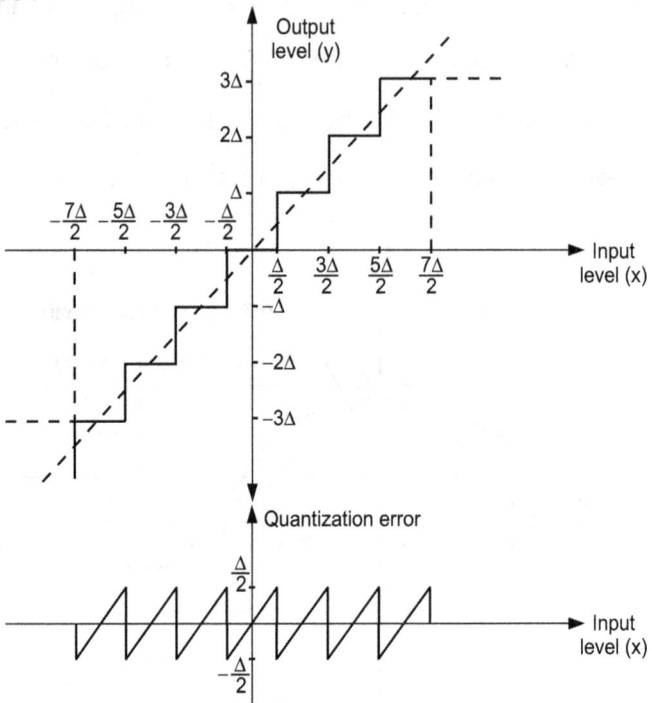

(b) Midrise type :

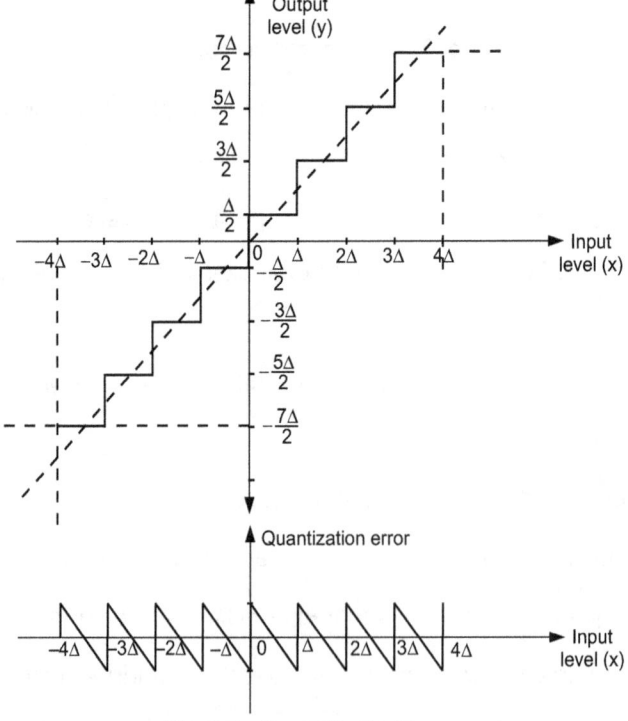

Fig. 2.4 : Quantization types

- The input signal level to quantizer is represented by x and output level is y.
- The error signal which is difference between input and output is shown for midtread type quantizer.
- The error will always be less than or equal to $\Delta/2$.
- Fig. 2.5 illustrates the quantization error resulting from quantization process.
- The signal x(t) is input to the quantizer with quantization levels, 0, ±2, ±4.
- The quantized signal $x_q(t)$ is output from the quantizer.
- The error signal $e(t) = x(t) - x_q(t)$ is random signal hence termed as quantization noise.
- Note that the quantization process shown in Fig. 2.3 was for the case if the input quantizer is set of equispaced samples of x(t). In that case, output was also sequence of equispace samples. It can be implemented using digital processor.
- The quantization process shown in Fig. 2.5 uses Analog to Digital Converter (ADC).

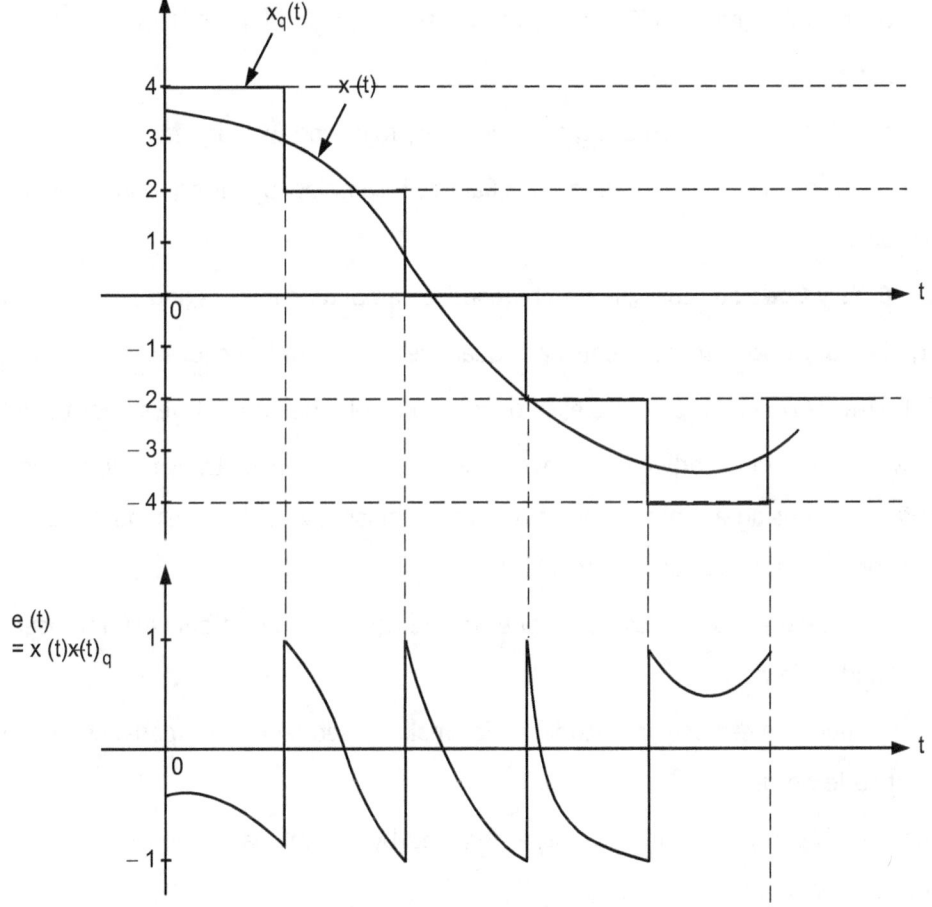

Fig. 2.5 : Quantization process

Comparison of Midrise and Midtread Quantizer :

- When there is no input (zero input level) to quantizer the output of midtread will be zero whereas midrise output will be $\pm \Delta/2$. This situation can arise in telephony when there is silence in speech or handset is covered for some purpose.

- The average noise power during zero input condition in will be $\Delta^2/4 \left[\frac{1}{2}\left(\frac{\Delta}{2}\right)^2 + \frac{1}{2}\left(-\frac{\Delta}{2}\right)^2 \right]$ in case of midrise and it will be zero for midtread. Hence, midtread is better in terms of performance.

- The number of quantization levels in case of midrise will be even and for midtread will be odd. But for encoding these levels should be even.

2.2.4 Encoding

- The quantized signal x_q (nT_s) can be converted into digital format. This process is called encoding.

- The signal can be encoded using any one of the following techniques.

- It is one-to-one representation of quantized samples by using code elements or symbols.

    (i) Binary Code : It represents each quantized amplitude into 0's and 1's.

    (ii) Ternary Code : It represents each quantized level into three levels.

    (iii) M-ary Code : It represents each quantized amplitude into M levels (mor than 3).

- However, maximum advantages over the effect of noise in transmission medium is obtained by using a binary code. It is because binary symbols withstand relatively high level of noise and are easy to regenerate.

- There are several ways to establish one-to-one correspondence between representation level and code word.

- For example, we can use an encoder which makes n sequential comparisons to generate n-bit code word.

- The level is compared with a voltage obtained by a combination of reference voltages proportional to 2^7, 2^6, 2^5, ..., 2^0.

- Hence, if we are using 3-bit PCM, then we can have $2^3 = 8$ quantization levels into which we have to divide the signal amplitudes $-A_{max}$ to $+A_{max}$. The quantized output can be encoded in 3-bit format as follows :

Quantized Level	Encoder Output
$-A_{max}\left(-\dfrac{7\Delta}{2}\right)$	000
$-3A_{max}/4\left(-\dfrac{5\Delta}{2}\right)$	001
$-2A_{max}/4\left(-\dfrac{3\Delta}{2}\right)$	010
$-A_{max}/4\left(-\dfrac{\Delta}{2}\right)$	011
$+A_{max}/4\left(+\dfrac{\Delta}{2}\right)$	100
$+2A_{max}/4\left(+\dfrac{3\Delta}{2}\right)$	101
$+3A_{max}/4\left(+\dfrac{5\Delta}{2}\right)$	110
$+A_{max}\left(+\dfrac{7\Delta}{2}\right)$	111

- The number of bits required for encoding a sample depends on number of quantization levels.

- If there are L quantization levels, then number of bits required for encoding a sample will be $\log_2 L$.

- In other words, if we use v bits for encoding there will be 2^v quantization levels.

  i.e. $\boxed{L = 2^v}$ or $\boxed{v = \log_2 L}$ ... (2.1)

- Consider the following example shown in Fig. 2.6.

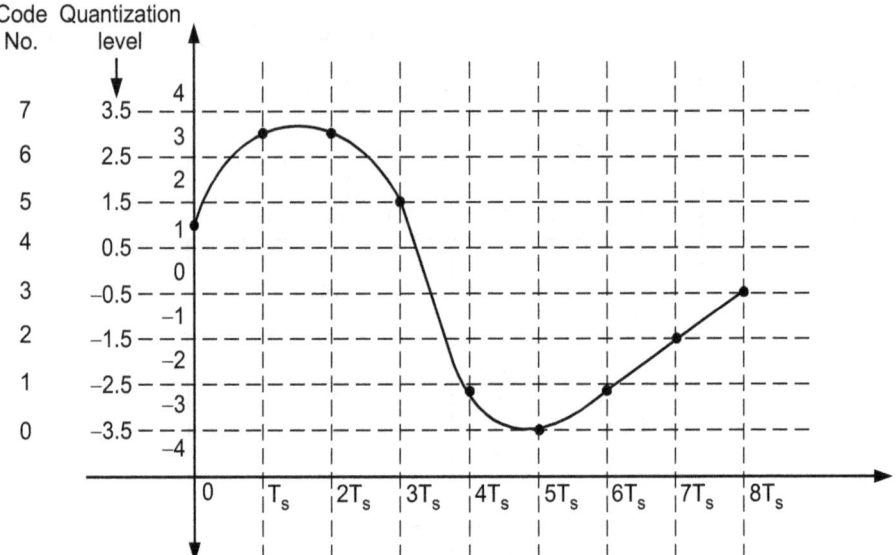

Fig. 2.6 : Encoding

Natural sample values	1	2.8	2.9	1.5	−2.9	−3.3	−2.6	−1.6	−0.7
Quantized values	1.5	2.5	2.5	1.5	−2.5	−3.5	−2.5	−1.5	−0.5
Code number	5	6	6	5	1	0	1	2	3
PCM output	101	110	110	101	001	000	001	010	011

2.2.5 Regeneration

- The most important feature of PCM system lies in ability to control distortion and noise.
- This is achieved by reconstructing the PCM signal by means of chain of regenerative repeaters located at sufficiently close spacing.
- It consists of circuit which reshapes the distorted signal into clean pulses.
- Fig. 2.7 shows block diagram of regenerative repeaters.

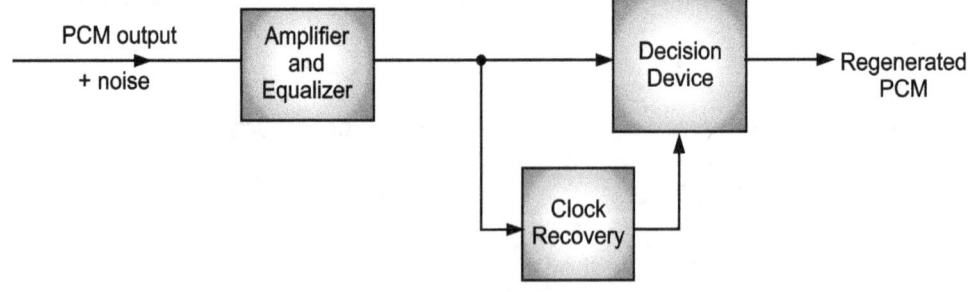

Fig. 2.7 : Regenerative repeater

- The three basic functions performed by regenerative repeater are :
  - (i)   Equalization
  - (ii) Clock Recovery (Timing)
  - (iii) Decision-making.
- When the PCM signal is transmitted through channel it undergoes amplitude and phase distortion. Equaliser is used to compensate for these distortions.
- The receiver pulses are to be sampled at every bit duration to recover the clock from them for timing purpose. The clock recovery circuit or timing circuit does this.
- The decision device is used to decide in every bit interval, the received bit (1/0) based on received sample of the pulse and preset threshold.

2.2.6 Decoding

- The first operation in the receiver is to regenerate the received pulses (1's and 0's).
- These pulses are regrouped into code words and decoded into quantized signal.
- The decoding process involves generating a pulse whose amplitude is linear sum of 1's and 0's in the codeword (similar to binary to decimal conversion).
- This process is also called Digital to Analog Conversion (DAC).

2.2.7 Reconstruction Filters

- The decoded output (DAC output) is staircase waveform.
- A low pass filter whose cut-off frequency is equal to message bandwidth W Hz is used to smoothen out the DAC output.

2.2.8 Bandwidth Requirement of PCM

- How much bandwidth is required for transmission of PCM signal ?
- If the signal bandwidth is W Hz, then it requires to be sampled at a rate 2W samples per second.

  If each sample is encoded into v bits then the bit rate i.e. number of bits per second will be,

$$\text{Bit rate (r)} = \text{Number of samples per second} \times \text{Number of bits per sample}$$

$$\therefore \qquad r = f_s \times v$$

$$\therefore \qquad \boxed{r = vf_s} \qquad\qquad\qquad \text{... (2.2)}$$

- Therefore, bandwidth needed for PCM will be,

$$B_T = \frac{1}{2} \times r = \frac{1}{2} vf_s$$ ... (2.3)

- The minimum bandwidth requirement for transmission of PCM signal will be when $f_s = 2W$

$$\therefore \qquad (B_T)_{min} = \frac{1}{2} v \times 2W = v \times W$$ ... (2.4)

Example 2.1 : An analog signal with maximum frequency 3 kHz is transmitted using binary PCM. The number of quantization levels used are 16. Find minimum bandwidth requirement.

Solution : Given :   W = 3 kHz

Number of quantization levels = L = 16

$\qquad \therefore$ Sampling rate f_s = $2 \times W$

$\qquad\qquad\qquad\qquad = 2 \times 3 = 6$ kHz

Since, $L = 2^v$

Number of bits per sample (v) = $\log_2 L$

$\qquad\qquad\qquad\qquad = \log_2 16$

$\qquad\qquad\qquad\qquad = 4$

$\therefore$ Bit rate of this system

$\qquad\qquad r$ = $v \times f_s$ = 4×6 kHz

$\qquad\qquad\qquad = 24$ kbps

Minimum bandwidth required

$\qquad\qquad (B_T)_{min}$ = $\frac{1}{2} \times v \times 2W$

$\qquad\qquad\qquad\qquad = \frac{1}{2} \times 24$

$\qquad\qquad\qquad\qquad = 12$ kHz

2.3 QUANTIZATION NOISE

- The process of quantization introduces quantization error in the PCM signal. This is because sampled output is approximated to nearest level.

- If signal x (t) is sampled at a rate $\dfrac{1}{T_s}$ then x (nT_s) will be the sample at t = nT_s.

- Let us say that it is approximated to x_q (nT_s) after quantization. The error difference q = x (nT_s) – x_q (nT_s) is called quantization noise.

Quantizer output for a typical input signal is shown in Fig. 2.8 (a). The plot of quantization error alongwith the quantized signal is shown in Fig. 2.8 (b).

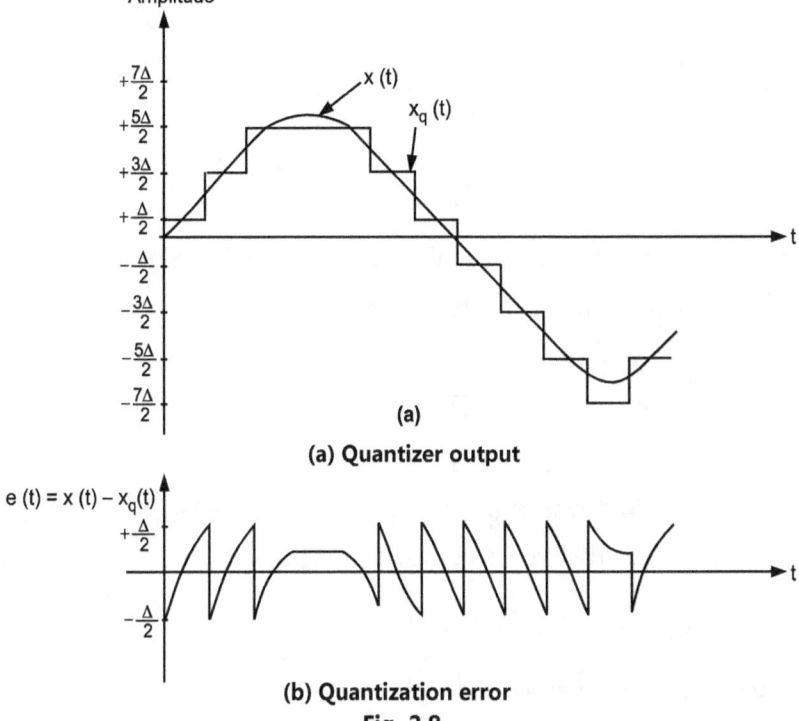

(a)

(a) Quantizer output

(b) Quantization error

Fig. 2.8

- It can be seen from the quantization error graph that the quantization error takes on any value between + Δ/2 and – Δ/2.

- Thus, it is uniformly distributed random variable with zero mean. Let us denote this variable as Q.

- The probability density function for Q is plotted in Fig. 2.9.

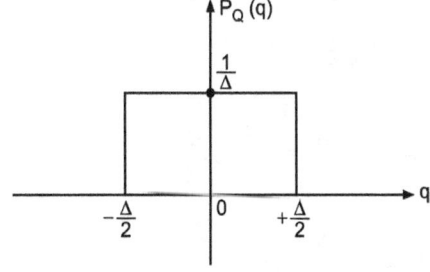

Fig. 2.9 : PDF of Quantization error

Hence,
$$P_Q(q) = \begin{cases} \dfrac{1}{\Delta} & ; \quad -\dfrac{\Delta}{2} \le q \le +\dfrac{\Delta}{2} \\ 0 & ; \quad \text{Otherwise} \end{cases}$$
... (2.5)

The variance can be calculated as,

$$\sigma_Q^2 = \int_{-\Delta/2}^{\Delta/2} q^2\, P_Q(q)\, dq = \int_{-\Delta/2}^{\Delta/2} q^2 \times \frac{1}{\Delta}\, dq$$

$$= \frac{1}{\Delta}\left[\frac{q^3}{3}\right]_{-\Delta/2}^{\Delta/2}$$

$$= \frac{\Delta^2}{12} \qquad\qquad\qquad \text{... (2.6)}$$

- This variance is mean square value of quantization noise. Since mean value is zero, $(E[X^2] = \sigma_X^2 - m_X^2)$. Hence, this is quantization noise power.

- ∴   Quantization noise power,

$$\boxed{P_{Nq} = \frac{\Delta^2}{12}}$$

- Let us consider an input whose amplitude ranges from $-A_{max}$ to $+A_{max}$. Assuming uniform quantizer of midrise type, step size is given by,

$$\Delta = \frac{2\,A_{max}}{L} \qquad\qquad \text{... (2.7)}$$

where, L is the number of representation levels.

- Let v be number of bits per sample.

∴ $\qquad\qquad\qquad L = 2^v$

or $\qquad\qquad\qquad v = \log_2 L$

∴ $\qquad\qquad\qquad \Delta = \dfrac{2\,A_{max}}{2^v} \qquad\qquad \text{... (2.8)}$

- Hence, quantization noise will be,

∴ $\qquad P_{Nq} = \dfrac{\Delta^2}{12} = \dfrac{4\,A_{max}^2}{2^{2v} \times 12} = \dfrac{A_{max}^2}{3L^2}$

$$\boxed{P_{Nq} = \frac{A_{max}^2}{3 \times 2^{2v}}} \qquad\qquad \text{... (2.9)}$$

- Therefore, the output signal-to-noise ratio of uniform quantizer will be,

$$\left(\frac{S}{N}\right)_0 = \frac{P_s}{P_{Nq}} \qquad \text{[P_s is signal power]}$$

$$\boxed{\left(\frac{S}{N}\right)_0 = \left(\frac{3 P_s}{A_{max}^2}\right) \times 2^{2v}} \qquad \text{... (2.10)}$$

- This equation shows that signal-to-noise ratio is proportional to bits per sample v.

- This is obvious from the fact that more number of bits per sample will increase number of levels which in turn will decrease step size. But then this will require more bandwidth as, $B_T = \frac{1}{2} v f_s$.

- If input signal is a sinusoidal signal, then signal power is,

$$P_s = \frac{A_{max}^2}{2}$$

$$\therefore \quad \left(\frac{S}{N}\right)_0 = \frac{3 \times A_{max}^2/2}{A_{max}^2} \times 2^{2v}$$

$$\left(\frac{S}{N}\right)_0 = \frac{3}{2} 2^{2v} \qquad \text{... (2.11)}$$

Or

$$\left(\frac{S}{N}\right)_0 = \frac{3L^2}{2}$$

$$\therefore \quad \left(\frac{S}{N}\right)_0 \text{ in dB} = 10 \log_{10}\left(\frac{3}{2} 2^{2v}\right)$$

$$= 10 \log_{10} \frac{3}{2} + 10 \log_{10} 2^{2v}$$

$$= 1.8 + 20 \, v \times \log 2$$

∴ For sinusoidal input

$$\left(\frac{S}{N}\right)_0 \text{ in dB} = 1.8 + 6 \, v \text{ dB} \qquad \text{... (2.12)}$$

Following table shows various values of L and v with corresponding $(SNR)_0$.

L (Levels)	v (bits/sample)	SNR (dB)
256	8	49.8
128	7	43.8
64	6	37.8
32	5	31.8

- For non-sinusoidal signals, such as voice, music etc. the signal to noise ratio is specified in terms peak signal power to average quantization noise power.

- The average quantization noise power

$$N_q = \frac{\Delta^2}{12}$$

- The peak signal power = A_{max}^2

But,
$$A_{max} = \frac{\Delta \times L}{2}$$

$\therefore$
$$A_{max}^2 = \frac{\Delta^2 L^2}{4}$$

$\therefore$ Peak signal power to average quantization noise power is,

$$\left(\frac{S}{N}\right)_{0\ peak} = \frac{\Delta^2 L^2 / 4}{\Delta^2 / 12}$$

$$\left(\frac{S}{N}\right)_{0\ peak} = 3L^2$$

- Thus, it can be seen that the signal to quantization noise ratio in PCM depends on L (number of levels).

- As $L \to \infty$, signal to noise ratio will be infinite. It means with infinite quantization levels (N_o quantisation) there will be no quantization noise.

- Thus, we have following results.

(i) Average signal power to average quantization noise power ratio is given by :

$$\left(\frac{S}{N}\right)_0 = \frac{P_s}{N_q} = \frac{P_s}{\Delta^2 / 12} = \frac{3P_s}{A_{max}^2} \times 2^{2V}$$

(ii) Average signal power to average quantization noise power ratio **if signal is sinusoidal** is given by,

$$\left(\frac{S}{N}\right)_0 = \frac{3L^2}{2} = \frac{3}{2} 2^{2V}$$

$$\left(\frac{S}{N}\right)_0 \text{ in dB} = 1.8 + 6v$$

(iii) Peak signal power to average quantization noise power ratio **for non-sinusoidal signal** is given by,

$$\left(\frac{S}{N}\right)_{0\ peak} = \frac{A_{max}^2}{\Delta^2/12} = \frac{\Delta^2 L^2/4}{\Delta^2/12} = 3L^2 = 3L^2 = 3 \times 2^{2v}$$

$\therefore$
$$\left(\frac{S}{N}\right)_{0\ peak\ in\ dB} = 4.8 + 6v$$

(iv) If P_s is average signal power and A_{max}^2 is peak signal power.

Then peak to average signal power is $\dfrac{A_{max}^2}{P_s}$

The average signal power to quantization noise power

$$\left(\frac{S}{N}\right)_0 = \frac{3P_s}{A_{max}^2} \times 2^{2V}$$

$$= \frac{3 \times 2^{2V}}{A_{max}^2/P_s}$$

$$= \frac{3L^2}{A_{max}^2/P_s}$$

$\therefore$
$$\left(\frac{S}{N}\right)_0 \text{ in dB} = 4.8 + 6v - \alpha$$

where,
$$\alpha = 10 \log_{10} \frac{A_{max}^2}{P_s} \text{ is peak to average signal power ratio}$$

For sinusoidal signal $\qquad\qquad \alpha \cong 3 \text{ dB}$

For voice signal $\qquad\qquad\qquad \alpha \cong 10 \text{ dB (due to large crest factor)}$

Note : Analog signals such as voice, music etc. are specified in terms crest factor which is defined as,

$$\text{Crest factor} = \frac{|x(t)|_{max}}{\sigma_x}$$

$\sigma_x^2 << 1$ implies large crest factor.

2.4 MULTIPLEXING AND SYNCHRONIZATION

- One of the advantages PCM has is, number of signals can be simultaneously transmitted over a single channel.
- This is possible with time division multiplexing of the signals.

- There is a time available between two samples of same source where we can accommodate samples from other sources.
- Of course, the signaling rate (bit rate) will increase and bandwidth requirement also.
- Consider a case of N identical sources having maximum frequency W Hz.
- If these sources are sampled at rate f_s and then multiplexed then the signaling rate will be,

$$r = N \times v \times f_s \text{ bps}$$

where, v is the number of bits used per sample.

- Hence, bandwidth requirement will be,

$$B_T = \frac{1}{2} \times r = \frac{1}{2} N \times v \times f_s \text{ Hz} \qquad \qquad \text{... (2.13)}$$

- The minimum bandwidth required will be for

$$f_s = 2W$$

$$\therefore \qquad (B_T)_{min} = \frac{1}{2} \times N \times v \times 2 \times W$$

$$= N \times v \times W \text{ Hz} \qquad \qquad \text{... (2.14)}$$

- But multiplexing requires timing operations at transmitter and receiver to be synchronized properly.
- Hence, we require a local clock at the receiver to keep the same time as that of clock at the transmitter.

Example 2.2 :

The bandwidth of TV video plus audio signal is 4.5 MHz. If this signal is converted to PCM bit stream with 1024 quantization levels. Determine number of bits/sec. generated by the PCM system. Assume that the signal is sampled at a rate 20% above Nyquist rate. **[Dec. 99, 2001]**

Solution : Given :

$$W = 4.5 \text{ MHz}$$

$$L = 1024$$

Now,

$$v = \log_2 L$$

$$\therefore \qquad v = \log_2 1024 = 10\text{-bits}$$

$$\text{Nyquist rate} = 2 \times W$$

$$= 2 \times 4.5$$

$$= 9 \text{ MHz}$$

$$\text{Sampling rate} = 9 + 0.2 \times 9$$
$$= 10.8 \text{ MHz}$$

$$\therefore \qquad \text{Bit rate} = \frac{1}{2} \times v \times f_s$$

$$= 10 \times 10.8 \times 10^6 \text{ bit/sec.}$$

$$= 108 \times 10^6 \text{ bits/sec.} = 108 \text{ Mbps}$$

Example 2.3 :

The output signal-to-noise ratio of 10-bit PCM was found to be 40 dB. The desired SNR is 42 dB. It was decided to increase SNR to desired level by increasing number of quantization levels. Find fractional increase in transmission bandwidth required for this increase in SNR.

[Dec. 2000]

Solution : Given :

$$\left(\frac{S}{N}\right)_{01} = 40 \text{ dB}$$

$$v_1 = 10$$

$$\therefore \qquad \left(\frac{S}{N}\right)_{01} = 10000$$

Desired SNR

$$\left(\frac{S}{N}\right)_{02} = 42 \text{ dB} = 15,849$$

Now,

$$\left(\frac{S}{N}\right)_{01} = \frac{3 P_S}{A_{max}^2} \times 2^{2V_1}$$

and

$$\left(\frac{S}{N}\right)_{02} = \frac{3 P_S}{A_{max}^2} \times 2^{2V_2}$$

$$\therefore \qquad \frac{10,000}{15,849} = \frac{2^{2V_1}}{2^{2V_2}}$$

$$0.63095 = \frac{2^{2V_1}}{2^{2V_2}}$$

$$0.63095 \times 2^{2V_2} = 2^{2V_1}$$

$$\log_2 0.63095 + 2 v_2 = 2 v_1$$

$$- 0.6644 + 2 v_2 = 20$$

$$v_2 = 10.33322$$

$$\therefore \qquad v_2 \simeq 11$$

$$\text{Bandwidth required for first case} = \frac{10 \, f_s}{2}$$

$$\text{Bandwidth required for second case} \quad = \frac{11\,f_s}{2}$$

$$\therefore \quad \text{Fractional increase in BW} \quad = \frac{11 - 10}{10}$$

$$= 0.1$$

$$\therefore \quad \text{Fractional increase in BW} \quad = 10\%$$

Example 2.4 :

A telephone signal with cut-off frequency of 4 kHz is digitized into 8-bit PCM sampled at Nyquist rate. Calculate baseband transmission bandwidth and quantization S/N ratio.

[May 2001]

Solution : Given :

$$W = 4 \text{ kHz}$$

$$v = 8$$

$$\therefore \qquad f_s = 8 \text{ kHz}$$

$$\text{Bit rate } r = v f_s$$

$$= 8 \times 8$$

$$= 64 \text{ kbps}$$

$$\therefore \qquad \text{Bandwidth } B_T = \frac{1}{2} r$$

$$= \frac{1}{2} \times 64 \text{ kHz}$$

$$= 32 \text{ kHz}$$

The peak signal power to average quantization noise ratio.

$$\text{For voice signal,} \qquad \left(\frac{S}{N}\right)_0 = 4.8 + 6\,v$$

$$= 4.8 + 6 \times 8$$

$$= 52.8 \text{ dB}$$

Example 2.5 :

A signal m(t) bandlimited to 3 kHz is sampled at a rate $33\frac{1}{3}$ % higher than Nyquist rate. The maximum acceptable error in the sample amplitude (the minimum quantization error) is 0.5% of peak amplitude m_p. The quantized samples are binary coded. Find minimum bandwidth of a channel required to transmit the encoded binary signal. If such 24 channels are time division multiplexed, determine minimum transmission bandwidth.   **[Dec. 2003, May 2007]**

Solution : Given : $\qquad W = 3 \text{ kHz}$

$\therefore$ $\qquad$ Nyquist rate $= 6$ kHz

$\therefore$ $\qquad$ Sampling rate $= 6$ kHz $+ 33\frac{1}{3}\%$ of 6 kHz

$\qquad = 6 + 2$

$\qquad = 8$ kHz

Maximum quantization error $= \pm\dfrac{\Delta}{2}$

$\therefore$ $\qquad \dfrac{\Delta}{2} = 5\%$ of A_{max}

$\therefore$ $\qquad \dfrac{\Delta}{2} = 0.005\, A_{max}$

$\qquad \Delta = 0.01\, A_{max}$

Now, $\qquad L = \dfrac{2\, A_{max}}{\Delta}$

$\therefore$ $\qquad L = \dfrac{2\, A_{max}}{0.01 \times A_{max}}$

$\qquad = 200$

$\therefore$ $\qquad v = \log_2 L$

$\therefore$ $\qquad v = \log_2 200$

$\qquad \approx 7.6$

$\therefore$ $\qquad v = 8$

Transmission bandwidth requirement (minimum),

$\qquad (B_T)_{min} = v \times W = 8 \times 3$

$\qquad = 24$ kHz

If 24 channels are multiplexed then, bandwidth requirement,

$\qquad B_T = N \times v \times W = 24 \times 18 \times 3$

$\qquad = 576$ kHz

Example 2.6 :

An audio signal has its spectral components limited to frequency band of 0.3 to 3.3 kHz. A PCM signal is generated with sampling rate of 8000 samples/sec. The required output peak signal power to average quantizing noise power ratio is 30 dB.

(i)   Calculate the minimum number of uniform quantization levels required ?

(ii) How many minimum number of bits per sample needed ?

(iii) Calculate minimum system bandwidth required.   **[May 2004]**

Solution : Given :   W = 3.3 kHz (Maximum frequency)

f_s = 8 kHz

We have, peak signal power to average quantization noise power

$$\left(\frac{S}{N}\right)_{peak\ dB} = 4.8 + 6v$$

∴   30 = 4.8 + 6v

∴   v = 4.2-bits

∴   v = 5-bits   **... Ans. (ii)**

Number of levels = 2^v

= 2^5

= 32   **... Ans. (i)**

Minimum transmission bandwidth required,

$$(B_T)_{min} = v \times W$$

= 5 × 3.3

= 16.5 kHz   **... Ans. (iii)**

2.5 NON-UNIFORM QUANTIZATION AND COMPANDING

- In case of uniform quantizer, the representation levels are uniformly spaced   i.e. step-size remains constant for the entire range.

- For a uniform quantizer the SNR = $\dfrac{12\ \sigma_x^2}{\Delta^2}$; where, Δ is constant. Hence, SNR is decided by signal power.

- In case of music and speech signals the range of voltage variations is very high because of loud talks and weak talks.

- In other words, the crest factor of these signals is very large. If uniform quantization is used in such signals, the weak passages will have more quantization errors compared to loud passages.

- Also for a person with loud tone the system will provide better SNR (say 40 dB) compared to person with soft tone (below 10 dB).

- Non-uniform quantization can be used in such signals, so that weak passages are given protection at the expense of loud passages.

- One way of achieving non-uniform quantization is to have characteristic of the quantizer as shown in Fig. 2.10 (a).

- The step-size is increased as the separation of the input-output amplitude characteristic is increased.

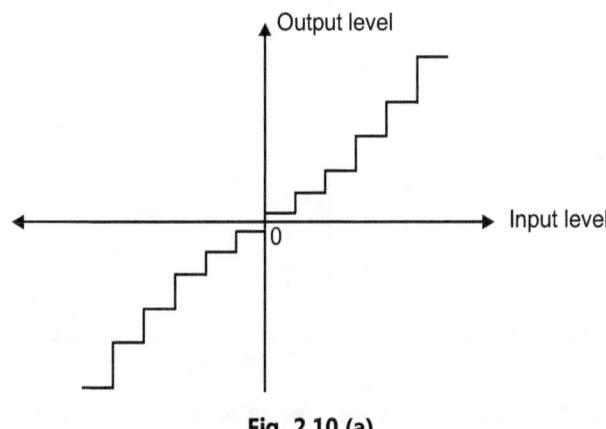

Fig. 2.10 (a)

- Another approach is to use logarithmic compression and then use uniform quantizer as shown in Fig. 2.10 (b).

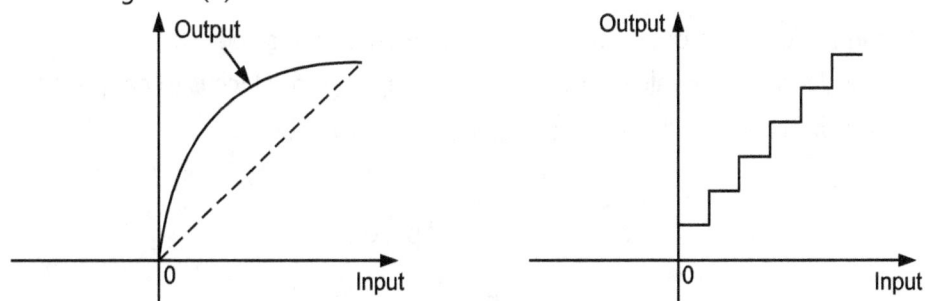

Fig. 2.10 (b) : Logarithmic compression and uniform quantizer

- Quantization noise depends on step size.
- The non-uniform quantization will introduce least noise for weak signals because step size for weak signals will be small compared to loud signals.
- The non-uniform quantization makes signal-to-noise ratio a constant for all signals within the input range.
- At the receiver, an inverse compression characteristic called expansion is used.
- The pair compression at transmitter and expansion at receiver is called companding.
- Since the step size is variable the quantization error $x\,(nT_s) - x_q\,(nT_s)$ will not be bounded between $-\dfrac{\Delta}{2}$ to $+\dfrac{\Delta}{2}$.
- The non-uniform quantizer will have different steps sizes divided in different intervals.
- For example, in the ith interval ranging from a_i to b_i the step size will be $\Delta_i = b_i - a_i$.

- The Probability distribution function for a typical signal will be as shown in Fig. 2.11. Note that the signal is normalized between −1 to +1. (from −X_{max} to +X_{max}).

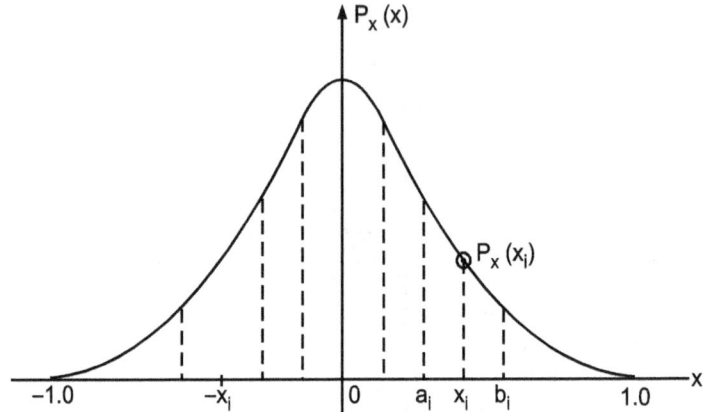

Fig. 2.11 : Message PDF with non-uniform quantization bands

- The quantization levels are closely spaced near x = 0 and widely spaced for large values of $|x(t)|$ as shown in Fig. 2.10 (a).

- The quantization noise power in this case can be calculated as below.

- If we consider a sample value $x(nT_s)$ in the band $a_i < x < b_i$ which is to be quantized to x_i, the quantization error will have mean squares value given by,

$$\overline{q_{ei}^2} = \int_{a_i}^{b_i} (x_i - x)^2 \, p_x(x) \, dx \qquad \qquad ...(2.15)$$

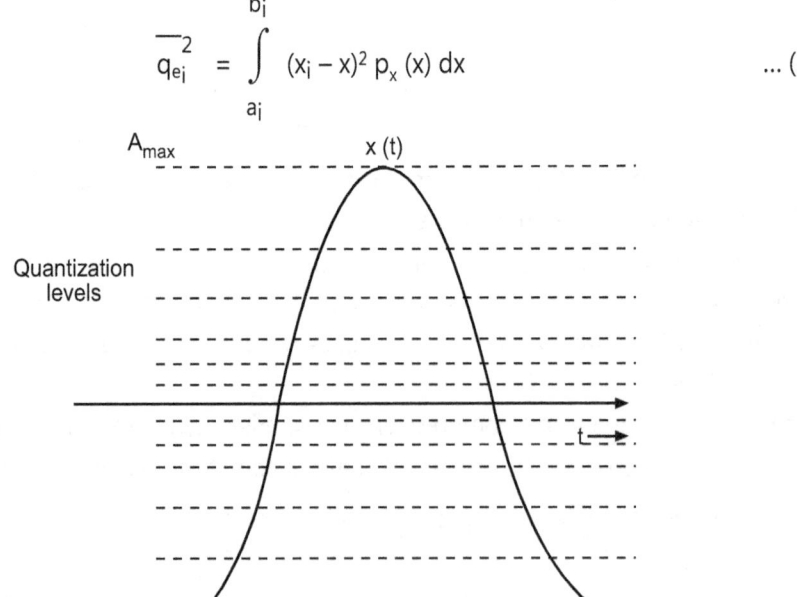

Fig. 2.12 : Non-uniform quantization

- If there are total L levels, then the quantization noise will be sum of all mean square values given by,

$$\sigma_q^2 = 2 \sum_{i=1}^{L/2} \overline{q_{e_i}^2} \qquad \qquad ...(2.16)$$

$b_i - a_i = \Delta_i$ is small enough for the approximation,

$$P_X(x) \simeq P_X(x_i) \qquad \qquad \text{Over each integration band}$$

$$\therefore \qquad \overline{q_{e_i}^2} = P_X(x_i) \int_{x_i - \Delta_i/2}^{x_i + \Delta_i/2} (x_i - x)^2 \, dx \qquad \qquad ...(2.17)$$

$$= P_X(x_i) \times \frac{\Delta_i^3}{12} \qquad \qquad ...(2.18)$$

$$\text{and} \qquad \sigma_q^2 = \frac{1}{6} \sum_{i=1}^{L/2} P_X(x_i) \Delta_i^3 \qquad \qquad ...(2.19)$$

If all the intervals are equal i.e. for uniform quantizer,

$$\Delta_i = \frac{2}{L} \qquad \qquad P_X(x_i) = \frac{1}{2}$$

$$\therefore \qquad \sigma_q^2 = \frac{1}{6} \times \frac{1}{2} \times \left(\frac{2}{L}\right)^3 \times \left(\frac{L}{2}\right) \qquad \qquad ...(2.20)$$

$$= \frac{1}{3L^2} = \frac{1}{3} \times \frac{1}{\left(\frac{2}{\Delta_i}\right)^2} = \frac{\Delta_i^2}{12}$$

which is quantization noise for uniform quantizer.

2.5.1 Compander

- It is possible to minimize quantization noise by proper selection of a_i, b_i and x_i. But, then this will require knowledge of signals PDF.

- This will also require custom tailored hardware. Hence, in practice a compressed signal is applied to uniform quantizer.

- The compression characteristics are shown in Fig. 2.13 (a).

- The horizontal axis is normalised input signal $|x(t)|/x_{max}$. The vertical axis is output signal.

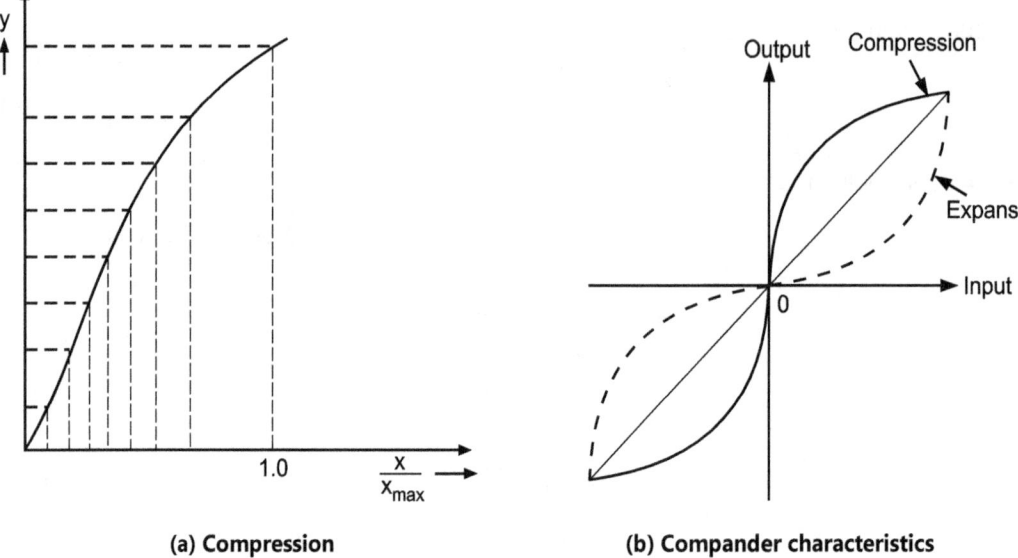

(a) Compression   (b) Compander characteristics

Fig. 2.13 : Compression characteristics

- The compressed sample must be restored to their original values at receiver by using an expander with complimentary characteristics of compressor. Fig. 2.13 (b) shows the characteristics of compander.

- The compressor and expander together are called compander.

- One important point here is that when we compress a signal its bandwidth will increase. But we are not compressing the original analog signal but the sampled version of analog signal, and as long as number of samples per second do not change, there will be no change in bandwidth. The post detection signal to noise ratio for companded PCM will be P_s/σ_q^2, where, σ_q^2 is given by equation (2.19) rewritten here,

$$\sigma_q^2 = \frac{1}{6} \sum_{i=1}^{L/2} p_X(x_i) \, \Delta_i^3$$

- Let us now find σ_q^2 for the compressor curve. The curve is drawn in Fig. 2.14.

- It is a normalised curve and shows positive part only since it is odd symmetric. [i.e. $y(x) = -y(|x|)$].

- The slope of this curve is $y'(x) = \dfrac{dy(x)}{dx}$.   ... (2.21)

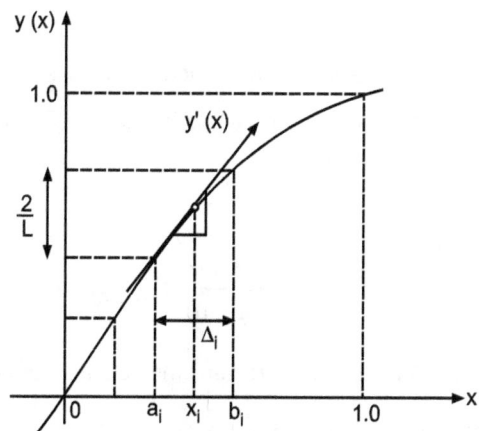

Fig. 2.14 : Compressor curve

- The value of slope at $x = x_i$ can be given by,

$$y'(x_i) = \frac{(2/L)}{\Delta_i} \qquad \text{... (2.22)}$$

$$\therefore \quad \Delta_i^2 = \frac{(2/L)^2}{[y'(x_i)]^2}$$

$$= \frac{4}{L^2 [y'(x_i)]^2} \qquad \text{... (2.23)}$$

- Hence, equation (2.19) becomes,

$$\sigma_q^2 = \frac{1}{6} \sum_{i=1}^{L/2} p_X(x_i) \times \frac{4}{L^2 [y'(x_i)]^2} \times \Delta_i$$

$$= \frac{2}{3 L^2} \sum_{i=1}^{L/2} \frac{p_X(x_i)}{[y'(x_i)]^2} \times \Delta_i$$

$$\approx \frac{2}{3 L^2} \int_0^1 \frac{p_X(x)}{[y'(x)]^2} dx \qquad \text{... (2.24)}$$

   [For large L, Converting summation to integration as $\Delta_i \rightarrow dx$]

$$\therefore \quad \left(\frac{S}{N}\right)_0 = \frac{P_s}{\sigma_q^2} = \frac{3 L^2 \times P_s}{I_y} \qquad \text{... (2.25)}$$

   where,

$$I_y = 2 \int_0^1 \frac{p_X(x)}{[y'(x)]^2} dx \qquad \text{... (2.26)}$$

- It can be seen from above expression that if $I_y < 1$, then $\left(\dfrac{S}{N}\right)_0 > 3 L^2 P_s$ meaning, companding improves PCM performance by reducing quantization noise.

A-Law and μ-Law :

- In practice, there are two compression laws which are in use viz. μ-law and A-law; μ-law is used in North America and Japan and A-law is used in Europe and rest of the world and international routes.

- The μ-law is defined as,

$$y(x) = \frac{\log_e (1 + \mu|x|)}{\log_e (1 + \mu)} \, \text{sgn}(x) \; ; \;\; 0 \le |x| \le 1$$

- μ is called compression parameter which determines degree of compression.

- The plot of y (x) against x is shown in Fig. 2.15.

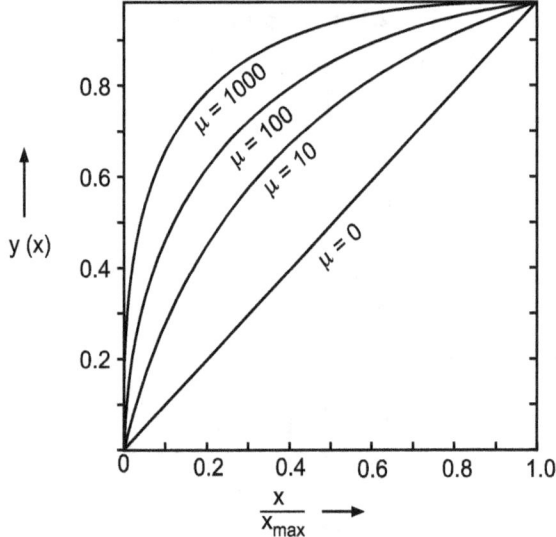

Fig. 2.15 : μ-Law characteristics

- μ = 0 represents uniform quantization.

- For better performance, values of μ above 100 are preferred. An optimum value of μ = 255 is used in practice.

We can find y' (x) to find $\left(\dfrac{S}{N}\right)_0$ of μ-law compander.

$$y' (x) = \frac{\mu}{\log_e (1 + \mu)} \times \frac{1}{1 + \mu|x|} \qquad\qquad\qquad ... (2.27)$$

where, $|x|$ is normalised input i.e. $|x| \le 1$.

Substituting equation (2.27) in equation (2.26),

Ch. 2 | 2.28

$$I_y = 2 \int_0^1 P_x(x) \times \frac{[\log(1+\mu) \cdot (1 + \mu |x|)]^2}{\mu^2} \, dx$$

$$= \frac{[\log(1+\mu)]^2}{\mu^2} \times 2 \int_0^1 P_x(x)(1 + 2\mu |x| + \mu^2 x^2) \, dx$$

$$= [\log(1+\mu)]^2 \times \left[2 \int_0^1 P_x(x) \, dx + 4\mu \int_0^1 |x| \, P_x(x) \, dx \right.$$

$$\left. + 2\mu^2 \int_0^1 x^2 \, P_x(x) \, dx \right]$$

$$\therefore \qquad I_y = \frac{[\log_e(1+\mu)]^2}{\mu^2} \times (1 + 2\mu \times m_x + \mu^2 \, \sigma_x^2) \qquad \ldots (2.28)$$

Substituting equation (2.28) in equation (2.24),

$$\therefore \qquad \sigma_q^2 = \frac{1}{3L^2} \left[\frac{\log_e(1+\mu)}{\mu^2} \right]^2 (1 + 2\mu m_x + \sigma_x^2)$$

$$\therefore \qquad \left(\frac{S}{N} \right)_0 = \frac{\sigma_x^2}{\sigma_q^2}$$

$$= \frac{3L^2}{[\log_e(1+\mu)]^2} \times \frac{\mu^2 \times \sigma_x^2}{(1 + 2\mu m_x + \sigma_x^2)}$$

$$\therefore \qquad \left(\frac{S}{N} \right)_0 = \frac{3L^2}{[\log_e(1+\mu)]^2} \times \frac{1}{\left(1 + \dfrac{2m_x}{\mu \sigma_x^2} + \dfrac{1}{\mu^2 \sigma_x^2} \right)} \qquad \ldots (2.29)$$

Since $|x|$ is normalised m_x and σ_x^2 are both less than one. Hence, the second term can be neglected.

$$\therefore \qquad \boxed{\left(\frac{S}{N} \right)_0 = \frac{3L^2}{[\log_e(1+\mu)]^2}} \qquad \ldots (2.30)$$

$$\boxed{\left(\frac{S}{N} \right)_0 \, dB = 4.8 + 6v - \alpha} \qquad \ldots (2.31)$$

where, $\alpha = 20 \log_{10} [\log_e(1+\mu)]$

We need m_x and P_s to find exact $\left(\dfrac{S}{N} \right)_0$ of μ-law.

- Experimentally it is observed that PDF of voice signal is given by,

$$p_X(x) = \frac{\lambda}{2} e^{-\lambda|x|}$$

$$\therefore \qquad P_s = \sigma_X^2 = \frac{2}{\lambda^2} \qquad \text{and } m_X = E[X] = \frac{1}{\lambda}$$

$$= \sqrt{\frac{P_s}{2}}$$

For $\mu = 255$, if we substitute above values in equation (2.28), we get,

$$I_y = 4.73 \times 10^{-4} (1 + 361 \sqrt{P_s} + 65{,}025 \, P_s)$$

- If we plot $\left(\dfrac{S}{N}\right)_0$ against P_s it can be seen that it remains constant over wide range of P_s as shown in Fig. 2.16. The figure also shows $\left(\dfrac{S}{N}\right)_0$ graph without companding for comparison. It means with companding the output SNR remains almost constant even if there is variation in the input signal power.

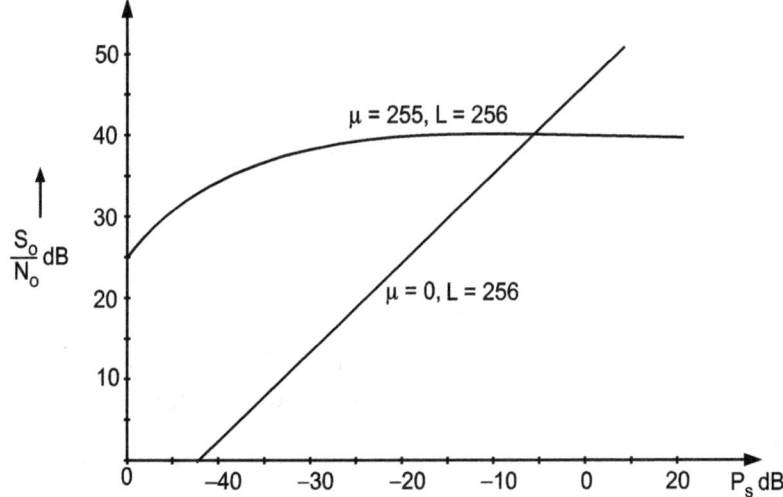

Fig. 2.16 : Signal to quantization-noise ratio in PCM with and without compression

Thus, μ-law companding provides fixed value of $\left(\dfrac{S}{N}\right)_0$ despite wide variations in P_s.

- The **A-Law** compander is defined as,

$$y(x) = \frac{A|x|}{1 + \log_e A} \qquad \text{Sgn}(x) \; ; \; 0 < |x| < \frac{1}{A}$$

$$= \frac{1 + \log_e (A|x|)}{1 + \log_e A} \qquad \text{Sgn}(x) \; ; \; \frac{1}{A} < |x| < 1$$

- A is called compression parameter and its practical values are near 100.
- For uniform quantization A = 1.
- The plot of y (x) against normalised input |x| is shown in Fig. 2.17.

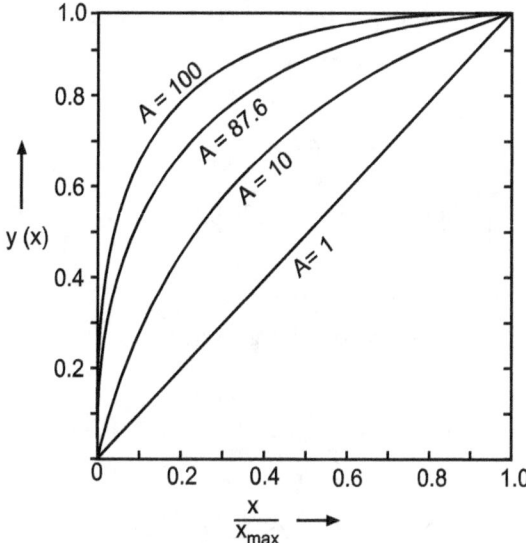

Fig. 2.17 : A-law characteristics

- The signal to noise ratio for A-law compander is given by,

$$\left(\frac{S}{N}\right)_0 = \frac{3L^2}{[\log_e (1 + A)]^2} \qquad \text{... (2.32)}$$

$$\left(\frac{S}{N}\right)_0 \text{ in dB} = 4.8 + 6v - \alpha \qquad \text{... (2.33)}$$

where, $\alpha = 20 \log_{10} (1 + \log_e A)$

- The logarithmic compressors like A-law and μ-law are implemented in practice using semiconductor diodes, as their V-I characteristic resembles compressor.
- Another approach is to use linear approximation to the logarithmic characteristic.

Example 2.7 :

A signal of bandwidth 4 kHz is transmitted using a binary companded PCM with μ = 100. Calculate transmission bandwidth and output signal to noise ratio for –

(i)   64 quantization levels.

(ii) 256 quantization levels.

Comment on the results of transmission bandwidth and output SNR.   **[May 2002]**

Solution : Given :   W   = 4 kHz

                                          μ   = 100

(i)   L = 64, v = 6

SNR ratio for PCM with μ-law is given by,

$$\left(\frac{S}{N}\right)_0 = \frac{3 \times L^2}{[\log_e (1 + \mu)]^2}$$

$$= \frac{3 \times 64 \times 64}{(\log 101)^2}$$

$$= 576.92$$

∴ $$\left(\frac{S}{N}\right)_0 \text{ in dB } = 10 \log 576.92$$

$$= 27.49 \text{ dB}$$

Bandwidth requirement (B_T) = 6 × 4 = 24 kHz

(ii) L = 256, v = 8

$$\left(\frac{S}{N}\right)_0 = \frac{3 \times L^2}{[\log_e (1 + \mu)]^2}$$

$$= \frac{3 \times 256 \times 256}{[\log_e (101)]^2}$$

$$= 9230.71$$

$$\left(\frac{S}{N}\right)_0 \text{ in dB } = 39.65 \text{ dB}$$

Bandwidth requirement B_T = n × W = 8 × 4 = 32 kHz

In case of L = 256, V = 8 the SNR improvement of 12.16 dB comes at the cost of increase in bandwidth of 8 kHZ. (33% increases).

2.6 PCM WITH NOISE

- The analog signal received at the receiver end of PCM system is corrupted by noise. Two types of noises are present in it.

    (i)   Quantization noise caused by quantizer at the transmitter. The detailed analysis of which is covered earlier.

    (ii) Bit errors in recovered PCM signal. The bit errors are caused by channel noise and improper channel filtering.

- In addition to this, there can be aliasing noise caused by filtering at transmitter end done purposely when the signal is not strictly bandlimited. Another distortion like aperture effect might occur due to flat-top sampling.

2.6.1 Decoding Noise

- Due to channel noise an erroneous bit can occur in the codeword which will result in decoding of wrong quantization level. This error is termed as **decoding noise.**
- Let us analyse this noise for PCM with uniform quantization.

  Let P_e be bit error probability $<< 1$.

  v be number of bits in a codeword.
- The probability of one error in a word will be vP_e, when $P_e << 1$. Probability of two or more errors can be negligibly small.
- Consider a received codeword $b_0, b_1, b_2, ..., b_{v-1}$.
- An error in the mth bit shifts the decoded level by an amount $= \dfrac{2}{L} \times 2^m$. Hence, the mean square error over the v bit positions will be,

$$\overline{e_m^2} = \frac{1}{v} \sum_{m=0}^{v-1} \left(\frac{2}{L} \times 2^m \right)^2 \qquad \text{... (2.34)}$$

$$= \frac{4}{vL^2} \cdot \sum_{m=0}^{v-1} 4^m = \frac{4}{vL^2} \times (4^v - 1)/3$$

$$= \frac{4}{3v} \times \frac{L^2 - 1}{L^2} \qquad (\because 4^v = 2^{2v} = L^2)$$

$$\simeq \frac{4}{3v} \qquad \text{... (2.35)}$$

- The decoding noise power will be,

$$\sigma_d^2 = vP_e \times \overline{e_m^2}$$

$$\simeq v \times P_e \times \frac{4}{3v} \qquad \text{... (2.36)}$$

$$\simeq \frac{4}{3} P_e$$

- The quantization noise power

$$\sigma_q^2 = \frac{1}{3L^2} \qquad \text{... (2.37)}$$

- Total destination noise power

$$\therefore \qquad N_0 = \sigma_q^2 + \sigma_d^2 = \frac{1}{3L^2} + \frac{4}{3} P_e$$

$$= \frac{1 + 4L^2 P_e}{3L^2}$$

Ch. 2 | 2.33

If P_s is signal power.

$$\therefore \qquad \left(\frac{S}{N}\right)_0 = \frac{3L^2}{1 + 4L^2\, P_e}\, P_s \qquad \text{... (2.38)}$$

If $P_e << \dfrac{1}{4L^2}$

$$\left(\frac{S}{N}\right)_0 = 3L^2\, P_s \qquad \text{... (2.39)}$$

and $P_e >> \dfrac{1}{4L^2}$

$$\left(\frac{S}{N}\right)_0 = \frac{3}{4P_e}\, P_s \qquad \text{... (2.40)}$$

- Hence for small P_e quantization noise is more significant whereas for large P_e decoding noise dominates.

- The error probability P_e is determined from received signal-to-noise ratio $\left(\dfrac{S}{N}\right)_R$ i.e. $P_e = Q\left[\sqrt{\left(\dfrac{S}{N}\right)_R}\right]$.

- As $\left(\dfrac{S}{N}\right)_R$ falls below a particular threshold value, there is sharp decline in detected output signal-to-noise ratio $\left(\dfrac{S}{N}\right)_D$. This is called threshold effect. It is caused by increasing errors. Below the error threshold $P_e >> \dfrac{1}{4L^2}$, the errors occur frequently causing totally wrong reconstruction of waveforms.

2.6.2 Error Threshold

- The PCM error threshold level is the point where decoding noise $\left(\dfrac{S}{N}\right)_D$ falls by 1 dB. But it is not possible to analyse error threshold from this definition. Hence, we will assume that decoding errors are negligible if $P_e << 10^{-5}$. Then we can obtain condition on $\left(\dfrac{S}{N}\right)_R$ for polar M-ary signaling as,

$$P_e = 2\left(1 - \frac{1}{M}\right) Q\left[\sqrt{\frac{3}{M^2 - 1} \times \left(\frac{S}{N}\right)_R}\right] \leq 10^{-5}$$

- Solving for minimum value of $\left(\dfrac{S}{N}\right)_R$,

$$\left(\frac{S}{N}\right)_{Rth} = 6\,(M^2 - 1)$$

- This equation says if $\left(\frac{S}{N}\right)_R < 6\,(M^2 - 1)$ then PCM output cannot be reconstructed satisfactorily due to decoding noise.

- We also have analog transmission parameter.

$$v = \frac{S_R}{N_0\,W}$$

$$= \left(\frac{B_T}{W}\right) \times \left(\frac{S}{N}\right)_R$$

- For PCM, $B_T >> \dfrac{r}{2} \geq v\,W$

$\therefore$

$$v_{th} = \left(\frac{B_T}{W}\right)\left(\frac{S}{N}\right)_{Rth}$$

$$\cong 6 \times \frac{B_T}{W} \times (M^2 - 1)$$

$\therefore$ $$v_{th} = 6\,v\,(M^2 - 1)$$

- Hence, given v and M we can find v needed for PCM above threshold. This will help in comparing PCM with other methods.

2.5 COMPARISON OF PCM AND ANALOG MODULATION

1. Analog modulation methods like FM, PPM exhibit reduction of wideband noise above their threshold level.

   PCM also has the property of wideband noise reduction above the threshold.

   Let the sampling frequency be close to Nyquist rate 2W

   $\therefore$ $$B_T \simeq v\,W$$

   $$L = M^v \qquad \text{where, } M = 2 \text{ in case of binary PCM}$$

   $\therefore$ $$L = M^b \qquad \text{where, } b = \frac{B_T}{W} \text{ (bandwidth ratio)}$$

   Since, $$\left(\frac{S}{N}\right)_0 = 3\,L^2\,P_s$$

   $$\left(\frac{S}{N}\right)_0 = 3\,M^{2b}\,P_s$$

This expression shows that there is an exponential reduction of noise above threshold. The plot of various modulation types is shown in Fig. 2.18.

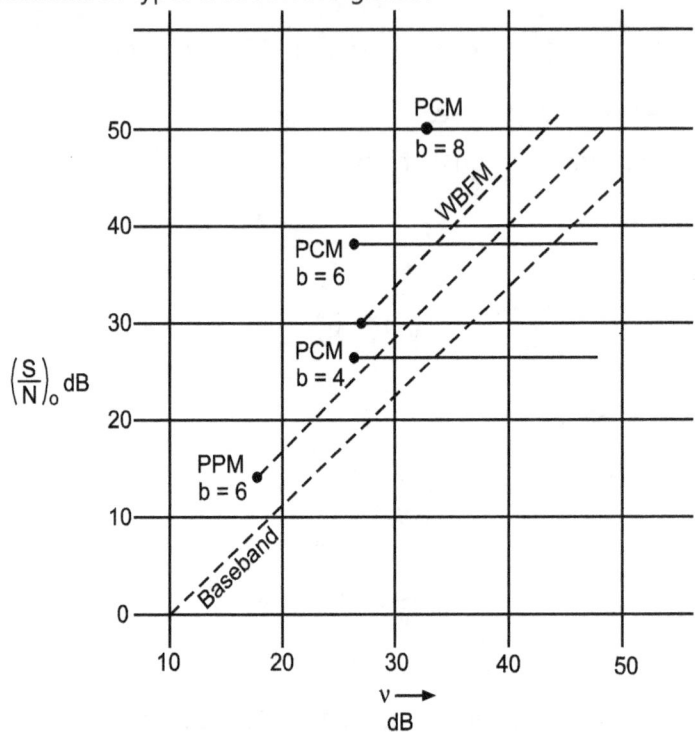

Fig. 2.18 : Performance of PCM and analog modulation

- It is seen that beyond threshold (indicated by dot) PCM does not offer any improvement in signal-to-noise ratio. Hence, PCM should be operated just above threshold for power efficiency. With same value of b PCM has better $\left(\dfrac{S}{N}\right)_0$ ratio near threshold.

2. PCM allows one of regenerative repeaters for reshaping the pulses for long distance transmission.

   Analog modulations do not offer this advantage.

3. Digital multiplexing is possible with PCM which offers advantage of transmission of signals from variety of sources (data, voice, images etc.) on same channel.

   Analog modulation schemes do not offer this advantage.

4. PCM is not suited for all application. e.g. in radio transmission a $\left(\dfrac{S}{N}\right)_0$ ratio of 60 dB is required. For this the bandwidth ratio required for PCM would be above 8 whereas, FM can offer this at b = 8. Moreover, FM has more simpler hardware at transmitter and receiver. In general, PCM is not suitable for most single channel applications because of bandwidth requirement and hardware complexity.

SOLVED PROBLEMS

Problem 2.1 :

A binary channel with r_b = 3600 bits/sec. is available for PCM voice transmission. Find appropriate values of bits/sample, number of quantization levels and sampling frequency if W = 3.2 kHz.

Solution :

$$f_s \geq 2W$$

$\therefore$

$$f_s \geq 2 \times 3.2 \geq 6.4 \text{ kHz}$$

(i) Now,

$$v \cdot f_s = r_b$$

$\therefore$

$$vf_s = 36000$$

$\therefore$

$$v \leq \frac{36000}{6400}$$

$\therefore$

$$v \leq 5.6$$

$\therefore$

$$v = 5$$

(ii)

$$L = 2^v$$

$$= 2^5$$

$$= 32$$

(iii) $\therefore$

$$f_s = \frac{r_b}{v} = \frac{36000}{5}$$

$$= \textbf{7.2 kHz}$$

Problem 2.2 :

A PCM system of video signal with f_s = 10 MHz requires signal-to-noise ratio of 50 dB for signal power = 1. Calculate signaling rate. Repeat above for signal power = 0.1.

Solution :   Given : f_s = 10 MHz

$$\left(\frac{S}{N}\right)_0 = 50 \text{ dB}$$

(i) $P_S = 1$

$\therefore$

$$\left(\frac{S}{N}\right)_0 = 3 L^2 P_S = 3 L^2$$

$$= 3 \times 2^{2v}$$

$$\left(\frac{S}{N}\right)_0 dB = 10 \log_e [3 \times 2^{2v}]$$

$$= 4.8 + 6 v$$

$$\therefore \qquad 50 = 4.8 + 6v$$

$$v = 7.583$$

$$\therefore \qquad v = 8$$

$$\therefore \qquad \text{Signaling rate } r = v \cdot f_s$$

$$= 8 \times 10 \times 10^6$$

$$= 80 \text{ Mbps}$$

(ii) $P_s = 0.1$

$$\left(\frac{S}{N_0}\right) = 3 L^2 \times P_s$$

$$= 3 \times 2^{2v} \times 0.1$$

$$\therefore \qquad \left(\frac{S}{N}\right)_0 \text{ in dB} = 10 \log (3 \times 2^{2v} \times 0.1)$$

$$= 4.8 + 6v - 10$$

$$50 = 4.8 + 6v - 10$$

$$\therefore \qquad v = 9.2$$

$$\therefore \qquad v = 10$$

$$\text{Signaling rate } r = v \cdot f_s$$

$$= 10 \times 10 \text{ MHz}$$

$$= 100 \text{ Mbps}$$

Problem 2.3 :

What is minimum size of memory required to store 10 minutes of sampled and quantized voice assuming peak signal-to-noise ratio is 35 dB and f_s = 8 kHz.

Solution : Given :

$$\left(\frac{S}{N}\right)_0 = 35 \text{ dB}$$

$$f_s = 8 \text{ kHz}$$

$$\text{Storage time} = 10 \text{ min.}$$

$$\left(\frac{S}{N}\right)_0 = 4.8 + 6v$$

$$35 = 4.8 + 6v$$

$$\therefore \qquad v = 5$$

$$\text{Signaling rate} = v \cdot f_s$$

$$= 5 \times 8 \times 10^3$$

$$= 40 \times 10^3 \text{ bps}$$

$\therefore$ Memory required for 10 min. storage

$$= 40 \times 10^3 \times 10 \times 60$$

$$= 24 \times 10^6 \text{ bits}$$

$$= 24 \text{ Mbits}$$

Problem 2.4 :

A television signal with a bandwidth of 4.2 MHz is transmitted using binary PCM. The number of quantization levels is 512. Calculate : (i) Code word length, (ii) Transmission bandwidth, (iii) Final Bit Rate (iv) $(SNR)_0$.   **(May 2009)**

Solution :

Given : Signal bandwidth W = 4.2 MHz

Number of quantization levels, L = 512

$\quad\therefore$ Sampling frequency, f_s = 2W = 8.4 MHz

(i)   Code word length, $v = \log_2 L = \log_2 512$

$$= 9$$

(ii)   Transmission bandwidth,

$$B_T = v \cdot f_s/2 = \frac{9 \times 8.4}{2} \times 10^6$$

$$= 37.8 \times 10^6 \text{ Hz} = 37.8 \text{ MHz}$$

(iii)   Final bit rate,

$$\text{Bit rate} = \text{Number of samples/sec} \times \text{No bit/Sample}$$

$$= f_s \times v = 8.4 \times 10^6 \times 9$$

$$= 75.6 \times 10^6 \text{ bps} = 75.6 \text{ Mbps}$$

(iii)   Peak signal power to swise ratio

$$\left(\frac{S}{N}\right)_0 \leq 4.8 + 6v$$

$$\leq 4.8 + 6 \times 9 = 58.8 \text{ dB}$$

Problem 2.5 :

A channel of 64 kHz is available for transmission of binary signal. If PCM system is to be used with 8-bit encoding per sample what is the maximum frequency of a cosine wave signal that can be transmitted ?

Solution : Given : Bandwidth, B_T = 64 kHz.

Number of bits per sample, v = 8.

We know required bandwidth for PCM.

$$B_T \geq \frac{v \cdot f_s}{2}$$

$\therefore\therefore$
$$f_s \leq \frac{2 \cdot B_T}{v}$$

$\therefore$
$$f_s \leq \frac{2 \times 64 \times 10^3}{8}$$

$$f_s \leq 16 \times 10^3 \text{ Hz}$$

$\therefore$
$$f_s \leq 16 \text{ kHz}$$

But,
$$f_s \geq 2 f_m$$

$\therefore$
$$f_m \leq \frac{f_s}{2}$$

$\therefore$
$$f_m \leq \frac{16 \times 10^3}{2}$$

i.e.
$$\boxed{f_m \leq 8 \text{ kHz}}$$

Problem 2.6 :

A binary channel with bit-rate of 56 kbps is available for uniform PCM voice transmission having signal bandwidth of 3.4 kHz.

Calculate :

(1) Sampling Frequency.

(2) Number of bits per sample.

(3) Quantization levels with step size.

Solution : Given :   Bit rate r_b = 56×10^3

Signal BW, W = 3.4 kHz

(i) Sampling Frequency, f_s = 2×3.4 = 6.8 kHz

(ii) r_b = $v \times f_s$

Bits/sample v = $\dfrac{r_b}{f_s} = \dfrac{56 \times 10^3}{6.8 \times 10^3} = 8.235 = 8$

[Lower value is selected otherwise bit rate will exceed 56 kbps]

(iii) Quantization Levels :

$$L = 2^v = 2^8$$
$$= 256$$

Problem 2.7 :

A PCM system uses a uniform quantizer followed by a 7-bit binary encoder. The bit rate of the system is equal to 50×10^6 b/s. What is the maximum message bandwidth for which the system operates satisfactorily ? Calculate output SNR when full load modulating wave of 1 MHz is applied at the input.   **(Nov. 2008)**

Solution :

Given : Bits/sample v = 7 bit

$$\text{Bit rate } r_b = 50 \times 10^6 \text{ bps}$$

$\therefore$ But, $$r_b = v \times f_s$$

$$f_s = r_b/v = \frac{50 \times 10^6}{7}$$

$\therefore$ Now, $$f_s \geq 2W$$

$$W \leq \frac{f_s}{2}$$

$$\leq \frac{50 \times 10^6}{7 \times 2}$$

$\therefore$ $$W \leq 3.57 \times 10^6$$

$\therefore$ $$W \leq 3.57 \text{ MHz}$$

$\therefore$ $$W_{max} = 3.57 \text{ MHz}$$

(ii) The SNR for sinusoidal signal input is

$$\left(\frac{S}{N}\right)_{dB} = 1.8 + 6v = 1.8 + 6 \times 7$$

$$= 43.8 \text{ dB}$$

SOLVED UNIVERSITY QUESTIONS

U.Q. 1 : Express μ law of companding. For μ = 225 determine the maximum advantage over linear quantizer if the peak power to average power ratio is 9 and dynamic range of input signal is 30 dB and quantizer uses 256 levels.   **(Dec. 2005)**

Solution : The μ law of companding is given by,

$$y(x) = \frac{\log_e (1 + \mu |x|)}{\log (1 + \mu)} \text{ Sng } (x) \; ; \; 0 \leq x \leq 1$$

Given : Peak to average signal power, $\alpha = \dfrac{A_{max}^2}{P_s} = 9$

$$L = 256$$

(i) For Linear quantizer :

$$\left(\frac{S}{N}\right)_0 = \frac{3L^2}{\alpha}$$

$$= \frac{8 \times 256}{9}$$

$$= 85.33$$

$$\left(\frac{S}{N}\right)_0 \text{ in dB} = 43.4 \text{ dB}$$

This will be maximum value of $\left(\frac{S}{N}\right)_0$.

Since dynamic range of input signal is 30 dB, the signal power can drop by 30 dB and the minimum value will be,

$$\left(\frac{S}{N}\right)_{0 \text{ min}} = 43.4 - 30$$

$$= 13.4 \text{ dB}$$

Now, for μ law compander,

$$\left(\frac{S}{N}\right)_0 = \frac{3L^2}{[\log (1 + \mu)]^2} \qquad \left[\because \ \frac{A_{max}^2}{\sigma_x^2} << \mu^2 \right]$$

$$= \frac{3 \times (256)^2}{[\log (1 + 255)]^2}$$

$$= 38.05 \text{ dB}$$

Hence, maximum advantage that will be over linear quantizer is

$$38.05 - 13.4 = 24.61 \text{ dB}.$$

U.Q. 2 : An analog waveform with bandwidth 15 kHz is to be quantized with 200 levels and transmitted via. binary PCM signal. Find rate of transmission and bandwidth required. If 10 such signals are to be multiplexed find the bandwidth requirement.

Solution :   **(May 2006)**

Given : Bandwidth,   W = 15 kHz

Number of levels,   L = 200

Number of channels,   N = 10

Minimum sampling frequency, f_s

$$= 2W = 2 \times 15$$

$$= 30 \text{ kHz}$$

Number of bits per sample, $\quad v = \log_2 L = \log_2 200$

$$\approx 8$$

The rate of transmission, $\qquad r = v \cdot f_s$

$$= 8 \times 30 \times 10^3 = 240 \times 10^3 \text{ bps}$$

$$= 240 \text{ kbps}$$

$\therefore$ Bandwidth requirement,

$$(B_T)_{min} = \frac{r}{2}$$

$$= 120 \text{ kHz}$$

The bandwidth required for N multiplexed signals,

$$(B_T)_{min} = \frac{N \cdot r}{2} = 1200 \text{ kHz}$$

$$= 1.2 \text{ MHz}$$

U.Q. 3 : A binary channel with bit rate 36 kbps is available for PCM voice transmission. Find appropriate values of number of quantization levels, number of bits per sample, and sampling frequency. Given that voice signal is band limited to 3.4 kHz.

(May 2006)

Solution : Given,

$\qquad$ Bandwidth of signal W $\ = 3.4$ kHz

$\therefore \qquad$ Sampling frequency $f_s \ \geq 2W$

$$\geq 6.8 \text{ kHz}$$

Let, $\qquad\qquad\qquad\qquad f_s = 6.8$ kHz

$\qquad$ Rate of transmission $= 36$ kbps $= 36 \times 10^3$ bps

Now, rate of transmission, $\qquad r = v \times f_s$

$\therefore \qquad\qquad 3600 \times 10^3 = v \times 6.8 \times 10^3$

Number of bits/sample,

$$\therefore \qquad\qquad v = \frac{36 \times 10^3}{6.8 \times 10^3} = 5.29$$

Let, $\qquad\qquad\qquad\qquad v = 5$

[The lower value is selected as rate should remain below 36 kbps].

$\therefore$ Number of quantization levels,

$$L = 2^v = 2^5 = 32$$

U.Q. 4 : A signal of bandwidth 3.5 KHz is sampled and quantized and coded by a PCM system. The coded signal is then transmitted over a transmission channel with transmission rate 50 kbps. Calculate the maximum signal to Noise ratio that can be obtained by the system. The input signal has peak to peak value of 4V and rms value of 0.2 V.   **(May 2007)**

Solution : Given :

Signal bandwidth, W = 3.5 kHz

Rate of transmission, r = 50 kbps

Peak-to-Peak Amp $2A_{max}$ = 4V

$\therefore$ A_{max} = 2V

r.m.s. value (Average value) = 0.2 V

Since, W = 3.5 kHz

Minimum sampling frequency, f_s = 7 kHz

Now, $r = v \cdot f_s$

$\therefore$ $v = \dfrac{r}{f_s} = \dfrac{50 \times 10^3}{7 \times 10^3}$

$= 7.14$ bits

Hence, we select, $v = 7$ bits

[Because v = 8 will increase rate of transmission beyond 50 kbps]

$\therefore$ Number of quantization

$L = 2^v$

$= 2^7$

$= 128$

The step size, $\Delta = \dfrac{2A_{max}}{L} = \dfrac{2 \times 2}{128}$

$= 0.03125$ v

$\therefore$ Quantization noise power,

$N_q = \dfrac{\Delta^2}{12}$

$= 8.1380 \times 10^{-5}$ Watt

Signal Power $P_s = (r.m.s.)^2 = (0.2)^2$

$= 0.04$

Signal-to-Noise Ratio (Maximum)

$$\left(\frac{S}{N}\right)_0 = \frac{0.04}{8.1380 \times 10^{-5}}$$

$$= 491.52$$

$$\left(\frac{S}{N}\right)_0 \text{ in dB} = 26.9154 \text{ dB}$$

U.Q. 5 : A signal having band of 300-3000 Hz is sampled at 8000 samples/sec and is coded for PCM. Assume that the ratio of peak signal power to average quantization noise required at the output is 30 dB.

(i) What is minimum number of quantization level needed ? Derive the formula used.   **(Dec. 2006, May 2008)**

(ii) Compute the bandwidth required for transmission.

(iii) Repeat (i) and (ii) for μ law compander with μ = 255.

Solution :

Given :

Maximum frequency, W = 3000 Hz

Sampling rate, f_s = 8000 samples/sec.

$$10 \log \frac{A_{max}^2}{N_q} = 30 \text{ dB}$$

∴
$$\frac{A_{max}^2}{N_q} = 1000$$

(i)   Now $$N_q = \frac{\Delta^2}{12} = \frac{4A_{max}^2}{L^2}$$

∴
$$\frac{A_{max}^2}{\frac{4_{max}^2}{L^2}} = 1000$$

$$L^2 = 4000$$

∴   Number of quantization Levels

$$L = 63.24$$

Let, L = 64

Number of bits / sample $v = \log_2 L = 5$

(ii)   The transmission bandwidth

$$B_T = \frac{v \cdot f_s}{2}$$

$$= \frac{6 \times 8000}{2}$$

$$= 24 \text{ kHz}$$

(iii)   For μ law compander with $\mu = 255$.

$$\left(\frac{S}{N}\right)_0 = \frac{3L^2}{[\log_3 (1 + \mu)]^2}$$

$\left(\frac{S}{N}\right)_0$ in dB is 30 dB. (Assuming it to be equal to Peak signal power to average quantization

noise power)

$$\therefore \qquad \left(\frac{S}{N}\right)_0 = 1000$$

$$\therefore \qquad 1000 = \frac{3L^2}{[\log_e (1 + 255)]^2}$$

$$\therefore \qquad L = 100$$

$$\therefore \qquad v = \log_2 L = 6.67$$

$$\approx 7 \text{ bits/sample}$$

Transmission bandwidth

$$B_T = \frac{v \cdot f_s}{2} = \frac{7 \times 8000}{2}$$

$$= 28 \text{ kHz}$$

U.Q. 6 : A signal band-limited to 1 MHz is sampled at a rate 50% higher than the Nyquist rate and quantized into 256 levels using a μ law quantizer with $\mu = 255$.

(i) Determine the signal to quantization noise ratio.

(ii) The SNR found in part (i) was unsatisfactory. It must be increased by atleast 10 dB. Would you be able to obtain the desired SNR without increasing the transmission bandwidth if it was found that a sampling rate 20% above the nyquist rate is adequate ? If so explain how. What is maximum SNR that can be realized in this way. **(Dec. 2007) (Marks 10)**

Solution :

Given : Signal bandwidth,

$$W = 1 \text{ MHz}$$

Sampling frequency 50% higher than 2W.

$$\therefore \quad f_s = 1.5 \times 2 \text{ MHz}$$
$$= 3.0 \text{ MHz}$$
$$L = 256$$
$$\mu = 255$$

(i)   The signal-to-noise ratio for μ law companding is,

$$\left(\frac{S}{N}\right)_0 = \frac{3L^2}{[\log_e (1 + \mu)]^2}$$

$$= \frac{3 \times (256)^2}{[\log_e (1 + 255)]^2}$$

$$= 6394$$

$$\therefore \quad \left(\frac{S}{N}\right)_0 \text{ in dB} = 38 \text{ dB}$$

(ii)   With $f_s = 3$ MHz

$$L = 256 \text{ i.e. } v = \log_2 L = 8 \text{ bits}$$

$$B_T = \frac{v \cdot f_s}{2}$$

$$= \frac{8 \times 3 \times 10^6}{2}$$

$$= 12 \times 10^6 \text{ Hz} = 12 \text{ MHz}$$

With $f_s = 20\%$ higher than 2W

i.e.
$$f_s = 1.2 \times 2 \times 10^6$$
$$= 2.4 \times 10^6 \text{ Hz}$$
$$= 2.4 \text{ MHz}$$

We want $B_T = 12$ MHz (same)

$$\therefore \quad \frac{v \cdot f_s}{2} = 12 \times 10^6$$

$$v = \frac{2 \times 12 \times 10^6}{2.4 \times 10^6}$$

$$= 10 \text{ bits}$$

i.e. the v has to be increased.

$$\therefore \quad L = 2^v$$
$$= 1024$$

$$\therefore \qquad \left(\frac{S}{N}\right)_0 = \frac{32^2}{[\log_e (1 + \mu)]^2} = \frac{3 \times (1024)^2}{[\log_e (1 + 255)]^2}$$

$$= 102303.45$$

$$\left(\frac{S}{N}\right)_0 \text{ in dB} = 50 \text{ dB}$$

Thus, SNR is increased by 12 dB.

Hence, if sampling frequency is reduced and number of bits per sample are increased SNR improves and bandwidth remains same.

The maximum signal to noise ratio will be when sample frequency is minimum.

When $\qquad f_s = 2W$

$$= 2 \times 1 \text{ MHz}$$

$$\therefore \qquad B_T = \frac{1}{2} v \cdot f_s$$

$$v = \frac{2 \times B_T}{f_s} = \frac{2 \times 12 \times 10^6}{2 \times 10^6}$$

$$= 12$$

$\therefore$ Number of quantization levels

$$L = 2^v = 12^{12}$$

$$= 4096$$

$$\therefore \qquad \left(\frac{S}{N}\right)_0 = \frac{32^2}{[\log_e (1 + \mu)]^2} = \frac{3 \times (4096)}{[\log_e (1 + 255)]^2}$$

$$= 1636855.2$$

$$\left(\frac{S}{N}\right)_0 \text{ in dB} = 62.1 \text{ dB}$$

U.Q. 7 : A PCM system uses a uniform quantizer followed by a 7-bit binary encoder, The bit rate of the system is equal to 50×10^6 b/s.

(i) What is the maximum message bandwidth for which the system operates satisfactorily ?

(ii) Determine the output signal-to-quantization) noise ratio when a full-load sinusoidal modulating wave of frequency 1 MHz is applied to the input.

(Dec. 2008)

Solution : Given : Number of bits per sample, v = 7.

$$\text{Bit rate, } r = 50 \times 10^6 \text{ bps}$$

Let message bandwidth = W Hz.

$$\therefore \qquad\qquad f_s \geq 2W$$

$$\therefore \qquad\qquad r = v \cdot f_s$$

$$50 \times 10^6 = 7 \times f_s$$

$$\therefore \qquad\qquad f_s = \frac{50}{7} \times 10^6 \text{ Hz}$$

But, $\qquad\qquad f_s \geq 2W$

$$\therefore \qquad\qquad W \leq \frac{f_s}{2}$$

$$\therefore \qquad\qquad W \leq \frac{50}{7 \times 2} \times 10^6 \text{ Hz}$$

$$\therefore \qquad\qquad W \leq 3.57 \text{ MHz}$$

Hence, maximum message, BW = 3.57 MHz.

(ii) The signal-to-quantization noise ratio for sinusoidal signal is given by,

$$\left(\frac{S}{N}\right)_0 = 1.8 + 6v = 1.8 + 6 \times 7$$

$$= 43.8 \text{ dB}$$

U.Q. 8 : Derive the expression for quantization error and signal to quantization noise ratio for a non-sinusoidal PCM system.   **(Dec. 2008)**

Solution : Refer Section 2.3.

$$\boxed{\text{May 2011}}$$

U.Q. 9 : In a 8-bit PCM scheme, the voice signal is sampled at a rate of 8 kHz. The maximum signal amplitude is 1V, voice signal bandwidth is 3.5 kHz. The quantisation noise signal amplitude is uniformly distributed as shown in Fig. 2.19. Calculate the signal to noise ratio of the system.   **(8)**

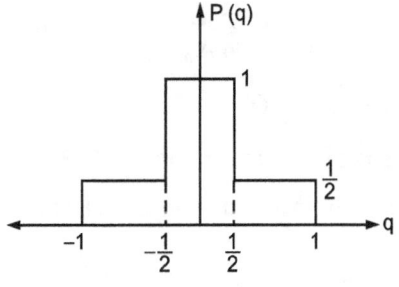

Fig. 2.19

Solution : Given: Number of bits v = 8

Sampling rate, f_s = 8 kHz

A_{max} = 1V

Signal bandwidth f_m = 3.5 kHz

The distribution of quantization noise given is incorrect as the area under the PDF should be 1. The problem can be solved using the formula of peak signal power to Avg quantization noise ratio is

$$\left(\frac{S}{N}\right)_{0 \text{ peak}} = 4.8 + 6v = 4.8 + 6 \times 8$$

$$= 52.8 \text{ dB}$$

Dec. 2011

U.Q. 10 : The information in an analog waveform, whose maximum frequency fm = 4000 Hz is to be transmitted using a 16-level PAM system. The quantization distortion must not exceed + 1% of the peak to peak analog signal.

(a) What is the minimum number of bits per sample that should be used in the transmission system?

(b) What is the minimum required sampling rate and bit rate of the system?

(c) What is the 16-ary PAM symbol transmission rate?   **(8)**

Solution : (a) Given: $\frac{\Delta}{2} \leq 0.01 \times 2A_{max}$

Now, $\Delta = \frac{2A_{max}}{L}$

∴ $L = \frac{2 A_{max}}{0.02 \times 2A_{max}}$

$L = \frac{2A_{max}}{0.04 A_{max}} = 50$

Select, L = 64

(b)   Therefore, number of bits per sample = $\log_2 L$ = 6. But since we are using 16-ary PAM, we have to use bits per sample in multiples of 8. Hence, here will be 2 symbols per sample.

∴   Bits/sample v = 8

(c)   Minimum sampling rate $f_s = 2f_m$

∴ $\quad\quad\quad\quad\quad\quad\quad f_s = 2 \times 4000 \text{ Hz} = 8000 \text{ Hz}$

$\quad\quad\quad\quad\quad\text{Bit rates} = v \times f_s$

$\quad\quad\quad\quad\quad\quad\quad\quad\quad = 8 \times 8000$

$\quad\quad\quad\quad\quad\quad\quad\quad\quad = 64 \text{ kbps}$

(d)   Symbol transmission rate will be

$\quad\quad\quad\quad\quad\quad = \text{Number of symbols per sample} \times \text{Number of}$ samples/sec.

$\quad\quad\quad\quad\quad\quad = 2 \times 8000$

$\quad\quad\quad\quad\quad\quad = 16 \text{ ksymbols/s}$

(b)   Explain how companding improves the signal to noise ratio of PCM system with respect to μ-law? **(8)**

Solution : Refer Section 2.5.

May 2012

U.Q. 11 : Consider an audio signal with spectral components limited to the frequency band of 500 Hz to 3 kHz. A PCM signal is generated with sampling rate of 8000 samples/sec. The required output signal to quantization noise ratio is 40 dB.

(i) How many number of levels and no. of bits/level are needed for uniform quantization.

(ii) Calculate the bandwidth requirement of the above system.

(iii) If A-law compander is used, what will be the changes in the number of levels, number of bits/sample and bandwidth? **(10)**

Solution : Given: $\quad\quad\quad\quad\quad\quad f_m = 3 \text{ kHz}$

$\quad\quad\quad\quad\quad\quad\quad\quad f_s = 8 \text{ kHz}$

$\quad\quad\quad\quad\quad\quad\quad\text{SNR} = 40 \text{ dB}$

(i)   For audio signal $\quad\quad\quad\text{SNR} = 6v + 4.8 \text{ dB}$

∴ $\quad$ Number of bits per single, $v = 5.86 \simeq 6$

∴ $\quad\quad\quad$ Number of levels, $L = 2^v = 64$

(ii) $\quad\quad\quad\quad$ BW requirement $= vf_s/2$

$\quad\quad\quad\quad\quad\quad\quad\quad = 6 \times 8 \text{ kHz}/2$

$\quad\quad\quad\quad\quad\quad\quad\quad = 24 \text{ kHz}$

(iii) SNR for A low compander is

$$SNR = \frac{3L^2}{[\log_e (1 + A)]^2}$$

$$SNR \text{ in dB} = 4.8 + 6v - \alpha$$

$$\alpha = 20 \log_{10} [1 + \log A]$$

$$\text{Using } A = 100$$

∴

$$v = 8$$

$$L = 256$$

$$B_T = v \cdot f_s/2$$

$$= 32 \text{ kHz}$$

Dec. 2012

U.Q. 12 : A signal m(t) band-limited to 3 kHz is sampled at a rate $33\frac{1}{3}$% higher than the Nyquist rate. The maximum acceptable error in the sample amplitude (the max. quantization error) is 1% of peak amplitude m_p. The quantized samples are binary coded. Find the minimum bandwidth of a channel required to transmit the encoded binary signal. If 24 such signals are time-division-multiplexed, determine the minimum transmission bandwidth required to transmit the multiplexed signal.   **(8)**

Solution : Refer Example 2.5.

U.Q. 13 : What is the necessity of companding? Explain the A law and μ law of companding graphically with expression.   **(8)**

Solution : Refer Section 2.5.

May 2013

U.Q. 14 : Consider a DM system designed to accommodate analog message signals limited to bandwidth W = 5 kHz. A sinusoidal test signal of amplitude A = 1 volt and frequency f_m = 1 kHz is applied to the system. The Sampling rate of the system is 50 kHz.

(i) Calculate the minimum step size Δ required to minimize slope overload.

(ii) Calculate signal to (quantization) noise ratio of the system for the specified sinusoidal test signal.   **(8)**

Solution : Refer U.Q. 6.9.

U.Q. 15 : A TV signal with a bandwidth of 4.2 MHz is transmitted using binary PCM. The number of quantization levels is 512. Calculate :   **(8)**

    (i)   Code word length   (ii) Transmission bandwidth

    (iii) Final bit rate   (iv) Output signal to quantization noise ratio.

Solution : Refer U.Q. 6.

U.Q. 16 :   A compact disc (CD) records audio signals digitally by PCM. Assume audio signal's bandwidth to be 15kHz. If signals are sampled at a rate 20% above Nyquist rate for practical reasons and the samples are quantized into 65,536 levels, determine bits/sec required to encode the signal and minimum bandwidth required to transmit encoded signal.   **(8)**

Solution : Given

$$f_m = 15 \text{ kHz}$$

$$\text{Nyquist rate} = 30 \text{ kHz}$$

$$\text{Sampling rate} = (30 + 0.2 \times 30) \text{ kHz}$$

$$= 36 \text{ kHz}$$

$$\text{Quantization levels,} \quad L = 65{,}536$$

$$\therefore \quad \text{Number of bits of sample} = \log 2^{65536}$$

$$v = 16$$

$$\therefore \quad \text{Bit rate} = v.f_s$$

$$= 16 \times 36 \text{ kHz}$$

$$r_b = 576 \text{ kbps}$$

$$\text{Minimum Bandwidth} = \frac{r_b}{2} = 288 \text{ kHz}$$

U.Q. 17 :   A voice signal band limited to 3.4kHz is to be transmitted using PCM system. The signaling rate of the PCM is not to exceed 36000bits/sec find.   **[8]**

    (a) The number of digit (bits) per word.

    (b) The number of quantization levels.

    (c) Range of sampling frequency

Solution : Given

$$f_m = 3.4 \text{ kHz}$$

$$r_b \leq 36 \text{ kbps}$$

$$\text{Nyquist rate} = 2f_m = 6.8 \text{ kHz}$$

$$\text{Minimum } f_s = 6.8 \text{ kHz}$$

Now
$$r_b = v.f_s$$

$\therefore$
$$v.f_s \leq 3.6 \times 10^3$$

Number of bits per word,
$$v \leq \frac{36 \times 10^3}{6.8 \times 10^3} \leq 5.29 \text{ bits}$$

Let
$$v = 5$$

Quantization level
$$L = 2^v = 32$$

Range of sampling frequency $= 6.8 \text{ kHz to } 7.2 \text{ kHz}$

SUMMARY

1. Pulse Code Modulation (PCM) system is used to transmit analog signal in digital form.

2. The transmitter of PCM consists of sampler, quantizer and encoder.

3. The receiver of PCM consists of decoder and reconstruction filter.

4. The quantization process gives rise to quantization noise.

5. The quantization noise power is $\frac{\Delta^2}{12}$.

6. The signal-to-quantization noise ratio in

$$\text{PCM is } \left(\frac{S}{N}\right)_0 = \frac{3P_s}{A_{max}^2} \times L^2$$

where, P_s is signal power.

L is number of quantization levels

A_{max}^2 is peak signal power.

7. For sinusoidal signal the signal-to-quantization noise ratio is,

$$\left(\frac{S}{N}\right)_0 = \frac{3}{2}L^2$$

$$\left(\frac{S}{N}\right)_{0 \text{ in dB}} = 1.8 + 6 V$$

8. For non-sinusoidal signal such as voice or audio signal, the peak signal power-to-quantization noise power ratio is

$$\left(\frac{S}{N}\right)_{0 \text{ peak}} = 3L^2$$

$$\left(\frac{S}{N}\right)_{0 \text{ in dB}} = 4.8 + 6V$$

9. The bandwidth requirement of PCM is,

$$B_T = \frac{v \cdot f_s}{2} \text{ Hz}$$

and minimum transmission bandwidth is,

$$(B_T)_{min} = \frac{v \cdot 2W}{2} = v \cdot W \text{ Hz}$$

10. The bandwidth required for multiplied PCM signal is,

$$B_T = N \times v \times f_s/2 \text{ Hz}$$

and $$(B_T)_{min} = N \times v \times W \text{ Hz}$$

11. Non-uniform quantization or companding is used to improve the performance of PCM in case of signals having large amplitude variations such as music or speech.

12. A-law and μ-law companding are used in practice.

13. The signal-to-quantization noise ratio of μ-law is,

$$\left(\frac{S}{N}\right)_0 = \frac{3L^2}{[\log(1 + \mu)]^2}$$

14. The decoding noise is a noise introduced due to bit errors caused by channel noise. It gives by

$$\sigma_d^2 = \frac{4}{3} P_e$$

EXERCISE

1. Compare along modulation techniques.

2. Explain the process of quantization in PCM.

3. Explain the need of low pass filter at the front end of PCM transmitter.

4. What is quantization noise. Derive the expression for signal-to-quantization noise power in PCM.

5. What is non-uniform quantizer ? Explain the process of companding in PCM.

6. Explain A-law and μ-law companding.

7. What is decoding noise in PCM. Derive the expression for decoding noise power in PCM.

8. Explain with suitable graph the performance of PCM with and without companding.

Chapter 3

DELTA MODULATION AND PREDICTIVE CODING

3.1 INTRODUCTION

- Most of the analog waveforms when sampled, have small change between two adjacent samples.

- We can make use of this fact to predict next sample value based on past sample values. This method of analog modulation is called predictive coding.

- These methods are more suitable for storage of audio and video signals in digital form. Some of these methods are –

  (i) Delta Modulation.   (ii)   Delta Sigma Modulation.

  (iii) Differential PCM.   (iv)   Adaptive Delta Modulation.

  (v) Linear Predictive Coding.

3.2 DELTA MODULATION (DM)

- It is a system in which corresponding to each sample we will have single encoded bit as opposed to n-bits in PCM.

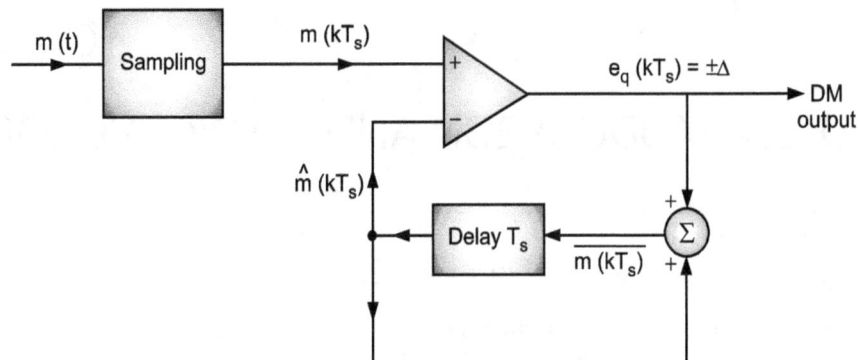

Fig. 3.1 : DM transmitter

- Delta modulator transmits binary output pulses whose polarity depends on difference between the modulating signal and feedback signal constituted from history of the signals previously sent.

- It has simple hardware and is less costly than PCM system.

- It is also more tolerant to transmission errors and does not need synchronization like PCM.

- But then all this comes with increased signaling rate (or sampling) and hence increased bandwidth requirements and possibility of slope-overload distortion.

The DM transmitter is shown in Fig. 3.1 below.

1. m(t) is the analog information signal.

2. $m(kT_s)$ is sampled version of m(t) at time kT_s, where k $=$ 0, 1, 2, ...

3. $e_q (kT_s)$ is the difference between current sample and predicted version of previous sample. $e_q (kT_s)$ is going to be either $+ \Delta$ or $- \Delta$.

4. Here $\hat{m} (kT_s) = \overline{m (k - 1) T_s}$ i.e. $\overline{m (kT_s)}$ delayed by one sampling time.

5. The waveforms are shown in Fig. 3.2.

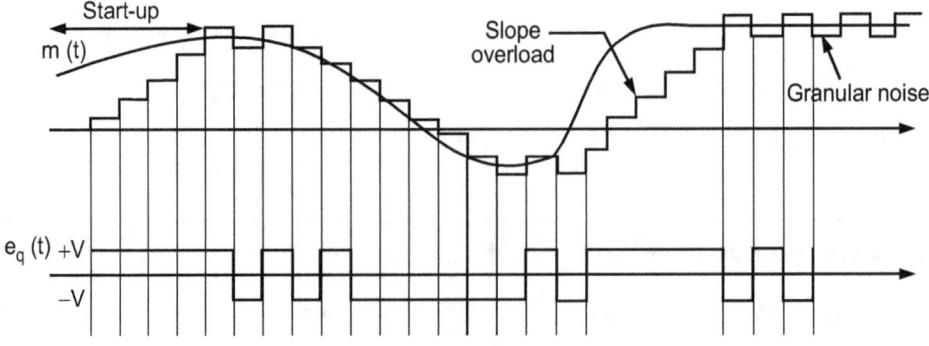

Fig. 3.2 : DM waveforms

6. It can be seen from the waveforms that whenever signal level m(t) is above $\hat{m}$ (kT$_s$), the output of DM is + Δ (bit 1) and if m (t) is below $\hat{m}$ (kT$_s$) output is – Δ (bit 0).

i.e. if   m(t) > $\hat{m}$ (kT$_s$)   output = + Δ

                   m(t) < $\hat{m}$ (kT$_s$)   output = – Δ

- When information signal m (t) is changing rapidly $\hat{m}$ (kT$_s$) cannot follow m(t) it is called slope overload effect. The error generated due this is called slope overload noise. It is shown in waveforms of Fig. 3.2.

- To avoid slope overload we can –

    (i)   Increase step size Δ.

    (ii)   Increase sampling frequency. i.e. reduce T$_s$.

- Increasing Δ will increase quantization noise, also called granular noise and increase in f$_s$ will require more transmission bandwidth.

- Thus, there are two types of quantization errors in DM :

    (i) Slope overload noise.

    (ii) Granular noise.

- Slope overload occurs when the step size is too small to follow fast rate changing part of waveform.

- Granularity occurs when the staircase function m(kT$_s$) hunts around a relatively slow varying part of waveform with large step size.

- Thus, a small value of Δ will give rise to slope overload and large value of Δ will increase granularity.

- The bit rate of DM is

$$r_b = \text{No. of samples/sec} \times \text{No. of bits/sample}$$

- Since DM has 1-bit per sample,

$$r_b = f_s$$

∴   Bandwidth requirement for DM is

$$\boxed{BW = \frac{r_b}{2} = \frac{f_s}{2}}$$

The DM receiver is shown in Fig. 3.3.

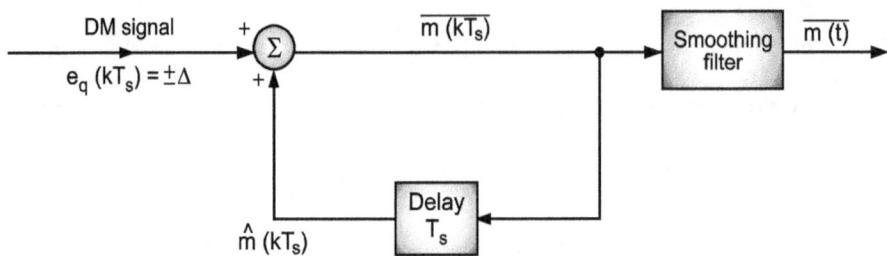

Fig. 3.3 : DM receiver

1. The accumulator will keep on accumulating the pulse ($\pm \Delta$) transmitted.

2. Hence $\overline{m}$ (kT_s) will be addition of received DM signal and delayed version of previous sample i.e. $\hat{m}$ (kT_s).

3. If the information signal m(t) remains constant for a long time or changing very slowly, $\overline{mkT_s}$ will hunt (fluctuate) and the resulting quantization noise becomes square wave with a period twice that of sampling period.

4. This is also called Idling noise or granular noise. This noise will be removed by smoothing filter (LPF) shown in DM receiver.

In practice, we can use a circuit shown in Fig. 3.4 to generate and reconstruct Delta modulator and demodulator. The first order predictor can be replaced by a low-cost (accumulator) integrator as shown in Fig. 3.4 (a).

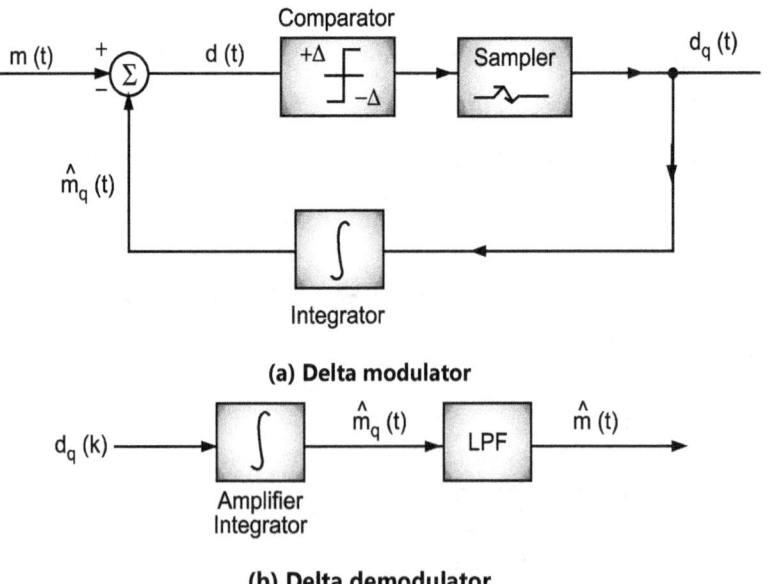

(a) Delta modulator

(b) Delta demodulator

Fig. 3.4

3.2.1 **Performance of Delta Modulator**

- Delta modulator can work well if the step size and T_s are sufficiently small.

- When m(t) increases or decreases too rapidly (as seen in the later part of waveform in Fig. 3.3) $\hat{m}_q$ (t) cannot catch up with m(t).

- This phenomenon is called slope overload. It gives rise to slope overload noise.

- This noise is basic limiting factor in the performance of delta modulator.

- Slope overload can be avoided by decreasing the step size and increasing f_s.

- But then this gives rise to another problem called granular noise.

- This effect is also shown in Fig. 3.3. When the signal varies too slowly, then there are alternate positive and negative pulses.

- This effect is more prominent if step size is small. Hence, we have to select optimum value for the step size.

- If the step size Δ and sampling time is T_s, then to avoid slope overload,

$$\max\left(\frac{dm\ (t)}{dt}\right) \leq \frac{\Delta}{T_s} \leq \Delta \times f_s \qquad \qquad ...(3.1)$$

Let,
$$m(t) = A_m \cos (2\pi f_m t) \qquad \qquad ...(3.2)$$

$\therefore$
$$\frac{dm\ (t)}{dt} = -2\pi f_m A_m \sin (2\pi f_m t) \qquad \qquad ...(3.3)$$

$$\max\left(\frac{dm\ (t)}{dt}\right) = 2\pi f_m A_m \qquad \qquad ...(3.4)$$

From equation (3.1) and (3.4), we can write,

$$2\pi f_m A_m \leq \Delta \times f_s$$

$$f_s \geq \frac{2\pi f_m A_m}{\Delta}$$

Hence to avoid slope overload,

$\therefore$
$$\boxed{f_s \geq \frac{2\pi f_m A_m}{\Delta}} \qquad \qquad ...(3.5)$$

Also,
$$\boxed{\frac{A_m}{\Delta} \leq \frac{1}{2\pi}\left(\frac{f_s}{f_m}\right)} \qquad \qquad ...(3.6)$$

- The step size Δ should be very small compared to peak-to-peak signal amplitude $2A_m$.

i.e.
$$\Delta \ll 2A_m$$

Ch. 3 | 3.5

$\therefore$ $$f_s \geq \pi \times f_m \left(\frac{2A_m}{\Delta}\right)$$

$\therefore$ $$f_s >> f_m$$

- Thus in DM, the sampling frequency required to avoid slope overload as very much larger than input signal frequency f_m. (In PCM we require $f_s = 2f_m$) or slightly more than that)

- The performance of DM depends on

  (i) Slope overload.

  (ii) Granular noise.

  (iii) Regeneration errors.

- Out of the three parameters granular noise is major parameter to be considered. It is nothing but quantization error and is defined as,

$$e\,(t) \;=\; \hat{m}_q\,(t) - m(t)$$

- The step size is Δ and hence the quantization error can be either $+\,\Delta$ or $-\,\Delta$.

Note that this error in case of PCM was $-\dfrac{\Delta}{2}$ to $\dfrac{\Delta}{2}$.

Hence, e(t) has uniform distribution over $-\,\Delta$ to $+\,\Delta$ as plotted in Fig. 3.5.

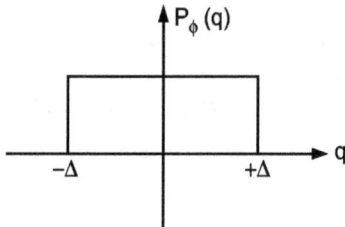

Fig. 3.5 : PDF of quantization error signal in DM

- Hence, the quantization noise or granular noise can be given by,

$$\sigma_q^2 \;=\; \int_{-\Delta}^{\Delta} q^2\,P_\phi\,(q)\,dq$$

$$=\; \int_{-\Delta}^{\Delta} q^2 \times \frac{1}{2\Delta}\,dq \;=\; \frac{1}{2\Delta}\left[\frac{q^3}{3}\right]_{-\Delta}^{\Delta} \;=\; \frac{\Delta^2}{3}$$

$\therefore$ $$\boxed{\sigma_q^2 = \frac{\Delta^2}{3}}$$ ... (3.7)

$\left(\text{In case of PCM this noise was } \dfrac{\Delta^2}{12}\right).$

- Let us now find the signal-to-noise ratio for DM.

- To find the noise power at the output of a low pass filter, we need the noise power spectral density.

- Experimentally, it is found that the power spectrum of granular noise is flat over a range extending beyond f_s, i.e.

$$S_{qn}(f) = \frac{\sigma_q^2}{2f_s} = \frac{\Delta^2}{3} \times \frac{1}{2f_s} , \text{ for } |f| \leq f_s \qquad \ldots (3.8)$$

Since σ_q^2 is mean square value (Average Power).

- But then this noise is filtered by LPF with cut-off frequency W Hz at the receiver. Hence, the noise power at the output of the filter will be,

$$N_q = \int_{-W}^{W} S_{qn}(f) \, df$$

$$= \int_{-W}^{W} \frac{\Delta^2}{3} \times \frac{1}{2f_s} \, df = \frac{\Delta^2}{3} \times \frac{1}{2f_s} \times 2W$$

$$= \frac{\Delta^2}{3} \times \frac{W}{f_s}$$

$$\therefore \boxed{N_q = \frac{\Delta^2}{3} \times \frac{W}{f_s}}$$

- Since granular noise is the most significant of the three noise types. Neglecting other two we can write the signal-to-noise ratio as,

$$\left(\frac{S}{N}\right)_0 = \frac{P_s}{N_q}$$

$$\therefore \left(\frac{S}{N}\right)_0 = \frac{P_s}{\frac{\Delta^2}{3} \times \frac{W}{f_s}}$$

$$\therefore \boxed{\left(\frac{S}{N}\right)_0 = \frac{3f_s}{\Delta^2 W} \times P_s} \qquad \ldots (3.9)$$

where, P_s is Average signal power $\overline{m^2(t)}$.

(Note that for PCM this expression was $3 L^2 P_s$).

Example 3.1 :

If input to linear delta modulator is $A_m \cos(2\pi f_m t)$, find the signal to quantization noise ratio if sampling frequency and stepsize is such that it is minimum value required to avoid slope overload.

Solution :

We know from equation (3.6) that to avoid slope overload in case of sinusoidal signal $A_m \cos(2\pi f_m t)$,

$$\frac{A_m}{\Delta} \leq \frac{1}{2\pi}\left(\frac{f_s}{f_m}\right)$$

Also from equation (3.6),

$$\left(\frac{S}{N}\right)_0 = \frac{3f_s}{\Delta^2 W} \times P_s$$

For sinusoidal signal,

$$P_s = \frac{A_m^2}{2}$$

$$\left(\frac{S}{N}\right)_0 = \frac{3f_s}{\Delta^2 W} \times \frac{A_m^2}{2} = \left(\frac{A_m}{\Delta}\right)^2 \times \frac{3f_s}{2W}$$

$$\therefore \qquad \left(\frac{S}{N}\right)_0 \leq \left(\frac{1}{2\pi}\times\frac{f_s}{f_m}\right)^2 \times \frac{3f_s}{2W}$$

$$\left(\frac{S}{N}\right)_0 \leq \frac{3}{8\pi^2}\times\frac{f_s^3}{f_m^2 \times W}$$

If $f_m = W$

$$\left(\frac{S}{N}\right)_0 = \frac{3}{8\pi^2}\left(\frac{f_s}{f_m}\right)^3$$

SNR for voice signal :

- Let us now consider the signal-to-noise ratio for voice signal.
- Let A_{max} be peak amplitude of voice signal $m(t)$. It has been shown that for voice signal, the maximum signal amplitude A_{max} that can be used to avoids slope overload is,

$$\therefore \qquad \left(\frac{S}{N}\right)_0 = \frac{3 \times f_s \times p_s}{\dfrac{A_{max}^2 \times \omega_r^2}{f_s^2} \times W}$$

$$= \frac{3 \times f_s^3 P_s}{A_{max}^2 \, \omega_r^2 \, W} = \frac{3 \times f_s^3 P_s}{A_{max}^2 \times 4\pi^2 \times (800)^2 \, W}$$

$$\therefore \qquad \left(\frac{S}{N}\right)_0 = \frac{3}{\pi^2} \times \left(\frac{f_s}{W}\right)^3 \times \frac{A_s}{A_{max}^2} \times \frac{W^2}{256 \times 10^4}$$

If $W = 4$ kHz

$$\left(\frac{S}{N}\right)_0 \cong \frac{18}{\pi^2} \left(\frac{f_s}{W}\right)^3 \times \frac{P_s}{A_{max}^2}$$

$$[A_{max}]voice = \frac{\Delta \times f_s}{\omega_r}$$

where, $\qquad \omega_r = 2\pi \times 800$

$$\therefore \qquad \left(\frac{S}{N}\right)_0 = \frac{3 \times f_s}{\Delta^2 \times W} \times P_s$$

Advantages of DM :

(i) Because one sample is represented by one bit hence no need to have word level synchronization at the input of demodulator and hardware is simple.

(ii) Less costly.

(iii) It is more tolerant to transmission errors. Because in DM each digit is separate whereas in PCM detection error depends on bit location.

Disadvantages of DM :

(i) Signaling rate is higher than PCM to take care of slope overload.

(ii) Slope overload distortion.

(iii) Granular noise.

(iv) Multiplexing of DM signal requires separate coder and decoder whereas in case of PCM single coder and decoder is shared by all channels.

Example 3.2 :

In a single integrator DM scheme, the voice signal is sampled at a rate of 64 kHz. The maximum signal amplitude is 1 volt, voice signal bandwidth is 3.5 kHz.

(i) Determine minimum value of step size to avoid slope overload.

(ii) Determine granular noise power N_0.

(iii) Assuming signal to be sinusoidal calculate signal power S_0 and Signal-to-Noise ratio.

(iv) Assuming that voice signal amplitude is uniformly distributed in the range $(-1, 1)$ determine signal power and signal to noise ratio.   **[Dec. 2000]**

Solution : Given :

$$f_s = 64 \text{ kHz}$$

$$f_m = W = 3.5 \text{ kHz}$$

$$A_{max} = 1 \text{ volt}$$

(i) We know to avoid slope overload, for sinusoidal signal.

$$f_s \geq \frac{2\pi f_m A_m}{\Delta}$$

∴ Step-size $\Delta \geq \dfrac{2\pi f_m A_m}{f_s}$

∴ $\Delta \geq \dfrac{2 \times \pi \times 3.5 \times 10^3 \times 1}{64 \times 10^3}$

∴ $\Delta \geq 0.34375 \text{ volt}$

To void slope overload for voice signal

∴ $A_{max} = \dfrac{\Delta \times f_s}{2\pi \times 800}$

∴ $\Delta = \dfrac{2\pi \times 800 \times 1}{64 \times 10^3} = 0.07854 \text{ volt}$

(ii) Granular noise power is given by,

For sinusoidal signal,

$$N_q = \frac{\Delta^2}{3} \times \frac{f_m}{f_s}$$

$$= \frac{(0.34375)^2}{3} \times \frac{3.5 \times 10^3}{64 \times 10^3}$$

$$= 2.154 \times 10^{-3} \text{ watt}$$

$$= 2.154 \text{ mW}$$

For voice signal

$$N_q = \frac{\Delta^2}{3} \times \frac{f_m}{f_s}$$

$$= \frac{(0.07854)^2 \times 3.5 \times 10^3}{3 \times 64 \times 10^3}$$

$$= 0.1124 \text{ mW}$$

(iii) If signal is sinusoidal, signal power is given by,

$$P_s = \frac{A_{max}^2}{2} = \frac{(1)^2}{2}$$

$$= 0.5 \text{ watt}$$

∴ $\left(\dfrac{S}{N}\right)_0 = \dfrac{P_s}{N_q}$

$$= \frac{0.5}{2.154 \times 10^{-3}}$$

$$= 232.126$$

(iv) Given that voice signal is uniformly distributed over (– 1, 1). Hence, signal power can be calculated by mean square value.

$$\sigma_x^2 \;=\; \int_{-1}^{1} x^2\, p_x\,(x)\, dx \;=\; \int_{-1}^{1} x^2 \times \frac{1}{2} \cdot dx$$

$$=\; \frac{1}{2} \times \left[\frac{x^3}{3} \right]_{-1}^{1}$$

$$=\; \frac{1}{3}$$

$$=\; 0.3333 \text{ watt}$$

$$\therefore \qquad\qquad P_S \;=\; 0.3333 \text{ watt}$$

Also, $\qquad\qquad A_{max} \;=\; 1$

Now, signal-to-noise ratio is,

$$\therefore \qquad \left(\frac{S}{N} \right)_0 \;=\; \frac{3 \times f_s}{\Delta^2 \times W}\, P_s \;=\; \frac{3 \times f_s \times p_s}{\left(\dfrac{A_{max} \times 2\pi \times 800}{f_s} \right)^2 \times W}$$

$$=\; \frac{3 \times 64 \times 10^3 \times 0.3333}{\left(\dfrac{1 \times 2\pi \times 800}{64 \times 10^3} \right)^2 \times 3.5 \times 10^3}$$

$$=\; 457.1$$

Example 3.3 :

1 kHz signal sampled by 8 kHz signal is to be encoded using –

(i) 12-bit PCM

(ii) DM systems

If 20 cycles of 1 kHz signal are digitized, state how many bits will be there in digital output signal in each case. State signaling rate and bandwidth in each case.

Solution : Given : $\qquad\qquad f_s \;=\; 8 \text{ kHz}$

$$W \;=\; f_m \;=\; 1 \text{ kHz}$$

(i) PCM System :

$$v \;=\; 12\text{-bit}$$

$$\text{Signaling rate } (r) \;=\; v \times f_s$$

$$=\; 12 \times 8 \times 10^3 \text{ bps} \;=\; 96 \text{ kbps}$$

$$1 \text{ cycle of 1 kHz} = 1 \text{ ms}$$

$$20 \text{ cycles of 1 kHz} = 20 \text{ ms}$$

$$\therefore \quad \text{Number of bits in 20 cycles} = 96 \times 10^3 \times 20 \times 10^{-3}$$

$$= 1920 \text{ bits}$$

Transmission bandwidth $\quad B_T = \dfrac{1}{2} \times r$

$$= \dfrac{1}{2} \times 96 \times 10^3$$

$$= 48 \text{ kHz}$$

(ii) DM System :

$$\text{Signaling rate} = f_s$$

$$= 8 \times 10^3 \text{ bps}$$

$$\therefore \quad \text{Number of bits in output} = 8 \times 10^3 \times 2 \times 10^{-3}$$

$$= 160 \text{ bits0}$$

Bandwidth requirement $\quad = \dfrac{r}{2} = \dfrac{8 \times 10^3}{2}$

$$= 4 \text{ kHz}$$

3.3 ADAPTIVE DELTA MODULATION (ADM)

- As we have seen in case of DM, to keep quantization noise and slope overload low, we should have high sampling rate.

- In fact it has to be many times the Nyquist rate i.e. $f_s >> 2f_m$.

- But this will require high bandwidth, which defeats very purpose of DM (1-bit PCM).

- To avoid slope overload, we can use variable step size.

- When the signal is varying slowly, we can have smaller step size; whereas when signal is varying faster, we can use higher step size.

- Such system is called Adaptive DM (ADM).

The block diagram of ADM transmitter is shown in Fig. 3.6 below.

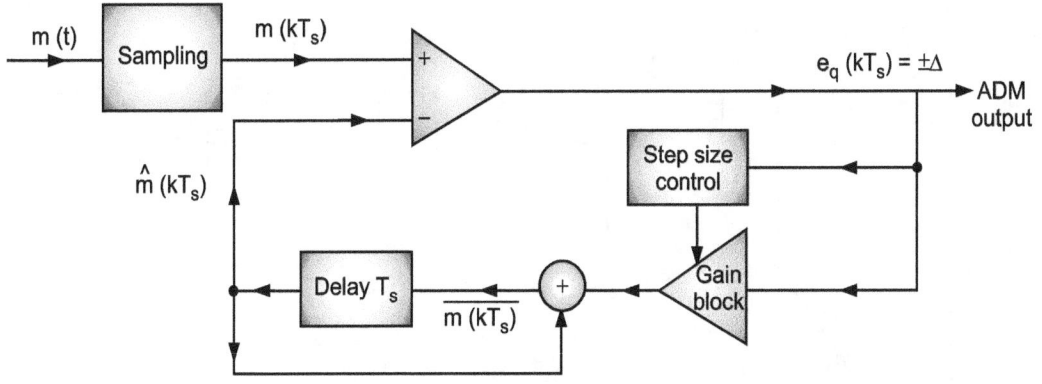

Fig. 3.6 : ADM transmitter

- he comparator at the input compares sample value of information signal $m(kT_s)$ and delayed predicted version of the previous sample $\hat{m}(KT_s)$.

If $\qquad\qquad m(kT_s) > \hat{m}(kT_s) \qquad\qquad$ output $= +\Delta$

$\qquad\qquad\qquad m(kT_s) < \hat{m}(kT_s) \qquad\qquad$ output $= -\Delta$

- The gain block controls the variable step size.
- The step size is varied based on past values of e_q. For example, if $e_q = +\Delta$ for several values of adjacent samples, it means m(t) is rising more rapidly than $\hat{m}(kT_s)$. It means we should increase step size.
- If e_q is alternating between $+\Delta$ and $-\Delta$, it means m(t) is slowly varying and we should decrease the step size in order to reduce quantization error or granular noise.
- Fig. 3.7 shows waveforms of ADM.
- The ADM algorithm for step size adjustment would be as below :
- The step size at time KT_s is given by

$$A(kT_s) = \begin{cases} A[(k-1)T_s] \cdot C, & \text{if } e_q(kT_s) = e_q(k-1)T_s \\ A[(k-1)T_s]/C, & \text{if } e_q(kT_s) = -e_q(k-1)T_s \end{cases}$$

where, C is a constant greater than 1.

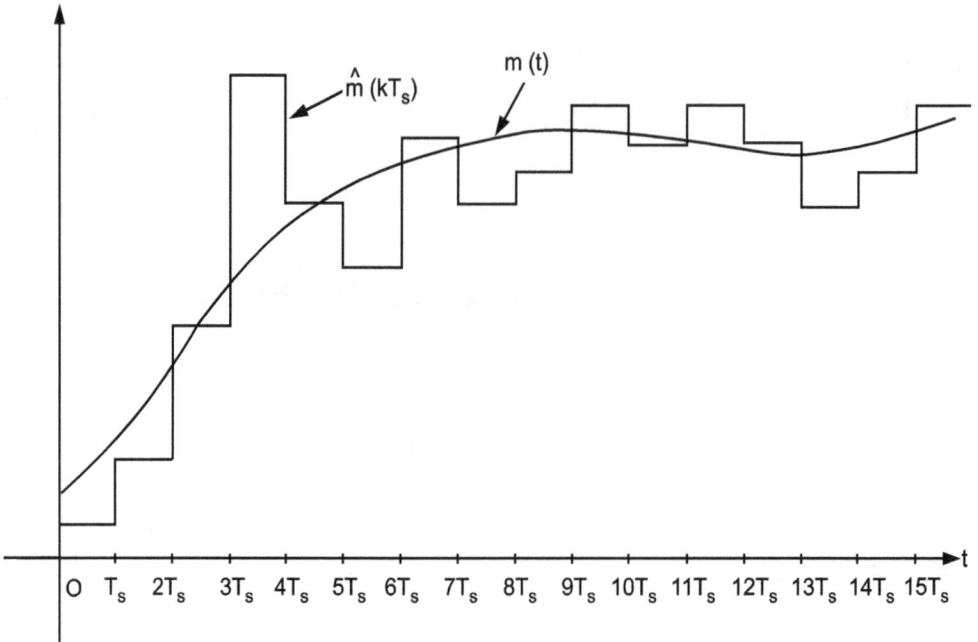

Fig. 3.7 : ADM waveform

- The ADM system reduces slope overload, but at the cost of increasing quantization noise.

- Since ADM uses large step sizes for wide variations in signal level and small step size for small variations in signal level, it has wide dynamic range compared to Delta Modulation.

- Hence ADM can operate at much lower bit rates than DM i.e. 32 kb/s even 16 kb/s with slight degradation in performance.

Advantages of ADM :

(i)   Dynamic range of ADM is better than DM because of variable step-size.

(ii) Because of reduction in slope overload, signal-to-noise ratio is improved.

(iii) Bandwidth requirement for ADM is reduced because slope overload is reduced.

(iv) Simple hardware implementation than PCM.

(v)   Less costlier than PCM.

(vi) 1-bit output per sample.

3.4 DELTA-SIGMA MODULATION

- In delta modulation which we have seen earlier we take derivative of incoming signal. Then at the receiver end we integrate (Accumulate) the signal.

- If this signal is added with noise then the demodulated signal is going to accumulate the errors due to noise. To overcome this drawback, we integrate the signal before delta modulation. This scheme is called Delta-Sigma Modulation, to be precise Sigma-Delta Modulation.

- It has following advantages :

  (i) We can eliminate the accumulator at the receiver and receiver circuit will be very simple.

  (ii) The low frequency contents of input signal are pre-emphasized.

  (iii) Adjacent samples of input given to delta modulator are more correlated with each other. It reduces variance of error signal improving system performance.

- Fig. 3.8 (a) shows the transmitter and receiver for delta-sigma modulator.

- The 1-bit DM signal is produced by multiplying pulse generator and the hard-limiter output because of integration used at the transmitter.

- We need a differentiator at the receiver end to compensate for the pre-emphasis. But then integrator-differentiator combination will cancel out each other and we need only low pass filter at the receiver. Similarly, we can combine the two integrators into one at the transmitter end.

- The modified block diagram is shown in Fig. 3.8 (b).

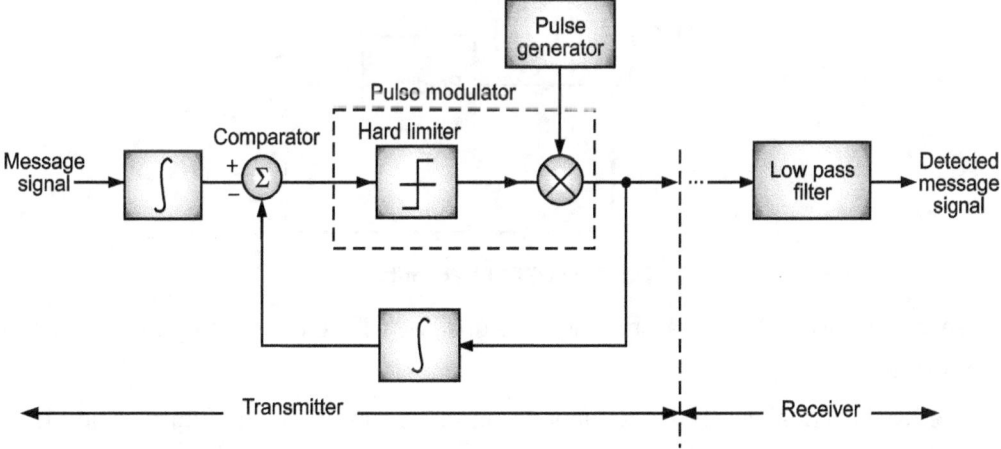

(a) Delta-sigma modulator-demodulator

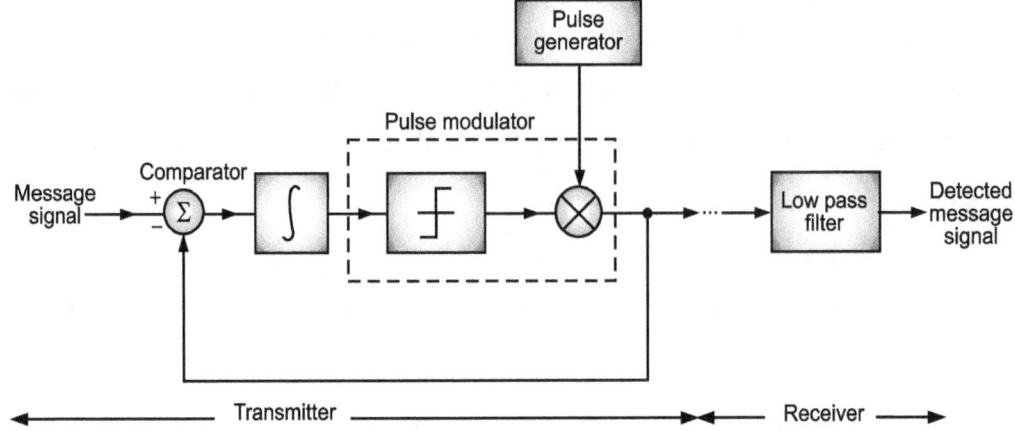

(b) Delta-sigma modulator-demodulator

Fig. 3.8

3.5 DIFFERENTIAL PCM (DPCM)

- Most of the time the samples of information signals are correlated with each other. In other words, there is lot of redundancy in the signal, meaning similar information resides in two or more samples.

- For example, when voice signal is sampled at a rate higher than Nyquist rate, adjacent samples do not change much.

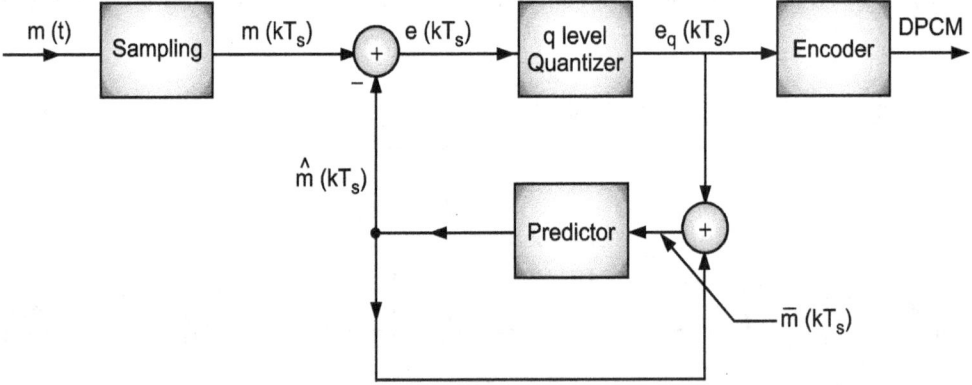

Fig. 3.9 : DPCM transmitter

- Hence, if we use PCM for transmitting the signal, we will be transmitting more redundant information.

- If we have a signal which has redundancy in it, we can predict its future value from its past values.

- Differential Pulse Code Modulation (DPCM) instead of transmitting encoded version of the sample, transmits encoded version of the difference between the two consecutive samples.
- Fig. 3.9 shows block diagram of the DPCM transmitter.
- $m(t)$ is the analog information signal and $m(kT_s)$ is sampled version of $m(t)$ at time kT_s, where $k = 0, 1, 2 \ldots$ $e(kT_s)$ is the error between actual value of $m(kT_s)$ and $\hat{m}(kT_s)$ which is predicted from previous samples. The error $e(kT_s)$ is quantized to generate $e_q(kT_s)$.
- The quantized signal $e_q(kT_s)$ is encoded and then transmitted.
- $\overline{m(kT_s)} = \hat{m}(kT_s) + e_q(kT_s)$ which is estimate of $m(kT_s)$. Following are the interrelations of the signal in the block diagram.

1. $e(kT_s) = m(kT_s) - \hat{m}(kT_s)$
2. $e_q(kT_s) = e(kT_s) + q_e(kT_s)$

   where, $q_e(kT_s)$ is quantization error.

3. $\overline{m(kT_s)} = \hat{m}(kT_s) + e_q(kT_s)$

4. $\overline{m(kT_s)} = \hat{m}(kT_s) + e(kT_s) + q_e(kT_s)$

Substituting in (1),

$$\therefore \qquad \overline{m(kT_s)} = \hat{m}(kT_s) + m(kT_s) - \hat{m}(kT_s) + q_e(kT_s)$$

$$\therefore \qquad \overline{m(kT_s)} = m(kT_s) + q_e(kT_s)$$

Thus $\overline{m(kT_s)}$ is almost equal to $m(kT_s)$ with small quantization error $q_e(kT_s)$.

- **Note :** if $\{m(kT_s)$ is correlated, then variance of $e(kT_s)$ would be less than $m(kT_s)$ and the step size Δ_e required to discretize $e(kT_s)$ would be smaller than the step size Δ_m required for $m(kT_s)$. Hence, $\dfrac{\Delta_e^2}{12} < \dfrac{\Delta_m^2}{12}$ and there would be improvement in signal to noise ratio.
- The DPCM receiver is shown in Fig. 3.10 below. It is identical to the predictor loop used in transmitter.
- The decoder converts received binary signal into quantized error signal $e_q(kT_s)$.
- This will be added to output $\hat{m}(kT_s)$ to generate $m(kT_s)$ as explained earlier.
- The reconstructed signal will be $\overline{m(t)}$ which is estimate of original signal $m(t)$.

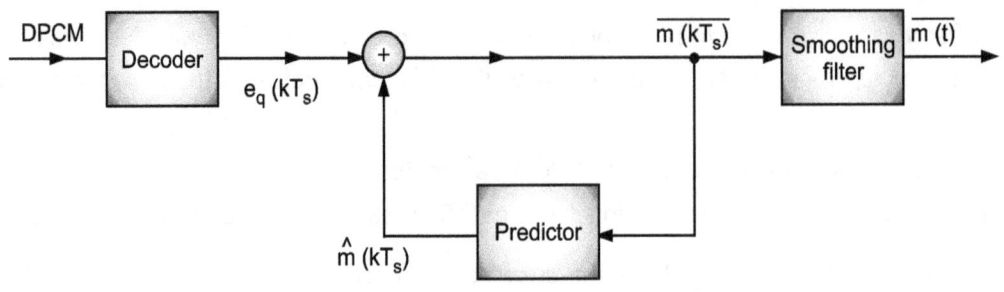

Fig. 3.10

- The predictor is DPCM transmitter and receiver is linear weighted sum of samples and can be implemented using shift registers as shown in Fig. 3.11 below.

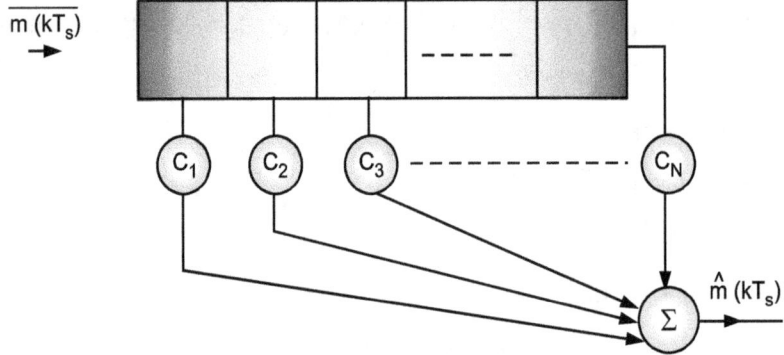

Fig. 3.11 : Predictor circuit

Signal-to-Noise Ratio for DPCM :

The signal-to-noise ratio of output of DPCM is given by,

$$(SNR)_0 = \frac{\sigma_m^2}{\sigma_q^2}$$

where, σ_m^2 is variance of original input signal m (k) and σ_q^2 is variance of quantization error.

We can write above equation as,

$$(SNR)_0 = \frac{\sigma_m^2}{\sigma_e^2} \times \frac{\sigma_e^2}{\sigma_q^2}$$

where, σ_e^2 is variance of prediction error.

$$\therefore \qquad (SNR)_0 = G_p \times \frac{\sigma_e^2}{\sigma_q^2}$$

where, G_p is called prediction gain or processing gain defined by,

$$G_p = \frac{\sigma_m^2}{\sigma_e^2}$$

If we use L levels for quantizing error signal e (k), then as already derived from PCM, SNR,

$$\frac{\sigma_e^2}{\sigma_q^2} = 3 L^2 \times P_s$$

Thus, signal-to-noise ratio for DPCM is given by,

$$\boxed{(SNR)_0 = G_p \times 3 L^2 P_s}$$

The SNR for DPCM is enhanced by prediction gain G_p.

The DPCM system and DM system are similar except that in DM we have one bit quantizer and there is single delay element instead of prediction filter. Thus, DM is 1-bit version of DPCM.

DPCM will suffer from slope overload for fast varying signal just like DM. DPCM has quantization noise similar to PCM.

Example 3.4 :

If DPCM predictor has predictor gain of the order of 6 dB show that DPCM word needs one less bit than that of binary PCM all other factors remaining same.

Solution : Given : $G_p = 6$ dB

$\therefore$ $G_p = 3.98 \approx 4$

SNR for PCM :

$$(SNR)_{PCM} = 3 L_1^2 \times P_s$$

L_1 is the number of quantization levels of PCM.

SNR for DPCM :

$$(SNR)_{DPCM} = G_p \times 3 L_2^2 P_s$$

L_2 is the number of quantization levels of DPCM.

$\therefore$ $3 L_1^2 \times P_s = G_p \times 3 L_2^2 P_s$

$$\frac{L_1^2}{L_2^2} = 4$$

$$\frac{L_1}{L_2} = 2$$

$$\therefore \qquad L_1 = 2 L_2$$

$$\therefore \qquad 2^{2V_1} = 2 \times 2^{V_2}$$

$$v_1 \log_2 2 \, v_1 = \log_2 (2 \times 2^{V_2})$$

$$\therefore \qquad v_1 = \log_2 2 + v_2 \log_2 2$$

$$v_1 = 1 + v_2$$

$\therefore$ Hence, number of bits of PCM is one more than number of bits of DPCM.

3.6 LINEAR PREDICTIVE CODER (LPC)

- Speech consists of a sequence of 'voiced' and 'unvoiced' sounds that are passed through a filter. Voiced sounds are generated by the vibrations of the vocal words. Unvoiced sounds are generated when speaker pronounces words with hissing sound.

- Linear Predictive Coding (LPC) is a method of representing speech signal into digital format. We need not transmit the actual speech waveform generated by a speaker.

- Instead we transmit the information related to synthesizing the waveform in encoded format. By doing this we will be operating at a very low bit rate of the order 3 to 8 kbps.

- Of course, the resulting reproduced voice is of artificial quality. Systems that generate speech in this manner are called **vocoders**.

- Thus, vocoders are simplified coding devices which extract, in efficient way, the significant components of speech waveform.

- Fig. 3.12 (a) shows speech synthesizer. It has two input generators, one for voiced sounds and another for unvoiced sounds, a variable gain amplifier and a filter in a feedback loop.

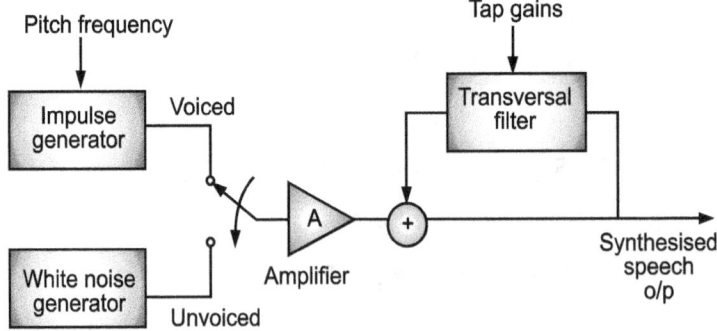

Fig. 3.12 : (a) Speech synthesizer

- The unvoiced sounds are generated by noise source and voiced sounds by an impulse generator.

- Impulse generator whose frequency is the fundamental frequency of vibration of vocal cords. The filter represents the effect of mouth, throat and nasal passages.
- Now let us consider the LPC transmitter shown in Fig. 3.12 (b).

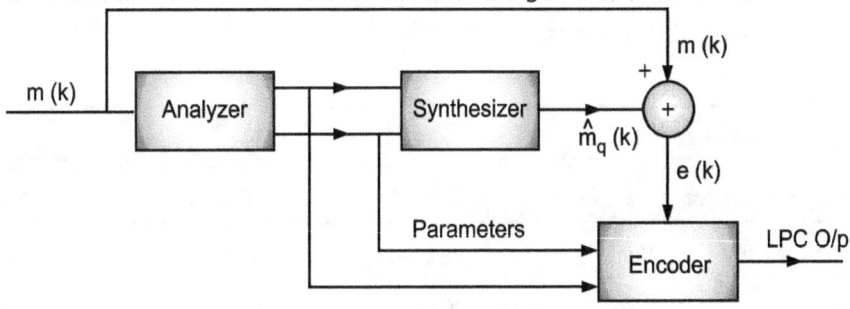

Fig. 3.12 : (b) LPC transmitter

- Speech signal from a speaker is analysed and the necessary parameters are generated, in every 10-25 ms frame.
- The synthesizer uses these parameters to generate approximate version of the signal.
- The synthesizer output $\hat{m}_q$ (k) and input signal m(k) are compared to generate error signal e(k).
- This error signal along with the parameters is encoded and transmitted as LPC signal.
- Fig. 3.12 (c) depicts receiver for LPC system.
- The decoder and synthesizer apply received filter coefficients to synthesizing filter which is excited with impulses at pitch frequency if voiced, or by white noise is unvoiced.
- The parameter values and quantized error are used to reconstruct the speech signal.

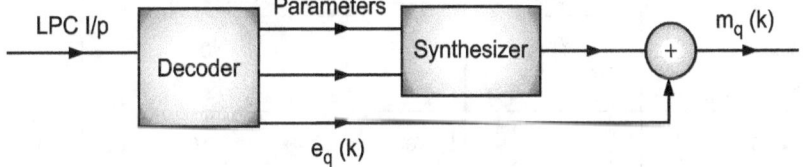

Fig. 3.12 : (c) LPC receiver

- An LPC codeword has 80-bits. They are distributed as below.

  1-bit for recognising voiced/unvoiced sound.

  6 bits for pitch frequency.

  5-bits for amplifier gain.

  6-bits each for 10 tap gains of the filter.

  and 8-bits for error.

- The filter has 10 tap gains.
- The parameters are updated every 10 to 25 ms.
- This is equivalent to sampling at 40 to 100 Hz. Hence, the LPC has bit rate equal to 80 × 40 (3200) to 80 × 100 (8000) bps.

3.7 COMPARISON

Parameter for comparison	PCM	ADPCM	DM	ADM
1. Bits per sample	Variable	Variable	One	One
2. Step-size	Fixed in simple PCM variable in companded PCM	Fixed	Fixed	Variable
3. Maximum Quantization error	$\pm\dfrac{\Delta}{2}$	$\pm\dfrac{\Delta}{2}$	$\pm\Delta$	$\pm\Delta$
4. Quantization Noise	$\dfrac{\Delta^2}{12}$	$\dfrac{\Delta^2}{12}$	$\dfrac{\Delta^2}{3}$	$\dfrac{\Delta^2}{3}$
5. Complexity of circuit	Complex	Complex	Less complex	More complex than DM
6. Bit rate for voice encoding (kbps)	56-64	32-48	64-128	48-64
7. Cost	Costly	Costly	Cheapest	Cheap
8. Synchronization requirement	Yes	Yes	No	No
9. Signaling rate	High	Lower than PCM	Lower if no slope overload, highest if slope overload	Lower than DM
10. Bandwidth requirement	Higher	Lower than PCM	Lower if no slope overload, highest if slope overload	Lower than DM
11. SNR	$3\,L^2\,P_s$	$G_p\,3\,L^2\,P_s$	$\dfrac{3}{\Delta^2}\times\dfrac{f_s}{W}\times P_s$	Better than DM.

SOLVED PROBLEMS

Problem 3.1 :

Find minimum sampling frequency to avoid slope overload when input signal cos (2π 800 t) and step size 0.1 V.

Solution : Given :

$$m(t) = \cos (2\pi\ 800\ t)$$

$$\Delta = 0.1$$

∴ $$f_m = 800\ Hz$$

$$A_m = 1$$

To avoid slope overload

$$f_s \geq 2\pi f_m \times \frac{A_m}{\Delta}$$

∴ $$f_s \geq 2 \times \pi \times 800 \times \frac{1}{0.1}$$

$$f_s \geq 50240\ Hz$$

Hence, minimum sampling frequency is 50.240 kHz.

Problem 3.2 :

If input to delta modulator is m(f) = 6 sin [(2π × 10³)t] + 4 sin [(4π × 10³)t] with t seconds. Determine the minimum rate that will percent slope overload if step size is 0.314.

Solution : Given :

$$\Delta = 0.314V$$

$$m(t) = 6 \sin [2\pi \times 10^3)\ t] + 4 \sin [(4\pi \times 10^3)]$$

∴ $$m'(t) = \frac{dm(t)}{dt} = 12\pi \times 10^3 \cos [(2\pi \times 10^3)\ t] + 16\pi \times 10^3$$

$$\cos [(4\pi \times 10^3)\ t]$$

$$(m'(t))_{max} = \frac{d'm(t)}{dt}\bigg|_{t=0}$$

∴ $$(m'(t))_{max} = 28\pi \times 10^3$$

To avoid slope overload

$$\Delta \times f_s \geq 28\pi \times 10^3$$

$$f_s \geq \frac{28\pi \times 10^4 \times 0.314}{0.314}$$

$$\geq 280 \times 10^3\ Hz$$

Hence, pulse rate will be 280 kHz.

Problem 3.3 :

A 1 kHz sine wave signal is sampled and transmitted using 12 bit PCM and DM systems. If 25 cycles of this signal are digitized find :

(i) Signalling rate.   (ii) Bandwidth required.   (iii) Total number of bit transmitted.

Solution :

1. For PCM :

Given : Sine wave frequency, f_m = 1 kHz

Bits per sample, v = 12

Sampling frequency, f_s = 4 kHz

(i) Signaling rate, $r = v \cdot f_s = 12 \times 4 \times 10^3$

$\qquad\qquad\qquad\qquad\qquad = 48$ Kbps

(ii) Bandwidth required, $B_T = \dfrac{r}{2} = \dfrac{48 \times 10^3}{2}$

$\qquad\qquad\qquad\qquad\qquad = 24$ kHz

(iii) Number of samples in 25 cycles

$\qquad\qquad\qquad\qquad = 25 \times$ Number of samples per cycle

$\qquad\qquad\qquad\qquad = 25 \times 4 = 100$

$\therefore$ Number of bits in 25 cycles

$\qquad\qquad\qquad\qquad =$ Number of samples $\times$ Number of bits per sample

$\qquad\qquad\qquad\qquad = 100 \times 12 = 1200$ bits

2. For D.M. system :

$\qquad\qquad$ Bits per sample $= 1$

(i)$\qquad\qquad$ Signaling rate $= v \cdot f_s = 1 \times 4 \times 10^3$

$\qquad\qquad\qquad\qquad\qquad = 4$ kHz

(ii) Bandwidth required, $B_T = \dfrac{r}{2} = \dfrac{4 \times 10^3}{2}$

$\qquad\qquad\qquad\qquad\qquad = 2$ kHz

(iii) No. of bits in 2.5 cycles $=$ Number of samples $\times$ Bits/Sample

$\qquad\qquad\qquad\qquad\qquad = 100 \times 1 = 100$ bits

Comment : It seems from above example that DM is better than PCM since bandwidth requirement is low for DM. But DM has the disadvantage of slope overload error. To avoid slope overload we have to increase f_s which increases bandwidth requirement of DM.

SOLVED UNIVERSITY QUESTIONS

U.Q. 1 : Delta modulator (DM) gives output pulse + p(t) or –p(t). The output of DM is +p(t) when instantaneous sample is larger than previous sample value and is –p(t) when instantaneous sample is smaller than previous sample value (last sample). The p(t) has 2 microsecond duration and 628 mV amplitude and repeats every 10 microsecond. Plot the input and output of DM on graph paper one below other to same scale if the input to DM is 1 Volt sine wave frequency 10 kHz for one cycle of input wave. What is the maximum frequency with 1 Volt amplitude that can be used in this system without slope overload distortion.

Solution : Given :

$$\text{Pulse width} = 2\mu s$$
$$\text{Pulse amplitude} = 628 \text{ mV}$$
$$\text{Sampling interval} = 10 \ \mu s$$

Input amplitude,   1V Frequency = 10 kHz

$$\therefore \qquad m(t) = \sin (2\pi \times 10000 \ t)$$

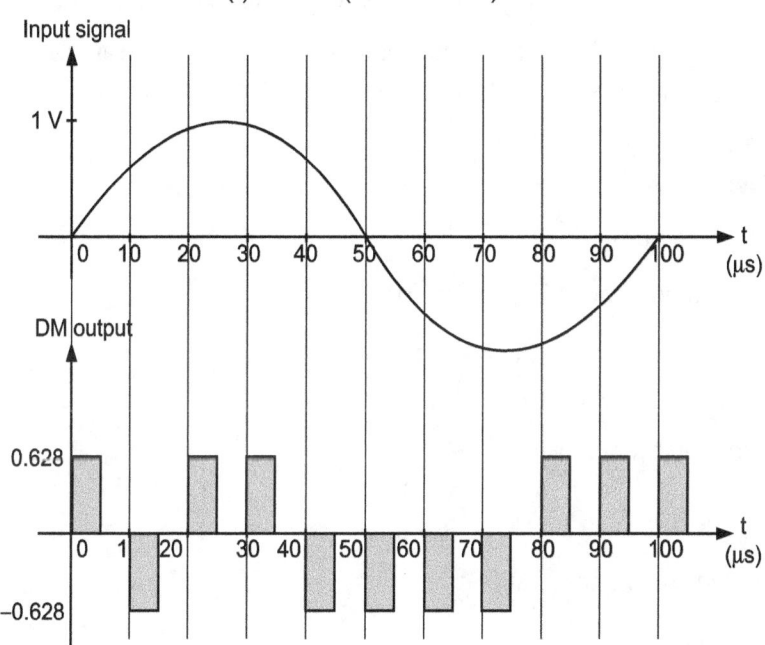

Fig. 3.13

t	0	10	20	30	40	50	60	70	80	90	100
m(t)	0	0.588	0.951	9.951	0.588	0	0.588	0.951	0.951	0.588	0

Here,
$$f_s = \frac{1}{10 \times 10^{-6}} = 100 \text{ kHz}$$

Slope of signal
$$m(t) = \sin(2\pi \times 10000\, t)$$

$$\frac{dm(t)}{dt} = 2\pi \times 1000 \cos(2\pi\, 1000\, t)$$

To avoid slope overload $2\pi f_m \cdot A_m \leq \Delta \times f_s$

$$\therefore \quad f_m \leq \frac{\Delta \times f_s}{2\pi \times A_m}$$

$$\leq \frac{0.628 \times 100 \times 10^3}{2\pi \times 1}$$

$$\leq 10000 \text{ Hz}$$

$$\leq 10 \text{ kHz}$$

Hence, maximum frequency of input signal to void slope overload is 10 kHz.

U.Q. 2 : A signal $\frac{m(t)}{2}$ band limited to B Hz has average power of m(t) and peak power of m_p^2 . Signal has maximum slope at $f_r = 800$ Hz. This signal is converted to digital by using delta modulation technique with sampling rate of f_x samples/second. Derive the relation for SNR (S/N) at the output of DM in terms of given data and transmission bandwidth B_T Hz.   **(Dec. 2005)**

Solution : Given :

Signal m(t) with Peak power m_p^2.

$$\text{Average power } (P_s) = \overline{m^2(t)}$$

$$\text{Bandwidth} = 3 \text{ Hz}$$

$$f_r = 800 \text{ Hz}$$

Quantization noise at the receiver will be,

$$N_q = \frac{\Delta^2}{3} \times \frac{B}{f_s}$$

$\therefore$ Signal-to-quantization noise ratio.

$$\left(\frac{S}{N}\right)_0 = \frac{P_s}{N_q}$$

$$= \frac{\overline{m^2(t)}}{\frac{\Delta^2}{3} \times \frac{B}{f_s}} = \frac{3 \times f_s \times \overline{m^2(t)}}{\Delta^2 \times B}$$

Since m_p in peak signal amplitude,

$$m_p = \frac{\Delta f_s}{\omega_r} \qquad\qquad \therefore\ \Delta = \frac{\omega_l m_p}{f_s}$$

$$\therefore \quad \left(\frac{S}{N}\right)_0 = \frac{3 \times f_s \times \overline{m^2(t)}}{\dfrac{\omega_2^2 \times m_p^2}{f_s^2} \times B}$$

$$= 3 \times \frac{f_s^3}{\omega_r^2} \times \frac{\overline{m^2(t)}}{m_p^2} \times \frac{1}{B}$$

But, $\qquad\qquad B_T = \dfrac{k \cdot f_s}{2}$

where, $1 < k < 2$

$$\therefore \quad \left(\frac{S}{N}\right)_0 = 3 \times \frac{\left(\dfrac{2B_T}{k}\right)^3}{\omega_r^2} \times \frac{\overline{m^2(t)}}{m_p^2} \times \frac{1}{B}$$

$$= 24 \left(\frac{B}{\omega_r}\right)^2 \times \left(\frac{B_T}{kB}\right)^3 \frac{\overline{m^2(t)}}{m_p^2}$$

$$= 24 \left(\frac{B}{2\pi \times 800}\right)^2 \times \left(\frac{B_T}{kB}\right)^3 \times \frac{\overline{m^2(t)}}{m_p^2}$$

$$= 15 \left(\frac{B_T}{kB}\right)^3 \left(\frac{\overline{m^2(t)}}{m_p^2}\right)$$

U.Q. 3 : Explain speech synthesis using LPC. **(6) (May 2006)**

Solution : Refer Section 3.6.

U.Q. 4 : Compare DM and ADM system. **(6) (May 2006)**

Solution : Refer Section 3.7.

U.Q. 5 : A speech signal band limited to 3.4 kHz having maximum amplitude 1V is delta modulated at 20 kbps. What is approximate step size for the same.

Solution : **(8) (Dec. 2006)**

Given : Signal bandwidth, $\quad W = 3.4$ kHz

$\qquad\qquad$ Amplitude, $A_m = 1V$

$\qquad\qquad$ Bit rate (r) $= 20$ kbps

Since in DM

$$r = f_s$$

$$f_s = 20 \text{ kHz}$$

To avoid slope overload

$$\frac{A_m}{\Delta} \leq \frac{1}{2\pi} \times \frac{f_s}{W}$$

∴

$$\Delta \geq \frac{2\pi \times W \times A_m}{f_s}$$

∴

$$\Delta \geq \frac{2 \times 3.142 \times 3.4 \times 10^3 \times 1}{20 \times 10^3}$$

$$= 1.068 \text{ volt}$$

U.Q. 6 : Derive an expression for signal to quantization noise ratio for delta modulation. Assume no slope overload distortion exists. **(May 2007)**

Solution : Refer Section 3.2.1.

U.Q. 7 : What are limitation of delta modulation ? How are they overcome in delta-sigma modulation and adaptive delta modulation ? Explain with necessary diagrams.

(8) (Dec. 2007)

Solution :

Limitations of Delta Modulation :

1. Slope overload.

2. Granular noise.

3. Accumulative errors due to noise.

Adaptive delta modulation can overcome slope overload (Refer Section 3.3) (Figs. 3.6 and 3.7).

Sigma Delta (or Delta Sigma) Modulation can eliminate the third drawback (Refer Section 3.4), Fig. 3.8.

U.Q. 8 : A DM systems is designed to operate at 3 times the Nyquist rate for the signal with 3 kHz bandwidth. The quantizing step size is 250 mV.

(i) Determine the maximum amplitude of 1 kHz input sinusoid for which the delta modulator does not show slope overload.

(ii) Determine the post filtered output signal-to-quantization ratio for the signal in part (i). **(8) (May 2008)**

Solution : Given :

Input signal bandwidth, $W = 3 \text{ kHz}$

Sampling rate, $f_s = 3 \times 2W$

$$= 3 \times 6$$

$$= 18 \text{ kHz}$$

Step size, $\Delta = 0.25 \text{ V}$

(i) Applied signal frequency, f_m = 1 kHz

To avoid slope overload,

$$\frac{A_m}{\Delta} \leq \frac{1}{2\pi} \times \frac{f_s}{f_m}$$

$\therefore$

$$A_m \leq \frac{1}{2\pi} \times \frac{\Delta \times f_s}{f_m}$$

$$\leq \frac{1}{2\pi} \times \frac{0.25 \times 18 \times 10^3}{1 \times 10^3}$$

$$\leq 0.716 \text{ V}$$

Hence, maximum amplitude in 716 mV.

(ii) Post filtered signal to noise ratio

We have,

$$f_m = 1 \text{ kHz}$$
$$W = 3 \text{ kHz}$$

To avoid slope overload

$$\frac{A_m}{\Delta} \leq \frac{1}{2\pi} \left(\frac{f_s}{f_m}\right)$$

$$\left(\frac{S}{N}\right)_0 = \frac{3f_s}{\Delta^2 W} \times P_s$$

where,

$$P_s = \frac{A_m^2}{2}$$

$\therefore$

$$\left(\frac{S}{N}\right)_0 = \frac{3f_s}{\Delta^2 W} \times \frac{A_m^2}{2} = \left(\frac{A_m}{\Delta}\right)^2 \frac{3f_s}{2W}$$

$$\left(\frac{S}{N}\right)_0 \leq \left(\frac{1}{\pi} \times \frac{f_s}{f_m}\right)^2 \frac{3f_s}{2W}$$

$$\leq \frac{3}{8\pi^2} \times \frac{f_s^3}{f_m^2 \times W}$$

$\therefore$

$$\left(\frac{S}{N}\right)_{0\,max} = \frac{3}{8\pi^2} \times \frac{(18 \times 10^3)^3}{(1 \times 10^3)^2 \times (3 \times 10^3)} = 4.56 \times 10^{-4}$$

i.e.

$$\left(\frac{S}{N}\right)_{0\,max} = -33.41 \text{ dB}$$

U.Q. 9 : Consider a DM system designed to accommodate analog message signals limited to bandwidth W = 5 kHz. A sinusoidal test signal of amplitude A = 1 volt and frequency f_m = 1 kHz is app[lied to the system. The sampling rate of the system is 50 kHz.   **(9 marks) (Dec. 2008)**

(i) Calculate step size required to avoid slope overload.

(ii) Calculate SNR.

Solution : Given :
$$W = 5 \text{ kHz}$$
$$A = 1 \text{ volt}$$
$$f_m = 1 \text{ kHz}$$
$$f_s = 50 \text{ kHz}$$

(i) To avoid slope overhead

$$\frac{A_m}{\Delta} \leq \frac{1}{2\pi}\left(\frac{f_s}{f_m}\right)$$

$$\therefore \qquad \Delta \geq 2\pi \times \frac{A_m \times f_m}{f_s}$$

$$\geq \frac{2 \times \pi \times 1 \times 1 \times 10^3}{50 \times 10^3}$$

$$\geq 0.1256 \text{ volt}$$

(ii) Signal-to-noise ratio

$$\left(\frac{S}{N}\right)_0 = \frac{3}{8\pi^2} \times \frac{f_s^3}{f_m^2 \times W}$$

$$= \frac{3 \times (50 \times 10^3)^2}{8 \times \pi^2 \times (1 \times 10^3) \times (5 \times 10^3)}$$

$$= 949.886 \text{ i.e. } 29.77 \text{ dB}$$

U.Q. 10 : Explain in detail principle of delta modulation system with block schematic and supporting waveforms. Derive expression for quantization noise in the same.

(9) (Nov. 2009)

Solution : Refer Sections 3.2 and 3.2.1.

U.Q. 11 : What is delta-sigma modulation ? Explain transmitter and receiver schemes of the same.   **(6) (May 2009)**

Solution : Refer Section 3.4.

U.Q. 12 : If a sinusoidal signal m(t) = A cos ($\omega_m t$) is applied to delta modulator with step size, show that slope overload distortion will occur if $A = \dfrac{\delta}{\omega_m}$ where $f_s = \dfrac{1}{T_s}$ is sampling frequency.   **(6) (May 2009)**

Solution : Refer Section 3.2.1.

Dec. 2010

U.Q. 13 : Draw the block diagram of DM transmitter and explain its working. Comment on the drawbacks of DM. Explain how the drawback of accumulation of noise is eliminated by Delta-Sigma modulator. **(10)**

Solution : Refer Sections 3.2 and 3.4.

U.Q. 14 : A signal having bandwidth 3 kHz is to be encoded using

(i) 8-bit PCM system

(ii) DM system

If 10 cycles of the signal are digitized, state how many bits will there in digitized, output in each case if sampling frequency is 10 KHz. Also find bandwidth required in each case. **(8)**

Solution : Given: Sampling frequency

$$f_s = 10 \text{ kHz}$$

Signal bandwidth $\quad f_m = 3 \text{ kHz}$

(i) For 8-bit PCM system

Number of bits per quantization level.

$$v = 8 \text{ bits}$$

∴ Signaling rate $r = v \times f_s = 8 \times 10 \text{ kHz} = 80 \text{ kbps}$

1 cycle of 3 kHz = 0.33 ms

∴ 20 cycles of 3 kHz = 6.6 ms

∴ Number of bits in 20 cycles $\quad = 80 \times 10^3 \times 6.6 \times 10^{-3}$

$$= 528 \text{ bits}$$

Transmission bandwidth $B_T = \dfrac{1}{2} \times r = \dfrac{1}{2} \times 80 \times 10^3 \text{ Hz} = 40 \text{ kHz}$

(ii) For DM system

Signalling rate $r = f_s = 10 \text{ kbps}$

Number of bits in 20 cycles $= 10 \times 10^3 \times 6.6 \times 10^{-3}$

$$= 66 \text{ bits}$$

Bandwidth requirement

$$B_T = \dfrac{1}{2} \times r = 5 \text{ kHz}$$

May 2011

U.Q. 15 : Explain LPC encoder and decoder in detail with help of block diagram. **(8)**

Solution : Refer Section 3.6

| May 2012 |

U.Q. 16 : What are the advantages of DM over PCM in terms of signaling rate and bandwidth requirement. Derive the output S/N ratio of delta modulator. Brief the condition to avoid slope overload error. **(8)**

Solution : Refer Sections 3.2 and 3.2.1

| Dec. 2012 |

U.Q. 17 : Consider a sinusoidal signal em (t) = A sin $(2\pi f_m t)$ applied to a delta modulator with representation level ±d. Show that in order to avoid slope overload disfortion it is necessary that: **(8)**

A < d/$(2\pi f_m T_s)$, where, Ts is sampling period.

Solution : Given: $\qquad e_m = A \sin (2\pi f_m t)$

For DM, if d is step size, to avoid slope overload,

$$\max\left(\frac{de_m}{dt}\right) = \frac{d}{T_s}$$

$$\frac{de_m}{dt} = 2A_m f_m \cdot \pi \cos (2\pi f_m t)$$

∴ $\qquad \max\left(\frac{de_m}{dt}\right) = 2A \cdot f_m \pi$

∴ $\qquad 2A \cdot f_m \cdot \pi \leq \frac{d}{T_s}$

∴ $\qquad A < \frac{d}{2A f_m \pi \cdot T_s}$

| May 2013 |

U.Q. 18 : Explain LPC encoder in detail with help of block diagram. **(8)**

Solution : Refer Section 3.6.

| Dec. 2013 |

U.Q. 19 : Compare PCM, DPCM, Delta modulation and Adaptive Delta modulation on the basis of Sampling Frequency, Bit rate and bandwidth requirement. **(8)**

Solution : Refer Section 3.7.

| May 2014 |

U.Q. 20 : Draw the block diagram of DM system and explain its working with waveforms. Comment on the drawbacks of DM. **(8)**

Solution : Refer Section 3.2.

SUMMARY

1. The modulation techniques which take advantage of correlation between adjacent samples are called predictive coding techniques.

2. Delta modulator transmits binary output, the polarity of which depends on difference between input signal and feedback signal constituted from history of previously sent samples.

3. Delta modulator has simple hardware.

4. Signaling rate of DM is equal to sampling frequency and bandwidth requirement is half of sampling frequency.

5. Delta modulator suffers from slope overload and granular noise.

6. Quantization noise (granular noise) for DM is $\dfrac{\Delta^2}{3}$.

7. To avoid slope overload in DM sampling frequency should be very much higher than signal bandwidth.

8. Signal to noise ratio of DM is given by, $\dfrac{\Delta^2}{3} \times \dfrac{W}{f_s}$.

9. Delta signal modulator is an improvement to DM which avoids accumulation of noise at the receiver by not having integrator.

10. Adaptive delta modulation is used to avoid slope overload and granular noise by using adaptive step size.

11. Continuously variable slope delta modulator uses variable gain amplifier which adjusts in the step-size according to variation of input signal. It has advantage of having constant $\dfrac{S}{N}$ ratio and reduced slope overload.

12. In differential PCM we transmit the differences between two adjacent samples by using PCM.

13. DPCM requires predictor which stores past values to predict next required increment.

14. Signal to noise ratio of DPCM is enhanced by prediction gain G_p and is given by

$$(SNR)_0 \ = \ G_p \times 3\, L^2\, P_s$$

15. Linear predictive coding is method of representing analog signal in digital format. It has the lowest bit rate.

EXERCISE

1. Using predictability theory, prove that transmission of encoded error signal (rather than encoded signal itself) is sufficient for reasonable reconstruction of signal. With the help of block schematic, suggest any one technique to transmit and receive encoded errors. What are limitations and advantages of such techniques with reference to linear or uniform PCM ?   **[Dec. 99] [May 03]**

2. Compare PCM, delta modulation and adaptive delta modulation on the basis of sampling rate, bit per sample, bit rate, area of application and simplicity/complexity in implementation. Draw necessary block diagrams of system.   **[May 2000]**

3. Write short notes on LPC.   **[May 2000] [Dec. 2002]**

4. What is differential PCM technique ? How it is different from PCM ?   **[May 2001]**

5. Explain with block schematic, the adaptive delta modulation technique for digitizing the voice signal. Its there any difference between APM and continuously variable slope delta modulation ?   **[Dec. 2001] [May 2004]**

6. Define start-up error and hunting in DM.

7. Explain with block diagram functional operation of vocoders.   **[May 2003]**

8. Explain with block diagram schematic LPC coder and decoder. State its advantages and disadvantages over other voice encoding methods.   **[Dec. 2003]**

9. Show that for DM the sampling frequency should be very much higher than input signal bandwidth to avoid slope overload.

10. Derive the expression for signal-to-noise ratio for DM ?

11. State merits and demerits of DM.

12. What is Delta-Sigma Modulator ? How it is different from DM.

13. What is continuously variable slope delta modulator ? Explain its operation.

14. Derive the expression for signal-to-noise ratio of DPCM.

CHAPTER 4
BASEBAND DIGITAL TRANSMISSION

4.1 MULTIPLEXERS

- Multiplexing is a technique of accommodating signals from number of sources for transmitting them on a single channel.
- Multiplexing helps in considerable reduction of cost of the communication system.
- The device that takes output from a number of terminals and combines the various data streams into one composite output signal is called as multiplexer. A similar device will be required at the receiver end to separate these signals. This device is called demultiplexer.
- Digital communication as has been seen earlier has the advantage of multiplexing signals from different types of sources such as voice, data, video, etc. It is possible

because digital signals are transmitted as a sequence of symbols. These symbols from different sources can be interleaved easily using time-division multiplexing.

4.1.1 Time-Division Multiplexing (TDM)

- It is a method of time interleaving of digital symbols from several sources so that the information from the sources can be transmitted serially over a single channel.

- TDM interleaves bits or characters from each source and transmits them at a higher speed over a wideband channel.

- Each source is assigned unique time slot that contains a predefined number of characters or bits.

- The allocation of time slot depends on bit rates of the sources to be multiplexed. Let us consider the two possible cases :

Case 1 : Bit rates of all sources are identical. We can either interleave bits or words from these sources. Fig. 4.1 (a) shows bit-by-bit interleaving whereas Fig. 4.1 (b) shows word-by-word interleaving.

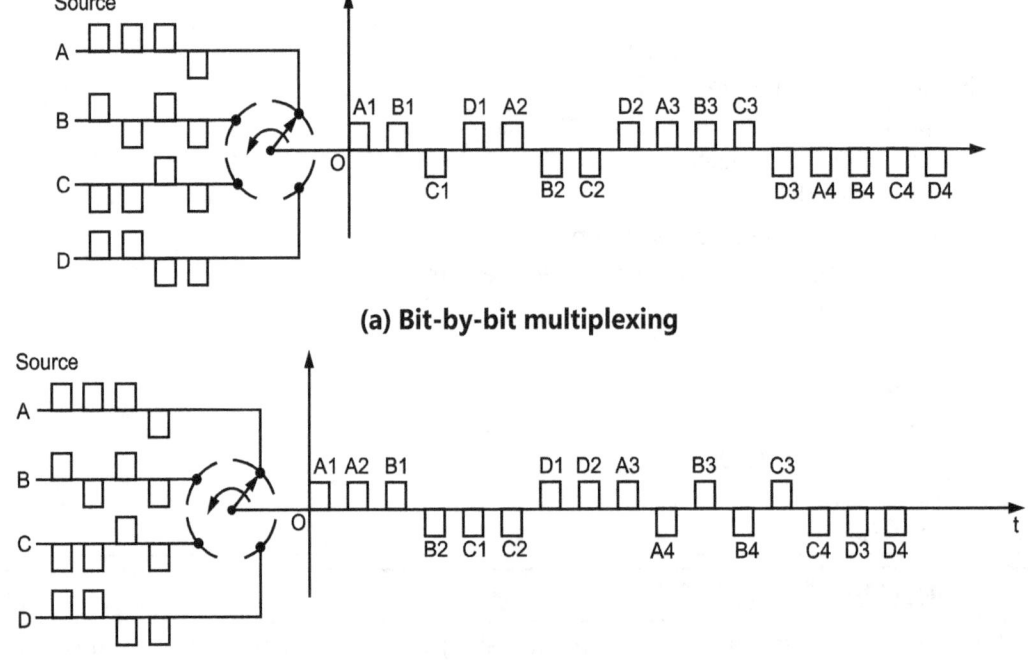

(a) Bit-by-bit multiplexing

(b) Word-by-word multiplexing

Fig. 4.1

Case 2 : Bit rates of sources are not identical. In this case, the source with high bit rate is allocated more time slots. Fig. 4.2 (a) and (b) shows the two schemes for interleaving sources A, B, C and D, where, A, B has bit rate r and C, D has bit rate r/2. The minimum length of multiplexed frame is multiple of lowest common multiple of incoming source bit rates.

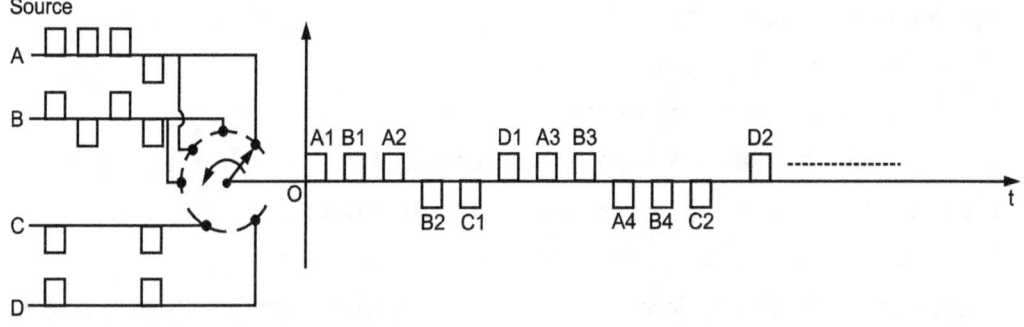

(a) Multiplexing with different bit rate (scheme 1)

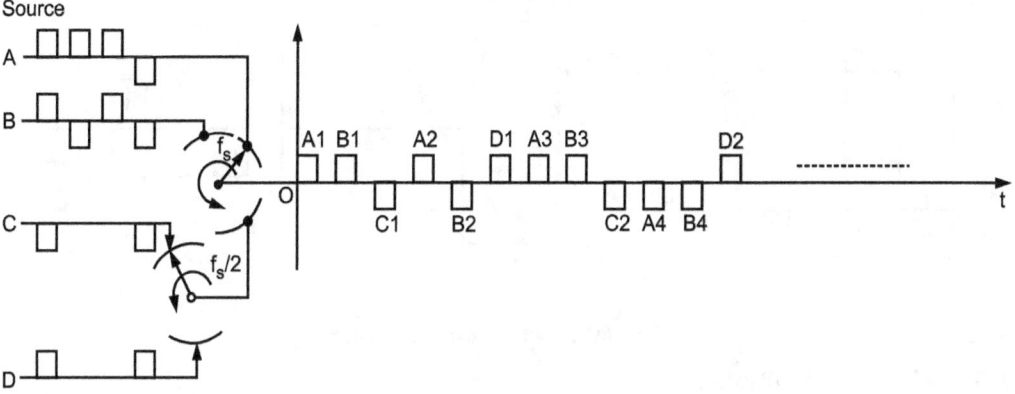

(b) Multiplexing with different bit rate (scheme 2)

Fig. 4.2

- At the receiving end, the incoming stream of bits/words must be divided and distributed to appropriate destinations.

- Apart from identifying the bit interval the frame interval also has to be known for this : framing and synchronization bits are added to data bits to identify the bit time and frame time.

4.1.2 Multiplexer Design Issues

The design of multiplexer depends on following factors :

1. Multiplexers must assign unique bit slots to each input in a frame.

2. There should be atleast one bit from each input in the frame.

3. It should insert additional bits for frame identification.

4. It should take care of variations in input bit rates.

Bit rate variations is a major problem in the design of multiplexers as seen earlier. Accordingly, multiplexers are categorised as below.

(i) Synchronous Multiplexers :

- There is a master clock which governs all sources.
- These systems have highest efficiency.
- But they require master-clock to be distributed to all levels.
- Each bit of data is clocked in synchronism with master clock.
- The synchronization signal is provided by separate clocking line.
- In addition to this, a higher level of synchronization is required to identify beginning and end of frame. A synchronous multiplexer is shown in Fig. 4.3 (a).

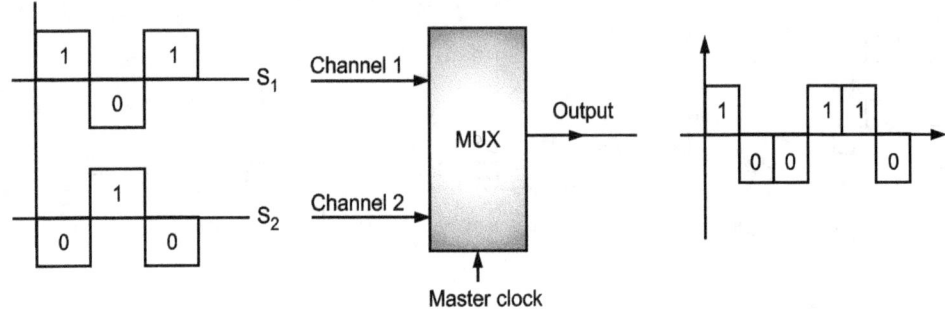

Fig. 4.3 : (a) Synchronous Multiplexer

(ii) Asynchronous Multiplexers :

- These are used where the traffic is bursty.
- The start and end of transmissions are marked by start and stop bits.
- This is called start-stop signaling.
- The receiver clock is started aperiodically and no synchronisation is required with master-clock.
- Keyboard terminals is an example of source which generates bursty traffic.
- Hence, A 7-bit character generated by these terminals is to be allotted with 1 start bit, 1 stop bit and 1 parity bit. It is shown in Fig. 4.3 (b).

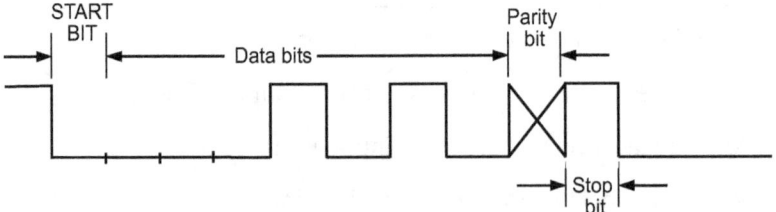

Fig. 4.3 : (b) Asynchronous transmission of a word

- Buffering and character interleaving can be used to multiplex these sources using synchronous multiplexing.

(iii) Quasi-Synchronous Multiplexers :

- They are used when the sources to be multiplexed are not synchronised in frequency i.e. there is slight variation in bit rates of these sources.

- In some applications, the input bit rates are not related with each other by a rational number.

- In such situations, to accommodate these asynchronous inputs, output clock rate has to be increased above nominal value.

- Some dummy bits are to be added called stuff bits when input is not available from input sources. This is illustrated in Fig. 4.3 (c).

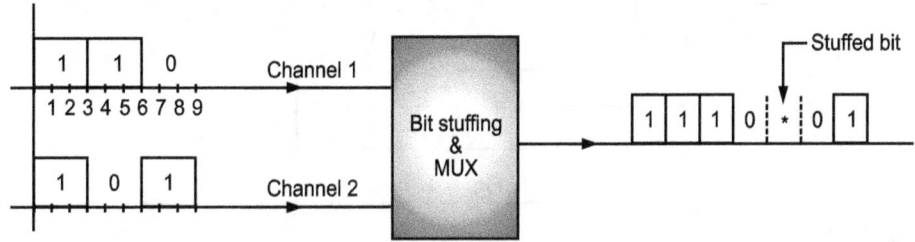

Fig. 4.3 : (c) Quasi Synchronous Multiplexer

Example 4.1 :

Design an efficient TDM telemetry system, which accepts five data channels with minimum sampling rates of 3000, 700, 600, 300 and 200 Hz. Use 8 : 1 multiplexer with sampling frequency f_s = 750 Hz one input of multiplexer is reserved for marker of the frame and remaining inputs are used to accommodate the data channels. Draw complete system block diagram. Find total output signaling rate and bandwidth.

Explain the operation of the system.   **[Dec. 2001]**

Solution : Given : f_s = 750 Hz

Channel	Minimum Sampling Rate	Actual f_s
1	3000 Hz	4 × 750 Hz
2	700 Hz	750 Hz
3	600 Hz	750 Hz
4	300 Hz	375 Hz
5	200 Hz	375 Hz

Hence, following inputs will be given to multiplexer.

1   Input from marker.

4   Inputs from channel 1.

1   Input from channel 3.

1   Inputs from channel 4 and 5 combined at previous stage with 2 : 1 MUX
     (f_s = 375 Hz).

This scheme is shown in Fig. 4.4.

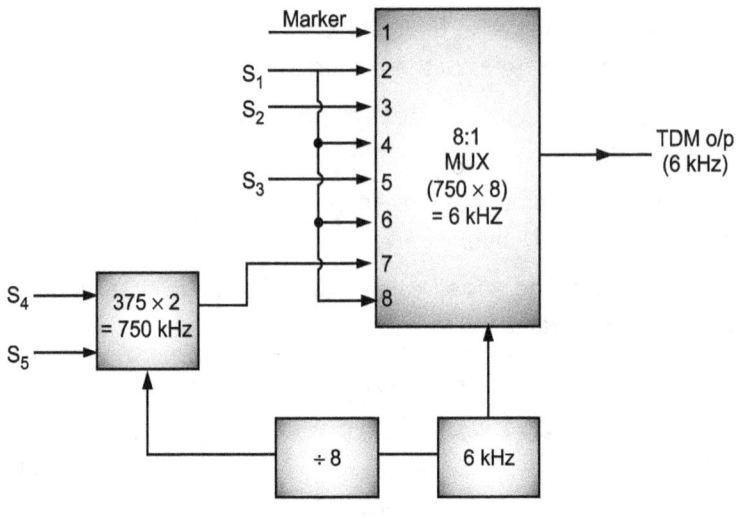

Fig. 4.4

Example 4.2 :

Given a 6 channel main multiplexer with f_s = 8 kHz, devise a telemetry system including a marker that accommodates six input signals having following bandwidth 8, 3.5, 2.0, 1.8, 1.5 and 1.2 kHz. Make sure that successive samples of each input signals are equispaced in time. Calculate the resulting baseband transmission bandwidth. Draw the block schematic of designed telemetry system.   **[Dec. 2003]**

Solution : Given : f_s = 8 kHz

Channel	Signal BW (kHz)	Nyquist Rate (kHz)	Actual f_s Used
1	8	16	2 × 8 kHz
2	3.5	7	1 × 8 kHz
3	2.0	4	4
4	1.8	3.6	4
5	1.5	3	4
6	1.2	2.4	4

Hence, following inputs will go to multiplexer.

1   Marker input

2   Inputs from channel 1.

1   Inputs from channel 2.

1   Input from channel 3 and 4 combined.

1   Input from channel 5 and 6 combined.

The scheme is shown in Fig. 4.5.

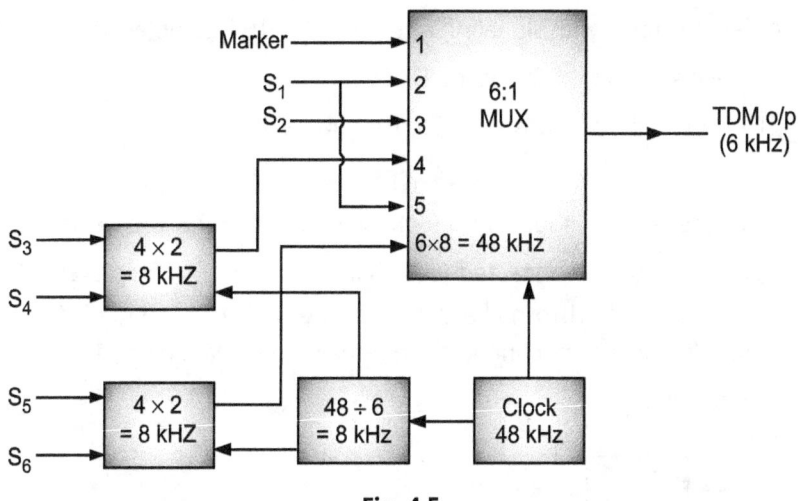

Fig. 4.5

$$\text{Signaling rate (r)} \quad = \quad 6 \times 8 \text{ kHz}$$
$$= \quad 48 \text{ kilo samples/sec.}$$
$$\text{Bandwidth requirement} \quad = \quad \frac{r}{2} = \frac{48}{2} = 24 \text{ kHz}$$

Example 4.3 :

Design a TDM multiplexer that will accommodate 11 sources whose specifications are given below.

Source 1 : Analog, 4 kHz bandwidth

Source 2 : Analog, 2 kHz bandwidth

Source 3 : Analog, 2 kHz bandwidth

Sources 4-11 : Digital, synchronous at 7.5 kbps 4 : 1

Assume that analog sources are converted 4 bit PCM signal. Also calculate total signaling rate and bandwidth required. Draw the system block diagram.

Solution :

Analog Source	Signal Frequency	Sampling Frequency
1	4 kHz	8 kHz
2	2 kHz	4 kHz
3	1 kHz	4 kHz
4	2 kHz	4 kHz

These signals can be multiplexed. Using 4 : 1 multiplexer with f_s = 4 kHz as below,

2   Inputs from channel 1.

1   Inputs from channel 2.

1   Input from channel 3.

The output PAM-TDM signal with signaling rate = $4 \times 4 = 16$ k samples/sec.

This output is converted in 4 bit PCM, using DAC

$\therefore$ PCM-TDM signal output rate $= 16 \times 10^3 \times 4$

                                 $= 64$ kbps

This output is multiplexed with sources 4-11 whose data rate is 7.5 kbps as below.

PCM-TDM output (64 kbps) is connected to 8 channels of 16 : 1 multiplexer with f_s = 8 kHz sources 4 to 11 are bit stuffed to make the data rate 8 kbps so that PCM-TDM output is multiple of it. These 8 sources are connected to remaining 8 channels of 16 : 1 multiplexer.

This scheme is shown in Fig. 4.6.

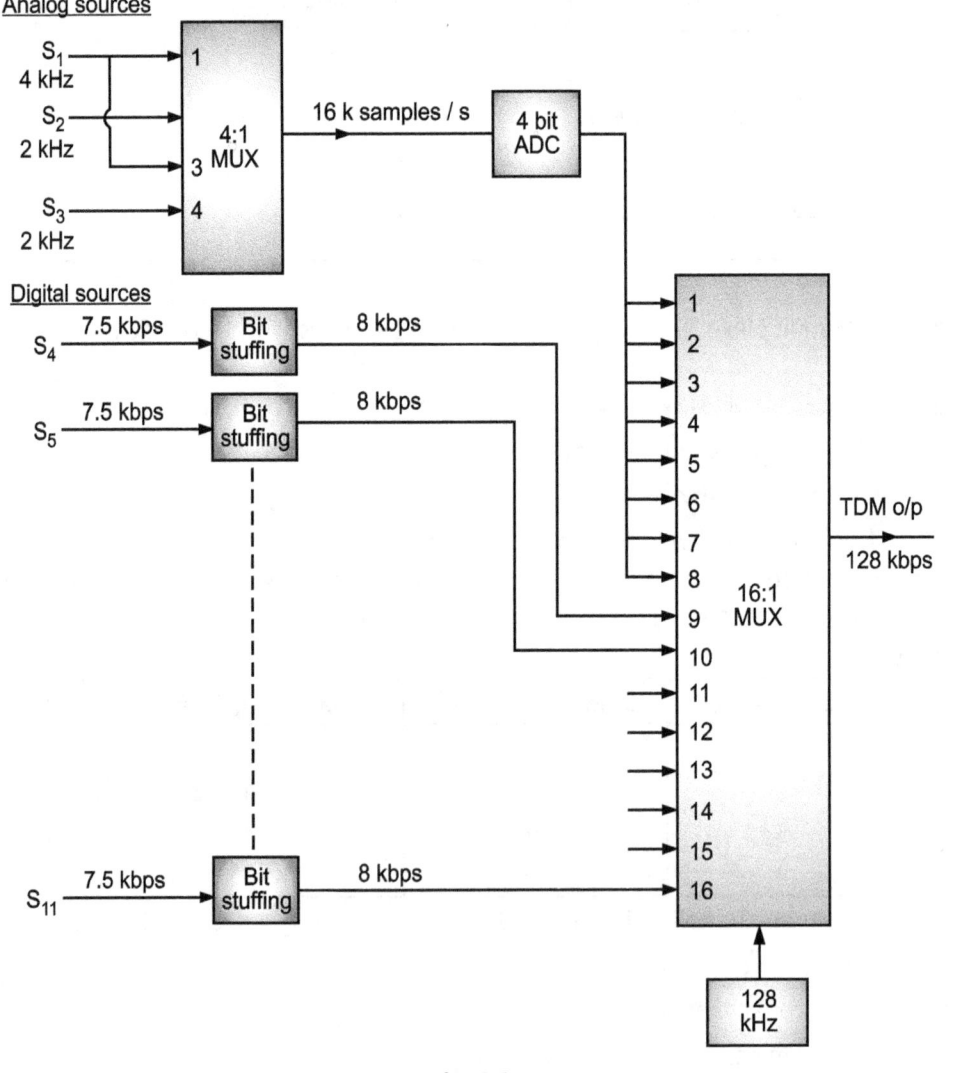

Fig. 4.6

$$\text{Signaling rate (r)} \quad = \quad 16 \times 8 \text{ kHz}$$

$$= \quad 128 \text{ kbps}$$

$$\text{Bandwidth requirement } B_T \quad = \quad \frac{r}{2}$$

$$= \quad 64 \text{ kHz}$$

4.2   MULTIPLEXING HIERARCHIES

There are two types of digital multiplexers.

(i) Low Speed Multiplexers :

- These are used with digital computer systems to merge digital signals from several sources.

- The output rates of these multiplexers are standardized to 1.2, 2.4, 3.6, 4.8, 7.2, 7.6 and 19.2 kbps. The output is designated as digital signal level 0 (DS0).

(ii) High Speed Multiplexers :

- They are used in commercial data transmission systems.

- Two different multiplexing standards have been adopted for digital communication.

- The AT & T hierarchy in North America and Japan and CCITT hierarchy in Europe and rest of world. Both hierarchies are based on 64 kbps voice PCM unit.

- Their structural layout is shown in Fig. 4.7.

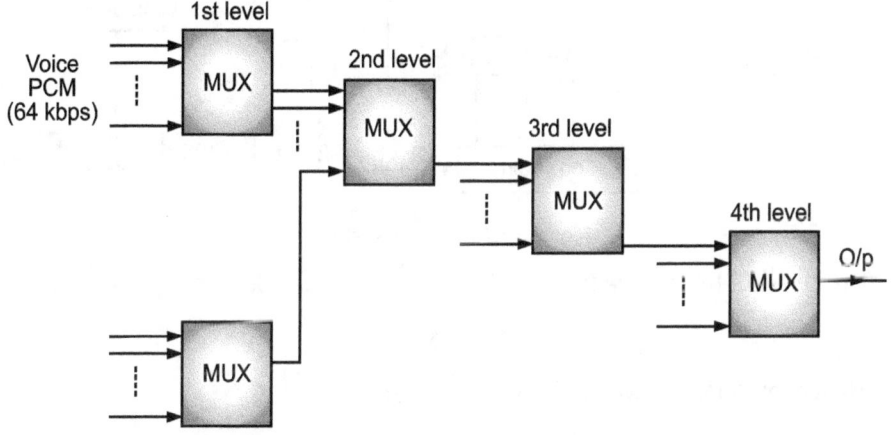

Fig. 4.7 : Structural layout of standard multiplexing schemes

- The telephone industry has standardised the bit rates to 1.544 Mbps, 6.312 Mbps, etc. and designates them as DS-1 (Digital Signal type 1) DS-2, etc.

- Thus, higher the DS level higher will be data rate. Different transmission medium is used for different DS levels.

- For example for higher DS - levels, fibre optic cables, microwave links are used.
- A single DS-1 signal is usually transmitted over a pair of twisted pair cables.
- This type of DS-1 transmission over a twisted pair medium is called T1-Carrier Systems.
- Similarly, the higher DS levels transmission are known as T2, T3, T4, carrier systems.

4.2.1 T1 Carrier System

- Fig. 4.8 shows basic T1 carrier system which is used to transmit 24 voice signals over a single DS-1 line.
- Two lines, one for transmission and another for reception are used in the system.
- Repeaters will be required if the T1 line is connecting telephone equipments over a large distance after every 2 km.

1. Sampling rate used, for each voice signal is 8 kHz.

2. Hence, frame length will be $\dfrac{1}{8000}$ = 125 μ-sec.

3. 8-bit PCM is used, hence frame length will be 24 × 8 = 192 bits.

4. 1-bit is added at the beginning of each frame for frame synchronisation. Hence, total bits in one frame = 193 bits.

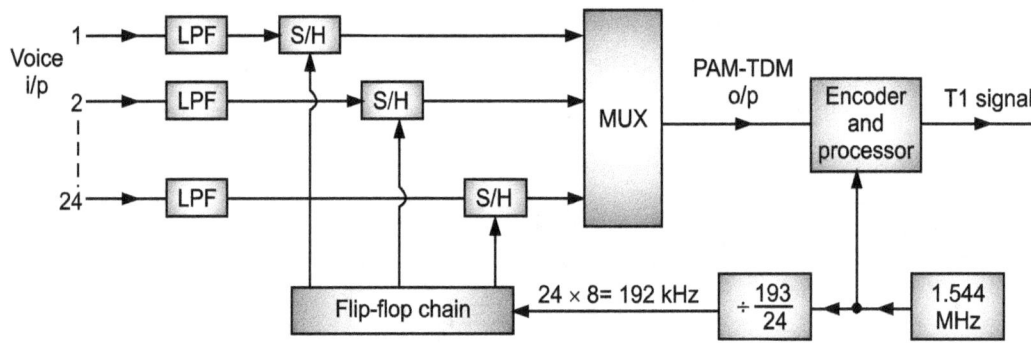

Fig. 4.8 : T1 carrier system

5.   Hence, the T1 data rate (r_b)   =   (193 bits/frame) × 8000 frames/sec.

$$= 1.544 \text{ Mbps}$$

Hence, bit duration will be 0.6488 μsec ($1/r_b$)

6. A telephone system must transmit speech as well as other signals related to call setup, termination etc. This is called signaling. After every 6 frames the 8th bit in every 24 channel is used for signaling purpose. Hence, the signaling data rate for each of 24 input channel is = (1 bit/6 frames) × 8000 frames/sec. = 1.333 kbps and a total equivalent signaling rate for 24 channels = 1.33 × 24 = 32 kbps.

7. T1 signals can be combined at an higher level multiplexer or transmitted directly over short distance links (upto 80 km).

8. It uses bipolar signal format.

9. The T1 transmission line is twisted pair cable.

10. Frame format for T1 system is shown in Fig. 4.9.

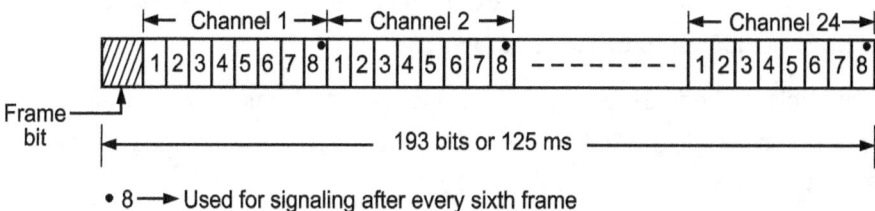

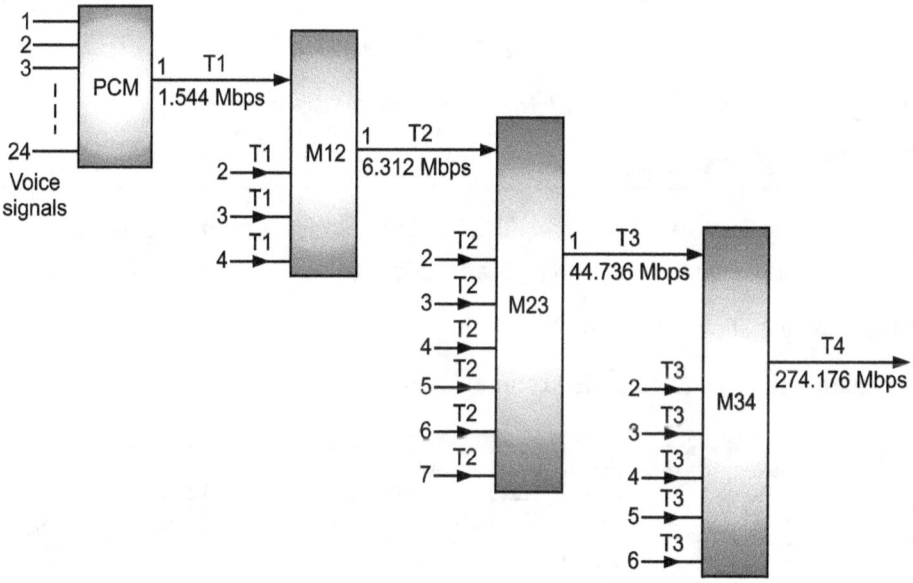

Fig. 4.9 : Frame format for t1 system

4.2.2 AT & T Hierarchy

*   Fig. 4.10 shows the AT&T multiplex hierarchy used in North America and Japan.

*   It shows transmission of voice, data from computer visual telephone and colour TV signals on a single T4 line.

Fig. 4.10 : AT & T hierarchy

1. T1 carrier line carries PCM voice or multiplexed digital data at a speed of 1.544 Mbps.

2. Four such T1 lines (referred as DS_1) are multiplexed by an M12 multiplexer generating T2 line.

3. M12 multiplexer adds 17 bits/frame synchronization and bits stuffing. Hence, number of bits/frame = $193 \times 4 + 17 = 789$ bits/frame.

$$\text{Hence, bit rate of T2 line} = 789 \text{ bits/frame} \times 8000 \text{ frames/sec.}$$

$$= 6.312 \text{ Mbps}$$

4. Seven T2 signals (Referred as DS-2) are multiplexed along with visual telephone signals using M23 multiplexer to generate T3 line.

5. M23 multiplexer adds 69 bits for synchronization and bits stuffing. Hence, number of bits/frame for a T3 line = $789 \times 7 + 69 = 5592$ bits/frame and signaling rate = $5592 \times 8000 = 44.736$ Mbps.

6. Six T3 lines (Referred as DS-3) are multiplexed by M34 multiplexer to generate T4 line. PCM encoded TV signals require a data rate of 90 Mbps. Hence, two T3 lines are allocated for this signal.

7. M34 multiplexer adds 720 bits for synchronization of bits stuffing. Hence, number of bits/frame for T4 line = $5592 \times 6 + 720 = 34{,}272$ bits/frame.

$$\text{And bit rate} = 34{,}272 \times 8000$$

$$= 274.176 \text{ Mbps}$$

8. The higher level multiplexors (M12, M23, M34) are quasisynchronous.

4.2.3 CCITT Hierarchy

*   In Europe and rest of the world, CCITT (Consultative Committee on International Telephony and Telegraphy) hierarchy is adopted.

*   This hierarchy is shown in Fig. 4.11.

*   It has data rate of 2.048 mbps/(30 channel) at first level.

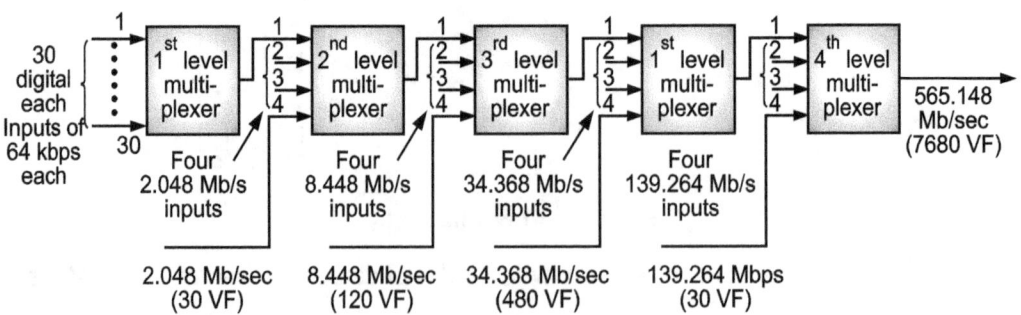

Fig. 4.11 : CCITT Digital TDM Hierarchy

Rest of the specifications are as below :

1. 30 voice frequency channels of 64 kbps are multiplexed at first level to generate 2.048 Mbps line.

2. Four 2.048 Mbps lines are multiplexed to generate 8.448 Mbps output rate at second level.

3. Four 8.448 Mbps line are multiplexed to generate 34.368 Mbps output line at 3rd level.

4. Four 34.368 lines are multiplexed to generate 139.264 Mbps output line at 4th level.

5. Four 139.264 Mbps lines are multiplexed to generate 565.148 Mbps output line at 5th level.

4.3 DATA FORMATS

- Till now, we have seen different methods of converting analog signals in digital format and how to multiplex these digital signals etc.

- Now is the time to transmit these signals over channel.

- We have a stream of 1s and 0s which can be transmitted using electrical pulses or waveforms which are called line codes or data formats or signaling formats.

- A number of waveform representations exist.

- Each representation has its own applications.

- There are two major categories :

    (i) turn-to-Zero (RZ).   (ii) Non-Return-to-Zero (NRZ).

- In RZ coding only half width pulse is used whereas in NRZ coding full width pulse is used.

- The waveforms for the line code may be further classified depending on the voltage levels used for representing 1's and 0's.

- They are –

    (i) On-off (unipolar).   (ii) Polar.

    (iii) Bipolar (Pseudoternary/AMI).   (iv) Manchester (v) Multilevel.

- Fig. 4.12 shows the various signaling formats for the data stream .

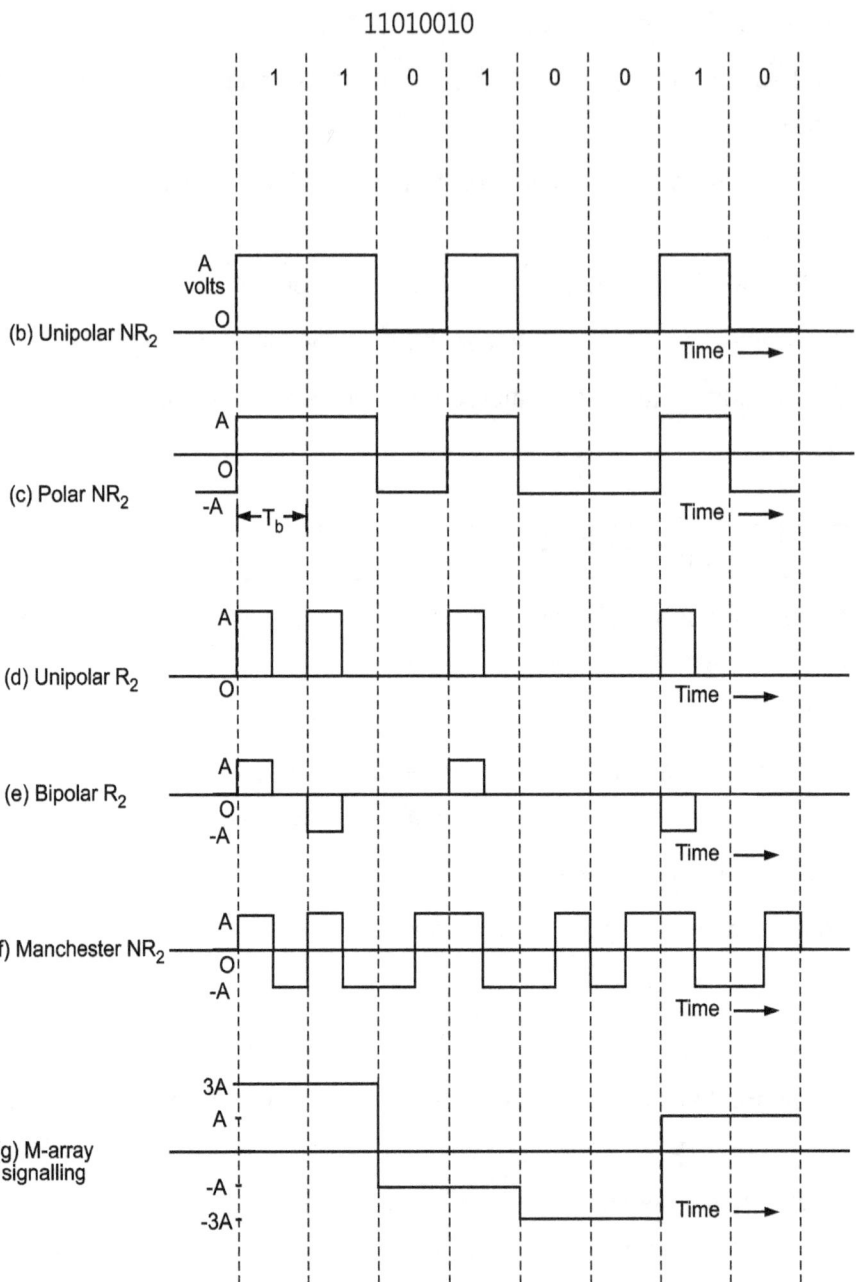

Fig. 4.12 : Line codes

1. Unipolar/On-off Signaling :

- 1 is represented by high level (+ A volt).
- 0 is represented by zero level (0 volt).
- When pulse occupies full duration, it is unipolar NRZ.

- When pulse occupies half duration, it is unipolar RZ.
- It has DC component which is undesirable.

2. Bipolar signaling (AMI/Psuedoternary) :

- 1 is represented by alternate positive and negative values (+ A/– A).
- 0 is represented by zero level.
- This is also called Alternate mark. Inversion (AMI).
- The name Psuedoternary is because of three levels of representation (+1, 0, –1).
- It can be of RZ or NRZ type.
- It has no DC component.
- It eliminates ambiguity that may arise because of polarity inversion.

3. Polar Signaling :

- 1 is represented by positive level (+ A volt).
- 0 is represented by negative level (– A volt).
- It has no DC component provided there are equal 1's and 0's.
- It is used in commercial PCM telephony.

4. Manchester Signaling :

- 1 is represented by positive half bit period followed by negative half bit period.
- 0 is represented by negative half bit period followed by positive half bit period.
- It has no DC component.
- It has built in synchronization capability.

5. Multilevel Signaling (M-ary) :

More than one bits are combined to represent them as multiple positive and negative levels. For example, if we combine 2 bits,

    00 represented as   – 3 A volt.
    01 represented as   – A volt.
    10 represented as   + A volt.
    11 represented as   + 3 A volt.

This is called with M-ary signaling with M = 4.

While selecting a particular line code for transmission in digital communication we have to analyse them on the following basis.

1. Power Efficiency : The transmitted power of the signal should be minimum for given bandwidth and error probability of detection of these signals at receiver end.

2. **Transmission Bandwidth :** It should be minimum. Some data formats such as multilevel codes, increase the efficiency of bandwidth utilization. For a given data rate, we require less bandwidth i.e. more information transmitted per bandwidth.

3. **DC Component :** If the transmitted signal has dc component, it contributes to D.C. energy to signal's power spectrum. If this signal is passed through a.c. coupled systems (repeaters) or used in magnetic recording system, the low frequency information will be lost. Hence, in such cases the D.C. component should not be present.

4. **Self Synchronisation :** Extraction of clock signal should be possible from received signal for synchronization purpose. The signal should have zero crossings at regular intervals.

5. **Error Detection :** A signal can have error detection or correction capability.

6. **Noise Immunity :** The signal should be more immune to noise. e.g. NRZ waveforms is more immune to noise than RZ.

7. **Transparency :** Any arbitrary symbol or bit pattern can be transmitted and received. That is there should be faithful reproduction of data whatever may be the sequence.

4.3.1 Spectral Attributes of Data Formats

- The data formats are selected on the basis of their spectral characteristics.

- It is one of the main criteria discussed above.

- The power spectral density of these waveforms can be obtained. Appendix A gives the detailed derivation of PSD's of various data formats.

- The PSD's and their plots are as below :

- We know (Refer Appendix A) the PSD of discrete amplitude waveform

$$d_T(t) \; = \; \sum_{n=-N}^{+N} a_n g(t - nT_s) \qquad \qquad ...(4.1)$$

is given by,

$$S_d(f) \; = \; \frac{|G(f)|^2}{T_s} \sum_{k=-\infty}^{\infty} R_k \, e^{j2\pi fkT_s} \qquad \qquad ...(4.2)$$

where, $R_k \; = \; E\,[a_n \cdot a_{n+k}] \; \overline{a_n \cdot a_{n+k}}$

and symbol pulse shape

$$g(t) \; \rightleftharpoons \; G(f)$$

1. Unipolar NRZ :

For unipolar NRZ, a_n can be either $+ A$ or 0. Assuming these values are equally likely and the data are independent. For $k = 0$,

$$R_0 = \sum_{i=1}^{2} (a_n \, a_n)_i \times P_i$$

$$= A^2 \times \frac{1}{2} + 0 \cdot \frac{1}{2} = \frac{1}{2} A^2$$

For $k \neq 0$ there are 4 possible values of $a_n \cdot a_{n+k}$ as $A \times A$, $A \times 0$, 0×0, $0 \times A$.

$$\therefore \quad R_k = \sum_{i=1}^{4} (a_n \, a_{n+k})_i \times P_i$$

$$= A \times A \times \frac{1}{4} + A \times 0 \times \frac{1}{4} + 0 \times 0 \times \frac{1}{4} + 0 \times A \times \frac{1}{4}$$

$$= \frac{1}{4} A^2$$

$$\therefore \quad R_k = \begin{cases} \dfrac{A^2}{2} & k = 0 \\[4mm] \dfrac{A^2}{4} & k \neq 0 \end{cases}$$

The basic NRZ unipolar pulse is,

$$g(t) = \text{rect}\left(\frac{t}{T_b}\right)$$

where, T_b is bit duration.

$$G(f) = T_b \, \text{sinc} \, (fT_b)$$

$$|G(f)|^2 = T_b^2 \, \text{sinc}^2 \, (fT_b)$$

$$\therefore \quad S_d(f) = \frac{T_b^2 \, \text{sinc}^2 \, (fT_b)}{T_b} \sum_{k=-\infty}^{\infty} R_k e^{j2\pi fkT_b}$$

$$= T_b \, \text{sinc}^2 \, (fT_b) \left[R_0 + \sum_{\substack{k=-\infty \\ k \neq 0}}^{\infty} R_k e^{j2\pi fkT_b} \right]$$

$$= T_b \, \text{sinc}^2 \, (fT_b) \left[\frac{A^2}{2} + \frac{A^2}{4} \sum_{\substack{k=-\infty \\ k \neq 0}}^{\infty} R_k e^{j2\pi fkT_b} \right]$$

$$= \frac{A^2 T_b}{2} \operatorname{sinc}^2 (fT_b) \left[1 + \frac{1}{2} \sum_{\substack{k = -\infty \\ k \neq 0}}^{\infty} e^{j2\pi f k T_b} \right]$$

$$= \frac{A^2 T_b}{2} \operatorname{sinc}^2 (fT_b) \left[\frac{1}{2} + \left(\frac{1}{2} + \frac{1}{2} \sum_{\substack{k = -\infty \\ k \neq 0}}^{\infty} e^{j2\pi f k T_b} \right) \right]$$

Combining last two terms in above expression

$$S_d (f) = \frac{A^2 T_b}{2} \operatorname{sinc}^2 (fT_b) \left[\frac{1}{2} + \frac{1}{2} \sum_{k = -\infty}^{\infty} e^{j2\pi f k T_b} \right]$$

(Note we have removed the restriction $k \neq 0$)

$$\therefore \qquad S_d (f) = \frac{A^2 T_b}{4} \operatorname{sinc}^2 (fT_b) \left[1 + \sum_{k = -\infty}^{\infty} e^{j2\pi f k T_b} \right]$$

Now using Porsson's Rules

$$\sum_{k = -\infty}^{\infty} e^{j2\pi f k T_b} = \frac{1}{T_b} \sum_{n = -\infty}^{\infty} \delta \left(f - \frac{n}{T_b} \right)$$

$$\therefore \qquad S_d (f) = \frac{A^2}{4} T_b \operatorname{sinc}^2 (fT_b) \left[1 + \frac{1}{T_b} \sum_{n = -\infty}^{\infty} \delta \left(f - \frac{n}{T_b} \right) \right] \qquad \ldots (4.3)$$

But $\qquad \operatorname{sinc}^2 (fT_b) = 0$ for $f = \pm \frac{1}{T_b}, \pm \frac{2}{T_b} \ldots$etc.

$$\therefore \qquad S_d (f) = \frac{A^2 T_b}{4} \operatorname{sinc}^2 (fT_b) + \frac{A^2}{4} \delta (f)$$

To compare PSD's of all data format formats we will normalize average power. So that the comparison will be fair. For unipolar NRZ, average power,

$$\frac{A^2 T_b}{2 T_b} = 1$$

$$\therefore \qquad A = \sqrt{2}$$

$$\therefore \qquad S_d (f) = 0.5 T_b \operatorname{sinc}^2 (fT_b) + \frac{1}{2} \delta (f) \qquad \ldots (4.4)$$

With this the plot of PSD of Unipolar NRZ signal is as shown in Fig. 4.13 (a). Note that the plot shows only first three lobes, actually it can be extended to infinity. Note that the plot shows only first three lobes, actually it can be extended to infinity.

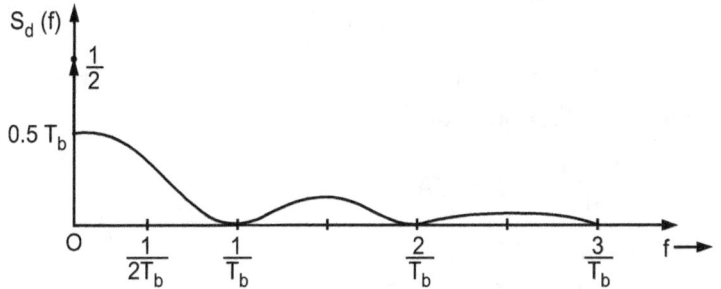

Fig. 4.13 : (a) PSD of unipolar NRZ

Observations :

1. There is dc component present in the spectrum which is waste of power.

2. There is dc wandering near low frequency area.

3. D.C. coupled circuits will be required for this.

4. Main lobe width is $\dfrac{1}{T_b}$. Which can be termed as bandwidth of the signal.

5. The unipolar NRZ signal is easy to generate.

6. It requires only one power supply.

7. There will be synchronisation problem if long stream of 1's or 0's occur.

2. Polar NRZ :

There are two possible levels in polar NRZ + A and − A which are assumed to be equally likely. The data are also assumed independent from bit to bit.

For k = 0

$$\therefore \quad R_0 \;=\; \sum_{i=1}^{2} (a_n \, a_n)_i \, P_i \;=\; A \times A \times \frac{1}{2} + (-A) \times (-A) \times \frac{1}{2}$$

$$= A^2$$

For $k \neq 0$

$$R_k \;=\; \sum_{i=1}^{4} (a_n \, a_{n+k})_i \, P_i$$

$$= A \times A \times \frac{1}{4} + A \times (-A) \times \frac{1}{4} + (-A) \times A \times \frac{1}{4} + (-A) \times (-A) \times \frac{1}{4}$$

$$= 0$$

$\therefore$ PSD for polar NRZ can be given by,

$$S_d (f) \;=\; \frac{\left| G(f) \right|^2}{T_b} \sum_{k=-\infty}^{\infty} R_k \, e^{j 2 \pi f k T_b} \;=\; \frac{T_b^2 \, \text{sinc}^2 (f T_b)}{T_b} \times R_0 \, e^{j 2 \pi f \times 0 \times T_b}$$

$$= T_b \, \text{sinc}^2 \, (fT_b) \times A^2$$

$$\therefore \qquad S_d \, (f) \;=\; A^2 \, T_b \, \text{sinc}^2 \, (fT_b) \qquad\qquad \dots (4.5)$$

Normalizing the power of NRZ polar signal i.e.

$$\frac{A^2 \, T_b}{T_b} \;=\; 1 \;\Rightarrow\; A = 1$$

The plot of PSD is shown in Fig. 4.13 (b).

$$\therefore \qquad S_d \, (f) \;=\; T_b \, \text{sinc}^2 \, (fT_b) \qquad\qquad \dots(4.6)$$

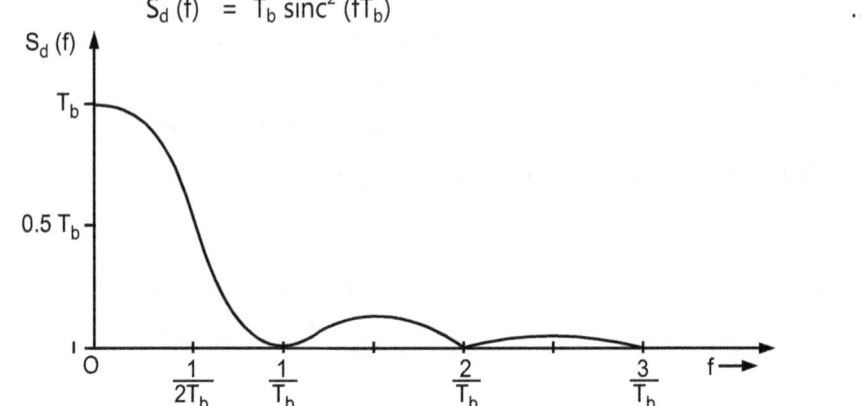

Fig. 4.13 : (b) PSD of polar NRZ

Observations :

1. It does not have DC component. Hence, no wastage of power and DC coupled circuit not required.
2. There is large PSD near dc.
3. Main lobe width is $\dfrac{1}{T_b}$ which can be termed as bandwidth of the signal.
5. Dual power supply will be required.

3. Unipolar RZ :

For RZ signaling pulse duration is $\dfrac{T_b}{2}$, $R_0 = \dfrac{A^2}{2}$ and $R_k \Big|_{k \neq 0} = \dfrac{A^2}{4}$

$$G \, (f) \;=\; \frac{T_b}{2} \, \text{sinc} \left(\frac{fT_b}{2} \right)$$

$$|G \, (f)|^2 \;=\; \frac{T_b^{\,2}}{4} \, \text{sinc}^2 \left(\frac{fT_b}{2} \right)$$

$$S_d \, (f) \;=\; \frac{\dfrac{T_b^{\,2}}{4} \, \text{sinc}^2 \left(\dfrac{fT_b}{2} \right)}{T_b} \left[R_0 + \sum_{\substack{k = -\infty \\ k \neq 0}}^{\infty} R_k e^{j2\pi fkT_b} \right]$$

$$= \frac{T_b \, \text{sinc}^2 \left(\frac{fT_b}{2} \right)}{4} \left[\frac{A^2}{2} + \sum_{\substack{k = -\infty \\ k \neq 0}}^{\infty} \frac{A^2}{4} e^{j2\pi fkT_b} \right]$$

$$= \frac{A^2 T_b \, \text{sinc}^2 \left(\frac{fT_b}{2} \right)}{16} \left[2 + \sum_{\substack{k = -\infty \\ k \neq 0}}^{\infty} e^{j2\pi fkfT_b} \right]$$

$$= \frac{A^2 T_b \, \text{sinc}^2 \left(\frac{fT_b}{2} \right)}{16} \left[1 + 1 + \sum_{\substack{k = -\infty \\ k \neq 0}}^{\infty} e^{j2\pi fkfT_b} \right]$$

$$= \frac{A^2 T_b \, \text{sinc}^2 \left(\frac{fT_b}{2} \right)}{16} \left[1 + \sum_{k = -\infty}^{\infty} e^{j2\pi fkT_b} \right]$$

$$= \frac{A^2 T_b \, \text{sinc}^2 \left(\frac{fT_b}{2} \right)}{16} \left[1 + \frac{1}{T_b} \sum_{n = -\infty}^{\infty} \delta \left(f - \frac{n}{T_b} \right) \right]$$

$$= \frac{A^2 T_b \, \text{sinc}^2 \left(\frac{fT_b}{2} \right)}{16} + \frac{A^2}{16} \delta (f)$$

$$+ \frac{A^2}{16} \delta \left(f - \frac{1}{T_b} \right) \text{sinc}^2 \left(\frac{1}{2} \right) \frac{A^2}{16} \delta \left(f - \frac{3}{T_b} \right) \text{sinc}^2 \left(\frac{3}{2} \right) + \dots$$

For normalized average power $\left(\frac{\frac{A^2 T_b}{2}}{2T_b} \right) = 1 \Rightarrow A = 2$

$\therefore$

$$S_d (f) = 0.25 \, T_b \, \text{sinc}^2 \left(\frac{fT_b}{2} \right) + 0.25 \, \delta (f) + 0.1013 \, \delta \left(f - \frac{1}{T_b} \right)$$

$$+ \, 0.01138 \left(f - \frac{3}{T_b} \right) + \dots \qquad \qquad \dots (4.8)$$

The PSD for unipolar RZ is plotted in Fig. 4.13 (c). If shows only two lobes, although it can be extended to infinity.

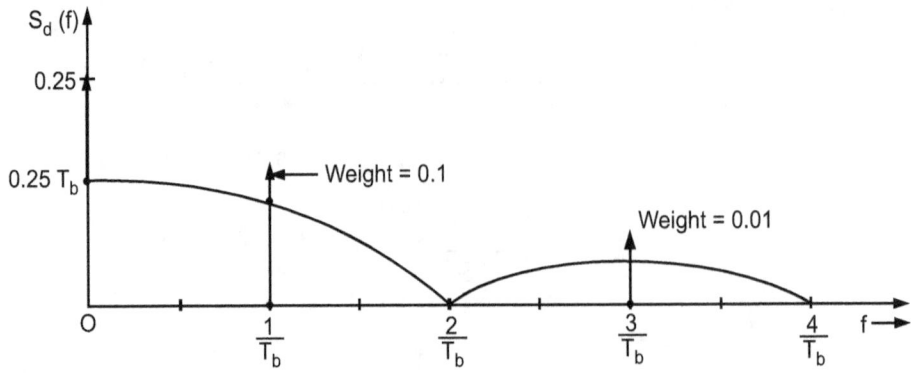

Fig. 4.13 : (c) PSD of unipolar RZ

Observations :

1. There is dc component present in the signal but its contribution to power is less compared to unipolar NRZ.

2. There is large PSD near dc but less than unipolar NRZ.

3. D.C. coupled circuits are required.

4. The main lobe width i.e. null to null bandwidth is $\dfrac{2}{T_b}$ which is twice the previous two cases.

5. There is a discrete impulse at $f = \pm \dfrac{n}{T_b}$ which shows that this periodic component can be used for clock recovery (synchronization).

6. It requires more signal power than polar signaling to achieve same error probability.

7. It is easy to generate and requires single power supply.

4. Bipolar RZ or AMI :

For k = 0 i.e same bit interval.

There are three possible values of a_n viz. + A, – A and 0. Hence, possible products are + A^2 and 0.

$$
\begin{aligned}
R_0 &= \sum_{i=1}^{2} (a_n\, a_n)_i\, P_i \\
&= A^2 \times \frac{1}{2} + 0 \times \frac{1}{4} \\
&= \frac{A^2}{2}
\end{aligned}
$$

For k = 1 i.e. adjacent intervals

Possible sequences are (1, 1), (0, 1), (1, 0), (0, 0) with products $- A^2$, 0, 0, 0 equally likely.

$$\therefore \qquad R_1 = \sum_{i=1}^{4} (a_n \, a_{n+1})_i \times P_i$$

$$= - A^2 \times \frac{1}{4} + 0 \times \frac{1}{4} + 0 \times \frac{1}{4} + 0 \times \frac{1}{4}$$

$$= - \frac{A^2}{4}$$

For k > 1 bits are not in adjacent interval.

Hence, possible sequence is (1, 1), (1, 0), (0, 1), (0, 0). With possible products $\pm A^2$, 0, 0, 0 occur with equal probability i.e. $+ A^2$ and $- A^2$ has probability $\frac{1}{8}$ each and 0, 0, 0 have probability $\frac{1}{4}$ each.

$$\therefore \qquad R_{k>1} = \sum_{i=1}^{5} (a_n \, a_{n+k})_i \, P_i$$

$$= (- A^2) \times \frac{1}{8} + (+ A^2) \times \frac{1}{8} + 0 \times \frac{1}{4} + 0 \times \frac{1}{4} + 0 \times \frac{1}{4}$$

$$= 0$$

$$\therefore \qquad R_k = \frac{A^2}{2} \qquad ; \qquad k = 0$$

$$= - \frac{A^2}{4} \qquad ; \qquad |k| = 1$$

$$= 0 \qquad ; \qquad |k| > 1$$

Using above result in equation (4.2) and considering the $G(f) = \frac{T_b}{2}$ sinc (fT_b), we get PSD of bipolar RZ as,

$$S_d (f) = \frac{A^2 \, T_b}{8} \, \text{sinc}^2 \left(\frac{fT_b}{2} \right) [1 - \cos (2\pi fT_b)]$$

$$S_d (f) = \frac{A^2 \, T_b}{4} \times \text{sinc}^2 \left(\frac{fT_b}{2} \right) \cdot \sin^2 (\pi fT_b) \qquad \qquad \text{... (4.9)}$$

If we normalize the average power with $\dfrac{A^2 T_b/2}{2T_b} = 1 \Rightarrow A = 1$

$$S_d (f) = T_b \, \text{sinc}^2 (fT_b) \sin^2 (\pi fT_b) \qquad \qquad \text{...(4.10)}$$

This is plotted in Fig. 4.13 (d) $\Rightarrow$ A = 2

Note that the plot shows only first two lobes, actually it can be extended to infinity.

i.e.   A = 2

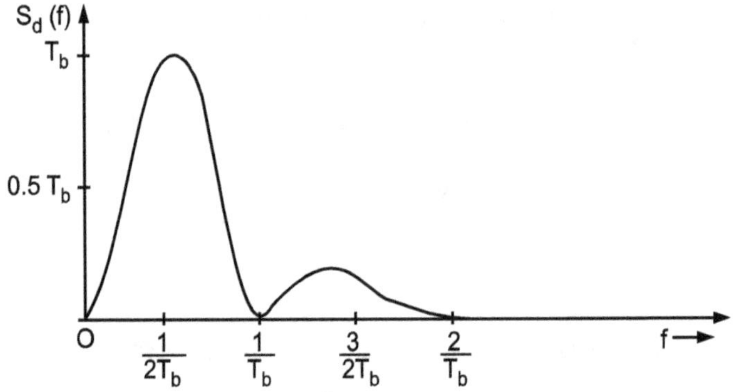

Fig. 4.13 : (d) PSD of bipolar RZ

Observations :

1. Bipolar signaling has zero value at dc hence ac coupled circuits can be used in the channel.

2. It has null to null bandwidth of $\dfrac{1}{T_b}$.

3. It does not have spectral components near dc.

4. It has a single error detection capability.

5. It is not transparent i.e. long stream of zeros and ones can cause synchronisation problem. Clock signal can be extracted from this waveform by using full-wave rectification which converts it into unipolar RZ.

6. It has to distinguish three levels + A, – A and 0.

7. It requires 3 dB more power than polar signal for same bit error probability.

5. Manchester (Split phase) Signaling :

The pulse shape of this signaling is,

$$g(t) = \text{rect}\left(\frac{t + T_b/4}{T_b/2}\right) - \text{rect}\left(\frac{t - T_b/4}{T_b/2}\right) \qquad \text{... (4.9)}$$

$$\therefore \qquad G(f) = \frac{T_b}{2}\text{sinc}(fT_b/2)\, e^{j2\pi fT_b/4} - \frac{T_b}{2}\text{sinc}(fT_b/2)\, e^{-j2\pi fT_b/4}$$

$$= \frac{T_b}{2}\text{sinc}(fT_b/2)\,[e^{j\pi fT_b/2} - e^{-j\pi fT_b/2}]$$

$$= j\,T_b\,\text{sinc}(fT_b/2)\cdot\sin(\pi fT_b/2) \qquad \text{... (4.10)}$$

Since + A and − A are possible levels which occur equally in each bit interval. It is similar to polar signaling. Hence,

$$R_k = A^2 \qquad\qquad k = 0$$
$$= 0 \qquad\qquad k \neq 0 \qquad\qquad ... (4.11)$$

∴ Using equation (4.10) and equation (4.11) in equation,

$$S_d(f) = \frac{|G(f)|^2}{T_s} \sum_{k=-\infty}^{\infty} R_k\, e^{j2\pi fkT_s}$$

we get PSD of Manchester signaling as,

$$S_d(f) = A^2 T_b\, \text{sinc}^2\left(\frac{fT_b}{2}\right) \sin^2(\pi fT_b/2)$$

The plot of this is shown in Fig. 4.13 (e) for normalized average power i.e. $\dfrac{A^2 T_b}{T_b} = 1$.

i.e.   A = 1

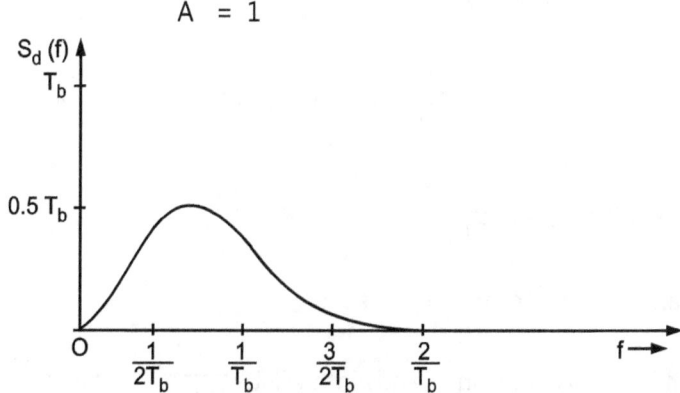

Fig. 4.13 : (e) PSD of manchester code

Observations :

1. It has null spectrum at dc.

2. It does not have spectrum near dc.

3. It has null-to-null bandwidth of $\dfrac{2}{T_b}$ which is twice that of bipolar RZ.

4. It is a transparent code, i.e. clock signal can be extracted.

6. Multi Level (M-ary) Signaling :

Let us consider specific case of multilevel signaling where, M = 4 coded as below.

$$\begin{array}{ll} 00 & -3A \\ 01 & -A \\ 10 & +A \\ 11 & +3A \end{array}$$

These are equally likely to occur.

For k = 0

$$\therefore \qquad R_0 = \sum_{i=1}^{4} (a_n)_i^2 \, p_i$$

$$= (-3A) \times (-3A) \times \frac{1}{4} + (-A) \times (-A) \times \frac{1}{4} + (A) \times (A) \times \frac{1}{4}$$

$$+ 3A \times 3A \times \frac{1}{4}$$

$$= 5A^2$$

For k ≠ 0

$$R_k = 0$$

Also, $\qquad G(f) = T_b \, \text{sinc} \, (2fT_b) \qquad\qquad [\because \text{ pulse with is } 2T_b]$

$$\therefore \qquad S_d \, (f) = \frac{|G(f)|^2}{T_s} \, (5A^2 + 0)$$

$$= \frac{4T_b^2}{2T_b} \, 5A^2 \times \text{sinc}^2 \, (2fTb) = 10A^2 \, T_b \, \text{sinc}^2 \, (2fT_b)$$

Observations :

1. Null bandwidth occurs at $\dfrac{1}{2T_b}$.

   Hence, bandwidth is $\dfrac{1}{2}$ of the binary signal.

2. In general for M-ary signaling bandwidth will be $\dfrac{1}{\log_2 M \times T_b} = \dfrac{R_b}{\log_2 M}.$

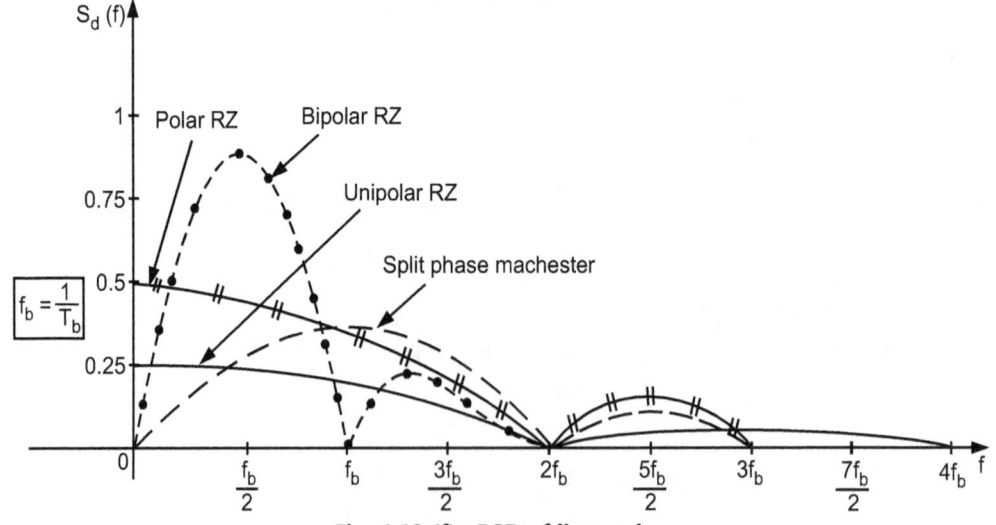

Fig. 4.13 (f) : PSD of line codes

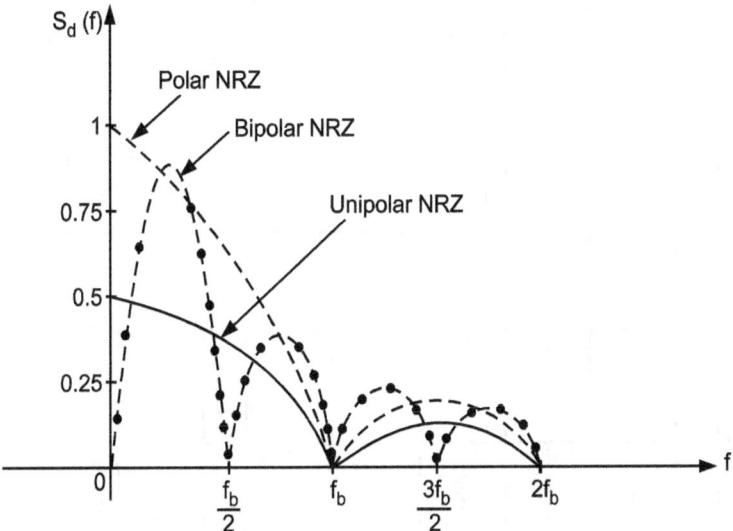

Fig. 4.13 (g) : PSD of line codes

4.3.2 Comparison of Line Codes

Sr. No.	Line code Parameter	Unipolar NRZ	Unipolar RZ	Polar NRZ	Polar RZ	Bipolar NRZ	Bipolar RZ	Split Phase Manchester	Multilevel
1.	D.C. component	Yes	Yes	Yes	Yes	No	No	No	Difficult
2.	Timing extraction	Difficult	Simple	Difficult	Rectify	Difficult	Rectify	Simple	Difficult
3.	Transparency	No.	No	No	No	No	No	Yes	No
4.	Error Detection	No	No	No	No	Yes	Yes	Yes	No
5.	First Null Bandwidth	f_b	$2f_b$	f_b	$2\,f_b$	$f_b/2$	f_b	$2\,f_b$	$\dfrac{f_b}{\log_2 M}$
6.	Relative power transmitted								
	Average	2	1	1	1/2	2	1	More	More
	Peak	4	4	1	1	4	4	More	More

Example 4.1 :

Represent the data 10011101 using following data formats.

1. Unipolar RZ.
2. Split phase Manchester.
3. M-ary format for M = 4.

Solution : The formats are shown in Fig. 4.14.

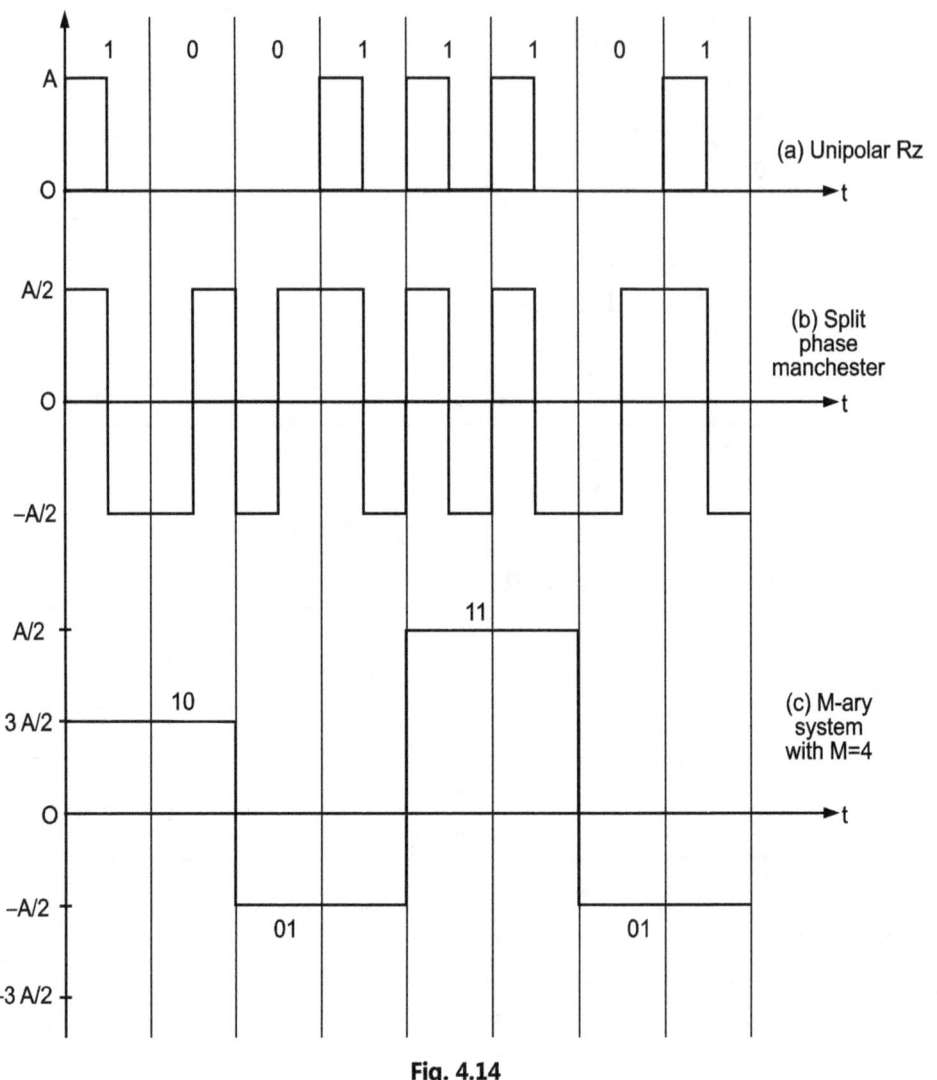

Fig. 4.14

Example 4.2 :

Sketch the following line encoding formats for the bit pattern 101011.

    (i)   Unipolar RZ

    (ii)   Unipolar NRZ

    (iii)   Polar RZ

    (iv)   Polar NRZ

    (v)   Bipolar RZ

    (vi)   Bipolar NRZ

Solution : The sketch is shown in Fig. 4.15.

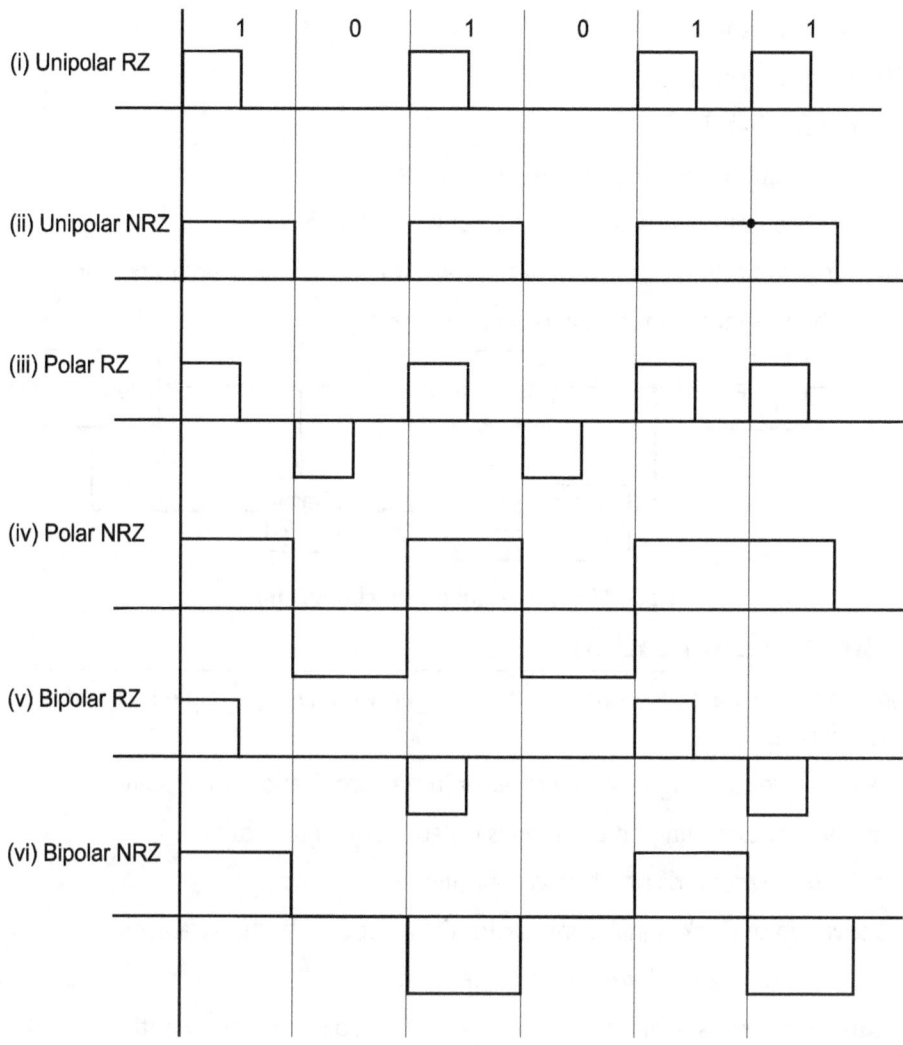

Fig. 4.15

4.4   SYNCHRONIZATION

- The timing operation at the receiver should closely follow the corresponding operation at the receiver.
- This is called synchronization between transmitter and receiver.
- For synchronization we require a clock signal at the receiver that should have a precise frequency and phase relationship with the received signal.
- Of course, some allowance has to be made to take into account propagation delay between transmitter and receiver.

- Digital communication needs three types of synchronizing signals.

  1. Bit synchronization.

  2. Frame synchronization

  3. Carrier synchronization

- Bit synchronization is required to identify the bit interval.

- Frame synchronization identifies a group of bits belonging to a time slot.

- Carrier synchronization extracts carrier signals timing with coherent detection.

- Fig. 4.16 shows synchronization in binary receiver.

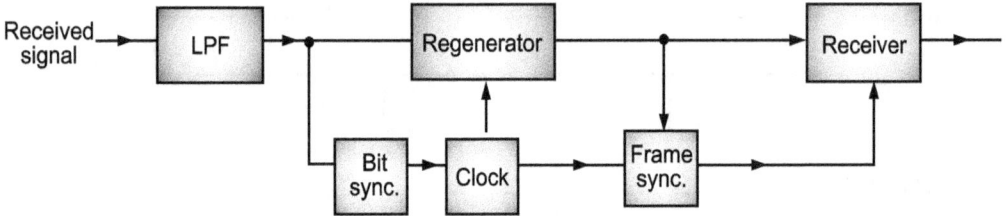

Fig. 4.16 : Frame and bit synchronization

4.4.1 Bit Synchronization

- In order to detect a binary signal at the receiver, we have to sample received signal at a precise instant.

- This will require clock signal at the receiver in synchronisation with receiver.

- The method of extracting bit duration is called bit synchronisation.

- There are three methods of bit synchronisation.

  1. Derivation of clock signal from master timing source both at transmitter and eceiver.

  2. Transmitting the clock from transmitter to receiver.

  3. Extracting clock signal from the signal itself called self-synchronisation.

- The first method is used for large volume of data and high-speed communication. Its cost is high.

- The second method uses channel capacity for transmission of clock. Hence, there should be spare capacity available.

- The third method is more efficient and used very often.

- Let us look into the method of self-synchronisation.

- If we have unipolar or on-off signaling format, it contains a discrete component of clock frequency. We apply this received signal to a resonant circuit (BPF) tuned to clock frequency. The output of resonant circuit will be a sinusoid cos $(2\pi f_b t + \phi)$, where, f_b is clock frequency. Hence, the output is required clock signal.

- For polar format, the signal is passed through a square law device. The resulting signal will be unipolar waveforms. It is shown in Fig. 4.17.

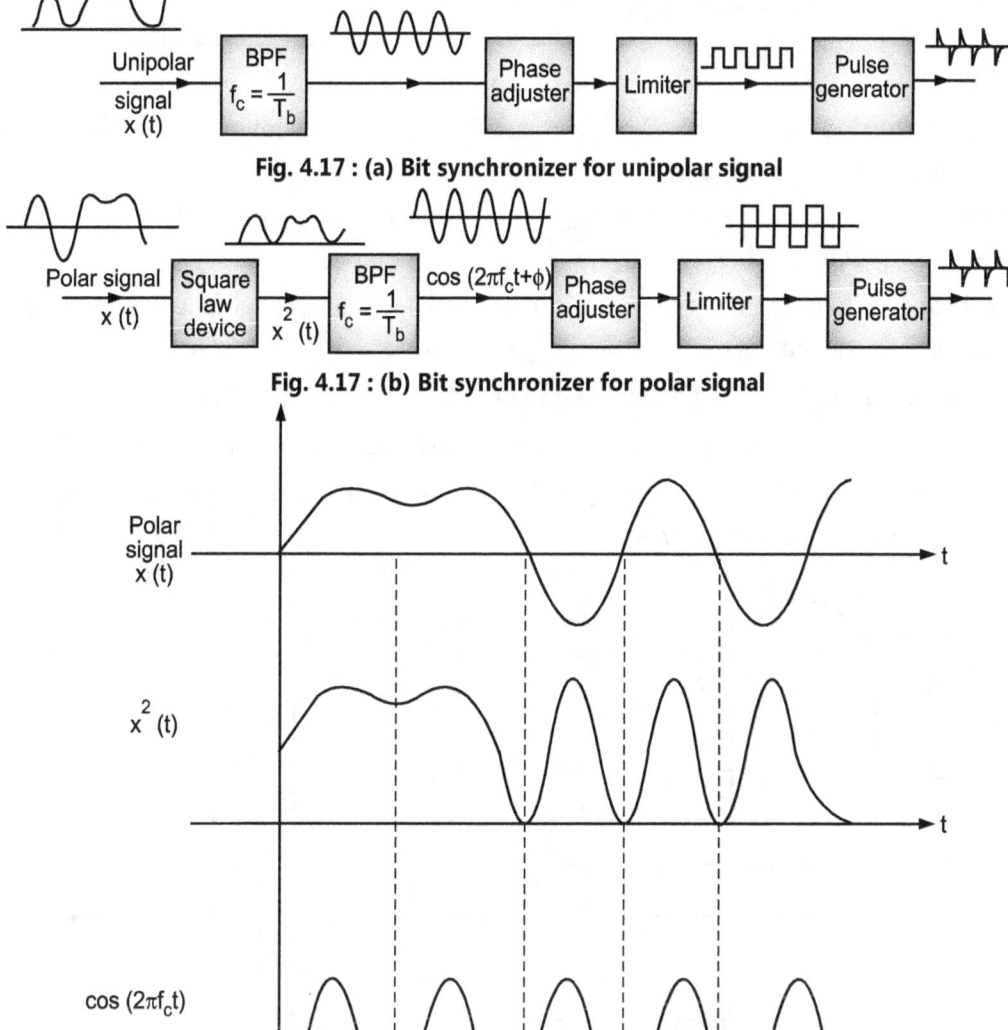

Fig. 4.17 : (a) Bit synchronizer for unipolar signal

Fig. 4.17 : (b) Bit synchronizer for polar signal

Fig. 4.17 : (c) Synchronisation waveforms

- The output of square law device is passed through band pass filter and phase adjuster to produce sinusoid of frequency f_b.

- This is amplified and passed through a limiter to produce clock signal.

- A closed loop bit synchroniser as shown in Fig. 4.18 (a) can be used to extract synchronisation signal from unipolar RZ waveform.

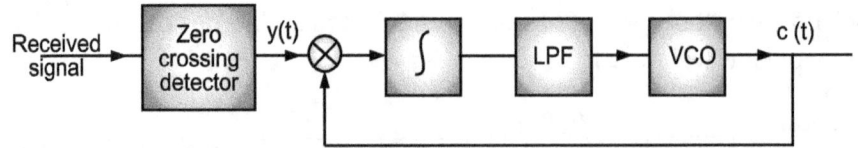

Fig. 4.18 : (a) Closed loop bit synchroniser

- A zero crossing detector gives out a rectangular pulse of duration $T_b/2$ at each zero crossing. (Refer Fig. 4.18 (b)).

- The pulse train is then multiplied with a clock signal generated by Voltage Controlled Oscillator (VCO).

- If there is difference in half duration of clock and $T_b/2$ the multiplication will yield two pulses of unequal duration.

- These pulses are integrated and filtered to generate VCO control voltage.

- This control voltage will speed up or slow down the clock accordingly.

- If the pulses are of equal duration ($T_b/4$), the control voltage will remain same keeping clock frequency constant at $1/T_b$.

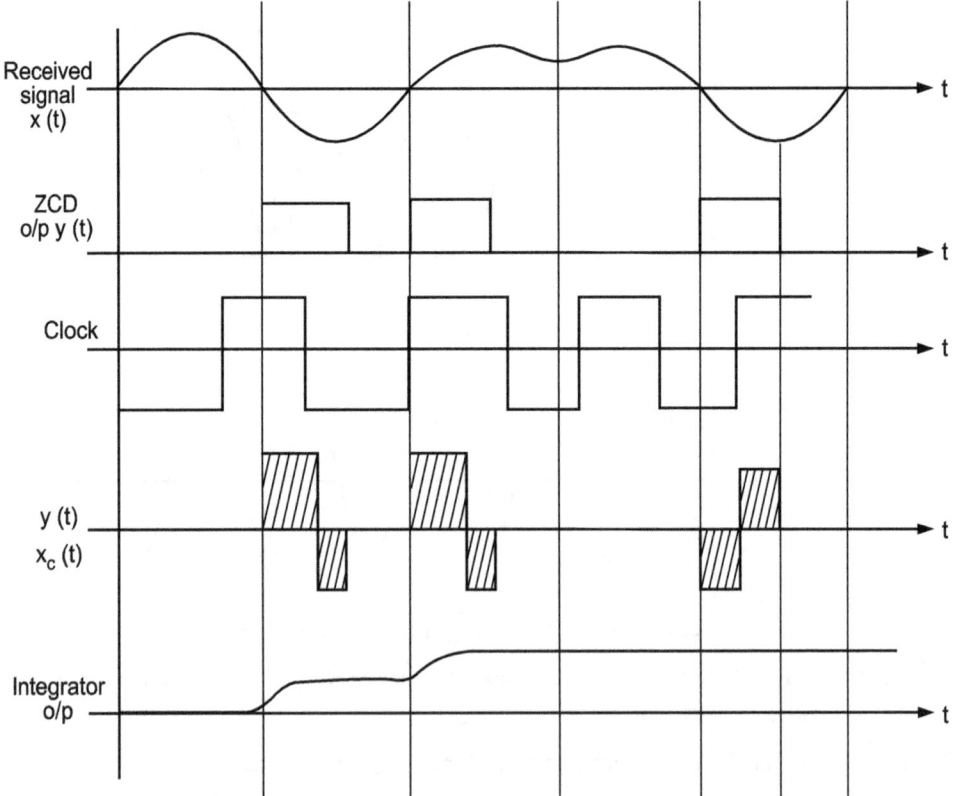

Fig. 4.18 : (b) Waveforms of closed loop bit synchroniser

- The above techniques work well if the zero crossings of received signal are spaced by integer multiple of T_b.

- Small random deviations in this will result (known as timing jitter) into loss of synchronisation.

- Another problem with above techniques is long stream of 1's and 0's will not have zero crossings.

- Hence, another technique which uses the fact that a filtered signal has peaks at optimum sampling time and is symmetric on either side as shown in Fig. 4.19 (a).

$$\left| y \, (nT_b - \Delta) \right| > \left| y \, (nT_b + \Delta) \right|$$

- If $t = nT_b$ is the sampling time and $\Delta < \dfrac{T_b}{2}$ and there is proper synchronisation at $t = nT_b$ then,

$$\left| y \, (nT_b - \Delta) \right| \simeq \left| y \, (nT_b - \Delta) \right| < y \, (nT_b)$$

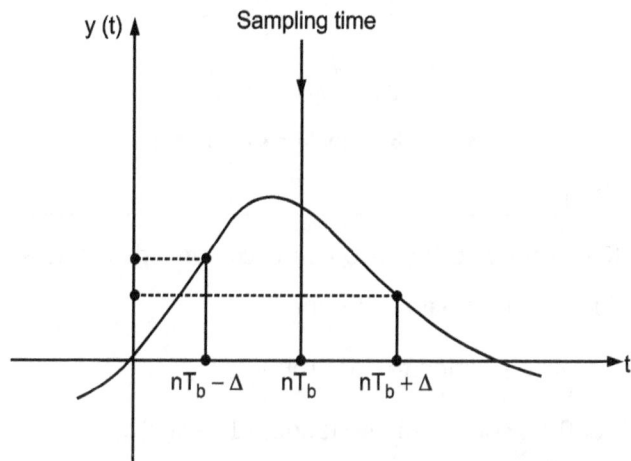

Fig. 4.19 : (a) Late synchronization signal

- If $\left| y \, (nT_b - \Delta) \right| > \left| y \, (nT_b + \Delta) \right|$ meaning the synchronisation signal is late and if $\left| y \, (nT_b - \Delta) \right| < \left| y \, (nT_b + \Delta) \right|$ means the synchronisation signal is early.

- This difference in outputs can be made use of to achieve synchronisation. The technique is called as Early-late synchronisation.

- As shown in Fig. 4.19 (b), a late synchronisation (sampling beyond peak) will result into increase in control voltage of VCO which will speed up the clock.

- An early synchronisation (sampling before peak) will cause control voltage to reduce resulting into slowing down of clock. A perfect synchronisation (sampling at peak) will keep control voltage constant in turn the clock frequency.

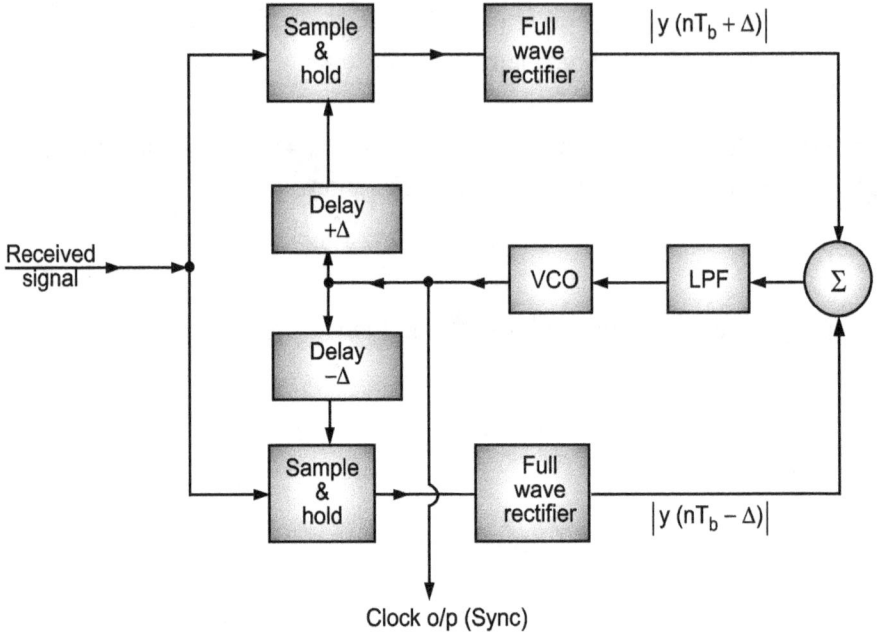

Clock o/p (Sync)

Fig. 4.19 : (b) Early late synchroniser

4.4.2 Scrambling

- The synchronisation technique based on zero crossing detectors suffers from loss of synchronisation due to long stream of 1's and 0's.

- Scrambling technique is a solution to this problem.

- A long stream 1's or 0's is converted into random 1's and 0's.

- This apart from helping synchronisation will also eliminate dc components in the power spectrum and avoid dc wandering.

- This requires a descrambling operation at the receiver end to get back the original sequence.

- A simple shift register and modulo-2 (EX-OR) adder arrangement as shown in Fig. 4.20 (a) can be used for scrambling and descrambling.

- The scrambler and descrambler circuits are shown in Fig. 4.20 (b) and (c).

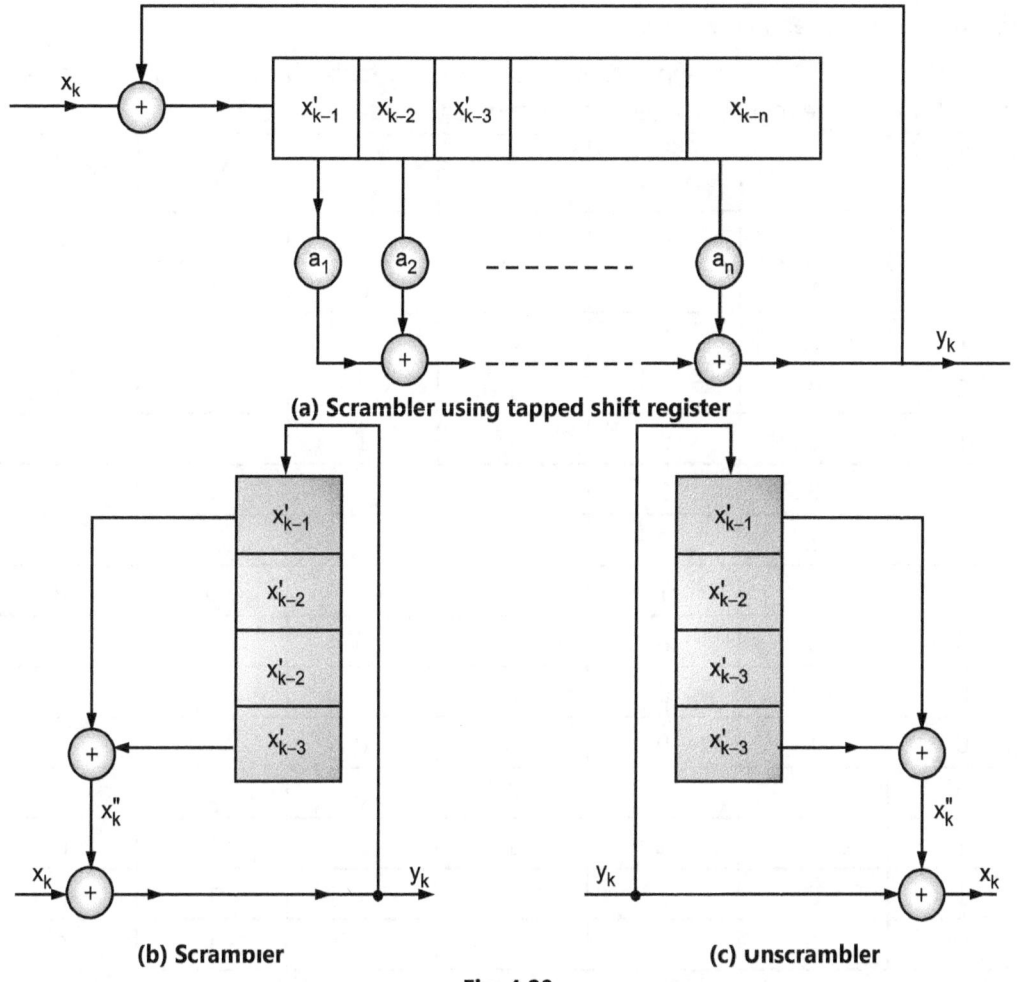

Fig. 4.20

- If Y is the output of the scrambler and X is the input sequence, then we can write,

$$y_k = a_1 x'_{k-1} + a_2 x'_{k-2} + ..., + a_n x'_{k-n}$$

- A scrambler with 4 shift registers is shown in Fig. 4.20 (b). Hence, we can write,

$$y_k = x''_k + x'_k = x_k + x'_{k-1} + x'_{k-3}$$

- The unscrambler shown in Fig. 4.20 (c) has reverse structure.
- Let us see how it reproduces original message. The unscrambled output can be written as,

$$x''_k + y_k = x''_k + (x_k + x''_k) \qquad \text{(Substituting } y_k = x_k + x''_k)$$

$$= x''_k + x''_k + x_k = x_k$$

which is sequence.

- Let us now consider an example.

Let 101010100000111 be the input sequence. Following table shows the output sequence obtained. Initially the register contents are assumed to be zeros.

Input (x_k)	x'_{k-1}	x'_{k-2}	x'_{k-3}	x'_{k-4}	x''_k	y_k (o/p)
1	0	0	0	0	0	1
0	1	0	0	0	1	1
1	1	1	0	0	1	0
0	0	1	1	0	0	0
1	0	0	1	1	1	0
0	0	0	0	1	1	1
1	1	0	0	0	1	0
0	0	1	0	0	0	0
0	0	0	1	0	0	0
0	0	0	0	1	1	1
0	1	0	0	0	1	1
0	1	1	0	0	1	1
1	1	1	1	0	1	0
1	0	1	1	1	1	0
1	0	0	1	1	1	0

- Thus, the output sequence has eliminated the long streams of zeros and also the initial periodic nature of the data stream.
- The disadvantage of this method is that if there is error in the transmitted bit y_k it is going to causes several errors at the receiver end i.e. error propagation occurs.

4.4.3 Frame Synchronisation

- The receiver should know when the transmission begins and when it ends.
- Otherwise when there is no transmission, noise signal will produce random bits.
- In case of time division multiplexing messages from various sources form a part of the frame.
- Thus, entire message has many subdivisions.
- These subdivisions are to be identified at the receiver end in order to distribute them at proper destinations.

- Hence, at the beginning of each transmission or each frame a particular bit pattern is used, which can be identified at the receiver end as start of transmission or start of frame. This is called frame synchronisation.

- A typical frame structure is shown in Fig. 4.21 (a).

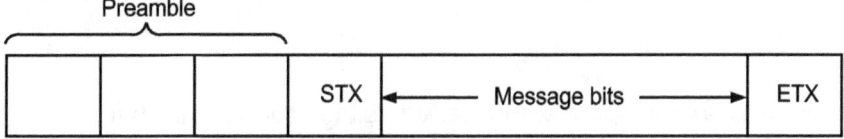

Fig. 4.21 : (a) A typical frame structure

- At the beginning of transmission several repetitions of a synchronisation word are transmitted to acquire bit synchronisation.

- Then start of message word is transmitted which tells the receiver that the message is following.

- When the transmission is over end of message word is sent to inform receiver that there is no more data available for transmission.

- In case of identification of frame, a synchronisation word is attached at the beginning of each frame.

- A frame synchroniser circuit is shown in Fig. 4.21 (b).

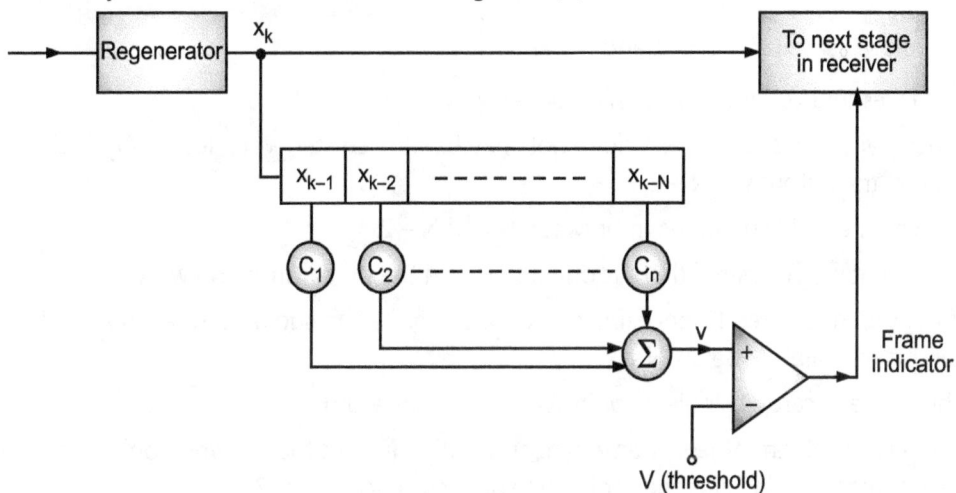

Fig. 4.21 : (b) Frame synchroniser

- The output of regenerator is reconstructed message sequence. It is stored in N-stage shift register.

- Where, N is number of bits in the synchronisation word to be identified.

- The bits are in polar format ($\pm$ 1).

- The tap gains of the shift register are adjusted depending on the synchronisation word.

- Let the synchronisation word be (S_1, S_2, ..., S_N) and the tap gains adjusted such that, i.e.

$$c_i = 2S_{N+1-i} - 1$$
$$c_1 = 2S_N - 1$$
$$c_2 = 2S_{N-1} - 1$$
$$\vdots$$
$$\vdots$$
$$c_N = 2S_1 - 1$$

- These tap gains are multiplied with received voltage collected in shift register and then added.
- This sum is compared with a preset threshold voltage V.
- The output of comparator will indicate whether the word in shift register is a valid synchronisation word or not.
- This is because when valid synchronisation word is present in the register, the voltage produced by the summer

$$V = \sum_{i=1}^{N} c_i \times x_{k-i}$$

will exceed the threshold voltage V. Otherwise it will remain below V.

- When the register word is same as synchronisation word. $x_{k-1} = c_i$.

- Therefore, $c_i \times x_{k-1} = c_i^2 = 1$ and $v = N$.

- The threshold voltage V is set slightly below N.

- When synchronisation word does not match with register word let us say it differs by one bit the output $v = N - 2$.

- Hence, threshold should be in between N and N − 2.

- Now what will happen if there is one bit error in the synchronisation word.

- It will go undetected ! Hence, instead of keeping the threshold between N and N − 2, it can be kept slightly below N − 2.

- This will take care of single error in synchronisation word.

- There is a problem of false frame synchronisation in case the synchronisation word is part of message. What is the probability of occurrence of this ?

- It will be equal to the probability that all N bits match or N − 1 bits match.

- Let the probability of 1 and 0 be equally likely, then the probability of false frame synchronisation is given by,

$$p_{ff} = \left(\frac{1}{2}\right)^N + \left(\frac{1}{2}\right)^{N-1}$$

all N bits
match

N − 1 bits
match

4.5 INTERSYMBOL INTERFERENCE (ISI)

- The bandwidth of flat top pulses is infinity.

- There are various filters in transmitter, channel and receiver of the communication systems.

- If these pulses are filtered improperly as they pass through a communication system, they will spread in time and the pulse for each symbol may be smeared into adjacent time slots and cause intersymbol interference as shown in Fig. 4.22.

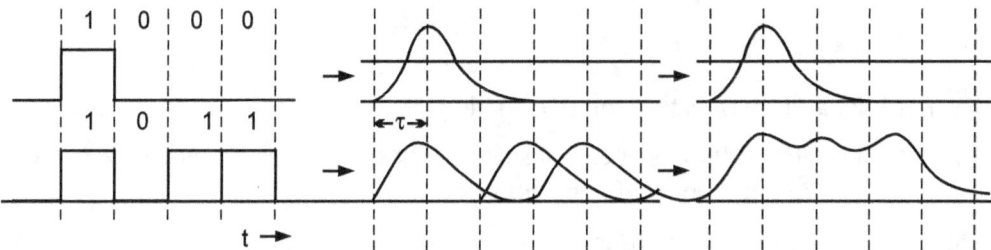

Fig. 4.22 : ISI problem

- The question is : How we can restrict bandwidth and still not introduce ISI ?

- With restricted bandwidth the pulses would have rounded tops.

- Thus our aim is to –

  (1) Study ISI problem.

  (2) Use baseband pulse shaping as solution to the problem.

4.5.1 Baseband Transmission of Binary Data

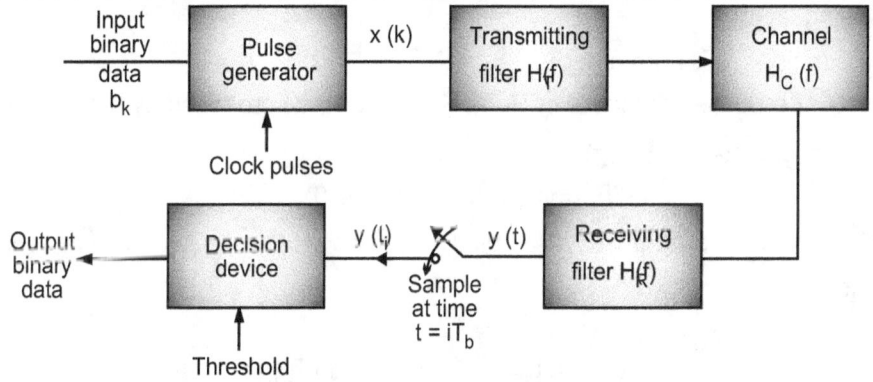

Fig. 4.23 : Binary PAM system

- For the baseband transmission of digital data, use of the discrete pulse amplitude modulation (PAM) provides the most efficient form of discrete pulse modulation in terms of power and bandwidth.

- The basic elements of binary PAM systems are shown in Fig. 4.23.

- The signal applied is the baseband binary data sequence {bk} with bit duration Tb seconds. bk is in the form of 1 and 0. This signal is applied to the pulse generator producing waveform.

$$x(t) \; = \; \sum_{k = -\infty}^{\infty} A_k \, g \, (t - kT_b) \qquad \qquad \text{... (4.12)}$$

g(t) – pulse shaping waveform.

where, g(0) = 1

and $\qquad\qquad A_k \; = \; \begin{cases} + a \text{ if input bit is 1} \\ - a \text{ if input bit is 0} \end{cases}$

- The PAM signal x(t) passes through transmitting filter with transfer function H_T (f).

- The resulting filter output defines transmitted signal, which is modified as a result of transmission through channel of transfer function H_c (f).

- The signal at the receiver input is passed through a receiving filter of transfer function H_R (f).

- This filter output is sampled synchronously with the transmitter and then these samples are used to reconstruct the original data sequence by means of a decision device.

4.5.2 The ISI Problem

- We assume the channel is noiseless. The receiving filter output may be written as,

$$y(t) \; = \; \mu \sum_{k = -\infty}^{\infty} A_k \, p \, (t - kT_b) \qquad\qquad \text{... (4.13)}$$

μ – Scaling factor

p(0) = 1 (pulse p(t) is normalised).

μ A_k p(t) – Response of cascade of H_T (f), H_R (f) and H_c (f) produced by the pulse A_k g(t).

∴   We may relate p(t) to g(t) as,

$$\mu \, P(f) \; = \; G(f) \, H_T \, (f) \, H_c \, (f) \, H_R \, (f) \qquad\qquad \text{... (4.14)}$$

- The receiving filter output y (t) is sampled at time t_i = iT_b (with i taking an integer values) yielding

$$y(t_i) \; = \; \mu \sum_{k = -\infty}^{\infty} A_k \, p \, [(i - k) \, T_b] \qquad\qquad \text{... (4.15)}$$

∴ $$y(t_i) \; = \; \mu A_i + \mu \sum_{\substack{k = -\infty \\ k \neq 0}}^{\infty} A_k \, p \, [(i - k) \, T_b] \qquad\qquad \text{... (4.16)}$$

- In above equation first term μA_i represents the contribution of the ith transmitted bits.
- The second term represents the residual effects of all other transmitted bits on the secondary of ith received bit, this residual effect is called **intersymbol interference (ISI)**.
- In absence of ISI, we observe that,

$$y(t_i) = \mu A_i$$

which shows that, under these ideal conditions the ith transmitted bit can be decoded correctly.

- The unavoidable presence of ISI in the system, however introduces errors in decision device at the receiver output.
- Therefore, in designing transmitting and receiving filters, the objective is to minimise the effect of ISI.
- Typically, the channel transfer function $H_c(f)$ and pulse spectrum $G(f)$ are specified, and the problem is to determine $H_T(f)$ and $H_R(f)$, so as to enable the receiver to correctly decode the receiving sequence of sample values $y(t_i)$.

4.5.3 Ideal Solution

- Control of ISI is achieved by controlling the function $p(t)$, or in the frequency domain by controlling $P(f)$.
- One signal waveform that produces zero intersymbol interference is defined by sinc function.

$$p(t) = \frac{\sin(2\pi B_0 t)}{2\pi B_0 t} = \text{sinc}(2B_0 t) \qquad \qquad ... (4.17)$$

where, $\qquad\qquad B_0 = \dfrac{1}{2T_b}$ $\qquad$ (Analogous with sampling theorem)

- It means if we make the overall impulse response of the system $P(t)$ as above by designing suitable filters at transmitter $H_T(f)$ and or reveiver $H_R(f)$ end there will be no ISI.
- The parameter B_0 is called Nyquist BW, it is minimum transmission BW for zero ISI equal to half the bit rate.

$$P(f) = \begin{cases} \dfrac{1}{2B_0} & 0 \le |f| \le B_0 \\ 0 & |f| \ge B_0 \end{cases} \qquad ... (4.18)$$

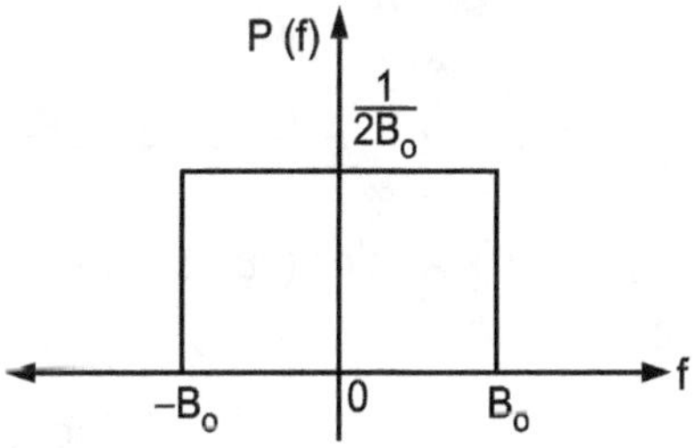

Fig. 4.24

- Thus, function p(t) is impulse response of ideal LPF with amplitude response $\frac{1}{2B_0}$ in the passband and BW = B_0. The function p(t) has its peak value at its origin and goes to zero at every integer multiplies of bit duration T_b.

- If y(t) is sampled at t = 0, $\pm T_b$, $\pm 2b$ …… then the pulses defined by $A_i\, p\, (t - iT_b)$ will not interfere with each other.

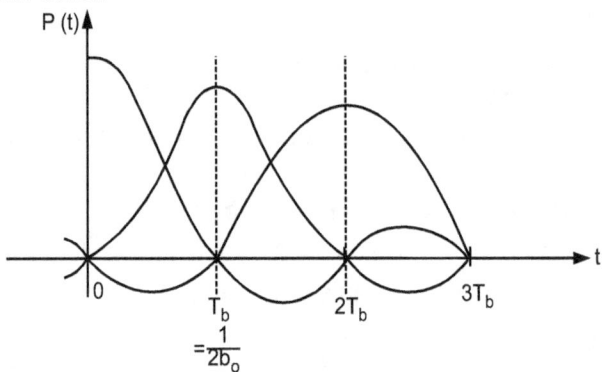

Fig. 4.25

- Although ideal choice of pulse shape solved ISI problem there are two difficulties that make its design impractical.

(i) It requires that frequency response P(f) be flat from $- B_0$ to B_0 and resolution elsewhere. This is physically unrealizable and very difficult to approximate in practice.

(ii) The time function p (t) decreases as $1/|t|$ for large $|t|$ resulting in slow rate of decay. This is caused by discontinuity of P(f) at $\pm B_0$. Accordingly, there is practically no margin of error in sampling times in the receiver. i.e. P(t) decays only as $1/|t|$ and is zero in adjacent time slots only when t is at exactly at correct sampling time. Thus, inaccurate synchronisation will cause ISI.

- To evaluate the effect of timing error, consider the sample y (t) at t = Δt. where, Δt is the timing error.

- To simplify the analysis we put the correct sampling time $t_i = 0$. We obtain,

$$y\,(\Delta t) \;=\; \mu \sum_{k=-\infty}^{\infty} A_k\, p\,(\Delta t - kT_b)$$

$$=\; \mu \sum_{k=-\infty}^{\infty} A_k\, \text{sinc}\,[2B_0\,(\Delta t - kT_b)] \qquad\qquad \ldots (4.19)$$

Since $2B_0T_b = 1$. $\qquad y\,(\Delta t) \;=\; \mu \sum_k A_k\, \text{sinc}\,(2B_0\,\Delta t - k)$

$$=\; \mu\, A_0\, \text{sinc}\,(2B_0 t) + \mu\, \frac{\text{sinc}\,(2\pi B_0 \Delta t)}{\pi} \times \sum_{\substack{k=-\infty \\ k \neq 0}}^{\infty} \frac{(-1)^k\, A_k}{2B_0\, \Delta t - k}$$

1st term – derived symbol.

Rest – ISI caused by timing error Δt in sampling y(t).

- The practical difficulties of ideal solution can be overcome by extending bandwidth from B_0 to an adjustable value between B_0 and $2B_0$.

- The solution is called Raised cosine spectrum.

4.5.4 Raised Cosine Waveform

- In Raised cosine spectrum, the overall frequency response P(f) decreases towards zero gradually rather than abruptly.

$$P(f) = \begin{cases} \dfrac{1}{2B_0} & ; 0 \le |f| < f_1 \\[2ex] \dfrac{1}{4B_0}\left\{1 - \sin\left[\dfrac{\pi\,(|f| - B_0)}{2B_0 - 2f_1}\right]\right\} & ; f_1 \le |f| < 2B_0 - f_1 \\[2ex] 0 & ; |f| > 2B_0 - f_1 \end{cases} \qquad \dots (4.20)$$

- The frequency f_1 and Nyquists BW B_0 are related by roll-off factor.

$$\alpha = 1 - \frac{f_1}{B_0}$$

- For $\alpha = 0$, $f_1 = B_0$

- The normalised plot is shown in Fig. 4.26 as follows.

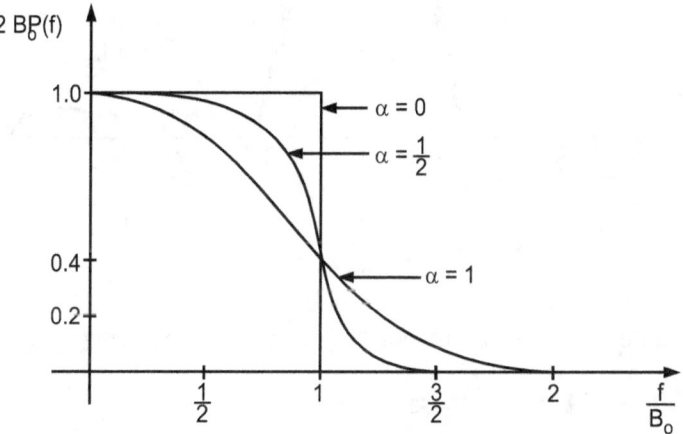

Fig. 4.26

- The time response p(t) i.e. inverse Fourier transform of P(f) is,

$$p(t) = \text{sinc}\,(2B_0t)\,\frac{\cos\,(2\pi\alpha B_0t)}{1 - 16\,\alpha^2 B_0 t^2} \qquad \dots (4.21)$$

- The time response p(t) has two parts :

  (i) The first part sinc ($2B_0t$) is ideal Nyquist solution which ensures zero crossings at t = iT_b.

  (ii) The second part decreases as $\dfrac{1}{|t|^2}$ for large t, which reduces the tails of pulse rapidly.

- For special case $\alpha = 1$.

$$p(t) \;=\; \frac{\text{sinc }(2B_0t)}{1 - 16\,B_0^2\,t^2}$$

- This time response has two interesting properties.

  (i) At t = $\pm\,T_b/2$ = $\pm\,1/4B_0$ we have p(t) = 0.5 i.e., the pulse width measured at half amplitude is = bit duration T_b.

  (ii) There are two zero crossings at t = $\pm\,3T_b/2$, $\pm\,5T_b/2$ in addition to normal zero crossings at t = $\pm\,T_b$, $\pm\,2T_b$.

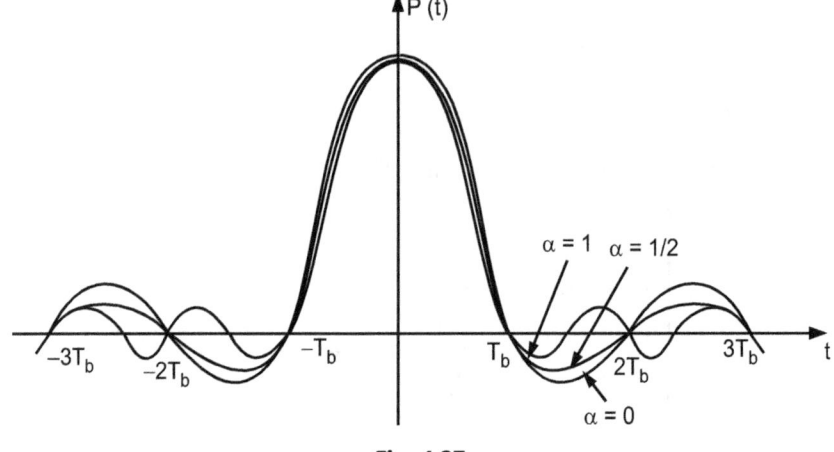

Fig. 4.27

- Note that a value of $\alpha = 1$, the response goes to zero, not only at zeros of $\dfrac{\sin(2\pi B_0t)}{2\pi B_0t}$.

  But also at midpoints between these samples.

- It is therefore possible to sample at the same rate as for ideal channel; with no resulting ISI.

- We note in the next section that the price paid for this is increased bandwidth which is $2B_0$ in case of $\alpha = 1$.

Limitations of Raised cosine spectrum :

(i)   The raised cosine filter have infinite impulse response.

(ii) The filters are non-causal and physically unrealizable.

(iii) Transmission bandwidth required is higher for practically realizable filter.

4.5.5 Transmission BW Requirement

- Raised cosine spectrum is limited to the interval $(0, 2B_0 - f_1)$ for positive frequency.
- The transmission BW required by raised cosine spectrum is given by,
$$B = 2B_0 - f_1$$

Using,
$$\alpha = 1 - \frac{f_1}{B_0}$$

$$B = B_0 (1 + \alpha) \qquad \qquad \text{... (4.22)}$$

B_0 – Nyquist BW, α – roll off factor.

1. When $\alpha = 0$ $B = B_0$
2. When $\alpha = 1$ $B = 2B_0$

Example 4.3 :

Transmission BW for T_1 carrier system.

Solution :

For T1 carrier system,

$$T_b = 0.647$$

$$R_b = \frac{1}{T_b} = 1.544 \text{ Mb/s}$$

$\alpha = 0$ $B_T = B_0 = \frac{1}{2T_b} = 772 \text{ kHz}$

$\alpha = 1$ $B_T = B = 2B_0 = 1.544 \text{ MHz}$

Example 4.4 :

What absolute bandwidth is required to transmit an information rate of 8 kbps using 64 level baseband signaling over a raised cosine channel with roll-off factor of 40% ?

Solution :

Given : $r_b = 8 \times 10^4 \text{ bps}$

                    Number of levels $= 64$

                                $\alpha = 0.4$

            Bit rate bit/sec $=$ Number of bits per symbol $\times$ Number of symbols per sec.

$$r_b = v \times f_s$$

$$f_s = \frac{r_b}{v} = \frac{8 \times 10^3}{\log_2 64}$$

$$= 1.333 \times 10^3 \text{ symbols/S}$$

$$\therefore \qquad B_0 = \frac{f_s}{2} = \frac{1.333}{2} \times 10^3$$

For raised cosine spectrum,

Transmission bandwidth,

$$B_T = B_0 (1 + \alpha)$$

$$= \frac{1.3333 \times 10^3}{2} (1 + 0.4)$$

$$= 933 \text{ Hz}$$

Example 4.5 :

A four level PAM pulse sequence has data rate 3600 bps. The system transfer characteristics consists of raised cosine spectrum with 100% excess bandwidth. Find minimum transmission bandwidth.

Solution :

Given :   Number of levels M $= 4$

$$\text{Data rate, } r_b = 3600 \text{ bps}$$

$$\text{Roll-off factor } \alpha = 1 \text{ (100% excess bandwidth)}$$

$$\text{Pulse rate, } R_s = \frac{r_b}{\log_e M} = \frac{3600}{2} = 1800 \text{ symbols/sec}$$

$$\therefore \qquad B_0 = \frac{1800}{2} = 900 \text{ Hz}$$

For raised cosine spectrum bandwidth,

$$B = B_0 (1 + \alpha) = 900 (1 + 1)$$

$$= 1800 \text{ Hz}$$

4.5.6 Causes of ISI

(i) We have seen that ISI occurs due to non-deal characteristics of channel. The transmitted pulses spread in time causing interference with adjacent pulses. The solution to this is pulse shaping through ideal or raised cosine spectrum.

(ii) The ISI can still occur with above suggested solutions due to timing inaccuracies in clock. If the sample time is not exactly at desired instant then ISI can occur.

(iii) The ISI can occur if the Nyquist bandwidth required for the pulse shaping is not sufficient.

(iv) For pulse shaping solution we should know the channel response exactly. The frequency characteristics of channel $H_c(f)$ can not be estimated exactly. This will give rise to incorrect solution and result into amplitude or pulse distortion.

(v) There can be phase distortion because different sine wave components in the transmitted signal undergo different amount of time delay through transmission medium.

4.5.7 Eye Pattern

- One way to study intersymbol interference in a PCM or data transmission system experimentally is to apply received wave to vertical deflection plates of an oscilloscope and a sawtooth wave at transmitted symbol rate 1/T to horizontal deflection plates.

- The successive symbol intervals are thereby translated into one interval on oscilloscope display.

- The effect of channel filtering and channel noise can be seen by observing the pattern.

- The resulting display is called eye pattern because of its resemblance with human eye.

- The Fig. 4.28 shows eye pattern for the three cases.

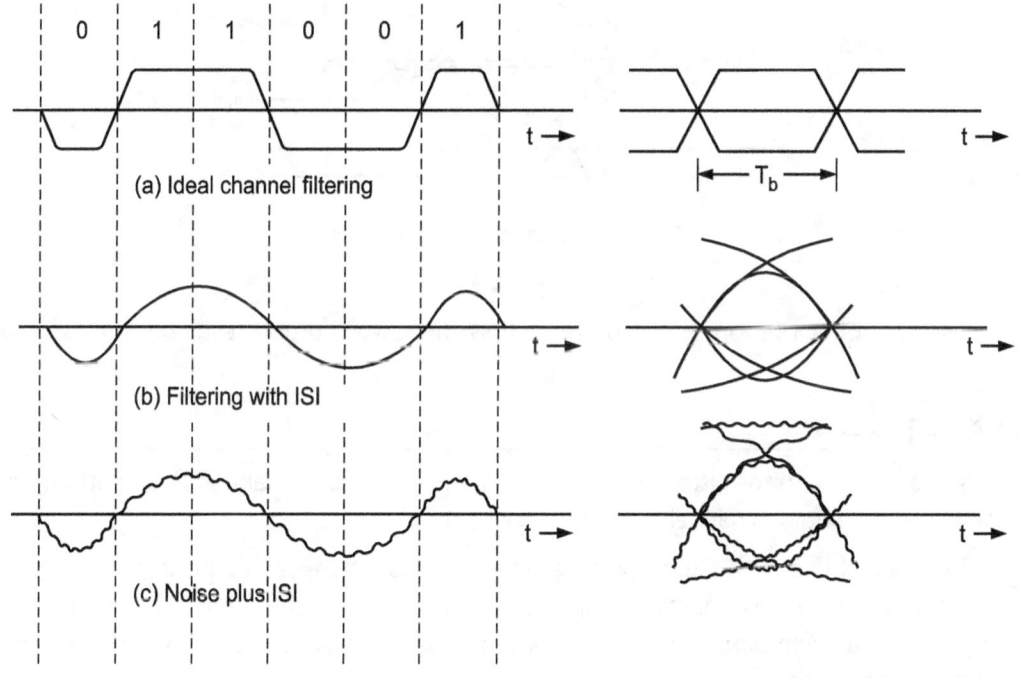

Fig. 4.28

Eye pattern gives information about –

1. The width of eye opening defines the time interval over which received wave can be sampled without error from ISI.

- Time for sampling – time at which is eye is open widest.

2. The sensitivity of the system to timing error is determined by rate of chosen of eye. [Slope of the open eye (evaluated near zero crossing point)].

3. Height of eye opening at specified sampling time, defines noise, margin.

4. Maximum distortion is given by the vertical width of the upper (or lower) portion of the eye at sampling time.

5. The range of amplitude differences (D_A) is a measure of distortion caused due to ISI.

6. The range of timing differences of zero crossings (J_T) is a measure of the timing jitter.

7. Measure of noise merging is M_N.

8. Sensitivity of timing error is S_T as shown in Fig. 4.29.

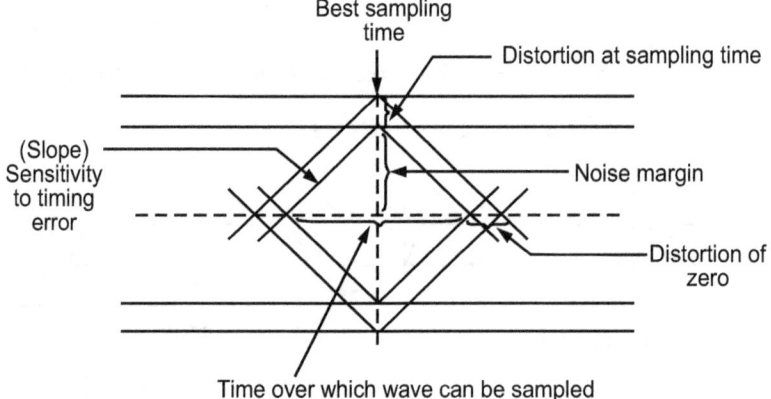

Fig. 4.29

For severe ISI upper portion of eye pattern cross the lower portion resulting in closure of eye.

4.5.8 Equalizers

- When a signal is transmitted through channel it undergoes changes in amplitude and phase depending on channel characteristics $H_c(f)$.

- If the channel has ideal filter type frequency response there will be no distortion in the signal. Ideal filter has constant amplitude response $|H_c(f)|$ and linear phase response $\angle H_c(f)$ over a given bandwidth. In this case no corrective action equalization is required at the receiver end.

- If the channel frequency response is not ideal, different frequency components will undergo different attenuation and different delay. The frequency response of such channel is such that the amplitude response is non constant (variable) and phase response is non-linear.

- In order to combat the effects of non-ideal frequency response we can use a filter at the front end of the receiver which has characteristics exactly opposite to that of channel filter. This is done in order to nullify or equalize the effects of channel filter. Hence filter is called as equalizer. If the channel has a frequency response $H_c(f)$ the equalizer will have frequency response.

$$H_{eq}(f) = \frac{1}{H_c(f)}$$

- The equalizers will also help in reducing the ISI.

- Since the channel conditions are changing especially in case of wireless channel, the channel, the channel frequency response is time varying. Hence the equalizers should also adopt to these changing conditions. Such equalizers are called adaptive equalizers.

- Following are few types of equalizers.

(i) Zero-forcing (ZF) equalizers

(ii) Minimum Mean Square Error Equalizers (MMSE)

(iii) Least square (LS) equalizers

(iv) Decision feedback equalizers.

SOLVED UNIVERSITY QUESTIONS

U.Q. 1 : In unipolar signaling (line code) scheme logic '1' is transmitted as +p(t) pulse and logic '0' as no pulse. Estimate the spectrum p(ω). Assume p(t) is half width rectangular pulse i.e. Rz. Plot P.S.D. $S_y(\omega)$. Comment on transmission bandwidth, error detection capability, favourable PSD or not, timing content and transparency. Given that for train of unit strength impulses are coded according to digital sequence x(t) with PSD.   **(Dec. 2005, 07)**

$$S_x(\omega) = \frac{1}{T_0} \sum_{n=-\infty}^{\infty} R_n e^{-jn\omega T_0}$$

$$= \frac{1}{T_0} \left[R_0 + \sum_{n=1}^{\infty} R_n \cos(n\omega T_0) \right]$$

$$T_0 = \text{Bit duration}$$

$$R_x(\tau) = \frac{1}{T_0} \sum_{n=-\infty}^{\infty} R_n \delta(\tau - nT_0)$$

$$R_n = \lim_{N \to \infty} \frac{1}{N} \sum_k a_n a_{n+k}$$

$$= \lim_{T \to \infty} \frac{T_0}{T} \sum_k a_n a_{n+k}$$

$$a_k = k^{th} \text{ impulse}$$

$$a_{k+n} = k + n^{th} \text{ impulse.}$$

Solution : Refer Section 4.6.1 (Unipolar NRZ and RZ).

U.Q. 2 : What are T1 multiplexing standards for (i) Rate, (ii) Number of voice channels, (iii) Mediums, (iv) Line code, (v) Repeater spacing, (vi) Max system length,   (vii) System BOR rate.   **(8) (Dec. 2005)**

Solution : Refer Section 4.4.1.

U.Q. 3 : Describe early-late synchronizer for polar NRZ signaling with the help of neat diagram.   **(10) (Dec. 2005, May 2010)**

Solution : Refer Section 4.4.3.

U.Q. 4 : Draw the line code formats for 10110100.   **(6) (May 2006)**

    (i)   RZ unipolar   (ii) NRZ polar

    (iii) AMI   (iv) Manchester

    (v)   RZ polar   (vi) Polar quaternary (NRZ)

Solution : The given format is 1 0 1 1 0 1 0 0.

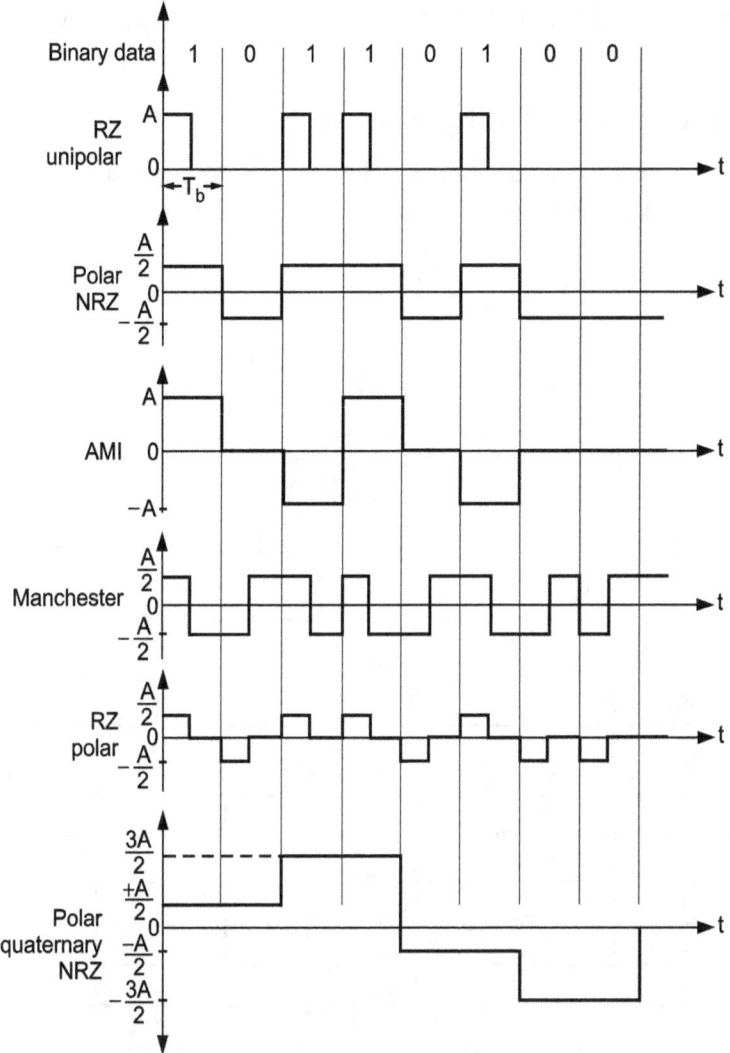

Fig. 4.22

U.Q. 5 : Explain need of scrambler. Show that unscrambler reproduces original sequence given to scrambler. **(10) (May 2006, 07)**

Solution : Refer Section 4.4.2.

U.Q. 6 : Explain multiplexing standards in detail. **(8) (Dec. 2006)**

Solution : Refer Section 4.4.1.

U.Q. 7 : Explain synchronous and quasi synchronous multiplexers. **(8) (Dec. 2006)**

Solution : Refer Section 4.3.

U.Q. 8 : Evaluate PSD of unipolar NRZ and polar RZ. Plot the spectrum. **(8) (Dec. 2008)**

Solution : Refer Section 4.4.

U.Q. 9 :   Explain the operation of Costas Loop synchronization to recover the carrier.

(8) (Dec. 2006)

Solution : Refer Section 4.4.1 (Closed loop synchronizer).

U.Q. 10 :   Why scrambler is needed in digital transmission ? The data stream 10101010001 is an input to scrambler shown in Fig. 4.23. Obtain the scrambled output.

(8) (Dec. 2006)

Solution :

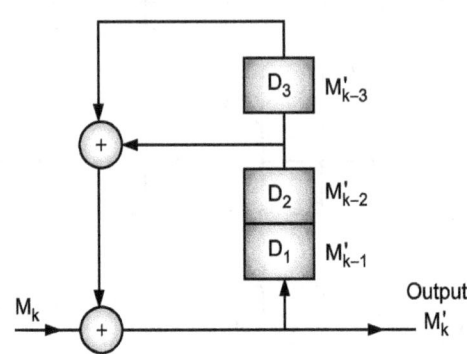

Fig. 4.23

(i) Need of scrambler : Refer Section 4.7.2.

Input	m'_{k-1}	m'_{k-2}	m'_{k-3}	m''_k	m'_k (o/p)
	0	0	0	0	
1	0	0	0	0	1
0	1	0	0	0	0
1	0	1	0	1	0
0	0	0	1	1	1
1	1	0	0	0	1
0	1	1	0	1	1
1	1	1	1	0	1
0	1	1	1	0	0
0	0	1	1	0	0

Hence, output scrambled is m'_k.

i.e. 10011110011.

U.Q. 11 : Explain properties of line codes and draw the PSD for various codes.

(8) (May 2007)

Solution : Refer Section 4.3.

U.Q. 12 : What is digital multiplexing ? Draw AT & T hierarchy and compare the output rate with CCITT hierarchy. **(8) (Dec. 2007)**

Solution : Refer Section 4.2.1.

U.Q. 13 : A scrambler is shown in Fig. 4.24. Design the corresponding unscrambler if a sequence is 101010100000111 is applied to the input, determine the output sequence T. Verify if this T is applied to the input the output is S. **(8) (Dec. 2007)**

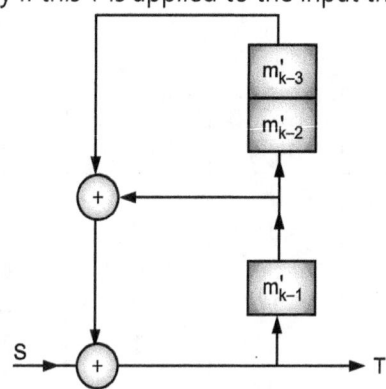

Fig. 4.24

Solution : The unscrambler will be as below.

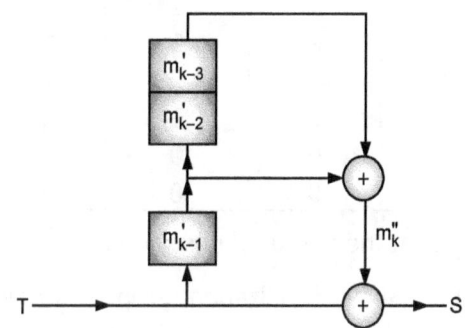

Fig. 4.25

The scrambling operation for given input is,

Input	m'_{k-1}	m'_{k-2}	m'_{k-3}	m''_k	T (o/p)
	0	0	0	0	
1	0	0	0	0	1
0	1	0	0	1	1
1	1	1	0	1	0
0	0	1	1	1	1
1	1	0	1	0	1
0	1	1	0	1	1

0	1	1	1	0	0
0	0	1	1	1	1
0	1	0	1	0	0
0	0	1	0	0	0
1	0	0	1	1	0
1	0	0	0	0	1
1	1	0	0	1	0

Thus, the scrambled output is,

1 1 0 1 1 1 0 1 0 0 0 1 0.

The unscrmabler output for the scrambler sequence.

Input	m'_{k-1}	m'_{k-2}	m'_{k-3}	m''_k	s'_s
	0	0	0	0	
1	0	0	0	0	1
1	1	0	0	0	0
0	1	1	0	0	1
1	0	1	1	1	0
1	1	0	1	0	1
1	1	1	0	1	0
0	1	1	1	0	0
1	0	1	1	1	0
0	1	0	1	0	0
0	0	1	0	0	0
0	0	0	1	1	1
1	0	0	0	0	1
0	1	0	0	1	1

Thus, we get original sequence at the output of unscrambler.

U.Q. 14 : What are the different synchronization techniques ? Draw the block diagram of synchronization in binary receiver and explain closed-loop bit synchronization techniques. **(8) (Dec. 2007)**

Solution : Refer Section 4.7.1.

U.Q. 15 : Draw diagram of digital multiplexing system that accommodates both analog and digital signals in a standard multiplexing hierarchy including the North American and CCITT. **(8) (May 2008)**

Solution : Refer Section 4.2.1.

U.Q. 16 : What is synchronizer ? Explain any one type of bit synchronizer. **(6) (Dec. 08)**

Solution : Refer Section 4.7.1.

U.Q. 17 : Write the functions performed by a multiplexer ? What are the three main categories of multiplexer ?   **(10) (Dec. 2008)**

Solution : Refer Section 4.2.

U.Q. 18 : What are desirable properties of line codes ? Compare RZ and NRZ line coding formats on the basis of above properties alongwith merits and demerits.

Solution : Refer Section 4.6.1.   **(6) (May 2009)**

Dec. 2010

U.Q. 19 : Explain T_1 carrier system and AT&T multiplexing hierarchy.   **(8)**

Solution : Refer Section 4.2.1.

U.Q. 20 : What is Inter Symbol Interference (ISI)? Explain the ideal solution to control ISI.   **(8)**

Solution : Refer Sections 4.5 and 4.5.3.

U.Q. 21 : What is bit synchronisation ? Explain closed loop bit synchroniser.   **(8)**

Solution : Refer Sections 4.4 and 4.4.1.

May 2011

U.Q. 22 : Describe Early-Late Synchronizer for polar NRZ signalling with help of neat diagram.   **(6)**

Solution : Refer Section 4.4.1.

U.Q. 23 : A scrambler is shown in Fig. 4.26 design the corresponding unscrambles if a sequence is 1010110 applied to the scrambler input determine the output. **(6)**

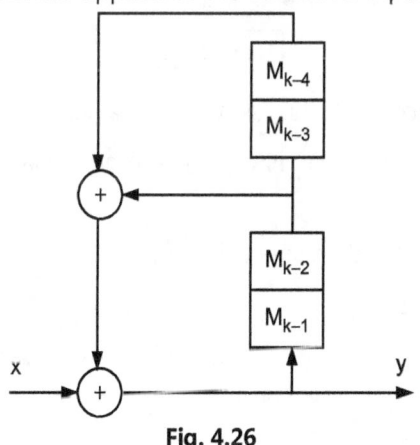

Fig. 4.26

Solution : The unscrambler will be

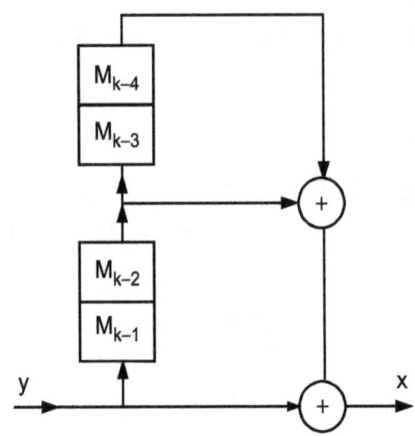

Fig. 4.27

The output corresponding to given input is shown below.

Input	m_{k-1}	m_{k-2}	m_{k-3}	m_{k-4}	Output
	0	0	0	0	
1	0	0	0	0	1
0	1	0	0	0	0
1	0	1	0	0	0
0	0	0	1	0	0
1	0	0	0	1	0
1	0	0	0	0	1
0	1	0	0	0	0

Hence, output will be 1000010.

U.Q. 24 : Explain T_1 carrier system and hence compare AT-T and CCIT hierarchy of multiplexing.   **(7)**

Solution : Refer Sections 4.2.1, 4.2.2 and 4.2.3.

Dec. 2011

U.Q. 25 : For the sequence 10111001, sketch the waveform using the following formats:

(i) Unipolar Rz, (ii) Polar NRz, (iii) Alternate Mark Inversion, (iv) Split phase Manchester coding.

Draw the corresponding spectrum of the above formats and explain.   **(10)**

Solution : Refer Section 4.3.

U.Q. 26 : What are the different types of multiplexers used in digital communication system? Explain quasi-synchronous multiplexer in detail with a neat sketch. **(8)**

Solution : Refer Section 4.1.

U.Q. 27 : Consider a sequence 10100001000000010 is applied to the scrambler shown in Fig. 4.28. Determine the output sequence '0'. Design the corresponding descrambler and verify whether its output matches with the given sequence. **(10)**

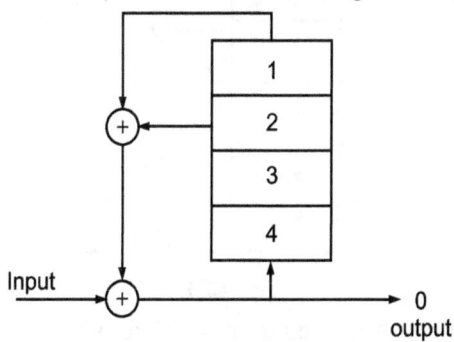

Fig. 4.28

Solution : The output of scrambler will be as below.

Input	X_1	X_2	X_3	X_4	Output
1	0	0	0	0	1
0	0	0	0	1	0
1	0	0	1	0	1
0	0	1	0	1	1
0	1	0	1	1	1
0	0	1	1	1	1
0	1	1	1	1	0
1	1	1	1	0	1
0	1	1	0	1	0
0	1	0	1	0	1
0	0	1	0	1	1
0	1	0	1	1	1
0	0	1	1	1	1
0	1	1	1	1	0
0	1	1	1	0	0
1	1	1	0	0	1
0	1	0	0	1	1

The scrambler will be as below.

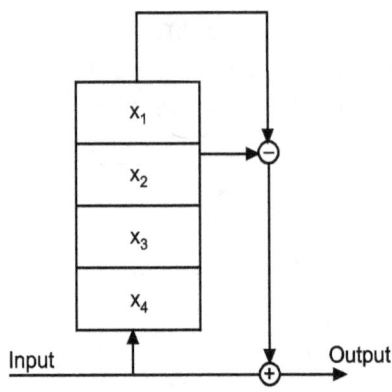

Fig. 4.29

The output of scrambler if applied to input of above descrambler, we get the original input as below.

Input	X_1	X_2	X_3	X_4	Output
1	0	0	0	0	1
0	0	0	1	0	0
1	0	1	0	1	1
1	1	0	1	1	0
1	0	1	1	1	0
1	1	1	1	1	0
0	1	1	1	0	0
1	1	1	0	1	1
0	1	0	1	0	0
1	0	1	0	1	0
1	1	0	1	1	0
1	0	1	1	1	0
1	1	1	1	1	0
0	1	1	1	0	0
0	1	1	0	0	0
1	1	0	0	1	1
1	0	0	1	1	0

May 2012

U.Q. 28 :   What are line codes and its characteristics? Compare the power spectral density of Unipolar NR2 and R2 formats by deriving suitable expressions.

Solution :   Refer Section 4.3.

U.Q. 29 :   Why synchronization is necessary in digital communication? Explain bit and frame synchronization using suitable sketch.   **(8)**

Solution :   Refer Sections 4.4, 4.4.1 and 4.4.3.

U.Q. 30 :   Consider the sequence of 1^s and 0^s.

(i) An alternate sequence of 1^s nad 0^s.

(ii) A continuous sequence of five 1^s followed by five 0^s.

(iii) A sequence of two 1^s followed by ten 0^s sketch the Manchester format representation for the above sequence and comment on the error detection capability.   **(8)**

Solution :   Refer Section 4.3.

U.Q. 31 :   What is intersymbol interference? Explain its causes and remedies to avoid it.**(8)**

Solution :   Refer Sections 4.5.1 , 4.5.3 and 4.5.4

Dec. 2012

U.Q. 32 :   Explain Inter Symbol Interference. With the help of baseband binary data transmission system derive expression of ISI.   **(10)**

Solution :   Refer Section 4.5, 4.5.1.

U.Q. 33 :   Consider the following sequences of 1's and 0's:

(i) An alternate sequence of 1's and 0's.

(ii) A long sequence of 1's followed by a long sequence of 0's.

(iii) A single "0" and then a long sequence of 1's. Sketch the waveform for each of these sequences using Unipolar RZ and Alternate Mark Inversion signaling

Solution :   Refer Section 4.3.

U.Q. 34 :   Derive and sketch the power spectral Density of polar RZ and polar NRZ signalling.   **(10)**

Solution :   Refer Section 4.4, 4.4.1 and 4.4.3.

U.Q. 35 :   What is a synchronizer? Explain any one type of bit synchronizer and need for frame synchronization with relevant diagram.   **(8)**

Solution :   Refer Section 4.4.

May 2013

U.Q. 36 :   What are the different types of multiplexers used in digital communication system? Explain quasi-synchronous multiplexer in detail with a neat sketch. **(10)**

Solution :   Refer Section 4.1.

U.Q. 37 :   Draw the line code formats and PSD waveform for 1 1 1 1 0 0 0 0 and comment on Power Spectral Density.

(i) RZ polar, (ii) NRZ polar, (iii) AMI, (iv) Manchester.   **(8)**

Solution :   Refer Section 4.3.

U.Q. 38 :   What is ISI? Hence explain the methods to eliminate the same.   **(8)**

Solution :   Refer Section 4.5, 4.5.3

U.Q. 39 : A scrambler is shown in Fig. 4.30. Design the corresponding descrambler. If a sequence S = 1010101000 is applied to the input of this scrambler, determine the output sequence T. Verify that if this T is applied to the input of the scrambler, the output sequence S. **(10)**

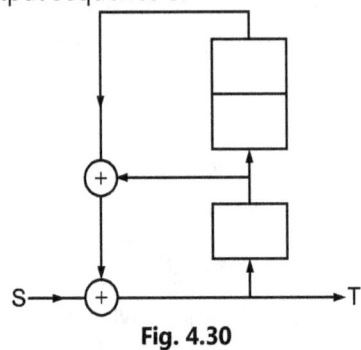

Fig. 4.30

Dec. 2013

U.Q. 40 : Explain need of Line coding. State its properties. Draw and give mathematical expression of Power Spectral Density for unipolar NRZ, Polar RZ, AMI, and Manchester. **(10)**

Solution : Refer Section 4.3

U.Q. 41 : A scrambler is shown in figure. Design the corresponding descrambler. If a sequence m_k=10110000000001 is applied to the input of this scrambler, determine the output sequence m_k'. Verify that if this m_k is applied to the input of the scrambler, the output sequence m_k. **[8]**

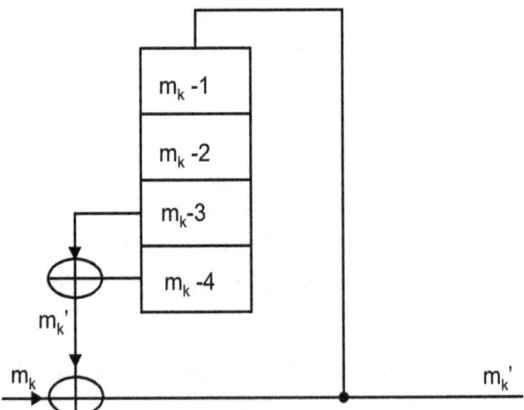

Fig. 4.31

U.Q. 42 : What is digital Hierarchy used in digital communication system? Explain anyone with a neat sketch. **[6]**

Solution : Refer Section 4.2.1

May 2014

U.Q. 43 : Explain important parameter of line codes with example. **(8)**

Solution : Refer Section 4.3.2

U.Q. 44 : What is a synchronizer? Explain any one type of bit synchronizer. **(8)**

Solution : Refer Section 4.4 and 4.4.1.

U.Q. 45 : Write short note on three preset equalizer and adaptive equalizer **(8)**

Solution : Refer Section 4.5.8.

U.Q. 46 : Three channels are to be multiplexed using TDM technique. The rate of each channel is 150 bytes per second. In TDM , one byte per channel is to be multiplexed. Draw the system block diagram and Calculate 1. Frame size   2. Frame duration   3. Frame rate and 4. Bit rate of TDM signal.

Solution : The multiplexer will be as below

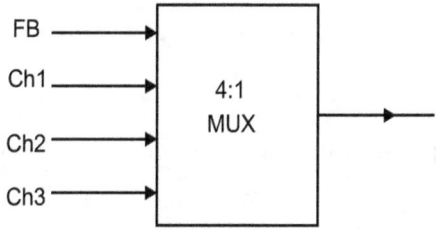

Fig. 4.32

FB is frame byte (for synchronization)

Number of bytes per frame = 4 (frame size in bytes)

4×15 = 600 bytes are to be accommodated in 1 sec.

$\therefore$ Number of frames per sec. = $\dfrac{600}{4}$ = 150

(Frame Rate)

$$\text{Frame duration} = \dfrac{4}{600} \text{ sec} = 6.67 \text{ ms}$$

$$\text{Bit rate} = 600 \times 8 = \text{ bits/sec}$$

$$= 4800 \text{ bits/sec}$$

SUMMARY

1. Multiplexing is a technique of accommodating signals from number of sources for transmitting them on single channel.

2. Time Division Multiplexers (TDM) interleave bits or characters from each source and transmit them at higher speed over a wideband channel.

3. There are three types of multiplexers :

    (i) Synchronous multiplexers

    (ii) Asynchronous multiplexers

    (iii) Quasi-synchronous multiplexers.

4. Multiplexing hierarchies are used to accommodate sources of different data rates on a single high speed channel.

5. Two different multiplexing hierarchies have been adapted for digital communication.

    (i) AT & T Hierarchy

    (ii) CCITT Hierarchy.

6. T_1 carrier system is used to transmit 24 voice signals over a single T_1 line whose speed is 1.544 Mbps.

7. Data multiplexers use message switching technique for transmission of data from one data source (computer) to another.

8. Various formats are used for transmission of digital data such as,

    (i) Unipolar RZ/NRZ   (ii) Polar RZ/NRZ

    (iii) Bipolar RZ/NRZ   (iv) Split Phase Manchester

    (v) M-ary

    They are called data formats/signaling formats/line codes.

9. The PSDs of various line codes are as below :

    (i) Unipolar NRZ $\text{sinc}^2 (fT_b) \left[1 + \dfrac{1}{T_b} \delta(f) \right]$

    (ii) Polar NRZ $A^2 T_b \, \text{sinc}^2 (fT_b)$

(iii) Unipolar RZ

$$\frac{A^2 T_b}{16} \, \text{sinc}^2 \, (fT_b/2) \left[1 + \frac{1}{T_b} \sum \delta \left(f - \frac{n}{T_b} \right) \right]$$

(iv) Bipolar RZ

$$\frac{A^2 T_b}{4} \, \text{sinc}^2 \, (fT_b/2) \, \sin^2 \, (\pi fT_b)$$

(v) Manchester

$A^2 T_b \, \text{sinc}^2 \, (fT_b) \, \sin^2 \, (\pi fT_b/2)$

(vi) Multilevel (M-ary)

$10 \, A^2 T_b \, \text{sinc}^2 \, (2fT_b)$

for M = 2 and levels + A, 3A, − A, − 3A

10. Synchronisation is proper timing operation between transmitter and receiver.

11. Two types of synchronisations are required in digital communication.

    (i) Bit Synchronisation

    (ii) Frame Synchronisation

12. There are three methods of bit synchronisation.

    (i)   Open loop method.

    (ii) Closed loop method.

    (iii) Early-late synchroniser.

13. Scrambling is a process of converting long stream of 1's and 0's into random bit so that synchronisation problem can be avoided.

14. Frame synchronisation is required to identify start/stop of transmission and to identify subdivisions of message.

EXERCISE

1. Write short notes on :

    (i)   Bit synchronisation and Frame synchronisation   **[Dec. 99]**

    (ii) Line Coding formats   **[May 2000] [May 2001] [Dec. 2002]**

    (iii) Multiplexing hierarchy for digital communication.

                              [May 2000] [May 2001] [May 2003] [May 2004]

2. What are the different types of digital multiplexers ? What are functional operations performed by digital multiplexers ? Explain any one digital multiplexer with block schematic.   **[Dec. 2000]**

3. What are desirable properties of line codes ? Compare RZ and NRZ line coding formats on the basis of above properties along with their merits and demerits.

[Dec. 2001] [Dec. 2003]

4. Discuss different types of synchronisation techniques used in digital communication system.   **[Dec. 99] [May 2003]**

5. Sketch the following line encoding formats for the bit pattern 11001010.

   (i)   Bipolar NRZ

   (ii) Polar RZ

   (iii) Split phase Manchester

   (iv) AMI

6. 34 voice channels of 4 kHz bandwidth each sampled at Nyquist rate and encoded into 8-bit PCM are multiplexed with 1-bit per frame as synchronisation bit. What is resultant bit rate at the output of multiplexer ? Sketch the configuration.   **[Dec. 99] [Dec. 2002]**

7. Draw the PSDs of the following line codes.

   (i)   Unipolar RZ   (ii) Unipolar NRZ

   (iii) Polar NRZ   (iv) AMI (Bipolar)

   (v)   Manchester

8. Derive the PSD of unipolar RZ.

9. Derive the PSD of unipolar NRZ.

10. Derive the PSD of polar NRZ.

11. Derive the PSD of AMI.

12. Derive the PSD of Manchester.

13. Explain how frame synchronisation is achieved.

14. Explain the need of frame and bit synchronisation.

CHAPTER 5
RANDOM PROCESSES

5.1 INTRODUCTION

- Random signals that occur in communication system are functions of time. They are called random processes.
- Random process is an extension of the concept of Random variable.
- In case of random variable, we map the outcome of random experiment into a number.
- Random signals like noise however are to be described as a function time.
- This random variable that is function of time is called **random process** or **stochastic process**.
- For example, noise voltages generated by number of identical resistors due to thermal electron motion. This voltage is random in nature. But it has to be denoted as function of time as v(t). Such random variable which is function of time is called random process.
- Let us look into this in more detail so that we can specify the random process mathematically. Fig. 5.1 shows thermal noise waveforms produced by large number of resistors.

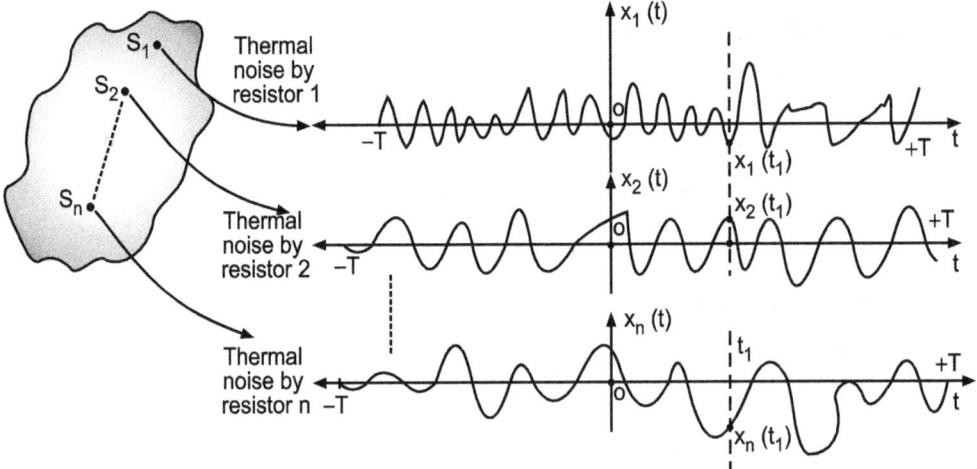

Fig. 5.1 : Thermal noise generated by n identical resistors

- The sample space S as shown in figure consists of n different waveforms.
- We assign a function $X(t, v_i)$ to each sample point (waveform).
- The collection of all such sample functions is called an **ensemble.**
- For simplification, let us denote $X(t, v_i)$ as $x_i(t)$.

i.e. $x_i(t) \equiv X(t, v_i)$

Thus, $x_1(t)$ represents first sample point.

           $x_2(t)$ represents second sample point and so on.

- The random process consisting of sample functions X (t, v_i) or x_i (t) is denoted as X (t, v) or simply as X(t).

- Thus, X(t) is a random process consisting of sample functions x_1 (t), x_2 (t), ..., x_n(t).

- Now, let us look into another way of representing random process.

- For this refer Fig. 5.1. For a time t, inside the observation interval – T to + T, we have a set of voltages x_1 (t_1), x_2 (t_1), x_3 (t_1), ..., x_n (t_1). Similarly, we can have number of sets like this at time t_2, t_3, ... Each set will now constitute a random variable. Thus, random process X (t) consists of ensemble of random variables {x_1 (t_j), x_2 (t_j), x_3 (t_j), ..., x_n (t_j)}; where, j = 1, 2, 3, ..., ∞.

- Thus, random process X(t) can also be thought as an ensemble of following random variables.

Random Variable 1 : X (t_1) = {x_1 (t_1), x_2 (t_1), x_3 (t_1), ..., x_n (t_1)}

Random Variable 2 : X (t_2) = {x_1 (t_2), x_2 (t_2), x_3 (t_2), ..., x_n (t_2)}

Random Variable 3 : X (t_3) = {x_1 (t_3), x_2 (t_3), x_3 (t_3), ..., x_n (t_3)}

$$\vdots$$
$$\vdots$$

so on upto ∞.

- This second view of random process is useful for analysis of random process.

- Let us now summarise the difference between Random Variable and Random Processes.

Random Variable	Random Processes
1. Outcome of random experiment is mapped into a number.	1. Outcome of random experiment is mapped into waveform that is function of time.
2. Random variable is a collection of a sample points.	2. Random process is a collection is infinite number of random variables.
3. e.g. Tossing of a coin thrice and number of heads noted.	3. e.g. Thermal noise generated by resistors.

Now, we will consider some more examples of random processes.

1. We record temperature of a city every day. The temperature recorded on one day (24 hours) will constitute a sample function. An ensemble of such sample functions will constitute a random process. There will be infinite number of sample functions in this random process.

2. We record the output of binary signal generator over an interval 0 to $5T_b$ where, T_b is bit duration. There will be an ensemble of 32 sample functions (waveforms). This ensemble will also be random process. It has finite number of sample functions.

3. An information source such a speech generates time varying signals whose contents are not known in advance. Here, random process will provide natural way to model information.

4. Reflection of radio waves from different layers of the ionospheres that make long-range broadcasting possible. Due to randomness of the reflection, the received signal can be modeled as random process.

5.2 MATHEMATICAL DEFINITION OF RANDOM PROCESS

- One important aspect that needs to be emphasised here is that, the random process X(t) will also have a probability associated with an observation of one of the sample functions of the random process.
- Thus, randomness is associated with the uncertainty as to which sample function (waveform) will occur in a given trial. Hence, we define the random process as below.

Definition :

A random process X(t) is defined as an ensemble of time functions together with probability rule that assigns a probability to any meaningful event associated with an observation of one of the sample functions of X(t).

- Here, meaningful event associated with an observation of sample function can be some statistical parameter. Thus, we need some quantitative measure to specify the random process.
- Consider an example of random process, $X(t) = A \cos (2\pi f_c t + \phi)$, where, ϕ is uniformly distributed over $(0, 2\pi)$.
- This analytical expression describes the random process completely.
- But this may not be always possible. In situation, where ensemble is obtained experimentally, we must find some quantitative measure that will specify the random process.
- Random process as we have seen earlier is a collection of random variables, which are generally dependent. We need joint Probability Distribution Functions (PDF) of these random variables.
- Let $X(t_1)$ be a random variable generated by observing all sample functions of X(t) at $t = t_1$.
- Let $X(t_2)$ be a random variable generated by observing all sample functions of X(t) at $t = t_2$ and so on upto $X(t_n)$.

- Then, the random process X(t) can be specified in terms of its joint PDF as

$$p_{X(t_1) X(t_2) X(t_3) \ldots X(t_n)} (x_1, x_2, x_3, \ldots, x_n) \text{ for all n (upto } \infty).$$

or

$$p_{X_1, X_2, \ldots, X_n} (x_1, x_2, \ldots x_n; t_1, t_2 \ldots t_n)$$

- Determining these PDFs is a difficult task. But most of the times we have to deal with first or second order statistics only.
- A complete statistical description of a random process X(t) is known if for any integer n and any choice of $(t_1, t_2, t_3 \ldots t_n)$ the joint PDF of $X(t_1), X(t_2), X(t_3) \ldots X(t_n)$ is given.
- A process X(t) is described by its mth order statistics if for all n ≤ m and all $(t_1, t_2, t_3 \ldots t_n)$ the joint PDF of $X(t_1), X(t_2), X(t_3) \ldots X(t_n)$ is given.
- Thus, to specify a random process we need ensemble statistics, which will give you idea of which sample function will occur in a given trial.

5.3   MEAN, CORRELATION AND COVARIANCE FUNCTION

- Since at any given time, the random process defines a random variable and at any given set of times it defines a random vector, we can define various statistical averages for the process.
- There are two types of averages : (i) Ensemble averages, (ii) Time averages.

5.3.1 Ensemble Averages

1. Mean :

For a random process X(t), we define mean as the expected value of random variable obtained by observing the process at some time t.

$$\therefore \qquad m_{X(t)} = \overline{X(t)} = E[X(t)] = \int_{-\infty}^{\infty} x \, p_{X(t)} (x) \, dx \qquad \ldots(5.1)$$

where, $p_{X(t)} (x)$ is first order probability density function of the random variable obtained by observing the process at some time t.

Note that there will be different values of $m_{X(t)}$ depending on observation time t. For example, $m_{X(t_1)}$ will be the mean value of random variable obtained by observing the process at time t_1.

$$\text{i.e.} \qquad m_{X(t_1)} = \overline{X(t_1)} = E[X(t_1)] = \int_{-\infty}^{\infty} x \, p_{X(t_1)} (x) \, dx \qquad \ldots(5.2)$$

Example 5.1 :

A random process defined by $X(t) = A \cos (2\pi f_c t + \phi)$ where ϕ is a random variable uniformly distributed on $[0, 2\pi]$ find the mean of the random process.

Solution :

Here, ϕ is a random variable. The plot of few sample functions of the random process are given in Fig. 5.2 below.

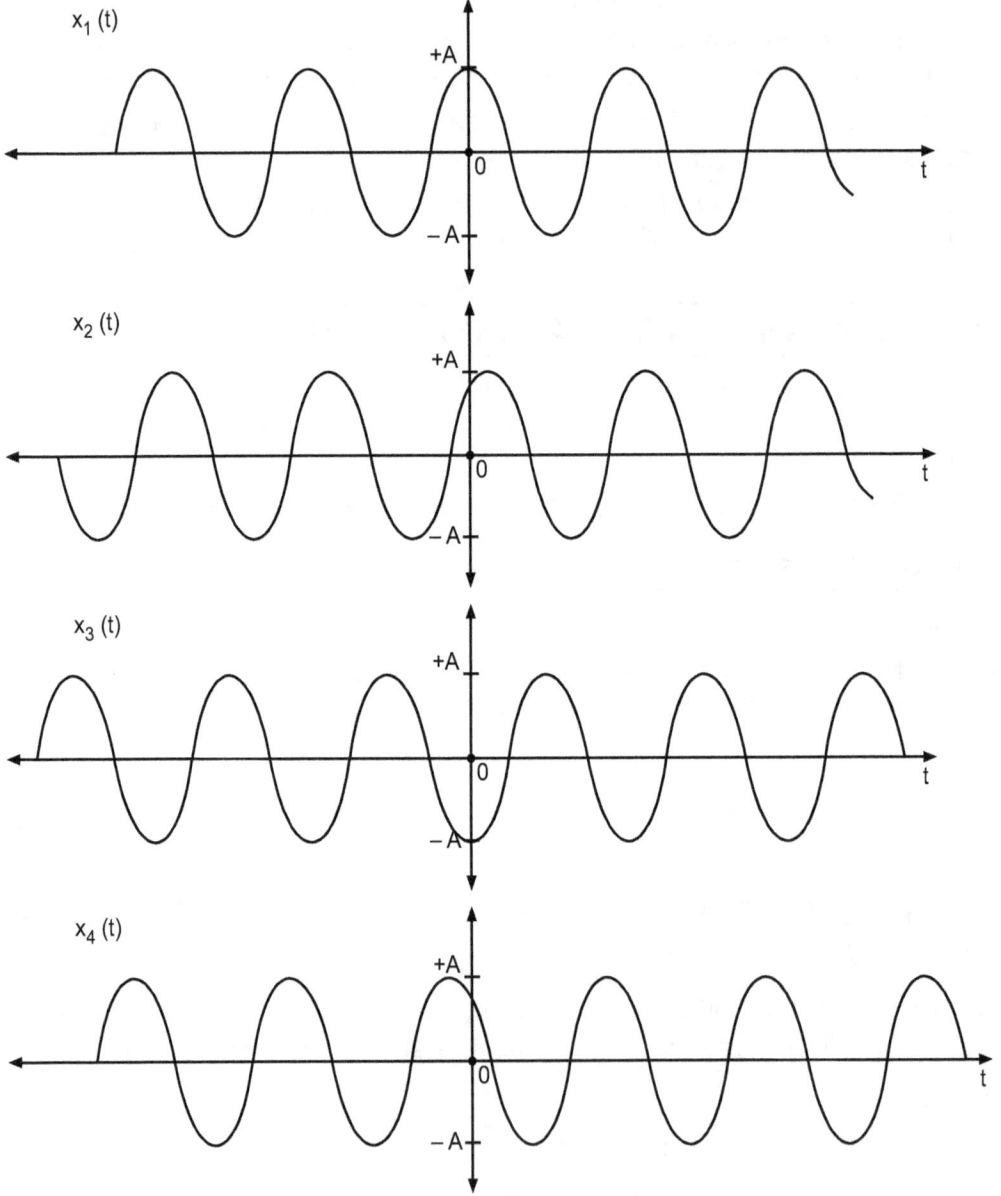

Fig. 5.2 : Sample functions of $X(t) = A \cos (2\pi fc + \phi)$

Given $\qquad P_\phi(\theta) = \dfrac{1}{2\pi}$; $\qquad 0 \le \theta \le 2\pi$

$\qquad\qquad\qquad\quad = 0$; $\qquad$ Otherwise

$\qquad\qquad X(t) = A \cos(2\pi f_c t + \phi)$

Randomness of $X(t)$ is due to ϕ.

We need to find the PDF $P_{X(t)}(x)$

Given $\qquad P_\phi(\theta) = \dfrac{1}{2\pi} \qquad 0 \le \theta \le 2\pi$

$\qquad\qquad\qquad\quad = 0 \qquad$ otherwise

As it can be seen from the waveforms. The amplitude at any instant t can be anything between $-A$ to $+A$ because of randomness of ϕ.

$\therefore \qquad\qquad P_{X(t)}(x) = \dfrac{1}{2A} \qquad -A \le x \le A$

$\qquad\qquad\qquad\qquad = 0 \qquad$ otherwise

$\therefore \qquad\qquad m_{X(t)} = E[X(t)] = \displaystyle\int_{-\infty}^{\infty} x\, P_{X(t)}(x)\, dx$

$\qquad\qquad\qquad = \displaystyle\int_{-A}^{A} \dfrac{1}{2A} x\, dx = \dfrac{1}{2A}\left[\dfrac{x^2}{2}\right]_{A}^{-A}$

$\qquad\qquad\qquad = 0$

This can also be calculated directly as below

$\therefore \qquad\qquad E[X(t)] = E[A\cos(2\pi f_c t + \phi)]$

$\qquad\qquad\qquad = \displaystyle\int_{-\infty}^{\infty} p_\phi(\theta) \cdot A \cdot \cos(2\pi f_c t + \theta)\, d\theta$

$\qquad\qquad\qquad = \displaystyle\int_{0}^{2\pi} \dfrac{1}{2\pi} A \cos(2\pi f_c t + \theta)\, d\theta$

$\qquad\qquad\qquad = \dfrac{1}{2\pi} \times \displaystyle\int_{0}^{2\pi} A \cos(2\pi f_c t + \theta)\, d\theta$

$\qquad\qquad\qquad = 0$

$\therefore \qquad\qquad m_{X(t)} = 0$

Hence, $m_{X(t_1)} = m_{X(t_2)} = m_{X(t_3)} = \ldots\, m_{X(t_n)} = 0$.

We observe that $m_X(t)$ is independent of t.

Example 5.2 :

The process X(t) is defined by $X(t) = X$ where, X is random variable uniformly distributed on $[-1, 1]$. Find mean of the process.

Solution :

The sample functions of the process will consists of DC functions taking any value between -1 to $+1$.

$$\therefore \qquad E[X(t)] = \int_{-\infty}^{\infty} x \, P_{X(t)}(x) \, dx$$

$$= \int_{-1}^{1} x \times \frac{1}{2} \, dx$$

$$= \frac{1}{2} \left[\frac{x^2}{2} \right]_{-1}^{1}$$

$$= \frac{1}{2} \left[\frac{1}{2} - \frac{1}{2} \right]$$

$$= 0$$

$$\therefore \qquad m_{X(t)} = 0$$

Hence, $m_{X(t_1)} = m_{X(t_2)} = m_{X(t_3)} = \dots m_{X(t_n)} = 0$.

We observe that $m_{X(t)}$ is independent of t.

2. **Autocorrelation :**

It is defined for a random process X(t) as product of expectation of two random variables $X(t_1)$ and $X(t_2)$ obtained by observing the process X(t) at time t_1 and t_2 respectively.

i.e.

$$R_X(t_1, t_2) = \overline{X(t_1) \cdot X(t_2)} = E[X(t_1) X(t_2)]$$

$$= \int_{-\infty}^{\infty} \int_{-\infty}^{\infty} x_1 x_2 \, P_{X(t_1) X(t_2)}(x_1, x_2) \, dx_1 \, dx_2 \qquad \dots(5.3)$$

where, $P_{X(t_1) X(t_2)}$ is second order probability density function of X(t). It is the joint probability distribution function.

Example 5.3 :

Find autocorrelation function of the random process X(t) given in Example 5.1.

Solution :

Given : $\qquad X(t) = A \cos(2\pi f_c t + \phi)$

and
$$P_\phi(\theta) = \frac{1}{2\pi} \qquad ; \qquad 0 \leq \theta \leq 2\pi$$
$$= 0 \qquad ; \qquad \text{Otherwise}$$
$$R_X(t_1, t_2) = E[A\cos(2\pi f_c t_1 + \phi) A\cos(2\pi f_c t_2 + \phi)]$$
$$= \frac{A^2}{2} E[\cos(2\pi f_c(t_1 - t_2)) + \cos(2\pi f_c(t_1 + t_2) + 2\phi)]$$
$$= \frac{A^2}{2} E[\cos(2\pi f_c(t_1 - t_2)) + \frac{A^2}{2}[\cos(2\pi f_c(t_1 + t_2) + 2\phi)]]$$
$$= \frac{A^2}{2} \cos[2\pi f_c(t_1 - t_2)] + 0 = \frac{A^2}{2} \cos[2\pi f_c(t_1 - t_2)]$$

Thus, autocorrelation function of given $X(t)$ depends only on observation of the difference $t_1 - t_2$.

Example 5.4 :

Find autocorrelation function of the random process given in Example 5.2.

Solution : Given :
$$X(t) = X$$
$$p_{X(t)}(x) = \frac{1}{2} \qquad ; \qquad -1 \leq x \leq 1$$
$$= 0 \qquad ; \qquad \text{Otherwise}$$
$$p_{X(t_1, t_2)} = E[X(t)X(t)]$$
$$= E[X^2]$$
$$= \int_{-\infty}^{\infty} x^2 \times p_X(x)\, dx = \int_{-\infty}^{\infty} x^2 \times \frac{1}{2}\, dx$$
$$= \frac{1}{3}$$

3.   Autocovariance :

It is defined for a random processes $X(t)$ as,
$$C_X(t_1, t_2) = E[(X(t_1) - m_{X(t_1)})(X(t_2) - m_{X(t_2)})] \qquad \qquad ...(5.4)$$

Note :

- Autocorrelation function is most important parameter of random process. It gives us spectral information of the random process. (Since Fourier transform of autocorrelation function is power spectral density function).

- The frequency contents of random process depends on how rapid is the change in amplitude with time. More rapidly the random process changes with time, more rapidly the autocorrelation function $R_X(t_1, t_2)$ will decrease from its maximum. Fig. 5.2 depicts this.

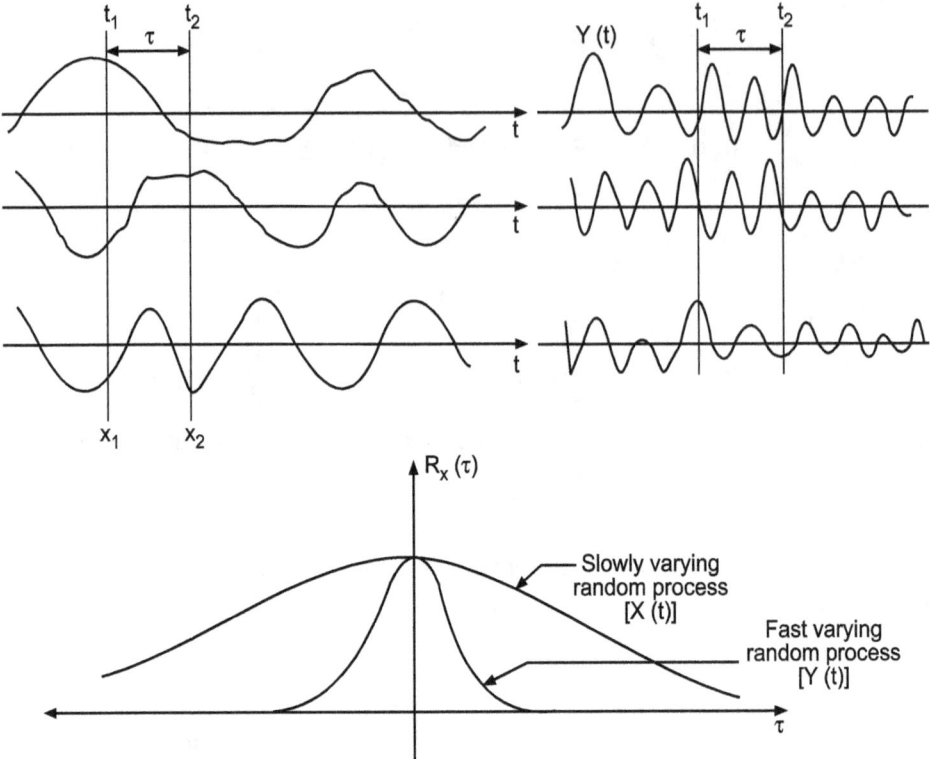

Fig. 5.3 : Autocorrelation functions of slowly and rapidly varying random processes

5.3.2 Time Averages

- The mean and autocorrelation functions seen above are called **ensemble averages.** They are the averages of Random variables.
- We can also associate **time averages** with random process. Time averages are taken along the time.

1. Mean :

The time mean value of X(t) is given by

$$m_X(T) = \overline{X(t)} = \lim_{T \to \infty} \frac{1}{T} \int_{-T/2}^{T/2} x_i(t)\, dt \qquad \qquad ...(5.5)$$

Thus, there will be time mean value of every sample function (waveform) $x_i(t)$.

2. Autocorrelation :

The time averaged autocorrelation functions is given by

$$R_X(\tau, T) = \overline{x(t)\, x(t+\tau)} = \lim_{T \to \infty} \int_{-T/2}^{T/2} x(t)\, x(t+\tau)\, dt \qquad \qquad ...(5.6)$$

- In time and ensemble averages we have seen only two averages viz. mean and autocorrelation. But there can be many more possible averages of higher order.

5.4   CLASSIFICATION OF RANDOM PROCESSES

- Till now we have seen two methods to describe random process : (i) Analytical and (ii) Statistical.

- Statistical description can be complete description or n^{th} order description.

- Second order statistical description may be adequate to describe a random process if not we can go for higher order description.

  Depending on ensemble statistics the random processes can be classified as

  (i)   Stationary process   (ii)   Non-stationary process

  (iii)   Wide-sense (or weakly) Stationary Process   (iv)   Ergodic Process

5.4.1 Stationary Process

- A random process X(t) is called stationary, if its statistical characteristics do not change with shift of time origin. In other words, statistical characterisation of the stationary random process is time invariant.

- The processes whose statistical properties are time independent are called **Stationary processes**.

- If $x(t_1)$, $x(t_2)$, ..., $x(t_n)$ are random variables obtained by observing the random process at time t_1, t_2, ..., t_n. The joint probability density function of this set of random variables is given by

  $$p_{X(t_1) X(t_2) ... X(t_n)} (x_1, x_2, ..., x_n)$$

- If we shift all observation times a fixed time τ, we obtain another set of random variables $x(t_1 + \tau)$, $x(t_2 + \tau)$ $x(t_3 + \tau)$, ..., $x(t_n + \tau)$. The observation times are $t_1 + \tau$, $t_2 + \tau$, ..., $t_n + \tau$. Let the joint probability density function of this set of random variables be

  $$p_{X(t_1 + \tau) X(t_2 + \tau), ..., X(t_n + \tau)} (x_1, x_2, ..., x_n)$$

- The random process X(t) is said to be **strictly stationary**, if

  $$p_{X(t_1) X(t_2), ..., X(t_n)} (x_1, x_2, ..., x_n)$$

  $$= p_{X(t_1 + \tau) X(t_2 + \tau), ..., X(t_n + \tau)} (x_1, x_2, ..., x_n) \quad ...(5.7)$$

  For all time shifts, all n and all possible choices of observation times t_1, t_2, ..., t_n.

- Thus, a random process X(t) initiated at $t = -\infty$ is strictly stationary if joint probability density function of any set of random variables obtained by observing random process X(t) is invariant with respect to the location of origin $t = 0$.

- What this means is, if we determine $p_{X(t_1)}(x_1)$ i.e. PDF of Random Variable $X(t_1)$ and shift the origin by τ and determine $p_{X(t_1 + \tau)}(x_1)$ the two PDFs must be same for stationary random process.

  i.e. for n = 1 in equation (5.7) for all τ,

$$p_{X(t)}(x) = p_{X(t + \tau)}(x) = p_x(x) \qquad \qquad ...(5.8)$$

  Similarly,

  for n = 2 and $\tau = -t_1$

$$p_{X(t_1) \times (t_2)}(x_1, x_2) = p_{X(0) \times (t_2 - t_1)}(x_1, x_2) \qquad \qquad ...(5.9)$$

  For all t_1 and t_2

- Thus, second order distribution function of a stationary random process depends only on time difference between the observation times t and t + τ.

Mean :

- Mean value for random process is defined as

$$m_{X(t)} = \overline{X(t)} = E[X(t)] = \int_{-\infty}^{\infty} x \, p_{X(t)}(x) \, dx$$

- For stationary process from equation (5.8)

$$p_{X(t)}(x) = p_{X(t + \tau)}(x) = p_x(x)$$

  for all τ

  i.e. $\qquad\qquad p_{X(t_1)}(x) = p_{X(t_2)}(x) = ... = p_{X(t_n)}(x) \qquad \qquad ...(5.10)$

  $\therefore \qquad\qquad m_{X(t_1)} = m_{X(t_2)} = ... = m_{X(t_n)} = m_X \qquad \qquad ...(5.11)$

- Hence, mean of a stationary random process is constant.

Autocorrelation :

- Autocorrelation for random process is defined as,

$$R_X(t_1, t_2) = \int_{-\infty}^{\infty} \int_{-\infty}^{\infty} x_1 x_2 \, p_{X(t_1) x(t_2)}(x_1, x_2) \, dx_1 \, dx_2$$

- For a stationary process from equation (5.9),

$$p_{X(t_1) \times (t_2)}(x_1, x_2) = p_{X(0) \times (t_2 - t_1)}(x_1, x_2)$$

$$\therefore \qquad R_X(t_1, t_2) = R_X(t_2 - t_1) \qquad \text{for all } t_1 \text{ and } t_2$$

$$= R_X(\tau)$$

where, $\qquad t_2 = t_1 + \tau$ ...(5.12)

- Thus, Autocorrelation function can also be written as,

$$R_X(\tau) = E[X(t)\,X(t+\tau)] \qquad ...(5.13)$$

- Hence, autocorrelation function of a stationary process depends only on the observation time difference $t_2 - t_1$.

Autocovariance :

- For a random process it is specified as,

$$C_X(t_1, t_2) = E[(X(t_1) - m_{X(t_1)})\,(X(t_2) - m_{X(t_2)})]$$

- For stationary process it is given by,

$$C_X(t_1, t_2) = R_X(t_2 - t_1) - m_X^2 \qquad ...(5.14)$$

- The **non-stationary process** is the random process whose ensemble statistics depends on time.

- Example of stationary process is noise process because its statistical parameters do not change with time.

- Example of non-stationary process can be temperature of a city. Its ensemble statistics depends on time.

- The two conditions listed above for mean and autocorrelation for stationary process are not sufficient to guarantee that random process is strictly stationary.

- If the two conditions are satisfied by any process then it is called wide-sense stationary or weakly stationary.

- For a process to be strictly stationary condition 5.7 needs to be satisfied.

- Strictly stationarity is a very strong condition that only a few processes may satisfy.

5.4.2 Wide-Sense or Weakly Stationary Process

- As discussed earlier a random process may not be strictly stationary but if it satisfies the two condition for mean and autocorrelation given by equations (5.11) and (5.12), then it is called Wide-sense or weakly stationary process.

- The two conditions are listed below.

    (i) $m_{X(t_1)} = m_{X(t_2)} = m_{X(t_3)} = \ldots\ldots = m_{X(t_n)} = m_X$ i.e. $m_{X(t)}$ is independent of t.

    (ii) $R_X (t_1, t_2) = R_X (t_2 - t_1) = R_X (\tau)$ i.e. $R_X (t_1, t_2)$ depends on the time difference $\tau = t_1 - t_2$ and not on t_1 and t_2 individually.

- All stationary processes are wide-sense stationary but converse is not necessarily true.

5.4.3 Properties of Autocorrelation Function of Stationary Process

- We have defined autocorrelation function as,

$$R_X (\tau) \;=\; E\,[X(t + \tau)\,X(t)] \quad ; \quad \text{for all t} \;\;\ldots(5.15)$$

This function has some important properties as listed as follows.

1. The mean square value of the process can be obtained by putting $\tau = 0$ in (5.15) (or $t_1 = t_2 = t$ in (5.3)) as,

$$R_X (0) \;=\; E\,[X^2 (t)] \qquad\qquad\qquad \ldots(5.16)$$

2. The autocorrelation function is an even function of τ i.e.

$$R_X (\tau) \;=\; R_X (-\tau) \qquad\qquad (\because \quad R_X(\tau) = E\,[X(t)\,X\,(t - \tau)]\ \text{also}) \;\;\ldots(5.17)$$

3. The autocorrelation $R_X (\tau)$ has maximum magnitude at $\tau = 0$ i.e.

$$\left| R_X (\tau) \right| \;\le\; R_X (0) \qquad\qquad\qquad \ldots(5.18)$$

5.4.4 Cross-Correlation Function (Multiple Random Processes)

- If we have two random processes X(t) and Y(t) with their autocorrelation functions $R_X (t_1, t_2)$ and $R_Y (t_1, t_2)$ respectively. Then we define two cross-correlation functions as,

$$R_{XY} (t_1, t_2) \;=\; E\,(X (t_1)\,Y (t_2)] \qquad\qquad \ldots(5.19)$$

and $\qquad\qquad\qquad R_{YX} (t_1, t_2) \;=\; E\,[Y (t_1)\,X (t_2)] \qquad\qquad \ldots(5.20)$

where, t_1 and t_2 are two observation times.

- Thus, we have four correlation functions and can be displayed in matrix format as,

$$R\,(t_1, t_2) \;=\; \begin{bmatrix} R_X (t_1, t_2) & R_{XY} (t_1, t_2) \\ R_{YX} (t_1, t_2) & R_Y (t_1, t_2) \end{bmatrix} \qquad\qquad \ldots(5.21)$$

- Above matrix is called correlation matrix of X(t) and Y(t).

- For separately and jointly wide-sense stationary processes X(t) and Y(t) . This matrix can be written as,

$$R(\tau) = \begin{bmatrix} R_X(\tau) & R_{XY}(\tau) \\ R_{YX}(\tau) & R_Y(\tau) \end{bmatrix} \qquad ...(5.22)$$

where, $\qquad \tau = t_1 - t_2$

1. The cross-correlation function is not generally even function of τ.

2. It does not have maximum at $\tau = 0$.

3. But $R_{XY}(\tau) = R_{YX}(-\tau)$.

- The two processes X(t) and Y(t) are said to be uncorrelated if their cross-correlation function is product of their means i.e.

$$= \overline{X(t)} \; \overline{Y(t)}$$

$$R_{XY}(\tau) = E[X(t) Y(t + \tau)] = E[X(t)] \cdot E[Y(t)] \qquad ...(5.23)$$

- The two processes are said to be incoherent or orthogonal if,

$$R_{XY}(\tau) = 0$$

- Incoherent or orthogonal processes are uncorrelated if E [X(t)] and/or E [Y(t)] is equal to zero.

- Processes X(t) and Y(t) are independent random process if for any t_1 and t_2, random variables $x(t_1)$ and $y(t_1)$ are independent.

Example 5.5 :

Show that the random processes X(t) = A cos $(2\pi f_c t + \phi)$ where, ϕ is uniformly distributed in $(0, 2\pi)$ is a wide-sense stationary.   **(10 Marks) (Dec. 2005, May 06, 08)**

Solution :

Given process

$$x(t) = A \cos (2\pi f_c t + \phi)$$

Since ϕ is random and uniformly distributed over $(0, 2\pi)$. The process is random. Some sample functions of this random process are shown in Fig. 5.4 (a).

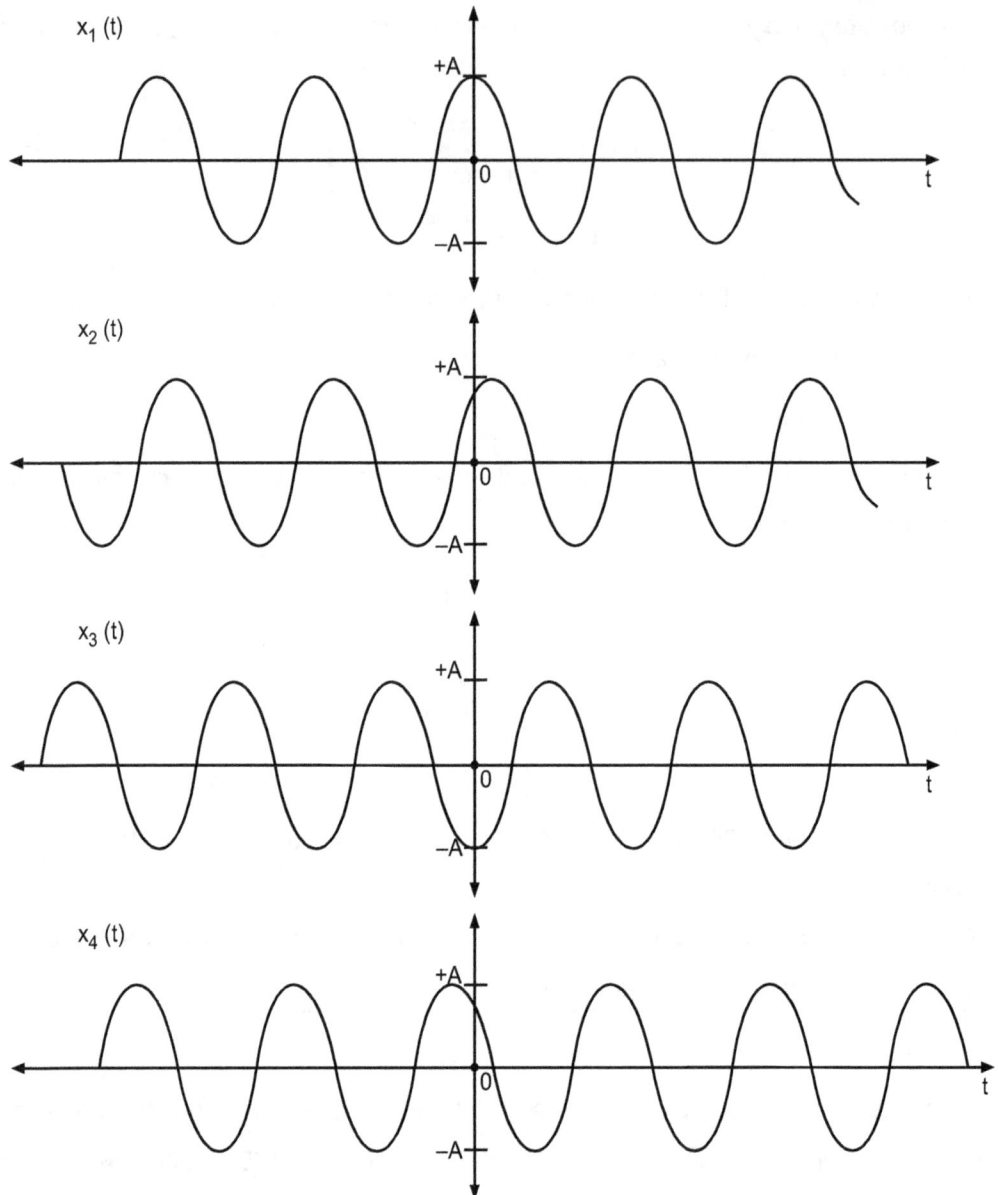

(a) Some sample functions of a cos ($2\pi f_c t + \phi$)

The distribution of ϕ is shown in Fig. 5.4 (b).

- Mean value of function of R.V. which is function of x is given by,

$$\overline{g(x)} = E[g(x)] = \int_{-\infty}^{\infty} g(x) \, p_X(x) \, dx \qquad \ldots(5.24\ a)$$

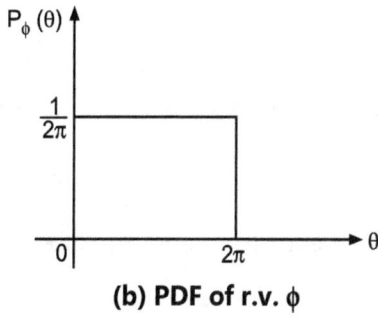

(b) PDF of r.v. ϕ

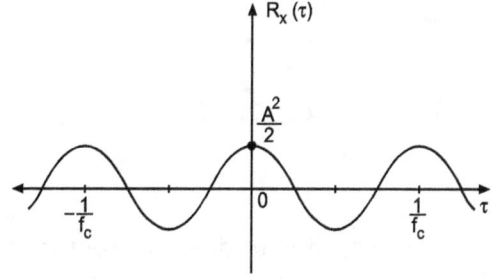

(c) Autocorrelation of function of A cos $(2\pi f_c t + \phi)$

Fig. 5.4

- $X(t)$ is a function of random variable ϕ.

$\therefore$ Mean value of $x(t)$ will be,

$$\overline{A \cos (2\pi f_c t + \phi)} = E\,[A \cos (2\pi f_c t + \phi)]$$

$$= \int_{-\infty}^{\infty} A \cos (2\pi f_c t + \theta)\, p_\phi (\theta)\ d\theta$$

$$= \int_{0}^{2\pi} A \cos (2\pi f_c t + \theta) \times \frac{1}{2\pi}\ d\theta$$

$$= \frac{1}{2\pi} \int_{0}^{2\pi} A \cos (2\pi f_c t + \theta)\ d\theta$$

$$= 0$$

- Hence, mean value of given random process is zero. Hence, ensemble mean of sample function amplitudes at any instant t is zero.

- Autocorrelation function of $x(t)$ is given by,

$$R_X (t_1, t_2) = E\,[x(t_1) \cdot x(t_2)]$$

$$= E\,[A \cos (2\pi f_c t_1 + \phi) \cdot A \cos (2\pi f_c t_2 + \phi)]$$

$$= A^2\, E\,[\cos (2\pi f_c t_1 + \phi)]\cos (2\pi f_c t_2 + \phi)]$$

$$= \frac{A^2}{2} \{ \overline{\cos [2\pi f_c (t_1 + t_2) + 2\phi]} + \overline{\cos [2\pi f_c (t_2 - t_1)]} \}$$

$$...(5.24\ b)$$

- The first term is function of random variable ϕ, and as seen earlier its mean value will be zero.

i.e. $\overline{\cos\left[2\pi f_c\,(t_1 + t_2) + 2\phi\right]} = \dfrac{1}{2\pi}\displaystyle\int_0^{2\pi} \left[\cos\left(2\pi f_c\,(t_1 + t_2) + 2\theta\right)\right] d\theta$ ...(5.24 c)

$$= 0$$

- The second term does not contain random variable hence it is constant. Substituting equation (5.24 c) in equation (5.24 b), we get,

$$R_X\,(t_1,\,t_2)\ =\ \frac{A^2}{2}\cos\left[2\pi f_c\,(t_2 - t_1)\right]$$ ... (5.25)

$\therefore$ $R_X\,(\tau)\ =\ \dfrac{A^2}{2}\cos 2\pi f_c \tau$

where, $\tau\ =\ t_1 - t_2$

- This function is plotted in Fig. 5.4 (c).
- Thus, the Autocorrelation of the given process is a function of time difference of observation times.

  Hence, given process is wide-sense stationary.

5.4.5 Ergodic Process

- We have seen that there are two types of averages of random process via. ensemble averages and time averages.

- Ensemble averages are for amplitudes of sample functions at sometime t.

- The averages are for each sample function.

- If all time averages are equal to the corresponding statistical averages, then stationary process is ergodic.

- Hence, the various statistical averages of ergodic process can be measured with only one sample function of the process, instead of considering number of functions and averaging over them.

- Testing for ergodicity of a random process is usually very difficult. A reasonable assumption in the analysis of most of communication signals is that random waveforms are ergodic in mean and in the autocorrelation.

- Let us consider a sample function x(t) of a random process X(t).

- The time averaged mean of the sample function $x(t)$ is defined as,

$$m_X (T) = \overline{x} = <x(t)> = \lim_{T \to \infty} \frac{1}{T} \int_{-T/2}^{T/2} x(t) \, dt \qquad \dots (5.26)$$

- Similarly, the time averaged autocorrelation of the sample function $x(t)$ is defined as,

$$R_X (T) = <x(t) \, x \, (t + \tau)> = \lim_{T \to \infty} \frac{1}{T} \int_{-T/2}^{T/2} x(t) \, x(t + \tau) \, dt$$

$$\dots (5.27)$$

- Note that $m_X (T)$ and $R_X (\tau, T)$ are random variables, whose values depend on which sample function of $X(t)$ is used.

- If $X(t)$ is stationary then,

$$E[m_X (T) = \left[\lim_{T \to \infty} \frac{1}{T} \int_{-T/2}^{T/2} x(t) \, dt \right]$$

$$= \lim_{T \to \infty} \frac{1}{T} \int_{-T/2}^{T/2} E[x(t)] \, dt$$

$$= m_X$$

$$= E[X(t)] \qquad \dots (5.28)$$

- Hence, for stationary random process the expected value of time averaged mean is equal to ensemble mean.

- Now, the expected value of $R_X (\tau, T)$ will be,

$$E[R_X (T)] = E\left[\lim_{T \to \infty} \frac{1}{T} \int_{-T/2}^{T/2} x(t) \, x(t + \tau) \, dt \right]$$

$$= \lim_{T \to \infty} \frac{1}{T} \int_{-T/2}^{T/2} E[x(t) \, x(t + \tau)] \, dt$$

$$= R_X (\tau, T) \qquad \dots (5.29)$$

- This indicates that the expected value of time averaged autocorrelation is equal to the ensemble autocorrelation.

- A stationary process X(t) is called ergodic in mean if,

  (i) $<x(t)> = E[X(T)]$ ... (5.30)

  (ii)   Variance of $<x(t)> = 0$

- A stationary process x(t) is called ergodic in autocorrelation if

  (i) $<x(t)\, x(t + \tau) = E[X(t)\, X(t + \tau)]$ ... (5.31)

  (ii)   Variance of $<x(t)\, x(t + \tau)> = 0$

- Fundamental electrical parameters, such as dc value, root-mean-square value, average power can be related to moments of ergodic random process as below.

1. $\bar{x} = <x(t)>$ is equal to dc level of signal.

2. $[\bar{x}]^2 = <x(t)>^2$ is equal to normalized power in dc component.

3. $R_X(0) = <x^2(t)> - <x(t)>^2$ is equal to total average normalized power.

4. $\sigma_{X_T}^2 = <x^2(t)> - <x(t)>^2$ is average normalized power in time varying or dc component of signal.

5. σ_{X_T} is rms value of ac component of the signal.

- We must test all possible higher order statistics of the process to determine whether a process is ergodic or not, but it is going to be much much difficult task. In practice however, we find that many of stationary processes are ergodic upto second-order averages.

- One more important thing to note here is that for a random process to be ergodic it has to be wide-sense stationary; but the converse is not necessarily true. If a process is known to be ergodic then we need to find ensemble average of one sample function only.

- From the classifications of random processes made above we can conclude that –
  This is depicted in Fig. 5.5.

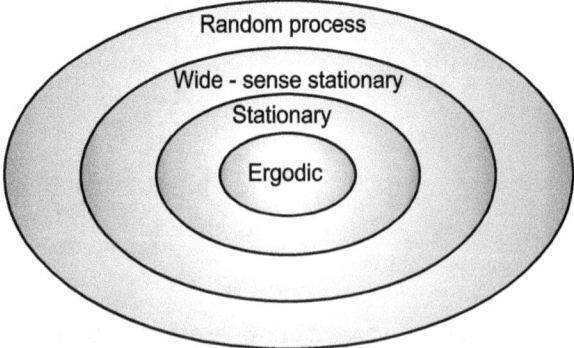

Fig. 5.5 : Classification of random processes

Example 5.6 :

Show that the random processes $X(t) = A \cos (2\pi f_c t + \phi)$ is ergodic in   mean and autocorrelation on where, ϕ is a random variable uniformly distributed in the range $(0, 2\pi)$.

Solution :

We have already established that given processes is wide-sense stationary and its ensemble averages.

$\therefore$ $$m_X = 0$$

and $$R_X (\tau) = \frac{A^2}{2} \cos (2\pi f_c \tau)$$

Now let us find the time averages.

Since $$x(t) = A \cos 2\pi f_c t + \phi$$

$$m_X (T) = \frac{1}{2T} \int_{-T}^{T} A \cos (2\pi f_c t + \phi) \, dt$$

$$= \frac{1}{2T} \left[\frac{A \sin (2\pi f_c t + \phi)}{2\pi f_c} \right]_{-T}^{T}$$

$$= \frac{1}{2T} \times \frac{A \sin (2\pi f_c T + \phi) + A \sin (2\pi f_c T + \phi)}{2\pi f_c}$$

$$= \frac{1}{2T} \frac{2A \sin (2\pi f_c T + \phi)}{2\pi f_c}$$

$$= \frac{A \sin (2\pi f_c T + \phi)}{2\pi f_c T}$$

$\therefore$ $$\lim_{T \to \infty} m_X (T) = 0$$

Thus,

$$m_X (T) = m_X = 0$$

Now, let us find autocorrelation function of $x(t)$

$$R_X (\tau, T) = \frac{1}{2T} \int_{-T}^{T} x(t) \, x(t + \tau) \, dt$$

$$= \frac{1}{2T} \int_{-T}^{T} A \cos (2\pi f_c t + \phi) + A \cos (2\pi f_c (t + \tau) + \phi) \, dt$$

$$= \frac{A^2}{2T} \int_{-T}^{T} \frac{1}{2}[\cos [(4\pi f_c (t + \tau) + 2\phi] + \cos (2\pi f_c \tau)] \, dt$$

$$= \frac{A^2}{4T} \int_{-T}^{T} \cos (4\pi f_c (t + \tau) + 2\phi) \, dt + \frac{A^2}{4T} \int_{-T}^{T} \cos 2\pi f_c \tau \, dt$$

First integral is zero as seen above.

$$\therefore \qquad R_X (\tau, T) = \frac{A^2}{4T} \cdot \cos 2\pi f_c \tau \, [2T]$$

$$= \frac{A^2}{2} \cos \cos (2\pi f_c \tau)$$

Thus,

$$R_X (\tau, T) = R_X (\tau)$$

Hence, given process x (t) is ergodic in mean and autocorrelation.

5.5 TRANSMISSION OF RANDOM PROCESS THROUGH LTI FILTER

- If a random process X(t) is passed through a linear time-invariant (LTI) filter having impulse response h(t) we will have another random process at the output this filter. Let this process be Y(t). This is depicted in Fig. 5.6.

X (t) ⟶ LTI filter h (t) ⟶ Y (t)

Fig. 5.6 : Transmission of random process through LTI filter

- Let X(t) be wide-sense stationary random process.

- The output Y(t) is given by,

$$Y(t) = \int_{-\infty}^{\infty} h (\lambda_1) \cdot X (t - \lambda_1) \, d\lambda_1 \qquad \qquad ...(5.32)$$

- Hence, the mean of output random process will be,

$$m_Y(t) = E[Y(t)]$$

$$= E\left[\int_{-\infty}^{\infty} h(\lambda_1) X(t-\lambda_1) d\lambda_1\right] \qquad \ldots(5.33)$$

- Interchanging order of expectation and integration,

$$m_Y(t) = \int_{-\infty}^{\infty} h(\lambda_1) E[X(t-\lambda_1)] d\lambda_1$$

$$\therefore \qquad m_Y(t) = \int_{-\infty}^{\infty} h(\lambda_1) m_X(t-\lambda_1) d\lambda_1 \qquad \ldots(5.34)$$

- Since, X(t) is wide-sense stationary,

$$m_X(t) = m_X(t-\lambda_1) = m_X \text{ (constant)}$$

$$\therefore \qquad m_Y(t) = m_X \int_{-\infty}^{\infty} h(\lambda_1) d\lambda_1$$

Using property of F.T. If G(f) is F.T. of g(t)

then

$$\int_{-\infty}^{\infty} g(t) dt = G(0)$$

$$= m_X H(0) \qquad \ldots(5.35)$$

where, H(0) is dc value of response of the system.

- Thus, the mean value of Y(t) is equal to mean value of X(t) multiplied by d.c. response of the system.

- The autocorrelation function of output random process Y(t) will be given by,

$$R_Y(t_1 t_2) = E[Y(t_1) \cdot Y(t_2)] \qquad \ldots(5.36)$$

$$\therefore \qquad R_Y(t_1, t_2) = E\left[\int_{-\infty}^{\infty} h(\lambda_1) X(t_1-\lambda_1) d\lambda_1 \cdot \int_{-\infty}^{\infty} h(\lambda_2) X(t_2-\lambda_2) d\lambda_2\right]$$

$$\ldots(5.37)$$

- Interchanging the order of expectation and integration w.r.t. λ_1 and λ_2, we get,

$$R_Y(t_1, t_2) = \int_{-\infty}^{\infty} d\lambda_1\, h(\lambda_1) \int_{-\infty}^{\infty} d\lambda_2\, h(\lambda_2) \cdot E\,[X(t_1 - \lambda_1) \cdot X(t_2 - \lambda_2)]$$

...(5.38)

- Since X(t) is wide-sense stationary process, the autocorrelation function of   X(t) is only a function of difference between the observation times $t_1 - \lambda_1$ and $t_2 - \lambda_2$.

$$\therefore \qquad R_Y(t_1, t_2) = \int_{-\infty}^{\infty} d\lambda_1\, h(\lambda_1) \int_{-\infty}^{\infty} d\lambda_2\, h(\lambda_2)\, R_X(t_1 - \lambda_1, t_2 - \lambda_2) \qquad ...(5.39)$$

- Put $\tau = t_1 - t_2$ in above equation we get,

$$R_Y(\tau) = \int_{-\infty}^{\infty} \int_{-\infty}^{\infty} h(\lambda_1)\, h(\lambda_2)\, R_X(\tau - \lambda_1 + \lambda_2)\, d\lambda_1\, d\lambda_2 \qquad ...(5.40)$$

- The above expression for $R_Y(\tau)$ shows that the autocorrelation function of output random process Y(t) is a function of difference between observation times ($\tau = t_1 - t_2$). hence, the output process is a wide-sense stationary process.

- The mean square value of the random process (E $[Y^2(t)]$) can be obtained by putting $\tau = 0$ in above equation. (Property of autocorrelation function).

$$\therefore \quad E\,[Y^2(t)] = R_Y(0) \qquad = \int_{-\infty}^{\infty} \int_{-\infty}^{\infty} h(\lambda_1)\, h(\lambda_2)\, R_X(\lambda_2 - \lambda_1)\, d\lambda_1\, d\lambda_2 \qquad ... (5.41)$$

- It shows that mean square value of output random variable processes Y(t) is constant.

5.6 POWER SPECTRAL DENSITY

- In the last section, we have seen how wide-sense stationary process is characterised in time domain.

- Now, we will see the frequency domain description of the random process in linear system.

- Impulse response of LTI filter is given by,

$$h(t) \;=\; \int\limits_{-\infty}^{\infty} H(f)\, e^{j2\pi ft}\, df \qquad\qquad\dots(5.42)$$

$$\therefore \qquad h(\lambda_1) \;=\; \int\limits_{-\infty}^{\infty} H(f)\, e^{j2\pi f\lambda_1}\, df \qquad\qquad\dots(5.43)$$

We know that, (from 5.41)

$$E\,[Y^2(t)] \;=\; \int\limits_{-\infty}^{\infty}\int\limits_{-\infty}^{\infty} h(\lambda_1)\, h(\lambda_2)\, R_X\,(\lambda_2 - \lambda_1)\, d\lambda_1\, d\lambda_2 \qquad\qquad\dots(5.44)$$

Substituting 5.43 in 5.44

$$\therefore \qquad E\,[Y^2(t)] \;=\; \int\limits_{-\infty}^{\infty}\int\limits_{-\infty}^{\infty} \left[\int\limits_{-\infty}^{\infty} H(f)\, e^{j2\pi f\lambda_1}\, df\right] h(\lambda_2)\, R_X\,(\lambda_2 - \lambda_1)\, d\lambda_1\, d\lambda_2 \quad\dots(5.45)$$

$$= \int\limits_{-\infty}^{\infty} df\, H(f) \int\limits_{-\infty}^{\infty} d\lambda_2\, h(\lambda_2) \int\limits_{-\infty}^{\infty} R_X\,(\lambda_2 - \lambda_1)\, e^{j2\pi f\lambda_1}\, d\lambda_1 \qquad\dots(5.46)$$

Put $\lambda \;=\; \lambda_2 - \lambda_1$

$$\therefore \qquad E\,[Y^2(t)] \;=\; \int\limits_{-\infty}^{\infty} df\, H(f) \int\limits_{-\infty}^{\infty} d\lambda_2\, h(\lambda_2)\, e^{j2\pi f\lambda_2} \int\limits_{-\infty}^{\infty} R_X\,(\lambda)\, e^{-j2\pi f\lambda}\, d\lambda$$

$$= \int\limits_{-\infty}^{\infty} df\, H(f) \cdot H^{*}\,(f) \int\limits_{-\infty}^{\infty} R_X\,(\lambda)\, e^{-j2\pi f\lambda}\, d\lambda$$

$$= \int\limits_{-\infty}^{\infty} \left|H(f)\right|^2 df \times \int\limits_{-\infty}^{\infty} R_X\,(\lambda)\, e^{-j2\pi f\lambda}\, d\lambda \qquad\qquad\dots(5.47)$$

- Since Fourier transform of autocorrelation function is Power Spectral Density function,

$$R_X\,(\tau) \rightleftharpoons S_X\,(f) \qquad\qquad\dots(5.48)$$

∴   P.S.D. is given by

$$S_X(f) = \int_{-\infty}^{\infty} R_X(\tau)\, e^{-j2\pi f\tau}\, d\tau \qquad ...(5.49)$$

∴

$$E[Y^2(t)] = \int_{-\infty}^{\infty} |H(f)|^2\, S_X(f)\, df \qquad ...(5.50)$$

- This is the mean-square value of the output random process Y(t) in frequency domain.

- What is physical significance of Power Spectral Density (PSD) ? To get an answer to this question, let us pass a random processes X(t) through an ideal narrow-band filter having frequency response shown in Fig. 5.7.

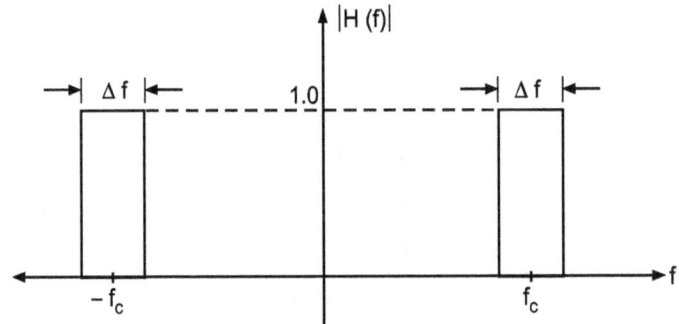

Fig. 5.7 : Frequency response of a filter

- Hence, $|H(f)| = 1$ for the range Δf around f_c.

- From equation, $E[Y^2(t)] = \displaystyle\int_{-\infty}^{\infty} |H(f)|^2\, S_X(f)\, df \qquad ...(5.51)$

$$= 2\int_{0}^{\Delta f} 1 \cdot S_X(f)\, df \qquad ...(5.52)$$

- If $S_X(f)$ is assumed to be constant over the range Δf, then we can write,

$$E[Y^2(t)] = 2 \times \Delta f \times S_X(f_c) \qquad ...(5.53)$$

- Since, the filter only passes frequency components of X(t) in the range Δf, $S_X(f_c)$ represents frequency density of the average power in the random process X(t) evaluated at $f = f_c$.

5.6.1 Properties of Power Spectral Density

- The power spectral density forms a Fourier transform pair with autocorrelation function. Hence, we write the two expressions as below.

$$S_X(f) = \int_{-\infty}^{\infty} R_X(\tau) \, e^{-j2\pi f \tau} \, d\tau \qquad \qquad ...(5.54)$$

$$R_X(\tau) = \int_{-\infty}^{\infty} S_X(f) \, e^{j2\pi f \tau} \, df \qquad \qquad ...(5.55)$$

- Above two equations are basic relations in spectral analysis of random processes.
- These expressions are also known as Einstein-Wiener-Khintchine relations. Using these relations, let us explore some properties of P.S.D.

Property 1 :

The total area under the autocorrelation function graph is equal to the value of P.S.D. at zero frequency.

i.e.
$$S_X(0) = \int_{-\infty}^{\infty} R_X(\tau) \, df \qquad \qquad ... (5.56)$$

This can be proved by putting f = 0 in equation (5.54).

Property 2 :

The mean-square value of a wide-sense stationary random process equals that area under the graph of P.S.D.

$$E[X^2(t)] = \int_{-\infty}^{\infty} S_X(f) \, df \qquad \qquad ... (5.57)$$

We know that,
$$R_X(\tau) = \int_{-\infty}^{\infty} S_X(f) \, e^{j2\pi f \tau} \, df \qquad \qquad ... (5.58)$$

Put $\tau = 0$
$$R_X(0) = \int_{-\infty}^{\infty} S_X(f) \, df \qquad \qquad ... (5.59)$$

Since
$$R_X(0) = E[X^2(t)]$$

$\therefore$
$$E[X^2(t)] = \int_{-\infty}^{\infty} S_X(f) \, df \qquad \qquad ... (5.60)$$

Property 3 :
- The PSD of wide-sense stationary random process is always non-negative

  i.e. $\qquad S_X(f) \geq 0 \quad ; \quad$ for all f $\qquad$ ... (5.61)
- We know that $\quad E[Y^2(t)] = 2\Delta f\, S_X(f_c)$
- Since, $E[Y^2(t)]$ is always non-negative $S_X(f)$ must also be non-negative for all f.

Property 4 :
- The P.S.D. of a real valued random process is an even function of f.

  i.e. $\qquad S_X(-f) = S_X(f) \qquad$ ... (5.62)

- We know that, $\qquad S_X(f) = \displaystyle\int_{-\infty}^{\infty} R_X(\tau)\, e^{-j2\pi f\tau}\, d\tau$

$$\text{Put } f = -f$$

$$S_X(-f) = \int_{-\infty}^{\infty} R_X(\tau)\, e^{j2\pi f\tau}\, d\tau$$

- Now put $\tau = -\tau \qquad d\tau = -d\tau$

$$S_X(-f) = \int_{-\infty}^{\infty} R_X(-\tau)\, e^{-j2\pi f\tau}\, (-1)\, d\tau$$

- Limits of integration will change but again can be restored by cancelling the negative sign and using the property $R_X(-\tau) = R_X(\tau)$ we can write,

$$S_X(-f) = \int_{-\infty}^{\infty} R_X(\tau)\, e^{-j2\pi f\tau}\, d\tau$$

$$= S_X(f)$$

Property 5 :
- The approximately normalised P.S.D. has properties of Probability Density Function (PDF).

- The normalise spectral density function is given by,

$$\frac{S_X(f)}{\displaystyle\int_{-\infty}^{\infty} S_X(f)\, df} \qquad \text{... (5.63)}$$

- Since, denominator gives total power and the numerator power contribution by the frequency f. Hence, above expression will be less than one and from property 2 and 3 it will be greater than or equal to 0. Hence, we can write,

$$p_X(f) = \frac{S_X(f)}{\int\limits_{-\infty}^{\infty} S_X(f)\, df} \qquad \qquad \ldots (5.64)$$

Example 5.7 :

Find the power spectral density of random process $X(t) = A \cos(2\pi f_c t + \phi)$ where, ϕ is uniformly distributed random variable over the integral $(0, 2\pi)$.

Solution :

The autocorrelation function of this random process is given by,

$$R_X(\tau) = \frac{A^2}{2} \cos(2\pi f_c \tau) \qquad \qquad \text{(Refer Example 5.3)}$$

- Since Fourier transforms of autocorrelation function is P.S.D. We find Fourier transform of above function.

$$R_X(\tau) = \frac{A^2}{2} \cos(2\pi f_c \tau) = \frac{A^2}{2}\left[\frac{e^{-j2\pi f_c \tau} + e^{j2\pi f_c \tau}}{2}\right]$$

$$= \frac{A^2}{4}[e^{-j2\pi f_c \tau} + e^{j2\pi f_c \tau}]$$

$$\therefore \qquad S_X(f) = \frac{A^2}{4}[\delta(f - f_c) + \delta(f + f_c)]$$

- The plot of this P.S.D. function is shown in Fig. 5.8.

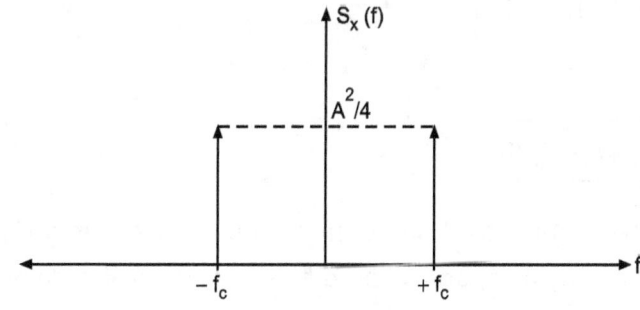

Fig. 5.8

5.6.2 Power Spectral Density Response of LTI Filter to Random Process

- When a wide-sense random process X (t) is transferred through LTI filter then autocorrelation of output random process is given by,

$$R_Y(\tau) = \int\limits_{-\infty}^{\infty} \int\limits_{-\infty}^{\infty} h(\lambda_1)\, h(\lambda_2)\, R_X(\tau - \lambda_1 + \lambda_2)\, d\lambda_1\, d\lambda_2 \qquad \dots (5.65)$$

- Now, the P.S.D. is given by,

$$S_Y(f) = \int\limits_{-\infty}^{\infty} R_Y(\tau)\, e^{-j2\pi f\tau}\, d\tau$$

$$= \int\limits_{-\infty}^{\infty} \int\limits_{-\infty}^{\infty} \int\limits_{-\infty}^{\infty} h(\lambda_1)\, h(\lambda_2)\, R_X(\tau - \lambda_1 + \lambda_2)\, e^{-j2\pi f\tau}\, d\lambda_1\, d\lambda_2\, d\tau \qquad \dots (5.66)$$

- Let $\tau - \lambda_1 + \lambda_2 = \lambda_0$

$$\therefore \qquad \tau = \lambda_0 + \lambda_1 - \lambda_2$$

$$\therefore \qquad S_Y(f) = \int\limits_{-\infty}^{\infty} \int\limits_{-\infty}^{\infty} \int\limits_{-\infty}^{\infty} h(\lambda_1)\, h(\lambda_2)\, R_X(\lambda_0)\, e^{-j2\pi f(\lambda_0 + \lambda_1 - \lambda_2)}\, d\lambda_1\, d\lambda_2\, d\lambda_0 \qquad \dots (5.67)$$

$$= \int\limits_{-\infty}^{\infty} d\lambda_1\, h(\lambda_1)\, e^{-j2\pi f\lambda_1} \cdot \int\limits_{-\infty}^{\infty} d\lambda_2\, h(\lambda_2)\, e^{-j2\pi f\lambda_2} \cdot \int\limits_{-\infty}^{\infty} d\lambda_0\, R_X(\lambda_0)\, e^{-j2\pi f\lambda_0}$$

$$\dots (5.68)$$

$$= H(f) \cdot H^*(f)\, S_X(f) \qquad \dots (5.69)$$

$$= \left| H(f) \right|^2 S_X(f) \qquad \dots (5.70)$$

- Thus, $\boxed{S_Y(f) = \left| H(f) \right|^2 S_X(f)} \qquad \dots (5.71)$

- Thus, power spectral density of output random processes from a LTI filter is equal to power spectral density of input multiplied by square of magnitude of transfer function of the filter.

Example 5.8 :

If the process $X(t) = A \cos(2\pi f_c t + \phi)$ where, ϕ is a random variable uniformly distributed in the range $(0, 2\pi)$ is passed through a filter with $H(f) = j2\pi f$. Find the output P.S.D.

Solution :

We have found in Example 5.7, that the P.S.D. for the given process $X(t)$ is given by,

$$S_X(f) = \frac{A^2}{4}[\delta(f - f_c) + \delta(f + f_c)]$$

We have output P.S.D. $\quad S_Y(f) = \left|H(f)\right|^2 S_X(f)$

Since, $\quad\quad\quad\quad\quad H(f) = j2\pi f$

$$\left|H(f)\right|^2 = 4\pi^2 f^2$$

$\therefore\quad\quad\quad S_Y(f) = 4\pi^2 f^2 \left[\frac{A^4}{4}\delta(f - f_c) + \frac{A^2}{4}\delta(f + f_c)\right]$

$$= A^2 \pi^2 f^2 [\delta(f - f_c) + \delta(f + f_c)]$$

Since $\quad\quad g(t)\,\delta(t - t_0) = g(t_0)\,\delta(t - t_0)$

$\therefore\quad\quad\quad S_Y(f) = A^2 \pi^2 f_c^2 [\delta(f - fc) + \delta(f + f_c)]$

Example 5.9 :

If the process $X(t) = X$ where X is random variable uniformly distributed in the range $-1, 1$, is passed through a differentiator $H(f) = j2\pi f$. Find output PSD and cross spectral density $S_{XY}(f)$.

Solution : $\quad\quad\quad S_Y(f) = |H(f)|^2 \cdot S_X(f)$

From Example 5.3, we know,

$$R_X(\tau) = \frac{1}{3}$$

$\therefore\quad\quad\quad S_X(f) = \frac{1}{3}\delta(f)$

$\therefore\quad\quad\quad S_Y(f) = (4\pi^2 f^2)\frac{1}{3}\delta(f)[\because \text{a}(f)\,\delta(f) = G(0)\,\delta(t)] \text{ Here a }(f) = \frac{1}{3}(4\pi^2 f^2)$

$$= 0$$

$\quad\quad\quad S_{XY}(f) = S_X(f) \cdot H^*(f) \quad\quad\quad\quad\quad [\because R_{XY}(\tau) = R_X(\tau) \cdot h(-\tau)]$

$$= \frac{1}{3}\delta(f) \cdot (-j2\pi f)$$

$$= 0$$

5.7 GAUSSIAN PROCESS

- It is an important family of Random processes. Gaussian processes are very much useful in communication systems.

- It is because thermal noise produced by the system devices can be modeled as Gaussian process.

- Each electron's movement in the device is random in nature and acts as a source of current independently.

- Hence, total current is sum of large number of random variables. According to Central Limit Theorem, this sum will be Gaussian distributed. Moreover, some properties of Gaussian process help in analysing a system with ease.

Definition :

A random process X (t) is a Gaussian process if for all n and all $(t_1, t_2, ..., t_n)$ the random variables {X (t_i)} have jointly Gaussian density function.

- From above definition, it can be seen that, at any instant to the random variable $X(t_0)$ is Gaussian.

- At any two points, t_1, t_2 random variable $(X(t_1), X(t_2))$ are distributed according to a two-dimensional Gaussian variable.

- We say that the random variable Y has a Gaussian distribution if its probability density function has the form,

$$p_Y(y) = \frac{1}{\sqrt{2\pi\sigma_y^2}} e^{-(y - m_y)^2/2\sigma_y^2}$$

where, m_y is mean and σ_y^2 is the variance Y. The plot of PDF is shown in Fig. 5.9.

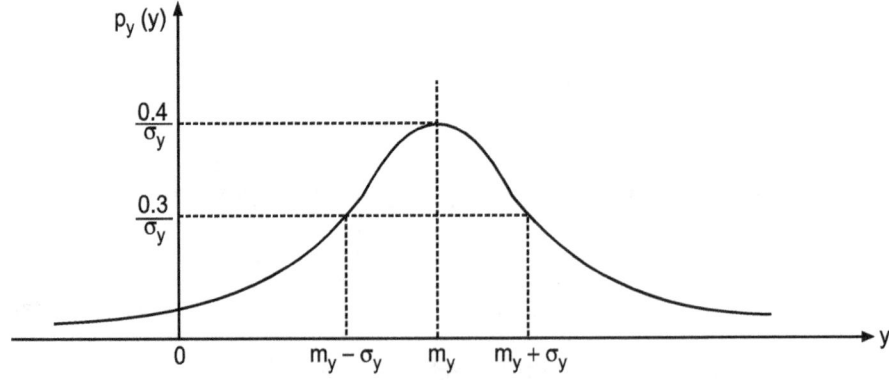

Fig. 5.9 : Gaussian distribution function

5.7.1 Properties of Gaussian Process

- There are some useful properties of Gaussian process which makes analysis of communication system easier.

Property 1 :

If a Gaussian process X(t) is applied to a stable linear filter, then the random process Y(t) developed at the output of the filter is also Gaussian.

To prove this, we write,

$$Y(t_i) = \int_{-\infty}^{\infty} X(\tau) \, h(t_i - \tau) \, d\tau$$

where, h(t) is response of the filter.

Y(t_i) can be written in terms of summation

$$Y(t_i) = \lim_{\substack{N \to 0 \\ \Delta \to 0}} \sum_{j=-N}^{N} X(j\Delta) \, h(t_i - j\Delta)$$

Since {X(jΔ)} is a Gaussian vector, Y(t_i) becomes linear combinations of these vectors hence, we can conclude that {Y(t_i)} are jointly Gaussian.

This property is useful to describe output of filter if it is known that input is Gaussian. It needs to be known only mean and autocorrelation function of output.

Property 2 :

If a process X(t) is Gaussian then, the set of random variables obtained by observing at t_1, t_2, t_3, ..., t_n for any n are jointly Gaussian and they can be completely described by specifying means and autocovariances as below.

$$m_{X(t_i)} = E[X(t_i)] \qquad i = 1, 2, ..., n$$

$$C_X(t_k, t_i) = E[(X(t_k) - m_{X(t_k)})(X(t_i) - m_{X(t_i)})]$$

$$k, i = 1, 2, ..., n$$

This property is with reference to the basic definition of Gaussian process.

Property 3 :

If a Gaussian process is wide-sense stationary then, it is also strictly stationary. This property follows from property 2.

Property 4 :

If the random variables obtained by observing a Gaussian process at t_1, t_2, t_3, ..., t_n are uncorrelated i.e.

$$E\ [(X(t_k) - m_{X(t_k)})\ (X(t_i) - m_{X(t_i)})] = 0 \quad i \neq k$$

Then, these random variables are statistically independent.

SOLVED EXAMPLES

Problem 5.1 :

Consider a random process $X(t) = A \cos (2\pi f_c t + \theta)$ where f_c and θ are constants and A is random variable. Determine whether X(t) is WSS.   **(U.Q. (4 marks) [Dec. 2008]**

Solution : $m_{X(t)}$ = E[X(t)]

$$= E[A \cos (2\pi f_c t + \theta)] = \cos (2\pi f_c t + \theta) \cdot E[A]$$

The value of $m_X(t)$ depends on E[A].

(i)   Hence, X(t) is not constant unless E[A] = 0

$$R_X(\tau) = E[X(t)\ EX(t + \tau)]$$

$$= E[A^2 \cos (2\pi f_c t + \theta) \cos (2\pi f_c (t_1 + \tau) + \theta)]$$

$$= \frac{1}{2} [\cos (2\pi f_c t + 2\theta + 2\pi f_c \tau) + \cos (2\pi f_c \tau)] \cdot E[A^2]$$

(ii) $R_X(\tau)$ is not function of τ above.

Hence, from (i) and (ii) we can conclude X(t) is not WSS.

Problem 5.2 :

Consider a random process $X(t) = A \cos (2\pi f_c t) + B \sin (2\pi f_c t)$ where f_c is constant and A and B are random variables.

(i)   Show that if E[A] = E[B] = 0, then X(t) is stationary.

(ii)   That X(t) is WSS if and only if random variables A and B are uncorrelated with equal variance i.e. E[AB] = 0 and $E[A^2] = E[B^2] = \sigma^2$.

Solution :

For X(t) to be stationary, $m_{X(t)}$ has to be independent of t.

(i) $m_{X(t)}$ = [X(t)]

$$= E[A \cos (2\pi f_c t) + B \sin (2\pi f_c t)]$$

$$= E[A] \cdot \cos (2\pi f_c t) + E[B] \sin (2\pi f_c t)$$

If $m_{X(t)}$ has to be independent of t, it has to be equal to 0. But it is possible only if E[A] = E[B] = 0.

(ii)   X(t) = A cos $(2\pi f_c t)$ + B sin $(2\pi f_c t)$

$$X(0) = A$$

∴

$$E[X^2(0)] = E[A^2]$$

$$E\left[X^2\left(\frac{1}{4f_c}\right)\right] = E[B]^2$$

If X(t) is W.S.S, then,

But,

$$E[X^2(0)] = E\left[X^2\left(\frac{1}{4f_c}\right)\right] = R_X(0) = \sigma_x^2$$

Hence,

$$E[A^2] = E[B^2] = \sigma_x^2 = \sigma^2$$

Now,

$$R_X(t, t + \tau) = E[X(t) \times (t + \tau)]$$
$$= E[A \cos(2\pi f_c t) + B \sin(2\pi f_c t))$$
$$(A \cos(2\pi f_c(t + \tau)) + B \sin(2\pi f_c(t + \tau)))]$$
$$= \sigma^2 \cos(2\pi f_c \tau) + E[AB] \sin(4\pi f_c t + 2\pi f_c \tau)$$

$R_X(t, t + \tau)$ will be function of τ only if E[AB] = 0.

Conversely, if

$$E[AB] = 0$$

and

$$E[A^2] = E[B^2] = \sigma^2$$

$$m_{x(t)} = 0$$

$$R_X(t, t + \tau) = \sigma^2 \cos(2\pi f_c \tau)$$

$$= R_X(\tau)$$

Hence, X(t) is WSS.

Problem 5.3 :

Consider a random process Y(t) given by,

$$Y(t) = \int_0^t X(\tau) \, d\tau$$

where, X(t) is given by X(t) = A cos $(2\pi f_c t)$.

where, f_c is constant and A is random variable with mean 0 and variance σ^2.

(i)   Determine PDF of Y(t) at t = t_1.

(ii)   Is Y(t) WSS ?

Solution :

Given :

$$Y(t) = \int_0^t X(t) \, d\tau$$

$$= \int_0^t A \cos (2\pi f_c \tau)$$

$\therefore$ $$Y(t_k) = \int_0^{t_k} A \cos (2\pi f_c \tau) \, d\tau$$

$$= \frac{\sin (2\pi f_c t_k)}{2\pi f_c} \times A$$

$$E[Y(t_k)] = \frac{\sin (2\pi f_c t_k)}{2\pi f_c} E[A] = 0$$

$$\sigma_y^2 = E[Y^2(t_k)] - E[Y(t_k)]$$

$$= E[Y^2(t_k)]$$

$$= \frac{\sin^2 (2\pi f_c t_k)}{2\pi f_c} \times \sigma^2$$

$\therefore$ P.D.F. of Y(t) will be,

$$p_{Y(y)} = \frac{1}{\sqrt{2\pi \sigma_y^2}} e^{-y^2/2\sigma_y^2}$$

where, σ_y^2 is given as above.

(ii) Since variance of Y(t) depends on t_k, Y(t) is not WSS.

Problem 5.4 :

A class of modulated random signal Y(t) is defined as,

$$Y(t) = A X(t) \cos (2\pi f_c t + \phi)$$

where, X(t) is random message signal with zero mean stationary process with autocorrelation $R_X(\tau)$ and PSD $S_Y(f)$. A cos $(2\pi f_c t + \phi)$ is carrier with A and f_c constant and ϕ is uniformly distributed over [0, 2π]. Assuming that X(t) and ϕ are independent, find the mean, autocorrelation and power spectrum of P(t).   **U.Q. (8 marks) (May 2007)**

Solution :

Given : $$Y(t) = A X(t) \cos (2\pi f_c t + \phi)$$

$$m_{Y(t)} = E[Y(t)] = E[A X(t) \cos (2\pi f_c t + \phi)]$$

$$= A E[X(t)] \cdot E[\cos (2\pi f_c t + \phi)]$$

$$= 0$$

$$R_Y(t, t + \tau) = E[Y(t) X(t + \tau)]$$
$$= E[A^2 X(t) X(t + \tau) \cos (2\pi f_c t + \phi) \cdot \cos (2\pi f_c (t + \tau) + \phi)]$$
$$= \frac{A^2}{2} E[X(t) X(t + \tau) E[\cos (2\pi f_c \tau) + \cos (2\pi f_c t + 2\pi f_c \tau + 2\phi)]$$
$$= \frac{A^2}{2} R_X(\tau) \cdot \cos (2\pi f_c \tau)$$

Since mean is constant and autocorrelation depends only on τ, Y(t) is WSS.

and
$$R_Y(\tau) = \frac{A^2}{2} R_X(\tau) \cos (2\pi f_c \tau)$$

$$S_Y(f) = F [R_Y(\tau)]$$

$\therefore$
$$S_Y(f) = \frac{A^2}{4} S_X(f) * [\delta(f - f_c) + \delta(f + f_c)]$$

$$= \frac{A^2}{4} [S_X (f - f_c) + S_X(f + f_c)]$$

Problem 5.5 :

Two random process X(t) and Y(t) are given below :   **(UQ May 2014)**
$$X(t) = A \cos (2\pi f_c t + \phi)$$
$$Y(t) = A \sin (2\pi f_c t + \phi)$$
where, A and f_c are constant and ϕ is uniform random variable over $[0, 2\pi]$ find cross correlation of X(t) and Y(t).

Solution :

Given :
$$X(t) = A \cos (2\pi f_c + \phi)$$
$$Y(t) = A \sin (2\pi f_c + \phi)$$
$$R_{XY}(t, t + \tau) = E[X(t) \cdot Y(t + \tau)]$$
$$= E[A^2 \cos (2\pi f_c t + \phi) \sin (2\pi f_c (t + \tau) + \phi)]$$
$$= \frac{A^2}{2} E [\sin (4\pi f_c t + 2\pi f_c \tau + 2\phi) - \sin (-2\pi f_c \tau)]$$

$\therefore$
$$R_{XY}(\tau) = \frac{A^2}{2} \sin (2\pi f_c \tau)]$$

Similalry,
$$R_{YX}(t, t + \tau) = E[Y(t) X(t + \tau)]$$
$$= E[A^2 \sin (2\pi f_c t) \cdot \cos (2\pi f_c (t + \tau) + \phi)]$$

$\therefore$
$$R_{YX}(\tau) = -\frac{A^2}{2} \sin (2\pi f_c \tau)$$

$$= R_{XY}(-\tau) = -\frac{A^2}{2} \sin (2\pi f_c \tau)$$

$\therefore$
$$R_{XY} (-\tau) = R_{YX}(\tau)$$

Problem 5.6 :

A WSS random process X(t) is passed through LTI system with impulse response h(t) = $3e^{-2t}$ u(t). Find mean value of output Y(t) if E[X(t)] = 2. **U.Q. (4 marks) (Dec. 2008)**

Solution :

Given :

$$h(t) = 3e^{-2t} u(t)$$

$$m_{X(t)} = 2$$

$$H(f) = 3 \cdot \frac{1}{2 + j2\pi f}$$

$$m_{Y(f)} = E[Y(t)] = m_{X(t)} H(0)$$

$$= 2 \times 3 \times \frac{1}{2 + 0}$$

$$= 3$$

Hence, mean value of output Y(t) is 3.

Problem 5.7 :

If a WSS random process X(t) with power spectrum $S_X(f)$ is passed through a filter shown in Fig. 5.10 below. Find power spectrum of output process Y(t).

Solution :

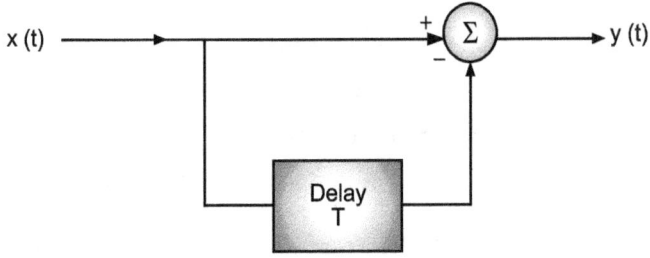

Fig. 5.10

The output Y(t) will be,   Y(t) = X(t) − X(t − T)

The impulse response of filter is,

$$h(t) = \delta(t) - \delta(t - T)$$

∴ $$H(t) = 1 - e^{-j2\pi f\tau}$$

Output power spectrum will be,

∴ $$S_Y(f) = |H(f)|^2 S_X(f) = |1 - e^{-j2\pi f\tau}| S_X(f)$$

$$= [(1 - \cos 2\pi f\tau)^2 + \sin^2 (2\pi f\tau)] S_X(f)$$

∴ $$S_Y(f) = 2 (1 - \cos 2\pi f\tau) S_X(f)$$

Problem 5.8 :

Consider a random process X(t) whose sample functions are constant with time i.e. x(t) = X where, X is random variable with PDF.

$$p_{X(x)} = 1 \quad ; \quad 0 \le x \le 1$$

$$= 0 \quad ; \quad \text{otherwise}$$

(i)   Is this process stationary ?

(ii) Is this process ergodic ?   **(8 marks) (Dec. 2007)**

Solution :

The random process assumes sample functions with constant value. Hence the sample function x(t) can be anything between 0 to 1. For example, say x(t) = 0.2 is one of the sample functions.

$$\therefore \qquad <x(t)> = \lim_{T \to \infty} \frac{1}{T} \int_{-T/2}^{T/2} x(t) \, dt$$

$$= \lim_{T \to \infty} \frac{1}{T} \int_{-T/2}^{T/2} 0.2 \, dt$$

$$= \lim_{T \to \infty} \frac{1}{T} [0.2 \, t]_{-T/2}^{T/2}$$

$$= \lim_{T \to \infty} \frac{0.2 \times T}{T}$$

$$= 0.2$$

If we take some other sample functions its time average will be different.

Now, the ensemble average,

$$E[X(t)] = \int_{-\infty}^{\infty} x \, p_x(x) \, dx = \int_{0}^{1} x \times 1 \, dx = \frac{1}{2}$$

(i)   The mean value is independent of t. Hence, the process is stationary.

(ii) But since the time average is not equal to ensemble average it is not ergodic.

Problem 5.9 :

Find mean and autocorrelation function of the waveform (random binary process) shown in Fig. 5.11 (a). Also find P.S.D. of it.

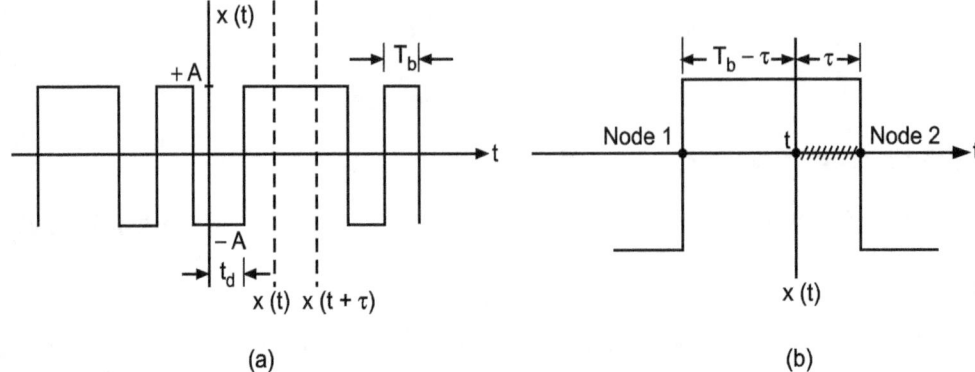

Fig. 5.11 : (a) Random binary wave

Solution :

Method 1 :

The Fig. 5.11 (a) shows a typical sample function of random binary process. There is randomness in states the signal can have (+ A or − A). Also the first node is equally likely to be situated at any instant from 0 to T_b from origin.

(i)   Since amplitude levels of signals are + A and − A, its mean value will be equal to 0.

$$\therefore \qquad\qquad m_X = E[X(t)] = 0$$

(ii) To find autocorrelation function $R_X(\tau) = R_X(t_1, t_2)$ we evaluate $E[x(t_1) x(t_2)]$ where, $X(t_1)$ and $X(t_2)$ are the random variables obtained by observing $X(t)$ at t_1 and t_2.

Let T_b the pulse duration. We have to consider two cases.

Case : 1 $\left| t_1 - t_2 \right| > T_b$

The random variables $x(t_1)$ and $x(t_2)$ occur in different pulse intervals hence they are independent of each other.

$$\therefore \qquad\qquad E[x(t_1) x(t_2)] = E[x(t_1)] \cdot E[x(t_2)]$$
$$= 0$$

Case 2 : $\left| t_1 - t_2 \right| < T_b$

The two random variables $x(t_1)$ and $x(t_2)$ occur in the same interval. T_b provided the delay t_d satisfies the condition $t_d < T_b - \left| t_1 - t_2 \right|$. Otherwise they will be in adjacent intervals.

If they lie in the same interval, the value $E[x(t_1) \cdot E(x(t_2)] = A^2$.

$$\therefore \quad E\left[x\,(t_1)\,x\,(t_2) \approx t_d\right] \;=\; A^2 \quad ; \quad t_d < T_b - \left|t_1 - t_2\right|$$

$$= 0 \quad ; \quad \text{elsewhere}$$

The probability density function of random variable T_d representing occurrence of starting time t_d of the first pulse for positive time is given by,

$$p_{T_d}(t_d) \;=\; \frac{1}{T_b} \quad ; \quad 0 \le t_d \le T_b$$

$$= 0 \quad ; \quad \text{otherwise}$$

$$\therefore \quad E\left[X(t_1)\,X(t_2)\right] \;=\; \int_{0}^{T_b - \left|t_1 - t_2\right|} A^2\, p_{T_d}(t_d)\, dt_d$$

$$= \int_{0}^{T_b - \left|t_1 - t_2\right|} \frac{A^2}{T_b}\, dt_d$$

$$= A^2\left(1 - \frac{\left|t_1 - t_2\right|}{T_b}\right) \quad ; \quad \left|t_1 - t_2\right| < T_b$$

$$= A^2\left(1 - \frac{\left|\tau\right|}{T}\right) \quad ; \quad \left|\tau\right| < T_b$$

$$\therefore \quad R_X(\tau) \;=\; \begin{cases} A^2\left(1 - \dfrac{\left|\tau\right|}{T}\right) & ; \quad \left|\tau\right| < T_b \\[2mm] 0 & ; \quad \text{otherwise} \left(\left|\tau\right| \ge T_b\right) \end{cases}$$

The Autocorrelation function is plotted in Fig. 5.11 (b).

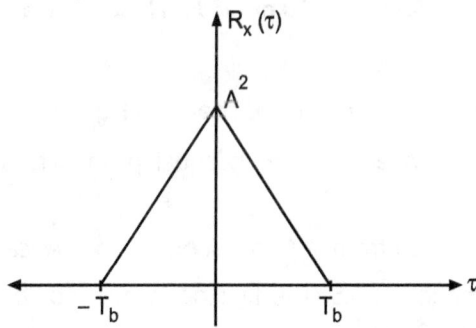

Fig. 5.11 : (b) Autocorrelation function of random binary wave

To find P.S.D. we take Fourier transform of autocorrelation function.

We have,

$$R_X(\tau) = \begin{cases} A^2\left(1 - \dfrac{|\tau|}{T_b}\right) & |\tau| < T_b \\ 0 & |\tau| \geq T_b \end{cases}$$

$$\therefore \qquad S_X(f) = f\,[R_X(\tau)] = \int_{-\infty}^{\infty} R_X(\tau)\, e^{-j2\pi f \tau}\, d\tau = \int_{-T_b}^{T_b} A^2\left(1 - \frac{|\tau|}{T_b}\right) e^{-j2\pi f \tau}\, d\tau$$

To evaluate this integral is difficult hence we make use of integration property of Fourier transform given in Chapter 1. We get the Fourier transform of triangular wave as sin c². Hence,

$$F\,[R_X(\tau)] = A^2\, T_b\, \text{sinc}^2\,(f\, T_b)$$

$$\therefore \qquad S_X(f) = A^2\, T_b\, \text{sinc}^2\,(f\, T_b)$$

This is plotted in Fig. 5.11 (c).

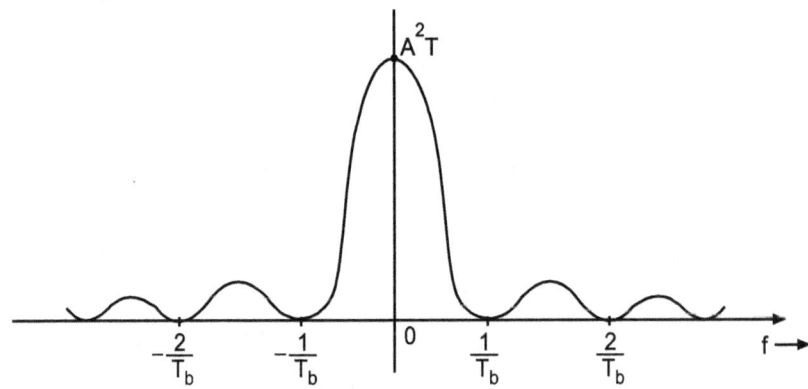

Fig. 5.11 : (c) PSD of random binary wave

Method 2 :

A sample function of random binary process is shown in Fig. 5.11 (a).

The signal has two values + A and − A with equal probabilities. Therefore, mean value $m_{X(t)} = 0$.

The state of the signal (transition from + A to − A or − A to + A) can occur every T_b sec. The probability of this state change is 0.5. The first node may not be starting exactly at time t = 0. It can start at time from 0 to T_b.

Let x (t_1) and x (t_2) be the random variables resulting from observing the process at time t = t_1 and at time t = t_2 respectively. They can take only two values + A and − A.

$\therefore$ $\quad\quad\quad\quad\quad\quad\quad R_X(\tau) = E[X(t_1) X(t_2)]$

$$= \sum_{x(t_1) \ x(t_2)} \sum x_1 x_2 \ P_{x(t_1) \ x(t_2)} (x_1, x_2)$$

$$= A^2 P_{x(t_1) \ x(t_2)} (+A, +A)$$

$$+ A^2 P_{x(t_1) \ x(t_2)} (-A, -A)$$

$$- A^2 P_{x(t_1) \ x(t_2)} (-A, A)$$

$$- A^2 P_{x(t_1) \ x(t_2)} (+A, -A)$$

Since first two and last two terms are symmetrical, we can write,

$\therefore$ $\quad\quad\quad\quad R_X(\tau) = 2A^2 \left[P_{x(t_1) \ x(t_2)} (A, A) \wedge P_{x(t_1) \ x(t_2)} (A, -A) \right]$

Using the result

$$P(A, B) = P(A) \cdot P(B|A)$$

$$R_X(\tau) = 2A^2 P_{x(t_1)} (A) [P_{x(t_2)|x(t_1)} (A|A)$$

$$- P_{x(t_2)|x(t_1)} (-A|A)]$$

Since $\quad\quad\quad\quad\quad P_{x(t_1)} = 0.5$

$$R_X(\tau) = A^2 [P_{x(t_2)|}P_{x(t_1)} (A|A) - P_{x(t_2)|x(t_1)} (-A|A)]$$

But $\quad\quad\quad P_{x(t_2)|x(t_1)} (A|A) = 1 - P_{x(t_2)|x(t_1)} (-A|A)$

$\therefore$ $\quad\quad\quad\quad\quad R_X(\tau) = A^2 [1 - 2 P_{x(t_2)|x(t_1)} (-A|A)]$

Now consider $P_{x(t_2)|x(t_1)} (-A|A)$

It is the probability of the event $X(t_2) = -A$ given $X(t_1) = A$. i.e. when $X(t_1)$ is observed there is a state change in the observation of $X(t_2)$. This state change will be dependent on whether the duration of observation is in same T_b or different T_b. Let us consider the case 1.

Case 1 : $t_2 - t_1 = \tau < T_b$.

$\therefore$ $\quad\quad P_{x(t_2)|x(t_1)} (-A|A) = P$ (A node lies in t to t + τ) × P (state change)

$$= \frac{1}{2} \times P \text{ (A node lies in t to t + τ)}$$

Fig. 5.11 (a) shows adjacent nodes node 1 and node 2 between which t lies. If t lies anywhere in the interval τ marked from node 2, then node 2 will lie within t to t + τ. But t is chosen arbitrarily between node 1 and node 2. Hence, it is equally likely to be at any instant over T_b and the probability that a node lies in t to t + τ = $\dfrac{\tau}{T_b}$.

$$\therefore \qquad P_{X\,(t_2)|X\,(t_1)}\,(-A|A) \;=\; \frac{1}{2}\times\left(\frac{\tau}{T_b}\right)$$

$$\therefore \qquad\qquad R_X\,(\tau) \;=\; A^2\left(1-\frac{\tau}{T_b}\right) \qquad\qquad ; \qquad \tau < T_b$$

Since $R_X\,(\tau)$ is even function

$$R_X\,(\tau)\,A^2\left(1-\frac{|\tau|}{T_b}\right) \qquad\qquad ; \qquad |\tau| < T_b$$

Case 2 : $\tau > T_b$

In this case, $x(t_1)$ and $x(t_2)$ occur in difference pulse intervals. Hence, they are independent of each other.

$$R_X\,(\tau) \;=\; E\,[x(t_1)\,x(t_2)] \;=\; 0 \; ; \qquad\qquad \tau > T_b$$

Considering above cases, we can write,

$$\therefore \qquad\qquad R_X\,(\tau) \;=\; \begin{cases} A^2\left(1-\dfrac{|\tau|}{T_b}\right) & ; \quad |\tau| < T_b \\[2ex] 0 & ; \quad |\tau| > T_b \end{cases}$$

The plot of $R_X\,(\tau)$ is shown in Fig. 5.11 (b).

The PSD of the given random process can be found by taking Fourier transform of $R_X\,(\tau)$. We know that Fourier transform of triangular pulse is sinc^2.

i.e. $A \wedge\left(\dfrac{t}{2T_b}\right) \Delta\ A\,T\ \text{sinc}^2\ (f\ T_b)$

$$F\,[R_X\,(\tau)] \;=\; A^2\,T_b\ \text{sinc}^2\ (f\ T_b)$$

$$\therefore \qquad\qquad S_X\,(f) \;=\; A^2\,T_b\ \text{sinc}^2\ (f\ T_b)$$

This is plotted in Fig. 5.11 (c).

Problem 5.10 :

Find the transfer function and output power spectral density for a filter given in Fig. 5.12.

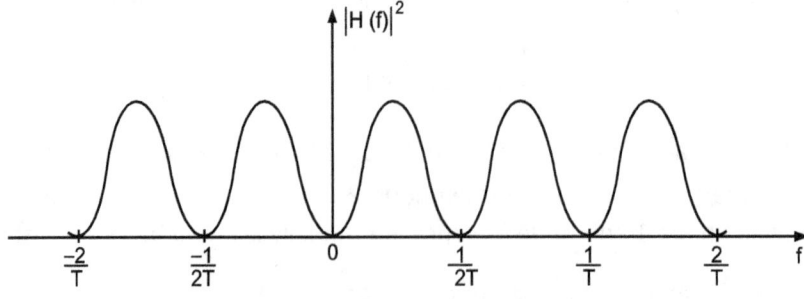

(a) Filter block diagram

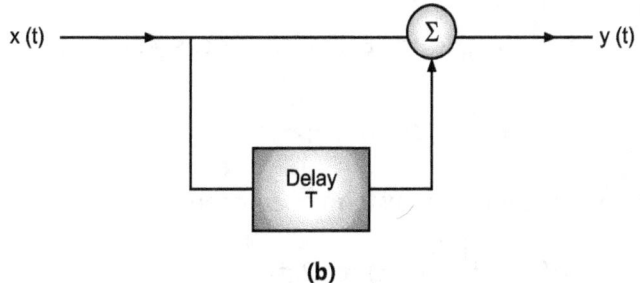

(b)

Fig. 5.12

Solution : We can write,

$$y(t) = x(t) - X(t-T)$$

$$\therefore \quad y(f) = x(f) - X(f)\, e^{-j2\pi fT}$$

$$\frac{Y(f)}{X(f)} = 1 - e^{-j2\pi fT}$$

$$H(f) = 1 - [\cos(2\pi fT) - j\sin(2\pi fT)]$$

$$H(f) = 1 - \cos(2\pi fT) + j\sin(2\pi fT)$$

$$\therefore \quad |H(f)|^2 = (1 - \cos 2\pi fT)^2 + (\sin^2(2\pi fT)$$

$$= 2[1 - \cos(2\pi fT)]$$

$$= 4\sin^2(\pi fT)$$

Therefore, the relationship between input and output power spectral density is given by,

$$S_Y(f) = |H(f)|^2 S_X(f)$$

$$\therefore \quad S_Y(f) = 4\sin^2(\pi fT)\, S_X(f)$$

Problem 5.11 :

Determine observation function and PSD of $Y(t) = X(t)\cos(2\pi f_c t + \phi)$ [DSB – SC – modulated process] where, $X(t)$ is wide-sense stationary random process and ϕ is an r.v. uniformly distributed over $(0, 2\pi)$ and independent of $X(t)$.

Solution : Given :

$$Y(t) = X(t)\cos(2\pi f_c t + \phi)$$

$$R_Y(\tau) = E[Y(t+\tau)\, Y(t)]$$

$$= E(X(t+\tau) \cdot \cos(2\pi f_c t + 2\pi f_c \tau + \phi) \cdot X(t) \cdot \cos(2\pi f_c t + \phi)]$$

$$= E[X(t+\tau)\, X(\tau)] \cdot E[\cos(2\pi f_c t + 2\pi f_c \tau + \phi) \cdot \cos(2\pi f_c t + \phi)]$$

$$= \frac{1}{2} \, R_X \, (\tau) \cdot E \, [\cos 2\pi f_c \tau + \cos (4\pi f_c t + 2\pi f_c \tau + \phi)]$$

$$= \frac{1}{2} \, R_X \, (\tau) \cos 2\pi f_c \tau$$

The power spectral density is fourier transform of autocorrelation function.

$$\therefore \qquad S_Y \, (f) \; = \; f \left[\frac{1}{2} R_X \, (\tau) \cos 2\pi f_c \tau \right]$$

$$= \; f \left[\frac{1}{4} R_X \, (\tau) \left(e^{j2\pi f_c \tau} + e^{-j2\pi f_c \tau} \right) \right]$$

$$= \; \frac{1}{4} \left[S_X \, (f - f_c) + S_X \, (f + f_c) \right]$$

Hence, the PSD of the output random process is shifted in frequency domain by f_c w.r.t. input PSD.

Problem 5.12 :

The random process X(t) = X where, X is a random variable uniformly distributed in the interval (– 1, 1). Find mean and autocorrelation function for the process and PSD.

Solution : Given : $X(t) \; = \; X$

$$p_X \, (x) \; = \; \frac{1}{2} \qquad ; \qquad -1 \le x \le 1$$

$$= \; 0 \qquad ; \qquad \text{otherwise}$$

$$m_X \; = \; E \, [X(t)] \; = \; E[X]$$

$$= \; \int_{-1}^{1} x \, f_X \, (x) \, dx$$

$$= \; \int_{-1}^{1} \frac{x}{2} dx$$

$$= \; \left[\frac{x^2}{4} \right]_{-1}^{+1}$$

$$= \; \frac{1}{2}$$

The autocorrelation function,

$$R_X(t_1, t_2) = E[X(t_1)X(t_2)]$$

$$= E[X^2]$$

$$= \int_{-1}^{+1} x^2 \, p_X(x) \, dx = \int_{-1}^{1} x^2 \times \frac{1}{2} \, dx$$

$$\therefore \qquad R_X(\tau) = \frac{1}{3}$$

To find P.S.D. we find inverse F.T. of $R_X(\tau)$.

Since,
$$R_X(\tau) = \frac{1}{3}$$

$$S_X(f) = F^{-1}\left[\frac{1}{3}\right]$$

$$= \frac{1}{3}\delta(f)$$

SOLVED UNIVERSITY QUESTIONS

U.Q. 1 : Show that if a wide sense stationary process X(t) is passed through a LTI filter with impulse response h(t), then its output has constant mean square value.

(8 marks) (Dec. 2006, May 2009)

Solution : Refer Section 5.5.

U.Q. 2 : Define autocorrelation function. State and explain any three properties of autocorrelation function. **(6 marks) (Dec. 2006)**

Solution : Refer Section 5.4.3.

U.Q. 3 : What are the conditions for random process to wide sense stationary ? What is ergodicity ?

Solution : Refer Sections 5.4.2 and 5.4.5.

U.Q. 4 : Define mean, correlation, covariance function for random process.

(6 marks) (May 2007)

Solution : Refer Section 5.3.2.

U.Q. 5 : What is power spectral density ? Derive expression of PSD when a random process is transmitted through a LTI filter ? **(8 marks) (Dec. 2007)**

Solution : Refer Section 5.6.

U.Q. 6 : With the help of mathematical expression explain stationary random process, non-stationary random process wide. Stationary process and ergodic processes.

(8 marks) (Dec. 08, May 2009)

Solution : Refer Section 5.4.

U.Q. 7 : Let $V(t) = X + 3t$ where, X is random variable with $\bar{X} = 0$ and $\bar{X^2} = 5$. Show that $\bar{V(t)} = 35$ and $R_v(t_1, t_2) = 5 + 9\, t_1 t_2$ where $R(t_1, t_2)$ is autocorrelation function and $\bar{V(t)}$ is mean value of $V(t)$.

Solution : Given : $\qquad V(t) = X + 3t$

where, X is random.

$$\therefore \qquad\qquad E[V(t)] = E[X] + E[3t]$$

$$z \qquad\qquad\qquad = 0 + 3t$$

$$= 3t$$

$$\therefore \qquad\qquad \bar{V(t)} = 3t$$

Now, $\quad R_v(t_1, t_2)$

$$= E[V(t_1)\, V(t_2)]$$

$$= E[(X + 3t_1)(X + 3t_2)]$$

$$= E[X^2 + 3X(t_1 + t_2) + 9\, t_1 t_2]$$

$$= E[X^2] + (t_1 + t_2)\, E[3X] = E[9\, t_1 t_2]$$

$$= 5 + (t_1 + t_2) \times 0 + 9 t_1 t_2$$

$$= 5 + 9 t_1 t_2$$

$$\therefore \qquad R_v(t_1, t_2) = 5 + 9 t_1 t_2$$

Dec. 2010

U.Q. 8 : Define random process. What are Time averages associated with random process?

(8)

Solution : Refer Sections 5.1 and 5.3.2.

U.Q. 9 : Find the mean square value of output random process when a WSS process is passed through an. LTI filter. **(8)**

Solution : Refer Section 5.4.2.

U.Q. 10 : What are conditions for a random process to be wide sense stationary? **(8)**

Solution : Refer Section 5.4.2.

U.Q. 11 : If X(t) = A cos (2πf$_c$t + φ) is random process with φ is a random variable uniformly distributed over (0, 2π). Prove that x(t) is ergodic in mean.   **(8)**

Solution : Refer Example 5.6

May 2011

U.Q. 12 : Explain classification of Random processes with Mathematical expressions.   **(6)**

Solution : Refer Section 5.2.

U.Q. 13 : A WSS random process X(t) is applied to the input of a LTI system with impulse response h (t) = a exp (–at) u (t). Find the mean value of the output Y(t) of the system if E [X (t)] = 6 and a = 2.   **(6)**

Solution : Given:
$$h(t) = ae^{-at} u(t)$$

∴
$$H(f) = \frac{a}{a + j2\pi f}$$

∴
$$H(0) = 1$$

Now,
$$Y(t) = \int_{-\infty}^{\infty} h(\lambda_1) \times (t - \lambda_1) \, d\lambda_1$$

The mean value of Y(t)
$$m_Y(t) = m_x H(0) = E[X(t)] \cdot H(0)$$
$$= 6 \times 1$$
∴
$$m_Y(t) = 6$$

U.Q. 14 : Two random processes z(t) and y (t) are given by
z (t) = A cos (ωt + θ)
y (t) = A sin (ωt + θ)
where A and ω are constants and θ is a uniform random variable over (0, 2π). Find the cross correlation of z (t) and y (t).   **(4)**

Solution : Refer Problem 5.5.

U.Q. 15 : Show that the output of LTI system is WSS if the input applied to it is WSS.   **(6)**

Solution : Refer Section 5.6.

U.Q. 16 : If the process X (t) = A cos (27πfct + φ), where φ is a random variable uniformly distributed in the range (0, 2π) is passed through a filter with H(f) = j2πf. Find the output PSD.   **(6)**

Solution : Refer Example 5.6.

U.Q. 17 : The random variable X has a uniform distribution over a 0 ≤ x ≤ 2 find mean and mean square value for the random process V (t) = 6e^X.   **(4)**

Solution : Given:
$$V(t) = 6e^X$$

$$p_x(x) = \frac{1}{2} \quad 0 \le x \le 2$$

$\therefore$

$$E[V(f)] = E[6e^X]$$

$$= \int_{-\infty}^{\infty} 6e^X p_x(x)\, dx = \int_0^2 6e^X \frac{1}{2}\, dx$$

$$= 3 \int_0^2 e^X\, dx = 3[e^2 - 1] = 19.17$$

$$e[V^2(t)] = E[V(t) \cdot V(t)] = E[36\, e^{2X}]$$

$$= \int_{-\infty}^{\infty} 36\, e^{2X} p_x(x)\, dx = \int_0^2 36\, e^{2X} \frac{1}{2}\, dx$$

$$= 18\, [e^4 - 1]$$

$$= 964.77$$

U.Q. 18 :   Derive an equation of PSD for ON-OFF signalling.   **(6)**

Solution :   Refer Section 7.3.1.

Dec. 2011

U.Q. 19 :   Explain in brief the different types of random processes with suitable examples.**(8)**

Solution : Refer Section 5.4.

U.Q. 20 :   Consider the random process $X(t) = A \cos 2\pi f_c t$, where the frequency 'fc' is constant and amplitude 'A" is uniformly distributed

$$f_A(a) = \begin{cases} 1 & 0 \le a \le 1 \\ 0 & \text{Otherwise} \end{cases}$$

Determine whether it is strictly stationary or not.   **(8)**

Solution : Refer Problem 5.1.

U.Q. 21 :   Show that if the wide sense stationary process $X(t)$ is passed through LTI system with impulse response $h(t)$, then its output has constant mean square value.   **(8)**

Solution : Refer Section 5.4.5.

U.Q. 22 :   What are the different properties of random process? A wide sense stationary random process $X(t)$ is applied to the input of LTI system with impulse response $h(t) = 3e^{-2t} u(t)$. Find the mean value of output $Y(t)$ of the system if $E[X(t)] = 2$. **(8)**

Solution : Given: $h(t) = 3e^{-2t} u(t)$

$$m_x(t) = \frac{3}{2 + j2\pi f}$$

$$m_y(t) = E[Y(t)] = m_x(t) \cdot H(0)$$

$$= 2 \times 3 \frac{1}{2 + 0}$$

$$= 3$$

Thus, mean value of Y(t) is 3.

May 2012

U.Q. 23 : Explain in detail about stationary, non-stationary, wide sense stationary and ergodic processes with suitable mathematical expressions and examples. **(8)**

Solution : Refer Sections 5.4.1, 5.4.2 and 5.4.5.

U.Q. 24 : Consider a random process $s(t) = \cos(\omega_0 t + \phi)$ where, 'ϕ' is a random variable with probability density

$$f(\phi) = \frac{1}{2\pi}; \; -\pi \le \phi \le \pi$$

$$= 0 \; ; \text{elsewhere}$$

(i) Show that the first and second moments of s(t) are independent of time.

(ii) If the random variable is fixed as ϕ_0, will the ensemble mean of s(t) be time independent? **(8)**

Solution : Refer equations 5.1 and 5.3.

U.Q.5.25 : Define the power spectral density and auto-correlation function of periodic signals. Show that both are related in frequency domain. **(8)**

Solution : Refer Section 5.6.

Dec. 2012

U.Q. 26 : Classify and explain different types of Random Processes. **(8)**

Solution : Refer Section 5.4.

May 2013

U.Q. 27 : Find the Power Spectral Density of random process X(t) defined by

$$X(t) = A \cos(2\pi f_c t + \phi)$$

Where ϕ is a uniform distributed random variable over the integral $(0, 2\pi)$ **(8)**

Solution : Refer Example 5.7.

U.Q. 28 : Define mean, correlation, standard deviation and variance of random process. **(8)**

Solution : Refer Section 5.3.

U.Q.5.29 : Let X(t) be a zero-mean, stationary, Gaussian process with autocorrelation function Rx(t). This process is applied to a square law device, which is defined by the input-output relation Y(t) = X(t) Where Y(t) is the output. Show that the mean of Y(t) is Rx(0).   **(8)**

Solution : Given: $Y(t) = X^2(t)$

∴ Mean value of Y(t) is

$$M_{Y(t)} = E[Y(t)] = E[X^2(t)] \qquad \ldots (1)$$

Now, $R_X(Y) = E[X(t + \tau) \, X(t)]$ is Autocorrelation function of X(t)

∴ $R_X(0) = E[X(t) \cdot X(t)] = E[X^2(t)] \qquad \ldots (2)$

Hence, from equations (1) and (2)

$$M_Y(t) = E[Y(t) = R_X(0)$$

U.Q. 30 : Explain stationary, non-stationary, wide sense stationary and Ergodic processes with the help of mathematical expression.   **(8)**

Solution : Refer Section 5.4.

Dec. 2013

U.Q. 31 : Show that a narrowband random process X(t) can be completely represented in terms of its in phase and Quadrature components.   **(8)**

Solution : Refer Section 5.4.

U.Q. 32 : Two random processes z(t) and y (t) are given by   [8]

$z(t) = A \cos (\omega_c t + \phi)$

$z(t) = A \sin (\omega_c t + \phi)$

Where A and ω_c are constant and ϕ is uniform random variable over (0,2 π). Find the auto correction and cross correlation of z(t) and y (t).

Solution : Refer Section 5.5.

U.Q. 33 : Explain Ergodic process. If X(t) = A cos (2π f_ct + φ) is random process with φ as a random variable uniformly distributed over (0, 2π). Prove that x(t) is ergodic in mean.   **(8)**

Solution : Refer Section 5.4.5 and refer Problem 5.4.

U.Q. 34 : What is a Wide Sense Stationary Process ? When A WSS R.P. X(t) is applied to input of LTI system with impulse response h(t) =3e^{-2t} u(t), Find the mean value of system if E [X (t)] = 2 and its autocorrection.   **(8)**

Solution : Refer Section 5.6.

May 2014

U.Q. 35 : Define the terms related to random processes   **[8]**

(a) Mean

(b) Auto correlation

(c) Power spectral density with mathematical formula

Solution : Refer Section 5.3.

U.Q. 36 : Two random processes x(t) & y(t) are given by   **(10)**

X(t) = Acos (ωt + θ) & y(t) = A sin (ωt + θ)

Where A & ω are constants & θ is a random variable having a uniform distribution over [0, 2π) , find the cross correlation of X(t)?

Solution : Refer Section 5.5.

U.Q. 37 : Define random process and with the help of mathematical expression explain

(1) Stationary random processes   **(10)**

(2) Non – stationary random processes

(3) Wide sense stationary processes

(4) Ergodic processes

Solution : Refer Section 5.4.

SUMMARY

1.   Random process consists of ensemble of time functions.

2.   Random process also consists of infinite number of Random variables and can be specified in terms of joint probability density functions of these random variables.

3.   Random process can be characterised by the ensemble statistics such as mean, autocorrelation etc.

4.   Random process can be classified as stationary, non-stationary, wide-sense stationary and ergodic process.

5.   A random process is strictly stationary if its statistical characteristics do not change with shift of time origin.

6.   A random process is said to be non-stationary if its statistical characteristics are dependent on time or change with shift of time origin.

---

7. A random process is said to be wide-sense stationary if its mean and autocorrelation functions do not change with shift of time origin.

8. A random process is said to be ergodic if its ensemble averages are same as time average.

9   When a random process X(t) is passed through a LTI filter of impulse response h(t). Then, the output random process Y(t) will be wide-sense stationary, if input X(t) is wide-sense stationary.

10. Power spectral density gives spectral information of a random process. It can be obtained by taking Fourier transform of autocorrelation function.

11. A random process X(t) is a Gaussian process if for all n, all $(t_1, t_2, ..., t_n)$ the random variables $\{X(t_i)\}$ have jointly Gaussian density function.

EXERCISE

1. Explain the following terms with reference to random process.

    (i)   Sample function   (ii) Ensemble   (iii) Ensemble statistics

2. Define random process. Explain random process with example.

3. What is stationary process ?

4. Explain wide-sense stationary process with example.

5. Define ergodic process. Explain the difference between ergodic process and stationary process.

6. Write a short note on ensemble statistics and wide-sense stationary process.

7. What is PSD ? Explain it with suitable derivation.

8. Derive the expression for autocorrelation function of output of LTI filter with impulse response h(t) if a random process X(t) is passed through it.

9. State and prove properties of PSD.

10. State and prove properties of autocorrelation function.

11. Explain what is Gaussian process.

12. State the properties of Gaussian process.

13. What is cross-correlation function ? What will be cross-correlation function of a wide-sense stationary process ?

Chapter 6

NOISE

6.1   INTRODUCTION

- Noise is unwanted signal which tends to interfere with transmission and processing of signals in communication systems. These signals are classified generally as human interference and naturally occurring noise.

- The human interference is produced by other communication systems, ignition, ac hum, etc.

- Naturally occurring noise is due to random electron motion, atmospheric disturbance, extraterrestrial radiation.

- Major task in a communication system design is to reduce the effects of these unwanted signals. For this we need to characterise noise in terms of its spectral components.

- Thermal motion of electrons in conducting media like wires, resistors, etc. generate noise which is unavoidable cause of electrical noise. This noise is called Thermal noise. This noise can be modelled as white noise with which we can analyse a system easily. We will be discussing this analysis along with bandpass (narrow-band) noise in this chapter.

6.2 THERMAL NOISE

- It is generated by random motion of charged particles (electrons) in conducting media.
- From kinetic theory, the average energy of particle is proportional to KT where, K – Boltzman's constant and T – Absolute temperature in °K.

- A metallic resistor R which is at temperature T produces a noise voltage $v_n(t)$ due to random motion of electrons at open terminals. According to central limit theorem, this v(t) will have Gaussian distribution with zero mean and mean square value given by,

$$\overline{v_n}^2 = \sigma_{vn}^2 = \frac{2\,(\pi\,KT)^2}{3h}\,R \;\; volt^2 \qquad\qquad ...\,(6.1)$$

where,
$$K = Boltzman's\ constant = 1.38 \times 10^{-33}\ J/k$$
$$h = Plank's\ constant = 6.62 \times 10^{-34}\ J/k$$

- At standard temperature i.e. 290°K, it is found that the power spectral density of thermal noise is given by

$$S_n(f) = 2KTR \;\; V^2/Hz \qquad\qquad ...\,(6.2)$$

- Thus, mean square voltage spectral density of thermal noise is constant or independent of frequency f.

- The noisy resistance R can be now replaced with mean square voltage generator and noiseless resistance as shown in Fig. 6.1 and Fig. 6.2 represented in terms of thevenin and Norton equivalent.

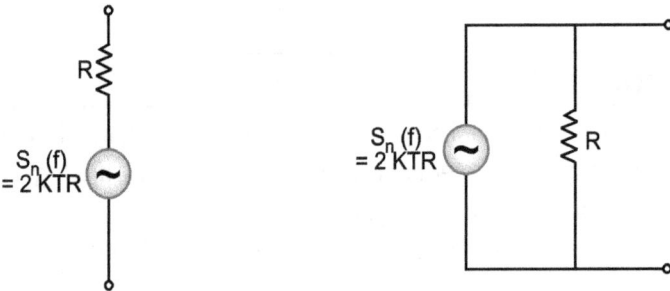

Fig. 6.1 : Thevenin equivalent of noisy resistor   **Fig. 6.2 : Norton equivalent of noisy resistor**

- If we connect a load across the noisy resistor the power available across this resistor will be given by maximum power transfer theorem.

$$P_a = \frac{<[V_n(t)/2]^2>}{R}$$

$$= \frac{<V_n(t)>^2}{4R} \qquad\qquad ...\,(6.3)$$

- Hence, the available power spectral density at load resistance will be,

$$S_a(f) = \frac{S_n(f)}{4R} = \frac{2KTR}{4R}$$

$$= \frac{1}{2}KT \;\; Watt/Hz.$$

It is shown in Fig. 6.3.

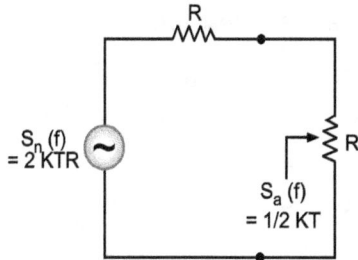

Fig. 6.3 : Available power

- Thus, a thermal resistor delivers maximum power density of $\dfrac{KT}{2}$ Watt/Hz to a matched load independent of value of R.
- Apart from thermal noise, many other types of noise sources are Gaussian and their power spectral density is constant over a wide range of frequency.
- It means these noise sources have all frequency components in equal proportion.
- Hence, it is called white noise. (Just like white light has all colours with equal proportion). Let us characterise this noise.

6.3   WHITE NOISE

- Noise in an idealised form is called white noise.
- In communication systems noise analysis is done using this idealised form of noise.
- The power spectral density of white noise is independent of frequency.
- The name white noise is used because it contains all frequency components with equal amount.
- If the probability distribution of white noise is Gaussian in nature hence it is called White Gaussian noise.
- The White Gaussian noise is denoted as W(t). Its power spectral density is given by,

$$S_W (f) \;=\; \frac{N_0}{2} \; \text{Watts/Hz} \qquad\qquad \text{... (6.4)}$$

- It is shown in Fig. 6.4 (a).

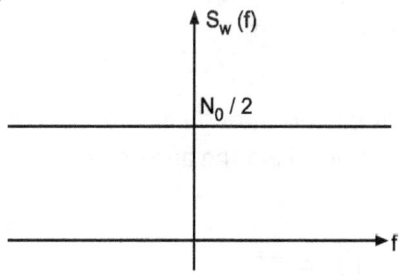

Fig. 6.4 : (a) PSD of white noise

$$N_0 \;=\; KT_e$$

- K is Boltzman's constant
- T_e is equivalent noise temperature of resistor.
- From the noise power spectral density we can find autocorrelation function $R_W(\tau)$ of white gaussian noise. By taking inverse Fourier transform
- Since, $1 \rightleftharpoons \delta(f)$

  and $\delta(t) \rightleftharpoons 1$

$$F^{-1}[S_W(f)] = \frac{N_0}{2} \times \delta(\tau) \qquad \text{... (6.5)}$$

$$\therefore \qquad R_W(\tau) = \frac{N_0}{2} \delta(\tau) \qquad \text{... (6.6)}$$

- The function is plotted in Fig. 6.4 (b).

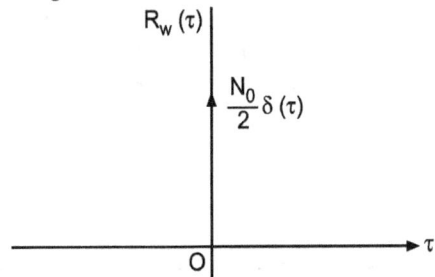

Fig. 6.4 : (b) Autocorrelation function

- Thus autocorrelation function of white noise is delta function weighted by a facts $\frac{N_0}{2}$ occurring at $\tau = 0$.
- From this we can conclude that any two different samples of white noise, no matter how closely together in time they are taken, are uncorrelated.
- If white noise W(t) is Gaussian then the two samples will also statistically independent. Thus, white gaussian noise is ultimate in randomness.
- White noise is physically not realisable. Its simplicity makes it useful in communication system analysis. Moreover any noise process can be modelled as white noise as long as its bandwidth is larger than the system.

Example 6.1 :

If a white gaussian noise W(t) is passed through an ideal low pass filter of bandwidth W and passband amplitude response as one. Find the autocorrelation function of output of the low pass filter.

Solution : Given : $S_W(f) = \frac{N_0}{2}$

Therefore, the output noise power spectral density function will be,

$$S_N(f) = |H(f)|^2 S_W(f) = \frac{N_0}{2}|H(f)|^2$$

But,
$$H(f) = 1 \qquad ; \qquad -W \le f \le W$$
$$= 0 \qquad ; \qquad \text{otherwise}$$

$$\therefore \qquad S_N(f) = \frac{N_0}{2} \qquad ; \qquad -W \le f \le W$$
$$= 0 \qquad ; \qquad \text{otherwise}$$

This function is plotted in Fig. 6.5 (a).

The autocorrelation function of output is inverse Fourier transform of output noise power spectral density $S_W(f)$.

$$\therefore \qquad R_N(\tau) = \int_{-\infty}^{\infty} S_N(f) \, e^{-j2\pi f\tau} \, df$$

$$= \int_{-W}^{W} \frac{N_0}{2} e^{-j2\pi f\tau} df$$

$$= \frac{N_0}{2}\left[\frac{e^{-j2\pi f\tau}}{-j2\pi\tau}\right]_{-W}^{W}$$

$$= \frac{N_0}{2\pi\tau}\left[\frac{e^{-j2\pi W\tau} + e^{+j2\pi W\tau}}{2j}\right]$$

$$= \frac{N_0}{2\pi\tau}\sin(2\pi W\tau)$$

$$= N_0 \times W \frac{\sin(2\pi W\tau)}{(2\pi W\tau)}$$

$$= N_0 W \operatorname{sinc}(2W\tau)$$

The function is plotted in Fig. 6.5 (b).

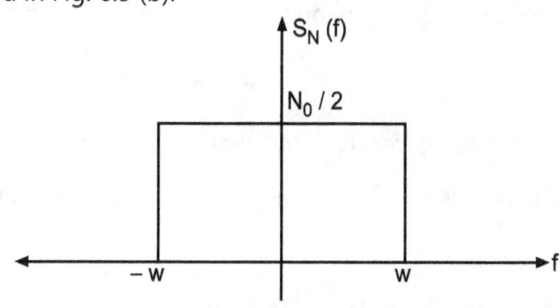

Fig. 6.5 : (a) PSD of filtered white noise

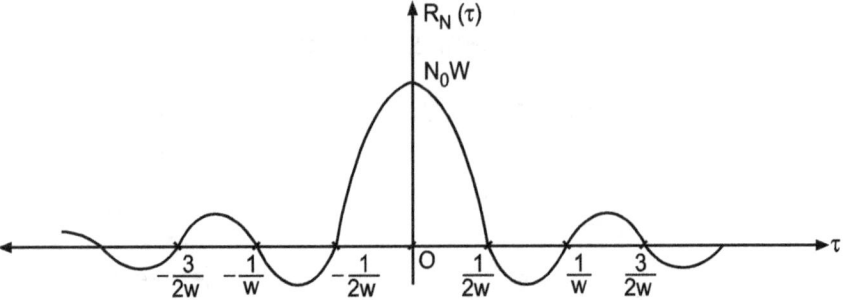

Fig. 6.5 : (b) Autocorrelation function of filtered white noise

6.4 NOISE EQUIVALENT BANDWIDTH

- Average output noise power P_{N_0} at the output of a linear system can be obtained by taking value of autocorrelation function at $\tau = 0$. e.g. output white noise power at the output of an ideal low pass filter will be obtained by putting $\tau = 0$ in

$$R_W(\tau) = N_0 \, \text{sinc}(2W\tau) \qquad \qquad ...(6.7)$$

$$\therefore \qquad P_{N_0} = N_0 W \qquad [\because \text{sinc}(0) = 1] \qquad ...(6.8)$$

- The average (ideal) output noise power is proportional to the bandwidth.
- Now consider any low-pass filter with transfer function H (f). If white noise of zero mean and PSD $\dfrac{N_0}{2}$ is applied at the input of this filter then average output noise power is given by,

$$P_{N_1} = \frac{N_0}{2} \int_{-\infty}^{\infty} |H(f)|^2 \, df$$

$$= N_0 \int_{0}^{\infty} |H(f)|^2 \, df \qquad ...(6.9)$$

- If the same source of white noise is connected to the input of an ideal low-pass filter of zero frequency response H (0) and bandwidth B_N. Then average output noise power is given by,

$$P_{N_2} = N_0 B_N H^2(0) \qquad ...(6.10)$$

- If this output average noise power (P_{N_2}) and that obtained at the output of normal filter P_{N_1} are same then the bandwidth B_N is called noise equivalent bandwidth.

$$N_0 B_N H^2(0) = N_0 \int_{0}^{\infty} |H(f)|^2 \, df \qquad ...(6.11)$$

$$\therefore \qquad B_N \;=\; \frac{\displaystyle\int_0^\infty \left|H(f)\right|^2 df}{H^2(0)} \qquad\qquad \text{... (6.12)}$$

This is depicted in Fig. 6.6.

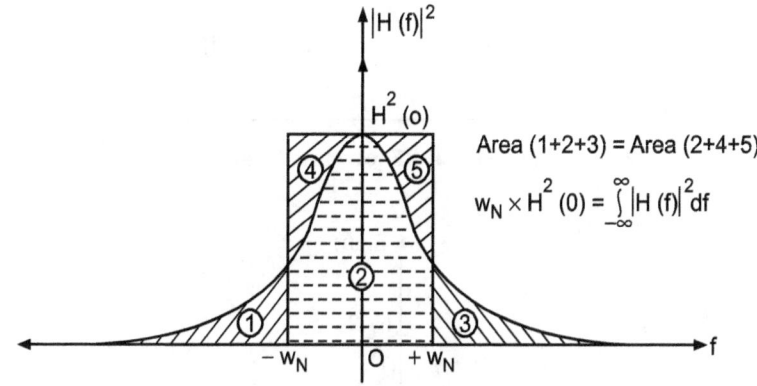

Fig. 6.6 : Noise equivalent bandwidth

- From equations (6.9) and (6.12), the filtered noise power will be,

$$P_{N_1} \;=\; N_0 \times H^2(0) \times B_N$$

- Thus, the filtering effect has two parts.
  1. Frequency selectivity described by B_N.
  2. Power gain or attenuation represented by $H^2(0)$.

Example 6.2 :

Find the noise equivalent bandwidth of RC low-pass filter. (Fig. 6.7 (a)).

Solution : The transfer function of an RC low-pass filter is given by,

$$H(f) \;=\; \frac{1}{1 + j2\pi fRC} \qquad\qquad \therefore \; \left|H(f)\right|^2 = \frac{1}{1 + (2\pi fRC)^2}$$

The P.S.D. of the noise n(t) at the output of this filter is given by,

$$S_N(f) \;=\; \left|H(f)\right|^2 S_W(f)$$

$$\therefore \qquad S_N(f) \;=\; \frac{N_0/2}{1 + (2\pi fRC)^2}$$

To find autocorrelation function we take inverse Fourier transform of above equation. For this, we the result,

$$e^{-a|t|} \;\Longleftrightarrow\; \frac{2a}{a^2 + (2\pi f)^2}$$

$$\text{Put } a \;=\; RC$$

$$\therefore \qquad R_N(\tau) = \frac{N_0}{4RC} e^{-|\tau|/RC}$$

The plot of $S_N(f)$ and $R_N(\tau)$ is shown in Fig. 6.7 (b) and (c) respectively.

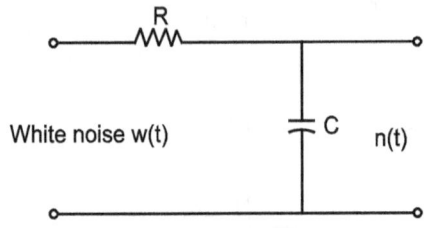

Fig. 6.7 : (a) RC low pass filter

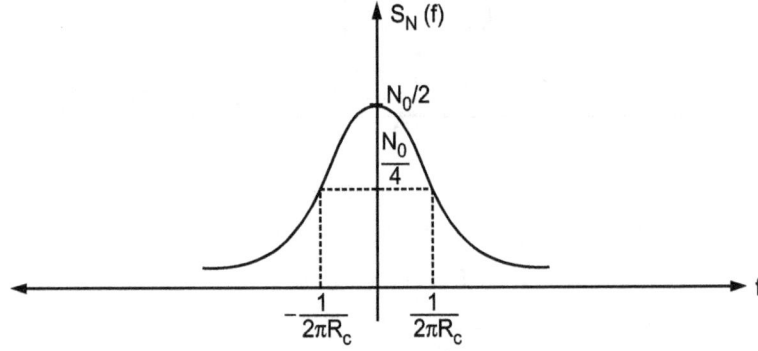

Fig. 6.7 : (b)

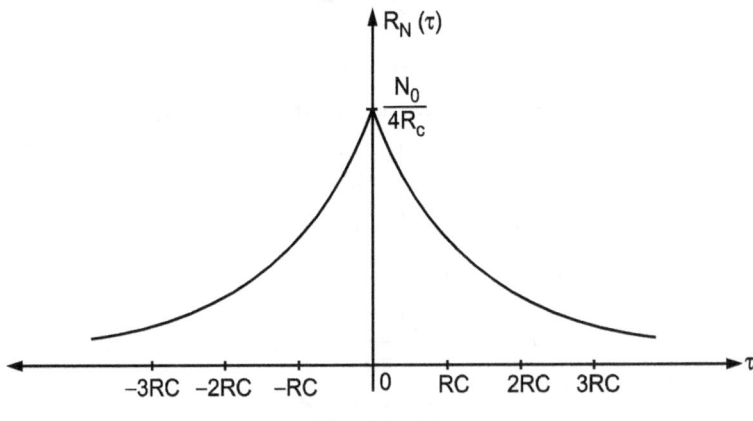

Fig. 6.7 : (c)

The average noise power at the output of RC low pass filter will be $R_N(0) = \dfrac{N_2}{4RC}$

$$\therefore \qquad N_0 B_N H^2(0) = \frac{N_0}{4RC}$$

$$\therefore \qquad N_0 \times B_N \times 1 \;=\; \frac{N_0}{4RC}$$

$$\therefore \qquad \text{Noise equivalent bandwidth } B_N \;=\; \frac{1}{4RC}$$

6.5 NARROWBAND NOISE

- A signal g(t) is said to be pass band signal if Fourier transform G(f) is non-negligible in the band of frequencies 2B centered around some frequency f_c.

- If this bandwidth 2B is very small compared to f_c, such signals are called narrow-band signals.

- Thus, narrow band signals are bandpass signals. Hence, before we characterise narrow-band noise let us study bandpass random process.

- A bandpass random process X(t) is represented as,

$$X(t) \;=\; X_i(t)\cos(2\pi f ct) + X_q(t)\sin(2\pi f_c t) \qquad\qquad \text{... (6.13)}$$

- The two terms $X_c(t)\cos(2\pi f_c t)$ and $X_s(t)\sin(2\pi f_c t)$ are called quadrature components.

- Equation (6.13) can be proved as below.

- Let there be a random process X(t) with PSD as shown in Fig. 6.8 (a).

- Let this bandpass process be passed through a system as shown in Fig. 6.8 (b).

- It has an ideal low pass filter $H_0(f)$ with impulse response $h_0(t)$.

- Let us find out the transfer function of this system. This can be done by calculating h(t). For this we have to give $\delta(t)$ as input to the system.

- In order to check time invariant nature of the systems we will give $\delta(t - t_0)$ as input instead of $\delta(t)$.

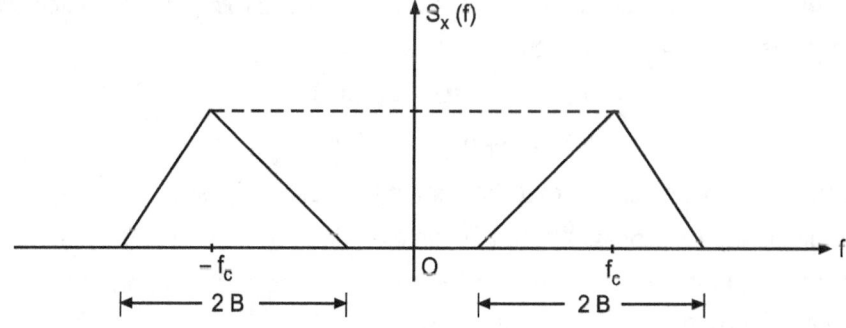

Fig. 6.8 : (a)

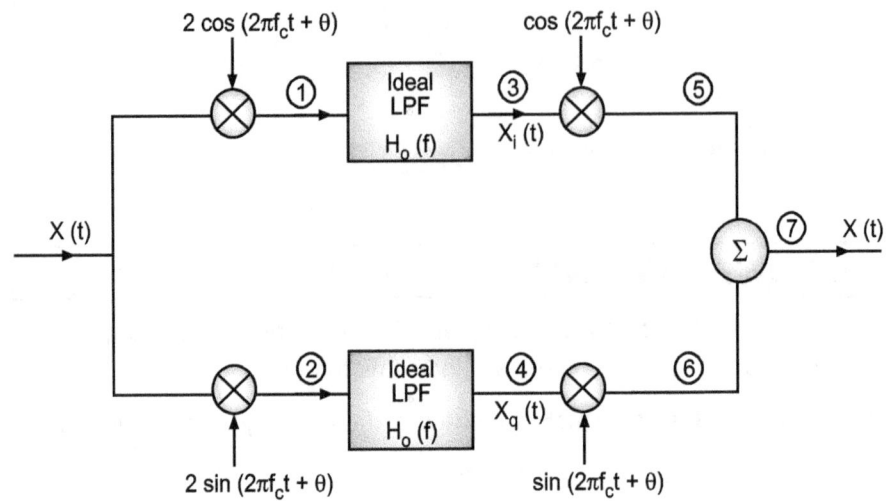

Fig. 6.8 : (b)

- Hence, the signals at various points in the system are as below :
- We will use the result $g(t) \delta(t - t_0) = g(t_0) \delta(t - t_0)$
- At point (1) $2 \cos(2\pi f_c t_0 + \theta) \delta(t - t_0)$
- At point (2) $2 \sin(2\pi f_c t_0 + \theta) \delta(t - t_0)$
- At point (3) $2 \cos(2\pi f_c t_0 + \theta) h_0(t - t_0)$
- At point (4) $2 \sin(2\pi f_c t_0 + \theta) h_0(t - t_0)$
- At point (5) $2 \sin(2\pi f_c t_0 + \theta) \cos(2\pi f_c t + \theta) h_0(t - t_0)$
- At point (6) $2 \sin(2\pi f_c t_0 + \theta) \sin(2\pi f_c t + \theta) h_0(t - t_0)$
- At point (7) $2 h_0(t - t_0) [\cos(2\pi f_c t_0 + \theta) \cos(2\pi f_c t + \theta)$

$$+ \cos(2\pi f_c t_0 + \theta) \sin(2\pi f_c t + \theta)]$$

$$= 2 h_0(t - t_0) \cos[2\pi f_c (t - t_0)]$$

- Hence, response to the signal $\delta(t - t_0)$ is $2 h_0(t - t_0) \cos 2\pi f_c(t - t_0)$ which shows the system is linear time invariant with

$$h(t) = 2 h_0(t) \cos(2\pi f_c t) \qquad \text{... (6.14)}$$

$$\therefore \qquad H(f) = H_0(f - f_c) + H_0(f + f_c) \qquad \text{... (6.15)}$$

- Above transfer function shows that the system is ideal bandpass filter.
- If we apply bandpass process X(t) to this system, the output will be X(t) itself.
- At point (3) and (4) we have outputs from low pass filters. If these outputs are denoted as $X_i(t)$ and $X_q(t)$, then we can write X(t) as,

$$X(t) = X_i(t) \cos(2\pi f_c t + \theta) + X_q(t) \sin(2\pi f_c t + \theta) \qquad \text{... (6.16)}$$

- X_i (t) and X_q (t) are low pass processes with bandwidth BHz. Since they are outputs of low pass filter of BW = B.

- Comparing equations (6.13) and (6.16), we can conclude that in equation (6.16), θ can take any value. Hence, put θ = 0.

- Let us now specify the two processes $X_{i(t)}$ and $X_{q(t)}$.

- X_i (t) is obtained by multiplying X (t) by 2 cos $(2\pi f_c t + \theta)$ and then passing it through LPF. Let θ be a random variable uniformly distributed over (0, 2π).

- Hence, the PSD of 2X (t) cos $(2\pi f_c t + \theta)$ will be,

$$4 \times \frac{1}{4} [S_X (f + f_c) + S_X (f - f_c)] \qquad \text{... (6.17)}$$

This PSD is S_X (f) shifted up and down by f_c. It shown in Fig. 6.8 (c).

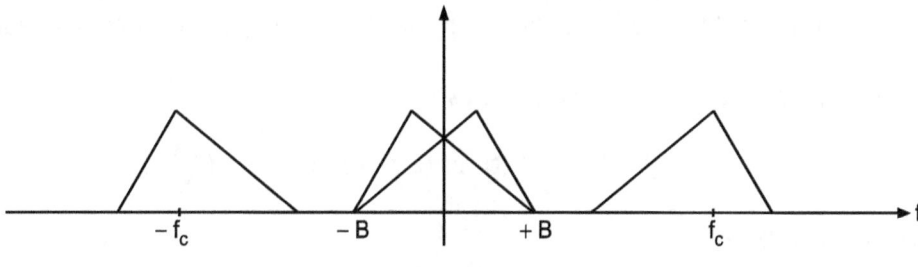

Fig. 6.8 : (c)

- When above PSD is passed through a LPF of bandwidth B. This will be PSD of X_i (t). The output PSD will be,

$$S_{X_i} (f) = \begin{cases} S_X (f + f_c) + S_X (f - f_c) & |f| < B \\ 0 & |f| > B \end{cases} \qquad \text{... (6.18)}$$

- Similarly, we can find S_{X_q} (f) which will be same as S_{X_i} (f) and plotted in Fig. 6.8 (d).

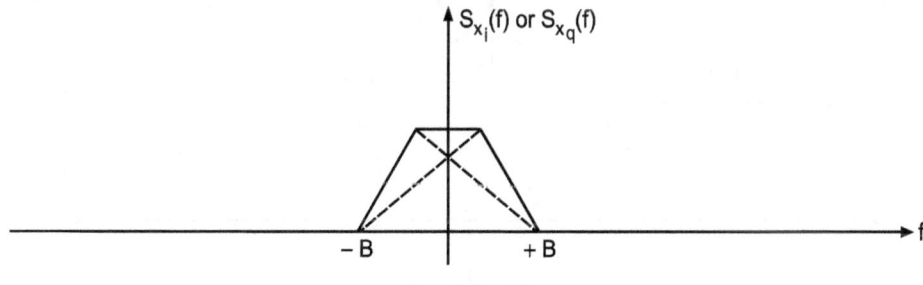

Fig. 6.8 : (d)

- Hence, we can conclude that PSDs of X (t), X_i (t) and X_q (t) are same. Hence, the area under the PSDs will be same.

- Hence,
$$\overline{X_i^2\ (t)} = \overline{X_q^2\ (t)} = \overline{X^2\ (t)} \qquad\qquad ... (6.19)$$

- i.e. mean square values of X (t), X_i (t) and X_q (t) are same.

6.5.1   Ideal Bandpass Filtered White Noise

- We know that the PSD of white noise W(t) is given by $\dfrac{N_0}{2}$.

- Hence, PSD of bandpass white noise is represented as shown in Fig. 6.9 (a).

- Let us now represent this bandpass filtered noise in terms of quadrature components.

∴   Bandpass process can be expressed as,

$$W(t) = W_i\ (t) \cos (2\pi fct) + W_q\ (t) \sin (2\pi fct)$$

- From equation (6.18),

$$S_{W_i}\ (f) = S_{W_q}\ (f) = \begin{cases} S_W\ (f + f_c) + S_W\ (f - f_c) & |f| < B \\ 0 & |f| > B \end{cases} \qquad ... (6.20)$$

∴
$$S_{W_i}\ (f) = S_{W_q}\ (f) = \begin{cases} N_0 & ; & |f| < B \\ 0 & ; & |f| > B \end{cases} \qquad ... (6.21)$$

- This is shown in Fig. 6.9 (b).

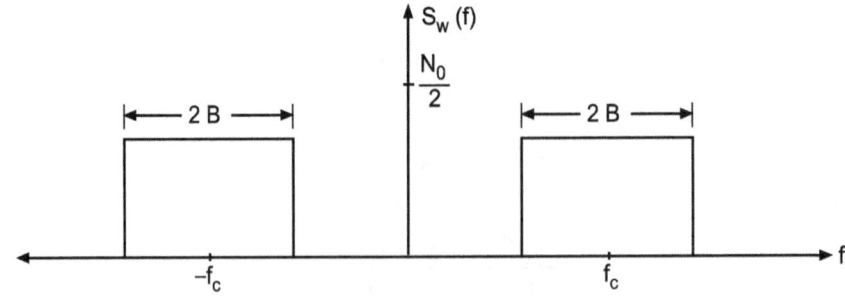

Fig. 6.9 : (a) PSD of bandpass white noise

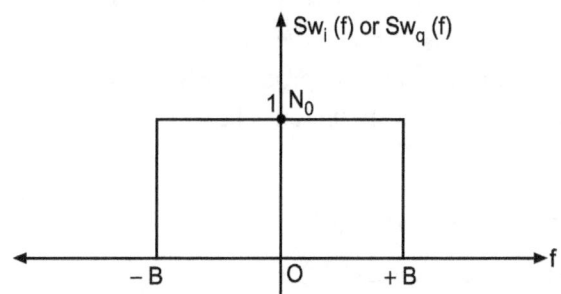

Fig. 6.9 : (b) PSD of quadrature components of white noise

$$\therefore \qquad \overline{W^2} = 2 \times \int_{f_C - B}^{f_C + B} \frac{N_0}{2} \, df$$

$$= 2 N_0 B \qquad \qquad \dots (6.22)$$

$$\therefore \qquad \overline{W_i^2} = \overline{W_q^2} = 2 \int_0^B N_0 \, df$$

$$= 2 N_0 B \qquad \qquad \dots (6.23)$$

$$\therefore \qquad \overline{W^2} = \overline{W_i^2} = \overline{W_q^2} = 2 N_0 B \qquad \qquad \dots (6.24)$$

- To find $R_W(\tau)$ we have to take inverse fourier transform of $S_W(f)$ shown in Fig. 6.9 (a).

$$\therefore \qquad R_W(\tau) = \int_{-f_C - B}^{-f_C + B} \frac{N_0}{2} e^{j2\pi f\tau} \, df + \int_{f - B}^{f_C + B} \frac{N_0}{2} e^{j2\pi f\tau} \, df$$

$$= N_0 B \, \text{sinc} \, (2B\tau) \, [e^{j2\pi f_C \tau} + e^{-j2\pi f_C \tau}]$$

$$\therefore \qquad R_N(\tau) = 2 N_0 B \, \text{sinc} \, (2B\tau) \cos(2\pi f_C \tau) \qquad \qquad \dots (6.25)$$

$$\therefore \qquad \overline{W^2} = R_W(0) = 2 N_0 B$$

- This result is same as (6.22).
- Similarly, we can find $R_{W_i}(\tau)$ and $R_{W_q}(\tau)$ from $S_{W_i}(f)$ or $S_{W_q}(f)$ by taking inverse fourier transform of these functions plotted in Fig. 3.9 (b).
- Since it is rectangular pulse its inverse fourier transform will be sinc.

$$\therefore \qquad R_{W_i}(\tau) = R_{W_q}(\tau) = 2 N_0 B \, \text{sin} \, c \, (2B\tau)$$

$$\therefore \qquad W_i^2 = W_q^2 = R_{W_i}(0) = R_{W_q}(0) = 2 N_0 B$$

- This result is same as (6.23).

6.5.2   Bandpass White Gaussian Random Process

- In the last chapter, we have seen that a random variable X(t) formed by sample function amplitudes at instant of t of a Gaussian process is Gaussian i.e. it has Gaussian PDF.
- A Gaussian random process with uniform PSD is called a white gaussian random process.
- Let us consider a white gaussian process W (t) with PSD $\frac{N_0}{2}$ centered at f_c with bandwidth 2B. Then, we can express W(t) as,

$$W(t) \;=\; W_i\,(t)\,\cos\,(2\pi f c t) + W_q\,(t)\,\sin\,(2\pi f_c t) \qquad\qquad \dots (6.26)$$

- ∴   From equation (6.21) we can write,

$$S_{W_i}\,(f) \;=\; S_{W_q}\,(f) \;=\; \begin{cases} N_0 & ; \quad |f| \geq B \\ 0 & ; \quad |f| > B \end{cases}$$

- Also from equation (6.24) we can write,

$$\overline{W^2} = \overline{W_i}^2 = \overline{W_q}^2 \;=\; 2N_0\,B \qquad\qquad \dots (6.28)$$

- The signal W (t) can be written in polar form as,

- $\left[\text{using } a\cos\theta + b\sin\theta = \sqrt{a^2 + b^2}\,\cos\left(\theta + \tan^{-1}\left(\frac{b}{a}\right)\right) \right]$

- $$W(t) \;=\; r(t)\,\cos\,(2\pi f_c t + \phi)$$

- where,

$$r\,(t) \;=\; \sqrt{W_i^2\,(t) + W_q^2\,(t)} \qquad\qquad \dots (6.29)$$

$$\phi \;=\; -\tan^{-1}\left[\frac{W_q\,(t)}{W_i\,(t)}\right] \qquad\qquad \dots (6.30)$$

- The two processes W_i (t) and W_q (t) are uncorrelated i.e.

$$R_{W_i\,W_q}\,(\tau) \;=\; 0$$

- They also have zero mean and variance $2N_0B$.
- ∴   Their probability density functions are identical and given by,

$$p_{W_i}\,(w) \;=\; p_W\,(w) = \frac{1}{\sigma_W^2\,\sqrt{2\pi}}\;e^{-\,w^2/2\sigma_W^2}$$

   where, $\sigma_W^2 \;=\; 2N_0\,B$

- We have seen that if we have two Gaussian random variables which are uncorrelated, then their polar combination generates Rayleigh distribution.
- Hence, r(t) will have Rayleigh distribution given by,

$$p_R\,(r) \;=\; \frac{r}{\sigma_W^2}\,e^{-\,r^2/2\sigma_W^2} \qquad\qquad \sigma_W^2 = 2N_0\,B$$

and ϕ is uniformly distributed over (0, 2π).

6.5.3 Sinusoidal Signal with Narrow Band Noise

- Let us now consider another interesting case of sinusoid plus a narrow-band gaussian noise given by,

$$y(t) = A \cos (2\pi f_c t + \theta) + W(t)$$

But,
$$W(t) = W_i(t) \cos (2\pi f_c t + \theta) + W_q(t) \sin (2\pi f_c t + \theta)$$

$\therefore$
$$y(t) = [A + W_i(t)] \cos (2\pi f_c t + \theta) + W_q(t) \sin (2\pi f_c t + \theta)$$
$$= r(t) \cos (2\pi f_c t + \theta + \phi(t)]$$

where,
$$r(t) = \sqrt{(A + W_i(t))^2 + W_q^2(t)}$$

$$\phi(t) = -\tan^{-1}\left(\frac{W_q(t)}{A + W_i(t)}\right)$$

$W_i(t)$ and $W_q(t)$ are Gaussian with variance = $2N_0 B$.

- Now –
1. The mean of $A + W_i(t)$ is A.
2. The mean of $W_q(t)$ is 0.

3. The variance of $W_q(t)$ and $W_i(t)$ is $2N_0 B = \sigma_w^2$.

- Hence, we can write using derivatives of Rayleighs density function,

$$p_{r\theta}(r, \theta) = \frac{r}{2\pi\sigma_w^2} e^{-(r^2 - 2Ar \cos \phi(t) + A^2)/2\sigma_w^2}$$

$\therefore$
$$p_R(r) = \int_{-\pi}^{\pi} p_R(r, \theta) \, d\theta$$

$$= \frac{r}{\sigma_w^2} e^{-(r^2 + A^2)/2\sigma_w^2} \left[\frac{1}{2\pi} \int_{-\pi}^{\pi} e^{(Ar/r^2) \cos \theta} \, d\theta \right]$$

- The integration in brackets is defined as $I_0\left(\frac{rE}{\sigma_w^2}\right)$ where, I_0 is modified zero-order Bessel function of the first kind.

- This is known as Rice density or rician density.

- For large sinusoidal signal ($A \gg \sigma_w$). It can be shown that,

$$I_0\left(\frac{Ar}{\sigma_w^2}\right) \cong \sqrt{\frac{\sigma_w^2}{2\pi Ar}} \, e^{Ar/\sigma_w^2}$$

and
$$p_R(r) \cong \frac{1}{\sigma\sqrt{2\pi}} e^{-(r-A)^2/2\sigma_w^2}$$

which is very nearly a Gaussian density function.
We can obtain $p_\phi(\theta)$ as

$$p_\phi(\theta) = \int_0^\infty p_{R_\phi}(r, \theta)\, dr$$

$$\therefore \quad p_\phi(\theta) = \frac{1}{2\pi} e^{-A/2\sigma_w^2}$$

$$\left\{ 1 + \frac{A}{\sigma_w}\sqrt{2\pi}\cos\theta\, e^{A^2\cos^2\theta/2\sigma_w^2}\left[1 - Q\left(\frac{A\cos\theta}{\sigma_w}\right)\right]\right\}$$

SOLVED EXAMPLES

Problem 6.1 :

Calculate the thermal noise voltage generated by a resistor connected across a capacitor C.

Solution : The Fig. 6.10 (a) shows RC circuit and its equivalent with thermal noise voltage is shown in Fig. 6.10 (b).

$$S_n(f) = 2KRT$$

where,
$$K = \text{Boltzman's constant} = 1.38 \times 10^{-23}$$
$$T = \text{Ambient temperature in } °K \text{ of circuit in Fig. 6.9 (b)}$$

The transfer function is given by,

$$H(f) = \frac{1}{1 + j2\pi fRC}$$

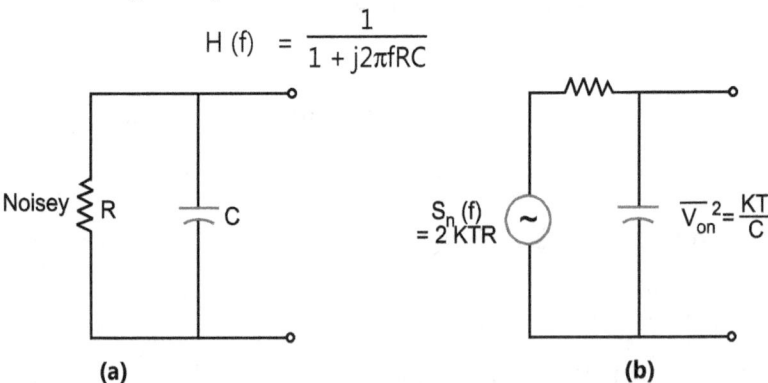

(a)	(b)

Fig. 6.10

Output PSD will be,

$$\therefore \quad S_{no}(f) = \left|H(f)\right|^2 S_n(f)$$

$$= \left|\frac{1}{1 + j2\pi fRC}\right| \times 2KTR$$

$$= \frac{2KRT}{(1 + (2\pi fRC)^2)} = \frac{2KTR}{1 + \left(\dfrac{f}{B}\right)^2}$$

where,
$$B = \frac{1}{2\pi RC}$$

The inverse Fourier transform of $S_{no}(f)$

$$R_{no}(\tau) = 2KRT\pi B \, e^{-2\pi B|\tau|} = 2KRT\pi \times \frac{1}{2\pi RC} e^{-2\pi \times \frac{1}{2\pi RC}|\tau|}$$

$$= \frac{KT}{C} e^{-|\tau|/RC}$$

$$\therefore \qquad V_{on}^2 = R_{on}(0)$$

$$\therefore \qquad V_{on} = \sqrt{\frac{KT}{C}}$$

Problem 6.2 :

Calculate the thermal noise voltage generated by resistor $R = 1\ k\Omega$ across a capacitor of 0.1 µF at room temperature.

Solution : Refer solution to Example 6.3.

$$V_{on} = \sqrt{\frac{KT}{C}}$$

$$\therefore \qquad \text{Given : } C = 0.1\ \mu F$$
$$T = 300°K$$
$$K = 1.38 \times 10^{-23}\ J/k$$

$$\therefore \qquad V_{on} = \sqrt{\frac{1.38 \times 300 \times 10^{-23}}{0.1 \times 10^{-6}}}$$

$$= 0.2\ \mu V$$

Problem 6.3 :

A random process X(t) with PSD shown in Fig. 6.11 (a) is passed through a bandpass filter shown in Fig. 6.10 (b). Determine PSDs and mean square values of quadrature components of output process. Assume centre frequency in representation to be 0.5 MHz.

Solution : A bandpass filter shown in Fig. 6.11 (b) is ideal bandpass filter. Hence, the PSDs of quadrature components are given by,

$$S_{X_i}'(f) = S_{X_q}'(f) = \begin{cases} S_X(f + f_c) + S_X(f - f_c) & ; \quad |f| \le B \\ 0 & ; \quad |f| > B \end{cases}$$

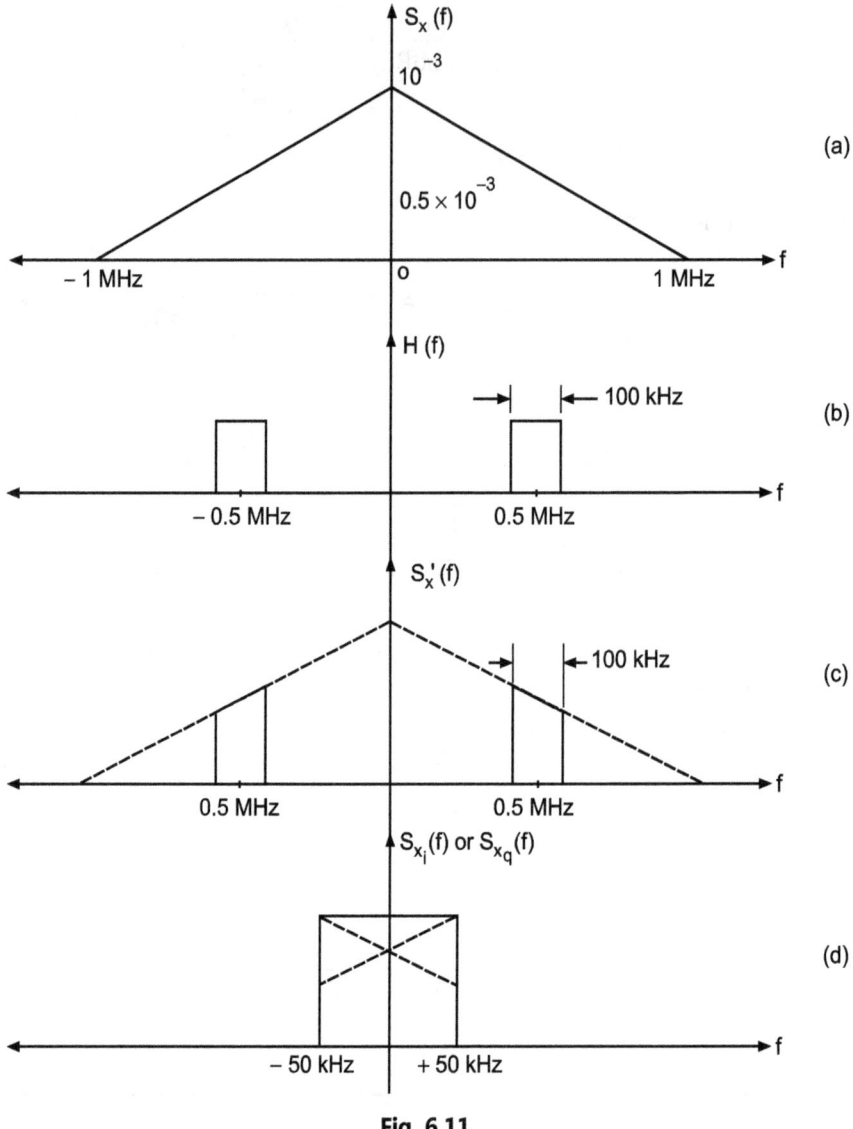

Fig. 6.11

where, $S_X'(f)$ is bandpass filtered PSD of X(t) whch is shown in Fig. 6.11 (c).

$$S_{X_i}'(f) = S_{X_q}'(f) = \begin{cases} 0.5 \times 10^{-3} & ; \quad |f| \leq 50 \\ 0 & ; \quad \text{Otherwise} \end{cases}$$

Mean square values are

$$\overline{X'^2} = \overline{X_i'^2} = \overline{X_q'^2} = 2 \times \int_0^{50} 0.5 \times 10^{-3} \, df$$

$$= 2 \times 0.5 \times 10^{-3} \times 50 = 50 \times 10^{-3} \text{ V}^2$$

$$= 0.05 \text{ V}^2$$

Ch. 6 | 6.18

SOLVED UNIVERSITY QUESTIONS

U.Q. 1 : Show that a random process X(t) can be represented in terms of its quadrature components. **(8 marks) (May 2006)**

Solution : Refer Section 6.5.

May 2012

U.Q. 2 : A random process g(t) has power spectral density G(f) = η/2 for −∞ ≤ f ≤ ∞. The random process is passed through a low pass filter with transfer function H(f) = 2 for −f_m ≤ f ≤ f_m and H(f) = 0 otherwise. Find the psd of the wave at the output of filter. **(8)**

Solution : Refer Example 6.1.

Dec. 2012

U.Q. 3 : Consider a Gaussian noise n(t) with zero mean and the power spectral density $S_N(f)$ shown in figure.
(i) Find the probability density function of the envelope of n(t).
(ii) What are the mean and variance of this envelope? **(8)**

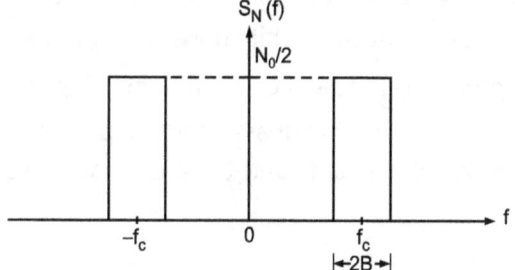

Fig. 6.12

Solution :   Refer Sections 6.5.1 and 6.5.2.

U.Q. 4 : Explain narrowband Noise and represent an narrowband noise in terms of inphase and quadrature components. **(8)**

Solution : Refer Section 6.5.

U.Q. 5 : A random telegraph signal x(t), characterized by the autocorrelation function Rx(τ) = exp (− 2v |τ|) where, v is constant is applied to the low-pass RC filter of figure. Determine the power spectral density and auto correlation function of the random process at the filter output. **(8)**

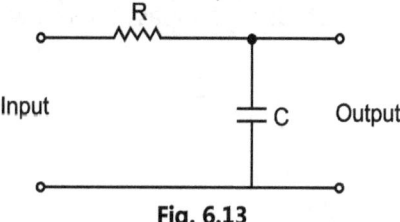

Fig. 6.13

Solution : Refer Example 6.2.

May 2014

U.Q. 6 : What is noise? Explain in detail different type of noise   **[8]**
Solution :   Refer Example 6.2 and 6.3.

SUMMARY

1. Noise is unwanted form of energy which tends to interfere with transmission and processing of signals.
2. Noise can be external or internal.
3. Short noise, thermal noise and examples of internal noise.
4. Noise is an idealised form is called white noise.
5. The PDF of white gaussian noise is specified as $S_w(f) = \dfrac{N_0}{2}$ and the autocorrelation function is given by $R_w(\tau) = \dfrac{N_0}{2}\delta(\tau)$.
6. The noise equivalent bandwidth is the bandwidth of an ideal 10 W pass filter with the same gain that would pass as much as white noise power as the filter under test.
7. A bandpass random process can be expressed in terms of quadrature components.
8. The power spectral densities of bandpass random process X(t) and its quadrature components $X_i(t)$ and $X_q(t)$ are same and the mean square values of $X_i(t)$, $X_q(t)$ and X(t) are also same.

EXERCISE

1. Explain why thermal noise is modelled as white noise.
2. Write short note on White Gaussian Noise.
3. What is Noise equivalent bandwidth ? Derive its expression.
4. Explain how bandpass process is expressed in terms of quadrature phase components.
5. Prove that PSDs and mean square values of bandpass process and its quadrature components are same.
6. Prove that mean square value of ideal bandpass filtered white noise is $N_0 B$ where, B is bandwidth of the filter.

CHAPTER 7
DETECTION THEORY AND SIGNAL SPACE

7.1 INTRODUCTION

Many signal processing applications involve decision making at some stage. The electronic signal processing systems such as communication, radar, image processing, speech etc. require detection of an event so that more information can be gathered further.

The problem of detection can be solved using statistical theory as there is randomness involved in the same. The statistical theory used to decide which event has occurred is known as detection theory, decision theory or hypotheses testing.

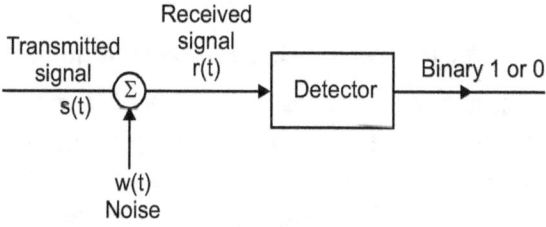

Fig. 7.1 (a) : Baseband receiver

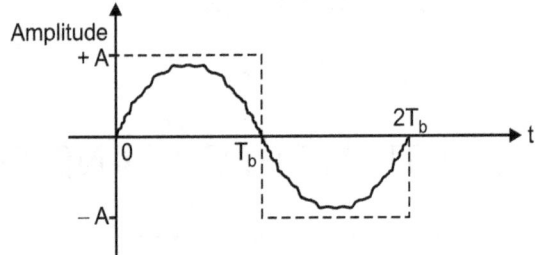

Fig. 7.1 (b) : Received waveform for binary 1 and 0

In digital communication, you have already studied the detection mechanism in case of baseband signal, BPSK, BFSK or QPSK receivers. In baseband receiver (Fig. 7.1), the task of the detector was to decide which of the two signals +A or −A was transmitted. The decision is to be made in presence of noise and distortion caused by channel.

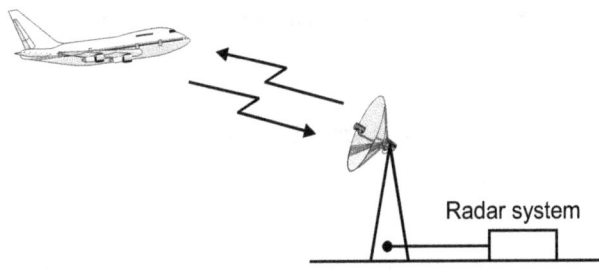

Fig. 7.2 (a) : Radar system

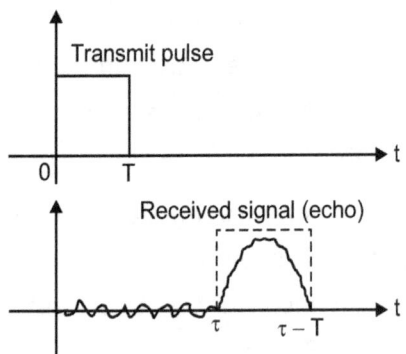

Fig. 7.2 (b) : Transmit and received waveform

In radar, we have to determine the presence or absence of target aircraft as shown in Fig. 7.2. The transmitted signal (pulse) is echoed by the target if present otherwise there will be no echo. The task of radar system is to decide whether the received signal is only noise (No target) or it is noise mixed with echo (Target present). Once the target is detected the further task can be estimation of speed, range etc. which comes under estimation theory.

The decision making in above two cases is between two events only. There can be problem of detection over multiple cases. For example, M-ary PSK where, we have to detect which of the M possible waveforms was transmitted. Another example can be identification of digits from '0' to '9' by a speaker.

In order to solve the problem, we need to have some data available to us. The signal will be available e.g. received signal added with noise in case of BPSK receiver. Since, we will be using digital signal processing technique, the waveform will be available in the form of digital signal i.e. data set or the time series $\{x[0], x[1], ..., x[N-1]\}$. Our task is to arrive at a function which satisfies the data set and then make a decision. As already, pointed out the data are random in nature, statistical approach is used to determine the function. It is called theory of statistical hypotheses testing.

The basic components of decision theory problem are shown in Fig. 7.3.

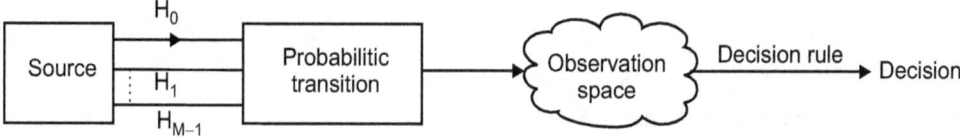

Fig. 7.3 : Components of decision theory problem

Source generates an output. These outputs are called hypotheses. The output can be anyone of the M hypotheses. $H_0, H_1, H_2, ..., H_{M-1}$. In simplest case, there will be two choices H_0 and H_1.

(i)   In radar system, we try to decide whether target is present (Hypotheses H_1) or target is absent (Hypotheses H_0).

(ii) In binary baseband, digital system when one is transmitted, we call it as H_1 and when zero is transmitted it will be H_0.

(iii) In speaker classification problem, if there are three speakers : Indian, Japanese, American and either male or female, there will be six hypotheses.

Probabilistic Transition : It is a device which knows which hypotheses is true. Based on this knowledge, it generates a point in the observation space according to some probability law.

After observing the outcome in observation space, the decision is made in favour of one of the hypotheses. For this, a decision rule needs to be formulated. The decision rule assigns each point in the observation space to one of the hypotheses.

7.2   LIKELIHOOD RATIO TESTING

We have seen that, hypotheses testing problem is nothing but deciding which of the M hypotheses are correct. Let us consider a simple hypotheses testing problem in which there are two hypotheses H_0 and H_1. Let the observed value in the observation space is denoted by y. In case of digital baseband system,

$$\text{Hypotheses } H_1 \; : \; \text{Transmission of one}$$
$$H_0 \; : \; \text{Transmission of zero} \qquad \text{... (7.1)}$$

The observed value y will be,

$$y \; = \; 1 + N$$
or $$y \; = \; 0 + N \qquad \text{... (7.2)}$$

where, N is noise component which is random in nature.

Thus, the observed value 'Y' can be any one of the range of values depending on noise added. The range of values y takes is observation space. Now, we need to decide what was transmitted signal. That is which of the two hypotheses H_0 and H_1 is correct. For this, we need some decision rules. This decision rule can be based on any one of the following criteria :

(i)   Maximum Aposteriori Probability (MAP).

(ii)   Likelihood Ratio Test (LRT).

(iii) Minimum Error Test.

Let us consider these tests one by one.

(i)   MAP :

The decision rule for selecting one of the two hypotheses is based on observed value y which is most likely.

Thus, the decision rule is

$$\text{Choose } H_0 \text{ if } p(H_0|y) > p(H_1|y) \qquad \text{... (7.3)}$$
$$\text{and choose } H_1 \text{ if } p(H_1|y) > p(H_0|y) \qquad \text{... (7.4)}$$

Above decision rule can be written as,

$$\text{Choose } H_0 \text{ if } \frac{p(H_1|y)}{p(H_0|y)} < 1 \qquad \text{... (7.5)}$$

$$\text{and choose } H_1 \text{ if } \frac{p(H_1|y)}{p(H_0|y)} > 1 \qquad \text{... (7.6)}$$

In short,

$$\boxed{\begin{array}{c} H_1 \\ \dfrac{p(H_1|y)}{p(H_0|y)} \; \begin{array}{c} > \\ < \end{array} \; 1 \\ H_0 \end{array}} \qquad \text{... (7.7)}$$

This criterion is called Maximum Aposteriori Probability (MAP) Test.

> **Note :** $p_{H_0|Y}(H_0|y)$ is probability of selecting hypotheses H_0 given observation y. This will be denoted as $p(H_0|y)$. Similarly, $p_{H_1|Y}(H_1|y)$ is probability of selecting by hypothesis H_1 given observation y. This will be denoted as $p(H_1|y)$.

(ii) LRT (Ideal Observer) :

Now, according to Bayes' Rule,

$$p(A|B) \; = \; \frac{p(B|A)\, p(A)}{p(B)} \qquad \qquad \text{... (7.8)}$$

Hence, we can write,

$$p(H_0|y) \; = \; \frac{p(y|H_0)\, p(H_0)}{p(y)} \qquad \qquad \text{... (7.9)}$$

and

$$p(H_1|y) \; = \; \frac{p(y|H_1) \cdot p(H_1)}{p(y)} \qquad \qquad \text{... (7.10)}$$

$$\therefore \quad \frac{p(H_1|y)}{p(H_0|y)} \; = \; \frac{p(y|H_1)}{p(y|H_0)} \cdot \frac{p(H_1)}{p(H_0)} \qquad \qquad \text{... (7.11)}$$

where, $p(H_0)$ and $p(H_1)$ are called priori probabilities and $p(y|H_0)$ and $p(y|H_1)$ are called **conditional probabilities**.

> **Note :** $p_{Y|H_0}(y|H_0)$ will be denoted as $p(y|H_0)$.
>
> and $p_{Y|H_1}$ will be denoted as $p(y|H_1)$.

From equations (7.7) and (7.11), we can write,

$$\therefore \quad \frac{p(y|H_1)}{p(y|H_0)} \cdot \frac{p(H_1)}{p(H_0)} \; \underset{H_0}{\overset{H_1}{\underset{<}{>}}} \; 1 \qquad \qquad \text{... (7.12)}$$

$$\therefore \quad \frac{p(y|H_1)}{p(y|H_0)} \; \underset{H_0}{\overset{H_1}{\underset{<}{>}}} \; \frac{p(H_0)}{p(H_1)} \qquad \qquad \text{... (7.13)}$$

Thus, we have two ratios.

$$\Lambda_1(y) \; = \; \frac{p(y|H_1)}{p(y|H_0)} \qquad \qquad \text{... (7.14)}$$

$$\Lambda_0(y) \; = \; \frac{p(y|H_0)}{p(y|H_1)} \qquad \qquad \text{... (7.15)}$$

We can write the criteria in equation (7.12) as below.

Choose H_1,   if $\dfrac{p(y|H_1)}{p(y|H_0)} > \dfrac{p(H_0)}{p(H_1)}$ ... (7.16)

i.e.   if $\Lambda_1(y) > \dfrac{p(H_0)}{p(H_1)}$ ... (7.17)

Choose H_0,   if $\dfrac{p(y|H_0)}{p(y|H_1)} > \dfrac{p(H_1)}{p(H_0)}$ ... (7.18)

i.e.   if $\Lambda_0(y) > \dfrac{p(H_1)}{p(H_0)}$ ... (7.19)

The ratios in equations (7.14) and (7.15) are called **Likelihood ratios**.

The decision rule based on these ratios given in equations (7.17) and (7.19) are called **Likelihood ratio tests**.

The receiver performing these tests is called **Ideal observer**.

This is equivalent to Maximum Aposteriori Probability (MAP) detection.

Instead of using two ratios Λ_1 and Λ_0, we will be using Λ_1 only and it will be denoted as $\Lambda(y)$.

If we take log of both sides of equation (7.13), we get,

$$ln\left(\frac{p(y|H_1)}{p(y|H_0)}\right) \underset{H_0}{\overset{H_1}{\underset{<}{>}}} ln\left[\frac{p(H_0)}{p(H_1)}\right] \qquad \text{... (7.20a)}$$

This is called log likelihood ratio test.

It is also written as

$$ln(\Lambda(y)) \underset{H_0}{\overset{H_1}{\underset{<}{>}}} ln(\eta) \qquad \text{... (7.20b)}$$

where, $\quad \Lambda(y) = \dfrac{p(y|H_1)}{p(y|H_0)}$ and $\eta = \dfrac{p(H_0)}{p(H_1)}$

(iii) Minimum Error Test :

We can use another decision rule based on minimum error criteria. In this case, γ is a threshold selected for decision making such that overall error probability is minimum.

Thus, decision rule is,

	Choose H_1,	if $y > \gamma$	... (7.21)
and	choose H_0,	if $y \le \gamma$	... (7.22)

The conditional probabilities, $p(y|H_0)$ and $p(y|H_1)$ are known to be Guassian distributed as shown in Fig. 7.4.

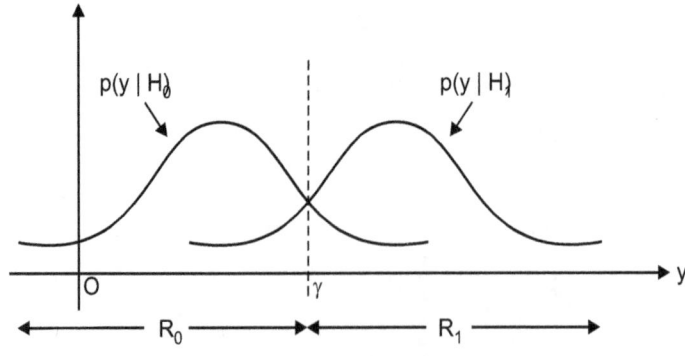

Fig. 7.4 : Conditional probabilities

The threshold γ divides the conditional probabilities in two regions R_0 and R_1. If the observation $y > \gamma$ decision will be made in favour of H_1 and if the observation $y < \gamma$ decision will be made in favour of H_0. The choice of γ has to be such that the chance of error is minimum. There can be two kinds of errors that can occur in this decision-making.

(i) If H_0 is true and we make decision in favour of H_1 because $y > \gamma$ i.e. observation y lies in region R_1.

(ii) If H_1 is true and we make decision in favour of H_0 because $y \leq \gamma$ i.e. observation y lies in region R_0.

The probability that $y > \gamma$ when H_0 is true is given by,

$$p(H_1|H_0) = p(y > \gamma|\ H_0) = p_{e_0} = \int_{R_1} p(y|H_0)\ dy \qquad \ldots (7.23)$$

$$\therefore \qquad p_{e_0} = \int_{\gamma}^{\infty} p(y|H_0)\ dy \qquad \ldots (7.24)$$

The probability that $y \leq \gamma$ when H_1 is true is given by,

$$p(H_0|H_1) = p(y \leq \gamma|H_1) = p_{e_1} = \int_{R_0} p(y|H_1)\ dy \qquad \ldots (7.25)$$

$$\therefore \qquad p_{e_1} = \int_{-\infty}^{\gamma} p(y|H_1)\ dy \qquad \ldots (7.26)$$

The total error probability is given by,

$$p_e = \text{Prob } \{H_0 \text{ is true and choose } H_1\} + \text{Prob } \{H_1 \text{ is true and choose } H_0\}$$

$$p_e = p(H_0) \cdot p_{e_0} + p(H_1)\ p_{e_1} \qquad \ldots (7.27)$$

We have, from equations (7.24), (7.26) and (7.27),

$$p_e = p(H_0) \int_{\gamma}^{\infty} p(y|H_0)\ dy + p(H_1) \int_{-\infty}^{\gamma} p(y|H_1)\ dy \qquad \ldots (7.28)$$

$$= p(H_0) \left[1 - \int_{-\infty}^{\gamma} p(y|H_0)\ dy \right] + p(H_1) \int_{-\infty}^{\gamma} p(y|H_1)\ dy$$

$$\ldots (7.29)$$

The minimum value of p_e can be obtained by setting $\dfrac{dp_e}{d\gamma} = 0$.

$$\therefore \qquad \frac{dp_e}{d\gamma} = 0 - p(H_0)\,p(\gamma|H_0) + p(H_1)\,p(\gamma_0|H_0) = 0 \qquad \text{... (7.30)}$$

$$\therefore \qquad p(H_0)\,p(\gamma|H_0) = p(H_1)\,p(\gamma|H_1) \qquad \text{... (7.31)}$$

$$\therefore \qquad \frac{p(\gamma|H_1)}{p(\gamma|H_0)} = \frac{p(H_0)}{p(H_1)} = \eta \qquad \text{... (7.32)}$$

Hence, the decision rule will be,

Choose H_1 if, $y > \gamma$

i.e. $\qquad \dfrac{p(y|H_1)}{p(y|H_0)} > \eta \qquad \qquad$ ... (7.33)

Choose H_0 if, $y \le \gamma$

i.e. $\qquad \dfrac{p(y|H_1)}{p(y|H_0)} \le \eta \qquad \qquad$ ... (7.34)

This criteria is same as Maximum Aposteriori Probability (MAP) and Likelihood Ratio Test. Hence, Minimum error criteria, MAP and LRT are similar.

SOLVED PROBLEMS

Example 7.1 :

Consider a binary digital communication system, which transmits signal over symbol interval (0, T). If received signal is corrupted by additive white Gaussian noise (AWGN), determine the threshold.

Solution :

The source in binary digital communication system generates two outputs say of amplitude a_0 and a_1. Hence, two hypotheses will be,

$$H_0 : y = a_0$$
$$H_1 : y = a_1$$

The received signal is corrupted by AWGN with zero mean and variance σ^2. Hence, the observed values will be,

$$H_0 : y = a_0 + N$$
$$H_i : y = a_1 + N$$

But N is random. Hence, the conditional probabilities of observation y under two hypotheses are given by,

$$p(y|H_1) = \frac{1}{\sqrt{2\pi\sigma^2}} e^{-(y-a_1)^2/2\sigma^2}$$

and $\qquad p(y|H_0) = \dfrac{1}{\sqrt{2\pi\sigma^2}} e^{-(y-a_0)^2/2\sigma^2}$

Hence, the likelihood ratio will be,

$$\frac{p(y|H_1)}{p(y|H_0)} = \frac{e^{-(y-a_1)^2/2\sigma^2}}{e^{-(y-a_0)^2/2\sigma^2}}$$

$$\therefore \quad \frac{p(y|H_1)}{p(y|H_0)} = e^{-\frac{(y-a_1)^2}{2\sigma^2} + \frac{(y-a_0)^2}{2\sigma^2}}$$

According to Likelihood ratio test,

$$\frac{p(y|H_1)}{p(y|H_1)} \mathop{\gtrless}_{H_0}^{H_1} \frac{p(H_0)}{p(H_1)} = \frac{P_0}{P_1}$$

$$\therefore \quad e^{-\frac{(y-a_1)^2}{2\sigma^2} + \frac{(y-a_0)^2}{2\sigma^2}} \mathop{\gtrless}_{H_0}^{H_1} \frac{P_0}{P_1}$$

Taking natural log of both sides,

$$-\frac{(y-a_1)^2}{2\sigma^2} + \frac{(y-a_0)^2}{2\sigma^2} \mathop{\gtrless}_{H_0}^{H_1} \ln\left(\frac{P_0}{P_1}\right)$$

$$\therefore \quad \frac{y(a_1-a_0)}{\sigma^2} - \frac{a_1^2 - a_0^2}{2\sigma^2} \mathop{\gtrless}_{H_0}^{H_1} \ln\left(\frac{P_0}{P_1}\right)$$

$$\therefore \quad y \mathop{\gtrless}_{H_0}^{H_1} \frac{\sigma^2}{a_1-a_0}\ln\left(\frac{P_0}{P_1}\right) + \frac{a_1+a_0}{2}$$

Thus, observed value y is compared with threshold $\gamma = \dfrac{\sigma^2}{a_1-a_0}\ln\left(\dfrac{P_0}{P_1}\right) + \dfrac{a_1+a_0}{2}$ to decide

whether H_1 or H_0 is true.

If $P_0 = P_1 = \dfrac{1}{2}$, then the decision rule becomes,

$$y \mathop{\gtrless}_{H_0}^{H_1} \frac{a_0+a_1}{2}$$

where threshold $\qquad\qquad \gamma = \dfrac{a_0+a_1}{2}$.

Example 7.2 :

In a binary digital communication system, verify that threshold $\gamma = \dfrac{a_0 + a_1}{2}$ gives minimum error probability. Also calculate the minimum error probability where a_0 and a_1 are amplitudes of two transmitted signals over the interval [0, T].

Solution :

As seen above in binary digital communication system, the received signal samples under two hypotheses are

$$H_0 : y = a_0 + N$$

$$H_1 : y = a_1 + N$$

where, N is AWGN with zero mean and variance σ^2.

There will be two kinds of errors that can occur i.e. when H_1 is true and H_0 is chosen or when H_0 true, H_1 is chosen. The total error probability will be,

$$p_e = p(H_0|H_1)\, p(H_1) + p(H_1|H_0) \cdot p(H_0)$$

Let y_0 be the threshold which divides the observation space into two regions R_0 and R_1.

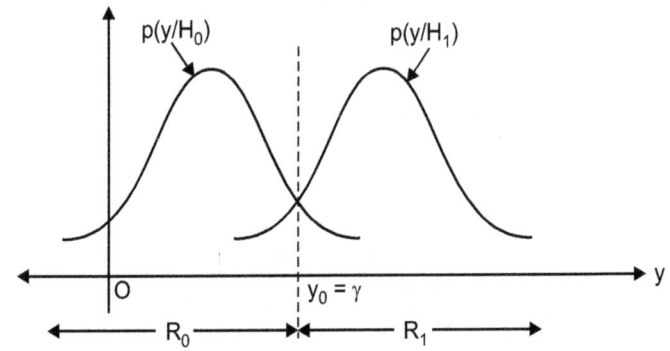

Fig. 7.5

$\therefore$

$$p_e = p(H_1) \cdot \int_{R_0} p(y|H_1)\, dy + p(H_0) \int_{R_1} p(y|H_0)\, dy$$

$$= p(H_1) \int_{\infty}^{y_0} p(y|H_1)\, dy + p(H_0) \int_{y_0}^{\infty} p(y|H_0)\, dy$$

$$= p(H_1) \int_{-\infty}^{y_0} p(y|H_1)\, dy + p(H_0) \left[1 - \int_{-\infty}^{y_0} p(y|H_0)\, dy \right]$$

For minimum p_e, we differentiate above equation w.r.t. y_0 and equate to 0.

$$\frac{dp_e}{dy_0} = p(H_1)\, p(y_0|H_1) + 0 - p(H_0)\, p(y_0|H_0) = 0$$

Let $y_0 = \gamma$

∴ $\qquad\qquad p(H_1)\, p(\gamma/H_1) = p(H_0)\, p(\gamma|H_0)$

∴ $\qquad\qquad \dfrac{p(\gamma|H_1)}{p(\gamma|H_0)} = \dfrac{p(H_0)}{p(H_1)}$

Let $p(H_0) = P_0 \quad p(H_1) = P_1$

∴ $\qquad\qquad \dfrac{e^{-(\gamma - a_1)^2/2\sigma^2}}{e^{-(\gamma - a_0)^2/2\sigma^2}} = \dfrac{p(H_0)}{p(H_1)} = \dfrac{P_0}{P_1}$

∴ $\qquad\qquad e^{\frac{-(\gamma - a_1)^2}{2\sigma^2} + \frac{(\gamma - a_0)^2}{2\sigma^2}} = \dfrac{P_0}{P_1}$

Taking natural log of both sides,

$$-\frac{(\gamma - a_1)^2}{2\sigma^2} + \frac{(\gamma - a_0)^2}{2\sigma^2} = \ln\left(\frac{P_0}{P_1}\right)$$

∴ $\qquad\qquad \dfrac{\gamma(a_1 - a_0)}{\sigma^2} - \dfrac{a_1^2 - a_0^2}{2\sigma^2} = \ln\left(\dfrac{P_0}{P_1}\right)$

∴ $\qquad\qquad \gamma = \dfrac{a_1 + a_0}{2} + \dfrac{\sigma^2}{a_1 - a_0}\ln\left(\dfrac{P_0}{P_1}\right)$

$$\text{If } P_0 = P_1 = \frac{1}{2}$$

$$\gamma = \frac{a_1 + a_0}{2}$$

Thus, the threshold for minimum error probability is $\gamma = \dfrac{a_1 + a_0}{2}$.

To calculate the minimum error probability substitute $\gamma = \dfrac{a_1 + a_0}{2}$ in the following equation.

$$P_{e_{min}} = p(H_1) \int_{-\infty}^{\frac{a_1 + a_0}{2}} p(y|H_1)\, dy + p(H_0) \int_{\frac{a_1 + a_0}{2}}^{\infty} p(y|H_0)\, dy$$

∴ $\qquad\qquad P_{e_{min}} = \dfrac{1}{2} I_1 + \dfrac{1}{2} \cdot I_2$

where,
$$I_1 = \int_{-\infty}^{\frac{a_1 + a_0}{2}} p(y|H_1)\, dy$$

and
$$I_2 = \int_{\frac{a_1 + a_0}{2}}^{\infty} p(y|H_0)\, dy$$

Now,
$$I_1 = \int_{-\infty}^{\frac{a_1 + a_0}{2}} \frac{1}{\sqrt{2\pi\sigma^2}}\, e^{-(y-a_1)^2/2\sigma^2}\, dy$$

Put
$$\frac{y - a_1}{\sigma} = z$$

$\therefore$
$$dy = \sigma dz$$

For $y = -\infty$, $z = -\infty$.

and $y = \dfrac{a_1 + a_0}{2}$ $z = \dfrac{a_0 - a_1}{2\sigma} = -\dfrac{a_1 - a_0}{2\sigma}$

$\therefore$
$$I_1 = \frac{1}{\sqrt{2\pi}} \int_{-\infty}^{-\frac{a_1 - a_0}{2\sigma}} e^{-z^2/2}\, dz = \frac{1}{\sqrt{2\pi}} \int_{\frac{a_1 - a_0}{2\sigma}}^{\infty} e^{-z^2/2}\, dz$$

$\therefore$
$$I_1 = Q\left(\frac{a_1 - a_0}{2\sigma}\right)$$

Since
$$Q(u) = \frac{1}{2}\,\text{erfc}\left(\frac{u}{\sqrt{2}}\right)$$

$$I_1 = \frac{1}{2}\,\text{erfc}\left(\frac{a_1 - a_0}{2\sqrt{2}\,\sigma}\right)$$

Now,
$$I_2 = \int_{\frac{a_1 + a_0}{2}}^{\infty} \frac{1}{\sqrt{2\pi\sigma^2}}\, e^{-(y-a_0)^2/2\sigma^2}\, dy$$

Put
$$z = \frac{y - a_0}{\sigma}$$

$\therefore$
$$dy = \sigma\, dz$$

For $y = \dfrac{a_1 + a_0}{2}$, $z = \dfrac{a_1 - a_0}{2\sigma}$

$y = \infty$, $z = \infty$

$$I_2 = \frac{1}{\sqrt{2\pi}} \int\limits_{\frac{a_1 - a_0}{2\sigma}}^{\infty} e^{-z^2/2}\, dz$$

$$I_2 = Q\left(\frac{a_1 - a_0}{2\sigma}\right)$$

or

$$I_2 = \frac{1}{2} \operatorname{erfc}\left(\frac{a_1 - a_0}{2\sigma}\right)$$

$\therefore$ $$P_{e_{min}} = \frac{1}{2} \times Q\left(\frac{a_1 - a_0}{2\sigma}\right) + \frac{1}{2} Q\left(\frac{a_1 - a_0}{2\sigma}\right)$$

$$P_{e_{min}} = Q\left(\frac{a_1 - a_0}{2\sigma}\right)$$

or $$P_{e_{min}} = \frac{1}{2} \operatorname{erfc}\left(\frac{a_1 - a_0}{2\sqrt{2}\,\sigma}\right)$$

Example 7.3 :

In a digital communication system, the source generates constant voltage A volt under hypotheses H_1 and 0 volt under hypotheses H_0. The observed signal is corrupted by an additive or received White Guassian noise of zero mean and variance σ^2.

(i)   Setup the Likelihood ratio test and determine decision regions.

(ii) Calculate probability of error and probability of detection.

Solution :

(i)   The observed/received signal under the two hypotheses are,

$$H_1 : y = A + N$$
$$H_0 : y = N$$

where N is Additive White Guassian noise with zero mean and variance σ^2. The conditional probabilities under H_1 and H_0 are,

$$p(y|H_0) = \frac{1}{\sqrt{2\pi\sigma^2}} e^{-(y^2/2\sigma^2)}$$

and $$p(y|H_1) = \frac{1}{\sqrt{2\pi\sigma^2}} e^{-(y - A)^2/2\sigma^2}$$

$\therefore$ $\qquad$ $\dfrac{p(y|H_1)}{p(y|H_0)} = e^{-(y-A)^2/2\sigma^2 + (y^2/2\sigma^2)}$

Hence, Likelihood ratio is $\qquad \Lambda(y) = \dfrac{p(y|H_1)}{p(y|H_0)} = e^{-\left(\dfrac{A^2 - 2Ay}{2\sigma^2}\right)}$

Taking natural log of both sides, we get log Likelihood ratio as

$$ln\,[\Lambda(y)] = \frac{Ay}{\sigma^2} - \frac{A^2}{2\sigma^2}$$

The log Likelihood ratio test is

$$ln\,[\Lambda(y)] \underset{H_0}{\overset{H_1}{\underset{<}{>}}} ln\,[\eta]$$

where, $\qquad\qquad\qquad \eta = \dfrac{p(H_0)}{p(H_1)}$

Hence, the Likelihood ratio test is

$$\frac{Ay}{\sigma^2} - \frac{A^2}{2\sigma^2} \underset{H_0}{\overset{H_1}{\underset{<}{>}}} ln\left[\frac{p(H_0)}{p(H_1)}\right]$$

$\therefore$ $\qquad\qquad y \underset{H_0}{\overset{H_1}{\underset{<}{>}}} \dfrac{\sigma^2}{A} ln\left[\dfrac{p(H_0)}{p(H_1)}\right] + \dfrac{A}{2}$

i.e. $\qquad\qquad y \underset{H_0}{\overset{H_1}{\underset{<}{>}}} \dfrac{\sigma^2}{A} ln\,(\eta) + \dfrac{A}{2} = \gamma$

The decision regions are shown in Fig. 7.6.

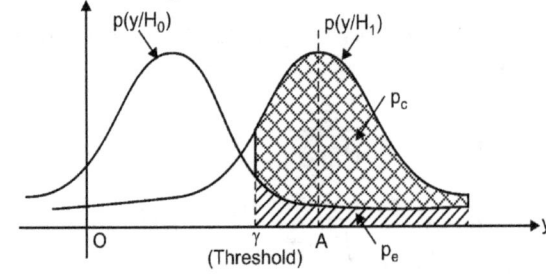

Fig. 7.6 : Decision regions

(ii) The error in this case will be when signal of 0 volt is transmitted (Hypotheses H_1) and decision is in favour of A volt (Hypotheses H_1). The probability of this happening is

$$p_e = p(H_0|H_1) = \int_\gamma^\infty p(y|H_1)\, dy$$

$$= \int_\gamma^\infty \frac{1}{\sqrt{2\pi\sigma^2}} e^{-y^2/2\sigma^2}\, dy$$

$$= Q\left(\frac{\gamma}{\sigma}\right)$$

The correct decision will be when signal of A volt is transmitted (hypotheses H_1) and A volt is detected (Hypotheses H_1).

$$\therefore \qquad p(H_1|H_1) = \int_\gamma^\infty p(y|H_1)\, dy$$

$$\therefore \qquad p_c = \int_\gamma^\infty \frac{1}{\sqrt{2\pi\sigma^2}} e^{-\frac{(y-A)^2}{2\sigma^2}}\, dy$$

$$p_c = Q\left(\frac{\gamma - A}{\sigma}\right)$$

Example 7.4 :

In a digital communication system, the source generates constant voltage A volt under hypotheses H_1 and 0 volt under hypotheses H_0. Before observation, the signal is corrupted by additive White Guassian noise. The received waveform or observed waveform is sampled to obtain 'K' sample values. Set up the Likelihood ratio test and determine decision region.

Solution :

Given :

$$H_1 : y_i = A + N_i \qquad\qquad i = 1, 2, ..., K$$
$$H_0 : y_i = N_i \qquad\qquad i = 1, 2, ..., K$$

The probability density of y_i under each hypotheses is given as,

$$p(y_i|H_0) = \frac{1}{\sqrt{2\pi\sigma^2}} e^{-y_i^2/2\sigma^2}$$

$$p(y_i|H_1) = \frac{1}{\sqrt{2\pi\sigma^2}} e^{-(y_i - A)^2/2\sigma^2}$$

Since, N_i are statistically independent the joint probability of y_i is simply the product of individual probabilities. Hence,

$$p(Y|H_0) = \prod_{i=1}^{K} \frac{1}{\sqrt{2\pi\sigma^2}} e^{(-y_i^2/2\sigma^2)}$$

$$p(Y|H_1) = \prod_{i=1}^{K} \frac{1}{\sqrt{2\pi\sigma^2}} e^{-(y_i - A)^2/2\sigma^2}$$

The Likelihood ratio will be

$$\Lambda(Y) = \frac{\displaystyle\prod_{i=1}^{K} \frac{1}{\sqrt{2\pi\sigma^2}} e^{-(y_i - A)^2/2\sigma^2}}{\displaystyle\prod_{i=1}^{K} \frac{1}{\sqrt{2\pi\sigma^2}} e^{-y_i^2/2\sigma^2}}$$

$$= \frac{e^{-\sum_{i=1}^{K} (y_i - A)^2/2\sigma^2}}{e^{-\sum_{i=1}^{K} y_i^2/2\sigma^2}}$$

$$= e^{-\sum_{i=1}^{K} \frac{(y_i - A)^2}{2\sigma^2} + \sum_{i=1}^{K} y_i^2/2\sigma^2}$$

$$= e^{\sum_{i=1}^{K} \frac{y_i A}{\sigma^2} - \sum_{i=1}^{K} \frac{A^2}{2\sigma^2}}$$

$$\therefore \qquad \Lambda(Y) = e^{\frac{A}{\sigma^2} \sum_{i=1}^{K} y_i - \frac{A^2 \cdot K}{2\sigma^2}}$$

Taking log of both sides,

$$\ln[\Lambda(Y)] = \frac{A}{2\sigma^2} \sum_{i=1}^{K} y_i - \frac{A^2 K}{2\sigma^2}$$

Hence the Likelihood ratio test is

$$\frac{A}{\sigma^2} \sum_{i=1}^{K} y_i - \frac{A^2 K}{2\sigma^2} \underset{H_0}{\overset{H_1}{\gtrless}} \ln(\eta)$$

where,

$$\eta = \frac{p(H_0)}{p(H_1)} = \frac{P_0}{P_1}$$

$$\therefore \qquad \sum_{i=1}^{K} y_i \underset{H_0}{\overset{H_1}{\gtrless}} \frac{\sigma^2}{A} \ln(\eta) + \frac{kA}{2} \qquad \dots \text{(i)}$$

Thus, threshold, $\gamma = \dfrac{\sigma^2}{A} \ln(\eta) + \dfrac{KA}{2}$

Thus, the processor will add the samples and compare it with the threshold to decide whether hypotheses H_1 is true or H_0 is true. The sum of data available is called sufficient statistics.

Equation (i) can also be written as,

$$\frac{1}{K} \sum_{i=1}^{K} y_i \underset{H_0}{\overset{H_1}{\underset{<}{>}}} \frac{\sigma^2}{KA} \ln(\eta) + \frac{A}{2}$$

i.e. $$\bar{Y} \underset{H_0}{\overset{H_1}{\underset{<}{>}}} \frac{\sigma^2}{KA} \ln(\eta) + \frac{A}{2} \qquad \ldots \text{(ii)}$$

Thus, we can take average of the samples and compare it with the threshold given on the right hand side of equation (ii).

7.3   SIGNAL SPACE REPRESENTATION

7.3.1 Representation of Signal

- Consider the conceptual model of a digital communication system shown in Fig. 7.7.

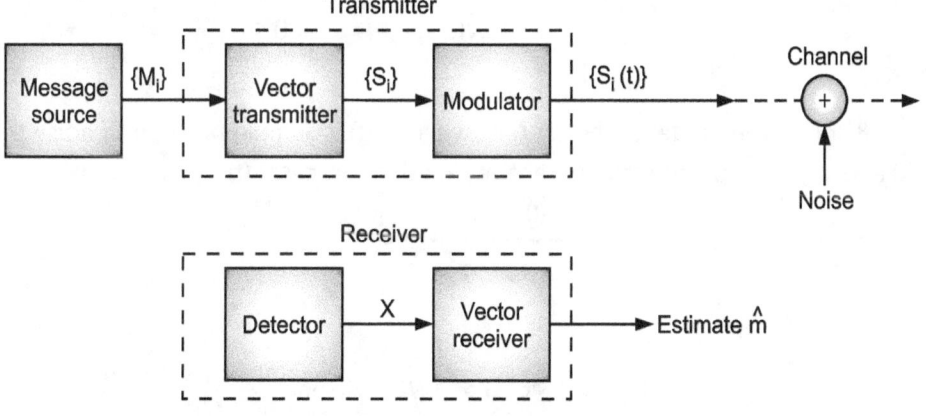

Fig. 7.7 : Conceptual Model of Digital Communication System

- At the transmitter the message source generates M symbols of duration T each.

- Let these symbols be $m_1, m_2, \ldots m_M$.

  e.g. In case of binary source there will be two symbols (1 and 0). In case of quaternary signal the symbols will be 00, 01, 10, 11.

- The vector transmitter produces a vector of real numbers.

$$\mathbf{s_i} = \begin{bmatrix} s_{i1} \\ s_{i2} \\ s_{i3} \\ \vdots \\ \vdots \\ s_{iN} \end{bmatrix} \quad i = 1, 2, 3, \dots, M$$

  where, $N \leq M$

- The modulator constructs the signal $s_i(t)$ of duration T seconds.
- The energy of the signal $s_i(t)$ is

$$E_i = \int_0^T s_i^2(t)\, dt \qquad\qquad i = 1, 2, \dots, M \quad \dots (7.35)$$

- The channel is assumed to have two characteristics :

  (i) It is linear with bandwidth that is large enough to accommodate the transmission of modulator output $s_i(t)$ without distortion.

  (ii) The transmitted signal $s_i(t)$ is affected by additive, zero-mean, stationary, while Gaussian noise process, denoted by w(t).

- The channel is known as Additive White Guassian Noise (AWGN) channel.
- The received random process is,

$$S(t) = S_i(t) + W(t) \qquad\qquad 0 \leq t \leq T$$
$$i = 1, 2, \dots, M \qquad \dots (7.36)$$

- Fig. 7.8 shows the model of the channel where w(t) is sample function of noise process w(t) and x(t) is simple function of received random process x(t).

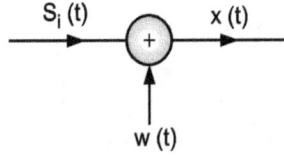

Fig. 7.8 : Model of AWGN Channel

- The receiver observes the received signal x(t) for a duration of T sec. and makes best estimate of the transmitted signal $s_i(t)$.

- Now, let us see how we can design M energy signal for the M symbols such that energy of each signal is limited within the symbol duration.

7.3.2 Gram-Schmidt Orthogonalization

- The principle of Gram-Schmidt Orthogonalization (GSO) states that, any set of M energy signals, {S$_i$(t)}, $1 \le i \le M$ can be expressed as linear combinations of N orthonormal basis functions, where N < M.

- If s$_1$(t), s$_2$(t), ..., s$_M$(t) are real valued energy signals, each of duration 'T' sec,

$$s_i(t) = \sum_{j=1}^{N} s_{ij}\, \phi_j(t); \begin{cases} 0 \le t \le T \\ i = 1, 2, \dots, M \ge N \end{cases} \qquad \dots (7.37)$$

where,

$$s_{ij} = \int_0^T s_i(t)\, \phi_j(t)\, dt; \begin{cases} i = 1, 2, \dots, M \\ j = 1, 2, \dots, N \end{cases} \qquad \dots (7.38)$$

- The ϕ_j(t) are the basis functions and 's$_{ij}$'-s are scalar coefficients. We will consider real-valued basis functions ϕ_j (t)'s which are orthonormal to each other, i.e.,

$$\int_0^T \phi_i(t) \cdot \phi_j(t)\, dt = \begin{cases} 1, \text{ if } i = j \\ 0, \text{ if } i \ne j \end{cases} \qquad \dots (7.39)$$

- Note that each basis function has unit energy over the symbol duration 'T'. Now, if the basis functions are known and the scalars are given, we can generate the energy signals, by following Fig. 7.8. Or, alternatively, if we know the signals and the basis functions, we know the corresponding scalar coefficients (Fig. 7.9).

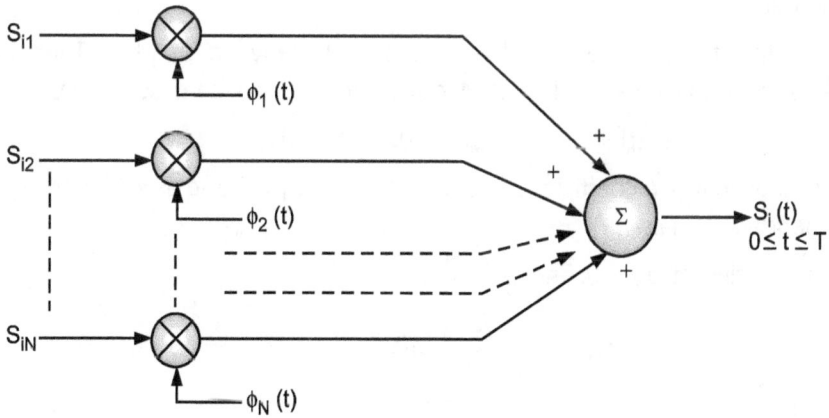

Fig. 7.9 : Pictorial Depiction of Equation (7.31)

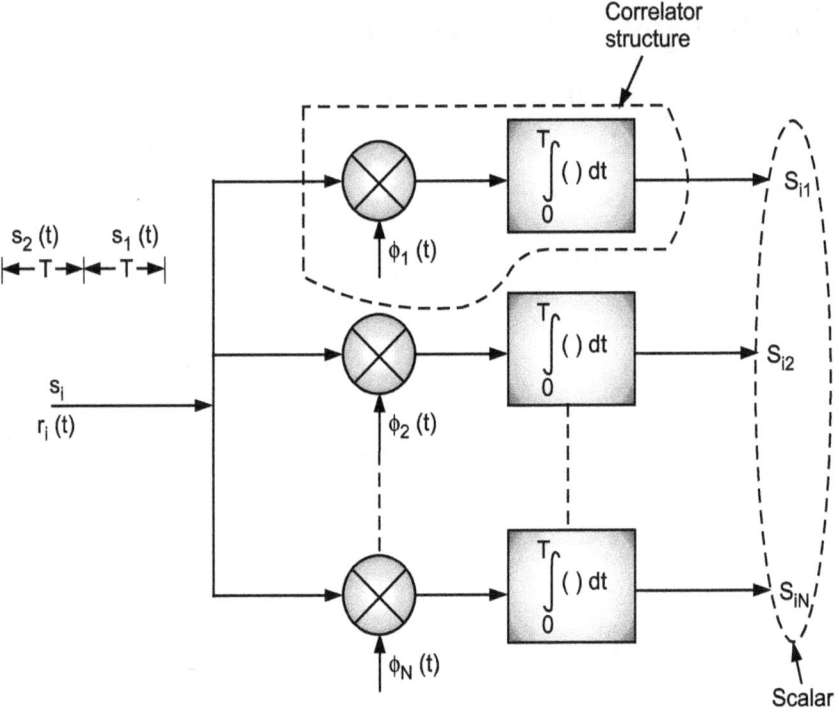

Fig. 7.10 : Pictorial Depiction of Equation (7.38)

Justification for G-S-O Procedure :

Stage – I :

- We show that any given set of energy signals, $\{s_i(t)\}$, $1 \leq i \leq M$ over $0 \leq t < T$, can be completely described by a subset of energy signals whose elements are linearly independent.

- To start with, let us assume that all $s_i(t)$ -s are not linearly independent. Then, there must exist a set of coefficients $\{a_i\}$, $1 < i \leq M$, not all of which are zero, such that,

$$a_1 s_1(t) + a_2 s_2(t) + \ldots + a_M s_M(t) = 0, \quad 0 \leq t < T \qquad \ldots (7.40)$$

- Verify that even if two coefficients are not zero, e.g. $a_1 \neq 0$ and $a_3 \neq 0$, then $s_1(t)$ and $s_3(t)$ are dependent signals.

- Let us arbitrarily set, $a_M \neq 0$. Then,

$$s_M(t) = -\frac{1}{a_M} [a_1 s_1(t) + a_2 s_2(t) + \ldots + a_{M-1} s_{M-1}(t)]$$

$$= -\frac{1}{a_M} \sum_{i=1}^{M-1} a_i s_i(t) \qquad \ldots (7.41)$$

Equation (7.41) shows that $s_M(t)$ could be expressed as a linear combination of other $s_i(t)$ – s, $i = 1, 2, .., (M-1)$.

- Next, we consider a reduced set with $(M - 1)$ signals $\{s_i(t)\}$, $i = 1, 2, ..., (M - 1)$.

- This set may be either linearly independent or not. If not, there exists a set of $\{b_i\}$, $i = 1, 2..., (M - 1)$, not all equal to zero such that,

$$\sum_{i=1}^{M-1} b_i s_i(t) = 0, \qquad\qquad 0 \le t < T \qquad\qquad ...(7.42)$$

- Again, arbitrarily assuming that $b_{m-1} \ne 0$, we may express $s_{M-1}(t)$ as,

$$s_{M-1}(t) = \frac{1}{b_{M-1}} \sum_{i=1}^{M-2} b_i s_i(t) \qquad\qquad ...(7.43)$$

- Now, following the above procedure for testing linear independence of the remaining signals, eventually we will end up with a subset of linearly independent signals. Let $\{s_i(t)\}$, $i = 1, 2, ..., N \le M$ denote this subset.

Stage – II :

- We now show that it is possible to construct a set of 'N' orthonormal basis functions $\psi_1(t), \psi_2(t), ..., \psi_N(t)$ from $\{s_i(t)\}$, $i = 1, 2, ..., N$.

- Let us choose the first basis function as, $\phi_i(t) = \dfrac{s_i(t)}{\sqrt{E_1}}$, where E_1 denotes the energy of the first signal $s_1(t)$, i.e.

$$E_1 = \int_0^T s_1^2(t)\, dt$$

$$\therefore \qquad\qquad s_1(t) = \sqrt{E_1} \cdot \phi_1(t) = s_{11}\phi_1(t) \qquad\qquad ...(7.44)$$

$$\text{where,} \qquad\qquad s_{11} = \sqrt{E_1}$$

- Now, from equation (7.38), we can write,

$$s_{21} = \int_0^T s_2(t)\, \phi_1(t)\, dt \qquad\qquad ...(7.45)$$

- Let us now define an intermediate function :

$$g_2(t) = s_2(t) - s_{21}\phi_1(t); \qquad\qquad 0 \le t < T \qquad\qquad ...(7.46)$$

- Note that,

$$\int_0^T g_2(t)\, \phi_1(t)\, dt = \int_0^T s_2(t)\, c_1(t)\, dt - s_{21} \int_0^T \phi_1(t)\, \phi_1(t)\, dt$$

$$= s_{21} - s_{21} = 0 \rightarrow g_2(t) \text{ Orthogonal to } \phi_1(t);$$

- So, we verified that the function $g_2(t)$ is orthogonal to the first basis function. This gives us a clue to determine the second basis function.

- Now, energy of $g_2(t)$,

$$= \int_0^T g_2^2(t) \, dt$$

$$= \int_0^T [s_2(t) - s_{21} \phi_1(t)]^2 \, dt$$

$$= \int_0^T s_2^2(t) \, dt - 2 \cdot s_{21} \int_0^T s_2(t) \phi_1(t) \, dt + s_{21}^2 \int_0^T \phi_1^2(t) \, dt$$

$$= E_2 - 2 \cdot s_{21}^2 + s_{21}^2 = E_2 - s_{21}^2 \qquad \text{... (7.47)}$$

- So, we now set,

$$\phi_2(t) = \frac{g_2(t)}{\sqrt{\int_0^T g_2^2(t) \, dt}} = \frac{s_2(t) - s_{21}\phi_1(t)}{\sqrt{E_2 - s_{21}^2}} \qquad \text{... (7.48)}$$

and $\qquad E_2 = \int_0^T s_2^2(t) \, dt$: Energy of $s_2(t)$

- Verity that,

$$\int_0^T \phi_2^2(t) = 1, \quad \text{i.e. } \phi_2(t) \text{ is a time limited energy signal of unit}$$

$$\text{energy}$$

and $\qquad \int_0^T \phi_1(t) \cdot \phi_2(t) \, dt = 0 \quad \text{i.e. } \phi_1(t) \text{ and } \phi_2(t) \text{ are orthonormal to each other.}$

- Proceeding in a similar manner, we can determine the third basis function, $\phi_3(t)$. For $i = 3$,

$$g_3(t) = s_3(t) - \sum_{j=1}^{2} s_{3j} \phi_j(t); \qquad 0 \le t < T$$

$$= s_3(t) - [s_{31} \phi_1(t) + s_{32} \phi_2(t)]$$

Ch. 7 | 7.22

where,

$$S_{31} = \int_0^T s_3(t) \, \phi_1(t) \, dt \quad \text{and} \quad S_{32} = \int_0^T s_3(t) \, \phi_3(t) \, dt$$

- It is now easy to identify that,

$$\phi_3(t) = \frac{g_3(t)}{\sqrt{\int_0^T g_3^2(t) \, dt}} \qquad \qquad \text{... (7.49)}$$

- Indeed, in general,

$$\phi_i(t) = \frac{g_i(t)}{\sqrt{\int_0^T g_i^2(t) \, dt}} = \frac{g_i(t)}{\sqrt{Eg_i}} \qquad \qquad \text{... (7.50)}$$

for i= 1, 2, ... , N, where

$$g_i(t) = s_i(t) - \sum_{j=1}^{i-1} s_{ij} \, \phi_j(t) \qquad \qquad \text{... (7.51)}$$

and

$$S_{ij} = \int_0^T s_i(t) \cdot \phi_j(t) \, dt \qquad \qquad \text{... (7.52)}$$

for 1 = 1, 2, ... , N and j = 1, 2, ..., M

- Let us summarize the steps to determine the orthonormal basis functions following the Gram-Schmidt Orthogonalization procedure :

(i)   If the signal set {$s_j(t)$} is known for j = 1, 2,....., M, $0 \le t < T$,

Derive a subset of linearly independent energy signals, {$s_i(t)$}, i = 1, 2,......,   N < M.

(ii) Find the energy of $s_1(t)$ as this energy helps in determining the first basis function $\phi_1(t)$, which is a normalized form of the first signal. Note that the choice of this 'first' signal is arbitrary.

(iii) Find the scalar 's_{21}', energy of the second signal (E 2), a special function '$g_2(t)$' which is orthogonal to the first basis function and then finally the second orthonormal basis function $\phi_2(t)$.

(iv) Follow the same procedure as that of finding the second basis function to obtain the other basis functions.

7.3.3 Conversion of Continuous AWGN of Channel into Vector Channel

- The received signal r(t) in Fig. 7.10 is given by,

$$r(t) = s_i(t) + w(t) \qquad 0 \le t \le T \qquad \ldots (7.53)$$

where, $i = 1, 2, 3, \ldots, M$

$s_i(t)$ is transmitted signal

$w(t)$ is sample function of white Guassian

Noise process $w(t)$ of zero mean and PSD $\dfrac{N_0}{2}$

- The correlator output is given by,

$$r_j = \int_0^T r(t)\, \phi_j(t)\, dt \qquad \ldots (7.54)$$

$$= s_{ij} + w_j \qquad j = 1, 2, 3, \ldots, N \qquad \ldots (7.55)$$

s_{ij} is due to $s_i(t)$

i.e.
$$s_{ij} = \int_0^T s_i(t)\, \phi_j(t)\, dt \qquad \ldots (7.56)$$

w_j is sample value of random variable w_j due to $w(t)$.

i.e.
$$w_j = \int_0^T w(t)\, \phi_j(t)\, dt \qquad \ldots (7.57)$$

- Let R(t) be random process whose sample function is received signal r(t).
- R_j is random variable whose sample value is correlator output $r_j = 1, 2, \ldots, N$.
- R(t) is a Guassian noise process. Hence, R_j is a Guassian random variable for j.
- The random variable wj has mean zero, Since w(t) has zero mean.
- Hence, mean of R_j depends on s_{ij}

$$\therefore \qquad m_{R_j} = E[R_j]$$
$$= E[sij + w_j]$$
$$= E[s_{ij}] + E[w_j]$$
$$= s_{ij} \qquad \ldots (7.58)$$

- Variance is R_j is,

$$\sigma_j^2 = \text{Var}\,[R_j]$$
$$= E[(R_j - s_{ij})^2]$$
$$= E[(w_j + s_{ij} - s_{ij})]$$
$$= E[(w_j + s_{ij} - s_{ij})]$$
$$= E[w_j^2] \qquad \ldots (7.59)$$

- But

$$w_j = \int_0^T w(t)\, \phi_j\, dt$$

-

$$\sigma_{x_j}^2 = E[w_j^2]$$

$$= E\left[\int_0^T w(t)\, \phi_j(t)\, dt \int_0^T w(x)\, \phi_j(x)\, dx\right]$$

$$= E\left[\int_0^T \phi_j(t)\, \phi_j(x)\, w(t)\, w(x)\, dt\, dx\right]$$

$$= \int_0^T \int_0^T \phi_j(t)\, \phi_j(x)\, E[w(t)\, w(x)]\, dt$$

$$= \int_0^T \int_0^T \phi_j(t)\, \phi j(x)\, R_w\,(t,\, x)\, dt\, dx \qquad\qquad ...(7.60)$$

But

$$R_w\,(t,\, x) = \frac{N_0}{2}\, \delta(t - x)$$

$$= \frac{N_0}{2} \int_0^T \int_0^T \phi_j(t)\, \phi_j(x)\, 8(t - u)\, dt\, du$$

$$= \frac{N_0}{2} \int_0^T \phi_j^2(t)\, dt$$

$$= \frac{N_0}{2} \qquad\qquad \text{for all } j \qquad\qquad ...(7.61)$$

- Thus, the correlator outputs (R_j) have variance equal to Power Spectral Density of AWGN i.e. $\frac{N_0}{2}$.

- Since each R_j is Gaussian random variable with mean s_{ij} and variance $N_0/2$, we have the Probability density function.

$$P_R\,(r_j/m_i) = \frac{1}{\sqrt{2\pi\sigma_{R_j}^2}}\, e^{-(r_j - m_{R_j})^2/2\sigma_{R_j}^2}$$

$$P_R\,(r_j/m_i) = \frac{1}{\sqrt{\pi N_0}}\, e^{-(r_j - s_{ij})^2/N_0}$$

$$i = 1, 2, 3, ..., N$$
$$j = 1, 2, 3, ..., M$$

- The probability density function of vector R given that $s_i(t)$ is transmitted is,

$$p_R(R/m_i) = \prod_{j=1}^{N} p_R(r_j/m_i)$$

$$= (\pi N_0)^{-N/2} e^{-\frac{1}{N_0} \sum_{j=1}^{N} (r_j - s_{ij})^2} \quad ... (7.62)$$

$$i = 1, 2, 3, ..., M$$

- Taking log of both sides we get log likelihood function

$$\ln[P_R(r/m_i)] = \ln\left[\frac{1}{\sqrt{\pi N_0}}\right] - \frac{1}{N_0} \sum_{j=1}^{N} (r_j - s_{ij})^2$$

- We can ignore the constant term $\ln\left[\dfrac{1}{\sqrt{\pi N_0}}\right]$ since it is independent of observation and has no relation with m_i.

- Hence the log like bood function is

$$L[m_i] = -\frac{1}{N_0} \sum_{j=1}^{N} (r_j - s_{ij})^2$$

where $i = 1, 2, ... m.$

- The received vector r can also be written as

$$\mathbf{r} = \mathbf{S_i} + \mathbf{W} \qquad i = 1, 2, 3, ...M$$

r is a N dimensional vector.

N is number of basis functions used to formulate the signal vector $\mathbf{s_i}$. Element of $\mathbf{s_i}$ and $\mathbf{w}$ are given as

$$s_{ij} = \int_0^T S_i(t) \, \phi_j(t) \, dt$$

$$w_{ij} = \int_0^T \omega(t) \, \phi_j(t) \, dt$$

7.3.4 Geometric Representation

- Let, for a convenient set of $\{\phi_j(t)\}$, $j = 1, 2, ..., N$ and $0 \leq t < T$

$$s_i(t) = \sum_{j=1}^{N} s_{ij} \phi_j(t), \quad i = 1, 2, ..., M \text{ and } 0 \leq t < T, \text{ such that}$$

$$s_{ij} = \int_0^T s_i(t) \, \phi_j(t) \, dt \qquad ... (7.63)$$

- Now, we can represent a signal $s_i(t)$ as a column vector whose elements are the scalar coefficients s_{ij}, $j = 1, 2, \ldots, N$.

$$s_i = \begin{bmatrix} s_{i1} \\ s_{i2} \\ \vdots \\ \vdots \\ s_{iN} \end{bmatrix} ; i = 1, 2, \ldots, M \qquad \ldots (7.64)$$

- These M energy signals or vectors can be viewed as a set of M points in an N − dimensional Euclidean space, known as the 'Signal Space' (Fig. 7.11). Signal Constellation is the collection of M signals points (or messages) on the signal space.

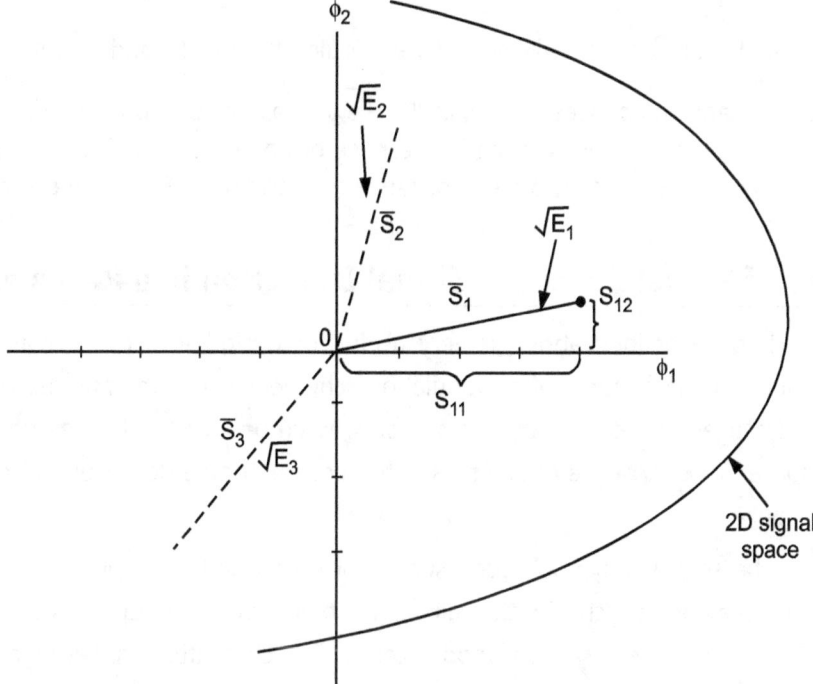

Fig. 7.11 : Sketch of a 2-dimentional-signal space showing three signal vectors, s_1, s_2 and s_3

- Now, the length or *norm* of a vector is denoted as $\| s_i \|$. The squared norm is the inner product of the vector

$$\| s_i \|^2 = (s_i, s_i) = \sum_{j=1}^{N} s_{ij}^2 \qquad \ldots (7.65)$$

- The cosine of the angle between two vectors is defined as

$$\cos (\text{angle between } s_i \text{ and } s_j) = \frac{(s_i, s_j)}{\| s_i \| \, \| s_j \|} \qquad \ldots (7.66)$$

∴ s_i and s_j are orthogonal to each other if (s_i) , $(s_j) = 0$

- If E_i is the energy of the ith signal vector,

$$E_i = \int_0^T s_i^2(t)\, dt = \int_0^T \left[\sum_{j=1}^N s_{ij}\, \phi_j(t)\right]\left[\sum_{k=1}^N s_{ik}\, \phi_k(t)\right] dt \qquad \ldots (7.67)$$

$$= \sum_{j=1}^N \sum_{k=1}^N s_{ij}\, s_{ik} \int_0^T \phi_j(t)\, \phi_k(t) \text{ as } \{\phi_j(t)\} \text{ forms an ortho-normal}$$

$$\text{set} \qquad\qquad \ldots (7.68)$$

- For a pair of signals $s_i(t)$ and $s_k(t)$, $\|s_i - s_k\|^2 = \sum_{j=1}^N (s_{ij} - s_{kj})^2 = \int_0^T [s_i(t) - s_k(t)]^2\, dt$

- It may now be guessed intuitively that we should choose $s_i(t)$ and $s_k(t)$ such that the Euclidean distance d_{ik} between them, i.e. $\|\overline{s_i} - \overline{s_k}\|^2$ is as much as possible to ensure that their detection is more robust even in presence of noise. For example, if $s_1(t)$ and $s_2(t)$ have same energy E, (i.e. they are equidistant from the origin), then an obvious choice for maximum distance of separation is, $s_1(t) = -s_2(t)$.

7.3.5 Use of Signal Space for Signal Detection in a Receiver

- The signal space defined above, is very useful for designing a receiver as well. In a sense, much of the features of a modulation scheme, such as the number of symbols used and the energy carried by the symbols, is embedded in the description of its signal space. So, in absence of any noise, the receiver should detect one of these valid symbols only.

- However, the received symbols are usually corrupted and once placed in the signal space, they may not match with the valid signal points in some respect or the other. Let us briefly consider the task of a good receiver in such a situation. Let us assume the following :

1. One of the M signals $s_i(t)$, i =1, 2, ... , M is transmitted in each time slot of duration 'T' sec.

2. All symbols are equally probable, i.e. the probability of occurrence of $s_i(t)$ = 1/M, for all 'i'.

3. Additive White Gaussian Noise (AWGN) processes W(t) is assumed with a noise sample function w(t) having mean = 0 and power spectral density [N_0 : single sided power spectral density of additive white Gaussian noise. Noise is discussed more in next two lessons].

4.   Detection is on a symbol-by-symbol basis.

- Now, if R(t) denotes the received random process with a sample function r(t), we may write,

$$r(t) = s_i(t) + w(t) \; ; \; 0 \le t < T \text{ and } i = 1, 2, \ldots, M$$

- The job of the receiver is to make "best estimate" of the transmitted signal $s_i(t)$ (or, equivalently, the corresponding message symbol m_i) upon receiving r(t).

- We map the received sample function r(t) on the signal space to include a 'received vector' or 'received signal point'. This helps us to identify a noise vector, w(t) ,also. The detection problem can now be stated as :

  'Given an observation / received signal vector $(\bar{r})$, the receiver has to perform a mapping from $\bar{r}$ to an estimate $\hat{m}$ for the transmitted symbol in a way that would minimize the average probability of symbol error'.

- Maximum Likelihood Detection scheme provides a general solution to this problem when the noise is additive and Gaussian.

Example 7.5 :

Consider the signal set as given in Fig. 7.12 representing polar NRZ codes.

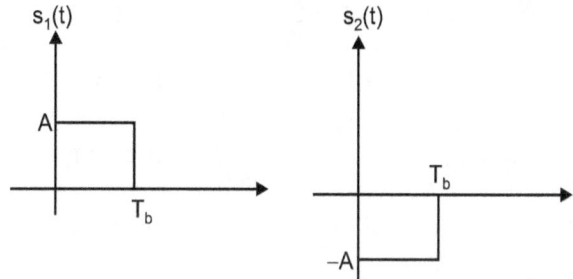

Fig. 7.12 : Polar NRZ signal set

Solution :

Given,

$$s_1(t) \quad = \quad +A \qquad\qquad 0 \le t \le T_b$$
$$\quad = \quad 0 \qquad\qquad \text{otherwise}$$
$$s_2(t) \quad = \quad -A \qquad\qquad 0 \le t \le T_b$$
$$\quad = \quad 0 \qquad\qquad \text{otherwise}$$

Energy of signal $s_1(t)$ $E_1 = A^2 T_b = E_b$

Energy of signal $s_2(t)$ $E_2 = A^2 T_b = E_b$

(1) Let $\phi_1(t) \quad = \quad \dfrac{s_1(t)}{\sqrt{E_b}}$ $\therefore \; A = \sqrt{\dfrac{E_b}{T_b}}$

$\therefore$ $\qquad$ $\phi_1(t) = \sqrt{\dfrac{1}{T_b}}$ $\qquad$ $0 \leq t \leq T_b$

$\qquad\qquad\qquad = 0$ $\qquad\qquad$ otherwise

$\therefore$ $\qquad$ $\boxed{s_1(t) = \sqrt{E_b}\, \phi_1(t)}$

$\therefore$ $\qquad$ $s_{11} = \sqrt{E_b}$

(2) Now $\qquad$ $s_{21} = \displaystyle\int_0^{T_b} s_2(t)\, \phi_1(t)\, dt$

$\qquad\qquad\quad = \displaystyle\int_0^{T_b} -A \times \sqrt{\dfrac{1}{T_b}}\ dt$

$\qquad\qquad\quad = \displaystyle\int_0^{T_b} -\sqrt{\dfrac{E_b}{T_b}} \times \sqrt{\dfrac{1}{T_b}}\ dt$

$\qquad\qquad\quad = -\sqrt{E_b}$

(3) Now $\qquad$ $g_2(t) = s_2(t) - s_{21}\phi_1(t)$

$\qquad\qquad$ $s_2(t) = -\sqrt{\dfrac{E_b}{T_b}}$ $\qquad$ $0 \leq t \leq T_b$

$\qquad\qquad\qquad = 0$ $\qquad\qquad$ otherwise

$\qquad$ $s_{21} \cdot \phi_1(t) = -\sqrt{E_b} \times \sqrt{\dfrac{1}{T_b}}$ $\qquad$ $0 \leq t \leq T_b$

$\qquad\qquad\qquad = 0$ $\qquad\qquad$ otherwise

$\therefore$ $\qquad$ $g_2(t) = 0$

$\therefore$ $\qquad$ $\phi_2(t) = \dfrac{g_2(t)}{\sqrt{E_{g_2}}} = 0$

$\therefore$ $\qquad$ $s_2(t) = s_{21}\phi_1(t)$

$\therefore$ $\qquad$ $\boxed{s_2(t) = -\sqrt{E_b}\, \phi_1(t)}$

Thus $s_1(t)$ and $s_2(t)$ can be represented using only we basis function $\phi_1(t)$. The Geometric representation will be as below.

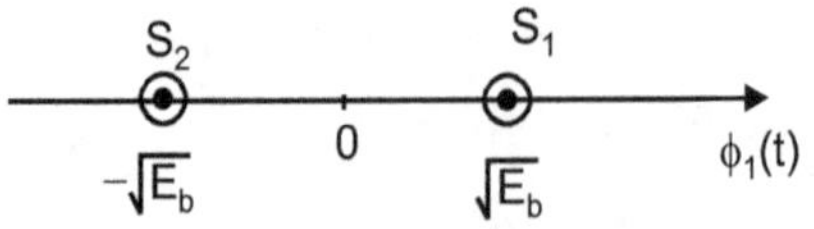

Fig. 7.13 : Geometric representation of polar NRZ signal set

Example 7.6 :

Consider the signal set as given in Fig. 7.14.

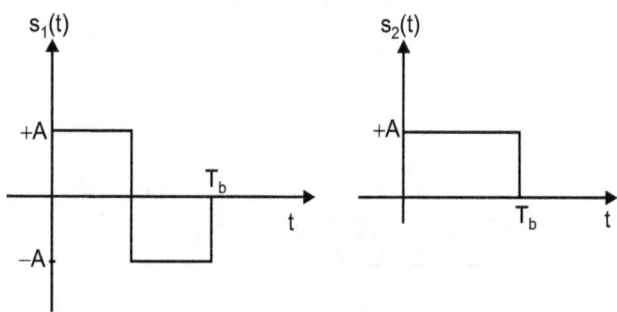

Fig. 7.14

(1)
$$E_1 = \frac{A^2 T_b}{2} + \frac{A^2 T_b}{2} = A^2 T_b \qquad E_2 = A^2 T_b$$

$$A = \sqrt{\frac{E_1}{T_b}} = \sqrt{\frac{E_2}{T_b}} = \sqrt{\frac{E}{T_b}}$$

$$\phi_1(t) = \frac{s_1(t)}{\sqrt{E}} \begin{cases} \dfrac{A}{\sqrt{E}} = \sqrt{\dfrac{1}{T_b}} & 0 \le t \le \dfrac{T_b}{2} \\[2mm] \dfrac{-A}{\sqrt{E}} = -\sqrt{\dfrac{1}{T_b}} & \dfrac{T_b}{2} \le t \le T_b \\[2mm] 0 & \text{otherwise} \end{cases}$$

$$\boxed{s_1(t) = s_{11}\phi_1(t) = \sqrt{E}\phi_1(t)}$$

(2)
$$s_{21} = \int_0^{T_b} s_2(t) \cdot \phi_1(t)\, dt = \int_0^{T_b} A \times \phi_1(t)\, dt$$

$$= \int_0^{T_b/2} A \times \sqrt{\frac{1}{T_b}}\, dt + \int_{T_b/2}^{T_b} A \times \left(\frac{1}{\sqrt{T_b}}\right) dt$$

$$= \frac{A}{\sqrt{T_b}} \times \frac{T_b}{2} - \frac{A}{\sqrt{T_b}} \times \frac{T_b}{2}$$

$$= 0$$

$$g_2 = s_2(t) - s_{21}\phi_1(t)$$

$$= s_2(t)$$

$$\phi_2(t) = \frac{g_2(t)}{\sqrt{\int_0^{T_b} g_2^2(t)\,dt}} = \frac{s_2(t)}{\sqrt{E}}$$

$$= \sqrt{\frac{1}{T_b}} \qquad\qquad 0 \le t \le T_b$$

$$= 0 \qquad\qquad\qquad \text{otherwise}$$

∴ $\boxed{s_2(t) = \sqrt{E}\,\phi_2(t)}$

$$s_{22} = \sqrt{E}$$

The signal space representation is given in Fig. 7.15.

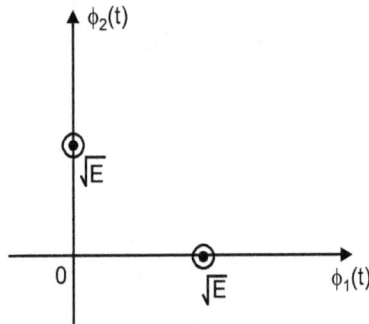

Fig. 7.15

Thus the signal set is orthogonal.

Example 7.7 :

Consider the signal set for unipolar NRZ signal given in Fig. 7.16.

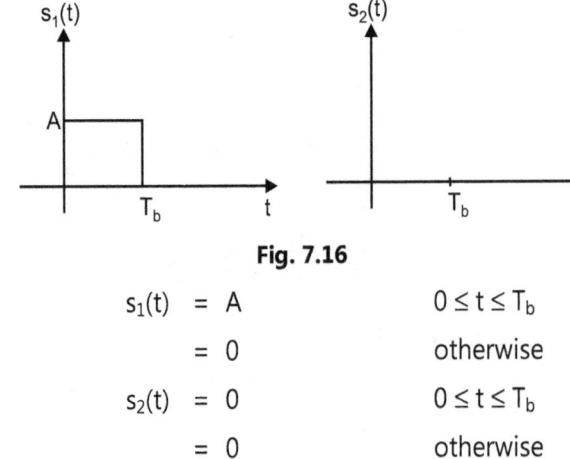

Fig. 7.16

$$s_1(t) = A \qquad\qquad 0 \le t \le T_b$$

$$= 0 \qquad\qquad\qquad \text{otherwise}$$

$$s_2(t) = 0 \qquad\qquad 0 \le t \le T_b$$

$$= 0 \qquad\qquad\qquad \text{otherwise}$$

Energy of $s_1(t)$	E_1	$= A^2 T_b = E_b$	$\therefore A = \sqrt{\dfrac{E_b}{T_b}}$
Energy of $s_2(t)$	E_2	$= 0$	

(1) Let

$$\phi_1(t) = \frac{s_1(t)}{\sqrt{E_b}}$$

$\therefore$

$$\phi_1(t) = \sqrt{\frac{1}{T_b}} \qquad 0 \le t \le T_b$$

$$= 0 \qquad \text{otherwise}$$

$\therefore$

$$s_1(t) = \sqrt{E_b}\,\phi_1(t)$$

and

$$S_{11} = \sqrt{E_b}$$

(2) Now

$$S_{21} = \int_0^{T_b} s_2(t)\phi_1(t)\, dt$$

$$= 0$$

(3)

$$g_2(t) = s_2(t) - S_{21}\phi_1(t)$$

$$= 0$$

$\therefore$

$$\phi_2(t) = 0$$

$\therefore$

$$\boxed{s_2(t) = 0.\phi_1(t)}$$

Thus $s_1(t)$ and $s_2(t)$ can be represented using only one basis function $\phi_1(t)$. The Geometric representation will be as below

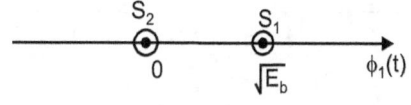

Fig. 7.17

Example 7.8 :

Suppose we have Polar NRZ signal which has two types of signals

$$S_1(t) = + A \qquad 0 \le t \le T$$

$$S_2(t) = - A \qquad 0 \le t \le T$$

The basis function for $S_1(t)$ and $S_2(t)$ will be a pulse normalized to have unit energy i.e.

$$\phi_1(t) = \frac{1}{\sqrt{T}} \qquad 0 \le t \le T$$

$$= 0 \qquad \text{sotherwise} \qquad \left[\because \int_{-\infty}^{\infty} \phi_1^2(t)\, dt = 1 \right]$$

Then the two signals can be written as

$$S_1(t) = A\sqrt{T}\,\phi_1(t) = \sqrt{A^2 T}\,\phi_1(t)$$

and

$$S_2(t) = -A\sqrt{T}\,\phi_1(t) = \sqrt{A^2 T}\,\phi_1(t)$$

$A^2 T$ is energy of the signal.

$\therefore$

$$S_1(t) = \sqrt{E_s}\,\phi_1(t)$$

$$S_2(t) = -\sqrt{E_s}\,\phi_2(t)$$

Thus the two signal vectors corresponding to $S_1(t)$ and $S_2(t)$ are

$$S_1 = [\sqrt{E_s}]$$

$$S_2 = [-\sqrt{E_s}]$$

The geometric representation of the two signals will be as shown in Fig. 7.18

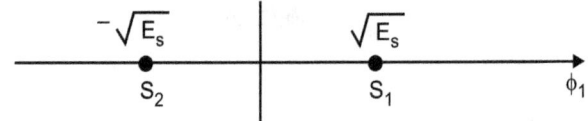

Fig. 7.18

Example 7.9 :

Consider the signals $S_1(t)$, $S_2(t)$, $S_3(t)$, and $S_3(t)$ shown in Fig. 7.19. Apply Gram Schmidt procedure to obtain the basis functions and represent the signals in the form of vectors.

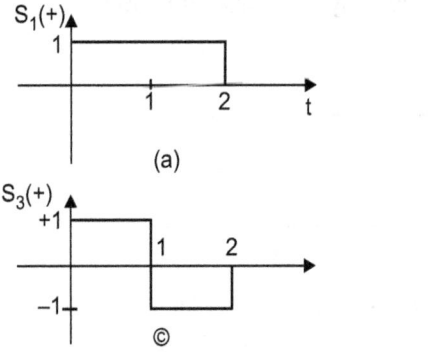
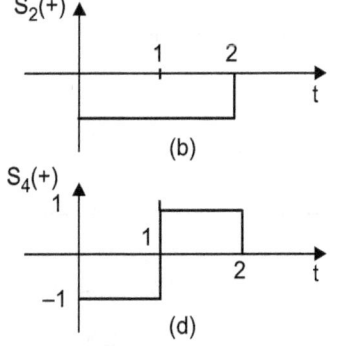

Fig. 7.19

(1)   Signal $S_1(t)$ has energy $E_1 = 2$

$$\left[\because \int_0^2 S_1^2(t)\,dt = 2\right]$$

$\therefore$

$$\phi_1(t) = \frac{S_1(t)}{\sqrt{E_1}} = \frac{1}{\sqrt{2}}\,S_1(t)$$

$\therefore$

$$\boxed{\phi_1(t) = \frac{1}{\sqrt{2}}\,S_1(t)}$$

(2) i = 2

$$\therefore \quad S_{21} = \int_0^T S_2(t)\, \phi_1(t)\, dt = \int_0^2 S_2(t) \times \frac{1}{\sqrt{2}} S_1(t)\, dt = -\sqrt{2}$$

$$g_2(t) = S_2(t) - S_{21} \cdot \phi_1(t)$$
$$= S_2(t) + \sqrt{2}\, \phi_1(t)$$
$$= S_2(t) + S_1(t) = 0$$

$$\therefore \quad \boxed{\phi_2(t) = 0}$$

(3) i = 3

$$S_{31} = \int_0^T S_3(t)\, \phi_1(t)\, dt = \int_0^2 \frac{1}{\sqrt{2}} S_3(t) \cdot S_1(t)\, dt = 0$$

$$S_{32} = \int_0^T S_3(t) \cdot \phi_2(t)\, dt = 0$$

$$g_3(t) = S_3(t) - S_{31}\, \phi_1(t) - S_{32}\, \phi_2(t)$$
$$= S_3(t)$$

$$\therefore \quad \phi_3(t) = \frac{g_3(t)}{\sqrt{\displaystyle\int_0^T g_3^2(t)\, dt}} = \frac{1}{\sqrt{2}} S_3(t)$$

$$\therefore \quad \boxed{\phi_3(t) = \frac{1}{\sqrt{2}} S_3(t)}$$

(4) i = 4

$$S_{41} = \int_0^1 S_4(t)\, \phi_1(t)\, dt = \frac{1}{\sqrt{2}} \int_0^2 S_4(t)\, S_1(t)\, dt = 0$$

$$S_{42} = \int_0^T S_4(t)\, \phi_2(t)\, dt = 0$$

$$S_{43} = \int_0^T S_4(t)\, \phi_3(t)\, dt = \frac{1}{\sqrt{2}} \int_0^2 S_4(t) \cdot S_3(t)\, dt = -\sqrt{2}$$

$$g_4(t) = S_4(t) - S_{41}\, \phi_1(t) - S_{42}\, \phi_2(t) - S_{43}\, \phi_3(t)$$

$$= S_4(t) - 0 - (-\sqrt{2}) \times \frac{1}{\sqrt{2}} S_3(t)$$

$$= S_4(t) + S_3(t) = 0$$

$$\therefore \quad \boxed{\phi_4(t) = 0}$$

Using above basis functions, we can write the four signals as

$$S_1(t) = S_{11} \phi_1(t) = \sqrt{2} \phi_1(t) \qquad\qquad [S_{12} = S_{13} = S_{14} = 0]$$

$$S_2(t) = S_{21} \phi_1(t) + S_{22} \phi_2(t) + S_{23} \phi_3(t) + S_{24} \phi_4(t)$$

$$\therefore \quad S_2(t) = -\sqrt{2} \phi_1(t)$$

$$S_3(t) = S_{31} \phi_1(t) + S_{32} \phi_2(t) + S_{33} \phi_3(t) + S_{34} \phi_4(t)$$

$$\therefore \quad S_3(t) = -\sqrt{2} \phi_3(t)$$

$$S_4(t) = S_{41} \phi_1(t) + S_{42} \phi_2(t) + S_{43} \phi_3(t) + S_{44} \phi_4(t)$$

$$\therefore \quad S_4(t) = -\sqrt{2} \phi_3(t)$$

Thus we have only two basis functions with which we can represent all four signal. Hence the dimensionally N = 2. The signal can be described with 2 vectors components as

$$S_1 = (\sqrt{2}\ \ 0) \quad S_2 = (-\sqrt{2}\ \ 0) \quad S_3 = (0\ \ \sqrt{2}) \quad S_1 = (0\ \ -\sqrt{2})$$

These are geometrically represented as shown in Fig. 7.20.

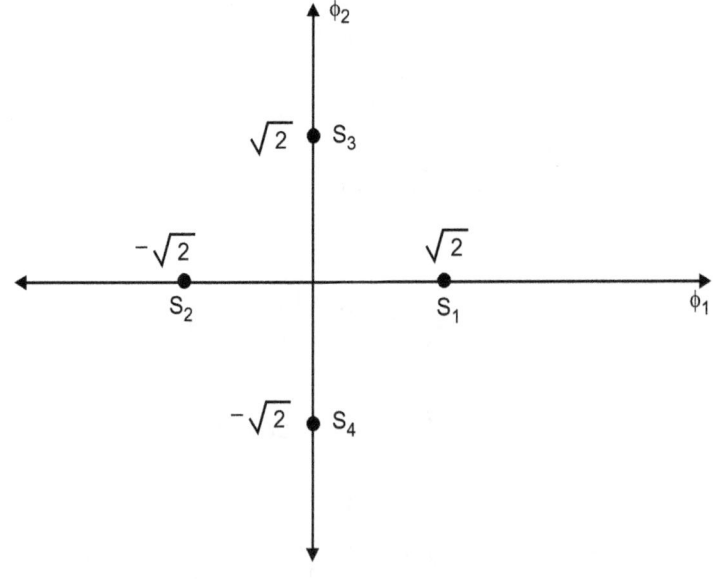

Fig. 7.20

SUMMARY

Estimation theory is used in number of applications such as radar systems, digital communication, speech and image processing etc.

- Estimation problem consists of
  - (i) Parameter space
  - (ii) Observation space
  - (iii) Estimation rule.

- Maximum Likelihood (ML) Estimation is used to estimate non-random parameters. To find maximum likelihood estimate and parameter θ, we take derivative of log likelihood function and set it zero.

$$\frac{\partial}{\partial \theta} \ln [P_{Y|\Theta} (y|\theta)] = 0$$

- An estimator is unbiased if $E[\hat{\theta}] = \theta$. If estimator is biased its bias is defined as $b(\theta) = E[\hat{\theta}] - \theta$.

- A good estimator should have minimum bias and variance of estimate minimum i.e. it should be Minimum Variance Unbiased (MVU) Estimator.

- The Crammer-Rao Lower Band (CRLB) sets limit on variance of any unbiased estimator. It can be used when it is difficult to obtain variance of estimate.

  According to CRLB theorem,

$$\text{Var} [\hat{\theta} - \theta|\theta] \geq \frac{-1}{E\left[\frac{\partial^2 \ln (p_{Y|\Theta} (y|\theta))}{\partial \theta^2}\right]}$$

  where, $\hat{\theta}$ is estimate of given observation $Y_1, Y_2, Y_3, ..., Y_K$.

- When the parameter θ is random, we use Bayes' estimation. But it requires priori knowledge of θ. In Bayes' estimation, we try to minimize the average cost or risk $\bar{C}$.

  i.e. $\bar{C} = E [C(\theta, \hat{\theta})]$

- Depending on cost function $C(\theta, \hat{\theta})$, there are three types of estimators.
  - (i) Minimum Mean Square (MMS) Estimator.
  - (ii) Minimum Mean Absolute Value of Error (MMAV) Estimator.
  - (iii) Maximum a Posteriori (MAP) Estimator.

- When PDF of data is not known, we can not use Minimum Variance Unbiased Estimation or Bayes' Estimation. In such situation, we limit the estimator to be linear function of the data and make sure that estimated value has minimum variance. This technique is called Best Linear Unbiased Estimation (BLUE).

- In Least Square (LS) Estimators, the criteria is to minimize squared difference between given observation (data and noise) and assumed signal data (reference).

- Kalman filter is a tool that can estimate the variables of wide range of processes having stationary as well as non-stationary data.

EXERCISE

1. What is hypothesis testing ? What are different criteria for hypothesis testing.

2. What is MAP ? What are its limitations in criteria in decision theory.

3. What is LRT criteria in detection theory. Derive the expression for LRT in case of binary digital communication system.

4. What is minimum error test ? Using minimum error test derive the expression for error probability of binary digital communication system in presence of AWGN.

5. What is signal space representation ? Explain with suitable example.

6. What is Gram-Schwidt orthogonalization procedure ? Give the steps.

7. What is utility of signal space representation in digital communication system ?

CHAPTER 8
DETECTION OF BASEBAND SIGNALS
IN PRESENCE OF NOISE

8.1   INTRODUCTION

- Baseband digital signal is a signal which is transmitted without any modulation.

- These baseband signals can either come from a data source like computer or from digital communication systems like PCM, DM, ADM etc.

- We have studied transmission and reception of such digital signals without considering the effect of noise on these signals. Noise is an important parameter to be considered while designing any communication system.

- The performance of receiver has to be evaluated in presence of noise. For the purpose of simplification, we will consider the noise to be white Gaussian Noise.

- Another parameter that affects is filtering at transmitter, channel and receiver resulting into Inter Symbol Interference (ISS).

- Our aim in designing the receiver should be to "Minimise the error probability of detection of signal".

- In this chapter, we are going to study the methods of minimising the error probability and improving performance of baseband signal receiver.

8.2 SIGNAL AND NOISE

- Electrical noise and interference is produced by variety of sources within the receiver as well as outside the receiver.

- The sources of noise include thermal noise, atmospheric noise, switching transients, intermodulation noise, interfering signals from other sources etc.

- With proper precaution we can minimize or eliminate effect of noise and interference entering the receiver except thermal noise.

- The thermal noise is caused due to thermal motion of electrons. The thermal motion produces thermal noise in transmitter and receiver circuits and it is additive in nature.

- Noise is random in nature. Hence, thermal noise will be expressed as random variable.

- The random signals are characterized with the help of their statistical parameters viz. mean, variance etc. and distribution.

- The thermal noise which results from the motion of electrons, have noise amplitudes Gaussian Distributed as shown below in Fig. 8.1.

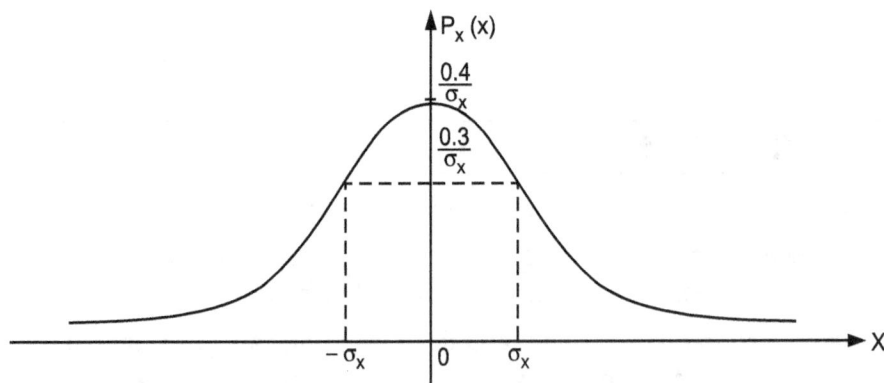

Fig. 8.1 : Distribution of amplitudes of thermal noise

- It means the noise has mean value 0 and variance σ_x^2. It has very few occurrences of large amplitude signals.

- The spectrum of a random signal is given in terms its Power Spectral Density (PSD).

- The PSD of the noise is given by,

$$S_n(f) = \frac{N_0}{2}$$

i.e. it is flat for all frequencies.

- It means thermal noise has same power for all frequencies. Hence, it is called white noise and denoted as w(t). It has PSD $S_w(f) = \frac{N_0}{2}$.

- Since it is additive it is called Additive White Gaussian Noise (AWGN) as shown in Fig. 8.2.

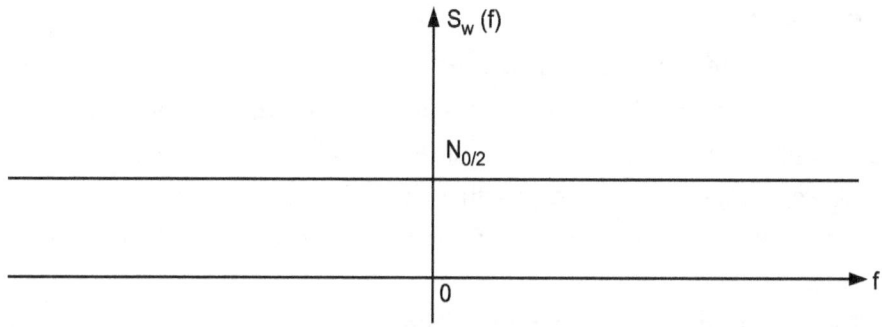

Fig. 8.2

8.3 BASEBAND SIGNAL DETECTION

- Consider a binary encoded signal S(t) defined as,

$$S(t) = + A \qquad\qquad \text{for Binary 1}$$
$$= - A \qquad\qquad \text{for Binary 0} \qquad ... (8.1)$$

- This signal is added with white Gaussian noise w(t). In the receiver circuit our aim is to detect whether + A was transmitted or − A was transmitted during a particular bit interval. The noise has effect of changing the signal S(t).

- The received signal r(t) is given by,

$$r(t) = S(t) + w(t) \qquad\qquad 0 \le t \le T \qquad ... (8.2)$$

where, T is symbol duration.

- In such situation, it will not be possible to detect the transmitted signal correctly. What best can be done is to reduce the probability of error in detection. This can be done by suppressing noise and emphasising the signal.

- One such circuit is an **integrate-and-dump** circuit shown in Fig. 8.3.

- The circuit has an integrator alongwith two switches.

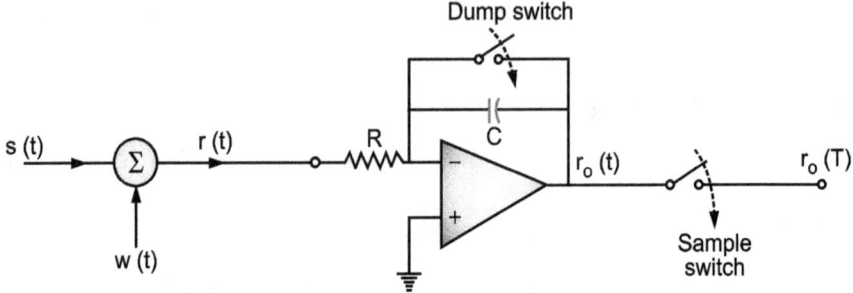

Fig. 8.3 : Integrate and dump circuit

Working of Circuit :

(i)   Integrator integrates the incoming input r(t).

(ii) Dump switch discharges the output of integrator at the beginning of each bit interval.

(iii) Sample switch samples the output of the integrator at the end of the bit interval.

- Hence, it must be clear to you that the switches are driven by bit synchroniser output. Let us analyse this circuit and see how exactly it fulfills our criteria of detection.

- The sampled output of integrator will be,

$$r_0(T) = \frac{1}{RC} \int_0^T [S(t) + w(t)] \, dt$$

$$= \frac{1}{RC} \int_0^T S(t) \, dt + \frac{1}{RC} \int_0^T w(t) \, dt \qquad \ldots (8.3)$$

- Thus, output sample is,

$$\boxed{r_0(T) = S_0(T) + n_0(T)}$$

There are two parts in the output sample,

(i)   Sample voltage due to signal given as,

$$S_0(T) = \frac{1}{RC} \int_0^T S(t) \, dt = \frac{1}{RC} (\pm A) T = \frac{\pm AT}{RC} \qquad \ldots (8.4)$$

(ii) Sample voltage due to noise given as,

$$n_0(T) = \frac{1}{RC} \int_0^T w(t) \, dt \qquad \ldots (8.5)$$

- We will be interested in a quantity called Peak pulse signal-to-noise ratio at the output which is given by,

---

Ch. 8 | 8.4

$$(SNR)_0 = \frac{E[S_0^2(T)]}{E[n_0^2(T)]} \qquad \text{... (8.6)}$$

- In order to find $E[n_0^2(t)]$, we will have to switch over to Power Spectral Density or Autocorrelation function, since $W(t)$ is a random process. Now $n_0(T)$ becomes a Gaussian random variable of the Gaussian random process $W(t)$.

- To find $E[n_0^2(T)]$, we need transfer function of integrator which is given by,

$$H(f) = \frac{1 - e^{-j2\pi f\tau}}{j2\pi f\, RC} \qquad \text{... (8.7)}$$

Let $\qquad\qquad RC = \tau$

$\therefore \qquad$
$$|H(f)|^2 = \left(\frac{T}{\tau}\right)^2 \left(\frac{\sin(\pi fT)}{\pi fT}\right)^2 \qquad \text{... (8.8)}$$

- The output noise power spectral density is given by,

$$S_N(f) = |H(f)|^2\, S_W(f) \qquad \text{... (8.9)}$$

and output noise power will be,

$$P_{n_0} = \int_{-\infty}^{\infty} S_N(f)\, df \qquad \text{... (8.10)}$$

Since, $\qquad\qquad S_W(f) = \dfrac{N_0}{2}$ N_0 is noise Power Spectral Density

$\therefore \qquad$
$$P_{n_0} = \frac{N_0}{2} \int_{-\infty}^{\infty} \left(\frac{T}{\tau}\right)^2 \left(\frac{\sin \pi Tf}{\pi Tf}\right)^2 df \qquad \text{... (8.11)}$$

$\therefore \qquad$
$$P_{n_0} = \frac{N_0}{2} \left(\frac{T}{\tau}\right)^2 \int_{-\infty}^{\infty} \left(\frac{\sin \pi Tf}{\pi Tf}\right)^2 df \qquad \text{... (8.12)}$$

Put $\qquad\qquad x = \pi fT$

$\therefore \qquad\qquad dx = \pi T df \qquad\qquad\qquad df = \dfrac{1}{\pi T} dx$

$$\therefore \qquad P_{n_0} = \frac{N_0}{2}\left(\frac{T}{\tau}\right)^2 \int_{-\infty}^{\infty}\left(\frac{\sin x}{x}\right)^2 \frac{1}{\pi T}\, dx \qquad \text{... (8.13)}$$

$$= \frac{N_0}{2\pi} \times \frac{T}{\tau^2} \int_{-\infty}^{\infty}\left(\frac{\sin x}{x}\right)^2 dx \qquad \text{... (8.14)}$$

But, $\qquad \displaystyle\int_{-\infty}^{\infty}\left(\frac{\sin x}{x}\right)^2 dx = \pi$

$$\therefore \qquad P_{n_0} = \frac{N_0 T}{2\tau^2} \qquad \text{... (8.15)}$$

- This output noise power is the expected value of

$$[n_0^2(T)] = \sigma_{no}^2 = E[n_0^2(T)] = \overline{n_0^2(T)}.$$

- Substituting equations (8.4) and (8.15) in equation (8.6), we get the peak pulse signal-to-noise ratio at the output of the integrate and dump circuit.

$$(SNR)_0 = \frac{\left(\pm\dfrac{AT}{\tau}\right)^2}{\left(\dfrac{N_0 T}{2\tau^2}\right)} \qquad \text{... (8.16)}$$

$$(SNR)_0 = \frac{2}{N_0} \times A^2 T \qquad \text{... (8.17)}$$

Thus, we can see from above equation that –

(1) The signal-to-noise ratio at the output of integrate-and-dump circuit increases with bit duration T.

(2) It also depends on $A^2 T$ which is normalised energy of the bit (symbol).

(3) Since $E[S_0^2(T)] = \dfrac{A^2 T^2}{\tau^2}$ and $E[n_0^2(T)] = \dfrac{N_0 T}{2\tau^2}$ the signal voltage increases linearly with T and the noise voltage (σ_{no}) increases slowly with $\sqrt{T}$. Hence, we can say that integrator enhances the signal more than the noise.

Fig. 8.4 shows the waveforms related to integrate-and-dump filter.

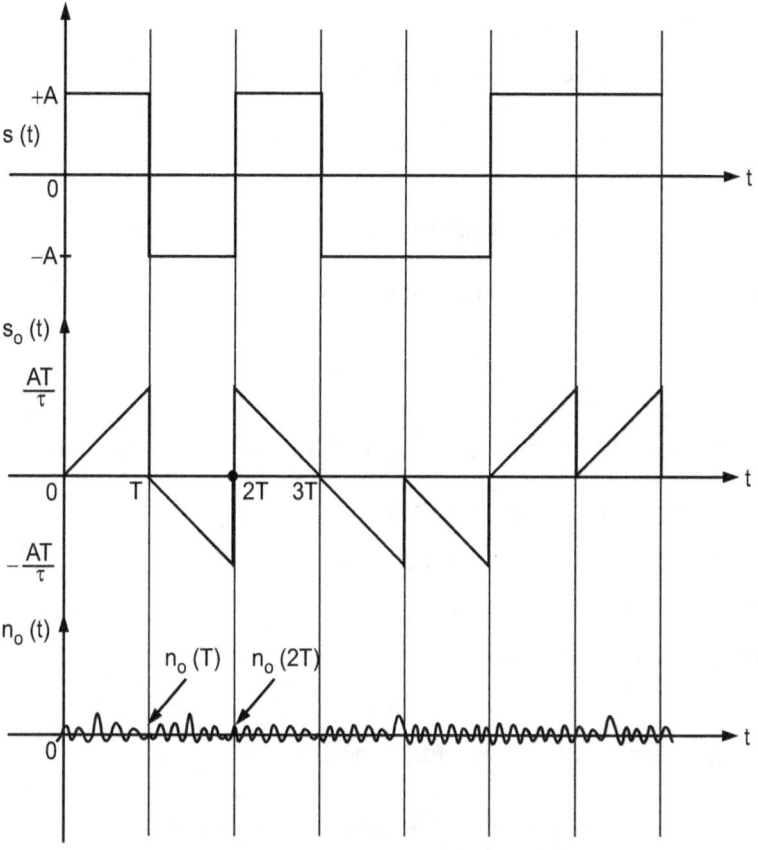

Fig. 8.4 : Waveforms of integrate-and-dump circuit

8.4 PROBABILITY OF ERROR

- In the last section, we have seen that the receiver has to make decision in favour of 1 or 0 with minimum error probability.

- Given integrate-and-dump circuit, we will be interested in finding this decision error probability. When the error will be made ? For this consider the received signal.

$$r(t) = S(t) + w(t) \qquad\qquad 0 \le t \le T \qquad\qquad ...(8.18)$$

- The output of integrate-and-dump circuit will be,

$$r_0(T) = S_0(T) + n_0(T) \qquad\qquad ...(8.19)$$

$$= \frac{\pm AT}{\tau} + n_0(T) \qquad\qquad ...(8.20)$$

where, $S_0(T)$ is the sample value due to input signal $S(t)$ at $t = T$.

and $n_0(T)$ is the sample due to noise input $w(t)$ and $t = T$.

- Now consider the two cases :

Case 1 : Input S(t) = + A (Binary 1 is transmitted)

$$r_0(T) \;=\; \frac{+\,AT}{\tau} + n_0(T) \qquad\qquad \text{... (8.21)}$$

If $n_0(T) < -\dfrac{AT}{\tau}$ there will be error, as decision will made in favour of 0.

Case 2 : Input S(t) = – A (Binary 0 is transmitted)

$$r_0(T) \;=\; \frac{-\,AT}{\tau} + n_0(T) \qquad\qquad \text{... (8.22)}$$

If $n_0(T) > \dfrac{AT}{\tau}$, there will be error as decision will be made in favour of 1.

- Hence, there are two kinds of error as below :

    1.   Symbol 0 is chosen when 1 was transmitted.

    2.   Symbol 1 is chosen when 0 was transmitted.

- Let us consider the case when 0 is sent.

$$\therefore \qquad\qquad r(t) \;=\; -A + w(t) \qquad\qquad \text{... (8.23)}$$

- Correspondingly the integrator-output will be,

$$r_0(T) \;=\; -\frac{AT}{\tau} + n_0(T)$$

- Since $n_0(T)$ is sample of filtered random process w (t), $r_0(T)$ represents sample value of a random variable.

- Let us denote the random variable as Y. This variable will be a Gaussian random variable. The Gaussian random variable is characterised by the probability function given by

$$p_Y(y) \;=\; \frac{1}{\sqrt{2\pi\sigma_y^2}} \times e^{-(y-m_Y)^2/2\sigma_y^2} \qquad\qquad \text{... (8.24)}$$

where, m_Y is mean value = E [Y]

$$\sigma_y^2 \text{ is variance } = E\,[(Y - m_Y)^2]$$

and $\qquad\qquad\qquad y \;=\; -\dfrac{AT}{\tau} + n_0(T)$

- Since, $n_0(T)$ is due to filtered white noise its mean value is zero.

- Hence, mean value of our random variable Y will be $-\dfrac{AT}{\tau}$

$$\therefore \qquad m_Y = -\frac{AT}{\tau} \qquad \qquad \qquad \text{... (8.25)}$$

- To find σ_y^2 we have,

$$\sigma_y^2 = E[(Y - m_Y)^2] \qquad \qquad \text{... (8.26)}$$

$$= E\left[\left(Y + \frac{AT}{\tau}\right)^2\right] \qquad \qquad \text{... (8.27)}$$

$$= E[n_0^2(T)] \qquad \text{Since } Y + \frac{AT}{\tau} = n_0(T) \qquad \text{... (8.28)}$$

- But $\qquad \qquad E[n_0^2(T)] = \frac{N_0 T}{2\tau^2} \qquad \qquad \text{(Refer equation (8.15))}$

$$\therefore \qquad \qquad \sigma_y^2 = \frac{N_0 T}{2\tau^2} \qquad \qquad \text{... (8.28)}$$

- Hence, the PDF of random variable Y is given by,

$$p_Y(y/0) = \frac{1}{\sqrt{\pi \dfrac{N_0 T}{\tau^2}}} \times e^{-(y + AT/\tau)^2 / \frac{N_0 T}{\tau^2}} \qquad \text{... (8.29)}$$

- The plot of this PDF is shown in Fig. 8.5 (a).

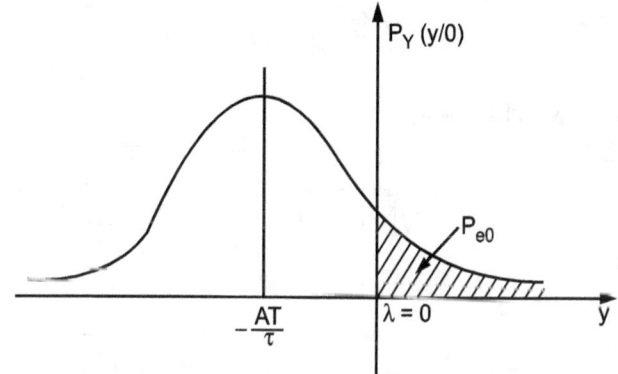

Fig. 8.5 : (a) PDF of rv y at integrator output when 0 is transmitted

- Let us denote this PDF as $P_Y(y/0)$. i.e. probability of receiving y given that 0 is transmitted. Now, if 0 is transmitted the output of integrator is given by,

$$y = -\frac{AT}{\tau} + n_0(T)$$

and there will be error in detection if $n_0(T) > \dfrac{AT}{\tau}$.

- Thus, error probability will be the probability that the value of $y > -\dfrac{AT}{\tau} + \dfrac{AT}{\tau}$ i.e. $y > 0$.

- The probability of occurrence of this can be found from equation (8.29) as,

- $$P_Y(y > 0|\text{symbol } 0 \text{ was sent}) = \int_0^\infty p_Y(y)\, dy \qquad \qquad \text{... (8.30)}$$

$$= \int_0^\infty \frac{1}{\sqrt{\pi \dfrac{N_0 T}{\tau^2}}} \, e^{-\left(y + \frac{AT}{\tau}\right)^2 \Big/ \left(\frac{N_0 T}{\tau^2}\right)}\, dy \qquad \qquad \text{... (8.31)}$$

- Let us call this probability as P_{e0}.

- Now, put $$z = \frac{y + \dfrac{AT}{\tau}}{\sqrt{\dfrac{N_0 T}{\tau^2}}}$$

- Hence, $$dz = \frac{1}{\sqrt{\dfrac{N_0 T}{\tau^2}}}\, dy$$

$$\therefore \qquad dy = \sqrt{\frac{N_0 T}{\tau^2}}\, dz$$

- Limits of integration will change as,

at $y = 0$ $$z = \frac{AT/\tau}{\sqrt{N_0 T/\tau^2}} = \sqrt{\frac{A^2 T}{N_0}} = \sqrt{\frac{E_b}{N_0}} \quad (E_b \text{ is energy per bit})$$

at $y = \infty$ $$z = \infty$$

$$\therefore \qquad P_{e0} = \int_{\sqrt{\frac{E_b}{N_0}}}^\infty \frac{1}{\sqrt{\pi N_0 T}\sqrt{\dfrac{}{\tau^2}}} \times e^{-z^2} \times \sqrt{\frac{N_0 T}{\tau^2}}\, dz \qquad \text{... (8.32)}$$

$$P_{e0} = \frac{1}{\sqrt{\pi}} \int_{\sqrt{\frac{E_b}{N_0}}}^\infty e^{-z^2}\, dz \qquad \qquad \text{... (8.33)}$$

- Above equation is of the standard complementary error function defined as,

$$\text{erfc (u)} = \frac{2}{\sqrt{\pi}} \int_{u}^{\infty} e^{-z^2} \, dz \qquad \text{... (8.34)}$$

- Hence, P_{e0} can be written in terms of this function as,

$$P_{e0} = \frac{1}{2} \times \frac{2}{\pi} \int_{\sqrt{\frac{E_b}{N_0}}}^{\infty} e^{-z^2} \, dz \qquad \text{... (8.35)}$$

$$\therefore \qquad P_{e0} = \frac{1}{2} \text{erfc}\left(\sqrt{\frac{E_b}{N_0}}\right) \qquad \text{... (8.36)}$$

- Now, consider the second case where symbol 1 is transmitted. The integrator output random variable will have an value $m_y = \dfrac{AT}{\tau}$ but the variance will remain the same i.e.

$$\sigma_y^2 = \frac{N_0 T}{2\tau^2}$$

- Hence, the PDF of this random variable can be given by,

$$p_Y(y|1) = \frac{1}{\sqrt{\pi \frac{N_0 T}{\tau^2}}} \times e^{-\left(y - \frac{AT}{\tau}\right)^2 \Big/ \left(\frac{N_0 T}{\tau^2}\right)} \qquad \text{... (8.37)}$$

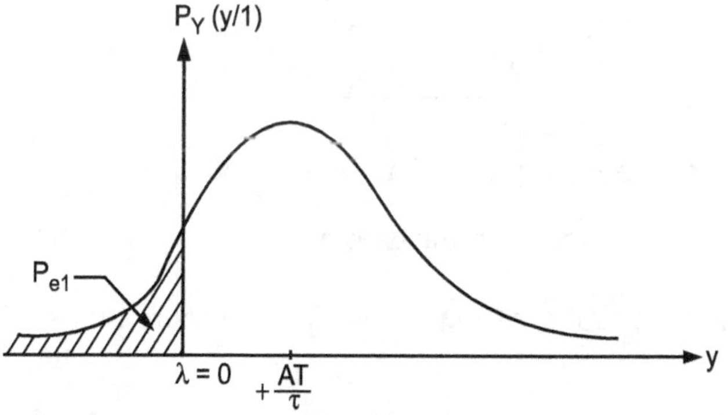

Fig. 8.5 : (b) PDF of rv y at integrator output when 1 is transmitted

- There will be error in decision-making if $n_0(T) < -\dfrac{AT}{\tau}$. The probability of this error will be denoted by P_{e1} and can be given by,

$$P_{e1} = p(y < 0 | \text{symbol 1 was sent})$$

$$= \int_{-\infty}^{0} \frac{1}{\sqrt{\pi \frac{N_0 T}{\tau^2}}} \times e^{-\left(y - \frac{AT}{\tau}\right)^2 \Big/ \left(\frac{N_0 T}{\tau^2}\right)} \qquad \text{... (8.38)}$$

Put
$$z = \frac{y - \frac{AT}{\tau}}{\sqrt{\frac{N_0 T}{\tau^2}}}$$

$$\therefore \qquad P_{e1} = \frac{1}{\sqrt{\pi}} \int_{\sqrt{\frac{E_b}{N_0}}}^{0} e^{-z^2} dz \qquad \text{... (8.39)}$$

$$P_{e1} = \frac{1}{2} \operatorname{erfc}\left(\sqrt{\frac{E_b}{N_0}}\right) \qquad \text{... (8.40)}$$

- Hence, both kinds of error probabilities are same. The average symbol error probability can be given by,

$$p_e = \frac{\text{Probability}}{\text{of transmitting 0}} \times \frac{\text{Error}}{\text{probability}} + \frac{\text{Probability}}{\text{of transmitting 1}} \times \frac{\text{Error}}{\text{probability}}$$

$$= p_0 \times p_{e0} + p_1 \times p_{e1}$$

If $\quad p_0 = p_1 = \frac{1}{2}$ $\qquad p_e = \frac{1}{2} \times \frac{1}{2} \operatorname{erfc}\left(\sqrt{\frac{E_b}{N_0}}\right) + \frac{1}{2} \times \frac{1}{2} \operatorname{erfc}\left(\sqrt{\frac{E_b}{N_0}}\right)$

$$\therefore \qquad \boxed{p_e = \frac{1}{2} \operatorname{erfc}\left(\sqrt{\frac{E_b}{N_0}}\right)} \qquad \text{... (8.41)}$$

- Thus, we see that the error probability depends on $\dfrac{E_b}{N_0}$ ratio. i.e. ratio of transmitted signal energy per bit to noise spectral density.

- The plot of p_e versus $\dfrac{E_b}{N_0}$ ratio is shown in Fig. 8.6. The figure shows –

(i)   As $\dfrac{E_b}{N_0}$ increases the error probability reduces.

(ii)   The maximum value of $P_e = \dfrac{1}{2}$. It means even if the signal is entirely lost in the noise, receiver can go wrong not more than half the times !

(iii)   There is rapid decrease of P_e with increase in E_b. (N_0 remaining same). Hence, a small increase in transmitted energy can make receiver almost error free.

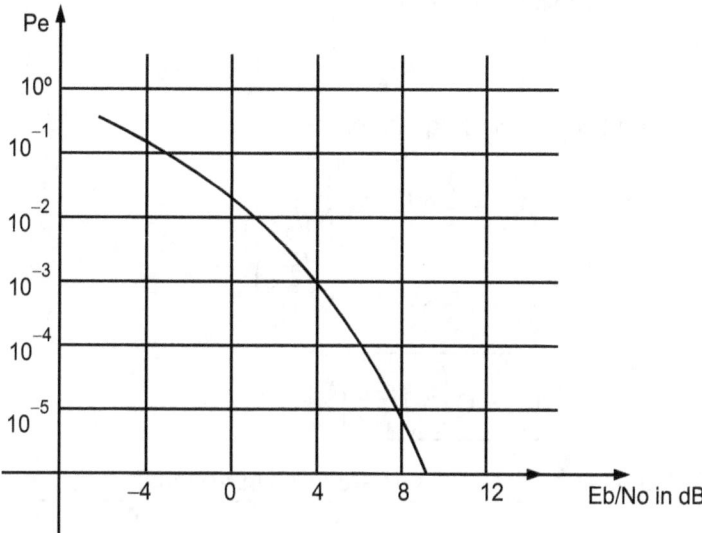

Fig. 8.6 : Variation of P_e against E_b/N_0

Note :

- Let us have a relook at the equation (8.41).

$$p_e = \frac{1}{2} \text{erfc}\left(\sqrt{\frac{E_b}{N_0}}\right)$$

- The error function is erf(u) = 1 − erfc(u) is a standard function whose tabulated values are available. They are given at Appendix − D.

- If we are given E_b and N_0 values we can find p_e by looking into the table.

- There is one more way of expressing the above formula. That is in terms of Q function which is defined as,

$$Q(u) = \frac{1}{\sqrt{2\pi}} \cdot \int_u^{\infty} e^{-x^2/2} \, dx$$

- We know

$$\text{erfc}(u) = \frac{2}{\sqrt{\pi}} \int_u^{\infty} e^{-x^2} \, dx$$

- Hence,

$$Q(u) = \frac{1}{2} \operatorname{erfc}\left(\frac{u}{\sqrt{2}}\right)$$

and

$$\operatorname{erfc}(u) = 2Q(\sqrt{2}\, u)$$

- Hence, the error probability equation,

$$p_e = \frac{1}{2} \operatorname{erfc}\left(\sqrt{\frac{E_b}{N_0}}\right)$$

$$= \frac{1}{2} \times 2 \cdot Q\left(\sqrt{\frac{2E_b}{N_0}}\right)$$

$$\therefore \qquad \boxed{p_e = Q\left(\sqrt{\frac{2E_b}{N_0}}\right)}$$

- The tabulated values of Q function are given in Appendix – C.

Example 8.1 :

A bipolar binary signal $S_i(t)$ is a + 1V or −1V pulse during the interval (0, T). Additive white Gaussian noise with power spectral density $\frac{N_0}{2} = 10^{-5}$ W/Hz is added to the signal. Determine the maximum bit rate that can be sent with a bit error probability of $p_e \leq 10^{-4}$.

(6 marks) (May 2006)

Solution :

Given :   Signal amplitudes

$$S_1(t) = + 1V$$

$$S_2(t) = -1V$$

$$\frac{N_0}{2} = 10^{-5} \text{ W/Hz}$$

$$\therefore \qquad N_0 = 2 \times 10^{-5} \text{ W/Hz}$$

$$p_e \leq 10^{-4}$$

To be calculated : Bit rate $\left(\frac{1}{T_b}\right)$.

For baseband the signal error probability is given by,

(I)
$$p_e = Q\left(\sqrt{\frac{2E_b}{N_0}}\right)$$

(II) $$p_e = \frac{1}{2} \text{erfc}\left(\sqrt{\frac{E_b}{N_0}}\right)$$

Let us solve it using both equations

(I) $$Q(u) = 10^{-4}$$

$$\therefore \quad u = 3.71$$

Now, $$p_e = Q\left(\sqrt{\frac{2E_b}{N_0}}\right) \qquad \textbf{(Refer Appendix – C)}$$

$$\therefore \quad 10^{-4} = Q\left(\sqrt{\frac{2A^2T_b}{N_0}}\right)$$

$$\therefore \quad \sqrt{\frac{2A^2T_0}{N_0}} = 3.71$$

$$\frac{2A^2T_b}{N_0} = (3.71)^2$$

$$\frac{2 \times 1 \times T_b}{2 \times 10^{-5}} = (3.71)^2$$

$$T_b = 13.76 \times 10^{-5} \text{ s}$$

$$\therefore \quad \text{Bit rate, } R_b = 7.26 \text{ kbps}$$

(II) Now using second formula,

$$p_e = \frac{1}{2} \text{erfc}\left(\sqrt{\frac{E_b}{N_0}}\right)$$

We require $$\frac{1}{2} \text{erfc}\left(\sqrt{\frac{E_b}{N_0}}\right) = 10^{-4}$$

But the table is erf table.

Now, $$\frac{1}{2} \text{erfc}(u) = 10^{-4}$$

$$\therefore \quad \text{erfc}(u) = 2 \times 10^{-4}$$

$$\therefore \quad 1 - \text{erf}(u) = 2 \times 10^{-4}$$

$$\therefore \quad \text{erf}(u) = 1 - 2 \times 10^{-4}$$

$$\therefore \quad \text{erf}(u) = 0.9998$$

Hence,

$$\frac{1}{2} \text{erfc}(u) = 10^{-4}$$

is equivalent to

$$\text{erf}(u) = 0.9998$$

From table for erf(u) = 0.9998, u = 2.63   **(Refer Appendix – D)**

For $\qquad \frac{1}{2}\text{erfc(u)} = 10^{-4}$

$$u = 2.63$$

$\therefore \qquad \sqrt{\frac{E_b}{N_0}} = 2.63$

$\therefore \qquad \sqrt{\frac{A^2T_b}{N_0}} = 2.63$

$$\frac{A^2T_b}{N_0} = (2.63)^2$$

$\therefore \qquad T_b = (2.63)^2 \times 2 \times 10^{-5}$

$$T_b = 13.83 \times 10^{-5}$$

$\therefore \qquad$ Bit rate, $r_b = 7.23$ kbps

Example 8.2 :

Find the error probability of a binary baseband which receiver the binary pulse $S_1(t) = +0.5$ V and -0.5 V with bit rate 1 kbps. The noise power spectral density is 10^{-5} W/Hz. What is the probability of error if the transmitted amplitudes are reduced by 50% ?

Solution :

Given :

$$S_1(t) = +0.5 \text{ V}$$

$$S_2(t) = -0.5 \text{ V}$$

$$r_b = 1 \text{ kbps}$$

$\therefore \qquad T_b = 1 \text{ ms}$

$$\frac{N_0}{2} = 10^{-5}$$

$\therefore \qquad N_0 = 2 \times 10^{-5}$

Method I :

We know,

$$p_e = \frac{1}{2}\text{erfc}\left(\sqrt{\frac{E_b}{N_0}}\right)$$

$$= \frac{1}{2}\text{erfc}\left(\sqrt{\frac{A^2T_b}{N_0}}\right)$$

$$= \frac{1}{2}\text{erfc}\left(\sqrt{\frac{(0.5)^2 \times 1 \times 10^{-3}}{2 \times 10^{-5}}}\right)$$

$$p_e = \frac{1}{2} \text{erfc}(3.535)$$

$$\frac{1}{2}\text{erfc}(31.535) = \frac{1}{2} - \frac{1}{2}\text{erf}(3.535)$$

$$= \frac{1}{2} - \frac{1}{2} \times 0.999999445$$

$$= 2.775 \times 10^{-7}$$

$$\therefore \qquad p_{e_1} = 2.775 \times 10^{-7}$$

Now, if transmitted amplitudes are reduced by 50%,

$$S_1(t) = 0.25 \text{ V}$$

$$S_2(t) = -0.25 \text{ V}$$

Hence,

$$p_e = \frac{1}{2}\text{erfc}\left(\sqrt{\frac{A^2 \times T_b}{N_0}}\right)$$

$$= \frac{1}{2}\text{erfc}\left(\sqrt{\frac{0.0625 \times 1 \times 10^{-3}}{2 \times 10^{-5}}}\right)$$

$$= \frac{1}{2}\text{erfc}(1.7677)$$

Now,

$$\frac{1}{2}\text{erfc}(1.77) = \frac{1}{2} - \frac{1}{2}\text{erf}(1.77)$$

$$= \frac{1}{2} - \frac{1}{2} \times 0.987691$$

$$= 6.15 \times 10^{-3}$$

$$= 0.00615$$

$$\therefore \qquad p_e = 0.00615$$

Method II :

$$p_e = Q\left(\sqrt{\frac{2E_b}{N_0}}\right)$$

$$= Q\left(\sqrt{\frac{2 \times A^2 T_b}{N_0}}\right)$$

For A = ± 0.5

$$p_e = Q\left(\sqrt{\frac{2 \times (0.5)^2 \times 1 \times 10^{-3}}{2 \times 10^{-5}}}\right)$$

$$= 3 \times 10^{-7}$$

For A = ± 0.25

$$p_e = Q\left(\sqrt{\frac{2 \times (0.25)^2 \times 1 \times 10^{-3}}{2 \times 10^{-5}}}\right)$$

$$= Q\left(\sqrt{6.25}\right)$$

$$= Q.(2.5)$$

$$= 0.0062$$

Example 8.3 :

Find error probability of Unipolar signaling.

Solution :

Consider the baseband unipolar signaling where,

$$S_1(T) = A \qquad 0 \le t \le T \qquad \text{For binary 1}$$

$$S_2(T) = 0 \qquad 0 \le t \le T \qquad \text{For binary 0}$$

The output of integrate-and-dump circuit will be,

$$r_0(T) = S_0(T) + n_0(T)$$

When input S(t) = +A, the output will be

$$r_0(T) = \frac{+AT}{\tau} + n_0(T)$$

When input S(t) = 0, the output will be

$$r_0(T) = 0 + h_0(T)$$

There are two kinds of error as below :

1. Symbol 0 is chosen when 1 was transmitted.

2. Symbol 1 is chosen when 1 was transmitted.

Case 2 : Symbol 1 is transmitted.

$$r(t) = A + w(t)$$

$$\therefore \qquad r_0(\tau) = \frac{AT}{\tau} + n_0(T)$$

It is random variable Say Y with mean :

$$m_Y = E[Y] \ = \ E\left[\frac{AT}{\tau} + n_0(T)\right]$$

$$= \ \frac{AT}{\tau}$$

and variance,

$$\sigma_y^2 \ = \ E[(Y - m_y)^2]$$

$$= \ E\left[\left(Y + \frac{AT}{\tau}\right)^2\right]$$

$$= \ E[n_0^2(T)]$$

$$\therefore \qquad \boxed{\sigma_y^2 = \frac{N_0 T}{2\tau^2}}$$

Hence, PDF of random variable Y will be

$$p_Y(y/1) \ = \ \frac{1}{\sqrt{\pi \times \dfrac{N_0 T}{\tau^2}}} \ e^{-(y - AT/\tau)^2 / \frac{N_0 T}{\tau^2}}$$

There will be error in detection if the output of integrator is below $\dfrac{AT}{2\tau}$ and this will happen if

$$n_0(T) > \frac{-AT}{2\tau} \text{ i.e. when } y < \frac{AT}{\tau} - \frac{AT}{2\tau} \text{ i.e. } y < \frac{AT}{2\tau}$$

Hence, the above equation becomes,

$$p_Y\left(y < \frac{AT}{2\tau}\right) \text{ Symbol 1 was sent i.e. } p_{e_1}$$

$$p_{e_1} \ = \ \int_{-\infty}^{AT/2\tau} \frac{1}{\sqrt{\pi \dfrac{N_0 T}{\tau^2}}} \ e^{-(y - AT/\tau)^2 / \frac{N_0 T}{\tau^2}}$$

Put

$$z \ = \ \frac{y - \dfrac{AT}{2\tau}}{\sqrt{\dfrac{N_0 T}{\tau^2}}}$$

$$\therefore \qquad P_{e_1} = \frac{1}{\sqrt{\pi}} \int_{-\infty}^{-\sqrt{\frac{A^2 T}{4N_0}}} e^{-z^2} dz = \frac{1}{\sqrt{\pi}} \int_{\sqrt{\frac{A^2 T}{4N_0}}}^{\infty} e^{-z^2} dz$$

But the energy per bit duration is

$$E_b = \frac{A^2 T}{2} \quad \text{(It is because for bit 1 pulse amplitude is +A and}$$

$$\text{bit 0 it is 0 hence, average will be } \frac{A^2}{2} \times T)$$

$$P_{e_1} = \frac{1}{\sqrt{\pi}} \int_{\sqrt{\frac{E_b}{2N_0}}}^{\infty} e^{-z^2} dz$$

$$P_{e_1} = \frac{1}{2} \operatorname{erfc} \left(\sqrt{\frac{E_b}{2N_0}} \right)$$

$$\therefore \qquad P_{e_1} = Q \left(\sqrt{\frac{E_b}{N_0}} \right)$$

Now for case 1 : When 0 is transmitted

$$r_0(T) = 0 + n_0(T)$$

The random output denoted by random variable Y will have,

$$m_Y = E[n_0(T)] = 0$$

and

$$\sigma_Y^2 = E[n_0^2(T)] = \frac{N_0 T}{2\tau^2}$$

$$\therefore \qquad p_Y(y/0) = \frac{1}{\sqrt{\pi \times \frac{N_0 T}{\tau^2}}} e^{-(y+0)^2 / \frac{N_0 T}{\tau^2}}$$

Hence, the error probability,

$$P_{e_0} = p_Y \left(y > \frac{AT}{\tau} / 0 \text{ is sent} \right)$$

$$= \int_{\frac{AT}{\tau}}^{\infty} \frac{1}{\sqrt{\pi \times \frac{N_0 T}{\tau^2}}} e^{-y^2 / \frac{N_0 T}{\tau^2}} \, dy$$

Put

$$z = \frac{y}{\sqrt{\frac{N_0 T}{\tau^2}}}$$

$$p_{e0} = \frac{1}{\sqrt{\pi}} \int_{\sqrt{\frac{A^2 T}{4N_0}}}^{\infty} e^{-z^2} \, dz$$

But

$$E_b = \frac{A^2 T}{2}$$

$\therefore$

$$p_{e0} = \frac{1}{\sqrt{\pi}} \int_{\sqrt{\frac{E_b}{2N_0}}}^{\infty} e^{-z^2} \, dz$$

$$= \frac{1}{2} \text{erfc} \left(\sqrt{\frac{E_b}{2N_0}} \right)$$

$$= Q \left(\sqrt{\frac{E_b}{N_0}} \right)$$

The overall error probability will be

$$p_e = p_0 \times p_{e0} + p_1 \times p_{e1}$$

$$p_e = \frac{1}{2} \times \frac{1}{2} \text{erfc} \left(\sqrt{\frac{E_b}{2N_0}} \right) + \frac{1}{2} \times \frac{1}{2} \text{erfc} \left(\sqrt{\frac{E_b}{2N_0}} \right)$$

$$p_e = \frac{1}{2} \text{erfc} \left(\sqrt{\frac{E_b}{2N_0}} \right)$$

$\therefore$

$$\boxed{p_e = Q \left(\sqrt{\frac{E_b}{N_0}} \right)}$$

8.5 THE OPTIMUM FILTER

- The integrate-and-dump circuit emphasizes signal output in comparison with the noise voltage. We have also seen that the error probability of this circuit is dependent on E_b/N_0 ratio. But then, is it an optimum value of probability that we get ?

- For this we need to know what is an optimum filter. Let us discuss about this filter first.

- There are two symbols in a binary signal which will be denoted as $S_1(t)$ and $S_2(t)$.

    Let $S_1(t)$ = + A   (Binary 1)

                     $S_2(t)$ = – A   (Binary 0)   ... (8.42)

- When the binary signal is transmitted it gets corrupted by noise which will be considered as Gaussian noise.

- The received signal r(t) will be,

$$r(t) = S(t) + n(t) \qquad \qquad ... (8.43)$$

- This received signal is filtered and sampled at end of sampling interval of symbol duration T as shown in Fig. 8.5. The filter output will be,

$$y(t) = S_0(t) + n_0(t) \qquad \qquad ... (8.44)$$

where, $S_0(t)$ is produced by signal $S(t)$ and $n_0(t)$ is due to n(t).

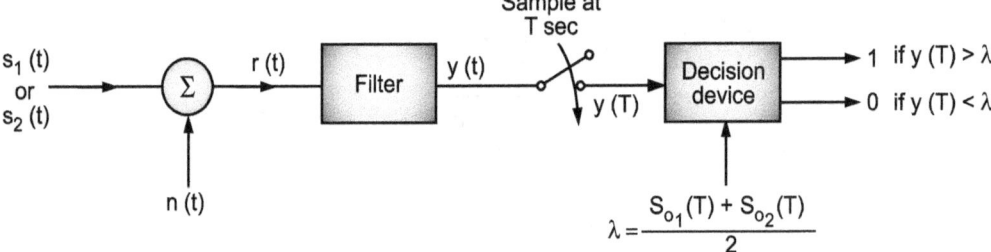

Fig. 8.7 : Optimum receiver

- Hence, sampled output will be,

$$y(T) = S_0(T) + n_0(T) \qquad \qquad ... (8.45)$$

- Now, in absence of noise, if input signal is $S_1(t)$, let the sampled output $y(T)$ be $S_{01}(T)$ and if input signal is $S_2(t)$, the sampled output be $S_{02}(T)$.

- When noise is present, the output signal $y(T)$ should be closer to $S_{01}(T)$ than $S_{02}(T)$ when $S_1(t)$ is transmitted. Similarly, output signal $y(T)$ should be closer to $S_{02}(T)$ than $S_{01}(T)$ when $S_2(t)$ is transmitted.

- As discussed in Chapter 7 using LRT or minimum error test criteria if the two symbols are equiprobable, the decision threshold can be kept as,

$$\lambda = \frac{S_{01}(T) + S_{02}(T)}{2} \qquad \qquad ... (8.46)$$

8.5.1 Error Probability of Optimum Filter

- In order to find error probability in this receiver, consider that $S_2(t)$ was transmitted.

- Let $n_0(T)$ be positive and $S_{01}(T) > S_{02}(T)$. If $n_0(T)$ is larger than $\lambda - S_{02}(T)$, error will be made in decision-making i.e. we will be deciding in favour of $S_1(t)$.

- Thus, error in detection occurs when,

$$n_0(T) \geq \lambda - S_{02}(T)$$

$$\geq \frac{S_{01}(T) + S_{02}(T)}{2} - S_{02}(T)$$

$$\geq \frac{S_{01}(T) - S_{02}(T)}{2} \qquad \qquad \text{... (8.47)}$$

- Since, $n_0(T)$ is a random variable. We will write PDF of $n_0(T)$ from which we can find the probability that $n_0(T)$ is greater than $\dfrac{S_{01}(T) - S_{02}(T)}{2}$ which will be error probability of detecting $S_1(t)$ when $S_2(t)$ is transmitted.

- Mean value of $n_0(T) = 0$

- Let variance $= \sigma_{no}^2$

- Let us denote this random variable $n_0(T)$ by X. Hence, PDF of $n_0(T)$ can be given by,

$$p_X(x) = \frac{1}{\sqrt{2\pi\sigma_{no}^2}} e^{-x^2/2\sigma_{no}^2} \qquad \qquad \text{... (8.48)}$$

The probability that $n_0(T)$ takes value above $\dfrac{S_{01}(T) - S_{02}(T)}{2}$ is given by,

$$p_{e_2} = \int\limits_{\frac{S_{01}(T) - S_{02}(T)}{2}}^{\infty} p_X(x)\, dx \qquad \qquad \text{... (8.49)}$$

$$\therefore \quad p_{e_2} = \int\limits_{\frac{S_{01}(T) - S_{02}(T)}{2}}^{\infty} \frac{1}{\sqrt{2\pi\sigma_{no}^2}} e^{-x^2/2\sigma_{no}^2}\, dx \qquad \qquad \text{... (8.50)}$$

Let

$$\frac{x^2}{2\sigma_{no}^2} = z^2$$

$\therefore$

$$dx = \sqrt{2\sigma_{no}^2}\, dz$$

When $\qquad x = \dfrac{S_{01}(T) - S_{02}(T)}{2}$ $\qquad z = \dfrac{S_{01}(T) - S_{02}(T)}{2\sqrt{2\sigma_{no}^2}}$

When $\qquad x = \infty$ $\qquad z = \infty$

$\therefore \qquad p_{e_2} = \displaystyle\int_{\frac{S_{01}(T) - S_{02}(T)}{2\sqrt{2\sigma_{no}^2}}}^{\infty} \dfrac{1}{\sqrt{2\pi\sigma_{no}^2}} \, e^{-z^2} \left(\sqrt{2\sigma_{no}^2}\right) dz \qquad \text{... (8.51)}$

$\qquad\qquad = \dfrac{1}{\sqrt{\pi}} \displaystyle\int_{\frac{S_{01}(T) - S_{02}(T)}{2\sqrt{2\sigma_{no}^2}}}^{\infty} e^{-z^2} \, dz$

$\therefore \qquad p_{e_2} = \dfrac{1}{2} \, \text{erfc}\left[\dfrac{S_{01}(T) - S_{02}(T)}{2\sqrt{2}\,\sigma_{no}}\right] = Q\left(\dfrac{S_{01}(T) - S_{02}(T)}{\sigma_{no}}\right) \qquad \text{... (8.52)}$

- Similarly when $s_1(t)$ is transmitted we can find the error probability p_{e_2} which comes out to be same as p_{e_1}

- The overall error probability $p_e = p_1 \cdot p_{e_1} + p_2 + p_{e_2}$ but $p_1 = p_2 = \dfrac{1}{2}$.

$\therefore \qquad p_e = \dfrac{1}{2} \, \text{erfc}\left[\dfrac{S_{01}(T) - S_{02}(T)}{2\sqrt{2}\,\sigma_{no}}\right] = Q\left[\dfrac{S_{01}(T)\,S_2(T)}{2\sigma_{no}}\right]$

- Thus, optimum filter has to maximize the ratio $\dfrac{S_{01}(T) - S_{02}(T)}{\sigma_{no}}$ in such a way that p_e becomes minimum.

8.5.2 Transfer Function of Optimum Filter

- In the previous section, we have obtained a condition for minimizing the error probability.

- Now, let us find the transfer function of filter which meets the criteria of maximising the ratio $\rho = \dfrac{S_{01}(T) - S_{02}(T)}{\sigma_{no}}$.

- The difference signal $S_{01}(T) - S_{02}(T)$ is going to decide the error probability which is going to be generated due to $S_1(t) - S_2(t)$.

- Let us call this signal as g(t) which will be assumed as input to optimum filter.

$\therefore \qquad g(t) = S_1(t) - S_2(t) \qquad\qquad \text{... (8.53)}$

- Hence, corresponding output signal will be,

$$\therefore \qquad g_0(t) = S_{01}(t) - S_{02}(t) \qquad \qquad \text{... (8.54)}$$

- Let

$$g(t) \rightleftharpoons G(f)$$

and

$$g_0(t) \rightleftharpoons G_0(f) \qquad \qquad \text{... (8.55)}$$

- If $H(f)$ is transfer function of optimum filter then,

$$G_0(f) = H(f) \cdot G(f) \qquad \qquad \text{... (8.56)}$$

$$\therefore \qquad g_0(t) = \int_{-\infty}^{\infty} H(f)\, G(f)\, e^{j2\pi ft}\, df \qquad \qquad \text{... (8.57)}$$

Put $t = T$

$$\therefore \qquad g_0(T) = \int_{-\infty}^{\infty} H(f)\, G(f)\, e^{j2\pi fT}\, df \qquad \qquad \text{... (8.58)}$$

Let the output noise power spectral density of filter be $S_{no}(f)$ which given by,

$$S_{no}(f) = \left| H(f) \right|^2 S_n(f) \qquad \qquad \text{... (8.59)}$$

where, $S_n(f)$ is input noise P.S.D.

$$\therefore \qquad \sigma_{no}^2 = \int_{-\infty}^{\infty} S_{no}(f)\, df \qquad \qquad \text{... (8.60)}$$

$$= \int_{-\infty}^{\infty} \left| H(f) \right|^2 S_n(f)\, df \qquad \qquad \text{... (8.61)}$$

$$\therefore \qquad \text{The ratio of our interest } \rho = \frac{S_{01}(T) - S_{02}(T)}{\sigma_{no}} = \frac{g_0(T)}{\sigma_{no}} \qquad \qquad \text{... (8.62)}$$

can be rewritten for our convenience as,

$$\rho^2 = \frac{g_0^2(T)}{\sigma_{no}^2} \qquad \qquad \text{... (8.63)}$$

Using equations (8.58) and (8.61) we can write,

$$\rho^2 = \frac{\left| \displaystyle\int_{-\infty}^{\infty} H(f)\, G(f)\, e^{j2\pi fT}\, df \right|^2}{\displaystyle\int_{-\infty}^{\infty} \left| H(f) \right|^2 S_n(f)\, df} \qquad \qquad \text{... (8.64)}$$

Our aim now is to find the transfer function H (f) which will maximize the above ratio. To find solution to this, we will use Schwarz's inequality which is as below.

If ϕ_1 (x) and ϕ_2 (x) are two complex functions in the real variables such that,

$$\int_{-\infty}^{\infty} |\phi_1 (x)|^2 \, dx \; < \; \infty$$

and

$$\int_{-\infty}^{\infty} |\phi_2 (x)|^2 \, dx \; \leq \; \infty$$

Then, we can write,

$$\left| \int_{-\infty}^{\infty} \phi_1 (x) \, \phi_2 (x) \, dx \right|^2 \; \leq \; \int_{-\infty}^{\infty} \left| \phi_1 (x) \right|^2 dx \cdot \int_{-\infty}^{\infty} \left| \phi_2 (x) \right|^2 dx$$

The equality holds good if and only if we have,

$$\phi_1 (x) \; = \; k \, \phi_2^{*} (x)$$

Now consider equation (8.64).

Let
$$\phi_1 (f) \; = \; \sqrt{S_n (f)} \times H(f) \qquad \qquad \text{... (8.65)}$$

and
$$\phi_2 (f) \; = \; \frac{1}{\sqrt{S_n (f)}} \cdot G(f) \, e^{j2\pi f\tau} \qquad \qquad \text{... (8.66)}$$

Hence,
$$\rho^2 \; = \; \frac{\left| \int_{-\infty}^{\infty} \phi_1 (f) \cdot \phi_2 (f) \, df \right|^2}{\int_{-\infty}^{\infty} \left| \phi_1 (f) \right|^2 df} \qquad \qquad \text{... (8.67)}$$

∴   Using Schwarz's inequality we can write,

∴
$$\rho^2 \; \leq \; \frac{\int_{-\infty}^{\infty} \left| \phi_1 (f) \right|^2 df \cdot \int_{-\infty}^{\infty} \left| \phi_2 (f) \right|^2 df}{\int_{-\infty}^{\infty} \left| \phi_1 (f) \right|^2 df} \qquad \qquad \text{... (8.68)}$$

$$\therefore \qquad \rho^2 \ \leq \ \int_{-\infty}^{\infty} \left| \phi_2 \, (f) \right|^2 \, df \qquad\qquad \dots (8.69)$$

Hence,
$$\rho_{max}^{2} \ = \ \int_{-\infty}^{\infty} \left| \phi_2 \, (f) \right|^2 \, df \qquad\qquad \dots (8.70)$$

$$= \ \int_{-\infty}^{\infty} \frac{\left| G(f) \right|^2}{S_n \, (f)} \, df \qquad\qquad \left[\therefore \ \left| e^{-2\pi f \tau} \right| = 1 \right] \dots (8.71)$$

Since the equality holds good for

$$\phi_1 \, (f) \ = \ k \, \phi_2^{*} \, (f)$$

$$\sqrt{S_n \, (f)} \ \cdot H \, (f) \ = \ k \cdot G^{*} \, (f) \, \infty \frac{1}{\sqrt{S_n \, (f)}} \ \ e^{-j2\pi f \tau} \qquad\qquad \dots (8.72)$$

$$\therefore \qquad H \, (f) \ = \ \frac{k \, G^{*} \, (f)}{S_n \, (f)} \ e^{-j2\pi f \tau} \qquad\qquad \dots (8.73)$$

This is the required transfer function of optimum filter, when the ratio $\dfrac{g_0^2 \, (T)}{\sigma_{no}^2}$ is maximum.

The ratio is given by equation (8.71).
Thus,

1. To maximize the ratio $\left[\dfrac{S_{01} \, (T) - S_{02} \, (T)}{\sigma_{no}} \right]^2$ the optimum filter should have transfer function.

$$H(f) \ = \ \frac{k \, G^{*} \, (f)}{S_n \, (f)} \ e^{-j2\pi f \tau} \qquad\qquad \dots (8.74)$$

2. The maximized ratio is,

$$\rho_{max}^{2} \ = \ \int_{-\infty}^{\infty} \frac{\left| G \, (f) \right|^2}{S_n \, (f)} \, df \qquad\qquad \dots (8.75)$$

8.6   MATCHED FILTER

- The optimum filter which we have considered in last section was with generalised Gaussian noise. An optimum filter which gives a maximum ratio $\rho^2 = \dfrac{g_0^2(T)}{\sigma_{no}^2}$ when input noise is white Gaussian noise, is called a matched filter.

- For AWGN, $S_n(f) = \dfrac{N_0}{2}$ ... (8.76)

- Using equation (8.76) in equation (8.74), we get,

$$H(f) = k\frac{G^*(f)}{\left(\dfrac{N_0}{2}\right)} e^{-j2\pi fT}$$ ... (8.77)

- This is the transfer function of matched filter.
- The impulse response of matched filter is given by,

$$h(t) = F^{-1}[H(f)] = \int_{-\infty}^{\infty} k\frac{G^*(f)}{\left(\dfrac{N_0}{2}\right)} e^{-j2\pi fT} e^{j2\pi ft} df$$

$$= \frac{2k}{N_0} \int_{-\infty}^{\infty} G^*(f) e^{-j2\pi fT} \cdot e^{j2\pi ft} df$$ ... (8.78)

- If g(t) is real valued signal

$$G^*(f) = G(-f)$$ ... (8.79)

$$\therefore \qquad h(t) = \frac{2k}{N_0} \int_{-\infty}^{\infty} G(-f) e^{-j2\pi f(T-t)} df$$ ... (8.80)

$$g(t) \rightleftharpoons G(f)$$ ... (8.81)

$$\therefore \qquad g(-t) \rightleftharpoons G(-f)$$ ... (8.82)

$$\therefore \qquad g[-(t-T)] \rightleftharpoons G(-f) e^{-j2\pi fT} \text{ ... (8.83)}$$

$$\therefore \qquad g(T-t) \rightleftharpoons G(-f) e^{-j2\pi fT} \text{ ... (8.84)}$$

- Using equation (8.84) in equation (8.80),

$$h(t) = \frac{2k}{N_0} g(T-t)$$ ... (8.85)

But, $\qquad g(t) = S_1(t) - S_2(t) \qquad$ (Assumed input signal)

$$\therefore \qquad h(t) = \frac{2k}{N_0} [S_1(T-t) - S_2(T-t)]$$ ... (8.86)

- The above equation is impulse response of matched filter. It shows that impulse response of matched filter is time reversed and delayed version of the input signal i.e. impulse response of matched filter is matched to the input.

Example 8.4 :

Show that peak pulse signal-to-noise ratio of matched filter depends only on signal energy to power spectral density of white noise at filter input.

Solution : Let $g(t)$ be an input signal to matched filter hence the impulse response of matched filter will be,

$$h(t) \quad = \quad \frac{2k_0}{N_0} \, g \, (T-t)$$

$$\therefore \qquad H(f) \quad = \quad \frac{2k}{N_0} \, G^* \, (f) \, e^{-j2\pi fT}$$

Let output of matched filter b $g_0 \, (t)$,

Now, if $\qquad\qquad\qquad g(t) \Longleftrightarrow G \, (f)$

and $\qquad\qquad\qquad g_0 \, (t) \Longleftrightarrow G_0 \, (f)$

$$G_0 \, (f) \quad = \quad H(f) \, G(f)$$

$$= \quad \frac{2k}{N_0} \, G^* \, (f) \, G \, (f) \, e^{-j2\pi fT}$$

$$= \quad \frac{2k}{N_0} \, \left| G \, (f) \right|^2 \, e^{-j2\pi fT} \quad \text{... (8.87)}$$

$$\therefore \qquad g_0 \, (t) \quad = \quad \int_{-\infty}^{\infty} G_0 \, (f) \, e^{+j2\pi ft} \, df$$

$$\therefore \qquad g_0 \, (T) \quad = \quad \int_{-\infty}^{\infty} G_0 \, (f) \, e^{+j2\pi fT} \, df$$

$$= \quad \frac{2k}{N_0} \int_{-\infty}^{\infty} \left| G \, (f) \right|^2 \, e^{-j2\pi fT} \cdot e^{j2\pi fT} \, df$$

$$= \quad \frac{2k}{N_0} \int_{-\infty}^{\infty} \left| G \, (f) \right|^2 \, df \qquad\qquad \text{... (8.88)}$$

Using Rayleigh's energy theorem,

$$\int_{-\infty}^{\infty} \left| G(f) \right|^2 df = \int_{-\infty}^{\infty} g^2(t)\, dt = E$$

$\therefore$ $\qquad\qquad g_0(T) = \dfrac{2k}{N_0} \times E$ $\qquad\qquad$ ... (8.89)

Now, $\qquad\qquad \sigma_{n0}^2 = \int_{-\infty}^{\infty} \left| H(f) \right|^2 \times \dfrac{N_0}{2}\, df$ $\qquad\qquad$ ... (8.90)

$$= \dfrac{N_0}{2} \int_{-\infty}^{\infty} \left| \dfrac{2k}{N_0} G^*(f)\, e^{-j2\pi fT} \right|^2 df$$

$$= \dfrac{N_0}{2} \times \dfrac{4k^2}{N_0^2} \int_{-\infty}^{\infty} \left| G(f) \right|^2 df$$

$\therefore$ $\qquad\qquad \sigma_{n0}^2 = \dfrac{2k^2}{N_0} \times E$ $\qquad\qquad$ ... (8.91)

Hence, $\qquad\qquad \rho_{max} = \dfrac{g_0^2(T)}{\sigma_{n0}^2}$

$$= \dfrac{\left(\dfrac{2k}{N_0} \times E \right)^2}{\dfrac{2k^2}{N_0} \times E}$$

$\therefore$ $\qquad\qquad \rho_{max} = \dfrac{2E}{N_0}$ $\qquad\qquad$ ... (8.92)

where, $\qquad\qquad E = \int_{-\infty}^{\infty} g^2(t)\, dt$

Thus, it can be seen from equation (8.92) that peak pulse signal-to-noise ratio of a matched filter depends only on the ratio of signal energy (E) and P.S.D. of white noise $N_0/2$.

8.6.1 Properties of Matched Filter

1. The spectrum of output signal of a matched filter with matched signal as input is proportional to energy density of input signal.

We have, $Y(f) = H(f) \cdot X(f)$

If input signal is $g(t)$, $X(f) = G(f)$

and
$$H(f) = \frac{2k}{N_0} G^*(f) e^{-j2\pi fT}$$

$\therefore$
$$Y(f) = \frac{2k}{N_0} G^*(f) e^{-j2\pi fT} \cdot G(f)$$

$$= \frac{2k}{N_0} |G(f)|^2 e^{-j2\pi fT} = \frac{2k}{N_0} \psi_g(f) e^{-j2\pi fT}$$

Hence, spectrum of output signal $[Y(f)]$ is proportional to its Energy Spectral Density $|G(f)|^2$.

2. The output signal of a matched filter is proportional to a shifted version of autocorrelation function of input signal to which the filter is matched.

We have
$$Y(f) = \frac{2k}{N_0} \psi_g(f) e^{-j2\pi fT}$$

Since,
$$R_g(\tau) \rightleftharpoons \psi_g(f)$$

$\therefore$
$$y(t) = \frac{2k}{N_0} \times R_g(t - T)$$

3. The output signal-to-noise ratio of matched filter depends only on the ratio of the signal energy to P.S.D. of white noise at filter input.

This property is already proved in equation (8.92).

Example 8.5 :

Find impulse function of filter for rectangular pulse given in Fig. 8.8 (a). Find output of matched filter.

Solution :
$$g(t) = A \, \text{rect}\left(\frac{t - T/2}{T}\right)$$

$g(-t)$ is shown in Fig. 8.8 (b).

$g[-(t-T)] = g(T-t)$ is shown in Fig. 8.8 (c).

We see that
$$g(T-t) = g(t) = A \, \text{rect}\left(\frac{t - T/2}{T}\right)$$

$\therefore$
$$h(t) = \frac{2k}{N_0} g(T-t) = \frac{2k}{N_0} A \, \text{rect}\left(\frac{t - T/2}{T}\right)$$

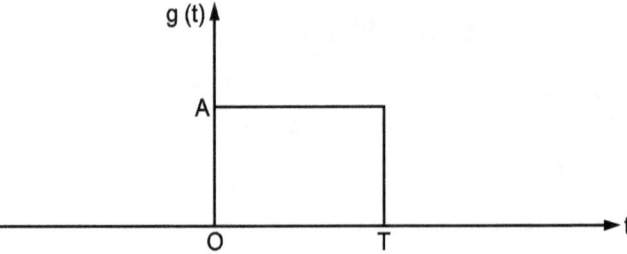

Fig. 8.8 : (a) Rectangular pulse g(t)

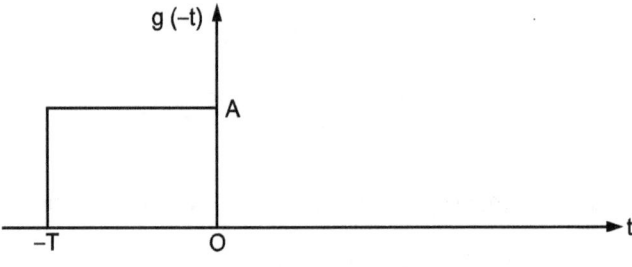

Fig. 8.8 : (b) g (– t)

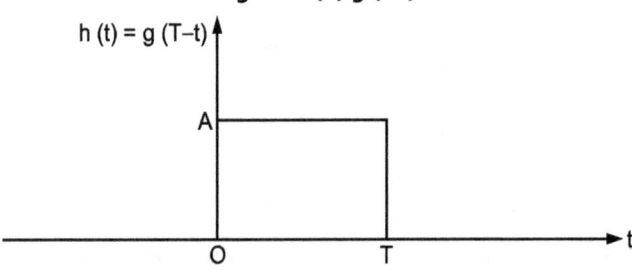

Fig. 8.8 : (c) g (T – t)

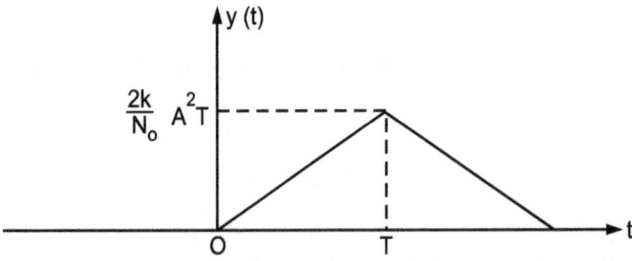

Fig. 8.8 : (d) Response of matched filter to rectangular pulse

The impulse response of matched filter for rectangular pulse input is same as rectangular pulse.

Output of matched filter can be found as input $g(t) = A \, \text{rect}\left(\dfrac{t - T/2}{T}\right)$.

$\therefore$ $y(t) = h(t) * g(t)$

$$A \, rect\left(\frac{t - T/2}{T}\right) \rightleftharpoons AT \, sinc \, (fT) \cdot e^{j\pi fT}$$

$\therefore$ $Y(f) = H(f) \cdot G(f)$

$$= \frac{2k}{N_0} \times AT \, sinc \, (fT) \cdot AT \, sinc \, (fT) \, e^{j2\pi fT}$$

$$= \frac{2k}{N_0} A^2 T^2 \, sinc^2 \, (fT) \, e^{j2\pi fT}$$

Taking inverse fourier transform of y (f), we get,

$$\therefore \; F^{-1}\left[\frac{2k}{N_0} \times A^2 T^2 \, sinc^2 \, (fT) \, e^{j2\pi fT}\right] = \frac{2k}{N_0} A^2 T \, \Delta\left(\frac{t - T}{2T}\right)$$

$\therefore$ $y(t) = \dfrac{2k}{N_0} A^2 T \, \Delta\left(\dfrac{t - T}{2T}\right)$

where Δ represents triangular pulse.

Hence, the output of matched filter is a triangular pulse of amplitude $A^2 T \times \dfrac{2k}{N_0}$ and width 2T.

Note that $A^2 T$ is energy of rectangular pulse of duration T and that this value occurs at the end of bit duration when we normally sample the signal for detection. If we consider the output for duration T, it will be output of integrate-and-dump filter. At the end of duration T, the filter can be dumped to start new integration in the next interval.

Example 8.6 :

Find the matched filter for polar NRZ signal. Also find output of the filter.

Solution : There are two signals used with polar NRZ waveform.

Let $S_1(t) = A \, rect\left(\dfrac{t - T/2}{T}\right)$ shown in Fig. 8.9 (a)

Fig. 8.9 : (a) $S_1(t) = rect\left(\dfrac{t - T/2}{T}\right)$

$$S_2(t) = -A\ \text{rect}\left(\frac{t-T/2}{T}\right) \text{ Shown in Fig. 8.9 (b)}$$

Fig. 8.9 : (b) $S_2(t) = -A\ \text{rect}\left(\dfrac{t-T/2}{T}\right)$

$\therefore$

$$g(t) = S_1(t) - S_2(t)$$

$$= 2A\ \text{rect}\left(\frac{t-T/2}{T}\right) \text{ shown in Fig. 8.9 (c)}$$

Fig. 8.9 : (c) $S_1(t) - S_2(t) = g(t)$

g (– t) is shown in Fig. 8.9 (d)

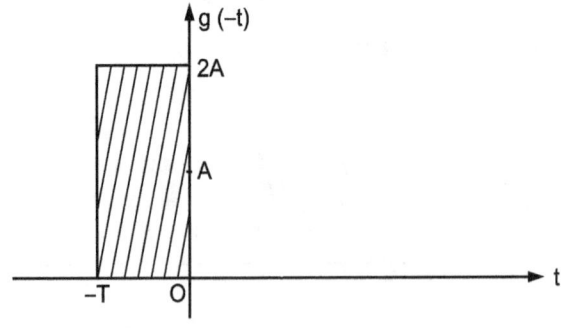

Fig. 8.9 : (d) g (– t)

$\therefore$ g [– (t – T)] is shown in Fig. 8.9 (e).

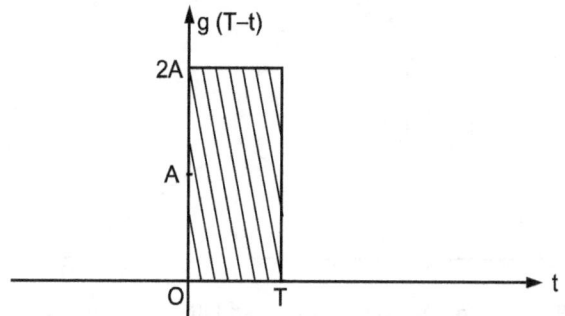

Fig. 8.9 : (e) g (T – t)

Hence, $$h(t) = \frac{2k}{N_0} \times 2A \; rect\left(\frac{t - T/2}{T}\right)$$

Thus, impulse response of matched filter for NRZ polar signal is a rectangular pulse of width T and amplitude 2A. It is shown in Fig. 8.9 (f).

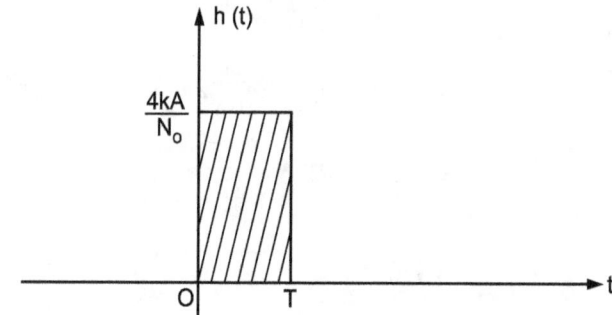

Fig. 8.9 : (f) Impulse Response h(t)

(i) For positive input pulse output of matched filter will be found as below.

$$S_1(t) = A \; rect\left(\frac{t - T/2}{T}\right)$$

$$h(t) = \frac{2k}{N_0} \times 2A \; rect\left(\frac{t - T/2}{T}\right)$$

$\therefore$ $$H(f) = \frac{2k}{N_0} \times 2 \; AT \; sinc(fT) \; e^{j\pi fT}$$

$$S_1(f) = AT \; sinc(fT) \; e^{j\pi fT}$$

$\therefore$ $$y(f) = H(f) \cdot S_1(f) = \frac{2k}{N_0} \times 2 \; A^2T^2 \; sinc^2(fT) \; e^{j2\pi fT}$$

$\therefore$ $$y(t) = \frac{4k}{N_0} A^2T \; \Delta\left(\frac{t - T}{2T}\right)$$

Plotted in Fig. 8.9 (g).

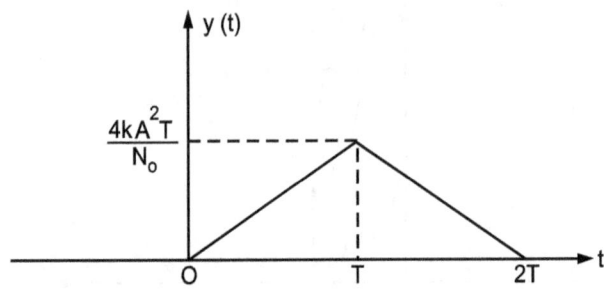

Fig. 8.9 : (g) Output of Matched Filter for Input S$_1$ (t)

(ii) For negative input pulse

$$S_2(t) = -A \, rect\left(\frac{t - T/2}{T}\right)$$

$$H(f) = \frac{2k}{N_0} \times 2AT \, sinc \, (fT) \, e^{j\pi fT}$$

$\therefore$ $$S_2(f) = -AT \, sinc \, (fT) \, e^{j\pi fT}$$

$\therefore$ $$Y(f) = H(f) \, S_2(f) = -\frac{2k}{N_0} 2 A^2 T^2 \, sinc^2 \, (fT) \, e^{j2\pi fT}$$

$$y(t) = -\frac{4k}{N_0} \times A^2 T \, \Delta\left(\frac{t - T}{2T}\right)$$

Plotted in Fig. 8.9 (h).

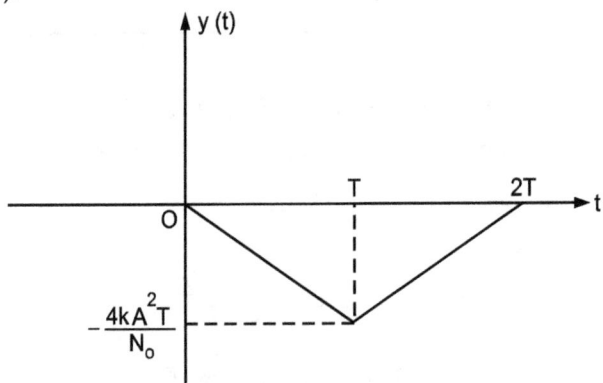

Fig. 8.9 : (h) Output of Matched Filter for Input S$_2$ (t)

Example 8.7 :

Find matched filter impulse response for the input shown in Fig. 8.10 (a) and (b).

Solution :

1. S_1 (t) and S_2 (t) are given hence.

2.   g (t) = S_1 (t) – S_2 (t) can be found. It is shown in Fig. 8.10 (c).

3.   g (– t) can be found and plotted in Fig. 8.10 (d).

4.   h (t) = g (T – t) is shown in Fig. 8.10 (e).

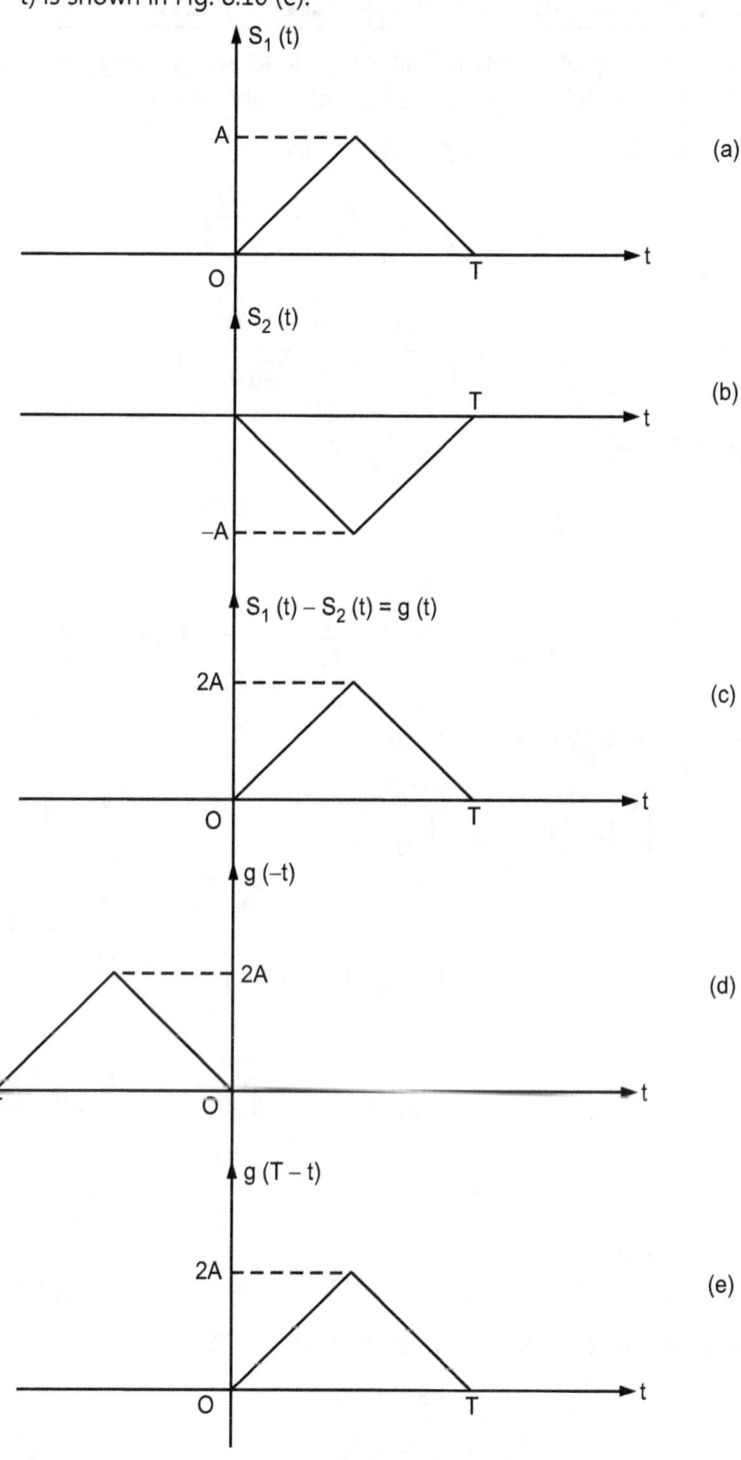

Fig. 8.10

8.7 ERROR PROBABILITY OF MATCHED FILTER

- The error probability of a matched filter can be found by using the result obtained for optimum filter. A matched filter is special case of optimum filter.

- For an optimum filter the error probability is given by,

$$P_e = \frac{1}{2} \, \text{erfc}\left[\frac{S_{01}(T) - S_{02}(T)}{2\sqrt{2}\,\sigma_{no}}\right] \qquad \text{... (8.93)}$$

$$\rho^2_{max} = \left[\frac{g_0^2(T)}{\sigma_{no}^2}\right] = \int_{-\infty}^{\infty} \frac{|G(f)|^2}{S_n(f)} \, df \qquad \text{... (8.94)}$$

- For a matched filter,

$$S_n(f) = \frac{N_0}{2}$$

$$\therefore \qquad \rho^2_{max} = \left[\frac{g_0^2(T)}{\sigma_{no}^2}\right] = \frac{2}{N_0} \int_{-\infty}^{\infty} |G(f)|^2 \, df \qquad \text{... (8.95)}$$

- Using Rayleigh's energy theorem, we get,

$$\int_{-\infty}^{\infty} |G(f)|^2 \, df = \int_{-\infty}^{\infty} g^2(t) \, dt$$

$$= \int_{0}^{T} [S_1(t) - S_2(t)]^2 \, dt$$

$$= \int_{0}^{T} S_1^2(t) \, dt + \int_{0}^{T} S_2^2(t) \, dt - 2\int_{0}^{T} S_1(t) \cdot S_2(t) \, dt$$

$$= E_1 + E_2 - 2E_{12} \qquad \text{... (8.96)}$$

E_1 – Energy of $S_1(t)$

E_2 – Energy of $S_2(t)$

E_{12} – Energy due to correlation between $S_1(t)$ and $S_2(t)$.

If $\qquad S_1(t) = -S_2(t)$

$$E_1 = E_2 = -E_{12} = E \qquad \text{... (8.97)}$$

$$\therefore \qquad \rho_{max}^2 = \frac{2}{N_0} \times (E + E - (-2E))$$

$$= \frac{2}{N_0} \times 4E$$

$$= \frac{8E}{N_0} \qquad \qquad ... (8.98)$$

$$\therefore \qquad \left[\frac{S_{01}(T) - S_{02}(T)}{\sigma_{n0}} \right]_{max}^2 = \frac{8E}{N_0} \qquad \qquad ... (8.99)$$

$$\therefore \qquad \left[\frac{S_{01}(T) - S_{02}(T)}{\sigma_{n0}} \right]_{max} = 2\sqrt{2} \sqrt{\frac{E}{N_0}} \qquad \qquad ... (8.100)$$

$$\therefore \qquad \left[\frac{S_{01}(T) - S_{02}(T)}{2\sqrt{2} \, \sigma_{n0}} \right]_{max} = \sqrt{\frac{E}{N_0}} \qquad \qquad ... (8.101)$$

- Minimum Error Probability of matched filter will be obtained by substituting equation (8.100) in equation (8.93).

$$\therefore \qquad = \frac{1}{2} \, erfc \left(\sqrt{\frac{E}{N_0}} \right) \qquad \qquad ... (8.101)$$

- Since this is error probability obtained for maximum value of $\left(\dfrac{E}{N_0} \right)$ it will be the minimum error probability value.

$$\therefore \qquad \boxed{ (P_e)_{min} = \frac{1}{2} \, erfc \left(\sqrt{\frac{E}{N_0}} \right) } \qquad \qquad ... (8.102)$$

- Now, let us go back to equation (8.41) where we obtained error probability for an integrator-and-dump circuit. The result obtained for matched filter and integrator-and-dump circuit are the same. Hence, we can conclude that **integrator-and-dump circuit is indeed a matched filter and gives minimum error probability value.**

- We will also verify whether the impulse response of matched filter for the signal defined as,

$$S_1(t) = +A \qquad ; \qquad 0 \le t \le T$$

$$S_2(t) = -A \qquad ; \qquad 0 \le t \le T$$

is same as integrator-and-dump filter or not.

- From equation (8.86), we can write,

$$h(t) = \frac{2k}{N_0} [S_1(T-t) - S_2(T-t)] \qquad \text{... (8.103)}$$

- $S_1(T-t) - S_2(T-t)$ will be a rectangular pulse with amplitude 2A and width T.

$$\therefore \qquad h(t) = \frac{2k}{N_0} \times 2A [u(t) - u(t-T)] \qquad \text{... (8.104)}$$

- The factor $\frac{2k}{N_0} \times 2A$ is amplification factor which is going to be applied both for signal

  and noise. Hence, has no effect on error probability.

$$\therefore \qquad h(t) = u(t) - u(t-T) \qquad \text{... (8.105)}$$

is actual impulse response of our interest.

- Taking Laplace transform, we get,

$$H(s) = \frac{1}{s} - \frac{e^{-sT}}{s} \qquad \text{... (8.106)}$$

- The first term $\frac{1}{s}$ is integration beginning at t = 0 and the second term $\frac{e^{-sT}}{s}$ is an
  integration beginning at t = T with reverse polarity.

- Hence, overall response is integration beginning at t = 0 and ending at t = T and zero response thereafter. This shows that the matched filter is an integrate-and-dump circuit.

8.8 CORRELATION

- Most often while detecting a signal at receiver end often a circuit called correlator is used which is combination of a multiplier and integrator.

- Thus, correlator is a receiving system used for coherent reception of binary digital modulated signals.

- Fig. 8.11 (a) shows a coherent system of signal reception which uses correlator.

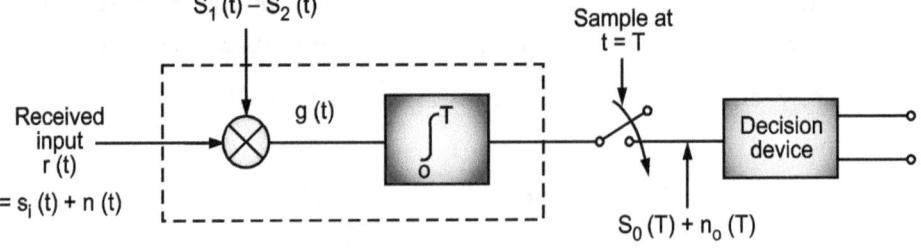

Fig. 8.11 : (a) Correlator

1.   The received signal $r(t) = S_i(t) + n(t)$ is multiplied with a locally generated waveform $S_1(t) - S_2(t)$. The received signal will have either $S_1(t)$ or $S_2(t)$ received alongwith noise $n(t)$.

2.   The output of multiplier $g(t)$ is passed through an integrator whose output is sampled at $t = T$.

3.   The sampled output can be given by,

$$S_0(T) = \frac{1}{\tau} \int_0^T S_i(t) [S_1(t) - S_2(t)] \, dt \qquad \text{... (8.107)}$$

$$n_0(T) = \frac{1}{\tau} \int_0^T n(t) [S_1(t) - S_2(t)] \, dt \qquad \text{... (8.108)}$$

where, $S_0(T)$ is sampled output due to input signal $S_i(t)$ and $S_0(T)$ is sampled output due to input noise $n(t)$.

- Now let us replace the correlator by a matched filter as shown in Fig. 8.11 (b).

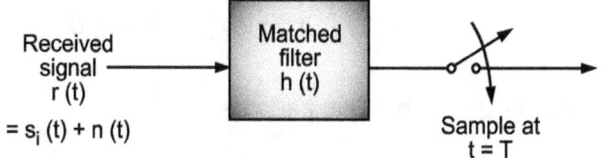

Fig. 8.11 : (b) Matched filter

- Let $h(t)$ be the impulse response of matched filter. Hence, output of matched filter can be given as,

$$g(t) = h(t) * r(t) \qquad \text{... (8.109)}$$

$$\therefore \qquad g(t) = \int_{-\infty}^{\infty} r(\lambda) \, h(t - \lambda) \, d\lambda \qquad \text{... (8.110)}$$

- Since filter response for bit interval T is required we write,

$$g(t) = \int_0^T r(\lambda) \, h(t - \lambda) \, d\lambda \qquad \text{... (8.111)}$$

- Now, matched filter impulse response for input signals $S_1(t)$ and $S_2(t)$ is given by equation (8.86) as,

$$h(t) = \frac{2k}{N_0} [S_1(T - t) - S_2(T - t)] \qquad \text{... (8.112)}$$

$\therefore \qquad\qquad h(t-\lambda) = \dfrac{2k}{N_0}[S_1(T-t+\lambda) - S_2(T-t+\lambda)] \qquad\qquad ...(8.113)$

- Putting this value in equation (8.111), we get output of matched filter as,

$$g(t) = \int_0^T r(\lambda) \times \dfrac{2k}{N_0}[S_1(T-t+\lambda) - S_2(T-t+\lambda)]\, d\lambda$$

$$= \dfrac{2k}{N_0}\int_0^T r(\lambda)[S_1(T-t+\lambda) - S_2(T-t+\lambda)]\, d\lambda \qquad ...(8.114)$$

Putting $r(\lambda) = S(\lambda) + n(\lambda)$

and $t = T$ in equation (8.114), we get,

$$g(T) = \dfrac{2k}{N_0}\int_0^T S(\lambda)[S_1(\lambda) - S_2(\lambda)]\, d\lambda$$

$$\qquad + \dfrac{2k}{N_0}\int_0^T n(\lambda)[S_1(\lambda) - S_2(\lambda)]\, d\lambda \qquad\qquad ...(8.115)$$

- Hence, the output matched filter has two parts below.

$$S_0(T) = \dfrac{2k}{N_0}\int_0^T S(\lambda)[S_1(\lambda) - S_2(\lambda)]\, d\lambda \qquad\qquad ...(8.116)$$

$$n_0(T) = \dfrac{2k}{N_0}\int_0^T n(\lambda)[S_1(\lambda) - S_2(\lambda)]\, d\lambda \qquad\qquad ...(8.117)$$

where, $\qquad\qquad g(T) = S_0(T) + n_0(T)$

- Comparing equations (8.116) and (8.117) with equations (8.107) and (8.108), we can conclude that output of correlator and matched filter are identical.

- Hence, performances of the two systems are same.

- Thus, if we have to synthesize a filter for inimizing error probability of receiver optimum filter) we can either use matched filter or correlator.

- The mathematical operation of matched filter is convolution whereas that of correlator is correlation. Still they behave in the same way.

- Impulse response of matched filter is input signal reversed in time. Now convolution also reverses the signal in time. This process as correlation.

- The correlator output and matched filter output are same only at t = T.

- For sine wave input the correlator output is linear ramp whereas matched filter output is amplitude modulated linear ramp as shown in Fig. 8.11 (c).

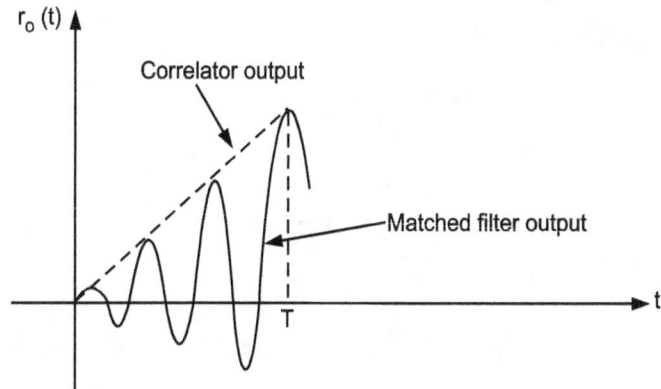

Fig. 8.11 (c) : Correlator and matched filter output

8.9 CALCULATION OF ERROR PROBABILITY USING SIGNAL SPACE AND DECISION THEORY

- From decision theory, applying CRT or minimum error test we know the minimum error probability is given by

$$p_e = Q\left(\frac{a_1 - a_0}{2\sigma}\right)$$

This is equivalent to our result obtained for optimum filter

$$p_e = Q\left(\frac{s_{01}(T) - s_{02}(T)}{2\sigma_{no}}\right)$$

- For AWGN

$$\sigma_{n_0}^2 = \frac{N_0}{2}$$

and

$$(s_{01}(T) - s_{02}(T))^2 = \int_0^{T_b} [s_1(t) - s_2(t)] \, dt = E_d$$

∴

$$\frac{s_{01}(T) - s_{02}(T)}{2\sigma_{n_0}} = \frac{1}{2}\sqrt{\frac{(s_{01}(T) - s_{02}(T))^2}{\sigma_{n_0}^2}}$$

$$= \frac{1}{2}\sqrt{\frac{2E_d}{N_0}} = \sqrt{\frac{E_d}{2N_0}}$$

- Hence error probability is given by

$$p_e = Q\left(\sqrt{\frac{E_d}{2N_0}}\right)$$

- For Polar NRZ signaling format,

$$s_1(t) = \sqrt{E_b}\,\phi_1(t)$$

$$s_2(t) = -\sqrt{E_b}\,\phi_2(t)$$

$$E_d = \int_0^{T_b} [s_2(t) - s_2(t)]\, dt$$

$$\therefore \quad E_d = \int_0^{T_b} s_1^2(t) + dt + \int_0^{T_b} s_2^2\, dt - 2\int_0^{T_b} s_1(t) \cdot s_2(t)\, dt$$

$$= E_b \int_0^{T_b} \phi_1^2(t)\, dt + E_b \int_0^{T_b} \phi_1^2(t)\, dt - 2\int_0^{T_b} (E_b)\phi_1^2(t)\, dt$$

$$= E_b + E_b + 2E_b$$

$$\therefore \quad p_e = Q\left(\sqrt{\frac{4E_b}{2N_0}}\right) = Q\left(\sqrt{\frac{2E_b}{N_0}}\right)$$

$$= 4E_b$$

- For unipolar NRZ signaling format

$$s_1(t) = \sqrt{E_b}\,\phi_1(t)$$

$$s_2(t) = 0$$

$$\therefore \quad E_d = \int_0^{T_b} [s_1(t) - s_2(t)]^2\, dt$$

$$= \int_0^{T_b} s_1^2(t)\, dt + \int_0^{T_b} s_2^2(t)\, dt - 2\int_0^{T_b} s_1(t)\, s_2(t)\, dt$$

$$= E_b + 0 + 0$$

$$= E_b$$

$$\therefore \quad P_e = Q\left(\sqrt{\frac{E_b}{2N_0}}\right)$$

- For orthogonal signaling format

$$s_1(f) = \sqrt{E_b}\phi_1(t)$$

$$s_2(f) = \sqrt{E_b}\phi_2(t)$$

$$\therefore \quad E_d = \int_0^{T_b} s_1^2(t)\, dt + \int_0^{T_b} s_2^2(t)\, dt - 2\int_0^{T_b} s_1(t)\, s_2(t)\, dt$$

$$= E_b + E_b - 2E_b \int_0^{T_b} \phi_1(t)\, \phi_2(t)\, dt = E_b + E_b - 2E_b \times 0$$

$$= 2E_b$$

$$\therefore \quad p_e = Q\left(\sqrt{\frac{2E_b}{2N_0}}\right) = Q\left(\sqrt{\frac{E_b}{N_0}}\right)$$

SOLVED EXAMPLES

Problem 8.1 :

Find frequency response of the filter which is matched to triangular pulse $\wedge$ (t – 1).

Solution :

Given : Input to matched filter.

$$g(t) = \Delta(t - 1)$$

The matched filter has frequency response.

$$H(f) = \frac{2k}{N_0} \times G^*(f) \cdot e^{-j2\pi f t_0}$$

For triangular pulse, width (T) is 1.

$$\therefore \quad H(f) = \frac{2k}{N_0}\, \text{sinc}^2(f)\, e^{+j2\pi f} \times e^{-j2\pi f} = \frac{2k}{N_0}\, \text{sinc}^2(f)$$

Problem 8.2 :

What is sampling instant signal-to-noise ratio at the output of a filter matched to a triangular pulse of height 10 mV and width 1.00 ms, if the noise at the input to the filter is white with PSD of 10 nV^2/Hz.

Solution :

Energy of input pulse is given by,

$$E_b = \int_0^{T_0} V^2(t)\, dt$$

$$= \int_0^{T_0/2} (20\,t)^2\, dt + \int_{T_0/2}^{T_0} [2 \times 10^{-2} - 20\,t]^2\, dt$$

$$= 400 \left[\frac{t^3}{3}\right]_0^{0.5 \times 10^{-3}} + 4 \times 10^{-4} \left[\frac{t}{1}\right]_{0.5 \times 10^{-3}}^{1 \times 10^{-3}}$$

$$- 80 \times 10^{-2} \left[\frac{t^2}{2}\right]_{0.5 \times 10^{-3}}^{1 \times 10^{-3}} + 400 \left[\frac{t^3}{3}\right]_{0.5 \times 10^{-3}}^{1 \times 10^{-3}}$$

$$= 0.33 \times 10^{-7}\ V^2 s$$

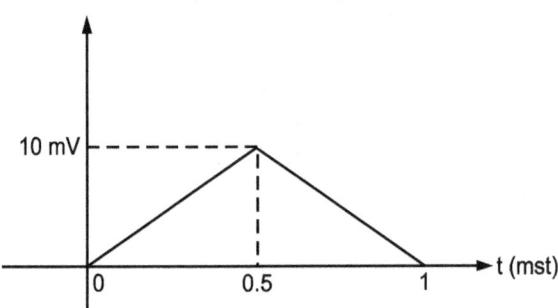

Fig. 8.22

The sampling instant SNR is,

$$\frac{S}{N} = \frac{2E_b}{N_0} = \frac{2 \times 0.33 \times 10^{-7}}{10 \times 10^{-9}}$$

$$= 6.67$$

$$\left(\frac{S}{N}\right)_{dB} = 10 \log 6.67 = 8.24\ dB$$

Problem 8.3 :

A bipolar binary system with $S_i(t) = \pm A$ uses integrate and dump filter for detection. If $p(S_1) = p(S_2) = \frac{1}{2}$, $\frac{N_0}{2} = 10^{-9}$ W/Hz and A = 10 mV with data rate 10^4 b/S.

(i) Find error probability.

(ii) If the bit rate is increased to 10^5 b/s what value of A is needed to attain the same p_e.

Solution :

(i)
$$\frac{2A^2T_b}{N_0} = \frac{A^2T_b}{N_0/2} = \frac{(0.01)^2 \times 10^{-4}}{10^{-9}} = 10$$

$\therefore$
$$p_e = Q\left(\sqrt{\frac{2A^2T_b}{N_0}}\right)$$

$$= Q(\sqrt{10})$$

$$= 7.8 \times 10^{-4}$$

(ii) Since we want $p_e = 7.8 \times 10^{-4}$

i.e.
$$7.8 \times 10^{-4} = Q\left(\sqrt{\frac{2A^2T_b}{N_0}}\right)$$

But,
$$Q(\sqrt{10}) = 7.8 \times 10^{-4}$$

$\therefore$
$$\frac{2A^2T_b}{N_0} = 10$$

$\therefore$
$$\frac{A^2T_b}{N_0/2} = 10$$

$\therefore$
$$\frac{A^2 \times 10^{-5}}{10^{-9}} = 10$$

$\therefore$
$$A^2 = 10 \times 10^{-4}$$

$$A = 31.62 \times 10^{-3}$$

$$= 31.62 \text{ mV}$$

SOLVED UNIVERSITY QUESTIONS

U.Q. 1 : Polar binary pulses are received with peak amplitude $A_p = 1$ mV. The channel noise rms amplitude is 192.3 micro volt. Threshold detection is used and logical '1' and '0' are equally likely. Find the detection error probability. **(8) (Dec. 2005)**

Solution : Given :

Peak amplitude, $A_p = 1$ mV

rms amplitude of channel noise,

$$\sigma_{n0} = 192.3 \ \mu V$$

$$p_e = \frac{1}{2} \text{erfc}\left(\frac{S_{o1}(T) - S_{o2}(T)}{2\sqrt{2} \ \sigma_{n0}}\right)$$

$$= Q\left(\frac{S_{o1}(T) - S_{o2}(T)}{2\sigma_{n0}}\right)$$

For polar signal,

$$S_{o1}(T) - S_{o2}(T) = A_p - (-A_p)$$

$$= 2A_p$$

$$\therefore \qquad p_e = Q\left(\frac{A_p}{\sigma_{n0}}\right)$$

$$\therefore \qquad = Q\left(\frac{1 \times 10^{-3}}{192.3 \times 10^{-6}}\right)$$

$$= Q\,(5.2)$$

$$= 10^{-7}$$

U.Q. 2 : Find the error probability for :

(i) On-off (unipolar) case and

(ii) Bipolar case

If pulses of same shape as in U.Q. 1 are used but amplitudes are adjusted so that transmission power is same as in U.Q. 1. **(8) (Dec. 2005)**

Solution :

On-off (Unipolar) case :

In earlier problem i.e. polar pulses,

$$A_p = 1\,mV$$

$$\sigma_{n0} = 193.3\,\mu V$$

To maintain same energy as in earlier problem,

$$A_p = \sqrt{2} \times 1\,mV$$

$$\text{Error probability, } p_e = Q\left(\frac{S_{o1}\,(T) - S_{o2}\,(T)}{2\sigma_{n0}}\right) = Q\left(\frac{\sqrt{2} \times 1 \times 10^{-3} - 0}{2 \times 193.3 \times 10^{-6}}\right)$$

$$= Q\,(3.68)$$

$$= 1.66 \times 10^{-4}$$

U.Q. 3 : A matched filter has time response given by,

$$h(t) = 1000\,t \text{ volts; for } 0 \le t \le 0.01\,ms$$

$$= 0 \qquad ; \qquad \text{otherwise}$$

(i) What should be the shape of input signal for this matched filter ?

(ii) What is sampling instance for decision ?

(iii) If $N_0 = 0.625 \times 10^{-10}$ W/Hz. Find p_e **(18) (Dec. 2005)**

Solution :

(i) Given : $\qquad\qquad h(t) = 1000\,t \qquad ; \qquad\qquad$ for $0 \le t \le 0.01\,ms$

$$= 0 \qquad ; \qquad \text{otherwise}$$

The plot will be,

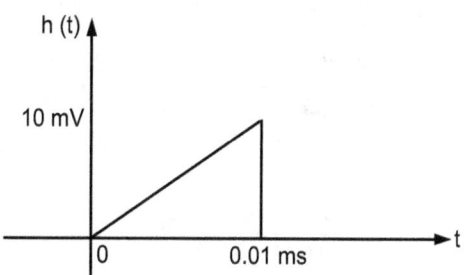

Fig. 8.23

Since input signal is, $\quad$ h(t) $\quad = \quad$ g(T – t)
The input signal g(t) will be as below.

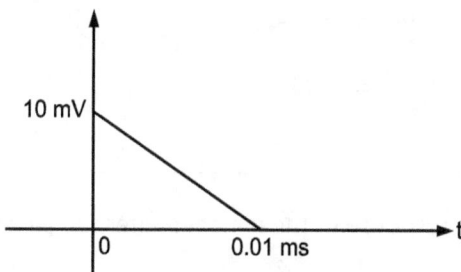

Fig. 8.24

(ii) The output of matched filter is,
$$y(t) \quad = \quad g(t) * h(t)$$

The output will be,

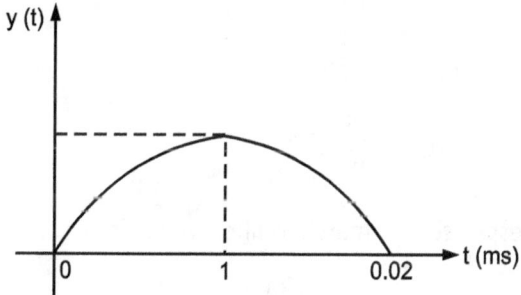

Fig. 8.25

Hence, best sampling time is t = 0.01 ms

(iii)
$$E_b^2 \quad = \quad \frac{1}{2} \Delta^2 \times T_b$$

$$= \quad \frac{1}{2} (10 \text{ mV})^2 \times (0.01 \text{ ms})$$

$$= \quad 0.5 \times 10^{-9} \text{ J}$$

$$\rho_{max}^2 = \frac{E_b^2}{\sigma_n^2}$$

$$= \frac{2E_b^2}{N_0}$$

$$= \frac{2 \times 0.5 \times 10^{-9}}{0.625 \times 10^{-10}}$$

$$= 16$$

$$\rho_{max} = 4$$

$$\therefore \qquad P_e = Q(\rho_{max})$$

$$= Q(4)$$

$$= 3 \times 10^{-5}$$

U.Q. 4 : Calculate impulse response of the matched filter for Gaussian pulse given by,

$$g(t) = e^{-\pi t^2} \qquad \text{(6) (May 2006)}$$

Solution : The impulse response of matched filter is given by,

$$h(t) = \frac{2k}{N_0} g(T - t)$$

But,

$$g(t) = e^{-\pi t^2}$$

$$\therefore \qquad h(t) = \frac{2k}{N_0} e^{-\pi(T - t)^2}$$

U.Q. 5 : Find impulse response of a matched filter whose input is given by,

$$g(t) = A \sin\left(\frac{2\pi t}{T}\right) \quad ; \qquad 0 < t < T$$

$$= 0 \qquad\qquad ; \qquad \text{otherwise} \qquad \text{(8) (May 2006)}$$

Solution : Let us find out graphically the impulse response of given input.

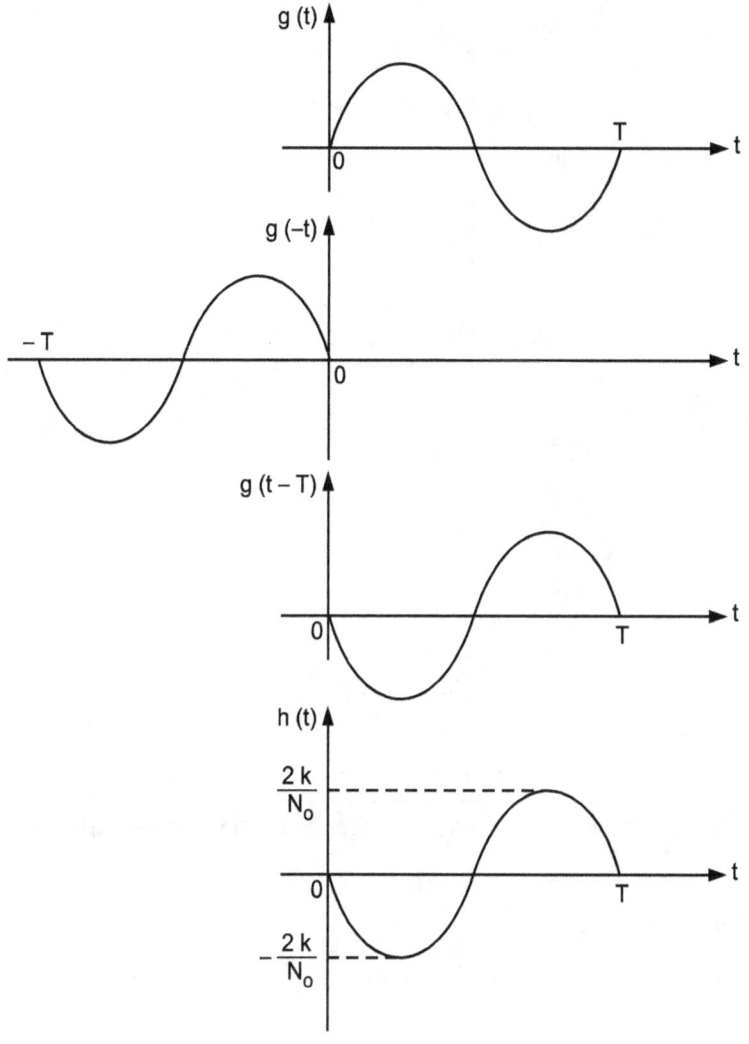

Fig. 8.26

$\therefore$

$$h(t) = -\frac{2k}{N_0} \sin\left(\frac{2\pi t}{T}\right) \quad ; \quad 0 < t \le T$$

$$= 0 \quad\quad\quad ; \quad \text{Otherwise}$$

U.Q. 6 : Explain operation of optimum receiver. **(8) (Dec. 2006)**

Solution : Refer Section 8.5.

U.Q. 7 : A received (binary) signal has amplitude $\pm$ 2V held for a time T. The signal is corrupted by White Gaussian noise having power spectral density 10^{-4} volt^2/Hz. If the signal is processed by integrate and dump filter, what should be minimum time T of the signal so that error probability is not above 10^{-4}.

Solution : Given : $\quad\quad\quad A = \pm 2V$

$$\frac{N_0}{2} = 10^{-4} \text{ volt}^2/\text{Hz}$$

$$N_0 = 2 \times 10^{-4} \text{ volt}^2/\text{Hz}$$

For polar signal error probability is,

$$p_e = \frac{1}{2} \text{erfc}\left(\sqrt{\frac{A^2 T_b}{N_0}}\right)$$

$$p_e = Q\left(\sqrt{\frac{2A^2 T_b}{N_0}}\right)$$

We require $p_e < 10^{-4}$

$\therefore$
$$Q(3.71) = 10^{-4}$$

$\therefore$
$$\sqrt{\frac{2A^2 T_b}{N_0}} = (3.71)$$

$$\frac{2A^2 T_b}{N_0} = (3.71)^2$$

$$T_0 = \frac{(3.71)^2 \times 2 \times 10^{-4}}{(\pm 2)^2 \times 2}$$

$$= 3.44 \times 10^{-4} \text{ s}$$

U.Q. 8 : State various properties of matched filter. Explain impulse response in detail.

(8) (Dec. 2006)

Solution : Refer Section 8.6.1.

U.Q. 9 : Derive expression for signal to noise ratio of integrator and dump filter.

(8) (May 2007)

Solution : Refer Example 8.3.

U.Q. 10 : Write short note on matched filter.   **(8) (May 2007)**

Solution : Refer Section 8.6.

U.Q. 11 : Show that for a matched filter maximum signal component occurs at t = T and has magnitude E i.e. energy of the signal.   **(8) (May 2007)**

Solution : Refer Example 8.4.

U.Q. 12 : Show that performance of correlator and matched filter are identical, with the help of suitable expression.   **(8 marks) (Dec. 2007, 2008)**

Solution : Refer Section 8.8.

U.Q. 13 : A binary data is transmitted at a rate 10 Mbps over a channel whose bandwidth is 8 MHz. Find signal energy per bit at receiver input for $p_e \leq 10^{-4}$. Assume $\frac{N_0}{2} = 10^{-10}$ Watt/Hz.   **(8 marks) (Dec. 2007)**

Solution : Given :
$$r_b = 10 \text{ Mbps}$$
$$BW = 8 \text{ MHz}$$
$$p_e \leq 10^{-4}$$
$$\frac{N_0}{2} = 10^{-10} \text{ Watt/Hz}$$

Now, $p_e = \frac{1}{2} \text{erfc}\left(\sqrt{\frac{E_b}{N_0}}\right)$

$\therefore \quad 10^{-4} = \frac{1}{2} \text{erfc}\left(\sqrt{\frac{E_b}{N_0}}\right)$

$2 \times 10^{-4} = \text{erfc}\left(\sqrt{\frac{E_b}{N_0}}\right)$

$1 - 2 \times 10^{-4} = 1 - \text{erfc}\left(\sqrt{\frac{E_b}{N_0}}\right)$

$0.9998 = \text{erfc}\left(\sqrt{\frac{E_b}{N_0}}\right)$

From table, $\text{erfc}(2.6) \simeq 0.9998$

$\therefore \quad \sqrt{\frac{E_b}{N_0}} = 2.6$

$\therefore \quad E_b = 1.35 \times 10^{-9} \text{ J}$

$p_e = Q\left(\sqrt{\frac{2E_b}{N_0}}\right)$

$10^{-4} = Q\left(\sqrt{\frac{2E_b}{N_0}}\right)$

$\therefore \sqrt{\frac{2E_b}{N_0}} = 3.7$

$\therefore \frac{2E_b}{N_0} = 13.69$

$\therefore E_b = \frac{13.69 \times 2 \times 10^{-10}}{2}$

$= 1.36 \times 10^{-9} \text{ J}$

U.Q. 14 : Show that the impulse response of a matched filter is a time reversed and delayed version of input signal.   **(8 marks) (May 2008)**

Solution : Refer Section 8.6.

U.Q.15 : For following signal S(t) shown in Fig. 8.27. Determine impulse response of matched filter. Find output also.   **(8 marks) (May 2008, Dec. 2008)**

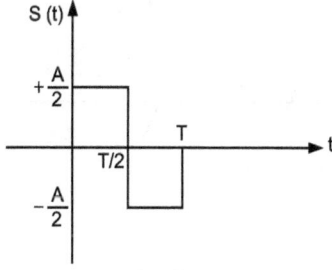

Fig. 8.27

Solution : The impulse response of matched filter is,

$$h(t) = \frac{2k}{N_0} S(T - t)$$

$\therefore$

$$h(t) = -\frac{A}{2} \quad ; \quad 0 \le t \le \frac{T}{2}$$

$$= \frac{A}{2} \quad ; \quad \frac{T}{2} \le t \le T$$

The output of matched filter is,

$$y(t) = s(t) * h(t)$$

Graphically shown as below.

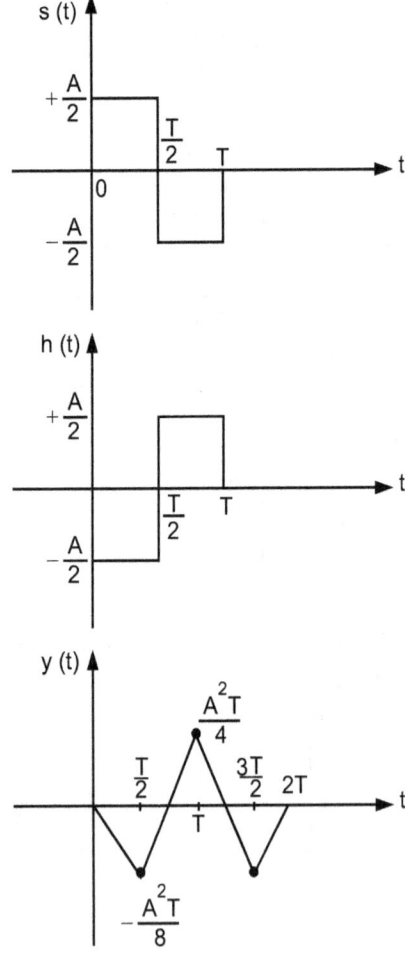

Fig. 8.28

Dec. 2010

U.Q. 16 :   A baseband receiver has received signal amplitude $\pm 2V$ held for a time T. The signal is corrupted by white Gaussian noise having Power Spectral density 10^{-4} volt^2/Hz. If the signal is processed by integrate and dump filter, what should be minimum Time T of the signal so that the error probability is not above 10^{-4}. (Given $Q(3.71) = 10^{-4}$). **(8)**

Solution :   **Given:** For baseband receiver,

$$S_1(t) = + 2V$$

$$S_2(t) = - 2V$$

Noise power spectral density

$$\frac{N_0}{2} = 10^{-4} \text{ volt}^2/\text{Hz}$$

$$\therefore \qquad N_0 = 2 \times 10^{-4} \text{ volt}^2/\text{Hz}$$

Error probability required

$$p_e \leq 10^{-4}$$

Now, for integrate and dump filter,

$$p_e = Q\left(\sqrt{\frac{2E_b}{N_0}}\right)$$

$$\therefore \qquad \sqrt{\frac{2E_b}{N_0}} \geq Q^{-1}(10^{-4}) = 3.71$$

$$\therefore \qquad \sqrt{\frac{2E_b}{N_0}} \geq 3.71$$

$$\therefore \qquad \frac{2E_b}{2 \times 10^{-4}} \geq (3.71)^2$$

$$\therefore \qquad E_b \geq (3.71)^2 \times 10^{-4} = 13.76 \times 10^{-4}$$

But, $$E_b = A^2 T_b$$

where, $$A = \pm 2V$$

$$\therefore \qquad A^2 T_b \geq 13.76 \times 10^{-4}$$

$$\therefore \qquad T_b \geq \frac{13.76}{4} \times 10^{-4}$$

$$T_b \geq 3.44 \times 10^{-4} \text{ s}$$

$\therefore$ Minimum time of signal is 0.344 ms.

U.Q. 17 :   Find the impulse response and output of matched filter for the given signal.   **(7)**

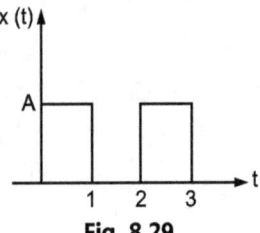

Fig. 8.29

Solution :   Given: $x(t) = \text{rect}\left(t - \frac{1}{2}\right) + \text{rect}\left(t - \frac{5}{2}\right)$

Now, the pulse has period T = 3.

∴   The matched filter will have impulse response.

∴ $h(t) = x(T - t) = x(3 - t)$

∴ $h(t) = \left[\text{rect}\left(\frac{5}{2} - t\right) + \text{rect}\left(\frac{1}{2} - t\right)\right]\frac{2k}{N_0}$

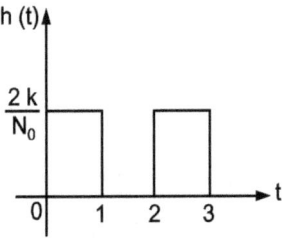

Fig. 8.30

Output of matched filter will be

$$y(t) = x(t) * h(t)$$

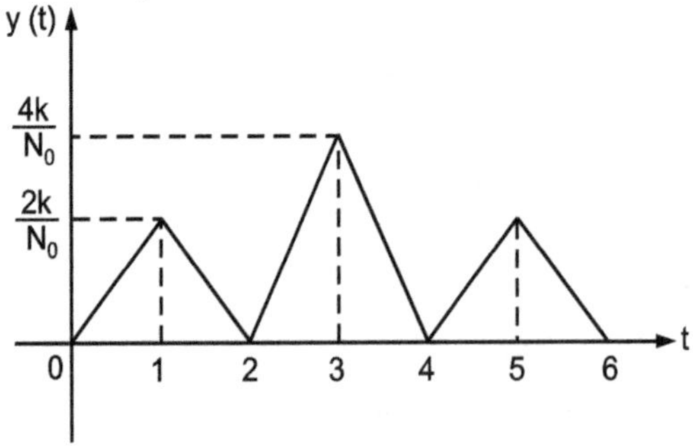

Fig. 8.31

U.Q. 18 :   Consider the signal s(t) in figure below: **(8)**

    (i) Determine the impulse response of a filter matched to this signal and sketch it as a function of time.

    (ii) Plot the matched filter output as a function of time.

    (iii) What is the peak value of the output?

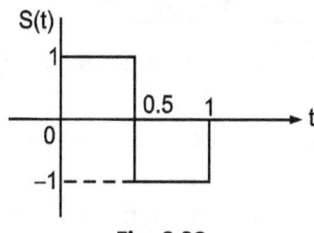

Fig. 8.32

Solution : Refer Problem U.Q. 13.

Dec. 2013

U.Q. 19 : Consider the signal S(t) shown in fig.   **(8)**

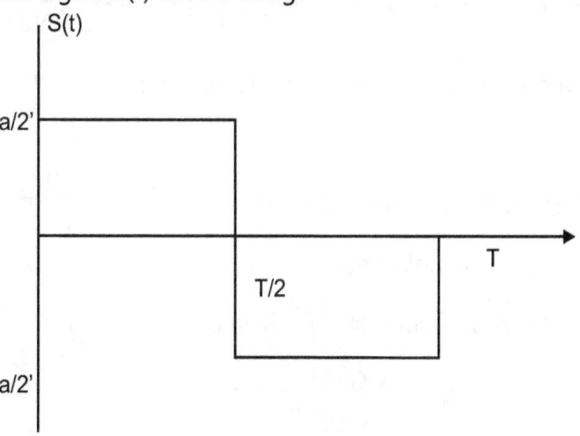

Fig. 8.34

Determine the impulse response of a filter matched to this signal and sketch it as a function of time, Plot the matched filter output as a function of time.

Solution : Refer U. Q. 13.

U.Q. 20 : What is Correlater? Compare its performance with Matched filter mathematically and relevant diagrams.   **(8)**

Solution : Refer Section 8.8.

May 2014

U.Q. 21 : State various properties of matched filer. Explain the impulse response in detail

                                                                        (8)

Solution : Refer Section 8.6.1.

SUMMARY

1. Integrate-and-dump circuit can be used for baseband signal detection.

2. The signal to noise ratio at the output of integrate and dump circuit is given by $\dfrac{2\,A2T}{N0}$.

3. Integrate and dump circuit enhances the signal more than that of noise.

4. The error probability of detection of binary signal for an integrate and dump circuit is $\dfrac{1}{2}$ erfc$\left(\sqrt{\dfrac{Eb}{N0}}\right)$.

5. The error probability of integrate and dump circuit reduces as $\dfrac{Eb}{N0}$ is increased.

6. An optimum filter is a detection circuit which minimises the error probability of detection.

7. The optimum filter maximises the ratio $\cdot$ max $= \left[\dfrac{S01\,(T) - S02\,(T)}{\cdot\,n0}\right]$ in such a way that error probability becomes minimum.

8. The transfer function of optimum filter is given by,

$$H(f) \;=\; \frac{k\,G^*\,(f)}{S_n\,(f)}\,c^{-j2\pi fr}$$

where, $G(f)$ is Fourier transform of input signal $g(t)$ to the filter and $S_n\,(f)$ is input noise power spectral density.

8. The value of maximised ratio $\rho_{max}^2 \;=\; \displaystyle\int_{-\infty}^{\infty} \frac{|G\,(f)|^2}{S_n\,(f)}$

10. An optimum filter which gives a maximum ratio of ρ^2 when input noise is white Gaussian it is called matched filter.

11. Impulse response of matched filter is given by,

$$h(t) \;=\; \frac{2k}{N_0}\,g\,(T - t)$$

where, $g\,(t)$ is input to the matched filter.

12. The ρ^2_{max} value (peak signal-to-noise ratio) for a matched filter $= \dfrac{2E}{N_0}$ where, E is signal energy.

13. The error probability of matched filter is given by,

$$P_e = \frac{1}{2} \, erfc \left(\sqrt{\frac{E}{N_0}} \right)$$

14. Integrate-and-dump filter and matched filter gives the same minimum error probability and integrate-and-dump circuit is a matched filter.

15. Correlator is a circuit which gives identical performance as that of matched filter in detection of binary signals.

16. Correlator and matched filters are two techniques of synthesizing the optimum filter.

EXERCISE

1. Explain the term Additive White Gaussian Noise. If the channel is a communication system is modelled as AWGN channel, suggest an optimum receiver for the transmission of two signals S_1 (t) and S_2 (t) such that S_1 (t) = $- S_2$ (t). Calculate probability of error and signal to noise ratio for receiver. Sketch the impulse response h (t) for the receiver by assuming suitable S_1 (t) and S_2 (t). Derive the expressions used.

[Dec. 1999]

2. Explain the terms optimum filter, matched filter and correlator.   **[May 2001]**

3. Explain the circuit for integrate and dump filter. State the expression for error probability of the same.   **[Dec. 2001]**

4. The matched filter and correlator are not simply two distinct, independent techniques of baseband digital signal detection, rather there are two methods of synthesizing the optimum filter transfer function. Justify.   **[Dec. 2002]**

5. Write short notes on :

   (i)   Matched filter   **[May 2000]**

   (ii)   Integrate and dump filter   **[May 2003]**

   (iii)   Integrate and dump receiver   **[May 2000]**

   (iv)   SNR of matched filter   **[Dec. 2002]**

6. Derive the expression for the transfer function and impulse response of the matched filter. Clearly indicate the assumptions you make.   **[May 2003] [May 2000]**

7. Derive the expression for the probability of error of integrate and dump receiver.

                                                                      [May 2001] [Dec. 2004]

8. Derive the expression for the probability of error of optimum filter.   **[Dec. 2001]**

9. Derive the expression for error probability of BPSK technique that makes use of matched filter detection.   **[Dec. 2003]**

10. How binary coded signals are detected by using integrate and dump receiver ? Derive the expression for its signal to noise ratio. How it can be minimised ?   **[May 2004]**

11. QPSK signal is detected by using matched filter. Derive the expression for it error probability.

Chapter 9

PASSBAND DIGITAL TRANSMISSION

9.1   INTRODUCTION

- In the chapter 4 and 8, we have seen transmission and detection of digital signal without any modulation (or frequency shift). This is called **baseband communication.**

- Following points are worth notable related to baseband signals.

1. These signals have significant power spectrum at low frequency hence, they can be transmitted over twisted pair cables, coaxial cables and fibre optic cables.

2. They cannot be transmitted over a radio link or satellites because this would require large sized antennas to take care of low frequency spectrum.

3. They can be used only over a short distance.

- Hence, for transmission of digital signals over long distance would require the spectrum of the signal to be shifted in high frequency region. This is called bandpass modulation.

- Thus, we have to modulate a carrier of frequency fc using baseband digital signal.

- The amplitude, phase or frequency of the carrier can be varied in accordance with the baseband signal. The resulting signal is bandpass signal and this type of transmission is called bandpass transmission.

- The bandpass modulation can also be used to separate different signals over single channel.

- When the amplitude of carrier is varied in accordance with baseband signal, it is called on-off keying (OOK) or Amplitude Shift Keying (ASK). As shown in Fig. 9.1 (b).

- When the phase of carrier is varied in accordance with baseband signal, it is called Phase Shift Keying (PSK). As shown in Fig. 9.1 (c).

- When the frequency of carrier is varied in accordance with baseband signal, it is called Frequency Shift Keying (FSK). As shown in Fig. 9.1 (d).

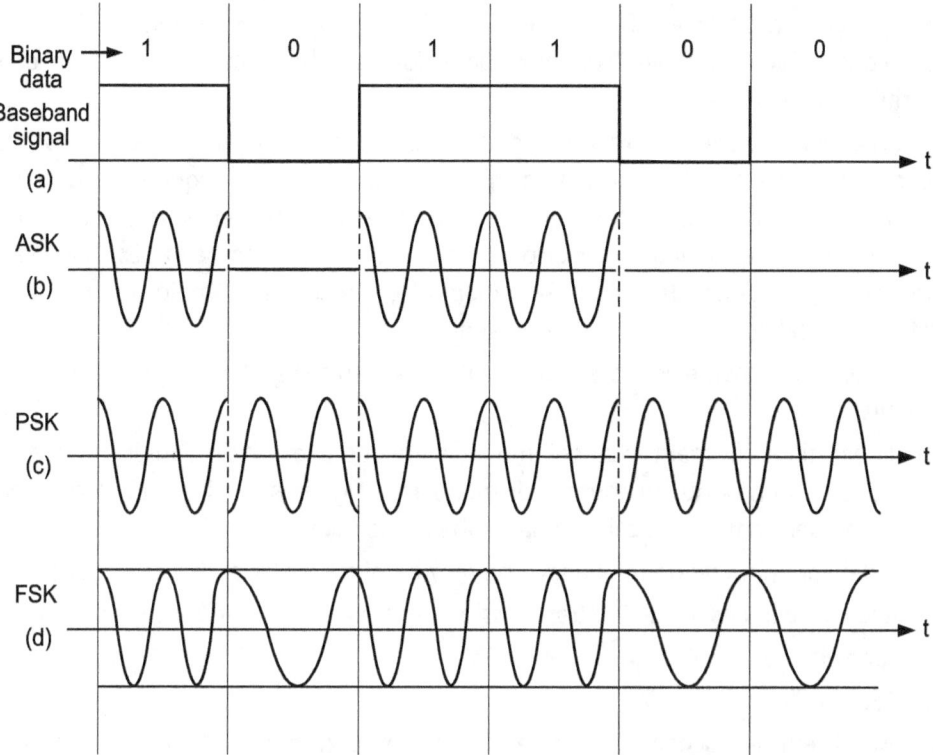

Fig. 9.1 : Basic Digital Modulation Techniques ASK, PSK, FSK

- In addition to these basic modulation schemes there are some modulation schemes that employ combination of amplitude and phase modulation. The details of these schemes are also discussed in this chapter.

- In each of these modulation schemes we require a modulator at the transmitter and a demodulator at the receiver to recover the baseband signal. Hence, for full-duplex transmission we need modulator and demodulator at both ends. This combination of modulator and demodulator is called modem.

- Ideally, PSK and FSK signals have a constant envelope as can be seen in Fig. 9.1. Due to this amplitude non-linearities encountered in microwave and satellite links do not cause detection problems. Whereas, ASK performance is poor in such applications. Hence, ASK is not used much in practice.

- The demodulation at the receiver can be done using two different methods.
   1. Coherent detection.
   2. Non-coherent detection.

- In coherent detection, the local carrier generated at the receiver is in synchronisation with the carrier at the transmitter. Thus, carrier at the receiver end is phase locked with the transmitter. Coherent detection is performed by correlating the received signal with locally generated carrier. This is also called synchronous detection. The modulation technique which employs coherent detection at the receiver is called coherent modulation technique.

- In non-coherent detection, knowledge of carrier wave's phase is not required or receiver need not be phase locked with transmitter. Since we do not require the carrier to be recovered or correlated with received signal the system becomes very simple. But the detection has poor quality i.e. error performance of the system degrades. This method is also called envelope detection. The modulation technique employing non-coherent detection is called non-coherent modulation.

- A modulation scheme is classified as either a narrowband modulation or wideband modulation.

- For linear time invariant channel model with additive white Gaussian noise, if the transmission bandwidth of the carrier-modulated signal is small (< 10%) compared to carrier frequency, then it is called a narrowband modulation.

- For wideband modulation the bandwidth may be of the order of carrier frequency.

- Modulation schemes for digital transmission system are also categorized as :

(i) Bandwidth efficient

(ii) Power efficient.

- Bandwidth efficient schemes are able to accommodate more information (bits/sec.) per unit transmission bandwidth (Hz). It is called spectral efficiency and specified in bits/sec.

- Bandwidth efficient schemes are preferred in digital terrestrial microwave radios, satellite communication and cellular telephony.

- Power efficient schemes are able to transmit information reliably at low energy per information bit.

- Power efficient schemes are preferred in some cellular telephony systems and some spread spectrum systems (FHSS).

- From the number of digital modulation schemes available for data transmission over a band-pass channel, which one to select ? The choice is made taking into account following design parameters.

(i)   Minimum use of channel bandwidth.

(ii) High data rate should be supported between the end users.

(iii) Minimum error probability.

(iv) Minimum transmission power should be used.

(v)   Maximum resistant to interfering signal and it should not cause interference beyond a limit.

(vi) Minimum circuit complexity and cost competitive.

- Some of these requirements are conflicting. Hence, some trade offs are to be made by the designer.

9.1.1 Band-Pass Transmission Model

- A band-pass signal S(t) is given as,

$$S(t) = x(t) \cos [2\pi f_c t + \phi(t)]$$

  where x(t) is envelope of band-pass signal and $\phi(t)$ is the phase of the signal, which are time varying.

- The band-pass signal can be expressed in terms of its inphase and quadrature phase components.

$$
\begin{aligned}
S(t) &= x(t) \cos (2\pi f_c t) \cos [\phi(t)] - x(t) \sin (2\pi f_c t) . \sin [\phi(t)] \\
&= x(t) \cos [\phi(t)] . \cos 2\pi f_c t - x(t) \sin \phi(t) . \sin (2\pi f_c t) \\
&= S_I(t) \cos (2\pi f_c t) - S_Q(t) \sin (2\pi f_c t)
\end{aligned}
$$

where $S_I(t) = x(t) \cos \phi(t)$

and $S_Q(t) = x(t) \sin \phi(t)$

are called in-phase and quadrature phase components.

- The complex envelope and phase of the band-pass signal can be written as,

$$x(t) = \sqrt{S_I^2(t) + S_Q^2(t)}$$

$$\phi(t) = \tan^{-1}\left[\frac{S_Q(t)}{S_I(t)}\right]$$

- The above representation of band-pass signal is used to generate and detect the band pass signals.

- Fig. 9.2 (a) gives the block diagram of generation of band-pass signal using in phase and quadrature components called as IQ generation.

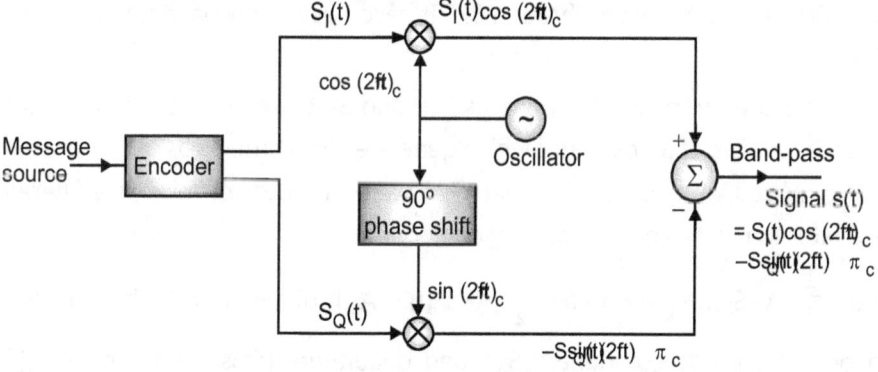

Fig. 9.2 (a) : Generation band-pass signal

- The data from message source is mapped by the encoder onto inphase and quadrature phase components. The mapping will decide type of band-pass signal generated.

- The band-pass signal is transmitted over a channel which can be assumed to be additive white Gaussian noise as shown in Fig. 9.2 (b) and assumed to have sufficient bandwidth for transmission of the signal.

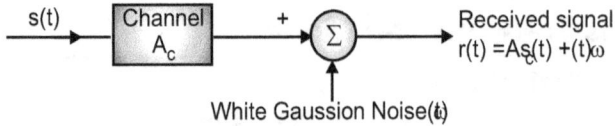

Fig. 9.2 (b) : Channel model for band-pass transmission

- The received signal is modified as

$$r(t) \;=\; A_c\, S(t) + W(t)$$

where A_c is attenuation introduced by the channel.

- The receiver for band-pass transmission is shown in Fig. 9.2 (c).

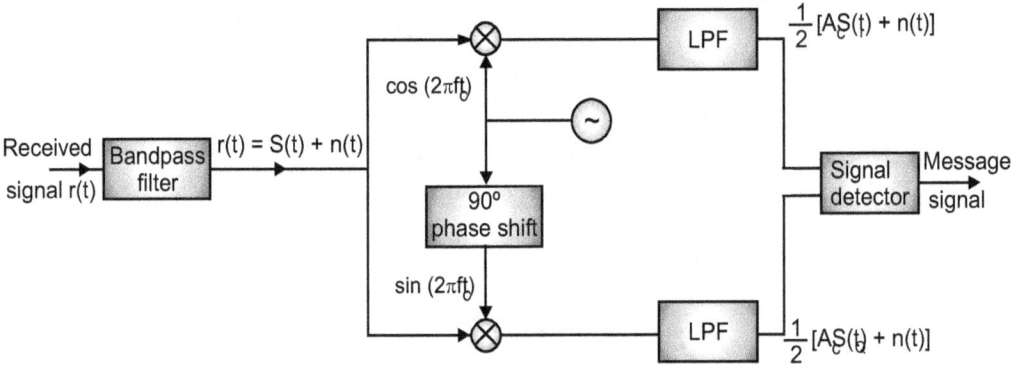

Fig. 9.2 (c) : Receiver model for band-pass signal transmission.

- The received signal is passed through a bandpass filter whose bandwidth is equal to that of transmitted signal. The output of this filter consists of signal S(t) along with narrow band noise n(t). (When W(t) is passed through BPF it becomes narrow band noise as seen in Chapter 6).

- The inphase and quadrature phase components $S_I(t)$ and $S_Q(t)$ are derived using the I.Q. down converter. It consists of an oscillator which generates the carriers $\cos(2\pi f_c t)$ and $\sin(2\pi f_c t)$ which are missed with signal. $r'(t) = s(t) + n(t)$. The outputs of mixer are filtered using low pass filter to remove high frequency components.

- The LPF outputs, $\dfrac{1}{2}\,[A_c\, S_I\,(t) + A_c\, n(t)]$ and $\dfrac{1}{2}\,[A_c\, S_Q(t) + A_c\, n(t)]$ are given to the detector, which based on the inphase component $S_I(t)$ and quadrature phase component $S_Q(t)$ estimate the transmitted message, $x(t) = S_I(t) + S_Q(t)$.

- There are number of considerations which are to applied for practical implementation of this model.

  (i) Practical receivers will include amplification stages which can amplify both signal and noise.

(ii) The receiver has to be synchronised in time with the transmitter. It is achieved using phase lock with incoming signal.

(iii) Some transmission strategies may use only in-phase signalling.

(iv) A receiver may perform non-coherent detection to avoid synchronisation problem.

(v) Some modern receivers do not use phase locking with incoming signal. Digital signal processing algorithms are used to eliminate the frequency and phase errors arising from loss of timing.

9.2 COHERENT BINARY PSK (BPSK)

- In Binary Phase Shift Keying System, the pair of time limited signals, $S_1(t)$ and $S_2(t)$ are used to represent 1 and 0. These signals are defined as,

$$S_1(t) = \sqrt{2P_s} \cos (2\pi f_c t) \qquad \qquad ... (9.1)$$

$$S_2(t) = \sqrt{2P_s} \cos (2\pi f_c t + \pi) \qquad \qquad ... (9.2)$$

- where, P_s is signal power given by,

$$P_s = \frac{A^2}{2} \qquad \text{(A being amplitude of signal i.e. } A = \sqrt{2P_s})$$

- Thus, when data is 1, the signal will have a fixed phase and when data is 0, it will have phase difference of 180° w.r.t. first signal.

- For narrowband transmission, $f_c > > \dfrac{1}{T_b}$. That is there will be multiple cycles of carrier sinusoid within one bit duration (T_b).

Generation of BPSK :

- We have to generate two signals $S_1(t)$ and $S_2(t)$ given in equations (9.1) and (9.2) corresponding to 1 and 0.

Now,

$$S_1(t) = \sqrt{2P_s} \cos (2\pi f_c t) \qquad \qquad ... (9.3)$$

$$S_2(t) = \sqrt{2P_s} \cos (2\pi f_c t + \pi)$$

$$= -\sqrt{2P_s} \cos (2f_c t) \qquad \qquad ... (9.4)$$

Now, we can write $S_1(t)$ and $S_2(t)$ as,

$$S(t) = b(t) \times \sqrt{2P_s} \cos (2\pi f_c t) \qquad \qquad ... (9.5)$$

where,
$$b(t) = +1 \qquad \text{when binary 1 is transmitted}$$
$$= -1 \qquad \text{when binary 0 is transmitted}$$

- Above equation suggests that BPSK signal can be generated by applying baseband signal in NRZ polar format and carrier signal to a balanced modulator (Product Modulator). Fig. 9.3 (a) shows the block diagram of BPSK generator.

- A commonly available balanced modulator (IC 1496) may be used as product modulator to actually generate modulated signal.

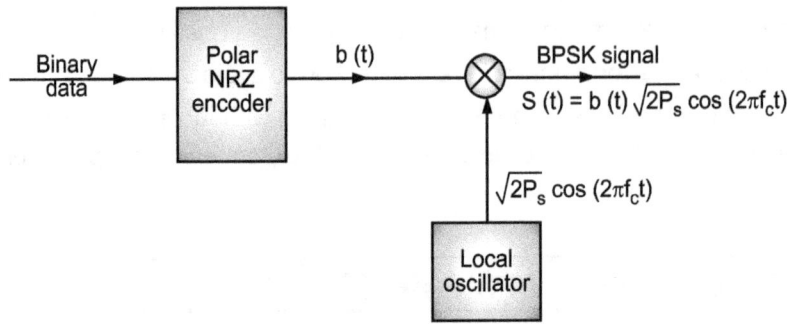

Fig. 9.3 : (a) BPSK Generation

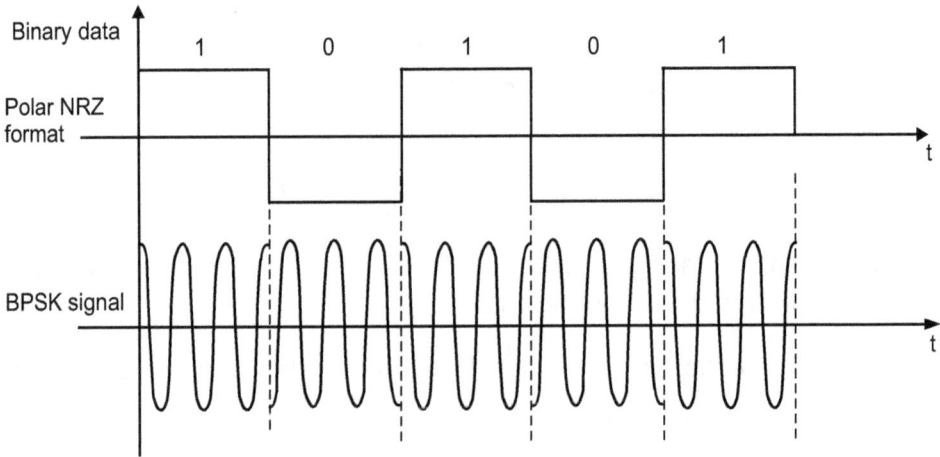

Fig. 9.3 (b) Wave from of BPSK

Reception of BPSK :

- The BPSK signal given by,

$$S(t) = b(t)\sqrt{2P_s}\cos(2\pi f_c t)$$

- When transmitted through a channel undergoes a phase change depending on propagation delay between transmitter and receiver. Hence, the received signal, without considering effect of noise can be written as,

$$r(t) = b(t)\sqrt{2P_s}\cos(2\pi f_c t + \theta) \qquad \qquad ... (9.6)$$

where, θ is fixed phase shift corresponding to propagation delay $\theta/2\pi f_c$.

- Since, we are using coherent detection, we have to generate carrier from the received signal. The demodulator for recovering the baseband signal is shown in Fig. 9.3 (c).

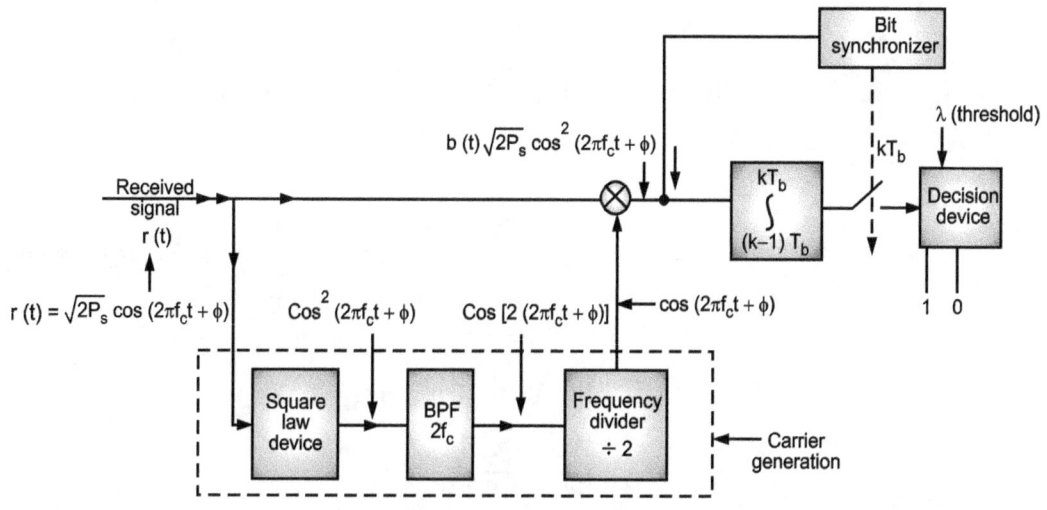

Fig. 9.3 : (c) BPSK Receiver

- The carrier generator part consists of square law device whose output will be,

$$\cos^2(2\pi f_c t + \phi) = \frac{1}{2} + \frac{1}{2}\cos[2(2\pi f_c t + \phi)]$$

- This is passed through a bandpass filter which eliminates the dc component $+\dfrac{1}{2}$. Hence, we get at the output of BPF,

$$\cos[2(2\pi f_c t + \phi)]$$

- This signal is given to frequency divider hence the output will be,

$$\cos(2\pi f_c t + \phi)$$

which is nothing but carrier shifted by phase ϕ.

- The synchronous demodulator (multiplier shown in diagram) multiplies carrier signal with received signal r(t). The output of multiplier will be,

$$
\begin{aligned}
r(t) &= b(t)\sqrt{2P_s}\cos(2\pi f_c t + \phi) \times \cos(2\pi f_c t + \phi) \\
&= b(t)\sqrt{2P_s}\cos^2(2\pi f_c t + \phi) \\
&= b(t)\sqrt{2P_s} \times \frac{1}{2}[1 + \cos[2(2\pi f_c t + \phi)]] \\
&= b(t)\sqrt{\frac{P_s}{2}}[1 + \cos[2(2\pi f_c t + \phi)]]
\end{aligned}
$$

- This signal is applied to an integrator and bit synchroniser. The integrator integrates the signal over one bit period. The timing (one bit period) is provided by bit synchroniser. At the end of one bit period output of integrator is sampled. e.g. in k^{th} bit interval the output of integrator will be,

$$S_o(t) = b(kT_b)\sqrt{\frac{P_s}{2}} \int_{(k-1)T_b}^{kT_b} [1 + \cos[2(2\pi f_c t + \phi)]\, dt$$

$$= b(kT_b)\sqrt{\frac{P_s}{2}} \int_{(k-1)T_b}^{kT_b} 1\, dt + \int_{(k-1)T_b}^{kT_b} \cos[2(2\pi f_c t + \phi)]\, dt$$

$$= b(kT_b)\sqrt{\frac{P_s}{2}}\, [t]_{(k-1)T_b}^{kT_b} + 0$$

$$= b(kT_b)\sqrt{\frac{P_s}{2}} \times T_b$$

$$= \sqrt{\frac{P_s}{2}} \times T_b \times b(kT_b) \qquad \qquad \dots (9.7)$$

- Thus, sampled output of integrator is proportional to $b(kT_b)$.

- This signal is given to a decision device to decide whether one was transmitted or zero by comparing it with some threshold value.

- e.g. if 1 is transmitted the detector output will be $\sqrt{\frac{P_s}{2}}\, T_b$ and if 0 is transmitted detector output will be $-\sqrt{\frac{P_s}{2}}\, T_b$. Hence by setting threshold at 0, we can detect correctly transmitted bit.

Spectrum of BPSK :

- The BPSK signal is given by,

$$S(t) = b(t)\sqrt{2P_s}\, \cos(2\pi f_c t)$$

$$= \sqrt{P_s}\, b(t) \times \sqrt{2}\, \cos(2\pi f_c t)$$

- Here, $\sqrt{P_s}\, b(t)$ is NRZ polar waveform whose amplitude varies from $+\sqrt{P_s}$ to $-\sqrt{P_s}$. Hence, PSD of this signal is given by,

$$S_b(f) = P_s T_b\, \text{sinc}^2(fT_b)$$

- Since NRZ waveform is multiplied by $\sqrt{2}\, \cos(2\pi f_c t)$, using the frequency shifting property, i.e. $g(t)\, e^{j2\pi f_c t} \;\Delta\; G(f - f_c)$ we can write PSD of BPSK waveform as,

$$S_{BPSK}(f) = \frac{P_s T_b}{2}\left[\text{sinc}^2[(f - f_c)T_b] + \text{sinc}^2[(f + f_c)T_b]\right] \qquad \dots (9.8)$$

- This PSD is plotted in Fig. 9.4 (a).

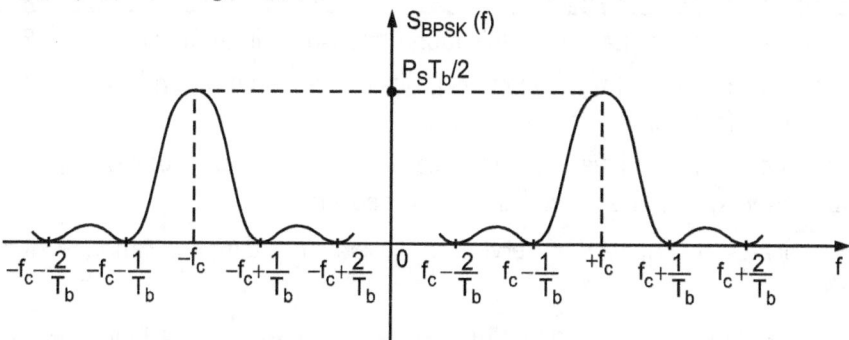

Fig. 9.4 (a) : PSD of BPSK Signal

- It is seen from the spectrum that it extends over wide frequency band.
- If we multiplex BPSK signals using different carrier frequencies, there would be overlap in spectra.
- This overlapping causes interchannel interference.
- To avoid this, we can keep the side lobes below specified levels.
- One way of doing this is to pass the NRZ baseband signal through a LPF to supress all side lobes.
- But then this spreads the signal in time giving rise to Intersymbol Interference (ISI). Equalizers are required to reduce ISI.

Bandwidth of BPSK :

From the power spectrum of BPSK plotted in Fig. 9.4, it can be seen that the null-to-null bandwidth of BPSK is,

$$\begin{aligned} BW &= \left(f_c + \frac{1}{T_b}\right) - \left(f_c - \frac{1}{T_b}\right) \\ &= f_c + \frac{1}{T_b} - f_c + \frac{1}{T_b} = \frac{2}{T_b} \\ &= 2f_b \end{aligned}$$

Thus, bandwidth of BPSK is twice the bit rate.

Disadvantages of BPSK :

- Coherent detection of BPSK requires both phase and timing synchronisation. Hence, the design of receiver becomes complicated.
- We cannot use non-coherent detection for BPSK because envelope of PSK is same for both 1 and 0. The solution to this is Differential Phase Shift Keying Method which will be discussed in Section 9.3.2.

9.3 BIT ERROR RATE (BER) AND SYMBOL ERROR RATE (SER)

- The performance of a digital communication is measured in terms of Bit Error Rate.
- It is defined as the ratio of total number of bits received in error and total number of bits received over a fairly large number of transmitted bits.
- Bit error rate is system-level performance. It is an indication of how good a digital communication system has been designed to perform.
- It also indicates the quality of service the users of a communication system should expect.
- It is not possible to have zero BER, but a system can ensure a BER below an 'acceptable' level.
- For example, a BER of 10^{-5} is acceptable for voice signal but not acceptable for a data service, where BER should be less than 10^{-7}.
- Symbol Error Rate (SER) is also used to describe performance of digital communication system. It is ratio of total number of the total symbols detected erroneously to the total number of symbols received.
- The performance of a digital communication system is also measured in terms of E_b/N_0 which is defined as,

$$\frac{E_b}{N_0} = \frac{\text{Energy received per bit of information}}{\text{One sides PSD of in-band noise}}$$

- $\frac{E_b}{N_0}$ is dimensionless and is also expressed in dB.
- We can express the bit error rate in terms of P_e called as error probability.
- For detection of a signal we can either use matched filter of correlator.
- We have seen that the performance of matched filter and correlator as same and can be expressed in terms of error probability.
- The knowledge of signal space is essential for calculation of error probability which is given in Appendix E for your reference.
- We will discuss various digital modulation schemes and their performance.

9.4 PERFORMANCE OF BINARY PHASE SHIFT KEYING

- In a coherent BPSK, we use pair of signals $s_1(t)$ and $s_2(t)$ for the two binary symbols 1 and 0 (M = 2).

$$s_1(t) = \sqrt{\frac{2E_b}{N_0}} \cos (2\pi f_c t \qquad \qquad \text{... (9.9)}$$

$$s_2(t) = -\sqrt{\frac{2E_b}{N_0}} \cos(2\pi f_c t) \qquad \ldots (9.10)$$

where, T_b is bit duration.

E_b is energy per bit

f_c is carrier frequency selected to be $\dfrac{n}{T_b}$.

9.4.1 Signal Space Representation

- The only basis function (N = 1) for the pair of signals will be

$$\phi_1(t) = \sqrt{\frac{2}{T_b}} \quad \cos(2\pi f_c t) \quad 0 \le t < T_b \qquad \ldots (9.11)$$

- Hence,

$$s_1(t) = \sqrt{E_b}\, \phi_1(t) \qquad \ldots (9.12)$$
$$s_2(t) = -\sqrt{E_b}\, \phi_1(t) \qquad \ldots (9.13)$$

- The co-ordinates of message points are

$$s_{11} = \int_0^{T_b} s_1(t)\, \phi_1(t)\, dt$$

$$= \int_0^{T_b} \sqrt{\frac{E_b}{T_b}} \times \cos(2\pi f_c t) \cdot \sqrt{\frac{2}{T_b}} \cos(2\pi f_c t)\, dt$$

$$= \sqrt{E_b}$$

$$s_{21} = \int_0^{T_b} s_2(t)\, \phi_1(t)\, dt$$

$$= -\sqrt{E_b}$$

- The message point corresponding to $s_1(t)$ is located at $s_{11} = +\sqrt{E_b}$ and message point corresponding to $s_2(t)$ is located at $s_{21} = -\sqrt{E_b}$ as shown in Fig. 9.5.

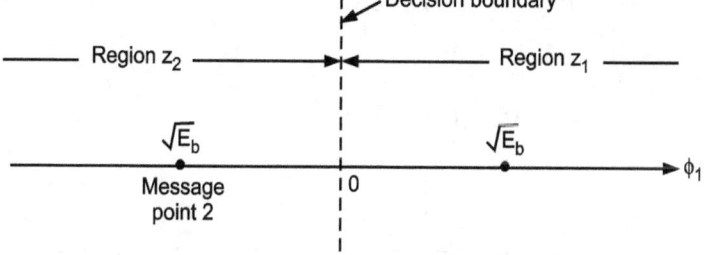

Fig. 9.5 : Signal Space for Diagram for Coherent BPSK

9.4.2 Error Probability of BPSK (Using Signal Space)

- The signal space can be partitioned into two regions Z_1 and Z_2.
- The decision boundary is mid point of joining these two points.
- The decision rule is to decide that $s_1(t)$ i.e. binary 1 was transmitted if the received signals falls in region Z_1 and decide that signal $s_2(t)$ i.e. binary 0 was transmitted if the received signal falls in region Z_2.
- Two kinds of errors can occur :

1. Signal $s_1(t)$ is transmitted but the noise is such that the received signal falls into region z_1 and receiver decides in favour of $s_1(t)$.

2. Signal $s_2(t)$ is transmitted but the noise is such that the received signal falls into region z_2 and receiver decides in favour of $s_2(t)$.

- Let us consider case 1 to calculate the probability of making error of the first kind. Let us call it as p_{e0}.

- The observation scalar or response generated by receiver is given by,

$$X_1 = \int_0^{T_b} r(t)\, \phi_1(t)\, dt \qquad \qquad \text{... (9.14)}$$

where, $r(t)$ is received signal given by

$$r(t) = s_2(t) + w(t)$$

- x_1 is value of random variable X_1 generated from response to signal $s_2(t)$.
- The conditional probability density function of random variable X_1 given that symbol 0 i.e. signal $s_2(t)$ was transmitted is given as,

$$p_{X_1}(x_1/0) = \frac{1}{\sqrt{2\pi\sigma_{n0}^2}}\, e^{-(x_1 - m_{X_1})^2/\sigma_{X_1}^2} \qquad \qquad \text{... (9.15)}$$

But,
$$m_{X_1} = E[X_1] = s_{21}$$

$$= \int_0^{T_b} s_2(t)\, \phi_1(t)\, dt$$

$$= -\sqrt{E_b} \qquad \qquad \text{... (9.16)}$$

and
$$\sigma_{X_1}^2 = \frac{N_0}{2} \qquad \qquad \text{... (9.17)}$$

$$\therefore \qquad p_{X_1}(x_1/0) = \frac{1}{\sqrt{2\pi \times \dfrac{N_0}{2}}} \times e^{-(x_1 + \sqrt{E_b})^2/2 \times \frac{N_0}{2}}$$

$$= \frac{1}{\sqrt{\pi N_0}} e^{-(x_1 + \sqrt{E_b})^2/N_0} \qquad \qquad \text{... (9.18)}$$

- Now probability that the decision will be made in favour of 1 will be probability that x_1 lies in region 1.

$$\therefore \qquad p_{eo} = \int_0^\infty p_{X_1}(x_1/0)\, dx_1$$

$$= \frac{1}{\sqrt{\pi N_0}} \int_0^\infty e^{-(x_1 + \sqrt{E_b})^2/N_0} \qquad \qquad \text{... (9.19)}$$

Put $\qquad \qquad z = \dfrac{x_1 + \sqrt{E_b}}{\sqrt{N_0}}$

$\therefore$ When $x_1 = 0$, $z = \sqrt{E_b}$ and $x_1 = \infty$, $z = \infty$

$$dz = \frac{1}{\sqrt{N_0}}\, dx_1$$

$$\therefore \qquad p_{eo} = \frac{1}{\sqrt{\pi}} e^{-z^2}\, dz$$

$$p_{eo} = \frac{1}{2}\, \text{erfc}\left(\sqrt{\frac{E_b}{N_0}}\right) \qquad \qquad \text{... (9.20)}$$

or $\qquad \qquad p_{eo} = Q\left(\sqrt{\frac{2E_b}{N_0}}\right) \qquad \qquad \text{... (9.21)}$

- Similarly, the probability of making second kind of error (let w call it as p_{e_1} will be,

$$p_{e_1} = \frac{1}{2}\, \text{erfc}\left(\sqrt{\frac{E_b}{N_0}}\right) \qquad \qquad \text{... (9.22)}$$

or $\qquad \qquad p_{e_1} = Q\left(\sqrt{\frac{2E_b}{N_0}}\right) \qquad \qquad \text{... (9.23)}$

- The average error probability will be,

$$p_e = p(0) \times p(1/0) + p(1) \times p(0/1)$$

$$= p_0 \times p_{eo} + p_1 \times p_{e_1}$$

$$\therefore \qquad p_e = \frac{1}{2} \times \frac{1}{2}\, \text{erfc}\left(\sqrt{\frac{E_b}{N_0}}\right) + \frac{1}{2} \times \frac{1}{2}\, \text{erfc}\left(\sqrt{\frac{E_b}{N_0}}\right)$$

$\therefore$

$$\boxed{p_e = \frac{1}{2}\,\text{erfc}\left(\sqrt{\frac{E_b}{N_0}}\right)} \qquad \ldots (9.24)$$

$$\boxed{p_e = Q\left(\sqrt{\frac{2E_b}{N_0}}\right)} \qquad \ldots (9.25)$$

- Thus, error probability depends on E_b and N_0.

- For specified N_0, when E_b is increased the message points corresponding to symbols 1 and 0 move further apart, and average probability of error p_e is reduced according to above equation.

9.4.3 Error Probability of BPSK using Optimum Filter Equation

- We can derive above equation using the formula of p_e for optimum filter. The error probability is given by,

$$p_e = \frac{1}{2}\,\text{erfc}\left[\frac{S_{o1}(T) - S_{o2}(T)}{2\sqrt{2}\,\sigma_{n0}}\right]$$

The optimum value of p_e will be when

$$\rho = \frac{S_{01}(T) - S_{02}(T)}{\sigma_{no}} \text{ is maximum}$$

$$\rho^2 = \frac{[S_{01}(T) - S_{02}(T)]^2}{\sigma_{n0}^2} = \frac{E_d}{N_0/2} \qquad \ldots (9.26)$$

where

$$E_d = \int_0^{T_b} (s_1(t) - s_2(t))^2 \, dt$$

$$= \int_0^{T_b} s_1^2(t)\, dt + \int_0^{T_b} s_2^2(t)\, dt - 2\int_0^{T_b} s_1(t)\, s_2(t)\, dt$$

$$= \int_0^{T_b} (\sqrt{E_b})^2\, \phi_1^2(t)\, dt + \int_0^{T_b} (\sqrt{E_b})^2\, \phi_1^2(t)\, dt$$

$$\qquad - \int_0^{T_b} (\sqrt{E_b})\,(-(\sqrt{E_b}))\, \phi_1^2(t)\, dt$$

$$= E_b + E_b + 2E_b$$

$$= 4E_b \qquad \ldots (9.27)$$

$\therefore$

$$\rho^2 = \frac{2E_d}{N_0} = \frac{8E_b}{N_0}$$

$\therefore$
$$\rho = 2\sqrt{2}\sqrt{\frac{E_b}{N_0}} \qquad\qquad ...(9.28)$$

$\therefore$
$$\boxed{p_e = \frac{1}{2}\,\text{erfc}\left(\sqrt{\frac{E_b}{N_0}}\right)} \qquad\qquad ...(9.29)$$

$\therefore$
$$\boxed{p_e = Q\left(\sqrt{\frac{2E_b}{N_0}}\right)} \qquad\qquad ...(9.30)$$

- This is the best possible error performance any BPSK system can achieve in presence of AWGN. Fig. 9.6 shows the plot of p_e against $\frac{E_b}{N_0}$.

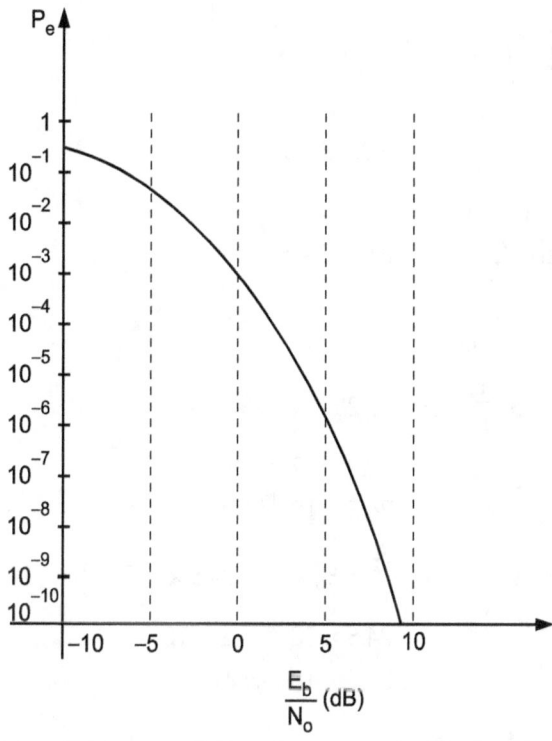

Fig. 9.6 : Optimum Error Performance of BPSK

Example 9.1 :

Binary data is transmitted using PSK at a rate 1 Mbps over RF link having bandwidth 3 MHz. Find signal power required at receiver input so that error probability is less than or equal to 10^{-6}. Assume Noise PSD to be 10^{-10} watt/Hz.

Solution :

Given :   Bandwidth = 3 MHz

$\qquad\qquad\qquad r_b = 1 \times 10^6$ bps

$$\frac{N_0}{2} = 10^{-10} \text{ Watt/Hz}$$

$$p_e \leq 10^{-6}$$

We know,

$$p_{e_{min}} = \frac{1}{2} \text{erfc}\left(\sqrt{\frac{E_b}{N_0}}\right)$$

$$\therefore \quad \frac{1}{2} \text{erfc}\left(\sqrt{\frac{E_b}{N_0}}\right) \leq 10^{-6}$$

$$\text{erfc}\left(\sqrt{\frac{E_b}{N_0}}\right) \leq 0.5 \times 10^{-6}$$

$$1 - \text{erfc}\left(\sqrt{\frac{E_b}{N_0}}\right) = 1 - 0.5 \times 10^{-6}$$

$$\text{erf}\left(\sqrt{\frac{E_b}{N_0}}\right) = 0.9999995$$

From the table given in appendix,

$$\text{erfc}(3.5) = 0.9999995$$

$$\therefore \quad \sqrt{\frac{E_b}{N_0}} \geq 3.5$$

$$\therefore \quad \frac{E_b}{N_0} \geq 12.25$$

$$\therefore \quad E_b \geq 12.25 \times 2 \times 10^{-10} \text{ J}$$

$$\therefore \quad E_b \geq 24.5 \times 10^{-10} \text{ J}$$

$$\therefore \quad \text{Average Power, } P = \frac{E_b}{T_b} = E_b \times r_b = 24.5 \times 10^{-10} \times 1 \times 10^6$$

$$= 24.5 \times 10^{-10} \times 1 \times 10^6$$

$$= 24.5 \times 10^{-4} \text{ watt}$$

9.5 COHERENT BINARY FSK

- Frequency shift keying is used in a low-cost applications for transmitting data at moderate or low rate over wired as well as wireless channels.
- In this modulation technique frequency of carrier is changed according to the baseband signal b(t).
- Since, there are two symbols to be transmitted, two different frequency sinusoidal signals are used as follows.
- **For Binary 1 :**

$$S_H(t) = \sqrt{2P_s} \cos [2\pi (f_c + f_1) t] \qquad \text{... (9.31)}$$

- **For Binary 0 :**

$$S_L(t) = \sqrt{2P_s} \cos [2\pi (f_c - f_1) t] \qquad \text{... (9.32)}$$

In general, we can write the FSK signal as,

$$S(t) = \sqrt{2P_s} \cos [2\pi (f_c + b(t) f_1) t] \qquad \text{... (9.33)}$$

where, $b(t) = +1$ for Binary 1

$\qquad\qquad\quad b(t) = -1$ for Binary 0

Thus, we have two carrier frequencies transmitted for the two symbols as,

$$f_H = f_c + f_1 \qquad \text{for Binary 1}$$

$$f_L = f_c - f_1 \qquad \text{for Binary 0}$$

- f_H is called mark frequency and f_L is called space frequency.
- The two frequencies are selected such that they are integer multiples of bit rate $1/T_b$.

Generation of BFSK :

- We need to generate two signals as,

$$S_H(t) = \sqrt{2P_s} \cos (2\pi f_H t) \qquad \text{... (9.34)}$$

$$= \sqrt{P_s T_b} \times \sqrt{\frac{2}{T_b}} \cos (2\pi f_H t)$$

$$S_L(t) = \sqrt{2P_s} \cos (2\pi f_L t) \qquad \text{... (9.35)}$$

$$= \sqrt{P_s T_b} \times \sqrt{\frac{2}{T_b}} \cos (2\pi f_L t)$$

- Above equations suggest we need two carriers of frequency $f_H = f_c + f_1$ and $\quad f_c - f_1$ to be generated. The block diagram of FSK receiver is shown in Fig. 9.7 (a).

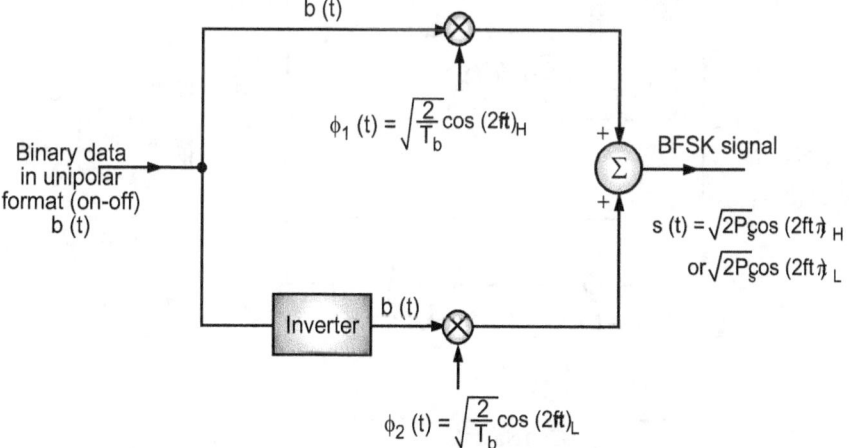

Fig. 9.7 : (a) Generation of BFSK Coherent

- The binary signal to be modulated has unipolar format and has amplitude $+\sqrt{P_s\,T_b}$ volt, for symbol 1 and zero volt for symbol 0.
- When Binary 1 is transmitted the signal in upper branch will be,

$$\sqrt{P_s\,T_b} \times \sqrt{\frac{2}{T_b}}\cos(2\pi f_H t)$$

Signal in lower branch will be,

$$0 \times \sqrt{\frac{2}{T_b}}\cos(2\pi f_L t) = 0$$

- Hence, the output BFSK signal will be,

$$S_H(t) = \sqrt{2P_s}\cos 2\pi f_H t$$

- When Binary 0 is transmitted the signal in upper branch will be,

$$0 \times \sqrt{\frac{2}{T_b}}\cos 2\pi f_H t$$

- Signal in lower branch will be,

$$\sqrt{P_s \infty T_b} \times \sqrt{\frac{2}{T_b}}\cos(2\pi f_L t)$$

- Hence, output BFSK signal will be,

$$S_H(t) = \sqrt{2P_s}\cos(2\pi f_L t)$$

Reception of BFSK :

- The block diagram of BFSK receiver is shown in Fig. 9.7 (b).

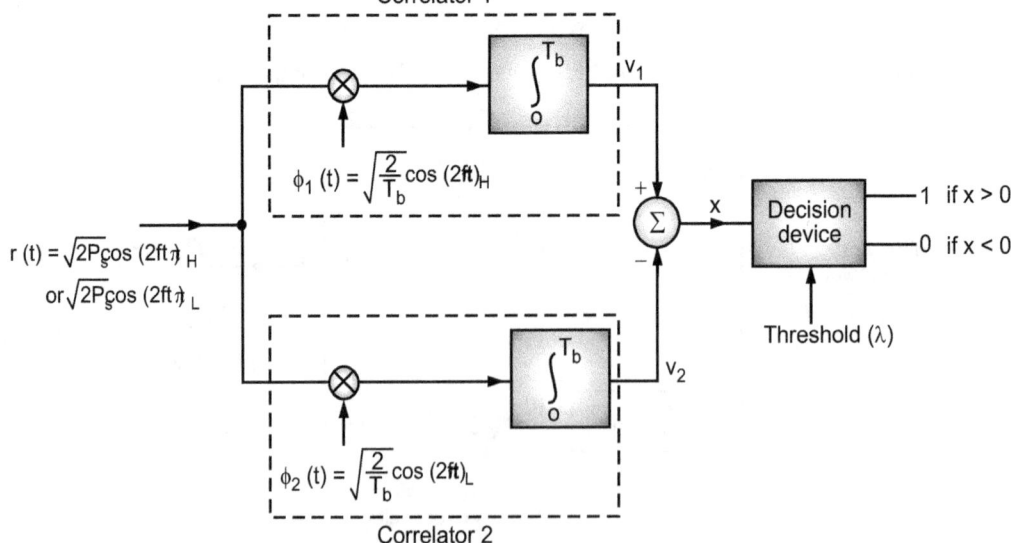

Fig. 9.7 : (b) Reception of Coherent BFSK

- It consists of two multipliers and integerators (correlators) which are supplied with common received input and locally generated coherent reference signals $\phi_1(t) = \sqrt{\dfrac{2}{T_b}}$ cos $(2\pi f_H t)$ and $\phi_2(t) = \sqrt{\dfrac{2}{T_b}}$ cos $(2\pi f_L t)$.

- The output of two correlators are subtracted and the difference is compared with same preset threshold by decision device to decide in favour of 1 or 0.

- When signal $S_H(t) = \sqrt{2P_s}$ cos $(2\pi f_H t)$ is received (corresponding to binary 1) it will have maximum correlation with $\phi_1(t)$. Hence, output v_1 will be more than v_2 making the difference positive and decision device will make decision in favour of 1.

- When signal $S_L(t) = \sqrt{2P_s}$ cos $(2\pi f_L t)$ is received (corresponding to binary 0) it will have maximum correlation with $\phi_2(t)$.

- Hence, output v_2 will be more than v_1, making the difference negative and decision device will make decision in favour of 0.

Spectrum of BFSK :

- The BFSK signal consists of two signals.

$$S_H(t) = \sqrt{2P_s} \text{ cos } (2\pi f_H t) \qquad \text{for Binary 1}$$
$$S_L(t) = \sqrt{2P_s} \text{ cos } (2\pi f_L t) \qquad \text{for Binary 0}$$

- Hence, combined BFSK signal can be written as,

$$S(t) = \sqrt{2P_s} \times b_H(t) \text{ cos } (2\pi f_H t) + \sqrt{2P_s}\, b_L(t) \text{ cos } (2\pi f_L t)$$

- Hence, when 1 is transmitted,

$$b_H(t) = 1 \qquad\qquad\qquad b_L(t) = 0$$

- When 0 is transmitted,

$$b_H(t) = 0 \qquad\qquad\qquad b_L(t) = 1$$

- Let us convert these coefficients $b_H(t)$ and $b_L(t)$ in polar format.

- Hence,
$$b_H(t) = \frac{1}{2} + \frac{1}{2} b_H'(t) \qquad\qquad \text{where, } b_H'(t) = +1/-1$$

$$b_L(t) = \frac{1}{2} + \frac{1}{2} b_L'(t) \qquad\qquad\qquad\qquad b_L'(t) = -1/+1$$

$$\therefore \qquad S(t) = \sqrt{2P_s}\left[\frac{1}{2} + \frac{1}{2} b_H'(t)\right]\cos(2\pi f_H t) \qquad \dots (9.36)$$

$$+ \sqrt{2P_s}\left[\frac{1}{2} + \frac{1}{2} b_L'(t)\right]\cos(2\pi f_L t) \qquad \dots (9.37)$$

$$\therefore \qquad S(t) = \sqrt{\frac{P_s}{2}}\cos(2\pi f_H t) + \sqrt{\frac{P_s}{2}}\cos(2\pi f_L t)$$

$$+ \sqrt{\frac{P_s}{2}}\, b_H'(t)\cos 2\pi f_H(t) + \sqrt{\frac{P_s}{2}}\, b_L'(t)\cos(2\pi f_L t)\dots (9.21)$$

- In above equation, first term and second term represent impulses at f_H and f_L respectively. The last two terms resemble with BPSK equation (b(t) $\sqrt{2P_s}$ cos $2\pi f_c t$). Hence, spectrum of BFSK signal will be,

$$S_{BFSK}(f) = \sqrt{\frac{P_s}{2}}\left\{\delta(f - f_H) + \delta(f + f_L) + T_b \text{ sinc}^2\left[(f - f_H)T_b\right] + T_b \text{ sinc}^2\left[(f - f_L)T_b\right]\right\} \dots(9.38)$$

- This PSD is plotted as shown in Fig. 9.8.

- Assuming $\qquad f_H - f_L = \dfrac{2}{T_b} = 2f_b$

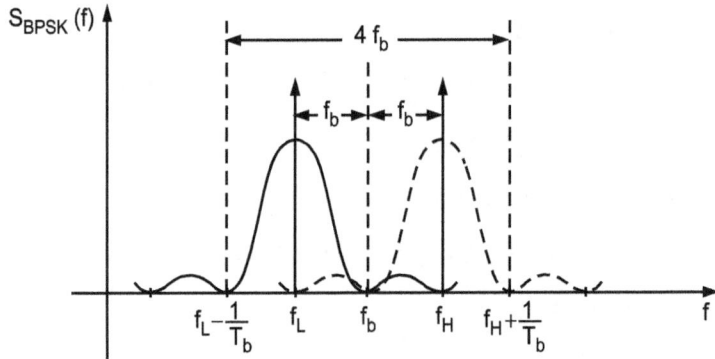

Fig. 9.8 : Power Spectrum of BFSK

Bandwidth of BFSK :

- As seen from the spectrum the total bandwidth is given by,

$$BW = \left(f_H + \frac{1}{T_b}\right) - \left(f_L - \frac{1}{T_b}\right)$$

$$BW = (f_H - f_L) + \frac{2}{T_b} = f_H - f_L + 2f_b \qquad \dots (9.39)$$

- For the case, $\qquad f_H - f_L = 2f_b$

- See that this is the minimum separation we should have between f_H and f_L

$$BW = 2f_b + 2f_b$$
$$= 4f_b$$

- Thus, bandwidth of BFSK is twice the BPSK.

9.6 BFSK (BINARY FREQUENCY SHIFT KEYING)

9.6.1 Signal Space Representation for BFSK

- If $S_1(t)$ and $S_2(t)$ are orthogonal, then orthonormal basis functions are,

$$\phi_1(t) = \sqrt{\frac{2}{T_b}} \cos (2\pi f_L t)$$

$$\phi_2(t) = \sqrt{\frac{2}{T_b}} \cos (2\pi f_H t) \qquad \text{... (9.40)}$$

Thus, M = 2 and N = 2 i.e. the system has two dimensional signal space with message points.

- The coefficients S_{ij} for 1 = 1, 2 and j = 1, 2 are defined by,

$$S_{ij} = \int_0^{T_b} S_i(t)\, \phi_j(t)\, dt \qquad \text{... (9.41)}$$

$$\therefore \qquad S_{11} = \sqrt{E_b}$$

$$S_{12} = 0$$

$$S_{21} = 0$$

$$S_{22} = \sqrt{E_b} \qquad \text{... (9.42)}$$

- The two message points are defined by,

$$S_1 = \begin{bmatrix} \sqrt{E_b} \\ 0 \end{bmatrix} \qquad \text{... (9.43)}$$

$$S_2 = \begin{bmatrix} 0 \\ \sqrt{E_b} \end{bmatrix} \qquad \text{... (9.44)}$$

- The signal space is shown in Fig. 9.9.

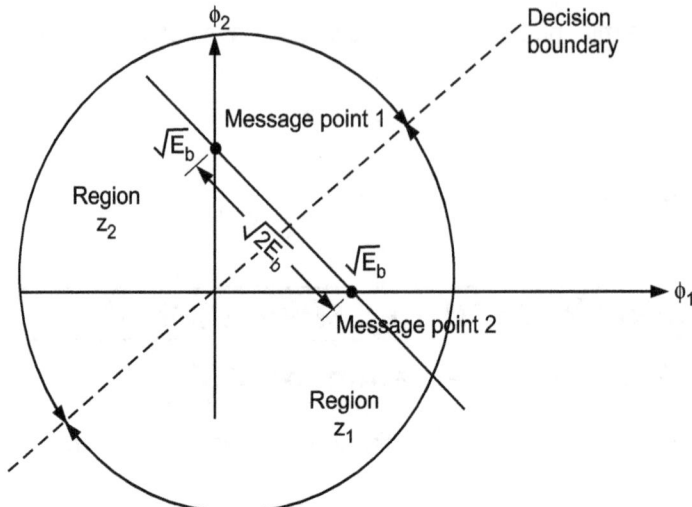

Fig. 9.9 : Signal Space Diagram for BPSK

9.6.2 Error Probability of BFSK using Signal Space

- The observation scalar has two elements r_1 and r_2 defined by,

$$r_1 = \int_0^{T_b} r(t)\, \phi_1(t)\, dt \qquad \qquad ...\,(9.45)$$

$$r_2 = \int_0^{T_b} r(t)\, \phi_2(t)\, dt \qquad \qquad ...\,(9.46)$$

where, r(t) is received signal.

- Now refer to Coherent demodulator for BFSK, discussed in section 9.6.

- If symbol 1 was transmitted

$$r(t) = S_1(t) + W(t) \qquad \qquad ...\,(9.47)$$

and if symbol 0 was transmitted

$$r(t) = S_2(t) + W(t) \qquad \qquad ...\,(9.48)$$

- The observation space is partitioned into two regions z_1 and z_2 as shown in Fig. 9.3.

- If $S_1(t)$ is transmitted and if noise is absent the output of upper correlator i.e. r_1 will be $\sqrt{E_b}$ and the output of the lower correlator will be zero. So we see that the intermediate parameter $x = (r_1 - r_2) > 0$.

- Similarly, if $S_2(t)$ is transmitted $x < 0$.

- If we consider additive noise, x represents a random variable whose mean value will be $+ \sqrt{E_b}$ when symbol 1 is transmitted and for symbol 0, the mean value of X will be $-\sqrt{E_b}$.

Thus,

$$E[X/1] = E[R_1/1] - E[R_2/1]$$

$$= +\sqrt{E_b} \qquad \qquad \text{... (9.49)}$$

and

$$E[X/0] = E[R_1/0] - E[R_2/0]$$

$$= -\sqrt{E_b} \qquad \qquad \text{... (9.50)}$$

where, R_1 and R_2 are random variable.

- The variance of random variable X is independent on the symbol transmitted since r_1 and r_2 are statistically independent with variance equal to $\dfrac{N_0}{2}$.

$$\text{Var}[X] = \text{Var}[R_1] + \text{Var}[R_2]$$

$$= \frac{N_0}{2} + \frac{N_0}{2}$$

$$\therefore \qquad \sigma_X^2 = N_0 \qquad \qquad \text{... (9.51)}$$

- Hence, the probability density function for the first case will be,

$$p_x(x/0) = \frac{1}{\sqrt{2\pi\sigma_X^2}} e^{-(x - m_X)^2/2\sigma_X^2}$$

$$= \frac{1}{\sqrt{2\pi \times N_0}} e^{-(x + \sqrt{E_b})^2/2 \times N_0} \qquad \qquad \text{... (9.52)}$$

- Since the condition $r_1 - r_2 > 0$ is equivalent to $x > 0$ the receiver will make decision in favour of 1 which will be error and the probability of this happening will be,

$$p_{e0} = p(x > 0/\text{Symbol 0 was transmitted})$$

$$= \frac{1}{\sqrt{2\pi N_0}} \int_0^\infty e^{-(x + \sqrt{E_b}^2)/2N_0} dx$$

Put

$$\frac{x + \sqrt{E_b}}{\sqrt{2N_0}} = z$$

When z = 0

$$z = \sqrt{\frac{E_b}{2N_0}}$$

x = ∞

$$z = \infty$$

$$dx = \sqrt{\frac{2N_0}{E_b}} dz$$

$$\therefore \qquad p_{e_0} = \frac{1}{\sqrt{\pi}} \int_{\sqrt{\frac{E_b}{N_0}}}^{\infty} e^{-z^2} dz$$

i.e.
$$p_{e_0} = \frac{1}{2} \text{erfc}\left(\sqrt{\frac{E_b}{2N_0}}\right) \qquad \ldots (9.53)$$

- Similarly, we can obtain the error probability for Case 2 where symbol 1 is transmitted and decision is made in favour of 0 will be,

$$p_{e_1} = \frac{1}{2} \text{erfc}\left(\sqrt{\frac{E_b}{2N_0}}\right) \qquad \ldots (9.54)$$

- The average error probability will be,

$$p_e = \frac{1}{2} \times p_{e_0} + \frac{1}{2} \times p_{e_1}$$

$\therefore$
$$\boxed{p_e = \frac{1}{2} \text{erfc}\left(\sqrt{\frac{E_b}{2N_0}}\right)} \qquad \ldots (9.55)$$

or
$$\boxed{p_e = Q\left(\sqrt{\frac{E_b}{N_0}}\right)} \qquad \ldots (9.56)$$

- Comparing this equation with error probability of BPSK, we see that, to obtain the same error probability as BPSK we have to double the energy per bit.
- This is because the Euclidean distance between two points in BPSK is $2\sqrt{E_b}$ whereas it is $\sqrt{2E_b}$ in case of BFSK.
- Hence, the performance of BPSK in better than BFSK.

9.6.3 Error Probability of BFSK using Optimum Filter Equation

- There is one more approach to find p_e for BFSK i.e. using optimum filter or correlator result obtained in Chapter .
- The binary FSK signal is represented as,

$$S_H(t) = \sqrt{2P} \cos(2\pi f_H t) \qquad \text{for binary 1}$$
$$S_L(t) = \sqrt{2P} \cos(2\pi f_L t) \qquad \text{for binary 0} \qquad \ldots (9.57)$$

where,
$$f_H = f_c + f_1$$
$$f_L = f_c - f_1$$

and $f_1 << f_H$ or f_c or f_L

Now
$$\rho^2 = \frac{[S_{01}(T) - S_{02}(T)]^2}{\sigma_{n_0}^2} \qquad \dots(9.58)$$

$$= \frac{2E_d}{N_0}$$

where
$$E_d = \int_0^{T_b} [s_1(t) - s_2(t)]^2 \, dt$$

$$= \int_0^{T_b} s_1^2(t) \, dt + \int_0^{T_b} s_2^2(t) \, dt - 2 \int_0^{T_b} s_1(t) \, s_2(t) \, dt$$

$$= \int_0^{T_b} \left(\sqrt{P_s T_b}\right)^2 \phi_1^2(t) \, dt + \int_0^{T_b} \left(\sqrt{P_s T_b}\right)^2 \phi_2^2(t) \, dt$$

$$- 2\int_0^{T_b} p_s \times T_b \phi_1(t) \, \phi_2(t) \, dt$$

$$= E_b + E_b - 2 P_s \int_0^{T_b} \cos(2\pi f_L t) \cdot \cos(2\pi f_H t) \, dt$$

$$= 2E_b - 2 P_s \times T_b \times \frac{1}{T_b}$$

$$\left[\int_0^{T_b} (\cos(2\pi(f_C + F_H) t) + \cos(2\pi(f_H - f_L) t) dt) \right]$$

Let
$$2f_c = f_H + f_L \text{ and } 2f_1 = f_H - f_L$$

$\therefore$
$$\rho^2 = 2E_b - 2E_b \times \frac{1}{T_b} \left[\int_0^{T_b} \cos(4\pi f_c t) \, dt + \int_0^{T_b} \cos(4\pi f_1 t) \, dt \right]$$

$$= 2E_b - 2E_b \left[\frac{\sin 2\pi f_c T_b}{4\pi f_c T_b} + \frac{\sin 4\pi f_1 T_b}{4\pi f_1 T_b} \right]$$

But $f_c \gg f_1$ hence we can neglect first term

$\therefore$
$$\rho^2 = 2E_b - 2E_b \cdot \frac{\sin 4\pi f_1 T_b}{4\pi f_1 T_b}$$

ρ^2 will be maximum when $\sin(4\pi f_1 T_b) = -1$

i.e. when
$$4\pi f_1 T_b = \frac{3\pi}{2}$$

$\therefore$
$$\rho_{max.}^2 = 2.42 E_b$$

Substituting above value in equation, we get,

$$\left[\frac{S_{01}(T) - S_{02}(T)}{\sigma_{no}}\right]^2 = 2.42 \frac{A^2 T}{N_0}$$

$$\therefore \quad \left[\frac{S_{01}(T) - S_{02}(T)}{\sigma_{no}}\right]^2 = 4.84 \times \frac{(A^2/2) T}{N_0}$$

$$\therefore \quad \frac{S_{01}(T) - S_{02}(T)}{\sigma_{no}} = \sqrt{\frac{4.84 \, E_b}{N_0}} \qquad \left[\therefore \quad \frac{A^2}{2} T = E_b\right]$$

$$\therefore \quad \left[\frac{S_{01}(T) - S_{02}(T)}{2\sqrt{2}\,\sigma_{no}}\right] = \frac{1}{2\sqrt{2}} \sqrt{\frac{4.84 \, E_b}{N_0}}$$

$$= \sqrt{\frac{4.84 \, E_b}{8 \, N_0}}$$

$$= \sqrt{\frac{0.6 \, E_b}{N_0}} \qquad \qquad \text{... (9.59)}$$

∴ Error probability of BFSK is given by,

$$P_e = \frac{1}{2} \, \text{erfc}\left[\frac{S_{01}(T) - S_{02}(T)}{2\sqrt{2}\,\sigma_{no}}\right]$$

$$= \frac{1}{2} \, \text{erfc}\left(\sqrt{\frac{0.6 \, E_b}{N_0}}\right) \qquad \text{... (9.60)}$$

It can be observed from above equation that error probability of BFSK is more than that of BPSK. To achieve same error probability as that of BPSK, the signal energy of BFSK has to be increased by about 2 dB. The reasons for superiority of PSK is that in PSK we have $S_1(t) = -S_2(t)$ whereas, in FSK, this condition is not met.

If the two basis functions $\phi_1(t)$ and $\phi_2(t)$ are orthogonal.

$$\rho^2 = E_b + E_b - \int_0^{T_b} S_1(t) \, S_2(t) \, dt$$

$$= 2E_b - \int_0^{T_b} P_s \, T_b \, \phi_1(t) \, \phi_2(t) \, dt$$

$$= 2E_b - 0 = 2E_b$$

$$\therefore \quad \boxed{P_e = \frac{1}{2} \, \text{erf}_c\left(\sqrt{\frac{E_b}{2N_0}}\right)} \qquad \text{...(9.61)}$$

$$\text{or} \quad \boxed{P_e = Q\left(\sqrt{\frac{E_b}{2N_0}}\right)} \qquad \text{...(9.62)}$$

Example 9.2 :

A FSK system transmits binary data at the rate of 2.5×10^6 bits per second. During the course of transmission, white Gaussian noise of zero mean and PSD 10^{-20} watt per Hz is added to the signal. In the absence of noise, the amplitude of the received sinusoidal wave for digit 1 or 0 is microvolt. Determine the average error probability assuming coherent detection.

Solution :

Given :

$$\text{Data rate, } r_b = 2.5 \times 10^6$$

$$\therefore \quad T_b = \frac{1}{r_b} = 0.4 \times 10^{-6} \text{ s}$$

$$N_0 = 10^{-20} \text{ watt/Hz}$$

$$\therefore \quad N_0 = 2 \times 10^{-10} \text{ watt/Hz}$$

$$\text{Amplitude of sinusoid, } A = 1 \times 10^{-6} \text{ V}$$

$$\therefore \quad E_b = \frac{A^2}{2} T_b = \frac{(1 \times 10^{-6})^2}{2} \times 0.4 \times 10^{-6}$$

$$= 0.2 \times 10^{-8} \text{ J}$$

$$\therefore \quad p_e = Q\left(\sqrt{\frac{E_b}{N_0}}\right)$$

$$= Q\left(\sqrt{\frac{0.2 \times 10^{-18}}{2 \times 10^{-20}}}\right) = Q\sqrt{0.1 \times 10^2}$$

$$= Q(3.16)$$

$$\approx 0.00082 \qquad \qquad \textbf{[Refer Appendix – C]}$$

9.7 QUADRATURE PHASE SHIFT KEYING

- This modulation scheme is expanded version of BPSK.

- It is a bandwidth conserving modulation scheme for transmission of digital data.

- It is an example of quadrature-carrier multiplexing system.

- The information carried by the signal is contained in phase.

- The phase of carrier is changed in four ways.

- Two successive bits are combined to form four distinct levels or symbols.

- When the level is changed, the phase of carrier is changed by $\pi/4$ radians (45°). Thus, the QPSK signal can be represented as,

$$S_i(t) = \begin{cases} \sqrt{2P} \cos\left[2\pi f_c t + (2i-1)\dfrac{\pi}{4}\right] & ; \quad 0 \le t \le T \\ 0 & ; \quad \text{otherwise} \end{cases} \qquad \text{... (9.63)}$$

where, $i = 1, 2, 3, 4$

and T is symbol duration = $2T_b$

P is average power of symbol.

$$f_c = n \times \frac{1}{T} = n\frac{1}{2T_b} \text{ is carrier frequency}$$

- Thus, the four waveforms are –

$$S_1(t) = \sqrt{2P} \cos\left(2\pi f_c t + \frac{\pi}{4}\right)$$

$$S_2(t) = \sqrt{2P} \cos\left(2\pi f_c t + \frac{3\pi}{4}\right)$$

$$S_3(t) = \sqrt{2P} \cos\left(2\pi fct + \frac{5\pi}{4}\right)$$

$$S_4(t) = \sqrt{2P} \cos\left(2\pi f_c t + \frac{7\pi}{4}\right) \qquad \text{... (9.64)}$$

- Equation (9.63) can also be written as,

$$S_i(t) = \sqrt{2P} \cos(2i-1)\frac{\pi}{4} \cos(2\pi f_c t)$$

$$-\sqrt{2P} \sin(2i-1)\frac{\pi}{4}\sin(2\pi f_c t) \quad 0 \le t \le T$$

$$= 0 \qquad\qquad\qquad\qquad \text{otherwise} \qquad \text{... (9.65)}$$

Thus, $$S_1(t) = +\sqrt{2P} \cos(2\pi f_c t) - \sqrt{2P} \sin(2\pi f_c t)$$
$$S_2(t) = -\sqrt{2P} \cos(2\pi f_c t) - \sqrt{2P}\sin(2\pi f_c t)$$
$$S_3(t) = -\sqrt{2P} \cos(2\pi f_c t) + \sqrt{2P} \sin(2\pi f_c t)$$
$$S_4(t) = +\sqrt{2P} \cos(2\pi f_c t) + \sqrt{2P} \sin(2\pi f_c t) \qquad \text{... (9.66)}$$

Generation of QPSK :

- Above equation (9.66) suggest the scheme of generation of QPSK signals.
- We can use two carriers which will be multiplied with input bits converted into polar formats.

- The block diagram is shown in Fig. 9.10 (a).

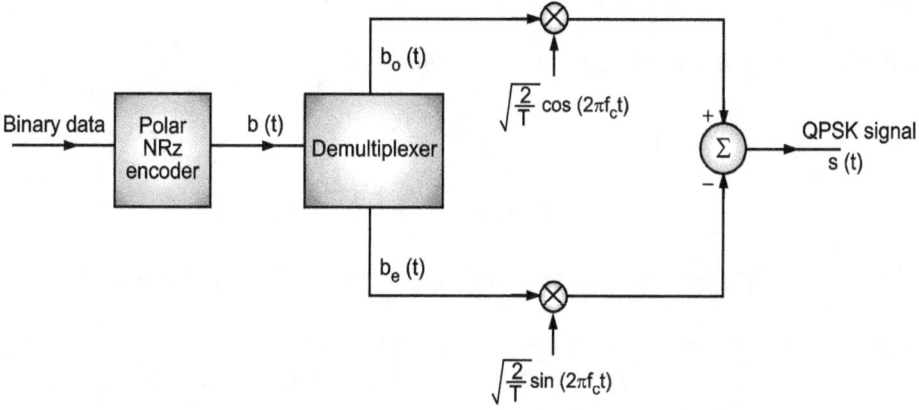

Fig. 9.10 : (a) Generation of QPSK

- The incoming binary wave in polar format is divided into two separate binary waves consisting of odd numbered and even numbered bits by means of a demultiplexer.
- Let us call these binary waves as $b_0(t)$ and $b_e(t)$.

Thus, $b_0(t)$ and $b_e(t)$ can be $+\sqrt{\dfrac{P \times T}{2}}$ or $-\sqrt{\dfrac{P \times T}{2}}$ depending on input bit stream.

e.g. if first two input bits are 1 and 0,

$$b_0(t) \;=\; +\sqrt{\dfrac{PT}{2}} \qquad \text{and} \quad b_e(t) \;=\; -\sqrt{\dfrac{PT}{2}}$$

$$\qquad\quad =\; +\sqrt{\dfrac{E}{2}} \qquad\qquad\quad =\; -\sqrt{\dfrac{E}{2}}$$

where, E is energy per symbol duration(t).
Following table shows all four combinations of $b_0(t)$ and $b_e(t)$.

Signal $S_i(t)$	Inputs Bits		Phase of QPSK	$b_0(t)$	$b_e(t)$
$S_1(t)$	1	0	$\pi/4$	$+\sqrt{\dfrac{PT}{2}}$	$-\sqrt{\dfrac{PT}{2}}$
$S_2(t)$	0	0	$3\pi/4$	$-\sqrt{\dfrac{PT}{2}}$	$-\sqrt{\dfrac{PT}{2}}$
$S_3(t)$	0	1	$5\pi/4$	$-\sqrt{\dfrac{PT}{2}}$	$+\sqrt{\dfrac{PT}{2}}$
$S_4(t)$	1	1	$7\pi/4$	$+\sqrt{\dfrac{PT}{2}}$	$+\sqrt{\dfrac{PT}{2}}$

- The odd numbered waveform is multiplied with carrier $\sqrt{\dfrac{2}{T}}\cos(2\pi f_c t)$ and even number

carrier is multiplied with $\sqrt{\dfrac{2}{T}}\sin(2\pi f_c t)$.

- These two are then added to generate QPSK waveform.

- e.g. if inputs bits are 1 and 0, the waveform generated will be –

$$S_0(t) \;=\; + \sqrt{\frac{PT}{2}} \times \sqrt{\frac{2}{T}} \cos(2\pi f_c t) - \sqrt{\frac{PT}{2}} \times \sqrt{\frac{2}{T}} \sin(2\pi f_c t)$$

$$\;=\; \sqrt{PT}\cos(2\pi f_c t) - \sqrt{PT}\sin(2\pi f_c t)$$

- This is same as $S_1(t)$. Similarly, other signals $S_2(t)$, $S_3(t)$ and $S_4(t)$ are generated.

- The BPSK waveform are shown in figure for an input bit pattern 10011100 in Fig. 9.10 (b).

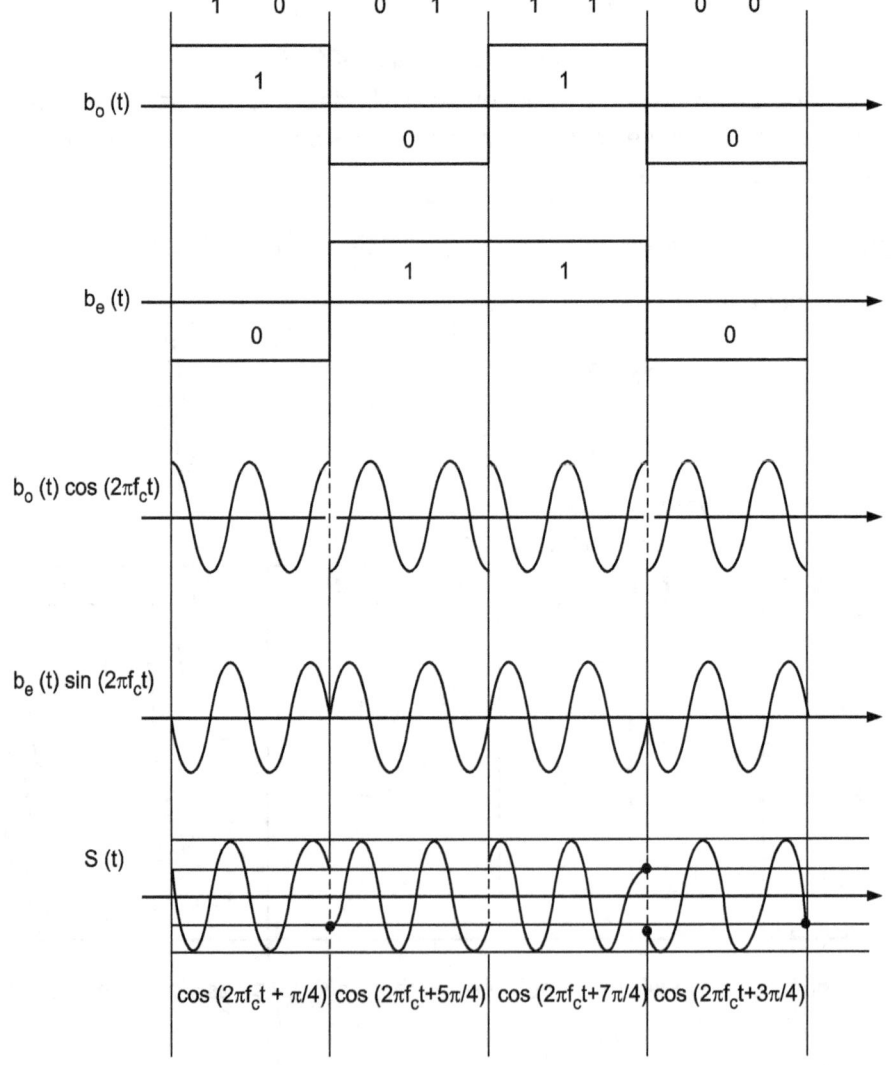

Fig. 9.10 : (b) QPSK Waveforms

Reception of QPSK :

- The QPSK receiver is shown in Fig. 9.10 (c).

- It consists of a pair of correlators with a common input r(t) and locally generated carriers $\sqrt{\frac{2}{T}} \cos 2\pi f_c t$ and $\sqrt{\frac{2}{T}} \sin (2\pi f_c t)$.

- The output of correlators (multiplier and integrator) v_1 and v_2 are compared with a threshold voltage (zero volt).

- If the output is positive, decision is made in favour of 1 and if output is negative, decision is made in favour of 0.

- These two bits from the two correlators are combined in a multiplexer to reproduce original binary sequence.

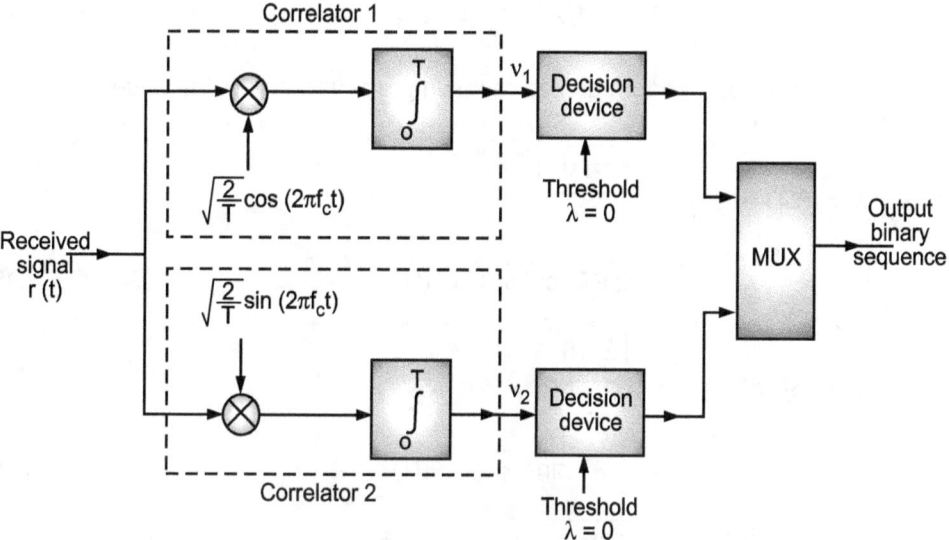

Fig. 9.10 : (c) QPSK Receiver

Spectrum of QPSK :

- The QPSK signal is represented as,

$$S_i(t) = \sqrt{2P} \cos (2\pi f_c t + \phi_i) \; ; \quad 0 \le t \le T$$

$$= 0 \qquad\qquad\qquad ; \quad \text{otherwise}$$

where, $\qquad\qquad \phi_i = (2i-1) \times \dfrac{\pi}{4}$

and $\qquad\qquad\qquad i = 1, 2, 3, 4$

$$S_i(t) = \left(\sqrt{2P}\cos\phi_i\right) \cdot \cos 2\pi f_c t$$

$$- \left(\sqrt{2P}\sin\phi_i\right)\sin 2\pi f_c t \quad ; \quad 0 \le t \le T$$

$$= 0 \quad\quad ; \quad \text{otherwise}$$

$$= \sqrt{2P}\cos\phi_i \; \text{rect}\left(\frac{t}{T}\right)\cos(2\pi f_c t) \quad\quad \dots (9.67)$$

$$- \sqrt{2P}\sin\phi_i \; \text{rect}\left(\frac{t}{T}\right)\sin(2\pi f_c t) \quad\quad \dots (9.68)$$

- Hence, PSD of above signal will be obtained by finding PSD of,

$$g_1(t) = \sqrt{2P}\cos\phi_i \; \text{rect}\left(\frac{t}{T}\right)$$

$$g_2(t) = \sqrt{2P}\sin\phi_i \; \text{rect}\left(\frac{t}{T}\right) \quad\quad \dots (9.69)$$

- But $\cos\phi$ and $\sin\phi$ are random processes assuming any four possible values.

$$S_{g_1}(f) = \text{PSD of } g_1(t) = \frac{\overline{\left|G_1(f)\right|}^2}{T}$$

$$= 2\,PT\,\overline{\cos^2\phi_i}\,\text{sinc}^2(fT) \quad\quad \dots (9.70)$$

$$S_{g_2}(f) = \text{PSD of } g_2(t) = \frac{\left|G_2(f)\right|^2}{T}$$

$$= 2\,PT\,\overline{\sin^2\phi_i}\,\text{sinc}^2(fT) \quad\quad \dots (9.71)$$

- But

$$\overline{\sin^2\phi_i} = \overline{\cos^2\phi_i}$$

$$= \frac{1}{2}$$

$$\therefore \quad S_{g_1}(f) = S_{g_2}(f) = PT\,\text{sinc}^2(fT) \quad\quad \dots (9.72)$$

- These spectra will be shifted by f_c due to multiplication of $\cos(2\pi f_c t)$ and $\sin(2\pi f_c t)$.

$$\therefore \quad\quad S_{QPSK}(f) = PT\,\text{sinc}^2[T(f-f_c)] + PT\,\text{sinc}^2[T(f+f_c)] \quad\quad \dots (9.73)$$

- Hence, the spectrum of QPSK signal will be centred around f_c as shown in Fig. 9.11.

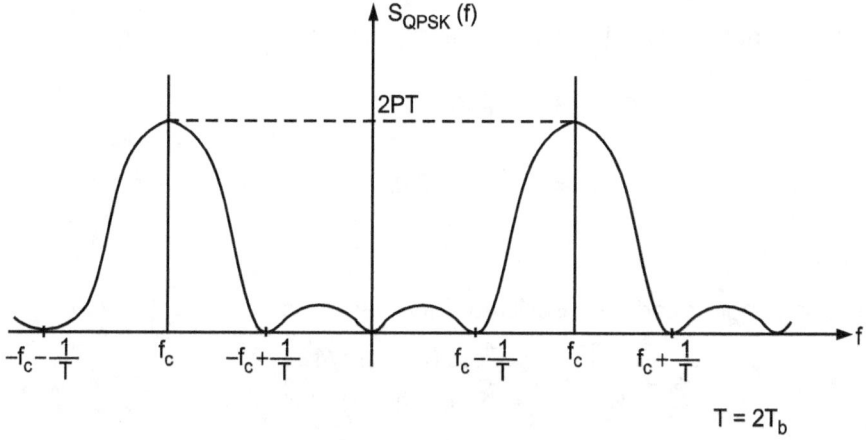

Fig. 9.11 : Spectrum of QPSK

Bandwidth of QPSK :

- As seen from the spectrum of QPSK (Fig. 9.11), the bandwidth will be,

$$BW = \left(f_c + \frac{1}{T}\right) - \left(f_c - \frac{1}{T}\right)$$

$$= \frac{2}{T}$$

- Since $\quad T = 2T_b$

- Bandwidth of QPSK is,

$$BW = \frac{2}{2T_b}$$

$$\boxed{BW = f_b} \qquad \qquad \dots (9.74)$$

- Thus, the bandwidth of QPSK is half of PSK.

9.7.1 Signal Space Representation of QPSK

- The QPSK signal is defined as,

$$s_i(t) = \sqrt{\frac{2E}{T}} \cos\left[2\pi f_c t + (2i - 1)\frac{\pi}{4}\right], \quad 0 \le t \le T$$

$$= 0 \qquad \qquad \text{Otherwise} \quad \dots (9.75)$$

where, i = 1, 2, 3, 4

E is energy per symbol duration

T is symbol duration.

- The two orthonormal basis function $\phi_1(t)$ and ϕ_2 for representing $s_i(t)$ are :

$$\phi_1(t) \;=\; \sqrt{\frac{2}{T}} \cos(2\pi f_c t) \qquad\qquad 0 \le t \le T$$

$$\phi_2(t) \;=\; \sqrt{\frac{2}{T}} \sin(2\pi f_c t) \qquad\qquad 0 \le t < T \qquad \dots (9.76)$$

There are

- Four message points and the associated signal vectors are

$$s_i = \begin{bmatrix} s_{i1} \\ s_{i2} \end{bmatrix} = \begin{bmatrix} \sqrt{E}\cos(2i-1)\,\pi/4 \\ -\sqrt{E}\cos(2i-1)\,\pi/4 \end{bmatrix} \qquad i = 1, 2, 3, 4$$

i.e.
$$s_1(t) = s_{11}\,\phi_1(t) + s_{12}\,\phi_2(t)$$

$$s_2(t) = s_{21}\,\phi_1(t) + s_{22}\,\phi_2(t)$$

$$s_3(t) = s_{31}\,\phi_1(t) + s_{32}\,\phi_2(t)$$

$$s_4(t) = s_{41}\,\phi_1(t) + s_{42}\,\phi_2(t) \qquad\qquad \dots (9.77)$$

- Thus, QPSK signal has two dimensional signal constellation (i.e. N = 2) and four message points (m = 4). It is given in Fig. 9.12.

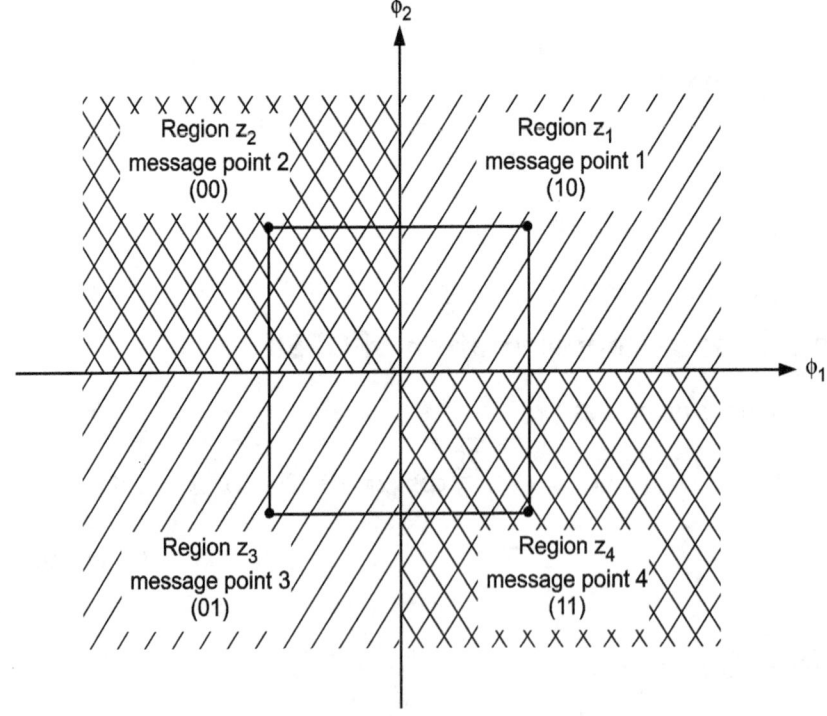

Fig. 9.12 : Signal-Space Diagram of QPSK

9.7.2 Error Probability of QPSK

- The received signal r(t) is defined as,

$$r(t) = s_i(t) + w(t) \qquad\qquad 0 \le t \le T; i = 1, 2, 3, 4$$

$$\dots (9.78)$$

where w(t) is sample function of white guassian noise process.
- The observation vector r has two elements r_1 and r_2 given by,

$$r_1 = \int_0^T r(t)\, \phi_1(t)\, dt = \sqrt{E} \cos\left[(2i - 1)\frac{\pi}{4} \right] + w_1$$

$$= \pm \sqrt{\frac{E}{2}} + w_1 \qquad\qquad \dots (9.79)$$

and

$$r_2 = \int_0^T r(t)\, \phi_2(t)\, dt$$

$$= -\sqrt{E} \sin\left[(2i - 1)\frac{\pi}{4} \right] + w_2 \qquad\qquad \dots (9.80)$$

$$= \mp \sqrt{E} + w_2$$

- Thus, r_1 and r_2 are sample values of independent Guassian random variables with mean $\pm \sqrt{\frac{E}{2}}$ and $\mp \sqrt{\frac{E}{2}}$ and variance $\frac{N_0}{2}$.

- The decision rule is

(i) $s_i(t)$ is transmitted if received signal point associated with observation vector s falls in region z_1.

(ii) $s_2(t)$ is transmitted if received signal point associated with observation vector s falls in region z_2.

(iii) $s_3(t)$ is transmitted if received signal point associated with observation vector s falls in region z_3.

(iv) $s_4(t)$ is transmitted if received signal point associated with observation vector s falls in region z_4.

- To calculate the symbol error probability, we can consider QPSK system equivalent to two coherent binary PSK systems working in parallel and using two carriers that are in quadrature phase as shown in Fig. 9.13.

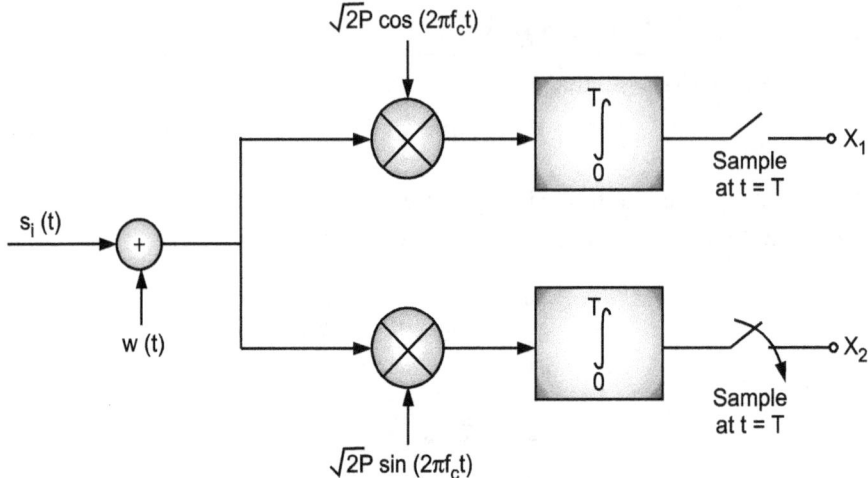

Fig. 9.13 : QPSK Receiver

- There are two outputs corresponding to one symbol. The in-phase output x_1 and quadrature channel output x_2 may be viewed as individual of two coherent BPSK.

- The energy per bit will be E/2 and noise PSD $N_0/2$. The error probability each channel of QPSK is,

$$p_{e_1} = p_{e_2} = \frac{1}{2}\,\mathrm{erfc}\left(\sqrt{\frac{E/2}{N_0}}\right)$$

$$= \frac{1}{2}\,\mathrm{erfc}\left(\sqrt{\frac{E}{2N_0}}\right) \qquad \ldots (9.81)$$

- The decision will be correct corresponding to a symbol if both bits are correct. The probability that both bits in symbol are correct will be,

$$p_c = (1 - P_{e_1})(1 - P_{e_2})$$

$$= \left[1 - \frac{1}{2}\,\mathrm{erfc}\left(\sqrt{\frac{E}{2N_0}}\right)\right]^2$$

$$= 1 - \mathrm{erfc}\left(\sqrt{\frac{E}{2N_0}}\right) + \frac{1}{4}\,\mathrm{erfc}^2\left(\sqrt{\frac{E}{2N_0}}\right) \qquad \ldots (9.82)$$

- Hence, average probability of symbol error.

$$p_e = (1 - p_c)$$

$$= \mathrm{erfc}\left(\sqrt{\frac{E}{2N_0}}\right) - \frac{1}{4}\,\mathrm{erfc}^2\left(\sqrt{\frac{E}{2N_0}}\right)$$

$$\simeq \mathrm{erfc}\left(\sqrt{\frac{E}{2N_0}}\right) \qquad \ldots (9.83)$$

where, E is energy for symbol duration T.

i.e. $\qquad\qquad E = \dfrac{A^2 T}{2}$

- The symbol error probability of QPSK is,

$$P_e = \text{erfc}\left(\sqrt{\frac{E}{2N_0}}\right) \qquad \qquad ...(9.84)$$

or

$$P_e = 2Q\left(\sqrt{\frac{E}{N_0}}\right) \qquad \qquad ...(9.85)$$

- Now since $E = 2E_b$, the average probability of symbol error in terms of E_b/N_0 ratio can be written as,

$$P_e = \text{erfc}\left(\sqrt{\frac{E_b}{N_0}}\right) \qquad \qquad ...(9.86)$$

where, E_b is energy per bit duration.

i.e. $\qquad \qquad E_b = \dfrac{A^2 T_b}{2}$

- Thus, bit error rate in each channel of QPSK can be given by,

$$P_{e_1} = P_{e_2} = \frac{1}{2}\text{erfc}\left(\sqrt{\frac{E_b}{2N_0}}\right) \qquad \qquad ...(9.87)$$

$$= Q\left(\sqrt{\frac{E_b}{N_0}}\right) \qquad \qquad ...(9.88)$$

- The above result is same as BPSK. Thus, QPSK has same performance as BPSK but uses half bandwidth. In other words, QPSK system transmits information at twice the bit rate of coherent BPSK for same bandwidth and same E_b/N_0 with same BER.

9.8 M-ARY PSK

- This is a family of two dimensional phase shift keying modulation schemes.

- Several bandwidth efficient schemes of this family are important for practical wireless applications.

- In this technique, the phase of carrier takes on one of M possible values.

- Hence, the M-ary PSK signal can be expressed as,

$$S_i(t) = \sqrt{2P}\cos(2\pi f_c t + \phi_i) \qquad \qquad ...(9.89)$$

$$i = 1, 2, 3, ..., M$$

where, $\qquad \qquad \phi_i = (2i-1)\dfrac{\pi}{M}$

(Note that QPSK is M-ary PSK with M = 4).

- The M possible signals are generated using M different phase values.

Generation of M-ary PSK :

- Fig. 9.14 shows transmitter of M-ary PSK.

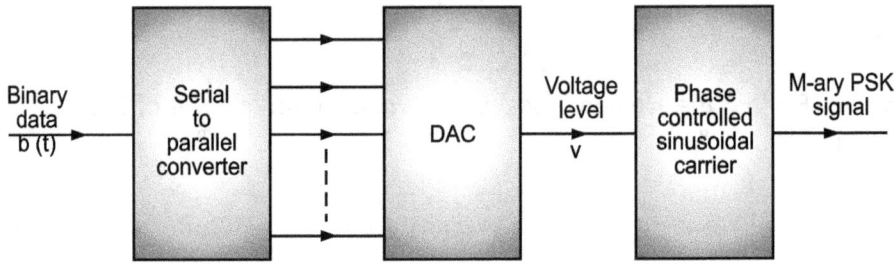

Fig. 9.14 : M-ary PSK transmitter

- It consists of a serial to parallel converter which takes N bits serially and presents it parallely to a Digital to Analog Converter (DAC).

- The DAC output will assume 2^N = M levels corresponding to N bit input.

- The DAC output v is used to determine the phase of sinusoidal signal to be transmitted.

- Thus, the N-bit symbol corresponds to particular phase of sinusoidal.

Reception of M-ary PSK :

- The optimum receiver for M-ary PSK is shown in Fig. 9.15.

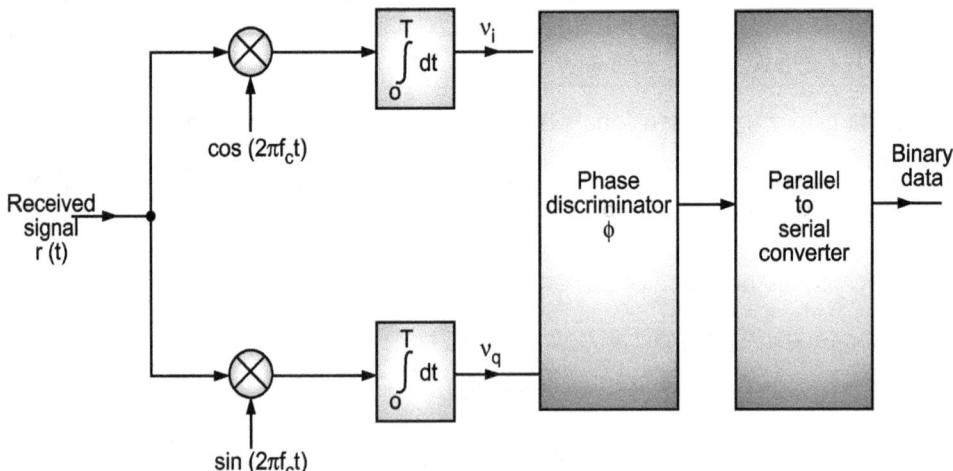

Fig. 9.15 : M-ary PSK Receiver

- It has a pair of correlators (Multiplier and Integrator) which are fed with received signal r(t) and carrier signals.

- The two correlators output v_i and v_q are given to a phase descriminator which estimates the phase.

$$\hat{\phi} = \tan^{-1}\left(\frac{v_q}{v_i}\right)$$

- Depending on this value, it selects one of the M possible N-bit bit patterns corresponding to the phase.

- The N bits are the converted into serial format by parallel to serial converter.

Spectrum of M-ary PSK :

- The M-ary PSK signal is represented in equation (9.89) can be rewritten as,

$$S_i(t) = \left(\sqrt{2P}\cos\phi_i\right)\cos(2\pi f_c t)$$
$$- (\sqrt{2P}\sin\phi_i)\sin(2\pi f_c t) \qquad \ldots (9.90)$$

- This signal representation is same as QPSK waveform. Except that here, we have $T = NT_b$ (whereas in case of QPSK we had $T = 2T_b$).

- Hence the power spectrum of M-ary PSK signal will be –

$$S_{\underset{PSK}{M\text{-ary}}}(f) = P \times T \ sinc^2\ [(f - f_c)\ T] + P \times T \ sinc^2\ [(f + f_c)\ T] \qquad \ldots (9.91)$$

$$= P \times NT_b \ sinc^2\ [(f - f_c)\ NT_b] + PNT_b \ sinc^2\ [(f + f_c)\ NT_b$$

$$\text{where, } T = NT_b$$

- The spectrum is plotted in Fig. 9.16.

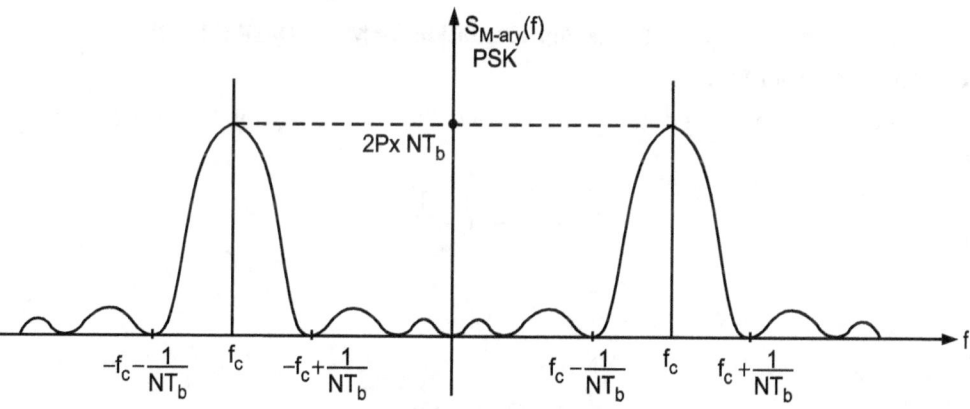

Fig. 9.16 : PSD of M-ary PSK

Geometrical representation of M-ary PSK :

- The M-ary PSK signal given in equation (9.38) suggests that we have two basis functions (having unit energy)

$$\phi_1(t) \;=\; \sqrt{\frac{2}{T}}\,\cos 2\pi f_c t \;;\; 0 \leq t \leq T$$

$$\phi_2(t) \;=\; \sqrt{\frac{2}{T}}\,\sin 2\pi f_c t \;;\; 0 \leq t \leq T$$

- The signal space diagram (signal constellation) is two dimensional with M message points given by $\sqrt{PT}\cos \phi_i$ and $\sqrt{PT}\sin \phi_i$. Fig. 9.17 shows M-ary PSK signal space diagram for M = 8.

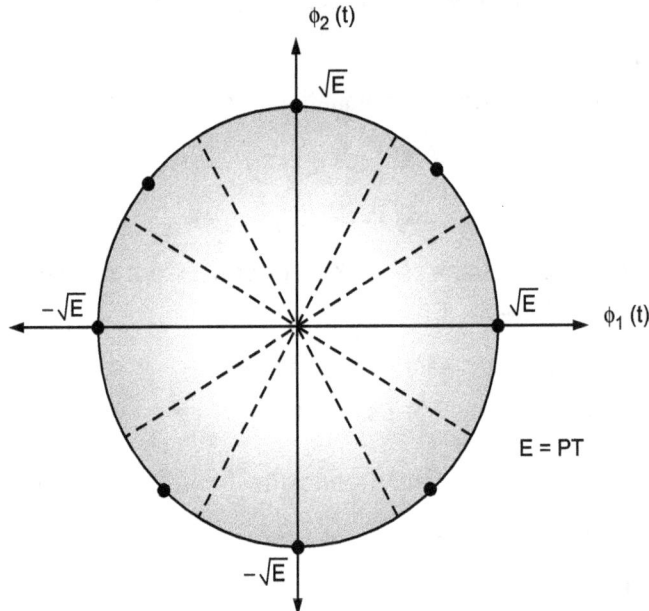

Fig. 9.17 : Signal Space Representation for M-ary QPSK (M = 8)

Bandwidth of M-ary PSK :

- From the spectrum plotted in Fig. 9.16 shows that the null-to-null bandwidth can given by,

$$\begin{aligned}
BW &= \left(f_c + \frac{1}{T}\right) - \left(f_c - \frac{1}{T}\right) \\[2mm]
&= \frac{2}{T}
\end{aligned}$$

Since,

$$= NT_b$$

$$W = \frac{2}{NT_b} = \frac{2f_b}{N} = \frac{2f_b}{\log_2 M} \qquad \qquad \ldots (9.92)$$

Hence, for M = 8,

$$W = \frac{2f_b}{\log_2 8} = \frac{2f_b}{3}$$

Merits and Demerits of M-ary PSK :

(i) The bandwidth requirement of M-ary PSK is small. Hence, data rate is high.

(ii) M-ary PSK (and BPSK, QPSK) systems transmit information through phase. The amplitude remains constant. Hence, these systems are useful where transmission medium causes variations in amplitude (fading channels).

(iii) Coherent M-ary PSK requires knowledge of carrier and phase of receiver to accurately synchronise transmitter. Hence, they are not suitable when carrier recovery at receiver is difficult.

(iv) As seen from the signal space diagram, the message points of M-ary PSK lie on circumference of a circle. These signal points are close together hence degrade the noise immunity.

9.8.1 Error Probability of M-PSK

- The error probability in terms of Euclidean distance for circularly symmetric signal constellation is given by,

$$P_e \leq \frac{1}{2} \sum_{\substack{k=1 \\ k \neq i}}^{M} \mathrm{erfc}\left(\frac{d_{ik}}{2\sqrt{N_0}}\right) \qquad \text{... (9.93)}$$

$$\therefore \quad P_e \simeq \frac{1}{2}\,\mathrm{erfc}\left(\frac{d_{12}}{2\sqrt{N_0}}\right) + \frac{1}{2}\,\mathrm{erfc}\left(\frac{d_{18}}{2\sqrt{N_0}}\right)$$

$$\simeq \mathrm{erfc}\left(\frac{d_{12}}{2\sqrt{N_0}}\right)$$

$$\simeq \mathrm{erfc}\left(\frac{2\sqrt{E}\sin\left(\frac{\pi}{8}\right)}{2\sqrt{N_0}}\right)$$

$$\boxed{P_e \simeq \mathrm{erfc}\left(\sqrt{\frac{E}{N_0}} \cdot \sin\left(\frac{\pi}{8}\right)\right)} \qquad \text{... (9.94)}$$

- In general for M-ary PSK

$$P_e = \mathrm{erfc}\left(\sqrt{\frac{E}{N_0}}\sin\left(\frac{\pi}{M}\right)\right) \qquad \text{... (9.95)}$$

- Hence, the symbol error probability,

For M = 4 i.e. QPSK $\quad P_e = \mathrm{erfc}\left(\sqrt{\frac{E}{2N_0}}\right) = 2Q\left(\sqrt{\frac{E}{N_0}}\right) \qquad \text{... (9.96)}$

For M = 8 $p_e = erfc\left(\sqrt{\dfrac{E}{N_0}}\sin\left(\dfrac{\pi}{8}\right)\right) = 2Q\left(\sqrt{\dfrac{2E}{N_0}}\sin\left(\dfrac{\pi}{8}\right)\right)$ ... (9.97)

For M = 16 $p_e = erfc\left(\sqrt{\dfrac{E}{N_0}}\sin\left(\dfrac{\pi}{16}\right)\right)$ ... (9.98)

- For large value of M we can approximate the above formula as below.
- The Euclidean distance between the two adjacent points for large M is given as,

$$d = \frac{2\pi \times \sqrt{E}}{M}$$ ... (9.99)

(Note that $\sqrt{E}$ is radius of circular constellation hence $2\pi \times \sqrt{E}$ is circumference of the circle).

$$\therefore \qquad d^2 = \frac{4\pi^2 \times E}{M^2} = \frac{4\pi^2 \times P \times T}{M^2}$$

$$= \frac{4\pi^2 \times P \times N \times T_b}{M^2}$$ ... (9.100)

$$= \frac{4\pi^2 \times NE_b}{M^2}$$

$$\therefore \qquad d = 2\pi\sqrt{\frac{NE_b}{M^2}} = 2\sqrt{\frac{\pi^2 NE_b}{M^2}}$$

- Taking into account only two nearest signal points to S_1 and using equation (9.93), we get,

$$p(e/S_1) = p_e \leq 2 \times \frac{1}{2}erfc\left(\sqrt{\frac{\pi^2 NE_b}{M^2 N_0}}\right)$$ ... (9.101)

where, $M = 2^N$

- Thus, $p_e = erfc\left(\sqrt{\dfrac{\pi^2 NE_b}{M^2 N_0}}\right)$ ... (9.102)

or $p_e = 2Q\left(\sqrt{\dfrac{\pi^2 NE_b}{M^2 N_0}}\right)$ ... (9.103)

- To keep p_e constant as number of bits per symbol N changes, we can have,

$$\frac{\pi^2 NE_b}{M^2 \times N_0} = \text{Constant} = K$$

$$\therefore \qquad \frac{E_b}{N_0} = \frac{K}{\pi^2} \times \frac{M^2}{N} = \frac{K}{\pi^2} \times \frac{2^{2N}}{N}$$

- Thus, signal energy-to-noise ratio increases nominally in exponential manner with N for constant p_e in M-ary PSK.

- The error probabilities of M-ary PSK are plotted in Fig. 9.18 for M = 2, 4, 8, 16, 32, 64.

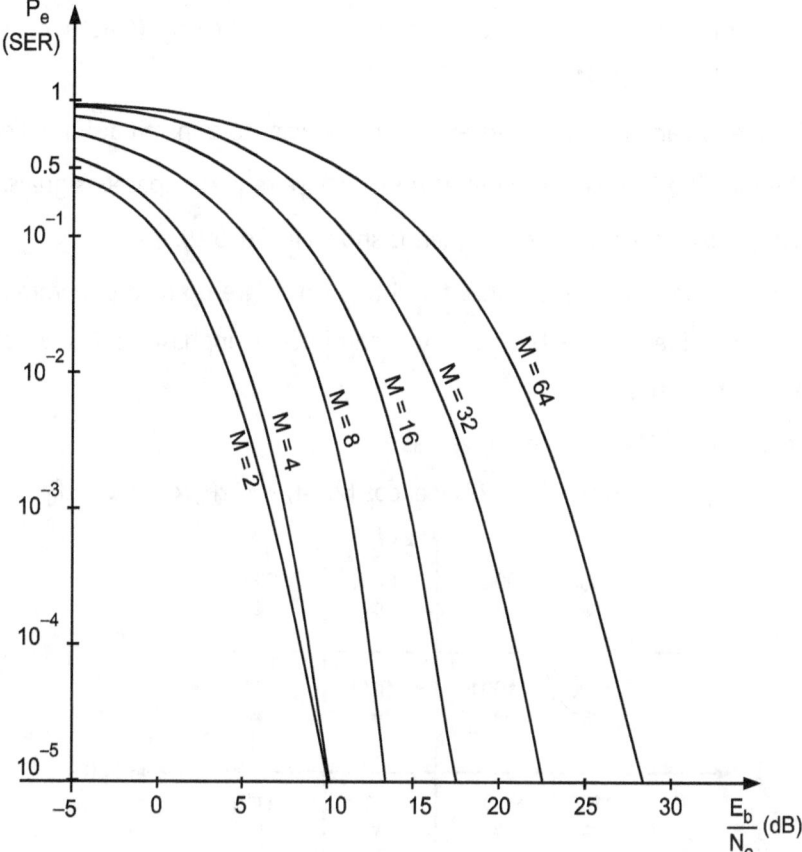

Fig. 9.18 : Symbol Error Probability for Coherent M-ary PSK

- It can be seen for above plot that for constant N_0, to achieve same error performance we have to put in more energy per symbol as M increases.

9.9   QUADRATURE AMPLITUDE MODULATION (QAM)

- In the last section, we have seen that amplitude of signal remains constant in case of BPSK, QPSK and M-ary PSK whereas phase varies.

- The constrained envelope (sample amplitude) of signal gives rise to a circular constellation for message points.

- Since these points are very near to each other, it gives rise to poor noise immunity.

- Hence, we can remove the amplitude constraint and make the amplitude also variable alongwith phase.

- Such a system is called Quadrature Amplitude Shift Keying (QASK) or Quadrature Amplitude Modulation (QAM).

- Let us consider a particular QAM system where we want to transmit a symbol every 4-bit.

- Hence, there will be 16 possible symbols for which we require separate signals.

- The signal space diagram for these signals is shown in Fig. 9.19.

- It can be seen from the diagram that the 4 bits which are used to generate a particular signal can be divided into 2 bits each to contribute to inphase and quadrature phase components of the signal.

- The general form of QAM signal is given as,

$$S_i(t) = \sqrt{2P_0} \times a_i \cos(2\pi f_c t) + \sqrt{2P_0} \times b_i \sin(2\pi f_c t) \quad \text{... (9.104)}$$

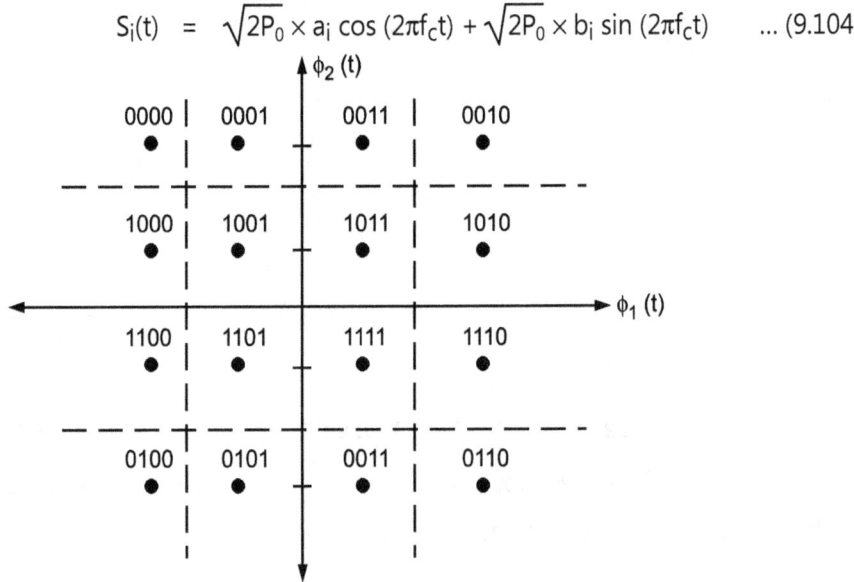

Fig. 9.19 : Signal Space Representation of QAM (M = 16)

where, P_0 is signal power of lowest amplitude signal. a_i and b_i decide the location of message points.

Transmitter and Receiver for QAM :

- The transmitter for QAM is shown in Fig. 9.16 (a).

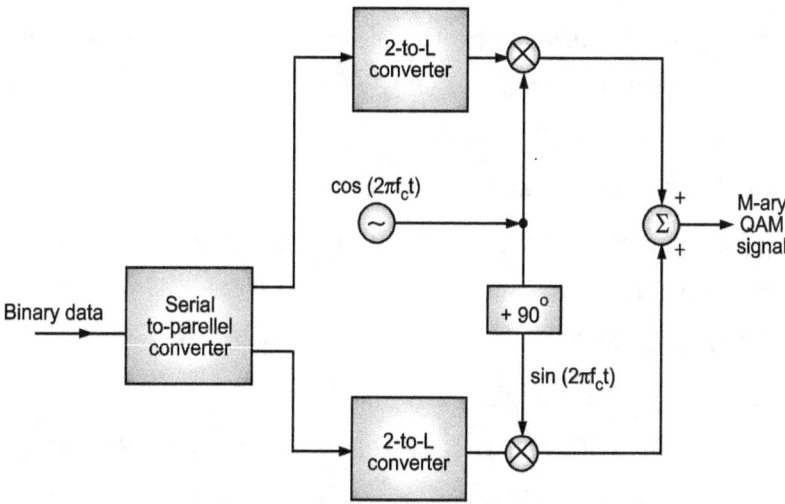

Fig. 9.20 : (a) QAM Transmitter

- It consists of a serial to parallel converter which converts N bit input data into 2 parallel binary sequences. (e.g. if 4-bit sequence 1001 is input, it is converted into 1 0 and 0 1).
- These binary sequences are given to 2 to L level converter.
- This converter converts these sequences into corresponding level.
- This output is multiplied with inphase and quadrature phase carrier which are combined by the adder to generate desired QAM signal.
- The receiver for QAM is shown in Fig. 9.20 (b).

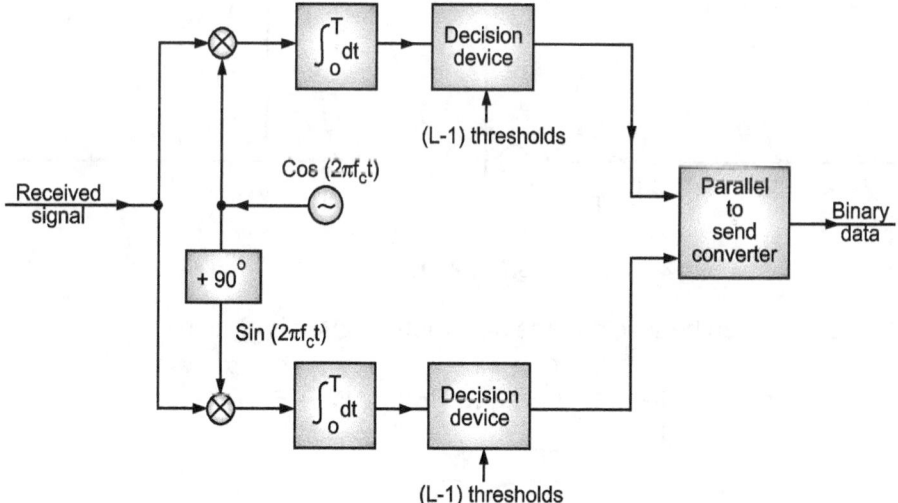

Fig. 9.20 : (b) QAM Receiver

- The received signal r(t) is given to two correlators (multiplier and integrator). The output of correlators is given to decision devices which is designed to compare the L level signals against L − 1 decision threshold.

- The decision devices give out two binary sequences based on the comparison.

- These sequences are combined by a parallel-to-serial converter to get back the original transmitted binary sequence.

Bandwidth of QAM Signal :

- The QAM/QASK signal is given by,

$$S_i(t) \;=\; \sqrt{2P_0} \times a_i \cos(2\pi f_c t) + \sqrt{2P_0} \times b_i \sin(2\pi f_c t)$$

- This equation is similar to M-ary PSK i.e. equation (9.38). Hence proceeding on the same line that of M-ary PSK we can write PSD of QAM as,

$$S_{QAM}(f) \;=\; \frac{PT}{2}\, \text{sinc}^2\,[(f - f_c)\,T] + \frac{PT}{2}\, \text{sinc}^2\,[(f + f_c)\,T] \qquad \dots (9.105)$$

where, T is symbol duration given by $T = NT_b$

- Hence, the plot of PSD of QAM is shown in Fig. 9.21.

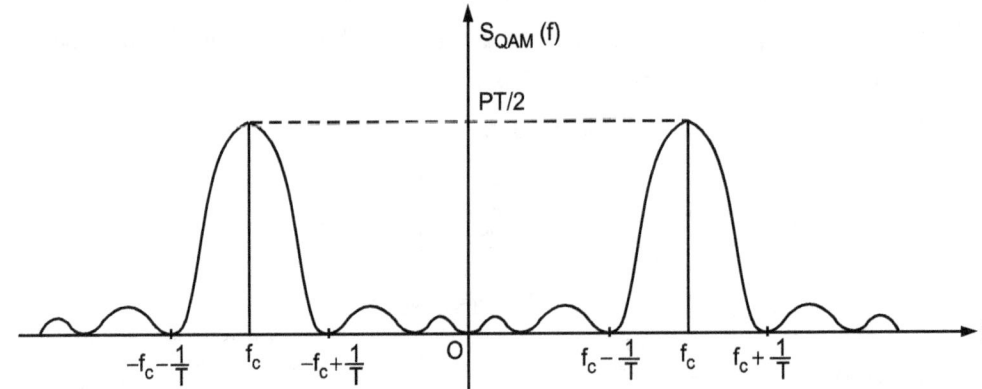

Fig. 9.21 : PSD of QAM

- From the plot, it can be seen that the bandwidth of QAM is given by,

$$BW \;=\; \left(f_c + \frac{1}{T}\right) - \left(f_c - \frac{1}{T}\right) = \frac{2}{T} = \frac{2}{NT_b}$$

$$=\; \frac{2f_b}{N} = \frac{2f_b}{\log_2 M} \qquad \dots (9.106)$$

- Hence, bandwidth of QASK/QAM and M-ary PSK is same.

- Thus, QASK/QAM system has an advantage of better noise immunity than M-ary PSK retaining the low bandwidth requirement.

Error probability of M-QAM

- The symbol error probability for M-QAM is given by

$$p_e \;=\; 4\left(1-\frac{1}{\sqrt{M}}\right) Q\left(\sqrt{\frac{E_o}{N_0}}\right)$$

where E_0 is energy of symbol with smallest amplitude.

- The error probability in terms of average energy is

$$p_e \;=\; 4\left(1-\frac{1}{\sqrt{M}}\right) Q\left(\sqrt{\frac{3E_{av}}{(m-1)\,N_0}}\right)$$

9.10 MINIMUM SHIFT KEYING (MSK)

- Linear modulation schemes such as QPSK, FSK etc. exhibit phase discontinuity in the modulated waveform.

- There is one more variant of QPSK called offset QPSK (OQPSK). In OQPSK odd and even bit streams do not change simultaneously as in case of QPSK. It results into a phase change of 90° instead of 180°. Hence, it eliminates the effect of abrupt phase change to some extent.

- The phase transitions cause problems for band limited and power efficient transmission especially in interference limited environment.

- The sharp phase changes in the modulated signal result into more power in side lobes of spectrum compared to the main lobe.

- In a cellular communication system, these sidelobes should be as small as possible.

- In power limited environment, a non-linear power amplifier alongwith a bandpass filter in the transmitter front-end results in phase distortion for the modulated signal waveform with sharp phase transitions.

- The abrupt phase transitions generate frequency components that have significant amplitudes. Thus, the resultant power in sidelobes cause co-channels and inter-channel interference.

- We can use high power amplifiers or non-linear amplifiers with extensive distortion compensation. However, high power amplifiers are to be operated in non-linear region. This results in power inefficiency.

- Continuous phase modulations, in which there is smooth phase change are preferred to counter these problems.

- Minimum Phase Shift Keying (MSK) is free from many of these problems mentioned above.

- MSK has following advantages :

   (i) Eliminates the abrupt phase changes.

   (ii) It makes main lobe wider making side lobes insignificant.

- The waveform of MSK are shown in Fig. 9.22. Let us understand the scheme through these waveforms.

1. Input waveform b(t) is divided into two waveforms $b_0(t)$ representing odd numbered bits and $b_e(t)$ representing even numbered bits. The duration of each bit $b_0(t)$ and $b_e(t)$ is $2T_b$. Fig. 9.22 (b) and (c).

2. There is staggering in $b_0(t)$ and $b_e(t)$ just like OQPSK of duration T_b.

3. Two waveforms $\sin [2\pi (t/4T_b)]$ and $\cos [2\pi (t/4T_b)]$ are generated at the MSK transmitter as shown in Fig. 9.22(d).

   Note that these waveforms are such that $\sin [2\pi (t/4T_b)]$ crosses zero at the end of the symbol time $b_e(t)$ and $\cos 2\pi (t/4T_b)$ crosses zero at the end of symbol time $b_0(t)$.

4. $b_0(t)$ and $b_e(t)$ are multiplied with the waveform $\sin [2\pi (t/4T_b)]$ and $\cos [2\pi (t/4T_b)]$ respectively to produce waveforms in Fig. 9.22 (e) and (f).

5. The original baseband waveform is converted into smoother waveforms (e) and (f) which are modulated using in-phase and quadrature phase carrier and the resultant MSK signal will be,

$$S(t) \quad = \quad \sqrt{2P}\left[b_e(t) \sin\left(\frac{2\pi t}{4T_b}\right)\right] \cos (2\pi f_c t) + \sqrt{2P}\left[b_0(t) \cos\left(\frac{2\pi t}{4T_b}\right)\right] \sin (2\pi f_c t) \quad ... (9.107)$$

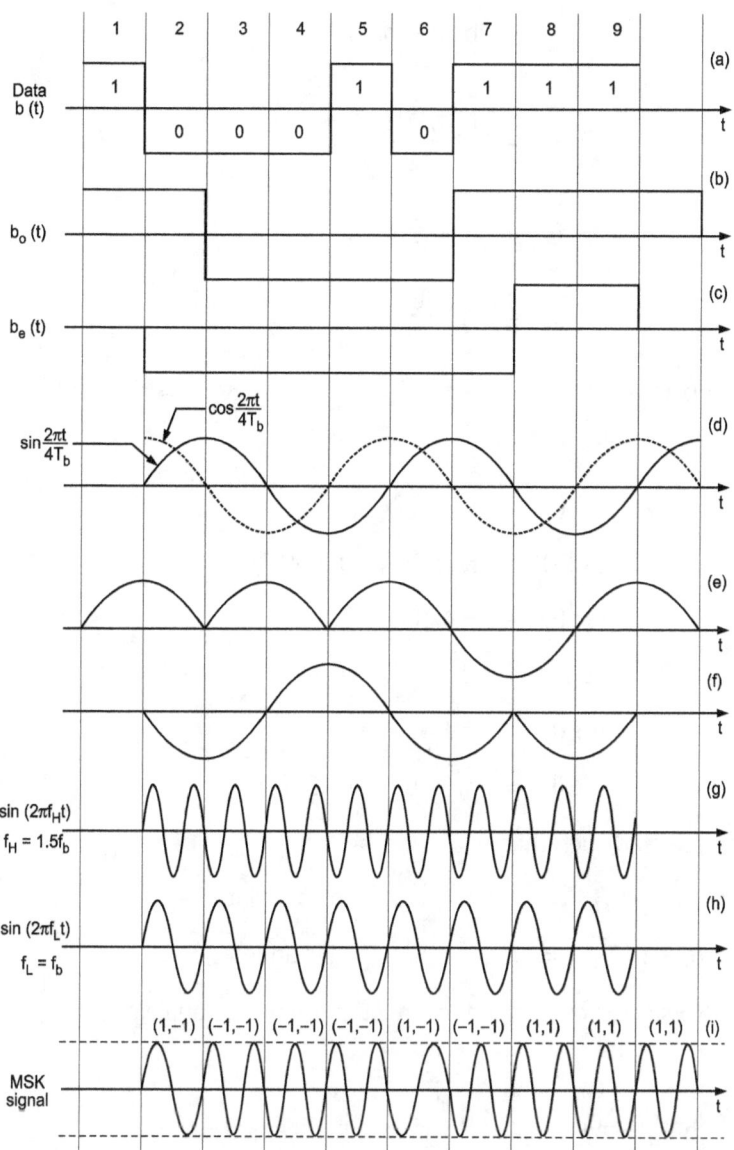

Fig. 9.22 : MSK Waveforms

$$\therefore \quad S(t) = \sqrt{2P}\left[\frac{b_0(t) + b_e(t)}{2}\right] \sin\left(2\pi f_c t + \frac{2\pi t}{4T_b}\right)$$

$$+ \sqrt{2P}\left[\frac{b_0(t) - b_e(t)}{2}\right] \sin\left(2\pi f_c t - \frac{2\pi t}{4T_b}\right) \qquad \dots (9.108)$$

$$\therefore \quad S(t) = \sqrt{2P} \cdot B_H(t) \sin(2\pi f_H t)$$

$$+ \sqrt{2P} \, B_L(t) \sin(2\pi f_L t) \qquad \dots (9.109)$$

where, $B_H(t) = \dfrac{b_0(t) + b_e(t)}{2}$

                  $B_L(t) = \dfrac{b_0(t) - b_e(t)}{2}$

                  $f_H = f_c + \dfrac{f_b}{4}$

                  $f_L = f_c - \dfrac{f_b}{4}$

6. When $b_0(t) = b_e(t)$

                  $B_H(t) = \pm 1$

                  $B_L(t) = 0$

$\therefore$ $S(t) = \sqrt{2P}\, B_H(t)\, \sin(2\pi f_H t)$ ... (9.110)

When $b_0(t) = -b_e(t)$

                  $B_H(t) = 0$

                  $B_L(t) = \pm 1$

$\therefore$ $S(t) = \sqrt{2P}\, B_L(t)\, \sin(2\pi f_L t)$ ... (9.111)

7. f_H and f_L are selected such that

          $2\pi(f_H + f_L)T_b = m\pi$ m is an integer

          $2\pi(f_H - f_L)T_b = n\pi$ n is an integer

Hence, the two signals $\cos 2\pi f_H t$ and $\sin 2\pi f_H t$ are orthogonal i.e.

$$\int_0^{T_b} \sin 2\pi f_H t\, \sin 2\pi f_L t\, dt = 0$$

$\therefore$ $2\pi\left(f_c + \dfrac{f_b}{4} + f_c - \dfrac{f_b}{4}\right) \times T_b = m\pi$

$\therefore$ $f_c = \dfrac{m f_b}{4}$

and $2\pi \times \left[\left(f_c + \dfrac{f_b}{4}\right) - \left(f_c - \dfrac{f_b}{4}\right)\right] \times T_b = n\pi$

$\therefore$ $2 \times \dfrac{f_b}{2} \times T_b = n$

$$\therefore \qquad n = 1$$

$$\therefore \qquad 2\pi(f_H - f_L)T_b = 1 \times \pi$$

$$\therefore \qquad f_H - f_L = \frac{1}{2T_b}$$

$$\therefore \qquad f_H - f_L = \frac{1}{2}f_b$$

- The name minimum shift keying has come from the fact that $f_H - f_L$ is minimum since $n = 1$. It is the minimum difference between f_H and f_L for which the signals are orthogonal.

8. The carrier frequency selected should be integer multiple of $f_b/4$.

i.e. $$f_c = \frac{mf_b}{4}$$

$$\therefore \qquad f_H = f_c + \frac{f_b}{4} = \frac{mf_b}{4} + \frac{f_b}{4}$$

$$= (m+1)\frac{f_b}{4}$$

$$f_L = f_c - \frac{f_b}{4}$$

$$= (m-1)\frac{f_b}{4}$$

- **Signal Space Representation of MSK :**

The MSK signal given by equation (9.109) can be rewritten as,

$$S(t) = \sqrt{PT} \times B_H(t)\sqrt{\frac{2}{T}}\sin(2\pi f_H t)$$

$$+ \sqrt{PT} \times B_L(t)\sqrt{\frac{2}{T}}\sin(2\pi f_L t) \qquad \text{... (9.112)}$$

Hence, the two basis functions are,

$$\phi_1(t) = \sqrt{\frac{2}{T}}\sin(2\pi f_H t)$$

$$\phi_2(t) = \sqrt{\frac{2}{T}}\sin(2\pi f_L t) \qquad \text{... (9.113)}$$

$$\therefore \qquad S(t) = B_H(t) \cdot \sqrt{PT}\,\phi_1(t) + B_L(t)\sqrt{PT}\,\phi_2(t) \qquad \text{... (9.114)}$$

- Depending $B_H(t)$ and $B_0(t)$ there will be four signal points as plotted in Fig. 9.23.

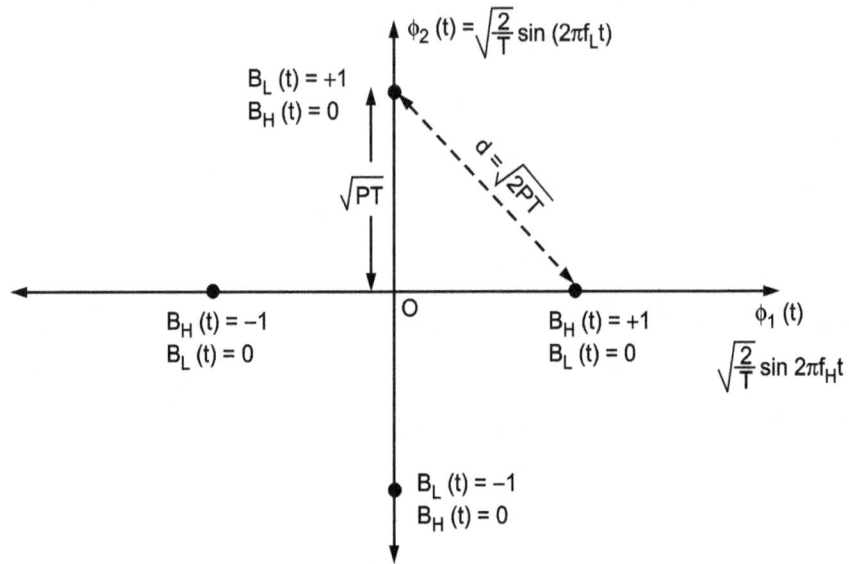

Fig. 9.23: Signal Space Diagram for MSK

- The distance between two nearest point will be,

$$d^2 = (\sqrt{PT})^2 + (\sqrt{PT})^2$$

∴
$$d = \sqrt{2PT}$$

Power Spectral Density :

- The MSK waveform is given by,

$$S(t) = \sqrt{2P}\, b_e(t) \sin\left(\frac{2\pi t}{4T_b}\right) \cos(2\pi f_c t)$$

$$+ \sqrt{2P}\, b_0(t) \cos\left(\frac{2\pi t}{4T_b}\right) \cdot \sin(2\pi f_c t) \qquad \dots (9.115\ a)$$

- Consider the waveform,

$$g(t) = \sqrt{2P}\, b_0(t) \cos\left(\frac{2\pi t}{4T_b}\right) \quad -T_b \le t \le T_b$$

- The PSD of above signal is,

$$S_g(f) = \frac{32\, E_b}{\pi^2}\left[\frac{\cos 2\pi f T_b}{1 - (4fT_b)^2}\right]^2 \qquad \dots (9.115\ b)$$

where,
$$E_b = \frac{PT}{2} \text{ (Energy per bit duration)}$$

- Hence, PSD of MSK will be,

$$S_{MSK}(f) = \frac{8}{\pi^2}E_b\left[\left\{\frac{\cos 2\pi(f - f_c)T_b}{1 - [4(f - f_c)T_b]^2}\right\}^2 + \left\{\frac{\cos 2\pi(f + f_c)T_b}{1 - [4(f - f_c)T_b]^2}\right\}^2\right]$$

$$\dots (9.116)$$

- This PSD is plotted in Fig. 9.24 for normalised power along with QPSK for comparison.

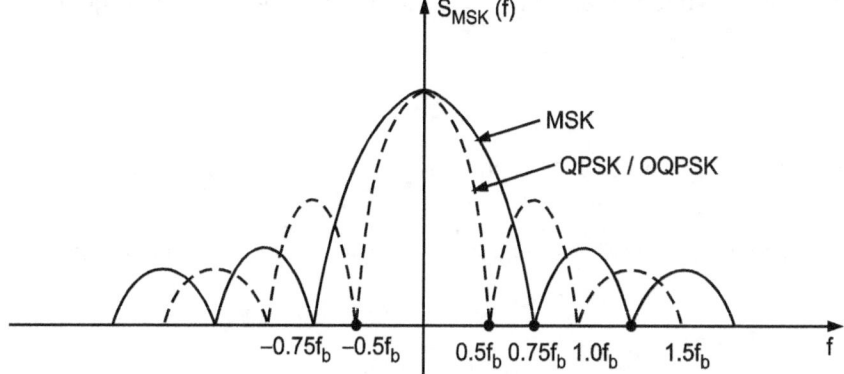

Fig. 9.24 : PSD of MSK along with PSD of QPSK

Bandwidth of MSK :

- It can be seen from Fig. 9.20 that the bandwidth of MSK is,

$$BW = \frac{3}{4} f_b - \left(-\frac{3}{4} f_b\right) = 1.5 \, f_b$$

- It can be seen that the main lobe width of MSK is larger than QPSK and has higher bandwidth.

Generation of MSK :

- The MSK transmitter block diagram is shown in Fig. 9.25 (a).

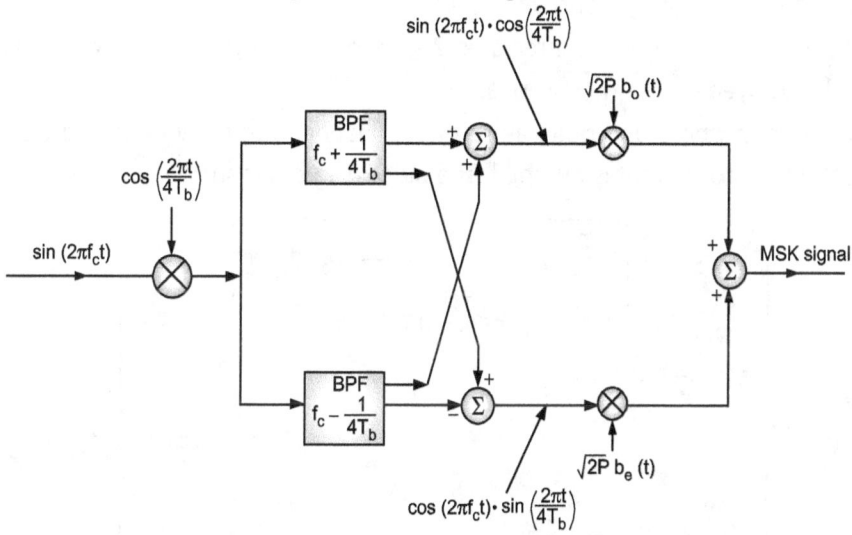

Fig. 9.25 : (a) Generation of MSK Signal

- The MSK signal is given by,

$$S(t) = \sqrt{2P} \, b_e(t) \sin\left(\frac{2\pi t}{4T_b}\right) \cdot \cos(2\pi f_c t)$$

$$+ \sqrt{2P} \, b_0(t) \cos\left(\frac{2\pi t}{4T_b}\right) \cdot \sin(2\pi f_c t) \qquad \ldots (9.117)$$

- First we generate $\sin(2\pi f_c t)$ and $\sin\left(\dfrac{2\pi t}{4T_b}\right)$ and use 90° phase shifter to get $\cos(2\pi f_c t)$ $\cos\left(\dfrac{2\pi t}{4T_b}\right)$.

- Then we use multiplier to get the terms $\sin\left(\dfrac{2\pi t}{4T_b}\right) \cdot \cos(2\pi f_c t)$ and $\cos\left(\dfrac{2\pi t}{4T_b}\right) \sin(2\pi f_c t)$.

- Another set of multiplier will generate $\sqrt{2P}\, b_e(t) \sin\left(\dfrac{2\pi t}{4T_b}\right) \cdot \cos(2\pi f_c t)$ and $\sqrt{2P}\, b_0(t) \cos\left(\dfrac{2\pi t}{4T_b}\right) \cdot \sin(2\pi f_c t)$.

- Then an adder adds these two terms to get the signal represented in equation (9.54).

Reception of MSK :

- The detection is performed by correlating received signal with two waveforms.

$$\phi_1(t) = \cos\left(\frac{2\pi t}{4T_b}\right) \sin(2\pi f_c t)$$

$$\phi_2(t) = \sin\left(\frac{2\pi t}{4T_b}\right) \cos(2\pi f_c t)$$

- The received signal r(t) is multiplied and integrated by the two separate correlators whose another input is $\phi_1(t)$ and $\phi_2(t)$.

- In both the cases integration interval is $2T_b$ seconds and the integration in quadrature channel is delayed by $T_b \cdot$ w.r.t. in-phase channel.

- The resulting in-phase and quadrature phase channel outputs v_1 and v_2 are stored and then the integrator output is dumped. The block diagram is shown in Fig. 9.25 (b).

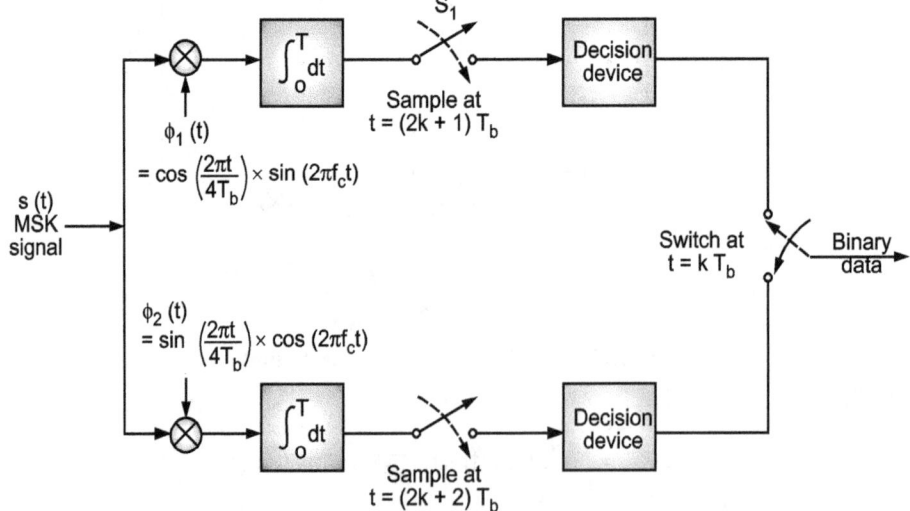

Fig. 9.25 : (b) MSK Receiver Block Diagram

Phase Continuity in MSK :

- The MSK signal is given by,

$$S(t) = \sqrt{2P}\left[\frac{b_0(t) + b_e(t)}{2}\right] \sin\left[2\pi\,(f_c + f_1)\,t\right]$$

$$+ \sqrt{2P}\left[\frac{b_0(t) - b_e(t)}{2}\right] \sin\left[2\pi\,(f_c - f_1)\,t\right]$$

- This equation can be rewritten as,

$$S(t) = b_0(t)\,\sqrt{2P}\,\sin\left[2\pi\,(f_c + b_0(t)\cdot b_e(t)\,f_1)\,t\right]$$

- Now, following table gives the MSK signal for various combinations of $b_0(t)$ and $b_e(t)$.

$b_0(t)$	$b_e(t)$	$S(t)$
+ 1	+ 1	$\sqrt{2P}\,\sin\left[2\pi\,(f_c + f_1)\,t\right]$ $= \sqrt{2P}\,\sin(2\pi f_H t)$
+ 1	− 1	$-\sqrt{2P}\,\sin\left[2\pi\,(f_c - f_1)\,t\right]$ $= -\sqrt{2P}\,\sin(2\pi f_L t)$
− 1	+ 1	$\sqrt{2P}\,\sin\left[2\pi\,(f_c - f_1)\,t\right]$ $= \sqrt{2P}\,\sin(2\pi f_L t)$
− 1	− 1	$\sin\left[2\pi\,(f_c + f_1)\,t\right]$ $= \sin(2\pi f_H t)$

- Accordingly the MSK waveforms for f_H and f_L are drawn in Fig. 9.18 (g) and (h) from the MSK waveforms drawn and referring above table we can observe the following things.

1. $b_0(t)$ and $b_e(t)$ do not change at the same time.

2. The product $b_0(t) \cdot b_e(t)$ will cause a change of phase $k\pi$ (where, k is integer) whenever it changes from + 1 to − 1 or − 1 to + 1.

3. $b_0(t)$ changes only at odd bit intervals i.e. T_b, $3T_b$, etc.

   $b_e(t)$ can change only at even bit intervals i.e. $2T_b$ $4T_b$, etc.

4. Change in $b_e(t)$ will change the phase by multiple of 2π. It is equivalent to no change of phase.

5. Change in $b_0(t)$ will cause a phase change of $k\pi$ since it changes at odd bit intervals. But $b_0(t)$ will further cause a phase change of π since it multiplies $\sqrt{2P}\,\sin\left[2\pi\,(f_c + b_0(t)\cdot b_e(t)\,f_1)\right]$. Hence, this will also result in phase change of multiple of 2π.

6. From (4) and (5) we can conclude that there is phase continuity in MSK signal.

Comparison of MSK and QPSK :

MSK	QPSK
1. It has continuous phase change in transmitted waveforms.	1. It has abrupt phase change in transmitted waveforms.
2. When filtered there is no amplitude variation.	2. When filtered they gives rise to amplitude variations.
3. Interchannel interference is very small due to small side lobes.	3. Interchannel interference is large due to large side lobes.
4. Main lobe is wider and has more than 95% energy in it.	4. Main lobe is narrow and has around 90% energy in it.
5. Bandwidth of MSK is 1.5 f_b.	5. Bandwidth of QPSK is f_b.
6. Generation and detection circuit is more complex.	6. Generation and detection circuit is less complex.
7. Receiver uses a coherent phase decoding process over two successive bits to recover original bit stream.	7. Receiver uses coherent phase decoding process over two successive bits to recover original bit stream.
8. While generating signal the baseband is modified first to make it smoother.	8. While generating QPSK signal original baseband signal is not modified.
9. The bit pattern is divided into odd and even pattern and there is offset of T_b in these patterns.	9. The bit pattern is divided into odd and even patterns but there may not be offset of T_b in these patterns.

9.11 NON-COHERENT BINARY MODULATION TECHNIQUES

- Coherent detection techniques seen in last section use carrier wave's phase reference.
- When it is not possible to have carrier recovered at the receivers end we use non-coherent detection.
- In this section, we will study these non-coherent detection techniques. viz. FSK, DPSK.
- Note that we cannot have non-coherent detection of PSK. Hence, we have DPSK technique used for non-coherent detection.

9.11.1 Non-coherent BFSK

- BFSK signal is represented as,

$$S_H(t) = \sqrt{2P_s} \cos (2\pi f_H t) \qquad \qquad \text{... (9.118)}$$

and
$$S_L(t) = \sqrt{2P_s} \cos (2\pi f_L t) \qquad \qquad \text{... (9.119)}$$

where,
$$f_H = f_c + f_1$$

and
$$f_L = f_c - f_1$$

- Even though they have same amplitude (envelope) the different carrier frequencies make non-coherent detection possible in BFSK.
- The receiver for non-coherent detection of BFSK is shown in Fig. 9.26. The received signal is applied to two bandpass filters with centre frequencies f_H and f_L.
- As we have seen f_H and f_L are selected such that $f_H - f_L = 2f_b$.
- Hence, the filter frequency ranges do not overlaps the main lobe can be filtered by each filter which will pass nearly all energy.
- The output of filters is given to envelope detector. Suppose that we have transmitted 1. Hence, the waveform received at the input of receiver will be,

$$r(t) = \sqrt{2P_s} \cos (2\pi f_H t)$$

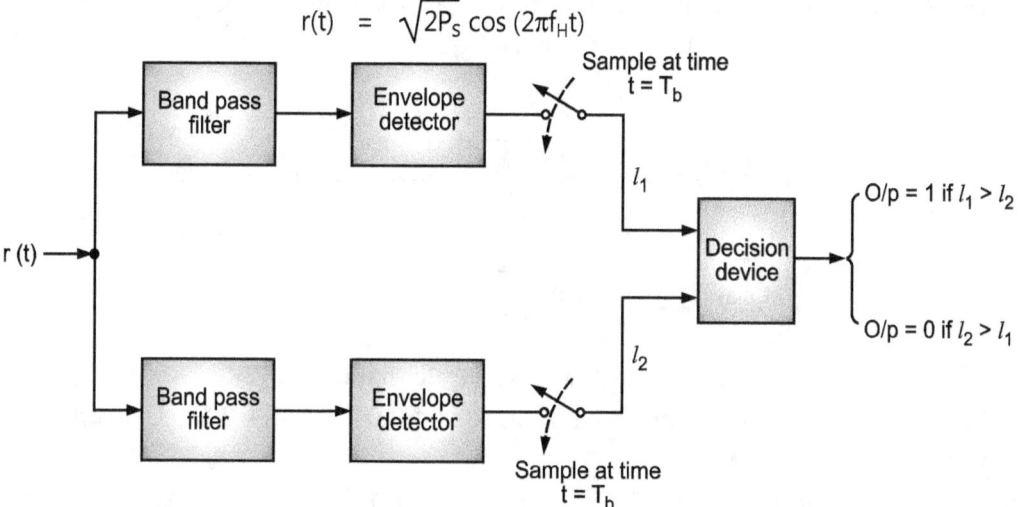

Fig. 9.26 : Non-coherent BFSK

- It is given to two bandpass filters.
- The output of upper bandpass filter will be $\sqrt{2P_s} \cos (2\pi f_H t)$ whereas lower bandpass filter will be zero. (This is assuming that there is no noise or distortion in the received waveform).
- The envelope detector output in the upper branch will be more than that of lower.
- Hence, the decision device which compares the two sampled outputs will be making decision in favour of 1. Similarly, when 0 is transmitted, lower branch is going to have higher specified output than upper.
- In presence of noise, the performance of the receiver is going to be affected depending on the signal energy and noise power which will be evaluated in the next chapter.

9.11.2 Differential Phase Shift Keying (DPSK)

- It is non-coherent version of PSK i.e. this modulation technique eliminates the synchronous carrier recovery at the receiver end simplifying the receiver circuit.

- There is one more problem associated with coherent PSK detection. We recover the carrier from received signal by squaring it. But then changing the sign of input signal will not alter the carrier. Hence, there is phase ambiguity of 180° in PSK detection. The DPSK technique eliminates this phase ambiguity.
- At the transmitter, it uses two basic operations :
  (i) Differential encoding of input binary wave.
  (ii) Phase Shift Keying.
- The block diagram of DPSK transmitter is shown in Fig. 9.27 (a). The data stream d(t) to be transmitted is applied to an EX-OR logic along with delayed version of output of EX-OR gate (feedback). Thus, the output of EX-OR gate can be expressed as,

$$b(t) \ = \ d(t) + b\,(t - T_b) \qquad\qquad \dots (9.120)$$

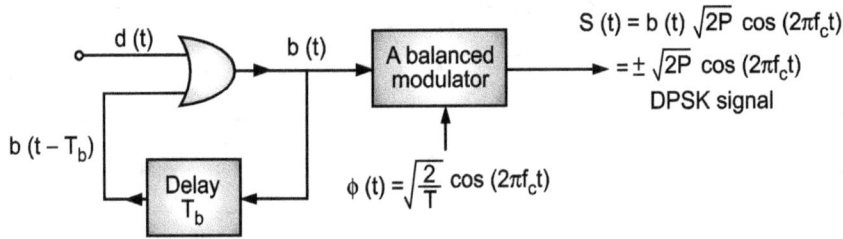

Fig. 9.27 : (a) Block Diagram for Generation of DPSK

- The waveforms corresponding to input bit stream 0 0 1 0 1 1 1 0 0 1 is shown in Fig. 9.27(b).

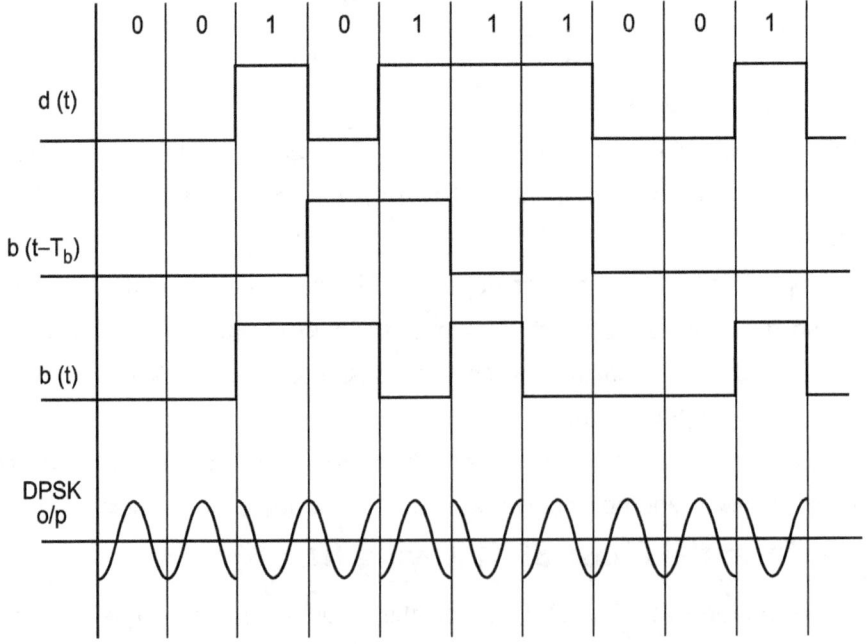

Fig. 9.27 : (b) DPSK Waveforms

- While drawing these waveforms the initial bit of b(t) is assumed to be 0.

- It can be seen from the waveforms that b(t) changes its level whenever the input bit d(t) = 1 and it remains same as previous whenever d(t) = 0.

- The output of EX-OR gate b(t) is applied to a balanced modulator (multiplier) which is applied with carrier cos $2\pi f_c t$ as other input. The output of balanced modulator will be,

$$S(t) = b(t)\sqrt{2P_s}\cos(2\pi f_c t)$$
$$= \pm\sqrt{2P_s}\cos(2\pi f_c t)$$

- Since b(t) varies whenever input 1 phase of carrier also changes when input is 1 by 180°.

- The receiver for DPSK as mentioned earlier is simple and is shown in Fig. 9.27 (c).

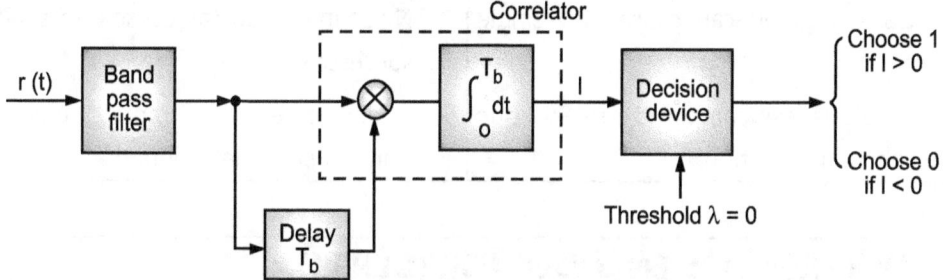

Fig. 9.27 : (c) DPSK Receiver

- Here, the received signal r(t) = b(t) $\sqrt{2P_s}$ cos $2\pi f_c t$ is multiplied with its delayed version. Hence, the output of multiplier will be,

b(t) b (t − T_b) · 2 P_s cos ($2\pi f_c t + \theta$) · cos [$2\pi f_c$ (t − T_b) + θ]

$$= P_s\, b(t)\, b\,(t - T_b) \left\{ \cos 2\pi f_c T_b + \cos\left[4\pi f_c \left(t - \frac{T_b}{2}\right) + 2\theta \right] \right\} \qquad \text{... (9.121)}$$

- This output is given to an integrator. As seen in case of BPSK, the integrator will suppress the second terms and if we select $2\pi f_c \times T_b = 2n\pi$ (or f_c is integral multiple of $1/T_b$), then the output of integrator will be b(t) · b (t − T_b).

- The transmitted data can be recovered from this product b(t) b (t − T_b) easily.

- When transmitted data,

$$d(t) = 0 \qquad\qquad b(t)\, b\,(t - T_b) = +1$$
and
$$d(t) = 1 \qquad\qquad b(t)\, b\,(t - T_b) = -1$$

- Hence, if the product b(t) b (t − T_b) is positive decision can be made in favour of 0 and if it is negative decision is made in favour of 1.

Comparison of PSK and DPSK :

PSK	DPSK
1. It is coherent modulation technique.	1. It is non-coherent modulation technique.
2. Local carrier needs to be generated at receiver which makes receiver circuit complex.	2. No carrier generated at receiver hence circuit is simple.
3. Transmitter does not require differential encoding of input binary stream.	3. Transmitter requires differential encoding to be done.
4. Noise in one bit can cause only single error.	4. Noise in one bit can cause errors in two successive bits.
5. Error rate is less compared to DPSK due to coherent detection.	5. Error rate is more due to non-coherent detection.

9.12 DIFFERENTIAL ENCODED PSK (DEPSK)

- This technique is modification of DPSK.

- The drawback of DPSK is that it requires a device (synchronous demodulator) which operates at high frequency (carrier).

- Differential Encoded PSK (DEPSK) eliminates this requirement.

- First we recover the signal b(t) using synchronous detector in as case of PSK. Then a decoder as shown in Fig. 9.28 is used to get back d(t).

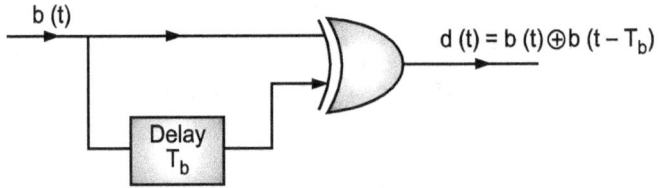

Fig. 9.28 : Decoder for DEPSK

- The output of decoder will be b(t) + b (t – T_b) which is nothing but original transmitted bit stream d(t).

i.e. when $b(t) = b(t - T_b)$ $d(t) = 0$

and $b(t) = \overline{b(t - T_b)}$ $d(t) = 1$

Comparison of DPSK and DEPSK :

DPSK	DEPSK
1. It employs non-coherent detection.	1. It is coherent modulation technique.
2. Transmitter has differential encoding of input data and PSK.	2. Transmitter has differential encoding of input data and PSK.
3. Receiver requires a device which operates at high frequency.	3. DEPSK eliminate need of such hardware.
4. DPSK receiver does not make hard decision in each bit interval.	4. DEPSK receiver makes hard decisions in each bit interval.
5. In DPSK receiver errors can occur in single or two bit intervals since the detection is based on comparison of received signal in two bit intervals.	5. In DEPSK errors always occur in pairs.

9.13 COMPARISON OF DIGITAL MODULATION TECHNIQUE

Table 9.1 shows the comparison of various digital modulation techniques.

Following Table 9.1 gives a few digital modulation schemes and their applications.

Table 9.1

Sr. No.	Modulation Scheme	Application
1.	BPSK	Telemetry and Telecommand
2.	QPSK	Satellite, Cellular Telephony, Digital Video Broadcasting.
3.	8-PSK	Satellite communication.
4.	16-QAM	Digital Video Broadcasting, Microwave Digital Radio Links.
5.	64-QAM	Digital Video Broadcasting, Multimedia Data Services, Set Top Boxes.
6.	FSK	Cordless Telephony, Paging.
7.	MSK	Cellular Telephony.

Following table gives bandwidth efficiency limits of the modulation schemes.

Table 9.2

Sr. No.	Modulation Scheme	Bandwidth Efficiency Bit/s/Hz
1.	BPSK	1
2.	QPSK	2
3.	8-PSK	3
4.	16-QAM	4
5.	32-QAM	5
6.	256-QAM	8
7.	MSK	1

Error probability of the digital modulation schemes :

- Let us see the error probabilities of various other digital modulation schemes without derivation.

(i) BPSK

$$p_e = \frac{1}{2} \text{erfc}\left(\sqrt{\frac{E_b}{N_0}}\right)$$

$$= Q\left(\sqrt{\frac{2E_b}{N_0}}\right)$$

(ii) BFSK (Non-orthogonal signal)

$$p_e = \frac{1}{2}\left(\sqrt{\frac{0.6\, E_b}{N_0}}\right)$$

$$= Q\left(\sqrt{\frac{1.2\, E_b}{N_0}}\right)$$

(iii) BFSK (orthogonal signal set)

$$p_e = \frac{1}{2} \text{erfc}\left(\sqrt{\frac{E_b}{N_0}}\right)$$

(iv) QPSK\

$$p_e = \frac{1}{2} \text{erfc}\left(\sqrt{\frac{E_b}{N_0}}\right)$$

$$= Q\left(\sqrt{\frac{2E_b}{N_0}}\right)$$

(v) M-ary PSK

$$p_e = 2Q\left(\sqrt{\frac{2E}{N_0}}\sin\left(\frac{\pi}{m}\right)\right)$$

$$= \mathrm{erfc}\left(\sqrt{\frac{E}{N_0}}\sin\left(\frac{\pi}{m}\right)\right)$$

(vi) M-ary QAM

$$p_e = 2\left(1-\frac{1}{\sqrt{m}}\right)Q\left(1-\frac{1}{\sqrt{m}}\right)\mathrm{erfc}\left(\sqrt{\frac{E_0}{N_0}}\right)$$

where E_0 is energy of smallest amplitude signal.

$$p_e = 4\left(1-\frac{1}{\sqrt{m}}\right)Q\left[\sqrt{\frac{E_{av}}{(m-1)N_0}}\right]$$

where E_{av} is average energy.

Comparison of digital modulation schemes :

The bit error rates of various digital modulation schemes are given below :

(a) Coherent BPSK, coherent QPSK, coherent MSK.

$$p_e = \frac{1}{2}\mathrm{erfc}\left(\sqrt{\frac{E_b}{N_0}}\right)$$

$$= Q\left(\sqrt{\frac{2E_b}{N_0}}\right)$$

(b) Coherent BFSK

$$p_e = \frac{1}{2}\mathrm{erfc}\left(\sqrt{\frac{E_b}{2N_0}}\right)$$

$$= Q\left(\sqrt{\frac{E_b}{N_0}}\right)$$

(c) DPSK

$$p_e = \frac{1}{2}e^{-E_b/N_0}$$

(d) Non-coherent BFSK

$$p_e = \frac{1}{2}e^{-E_b/2N_0}$$

The plot is shown in Fig. 9.29 below.

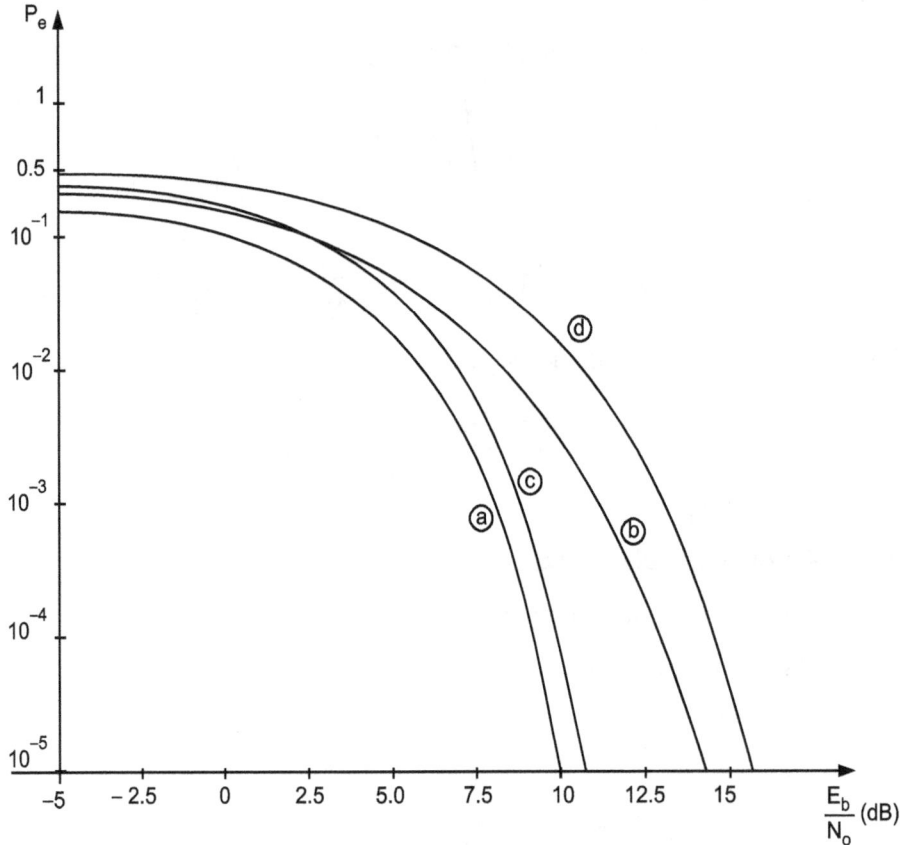

Fig. 9.29 : Comparison of Error Performance of PSK and FSK Schemes

Here are some observation based on the formulae and plots of BER's.

(i)   BER's decrease monotomically with increase in E_b/N_0 (Waterfall shape).

(ii) For all values of E_b/N_0 BPSK, MSK and QPSK have smaller BER than any other scheme.

(iii) Coherent BPSK and DPSK require E_b/N_0 approximately 3 dB less than corresponding values of coherent and non-coherent BFSK respectively to realize same BER.

(iv) The performance of DPSK and non-coherent BFSK is almost same for high values of E_b/N_0 for same BER and same E_b.

9.14 ORTHGONAL FREQUENCY DIVISION MULTIPLEXING (OFDM)

OFDM has been the most widely used communication technology in various applications.

(i)   Digital TV broadcasting : European DAB and DVB-T standards use OFDM.

(ii) HIPERLAN 2 standard is also using OFDM techniques and so is the 5 GHz extension of IEEE 802.11 standard.

(iii) ADSL and VDSL use OFDM. More recently, IEEE 802.16 has standardized OFDM for both Fixed and Mobile WiMAX.

(iv) The cellular world is not left behind either with the evolving LTE embracing OFDM.

One fundamental problem for communication systems is ISI. It is a fact that every transmission channel is time-variant. Two adjacent symbols are likely to experience different channel characteristics including time delays. This is particularly true in wireless channels and mobile terminals communicating in multipath conditions. For low bit rates (narrowband signal), the symbol rate is sufficiently long so that delayed versions of the signal all arrive with the same symbol. They do not spill over to subsequent symbols and therefore there is no ISI. As data rates go up and/or the channel delay increases (wideband signal), ISI starts to occur. Traditionally, this has been overcome by equalization techniques, linear predictive filters and rake receivers. This involves estimating the channel conditions. This works well if the number of symbols to be considered is low. Assuming BPSK, a data reate of 10 Mbps on a channel with a maximum delay of 10 μs would need equlization over 100 symbols. This would be too complex for any receiver. What could be a possible solution the ISI problem at higher bit rates ?

Initial proposals for OFDM were made in the 60s and the 70s. It has taken more than a quarter of a century for this technology to move from the research domain to the industry. The concept of OFDM is quite simple but the practicality of implementing it has many complexities. A single stream of data is split into parallel streams each of which is coded and modulated on to a subcarrier, a term commonly used in OFDM systems. Thus the high bit rates seen before on a single carrier is reduced to lower bit rates on the subcarrier. It is easy to see that ISI will therefore be reduced dramatically.

Basic Principles :

Orthogonal Frequency Division Multiplexing (OFDM) is very similar to the well-known and used technique of Frequency Division Multiplexing (FDM). OFDM uses the principles of FDM to allow multiple messages to be sent over a single radio channel. It is however in a much more controlled manner, allowing an improved spectral efficiency.

A simple example of FDM is the use of different frequencies for each FM (Frequency Modulation) radio stations. All stations transmit at the same time but do not interfere with each other because they transmit using different carrier frequencies. Additionally they are bandwidth limited and are spaced sufficiently far apart in frequency so that their transmitted signals do not overlap in the frequency domain. At the receiver, each signal is individually received by using a frequency tuneable band pass filter to selectively remove all the signals except for the station of interest. This filtered signal can then be demodulated to recover the original transmitted information.

OFDM is different from FDM in several ways. In conventional broadcasting each radio station transmits on a different frequency, effectively using FDM to maintain a separation between the stations. With an OFDM transmission such as DAB, the information signals from multiple stations is combined into a single multiplexed stream of data. This data is then transmitted using an OFDM ensemble that is made up from a dense packing of many subcarriers. All the subcarriers with in the OFDM signal are time and frequency synchronised to each other, allowing the interference between subcarriers to be carefully controlled. These multiple subcarriers overlap in the frequency domain, but do not cause Inter-Carrier Intereference (ICI) due to the orthogonal nature of the modulation. Typically with FDM the transmission signals need to have a large frequency guard-band between channels to prevent interference. This lowers the overall spectral efficiency. However with OFDM the orthogonal packing of the subcarriers greatly reduces this guard band, improving the spectral efficiency.

All wireless communication systems use a modulation scheme to map the information signal to a form that can be effectively transmitted over the communications channel. A wide range of modulation schemes has been developed, with the most suitable one, depending on whether the information signal is an analogue waveform or a digital signal. Some of the common analogue modulation schemes include Frequency Modulation (FM), Amplitude Modulation (AM), Phase Modulation (PM), Single Side Band (SSB), Vestigial Side Band (VSB), Double Side Band Suppressed Carrier (DSBSC). Common single carrier modulation schemes for digital communications include, Amplitude Shift Keying (ASK), Frequency Shift Keying (FSK), Phase Shift Keying (PSK) and Quadrature Amplitude Modulation (QAM).

Each of the carriers in a FDM transmission can use an analogue or digital modulation scheme. There is no synchronisation between the transmission and so one station could transmit using FM and another in digital using FSK. In a single OFDM transmission all the subcarriers are synchronised to each other, restricting the transmission to digital modulation schemes. OFDM is symbol based, and can be thought of as a large number of low bit rate carriers transmitting in parallel. All these carriers transmit in unison using synchronised time and frequency, forming a single block of spectrum. This is to ensure that the orthogonal nature of the structure is maintained. Since these multiple carriers form a single OFDM transmission, they are commonly referred to as 'subcarriers', with the term of 'carrier' reserved for describing the RF carrier mixing the signal from base band. There are several ways of looking at what make the subcarriers in an OFDM signal orthogonal and why this prevents interference between them.

Orthogonality :

Signals are orthogonal if they are mutually independent of each other. Orthogonality is a property that allows multiple information signals to be transmitted perfectly over a common channel and detected, without interference. Loss of orthogonality results in blurring between these information signals and degradation in communications. Many common multiplexing schemes are inherently orthogonal. Time Division Multiplexing (TDM) allows transmission of multiple information signlas over a single channel by assigning unique time slots to each separate information signal. During each time slot only the single from a single source is transmitted preventing any intereference between the multiple information sources. Because of this TDM is orthogonal in nature. In the frequency domain most FDM systems are orthogonal as each of the separate transmission signals are well spaced out in frequency preventing interference. Although these methods are orthogonal the term OFDM has been reserved for a special form of FDM. The subcarriers in an OFDM signal are spaced as close as is theoretically possible while maintain orthogonality between them.

OFDM achieves orthogonality in the frequency domain by allocating each of the separate information signals onto different subcarriers. OFDM signals are made up from a sum of sinusoids, with each corresponding to a subcarrier. The baseband frequency of each subcarrier is chosen to be an integer mutliple of the inverse of the symbol time, resulting in all subcarriers having an integer number of cycles per symbol. As a consequence the subcarriers are orthogonal to each other. Fig. 9.30 shows the construction of an OFDM signal with four subcarriers.

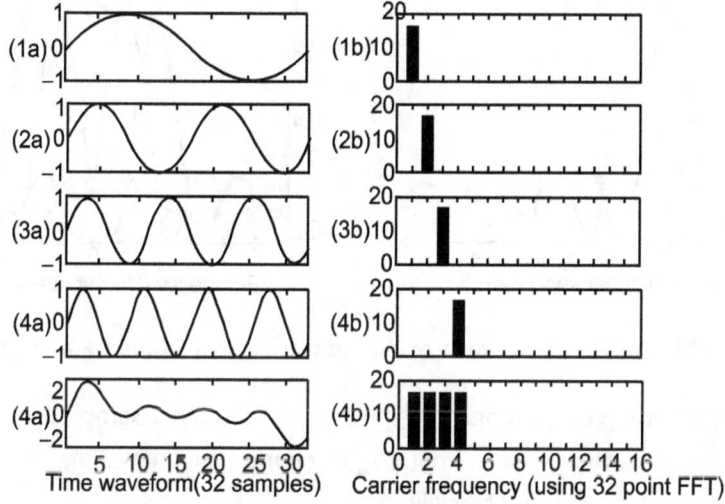

Fig. 9.30 : Time domain construction of an OFDM signal

(1a), (2a), (3a) and (4a) show individual subcarriers, with 1, 2, 3 and 4 cycles per symbol respectively. The phase on all these subcarriers is zero. Note, that each subcarrier has an integer number of cycles per symbol, making them cyclic. Adding a copy of the symbol to the end would result in a smooth join between symbols. (1b), (2b), (3b) and (4b) show the FFT of the time waveforms in (1a), (2a), (3a) and (4a) respectively. (4a) and (4b) shows the result for the summation of the 4 subcarriers.

Another way to view the orthogonality property of OFDM signals is to look at its spectrum. In the frequency domain each OFDM subcarrier has a sinc, sin (x)/x, frequency response, as shown in Fig. 9.31. This is a result of the symbol time corresponding to the inverse of the carrier spacing. As far as the receiver is concerned each OFDM symbol transmitted for a fixed time (T_{FFT}) with no tapering at the ends of the symbol. This symbol time corresponds to the inverse of the subcarrier spacing of $1/T_{FFT}$ Hz 1. This rectangular, boxcar, waveform in the time domain results in a sinc frequency response in the frequency domain. The sinc shape has a narrow main lobe, with many side-lobes that decay slowly with the magnitude of the frequency difference away from the centre. Each carrier has a peak at the center frequency and nulls evenly spaced with a frequency gap equal to carrier spacing.

The orthogonal nature of the transmission is a result of the peak of each subcarrier corresponding to the nulls of all other subcarriers. When this signal is detected using a Discrete Fourier Transform (DFT) the spectrum is not continuous as shown in Fig. 9.31 but has discrete samples. The sampled spectrum are shown as 'o's in the figure. If the DFT is time synchronised, the frequency samples of the DFT correspond to just the peaks of the subcarriers, thus the overlapping frequency region between subcarriers does not affect the receiver. The measured peaks correspond to the nulls for all other subcarriers, resulting in orthogonality between the subcarriers.

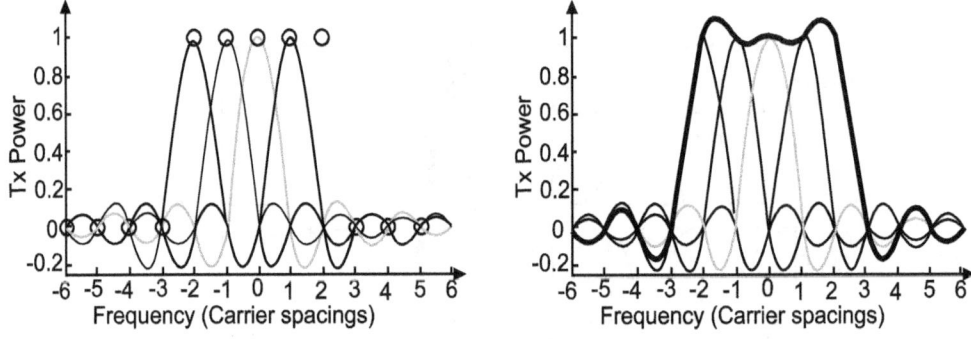

Fig. 9.31 : Frequency response of the subcarriers in a 5 tone OFDM signal

(a) Shows the spectrum of each carrier, and the discrete frequency samples seen by an OFDM receiver. Note, each carrier is sinc, sin (x)/x, in shape. (b) Shows the overall combined response of the 5 subcarriers (thick black line)

9.14.1 OFDM Generation and Reception

OFDM signals are typically generated digitally due to the difficulty in creating large banks of phase lock oscillators and receivers in the analog domain. Fig. 9.32 shows the block diagram of a typical OFDM transceiver. The transmitter section converts digital data to be transmitted, into a mapping of subcarrier amplitude and phase. It then transforms this spectral representation of the data into the time domain using an Inverse Discrete Fourier Transform (IDFT). The Inverse Fast Fourier Transform (IFFT) performs the same operations as an IDFT, except that it is much more computationally efficiency, and so is used in all practical systems.

In order to transmit the OFDM signal the calculated time domain signal is then mixed up to the required frequency.

The receiver performs the reverse operation of the transmitter, mixing the RF signal to base band for processing, then using a Fast Fourier Transform (FFT) to analyze the signal in the frequency domain. The amplitude and phase of the subcarriers is then picked out and converted back to digital data.

The IFFT and the FFT are complementary function and the most appropriate term depends on whether the signal is being received or generated. In cases where the signal is independent of this distinction then the term FFT and IFFT is used interchangeably.

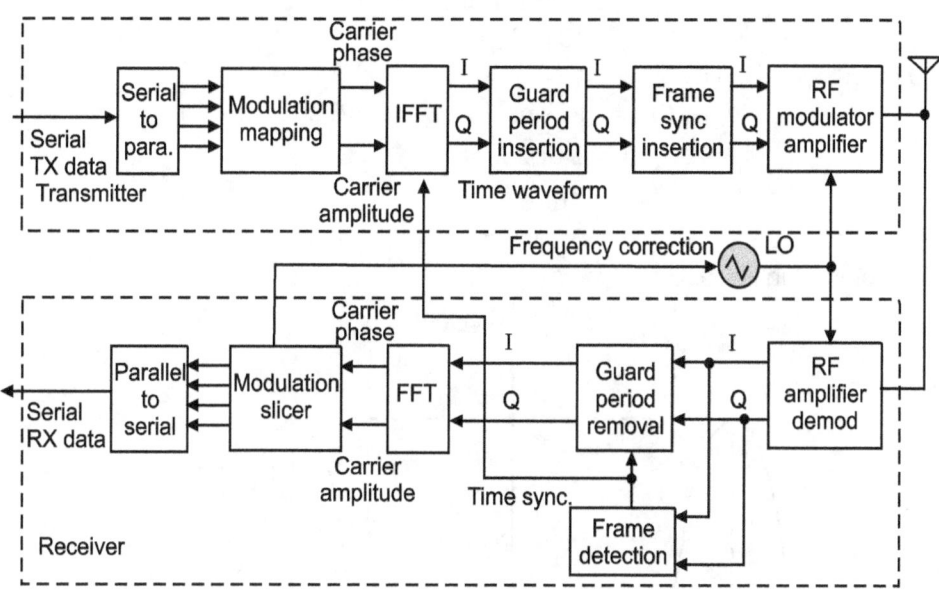

Fig. 9.32 : Block diagram showing a basic OFDM transceiver.

SOLVED PROBLEMS

Problem 9.1 :

In a QPSK system, bit rate of NRZ stream is 10 Mbps and carrier frequency is 1 GHz. Find symbol rate of transmission and bandwidth requirement of the channel. Sketch the PSD of QPSK signal.   **(Dec. 2002)**

Solution : Given :

$$r_b = 10 \text{ Mbps}$$

$$f_c = 1 \text{ GHz}$$

$$T_b = \frac{1}{r_b} = 0.1 \times 10^{-6} \text{ s}$$

Symbol duration for QPSK.

$$T = 2T_b$$
$$= 0.2 \times 10^{-6} \text{ s}$$

∴ Symbol rate

$$r = \frac{1}{T}$$
$$= 5 \times 10^{-6} \text{ symbol/sec.}$$

Bandwidth requirement

$$B = f_b \cdot \frac{1}{T_b} = \frac{1}{T_b}$$
$$= 10 \text{ MHz}$$

The PSD of QPSK is given by

$$S_{QPSK}(f) = PT \text{ sinc}^2 [(f - f_c) T] + PT \text{ sinc}^2 [(f + f_c) T]$$

Here,

$$f_c = 1 \text{ GHz}$$
$$T = 2T_b$$
$$= 0.2 \times 10^{-6}$$

The PSD is plotted in Fig. 9.33.

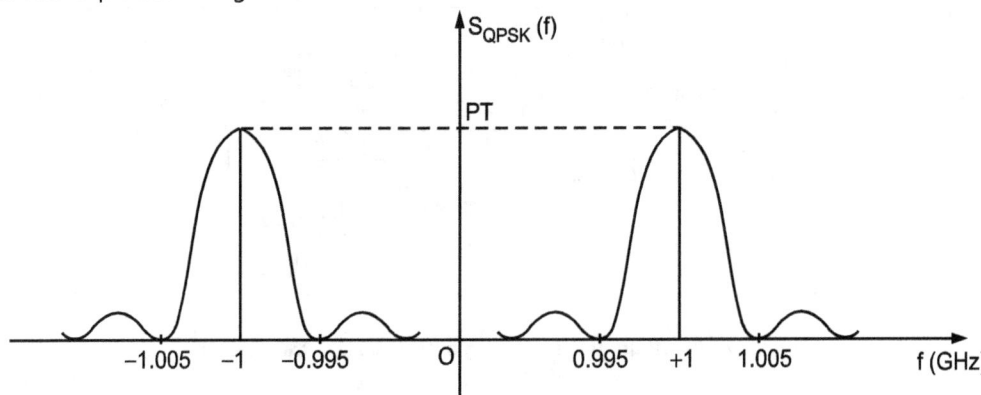

Fig. 9.33 : PSD of given QPSK Signal

Problem 9.2 :

For a BPSK modulator with a carrier frequency of 70 MHz and input bit rate of 10 Mbps. Draw the spectrum of output signal and determine the minimum Nyquist bandwidth.   **(May 2004)**

Solution : Given :

$$f_c = 70 \text{ MHz}$$
$$r_b = 10 \text{ Mbps}$$

The spectrum of output signal is given by,

$$S_{BPSK}(f) = \frac{PT_b}{2} [\text{sinc}^2 [(f - f_c) T_b] + \text{sinc}^2 [(f + f_c) T_b]$$

$$T_b = 0.1 \times 10^{-6} \text{ s}$$

$$f_b = 10 \text{ MHz}$$

The PSD is plotted in Fig. 9.34.

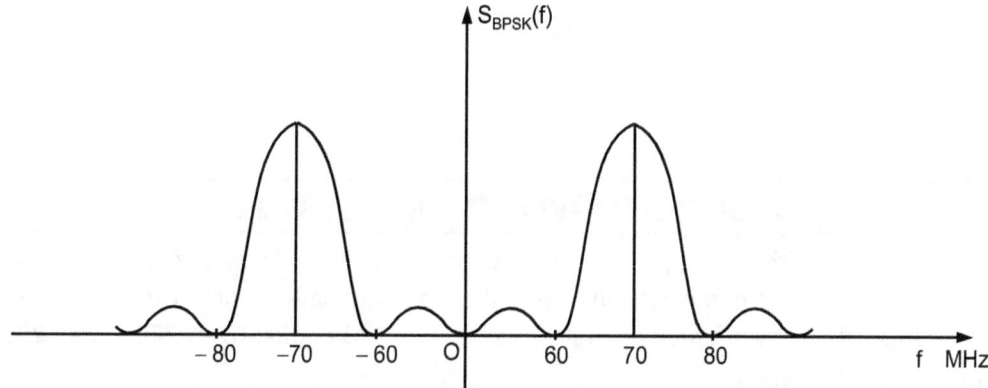

Fig. 9.34 : PSD of Given QPSK Signal

$$\text{Bandwidth} = 2f_b = 2 \times 10 \text{ MHz}$$
$$= 20 \text{ MHz}$$

Problem 9.3 :

Find the bit error rate for BPSK system with bit rate 1 Mbps. The received waveforms are :

$$s_1(t) = A \cos(\omega_0 t)$$
$$s_2(t) = -A \cos(\omega_0 t)$$

Coherently detected with a matched filter. Value of A is 10 mV. Given : Single sides power spectral density is 10^{-10} Watt/Hz and signal power and energy per bit are normalized relative to 1 Ω load.

Solution :

Given :

$$A = 10 \text{ mV}$$
$$N_0 = 10^{-10} \text{ Watt/Hz}$$
$$r_b = 1 \times 10^6 \text{ bps}$$
$$T_b = 1 \times 10^{-6} \text{ s}$$

For BPSK

$$P_e = Q\left(\sqrt{\frac{2E_b}{N_0}}\right)$$

$$E_b = \frac{A^2}{T} T_b$$

$$= \frac{(1 \times 10^{-3})^2}{2} \times 1 \times 10^{-6}$$

$$= 5 \times 10^{-11} \text{ J}$$

$$\therefore \qquad p_e = Q\left(\sqrt{\frac{2 \times 5 \times 10^{-11}}{10^{-10}}}\right)$$

$$= Q(\sqrt{10})$$

$$= Q(3.16)$$

$$= 8 \times 10^{-4}$$

SOLVED UNIVERSITY QUESTIONS

U.Q. 1 : Describe with the help of block diagram 16 point QAM system transmitter and receiver. Explain the working with the help of mathematical expressions. Also express bandwidth requirement. **(8 marks) (Dec. 2005, May 2008)**

Solution : Refer Section 9.9.

U.Q. 2 : A baseband pulses at the rate 2400 bits/sec. are transmitted over telephone channel using Nyquist first criterion and roll-off factor of 12.5%. Estimate the bandwidth before and after modulation. If 16 point QAM is used how much maximum data rate of transmission can be achieved. Explain the answer.

(10 marks) (Dec. 2005)

Solution : Given : Baseband pulse rate

$$r_b = 2400 \text{ bits/sec.}$$

$$\text{Roll-off factor } \alpha = 12.5 \%$$

$\therefore$ Bandwidth required

$$\text{B.W.} = \frac{r_b}{2}$$

$$= \frac{2400}{2}$$

$$= 1200 \text{ Hz}$$

With Nyquist first criteria

$$\text{B.W.} = (1 + \alpha) f_b$$

$$= (1 + 0.125) \, 1200$$

$$= 1350 \text{ Hz}$$

Bandwidth after modulation $\qquad = 2 \times$ bandwidth before modulation

$$= 2 \times 1350$$

$$= 2700 \text{ Hz.}$$

In QAM four bit sequence is combined to form a symbol. Hence, bandwidth requirement for 16-QAM is $\frac{f_b}{4}$. Hence, if a bandwidth of 1200 Hz is available we can transmit 4×1200 bits/sec. 600 bits/sec.

U.Q. 3 : Describe the scheme to recover the baseband signal in BPSK. With the help of block diagram and signals marked at input, output of these blocks. Also write the functional nones inside the blocks.   **(8 marks) (Dec. 2005, May 2007, Dec. 2008)**

Solution : Section 9.4.

U.Q. 4 : Derive the expression for frequency spectrum of binary FSK signal and plot it.

(8 marks) (May 2006, May 2009)

Solution : Refer Section 9.6.1.

U.Q. 5 : What is differential PSK ? Draw block diagram of DPSK transmitter and receiver.

(4 marks) (May 2006)

Solution : Refer Section 9.11.2.

U.Q. 6 : Give mathematical representation of QPSK signal. Draw the signal space diagram of QPSK signal. Write the expression of all the message points in the diagram.

(8 marks) (May 2006, May 2008)

Solution : Refer Section 9.7.1.

U.Q. 7 : With mathematical expression and block diagram, explain the operation of offset QPSK. Also express bandwidth requirement.   **(10 marks) (Dec. 2006)**

Solution : Refer Section 9.7.1.

U.Q. 8 : In a digital communication system the bit rate of NRZ data stream is 1 Mbps and carrier frequency of 100 MHz. Compute the symbol rate of transmission and bandwidth requirement of channel for (i) BPSK system, (ii) QPSK system.

(8 marks) (Dec. 2006)

Solution : Given :

$$\text{Bit rate, } f_b = 1 \text{ Mbps}$$
$$f_c = 100 \text{ MHz}$$

(i) BPSK system :

$$\text{Symbol rate} = f_b = \frac{1}{T_b} = 1 \text{ Mbps}$$

$$\begin{aligned}
\text{Bandwidth} &= 2f_b \\
&= 2 \times 1 \times 10^6 \text{ Hz} \\
&= 2 \text{ MHz}
\end{aligned}$$

(ii) For QPSK system :

$$\text{Symbol rate, } \frac{1}{T} = \frac{1}{2T_b} = \frac{1}{2} f_b$$

$$\begin{aligned}
&= \frac{1}{2} \times 1 \times 10^6 \\
&= 500 \times 10^3 \text{ symbols/sec.}
\end{aligned}$$

$$\text{Bandwidth, B.W.} = f_b$$
$$= 1 \times 10^6 \text{ Hz}$$
$$= 1 \text{ MHz}$$

U.Q. 9 : Draw the signal space representation of orthogonal and non-orthogonal BFSK signal.

(8 marks) (May 2007)

Solution : Refer Sections 9.6.1

U.Q. 10 : Write mathematical expression for M-ary PSK. Draw PSD and signal space representation and bandwidth of M-ary PSK. **(8 marks) (May 2007)**

U.Q. 11 : For rectangular pulses calculate the second null to null bandwidth of BPSK, QPSK, MSK, 16-PSK and 16-QAM. Discuss advantages and disadvantages of each method.

(8 marks) (Dec. 2007)

Solution : Refer Section 9.13

U.Q. 12 : State basic principles of MSK with block schematic and suitable waveforms.

(8 Marks) (Dec. 2007)

Solution : Refer Section 9.10

U.Q. 13 : Draw a neat diagram, explain how a coherent binary FSK wave can be generated and detected. **(8 Marks) (May 2008)**

Solution : Refer Section 9.5

U.Q. 14 : If a digital message input data rate is 8 Kbps and average energy per bit is 0.01 unit. Find.

(i) Bandwidth required for transmission of message through BPSK, QPSK, 16-MPSK orthogonal BFSK, MSK and 16-MFSK.

(ii) Put these schemes in order of their susceptibility to noise after calculating minimum separation in signal space. **(8 marks) (May 2008)**

Solution : Given :

$$\text{Data rate,} \qquad f_b = 8 \times 10^3 \text{ bps}$$
$$E_b = 0.01$$

(i) Bandwidth for

(a) BPSK BW $= 2f_b = 2 \times 8 \times 10^3 \text{ Hz} = 16 \text{ kHz}$

(b) QPSK BW $= f_b = 8 \times 10^3 \text{ Hz} = 8 \text{ kHz}$

(c) 16-MPSK   BW $= \dfrac{2f_b}{\log_2 M} = \dfrac{2 \times f_b}{\log_2 16} = \dfrac{f_b}{2}$

$$= \frac{8 \times 10^3}{2} \, Hz$$

$$= 4 \, kHz$$

(d) Orthogonal BFSK   BW $= 4f_b = 4 \times 8 \times 10^3 \, Hz$

$$= 32 \, kHz$$

(e) For MSK   BW $= 1.5 \, f_b = 1.5 \times 8 \times 10^3 \, Hz$

$$= 12 \, kHz$$

(f) For 16-MFSK   BW $= 2M \, f_b = 2 \times 16 \times 8 \times 10^3 \, Hz$

$$= 256 \, kHz$$

(ii) Minimum Separation in Signal space :

(a) BPSK $\Rightarrow 2\sqrt{E_b} = 0.2$

(b) QPSK $\Rightarrow 2\sqrt{E_b} = 0.2$

(c) 16-QPSK $\Rightarrow \sqrt{4N \, E_b \sin^2 (\pi/16)} = 0.0152$

(d) Orthogonal BFSK $\Rightarrow \sqrt{2E_b} = 0.1414$

(e) MSK $\Rightarrow 2\sqrt{E_b} = 0.2$

(f) 16-MFSK $\Rightarrow \sqrt{2NE_b} = 0.282$.

Order of susceptibility to noise 16 MFSK, MSK, BPSK, QPSK, BFSK, 16 QPSK.

U.Q. 15 :   Binary data is transmitted at a rate 10 Mbps over a channel whose bandwidth is 8 MHz. Find signal energy per bit at the receiver input for coherent BPSK and DPSK to achieve error probability $p_e \le 10^{-4}$.

         Assume $N_0/2 = 10^{-10}$ Watt/Hz   **(8 marks) (May 2006)**

Solution : Given : r_b $= $ 10 Mbps

$\therefore$ T_b $= $ $0.1 \times 10^{-6} \, S$

                          p_e $\le$ 10^{-4} Watt/Hz $N_0 = 10^{-10} \times 2$ Watt/Hz

(i) For BPSK : p_e $= $ $Q\left(\sqrt{\dfrac{2E_b}{N_0}}\right)$

            For $Q(x)$ $= $ 10^{-4}

                    x $= $ 3.70

$\therefore$ $\sqrt{\dfrac{2E_b}{N_0}}$ $= $ 3.70

$\therefore$ $\dfrac{2E_b}{N_0}$ $= $ $(3.70)^2$

                     E_b $= $ $\dfrac{(3.70)^2 \times 2 \times 10^{-10}}{2} = 1.36 \times 10^{-9} \, J.$

(ii) For DPSK :

$$p_e = \frac{1}{2} e^{-E_b/N_0}$$

$$\therefore \qquad 10^{-4} = \frac{1}{2} \times e^{-E_b/2 \times 10^{-10}}$$

$$\therefore \qquad \frac{E_b}{N_0} = 8.5$$

$$\therefore \qquad E_b = 8.5 \times 2 \times 10^{-10}$$

$$= 1.7 \times 10^{-9} \, J$$

U.Q. 16 : Derive the expression for error probability if BPSK signal is detected using optimum receiver.   **(8 marks) (December 2006)**

Solution : Refer Section 9.4.2.

U.Q. 17 : Derive the error probability expression for BPSK and BFSK.

                                                (10 marks) (December 2007)

Solution : Refer Section 9.4.2 and 9.6.2.

U.Q. 18 : It is required to transmit 2.08×10^6 binary digits per second with $p_b \times 10^{-6}$. Three possible schemes are considered : (i) Binary, (ii) 16-ary ASK, (iii) 16-ary PSK. The channel noise PSD is 10^{-8}. Determine the transmission bandwidth and signal power required at the receiver input in each case. **(10 marks) (December 2007)**

Solution : Given :

$$r_b = 2.08 \times 10^6 \text{ bps}$$

$$\therefore \qquad T_b = \frac{1}{r_b} = \frac{1}{2.08 \times 10^6} = 4.8 \times 10^{-7} \, S$$

$$\frac{N_0}{2} = 10^{-8} \text{ Watt/Hz}$$

$$\therefore \qquad N_0 = 2 \times 10^{-8} \text{ Watt/hz}$$

$$p_e \le 10^{-6}$$

(i) Binary i.e. baseband :

$$p_e = \frac{1}{2} \text{erfc} \left(\sqrt{\frac{E_b}{N_0}} \right)$$

$$\therefore \qquad 10^{-6} = \frac{1}{2} \text{erfc} \left(\sqrt{\frac{E_b}{N_0}} \right)$$

$$0.999998 = \text{erf} \left(\sqrt{\frac{E_b}{N_0}} \right)$$

$$\text{erf}(3.3) = 0.999998$$

$$\therefore \quad \sqrt{\frac{E_b}{N_0}} = 3.3$$

$$\frac{E_b}{N_0} = (3.3)^2$$

$$E_b = (3.3)^2 \times N_0$$

$$E_b \quad (3.3)^2 \times 2 \times 10^{-8}$$

$$\text{Signal Power, P} = \frac{(3.3)^2 \times 2 \times 10^{-8}}{4.8 \times 10^{-7}}$$

$$= 0.45375 \text{ Watt}$$

Bandwidth required :

$$B_T = \frac{r_b}{2}$$

$$= \frac{2.08 \times 10^6}{2}$$

$$= 1.04 \text{ MHz}$$

(ii) For 16-ary ASK :

For m-ary ASK, symbol error rate,

$$p_s = \text{erfc}\left(\sqrt{\frac{3NE_b}{M^2 N_0}}\right)$$

We are given bit error rate p_e.

$$\therefore \quad p_s = \text{Bit error rate} \times \text{Bits per symbol}$$

$$= p_e \times N$$

For 16-ary ASK

$$N = \log_2 M$$

$$= \log_2 16$$

$$= 4 \text{ bits/symbol}$$

$$\therefore \quad p_s = 10^{-6} \times 4$$

$$\therefore \quad 4 \times 10^{-6} = \text{erfc} \sqrt{\frac{3 \times 4 \times E_b}{(16)^2 \times 2 \times 10^{-8}}}$$

$$1 - 4 \times 10^{-6} = 1 - \text{erfc}\left(\sqrt{\frac{12\, E_b}{512 \times 10^{-8}}}\right)$$

$$\therefore \quad \text{erf}\left(\sqrt{\frac{12 E_b}{512 \times 10^{-8}}}\right) = 0.999996$$

$$\therefore \quad \text{But erf}(3.2) = 0.999996$$

$$\therefore \qquad \frac{12E_b}{512 \times 10^{-8}} = (3.2)^2$$

$$\therefore \qquad E_b = \frac{(3.2)^2 \times (512) \times 10^{-8}}{12}$$

$$= 4.37 \times 10^{-6}$$

$$\therefore \qquad \text{Signal Power, p} = \frac{NE_b}{NT_b}$$

$$= \frac{E_b}{T_b}$$

$$= \frac{4.37 \times 10^{-6}}{4.8 \times 10^{-7}}$$

$$= 9.1 \text{ Watt}$$

$$B_T = \frac{r_b}{4} = \frac{2.08 \times 10^6}{4} = 0.52 \times 10^6 \text{ Hz}$$

$$= 520 \text{ kHz}$$

(iii) For 16-ary PSK :

$$p_s = \text{erfc}\left(\sqrt{\frac{\pi^2 NE_b}{M^2 N_0}}\right)$$

We are given p_e $p_s = N \times p_e$

$$= 4 \times 10^{-6}$$

$$\therefore \qquad 4 \times 10^{-6} = \text{erfc}\left(\sqrt{\frac{\pi^2 N \times E_b}{M^2 N_0}}\right)$$

$$1 - 4 \times 10^{-6} = 1 - \text{erfc}\left(\sqrt{\frac{\pi^2 NE_b}{M^2 N_0}}\right)$$

$$\therefore \qquad \text{erf}\left(\sqrt{\frac{\pi^2 NE_b}{M^2 N_0}}\right) = 0.999996$$

$$\therefore \qquad \sqrt{\frac{\pi^2 NE_b}{M^2 N_0}} = 3.2$$

$$\therefore \qquad E_b = 1.328 \times 10^{-6}$$

$$\text{Signal Power} = \frac{E_b}{T_b} = \frac{1.328 \times 10^{-6}}{4.8 \times 10^{-7}}$$

$$= 2.766 \text{ Watt}$$

For M-ary PSK $B_T = \dfrac{r_b}{\log_2 M} = \dfrac{2.08 \times 10^6}{4}$

$$= 520 \text{ kHz}$$

$$\boxed{\text{Dec 2010}}$$

U.Q. 19 : Explain coherent BPSK transmitter and receiver. Derive the expression for receiver output considering effect of noise. Draw the spectrum of BPSK signal and comment on bandwidth required. **(8)**

Solution : Refer Section 9.6.

U.Q. 20 : Starting from signal expression of MSK find suitable values of f_H and f_L. **(8)**

Solution : Refer Section 9.10.

U.Q. 21 : Write signal expression for QPSK. Draw the block diagram of QPSK transmitter and receiver and explain the working. **(8)**

Solution : Refer Section 9.7.

U.Q. 22 : What is non-coherent version of BPSK? Explain with suitable block diagram and waveforms. **(8)**

Solution : Refer Sections 9.4

U.Q. 23 : Derive the expression for error probability of BPSK receiver. **(8)**

Solution : Refer Sections 9.4.2.

U.Q. 24 : Binary data is transmitted using PSK at a rate 2 Mbps over RF link having bandwidth 2 MHz, Find signal power required at receiver input so that error probability is less than or equal to 10^{-4}. Assume noise PSD to be 10^{-10} watt/Hz. $(Q(3.71) = 10^{-4})$. **(8)**

Solution : Given:

$$\text{Bandwidth} = 2\,\text{MHz}$$

$$\text{Data rate } r_b = 2\,\text{Mbps}$$

$$\text{Noise, PSD } \frac{N_0}{2} = 10^{-10}\,\text{watt/Hz}$$

$$\therefore \qquad N_0 = 2 \times 10^{-10}\,\text{watt/Hz}$$

Required error probability

$$p_e \leq 10^{-4}$$

For BPSK,

$$p_{e\,min} = Q\left(\sqrt{\frac{2E_b}{N_0}}\right)$$

$$\therefore \qquad Q\left(\sqrt{\frac{2E_b}{N_0}}\right) \leq 10^{-4}$$

$$\therefore \qquad \sqrt{\frac{2E_b}{N_0}} \geq Q^{-1}(10^{-4})$$

$$\therefore \qquad \frac{2 \times E_b}{2 \times 10^{-10}} \geq (3.71)^2$$

$$\therefore \qquad E_b \geq (3.71)^2 \times 10^{-10}$$

$$\therefore \qquad \text{Signal power, } P = \frac{E_b}{T_b} = E_b \times r_b$$

$$\therefore \qquad P = (3.71)^2 \times 10^{-10} \times 2 \times 10^6$$

$$= 2.75 \times 10^{-3} \text{ watt}$$

U.Q. 25 : Calculate the symbol error probability of QPSK receiver. (8)

Solution : Refer Section 9.7.2.

U.Q. 26 : Binary data is transmitted using M-ary PSK at a rate 2 Mbps over RF link having bandwidth 2 MHz. Find signal power required at receiver input so that bit error probability is less than or equal to 10^{-5}. The channel noise PSD is 10^{-8} watt/Hz. Calculate for M = 16 and M = 32

Given : erf (0.99996) = 3.1

erf (0.99995) = 3.2 **(8)**

Solution : Given:
Data rate, r_b = 2 Mbps

Bandwidth, B = 2 MHz

Error probability, $p_e \leq 10^{-5}$

$$\text{Noise PSD} = \frac{N_0}{2} = 10^{-8} \text{ watt/Hz}$$

Required $p_e \leq 10^{-5}$

(i) For M = 16

$$p_e = \text{erfc}\left(\sqrt{\frac{E}{N_0}} \sin\left(\frac{\pi}{M}\right)\right)$$

$$= 1 - \text{erf}\left(\sqrt{\frac{E}{N_0}} \cdot 0.2\right)$$

$$\therefore \qquad \text{erf}\left(0.2\sqrt{\frac{E}{N_0}}\right) \geq 1 - p_e = 0.99999$$

$$\therefore \qquad 0.2\sqrt{\frac{E}{N_0}} \geq 3$$

$$E \geq \frac{(3)^2 \times 2 \times 10^{-8}}{(0.2)^2}$$

$$\therefore \qquad E \geq 4.5 \times 10^{-6}$$

$$\therefore \qquad E_b \geq \frac{4.5 \times 10^{-6}}{\log_2 16} = 1.125 \times 10^{-6} \text{ J}$$

$$\therefore \qquad P = E_b \times r_b = 2.25 \text{ watt}$$

(ii)

$$p_e = \text{erfc}\left(\sqrt{\frac{E}{N_0}}\sin\frac{\pi}{M}\right)$$

$\therefore$

$$p_e = \text{erfc}\left(0.1\sqrt{\frac{E}{N_0}}\right)$$

$$= 1 - \text{erf}\left(0.1\sqrt{\frac{E}{N_0}}\right)$$

$$= 1 - \text{erf}\left(0.1\sqrt{\frac{E}{N_0}}\right)$$

$\therefore$

$$\text{erf}\left(0.1\sqrt{\frac{E}{N_0}}\right) \geq 1 - p_e = 0.99999$$

$\therefore$

$$0.1\sqrt{\frac{E}{N_0}} \geq 3$$

$\therefore$

$$E \geq \frac{(3)^2 \times 2 \times 10^{-8}}{(0.1)^2}$$

$$E \geq \frac{1.8 \times 10^{-5}}{\log_2 32} = 3.6 \times 10^{-5}$$

$$p \geq E_b \times r_b = 7.2 \text{ watt}$$

$$\boxed{\text{May 2011}}$$

U.Q. 27 : Draw the block diagram and with the help of mathematical expression explain in detail the QPSK transmitter and receiver. Diagram the geometric representation and draw its power spectral density, along with its expression thereby comment on its Euclidean distance and bandwidth. **(10)**

Solution : Refer Section 9.7.

U.Q. 28 : If the digital message input data rate is 10 kbps and average energy per bit is 0.02 unit find bandwidth and Euclidian distance for the following schemes.

(1) BPSK, (2) 16-MPSK, (3) MSK, (4) 16-QAM. **(6)**

Solution : Given: r_b = 10 kbps, f_b = 10 kHz

$$E_b = 0.02$$

(i) BPSK   BW = $2f_b$ = 20 kHz

Euclidean distance = $2E_b$ = 0.04

(ii) 16-PSK, $BW = \dfrac{2f_b}{N} = \dfrac{2 \times 10 \text{ kHz}}{\log_2 16} = 5 \text{ kHz}$

$$\text{Euclidean distance} = 2\sqrt{NE_b}\sin\left(\frac{\pi}{M}\right)$$

$$= 2\sqrt{4 \times 0.02} \times 0.195$$

$$= 0.11$$

(iii)   MSK BW $= 1.5\,f_b = 1.5 \times 10 = 15$ kHz

$$\text{Euclidean distance} = \sqrt{2E_b} = 0.2$$

(iv)   16 QAM, BW $= \dfrac{2f_b}{N} = \dfrac{2 \times 10}{4} = 5$ kHz

$$\text{Euclidean distance} = 2\sqrt{2E_b} = 0.4$$

U.Q. 29 : With a neat diagram, explain how a coherent binary FSK wave can be generated and detected.   **(6)**

Solution : Refer Section 9.5.

U.Q. 30 : Diagram the geometric representation of

(a) Orthogonal and non-orthogonal BFSK.

(b) M-ary FSK.

State the Euclidean distance of above mentioned systems by explaining the importance of Euclidean distance.   **(6)**

Solution : Refer Section 9.6.

U.Q. 31 : What is DPSK and DEPSK?   **(4)**

Solution : Refer Sections 9.11.2 and 9.12.

U.Q. 32 : Show that the probability of error of QPSK is same as that of BPSK for 1-bit duration.   **(8)**

Solution : Refer Section 9.7.7.

U.Q. 33 : A QPSK signal is received at the input of a coherent optimal receiver with amplitude 10 mV and frequency 2 MHz. The signal is corrupted with white noise of PSD 10^{-11} W/Hz. If data rate is 10^4 bits/sec find the probability of error, also find the probability of error for BPSK system if the local oscillator has a phase shift of $\pi/6$ rad with the input signal. Ref. Table 1.   **(8)**

Solution : Given: $A = 10$ mV

$$f = 2\,\text{MHz}$$

$$\frac{N_0}{2} = 10^{-11}\,\text{watt/Hz}$$

∴ $N_0 = 2 \times 10^{-11}\,\text{watt/Hz}$

$$r_b = 10^4\,\text{bits/sec.}$$

(i) For QPSK system

$$T_b = 1 \times 10^{-4}\,\text{s}$$

$$E_b = A^2 T_b = (0.01)^2 \times 1 \times 10^{-4} = 10^{-8}$$

$$p_e = Q\left(\sqrt{\frac{2E_b}{N_0}}\right)$$

$$= Q\left(\sqrt{\frac{2 \times 5 \times 10^{-8}}{10^{-11}}}\right)$$

$$= Q(\sqrt{2000})$$

Thus, from the given table, we can write

$$p_e \leq 1 \times 10^{-7}$$

(ii) For BPSK

$$p_e = Q\left(\sqrt{\frac{E_b \cos^2\phi}{N_0}}\right) \qquad\qquad (\phi = \pi/6)$$

$$= Q\left(\sqrt{\frac{5 \times 10^{-9} \times 0.75}{2 \times 10^{-11}}}\right)$$

$$= Q(\sqrt{87.5}) << 10^{-7}$$

U.Q. 34 : Derive the equations of probability of error for BPSK and BFSK.   **(8)**

Solution : Refer Sections 9.4.2 and 9.6.2.

U.Q. 35 : A system transmits binary data at the rate of 2.5×10^6 bits per second. During the course of transmission, white Gaussian noise of zero mean and power spectral density 10^{-20} W/Hz is added to the signal. In the absence of noise, the amplitude of the received sinusoidal wave for digit 1 or 0 is 1 mV. Determine the average probability of symbol error for the following system configuration

   (i) Coherent binary FSK.

   (ii) Non-coherent binary FSK.

   (iii) 16 MPSK. (Ref. Table 1).   **(8)**

Solution : Given: $\qquad\qquad r_b = 2.5 \times 10^6$ bps

$$\therefore \qquad\qquad T_b = \frac{1}{r_b} = 0.4 \times 10^{-6}\text{ s}$$

$$\therefore \qquad\qquad \frac{N_0}{2} = 10^{-20}\text{ watt/Hz}$$

$$N_0 = 2 \times 10^{-20}\text{ watt/Hz}$$

$$E_b = \frac{A^2 T_b}{2} = \frac{(1 \times 10^{-3})^2 \times 0.4 \times 10^{-6}}{2} = 0.2 \times 10^{-12}\text{ J}$$

(i) For BFSK

$$p_e = \frac{1}{2}\text{erfc}\left(\sqrt{\frac{0.6\,E_b}{N_0}}\right) = Q\left(\sqrt{\frac{1.2\,E_b}{N_0}}\right)$$

$$= Q\left(\sqrt{\frac{1.2 \times 0.2 \times 10^{-12}}{2 \times 10^{-20}}}\right)$$

$$= Q\sqrt{1.2 \times 10^{7}}$$

$$\cong 0$$

$$= Q\left(\sqrt{\frac{0.6 \times 0.2 \times 10^{-12}}{2 \times 10^{-20}}}\right)$$

$$= Q\left(\sqrt{6 \times 10^{4}}\right) \approx 0$$

(ii) Non-coherent BFSK

$$p_e = \frac{1}{2} e^{-E_b/2N_0} = \frac{1}{2} e^{-0.2 \times 10^{-12}/2 \times 10^{-20}}$$

$$\approx 0$$

(iii) For M-ary PSK

M = 16, N = log 16 = 4.

$$p_e = 2Q\left(\sqrt{\frac{\pi^2 N E_b}{M^2 N_0}}\right)$$

$$= 2Q\left(\sqrt{\frac{\pi^2 \times 4 \times 0.2 \times 10^{-12}}{(16)^2 \times 2 \times 10^{-20}}}\right) = 2Q\left(\sqrt{1.5 \times 10^{6}}\right)$$

$$\approx 0$$

Note : The error probability is almost zero because SNR (E_b/N_0) is very large

Dec. 2011

U.Q. 36 : Draw the constellation diagram of 16-ary PSK and 16 QAM. Compare them with respect to their Euclidean distance. What is the physical significance of Euclidean distance?   **(10)**

Solution : Refer Sections 9.10..

U.Q. 37 : What is coherent detection? Draw the block diagram of BPSK receiver and explain its operation with proper mathematical expressions.   **(8)**

Solution : Refer Sections 9.5.

U.Q. 38 : Explain the necessity of continuous PSK. State and explain the basic principles of MSK with block schematic and suitable waveforms.   **(10)**

Solution : Refer Section 9.10.

U.Q. 39 : In a digital communication system, the bit rate of NRz data stream is 1 Mbps and carrier frequency of transmission is 100 MHz. Find the symbol rate of transmission and band width requirement of the channel in the following cases.

(i) BPSK, (ii) QPSK, (iii) 16-ary PSK. **(8)**

Solution : Given:

$$r_b = 1 \text{ Mbps} = f_b$$
$$f_c = 100 \text{ MHz}$$
$$\therefore \quad T_b = 1 \times 10^{-6} \text{ s}$$

(i) BPSK

$$\text{Symbol rate, } r = 1 \text{ Mbps}$$
$$BW = 2f_b = 2 \text{ MHz}$$

(ii) QPSK

$$\text{Symbol rate } r = \frac{1}{T} = \frac{1}{2 \times T_b} = \frac{1}{2 \times 1 \times 10^{-6}}$$
$$BW = f_b = 1 \text{ MHz} = 0.5 \times 10^6 \text{ symbols/s}$$

(iii) 16 ary PSK

$$\text{Symbol rate, } r = \frac{1}{T}$$
$$= \frac{1}{NT_b} = \frac{1}{4 \times 1 \times 10^{-6}} \text{ symbols/s}$$
$$BW = \frac{2f_b}{N} = \frac{2 \times 10^6}{4} = 0.5 \text{ MHz}$$

U.Q. 40 : Find the bit error probability for a BPSK system with bit rate of 1 Mbps. The received waveforms $S_1(t) = A \cos \omega_0 t$ and $S_2(t) = -A \cos \omega_0 t$ are coherently detected with a matched filter. The value of A is 10 mV. Assume that noise power special density $N_0 = 10^{-11}$ W/Hz signal and that signal power and energy per bit are normalised relative to 10 load. **(8)**

Solution : Given:

$$A = 10 \text{ mV}$$
$$N_0 = 10^{-11} \text{ watt/Hz}$$
$$r_b = 1 \text{ Mbps}$$
$$\therefore \quad T_b = 1 \times 10^{-6} \text{ s}$$
$$E_b = \frac{A^2 T_b}{2} = (0.010)^2 \times 1 \times 10^{-6}/2$$
$$= 5 \times 10^{-11} \text{ J}$$

For BPSK

$\therefore$ $p_e = Q\left(\sqrt{\dfrac{2E_b}{N_0}}\right)$

$= Q\left(\sqrt{\dfrac{2 \times 5 \times 10^{-11}}{10^{-11}}}\right)$

$= Q\left(\sqrt{10}\right) = Q\,(3.16)$

$= 8 \times 10^{-4}$

U.Q. 41 : Derive the expression for the probability of error of a BFSK system.   **(8)**

Solution : Refer Section 9. 6.2.

U.Q. 42 : Prove that the error probability of MSK is same as that of QPSK system.   **(8)**

Solution : Out of syllabus.

May 2012

U.Q. 43 :   Explain M-ary PSK transmitter and receiver with suitable block diagram and waveforms. What are the advantages of M-ary PSK over M-ary FSK?   **(8)**

Solution :   Refer Section 9.10

U.Q. 44 :   Derive and draw the spectrum of BPSK, QPSK and BFSK signal and compare their bandwidths.   **(8)**

Solution :   Refer Sections 9.13

U.Q. 45 :   Explain the performance of MSK with suitable block schematic and also explain how phase continuity is maintained in this system?   **(8)**

Solution :   Refer Section 9.6

U.Q. 46 :   Explain BFSK transmitter and receiver with a proper sketch. What are the salient features of BFSK signal?   **(8)**

Solution :   Refer Section 9.6

U.Q. 47 :   A received signal of either +2V or –2V held for a duration 'T' is corrupted by white Gaussian noise of power spectral density 10^{-4} volts^2/Hz. If the signal is processed by integrate and dump receiver, what is the maximum duration 'T' during which the signal must be sustained if the probability of error is not to exceed 10^{-4}?   **(8)**

Solution : Given : $A = \pm 2V$

$\dfrac{N_0}{2} = 10^{-4}$

Required $p_e = 10^{-4}$

$$\text{Now, } p_e = Q\left(\sqrt{\frac{2E_b}{N_0}}\right) \leq 10^{-4}$$

$$\therefore \quad \sqrt{\frac{2E_b}{N_0}} \geq Q^{-1}(10^{-4})$$

$$\therefore \quad \sqrt{\frac{2E_b}{N_0}} \geq 3.71$$

$$\therefore \quad E_b \geq \frac{(3.71)^2}{2} \times 2 \times 10^{-4}$$

$$E_b \geq 13.76 \times 10^{-4}$$

$$\therefore \quad A^2 T_b \geq 13.76 \times 10^{-4}$$

$$T_b \geq \frac{13.76 \times 10^{-4}}{4} = 3.44 \times 10^{-4} \text{ s}$$

U.Q. 48 : Derive the relation between bit error rate and symbol error rate. **(8)**

Solution : Refer Section 9.5.

U.Q. 49 : Calculate the error probability in the detection of BPSK, QPSK and BFSK signals using signal space representation and compare their performance with respect to this criteria. **(8)**

Solution : Refer Section 9.4.2, 9.7.2 and 9.6.2.

Dec 2012

U.Q. 50 : Draw the block diagram of QPSK Receiver and explain the working detail with mathematical expressions. **(8)**

Solution : Refer Section 9.7.

U.Q. 51 : State advantages of MSK over QPSK and sketch the waveforms for I/P pattern 11010111. **(10)**

Solution : Refer Section

U.Q. 52 : Compare the performance of BPSK, FSK, M-ary PSK, M-ary FSK with respect to bandwidth, euclidian distance and probability of error.

Solution : Refer Section 9.13.

U.Q. 53 : For an input stream of 110100010 explain the encoding and decoding process for DPSK with the help of waveforms and expressions. **(8)**

Solution : Refer Section 9.11.2.

U.Q. 54 : Binary data has to be transmitted over a telephone link that has a usable bandwidth of 3000 Hz, and d maximum achievable signal-to-noise power ratio of 6 dB at its output.

(i) Determine the maximum signalling rate and probability of error of a coherent ASK scheme is used for transmitting binary data through this channel.

(ii) If the data is maintained at 300 bits/sec calculate the error probability.

$Q(3.4) = 0.0003$, $Q(6.4) = 10^{-10}$, $Q(5.25) = 10^{-7}$ **(8)**

Solution : Note: This equation is out of syllabus.

Given:

$$BW = 3 \text{ kHz}$$
$$(SNR)_0 = 6 \text{ dB}$$
$$SNR \text{ in dB} = 10 \log_{10}\left(\frac{S}{N}\right)$$

$\therefore$

$$\frac{S}{N} = 10^{6/10} = 3.98$$

$\therefore$ Maximum rate of transmission is

$$r_b = C = B \log\left(1 + \frac{S}{N}\right)$$
$$= 3 \times 10^3 \log_2 (1 + 3.98)$$
$$= 6.950 \text{ kbps}$$

$\therefore$

$$T_b = \frac{1}{6.950 \times 10^3}$$

For ASK

$$P_e = \frac{1}{2} \text{erfc}\left(\sqrt{\frac{E_b}{2N_0}}\right) = Q\left(\sqrt{\frac{E_b}{N_0}}\right)$$

Now,

$$\frac{S}{N} = \frac{E_b/T_b}{N_0 B} = \frac{E_b/N_0}{B \times T_b}$$

$\therefore$

$$\frac{E_b}{N_0} = \frac{S}{N} \times B \times T_b = 3.98 \times 3 \times 10^3 \times \frac{1}{6.950 \times 10^3} = 1.72$$

$\therefore$

$$P_e = Q\left(\sqrt{\frac{E_b}{N_0}}\right) = Q\left(\sqrt{1.72}\right) = Q(1.31) = 9.68 \times 10^{-2}$$

(ii)

$$r_b = 300 \text{ bits/sec}$$
$$T_b = \frac{1}{300}$$

$$\frac{E_b}{N_0} = \frac{S}{N} \times B \times T_b = 3.98 \times 3 \times 10^3 \times \frac{1}{300} = 40$$

$\therefore$

$$P_e = Q\left(\sqrt{\frac{E_b}{N_0}}\right) = Q(6.3) \approx 10^{-10}$$

U.Q. 55 :   Derive the expression for error probability for optimum filter.   **(8)**

Solution :   Refer Section 9.4.3.

U.Q. 56 :   A BPSK signal is received at the input of a coherent optimal receiver with amplitude 10 mV and frequency 10 kHz. The signal is corrupted with white noise of PSD 10^{-9} W/Hz. If data rate is 10^4 bits/sec.

(i) Find error probability.

(ii) Find error probability if the local oscillator has a phase shift of $\pi/6$ rad with input signal.

(iii) Find error probability if there is 10% mismatching in bit synchronization.

erfc (1.58) = 0.0254, erfc (1.36) = 0.0528, erfc (1.26) = .073 erfc (1.09) = 0.1214.**(8)**

Solution : Given:

$$A = \pm 10 \text{ mV}$$

$$f = 10 \text{ kHz}$$

$$\frac{N_0}{2} = 10^{-9} \text{ W/Hz}$$

$$\therefore \qquad N_0 = 2 \times 10^{-9}$$

$$r_b = 10^4$$

$$T_b = \frac{1}{10^4} \text{ s}$$

$$\frac{E_b}{N_0} = \frac{A^2 T_b}{2} = \frac{(0.01)^2}{2} \times \frac{1}{10^4} = 0.5 \times 10^{-8}$$

(i) $\therefore$

$$p_e = \frac{1}{2} \text{erfc} \left(\sqrt{\frac{E_b}{N_0}} \right)$$

$$= \frac{1}{2} \text{erfc} \left(\sqrt{\frac{0.5 \times 10^{-8}}{2 \times 10^{-9}}} \right)$$

$$= \frac{1}{2} \text{erfc} \left(\sqrt{2.5} \right)$$

$$= \frac{1}{2} \text{erfc} (1.58) = 0.0254$$

(ii)

$$p_e = \frac{1}{2} \text{erfc} \left(\sqrt{\frac{E_b}{N_0} \cos^2 \phi} \right)$$

$$= \frac{1}{2} \text{erfc} \left(\sqrt{\frac{0.5 \times 10^{-8} \times 0.75}{2 \times 10^{-9}}} \right)$$

$$= \frac{1}{2} \text{erfc} (1.369)$$

$$= 0.0528$$

(iii)
$$p_e = \text{erfc}\left(\sqrt{\frac{E_b}{N_0}\left(1 - \frac{21 + 8}{T_b}\right)^2}\right)$$

$$\text{erfc} = \left(\sqrt{\frac{0.5 \times 10^{-8}}{2 \times 10^{-9}} \times (1.2 \times 0.1)^2}\right)$$

$$= \text{erfc}(1.26) = 0.073$$

May 2013

U.Q. 57 : Explain block diagrams for generation and reception of M-ary PSK singals. With suitable mathematical expressions, signal space representation, Bandwidth and PSD. **(12)**

Solution : Refer Section 9.8.

U.Q. 58 : Draw signal space and spectral diagram of following digital CW modulation and state only the bandwidth requirement. 16 QAM, 16-ary PSK,QPSK and MSK. **(6)**

Solution : Refer Sections 9.13.

U.Q. 59 : Explain the working of QPSK coherent receiver. Sketch the waveform of the inphase and quadrature components of a QPSK signal for binary sequence 1011111010. **(10)**

Solution : Refer Section 9.7.

U.Q. 60 : Write a note on: **(8)**
(i) 16-ary QAM, (ii) DEPSK

Solution : (i)16-ary QAM: Refer Section 9.9.

(ii)DEPSK: Refer Section 9.12.

U.Q. 61 : Derive the expression for the probability of error of a BPSK system. **(8)**

Solution : Refer Section 9.4.2

U.Q. 62 : Find the error probability for coherent FSK when **(8)**

(i) frequency offset is small, (ii) frequencies used are orthogonal, (iii) also find error probability for non-coherent detection.

Given that amplitude of input at coherent optimal receiver is 10 mV and freq 1 MHz. The signal is corrupted with white noise of PSD 10^9 W/Hz. The data rate is 10^4 bits/see.

[erfc(1.01) = 0.1531, erfc(l.11) = 0.1164, erfc(1.22) = 0.0844, erfc(1.33) = 0.0599]

Solution :

Given:
$$A = 10 \text{ mV}$$
$$f_c = 1 \text{ MHz}$$
$$\frac{N_0}{2} = 10^{-9} \text{ W/Hz}$$

$$r_b = 10^4 \text{ bits/s} \qquad\qquad T_b = 10^{-4} \text{ s}$$

Error probability

$$p_e = \frac{1}{2} \text{erfc}\left(\sqrt{\frac{E_b}{2N_0}}\right)$$

$$E_b = \frac{A^2 T_b}{2} = \frac{(0.01)^2 \times 10^{-4}}{2} = 5 \times 10^{-9}$$

$$\therefore \qquad p_e = \frac{1}{2} \text{erfc}\left(\sqrt{\frac{5 \times 10^{-9}}{4 \times 10^{-9}}}\right)$$

$$= \frac{1}{2} \text{erfc}\left(\sqrt{1.25}\right)$$

$$= \frac{1}{2} \text{erfc}\,(1.11)$$

$$= \frac{1}{2} \times 0.1164$$

$$= 0.0582$$

U.Q. 63 : Binary data is transmitted using PSK at a rate 3 Mbps over RF link having bandwidth 10 MHz. Find signal power required at receiver input so that error probability is less than or equal to 10^{-4}. Assume noise PSD to be 10^{-10} watt/Hz. $(Q(3.71) = 10^{-4})$. **(8)**

Solution : Given:

$$r_b = 3 \times 10^6 \text{ bps}$$

$$BW = 10 \text{ MHz}$$

$$p_e \leq 10^{-4}$$

$$\frac{N_0}{2} = 10^{-10} \text{ W/Hz}$$

For BPSK
$$p_e = Q\left(\sqrt{\frac{2E_b}{N_0}}\right) \leq 10^{-4}$$

$$\therefore \qquad \sqrt{\frac{2E_b}{N_0}} \geq Q^{-1}(10^{-4})$$

$$\sqrt{\frac{2E_b}{N_0}} \geq 3.71$$

$$E_b \geq \frac{(3.71)^2}{2} \times 2 \times 10^{-10}$$

$$E_b \geq 1.38 \times 10^{-9} \text{ J}$$

Required signal power $= E_b \times r_b$

$$= 1.38 \times 10^{-9}$$

$$= 4.14 \text{ mW}$$

Dec . 2013

U.Q. 64 : Explain MSK with the help waveforms for input sequence 11000111 along with respective mathematical representation. Compare it with QPSK.   **[10]**

U.Q. 65 : In a digital CW communication system, the bit rate of NRZ data stream is 1Mbps and carrier frequency is 100MHz. Find the symbol rate of the transmission bandwidth requirement of the channel in the following cases.   **[8]**

(i) BPSK system   ii) QPSK system   iii) 16-ary PSK system.

U.Q. 66: Compare the Euclidian distance 'd' and Bandwidth of M-Ary PSK, M-Ary FSK and QAM with M= 2n for n=3,4.   **[10]**

U.Q. 67 : The following bit streams are to be transmitted using DPSK scheme   **[8]**

(i) 1011100011   (ii) 0101000111

Determine and sketch the encoded sequence and transmitted phase sequene.

May 2014

U.Q. 68: Describe with the help of block diagram BFSK system transmitter and receiver.**[8]**

Draw the spectrum of BFSK and State the bandwidth requirement.

Solution : Refer Section 9.6.

U.Q. 69 : Compare and contrast   **[8]**

(A) BPSK & BFSK

(B) 16 PSK & 16 QAM

Solution : Refer Section 9.13.

U.Q. 70 : With the help of mathematical expression and block diagram , Explain the operation of offset QPSK. Also express the bandwidth requirement ?

Solution : Refer Section 9.7.

U.Q. 71 : Explain MSK with suitable waveform and prove phase continuity in MSK.   **[8]**

Solution : Refer Section 9.10.

U.Q. 72 : Derive expresssion for the probability of error of BPSK system.   **[8]**

Solution : Refer Section 9.4.2.

U.Q. 73 : Binary data tranmitted using PSK at the rate of 2 Mbps over RF link having bandwidth 2Mhz. Find signal power required at receiver input so that error probability is less than or equal to 10^{-4}. Assume noise PSD to be 10^{-10}W/Hz $(Q(3.71)= 10^{-4}$.

U.Q. 74 : Derive the expression for the probability of error of a BFSK system.   **[8]**

SUMMARY

1. An optimum filter which gives a maximum ratio of ρ^2 when input noise is white Gaussian it is called matched filter.

2. Impulse response of matched filter is given by,

$$h(t) \;=\; \frac{2k}{N_0}\, g\,(T-t)$$

where, $g(t)$ is input to the matched filter.

3. The ρ_{max}^{2} value (peak signal-to-noise ratio) for a matched filter $= \dfrac{2E}{N_0}$ where, E is signal energy.

4. The error probability of matched filter is given by,

$$P_e \;=\; \frac{1}{2}\,\mathrm{erfc}\left(\sqrt{\frac{E}{N_0}}\right)$$

5. Integrate-and-dump filter and matched filter gives the same minimum error probability and integrate-and-dump circuit is a matched filter.

6. Correlator is a circuit which gives identical performance as that of matched filter in detection of binary signals.

7. Correlator and matched filters are two techniques of synthesizing the optimum filter.

8. The error probability of BPSK receiver is $P_e = \dfrac{1}{2}\,\mathrm{erfc}\left(\sqrt{\dfrac{E_b}{N_0}}\right)$.

9. Imperfect phase synchronisation increases the error probability of BPSK and is given by,

$$P_e \;=\; \frac{1}{2}\,\mathrm{erfc}\left(\sqrt{\frac{E_b \cos^2 \phi}{N_0}}\right)$$

10. Error probability of detection of BFSK signal is given by,

$$P_e \;=\; \frac{1}{2}\,\mathrm{erfc}\sqrt{\frac{0.6\,E_b}{N_0}}$$

11. Error probability of detection of BFSK when both the frequencies are orthogonal is given by,

$$P_e \;=\; \frac{1}{2}\,\mathrm{erfc}\left(\sqrt{\frac{E_b}{2N_0}}\right)$$

12. DPSK results in sub-optimum performance and has inferior performance than BPSK. It is due to lack of stable phase reference. It is given by,

$$P_e \;=\; \frac{1}{2}\,e^{-\,E_b/N_0}$$

13. The error probability of QPSK is given by $p_e = \frac{1}{2} \text{erfc}\left(\sqrt{\frac{E_b}{N_0}}\right)$ which is same as BPSK.

14. We can use signal space diagram to calculate error probability of digital modulation techniques since the error probability depends on distance between message points in the signal space.

15. Modulation of high frequency carrier signal using baseband digital signal is called bandpass communication technique.

16. There are three basic types of digital modulation techniques.
    (i) Amplitude Shift Keying/On-off Keying (ASK/OOK)
    (ii) Phase Shift Keying (PSK).
    (iii) Frequency Shift Keying (FSK).

17. Based on demodulation technique used at the receiver digital modulation techniques are classified as –
    (i) Coherent Modulation (Synchronous).
    (ii) Non-coherent Modulation (Asynchronous).

18. Binary Phase Shift Keying (BPSK) is a coherent modulation technique. It uses two different phases for transmission of 1 and 0. Its bandwidth requirement is $= 2f_b$. It cannot be demodulated using non-coherent detection.

19. Binary Frequency Shift Keying method uses two different frequency carriers for transmission of 1 and 0. Its bandwidth requirement is $4f_b$. It can be demodulated using both coherent and non-coherent detection techniques.

20. Quadrature Phase Shift Keying (QPSK) is a bandwidth conserving scheme which uses four different phases of carrier to transmit the digital signal which is converted into 2-bits (digits) sequences.
    Bandwidth requirement for QPSK is $= f_b$.
    It has same noise immunity as that of PSK. It suffers from Interchannel Interference.

21. M-ary PSK is an extension of QPSK which uses M different phases of carrier to transmit digital data which is converted into N-bit groups (where, $N = 2^M$). The bandwidth requirement of M-ary PSK is $= 2f_b/\log_2 M$. It has degraded noise immunity than PSK. It suffers from variations in amplitude and interchannel interference.

22. Quadrature Amplitude Shift Keying (QASK) or Quadrature Amplitude Modulation (QAM) modulated both phase and amplitude of carrier depending on input bit pattern to improve noise immunity. Bandwidth requirement of QASK is $= \dfrac{2f_b}{\log_2 M}$ where, M is the number of symbols formed from N bit pattern i.e. $M = 2^N$.

23. Minimum Shift Keying (MSK) is modification QPSK/OQPSK to eliminate the problems associated with QPSK. It makes the abrupt phase changes smoother by modifying the

baseband signal before modulation. Bandwidth requirement of MSK is $= 1.5f_b$. But it has more energy in the main lobe than QPSK thereby making side lobes insignificant.

24. Differential Phase Shift Keying (DPSK) is a non-coherent modulation technique for PSK. The baseband signal is differentially encoded before PSK modulation. This eliminates need of synchronous carrier at receiver end.

25. Differential Encoded Phase Shift Keying is modification of DPSK which uses baseband decoding at the receiver thereby eliminating need of high frequency device at the receiver. It is coherent modulation technique.

26. M-ary FSK is an extension of Binary FSK where, M different frequency carriers are transmitted corresponding to digital data grouped into N bits where, $N = \log_2 M$. The bandwidth requirement of M-ary FSK is $= 2^{N+1} f_b/\log_2 M$.

EXERCISE

1. Define BER and SER.

2. Derive the expression for error probability of BPSK.

3. Derive the expression for error probability of QPSK.

4. Derive the expression for error probability of BFSK.

5. Explain the effect of imperfect phase synchronization in BPSK.

6. Explain the effect of imperfect bit synchronization in BPSK.

7. Compare the performances of following systems :
   (a) QPSK, (b) BPSK, (c) BFSK.

8. Discuss Minimum Shift Keying Technique of digital CW Modulation with the help of expressions, necessary waveforms, signals space representation, generation/reception techniques etc. What is minimum in this technique ? How is the phase continuity maintained ?

9. With the help of expressions, signal space and spectral representations and necessary waveforms, explain Binary Phase Shift Keying technique of Digital CW modulation. Discuss the method of generate and receive the BPSK signal.

10. Explain Quadrature Phase Shift Keying technique of Digital CW modulation. Elaborate your answer with suitable expressions, signal space and spectral representations and necessary waveform. How is QPSK signal generated and received ? What is the difference between OQPSK and non-offset QPSK ?

11. Discus Minimum Shift Keying technique of digital CW modulation. Elaborate your answer with necessary waveforms, expressions, signal space representation, spectral diagrams etc. Explain with neat block diagram, the generation and reception of MSK signal.

12. With suitable block diagram, explain generation and reception of FSK signal in digital CW modulation system. Elaborate your answer with necessary waveforms and expressions. What is bandwidth requirement of FSK system ?

13. Sketch the power spectral density of BPSK signal and state the bandwidth occupied by BPSK signal.

14. State the advantages of digital CW modulation over baseband digital transmission.

15. Discuss the different techniques in brief to recover the carrier in coherent digital CW modulation system.

16. What is Differential Phase Shift Keying ? Discuss with block schematic the generation and reception of DPSK signal. State merits and demerits of DPSK system over PSK system.

17. In a QPSK system, the bit rate of NRZ stream is 10 Mbps and carrier frequency is 1 GHz. Find the symbol rate of transmission and bandwidth requirement of the channel. Sketch the power spectral density of the QPSK signal.

18. Explain generation and reception of BFSK signal with suitable block schematic. Sketch necessary waveforms, signal space representation and frequency spectrum of BFSK signal.

19. What is Gaussian MSK ? State area of application for the same.

20. For a BPSK modulator with a carrier frequency of 70 MHz and an input bit rate of 10 Mbps. Draw the spectrum of output signal and determine the minimum Nyquist bandwidth.

21. Write short notes on :
    (i)   16 QAM
    (ii) M-ary FSK
    (iii) Quadrature Amplitude Modulation
    (iv) Gaussian MSK
    (v)   Frequency Shift Keying
    (vi) Gaussian MSK
    (vii) M-ary PSK
    (viii) DPSK and DEPSK Modulation

22. Explain working of BFSK transmitter and receiver. Show signal space representation of the orthogonal and non-orthogonal BFSK signals.

CHAPTER 10
SPREAD SPECTRUM TECHNIQUES

10.1 INTRODUCTION

- Spectrum is the most precious resource in the communication system. All the techniques that we have discussed till now aim at minimizing the bandwidth requirement.
- The narrowband communication however has two major disadvantages.
(i) Because of the limited range of frequencies, it becomes easier for the unauthorized user to intercept and detect the transmitted signal.
(ii) It becomes very easy for a jammer to jam the signal because of very little redundancy in the transmitted signal.
- Thus, the transmitted narrowband signal is insecure especially for military and intelligence agencies.
- The spread spectrum techniques are used to overcome the above mentioned shortcomings.
- The idea of spread spectrum is exactly opposite of conserving the bandwidth. The signal is spread over a broader spectrum and then transmitted. By doing so the signal power gets distributed over a larger range of frequencies thus lowering the power spectral density.

- There are two types of spread spectrum techniques :
(i) Direct Sequence Spread Spectrum (DSSS)
(ii) Frequency Hop Spread Spectrum (FHSS)

Definition of Spread Spectrum

A digital communication technique in which a psuedo-noise (PN) code, independent of the information data is used as modulation waveform to "spread" the signal energy over a bandwidth much greater than the message bandwidth. At the receiver, the signal is despread using same PN code which is in synchronous with transmitted PN code.

Definition of Direct Sequence Spread Spectrum (DSSS)

A digital communication technique in which a PN code generated at the transmitter is used to spread the message signal energy over a bandwidth much greater than message bandwidth. The spreaded signal is modulated by M-PSK modulation so that the phase of PSK signal changes psuedo randomly at a chipping rate Rc.

Definition of Frequency Hop Spread Spectrum (FHSS)

A digital communication technique in which a PN code generated at transmitter is used in conjunction with M-ary FSK modulation to shift the carrier frequency of FSK signal psuedo randomly; at a hopping rate R_h.

10.2 PSEUDO-NOISE (PN) SEQUENCE

Both the techniques of spread-spectrum direct-sequence and frequency hop require a noise-like spreading code called as Pseudo-Noise (PN) sequence. A PN sequence is called as coded sequence of 1's and 0's with certain autocorrelation properties. It can be generated using linear feedback shift register. A shift register having 'm' flip-flops can generate a maximum length sequence with a period of

$$N = 2^m - 1$$

A pseudo-noise (PN) sequence is a periodic binary sequence with noise like waveform that is usually generated by means of feedback shift registers.

A general block diagram is shown below in Fig. 10.1 (a).

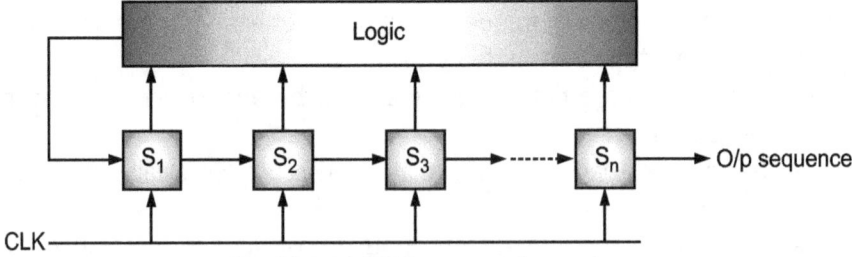

Fig. 10.1 (a) PN Sequence Generator

With each clock pulse logic, circuit computes a boolean function of states of flip-flops. This result in feedback to first flip-flop.

With total number of m flip-flops the number of possible states of shift registers is at most 2^m. The PN sequence becomes periodic after $2^m - 1$ states, zero state is not permitted.

Consider a linear feedback register shown below.

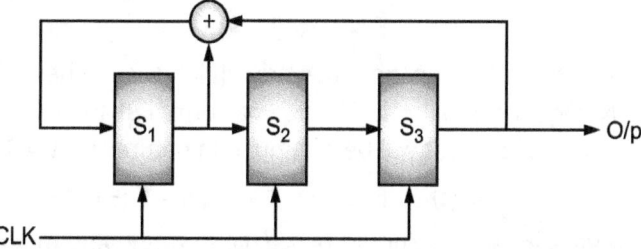

Fig. 10.1 (b) : PN sequence generator with m = 3 (N = 7)

Assuming initial states 100,

Table 10.1 : Different States

S_1	S_2	S_3
1	0	0
1	1	0
1	1	1
0	1	1
1	0	1
0	1	0
0	0	1
1	0	0

The output sequence is 00111010 which repeats with period $2^3 - 1 = 7$.

Properties of Maximum Length Sequence :

1.   Balance Property :

In each period of a maximum length sequence, the number of 1's are always one more than number of 0's.

2.   Run property :

Among the runs of 1's and 0's in each period of a maximum length sequence, one half the runs of each kind are of length 1, one fourth are of length two, one eighth are of length three and so on. For a maximum length sequence generated with on shift registers has $(N + 1)/2$ runs where, $N = 2^m - 1$.

3.   Correlation Property :

The autocorrelation function of a maximum length sequence is periodic and binary valued.

Period of PN sequence is, $N = 2^m - 1$

Let c(t) be the waveform representing maximum length sequence period of waveform c(t) is,

$$T_b = NT_c$$

T_c is chip duration.

∴ $$R_c(\tau) = \frac{1}{T_b} \int_{-T_b/2}^{+T_b/2} c(t)\, c(t - \tau)\, dt \qquad \qquad ...(10.1)$$

The autocorrelation function of random sequence is given,

$$R_C(\tau) = E[x(t) \cdot x(t + \tau)] \qquad ...(10.2)$$

We have already seen that this function has triangular form when $x(t) = \pm 1$. Hence, autocorrelation of PN sequences will also have same form. But then this sequence repeats after time $t = NT_C$. Hence, for $\tau < T_C$ it will be triangular in nature and $\tau = KT_C$.

$$R_C(\tau) = E[c(t) \cdot c(t + KT_C)] = E[-c(t + KT_C)] \qquad ...(10.3)$$

This is because if the PN sequence is shifted by K-chip duration and multiplied with original PN sequence we get inverted PN sequence. Now, $c(t + KT_C)$ will have an average value of $1/N$ since in N-chips there is one more 1 than 0.

$\therefore \qquad\qquad E[-c(t + KT_C)] = -\dfrac{1}{N}$

$\therefore \qquad\qquad R_C(\tau) = \begin{cases} 1 - \dfrac{N+1}{NT_C}\,|\tau| & ; \quad |\tau| \le T_C \\[3mm] -\dfrac{1}{N} & ; \quad \text{otherwise} \end{cases} \qquad ...(10.4)$

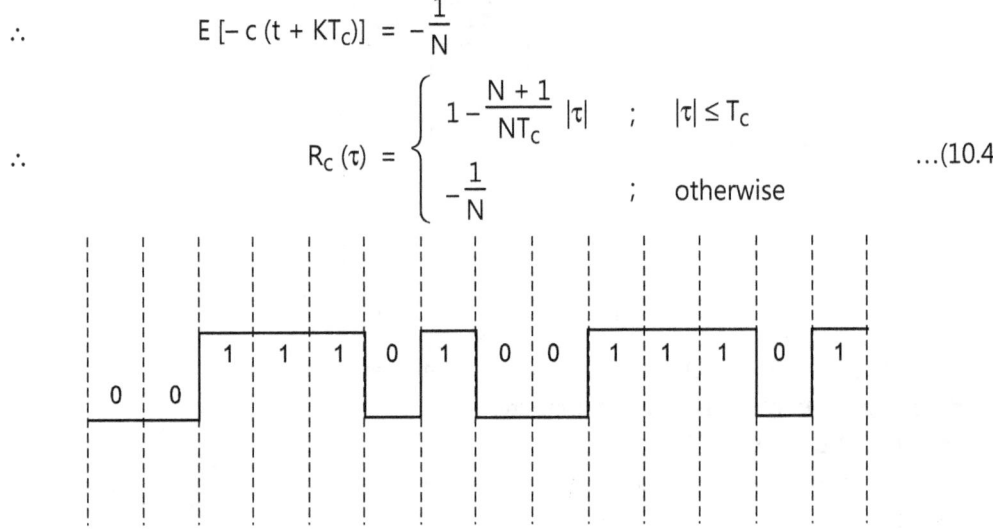

Fig. 10.2 : (a) PN Sequence

Fig. 10.2 : (b) Autocorrelation function of PN sequence

$\therefore$ PSD of PN sequence will be,

$$\therefore \qquad S_C(f) = \frac{1}{N^2}\delta(f) + \frac{1+N}{N^2}\sum_{\substack{n=-\infty \\ n \ne 0}}^{\infty} \text{sinc}^2\left(\frac{n}{N}\right)\delta\left(f - \frac{n}{NT_C}\right) \qquad ...(10.5)$$

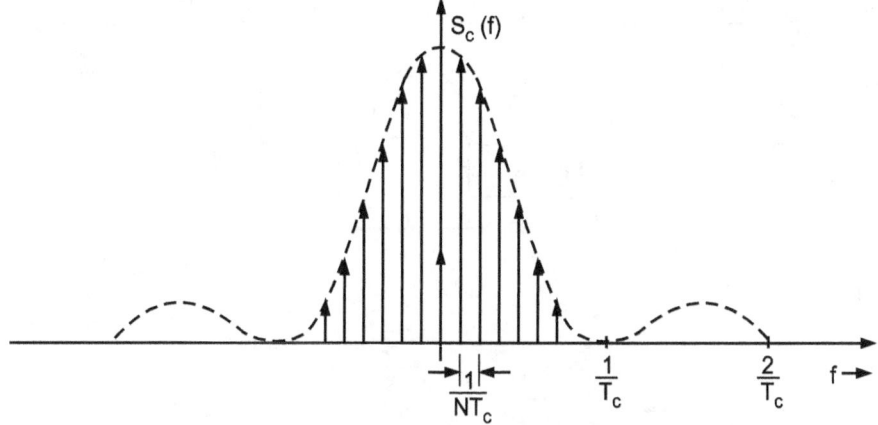

Fig. 10.2 : (c) PSD of PN sequence

Above waveforms show that,

(1) For a period of maximum length sequence the autocorrelation function $R_C(\tau)$ is somewhat similar to that of random binary wave.

Choosing maximum length sequence :

Following table gives feedback taps to be used for various PN sequences.

Table 10.2 : Shift Sequence Length and Feedback Taps

Shift Sequence Length (m)	Feedback Taps
2	(2, 1)
3	(3, 1)
4	(4, 1)
5	(5, 2) (5, 4, 3, 2) (6, 4, 2, 1)
6	(6, 1) (6, 5, 2, 1) (6, 5, 3, 2)
7	(7, 1) (7, 3) (7, 3, 2, 1)
	(7, 4, 3, 2) (7, 6, 4, 2)
8	(8, 4, 3, 2) (8, 6, 5, 3)
	(8, 6, 5, 2) (8, 5, 3, 1)

10.3 BASEBAND SPREAD SPECTRUM SYSTEM

Fig. 10.3 shows an idealized model of a baseband spread spectrum system.

The message signal occupied a bandwidth far in excess of the minimum bandwidth necessary to transmit it. This provides protection against jamming waveforms.

Data sequence d(t) modulates a wide-band PN sequence c(t) by applying both these sequences to a product modulator. Thus, if data sequence d(t) is narrowband and PN sequence c(t) is wideband, product signal q(t) will have a spectrum same as the PN sequence.

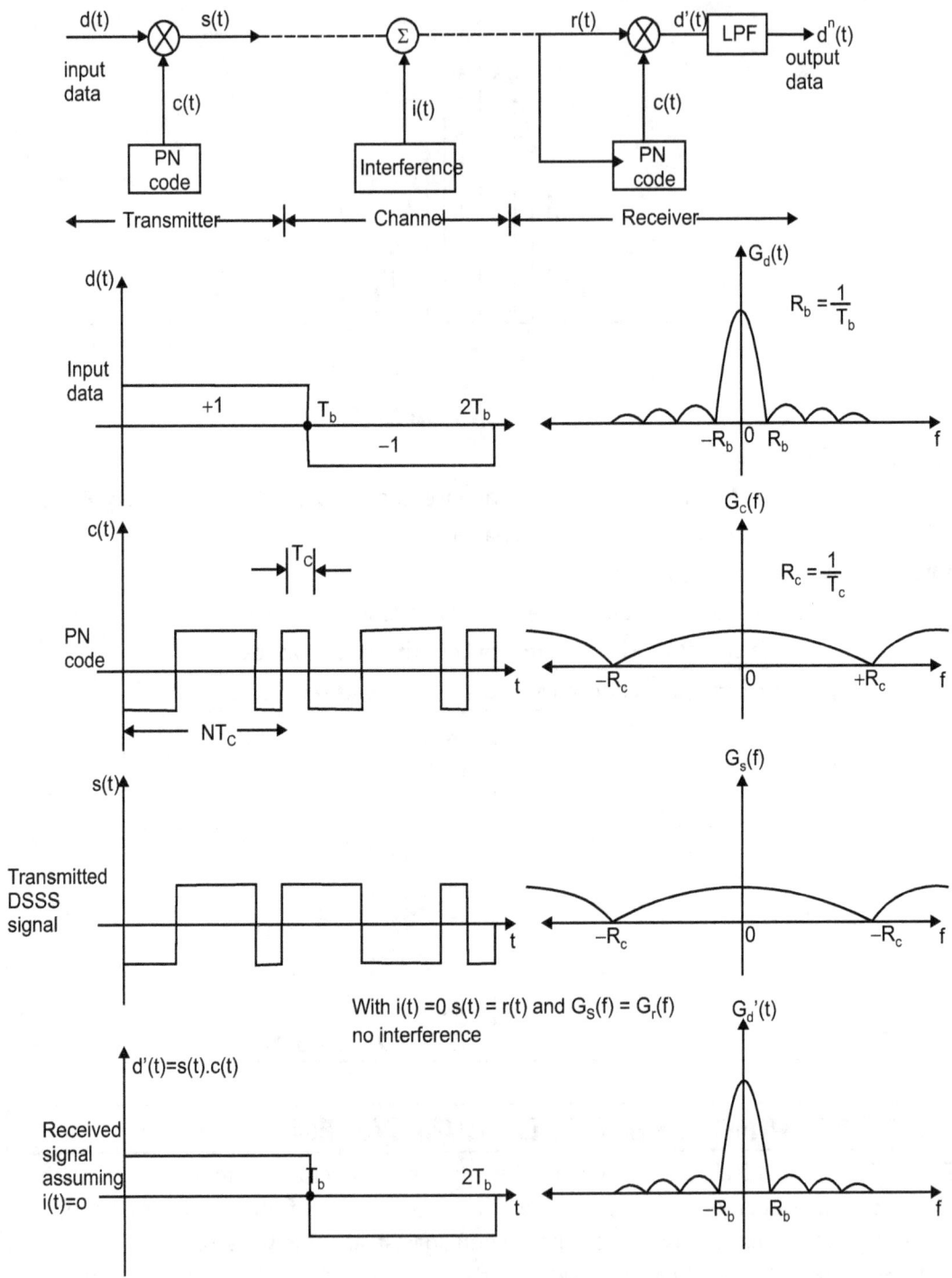

Fig. 10.3 : A baseband spread spectrum system

The transmitted signal s(t) = d(t) c(t) gets added with the channel interference signal i(t).

Thus, the received signal at the receiver side is,

$$r(t) = s(t) + i(t)$$

$$= d(t) \, c(t) + i(t) \qquad \qquad ...(10.6)$$

The receiver consists of a multiplier followed by a low pass filter. The received signal m(t) is multiplied by an exact replica of the PN sequence that was used at the transmitter. The demodulated signal is therefore given as,

$$d'(t) = c(t) \cdot r(t)$$

$$= c^2(t) \, d(t) + c(t) \, i(t) \qquad \qquad ...(10.7)$$

Both the sequences c(t) and d(t) are represented in the polar form. Hence, $c^2(t) = 1$.

$$\therefore \qquad \qquad \hat{d}(t) = d(t) + c(t) \, i(t) \qquad \qquad ...(10.8)$$

The interference signal gets widened as it is multiplied by the spreading code c(t). Hence, when d(t) passes through the LPF, data signal d(t) can easily be recovered. The effect of i(t) is considerably mitigated at the receiver output.

- Now let us see the effect of interference and how the DSS system takes case of it.

- We will consider how cases of interference viz narrowband and wideband.

- If narrowband interference is added in the channel, it gets added to the spreaded transmitted spectrum as shown in Fig. 10.4

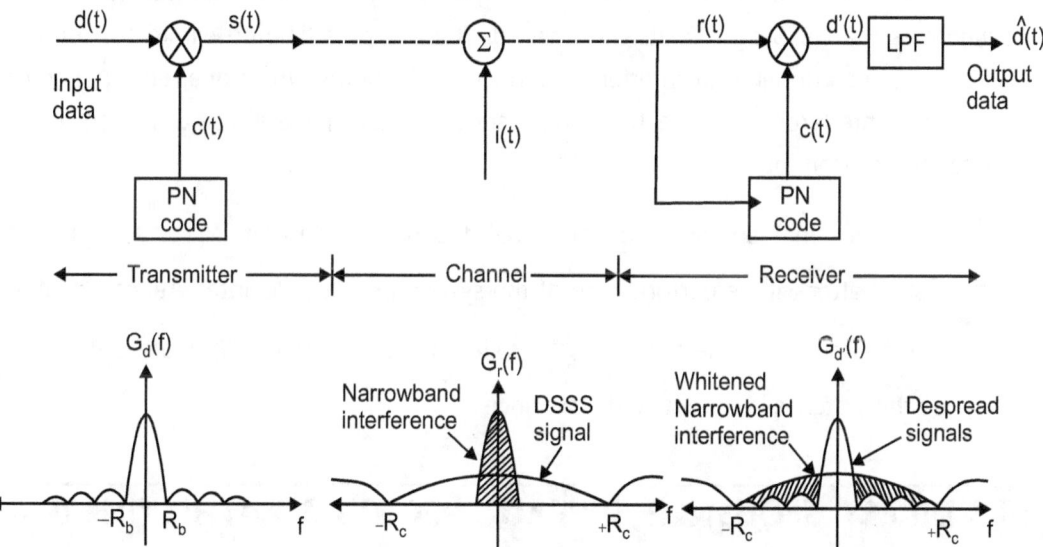

Fig. 10.4 : DSSS system with narrowband interference (whitened)

- At the receiver, the narrowband interference gets spreaded (whitened) in frequency domain as it gets multiplied by PN code where as the DSSS signal gets despreaded. The low pass filtering eliminates most of the energy of the interfering signal passing only the original message signal to the output.

- Now consider the case of wideband interference which can originate due to multiple users or Gaussian noise as shown in Fig. 10.5.

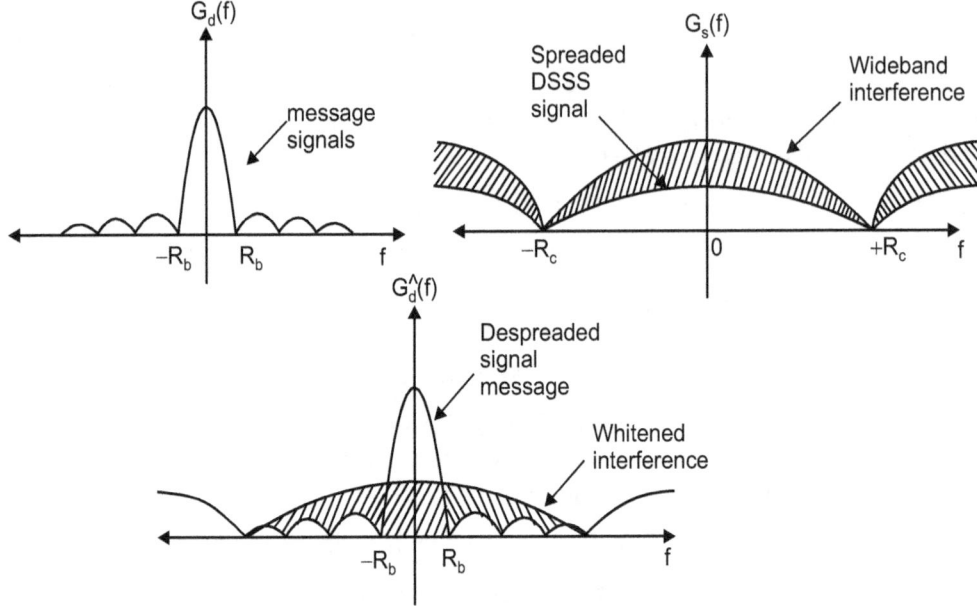

Fig. 10.5 : Spectra of DSSS with wideband interference

- At the receiver the wideband interference gets spreaded (whitened) due to PN code where as the DSSS signal gets despreaded. The low pass filtering eliminates the high frequency components of interference. Thus at the output the signal energy is more than the interference. Hence the spread spectrum technique is useful in combatting interference from other users.

- It can be seen that, spreading of the signal depends on chip rate $R_c = \dfrac{1}{T_c}$. Higher the chip rate, better will be performance of the system because the interference signal will be whitened properly. The ratio $\dfrac{T_b}{T_c} = \dfrac{R_c}{R_b}$ is called processing gain (PG). More is PG, better will be the system's immunity to interference.

10.4 DIRECT SEQUENCE SPREAD SPECTRUM WITH COHERENT BPSK

- We have discussed baseband DSSS system which can be implemented over passband by incorporating modulation scheme like Coherent BPSK. Fig. 10.6 shows the transmitter for DSSS with Coherent BPSK system.

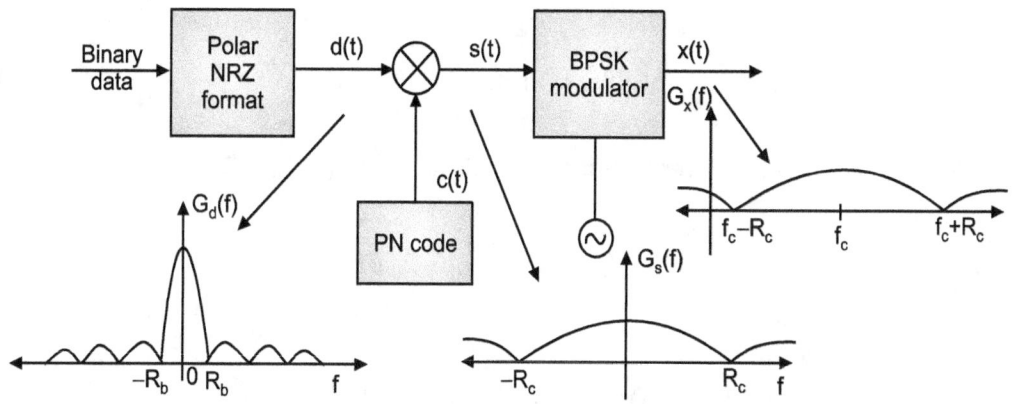

Fig. 10.6 : Transmitter for DSSS with Coherent BPSK System.

- The message signal $d(t)$ is multiplied by PN code sequence $c(t)$ to generate spreaded signal $s(t)$ (it is also called chipped message) as,

$$s(t) = d(t) \cdot c(t) \qquad \qquad \ldots(10.9)$$

- Expect signal $d(t)$ all other signals are random. Hence we have to analyse through their auto correlations and power spectral densities.

- We have seen that the PN sequence has auto correlate and PSD as

$$R_c(\tau) = \triangle\left(\frac{t}{T_c}\right) \qquad \qquad \ldots(10.10)$$

$$G_c(f) = T_c \, \text{sinc}^2\left(\frac{f}{R_c}\right) \qquad \qquad \ldots(10.11)$$

- The chipped message $s(t)$ can be thought as a random process whose average power can be given as

$$\sigma_s^2 = E[s^2(t)] = E[d^2(t) \cdot c^2(t)] \qquad \qquad \ldots(10.12)$$

$$= E[d^2(t)] \qquad \qquad [\because c^2(t) = 1]$$

$$= S_d$$

Thus the spreaded signal power will be same as average message signal power.

- Now, the frequency domain representation of the spreaded signal $s(t)$ will be obtained by taking convolution of their PSD's.

$$G_s(f) = G_d(f) * G_c(f) = \int_{-\infty}^{\infty} G_d(\lambda) \cdot G_c(f - \lambda) \, d\lambda \qquad \ldots(10.13)$$

But $G_d(f)$ exists over $f = -R_b$ to $+R_b$ only.

$$\therefore \qquad G_s(f) = \int\limits_{-R_b}^{R_b} G_d(\lambda)\, G_c(f-\lambda)\, d\lambda \qquad \qquad ...(10.14)$$

Since $G_c(f)$ is almost flat over the range $\lambda = -R_b$ to $+R_b$, $G_c(f-\lambda) \cong G_c(f)$

$$\therefore \qquad G_s(f) = G_c(f) \int\limits_{-R_b}^{R_b} G_d(\lambda)\, d\lambda \qquad \qquad ...(10.15)$$

But $\qquad \int\limits_{-R_b}^{R_b} G_d(\lambda) d\lambda = S_d \qquad \qquad ...(10.16)$

[PSD integrated over the entire frequency rage]

$$\therefore \qquad G_s(f) = S_d\, G_c(f). \qquad \qquad ...(10.17)$$

- Thus PSD of spreaded signal s(t) is same as the PSD of PN sequence c(t). Hence the bandwidth of PN sequence. The bandwidth of spreaded signal will be R_c. The bandwidth expansion factor $N = \dfrac{R_c}{R_b} = \dfrac{T_b}{T_c}$ decides the system's immunity to interference.

- Since the spreaded signal s(t) is modulated using BPSK, with carrier frequency f_c, the PSD of the resulting is denoted by $G_x(f)$ in Fig. 10.6. It is shifted version of $G_s(f)$ ground the carrier frequency f_c. Note that the transmission bandwidth required will be $2R_c$ which is much higher than message signal bandwidth R_b.

i.e. $B_T >> R_b$

- Fig 10.7 shows the receiver block diagram of DSSS BPSK system

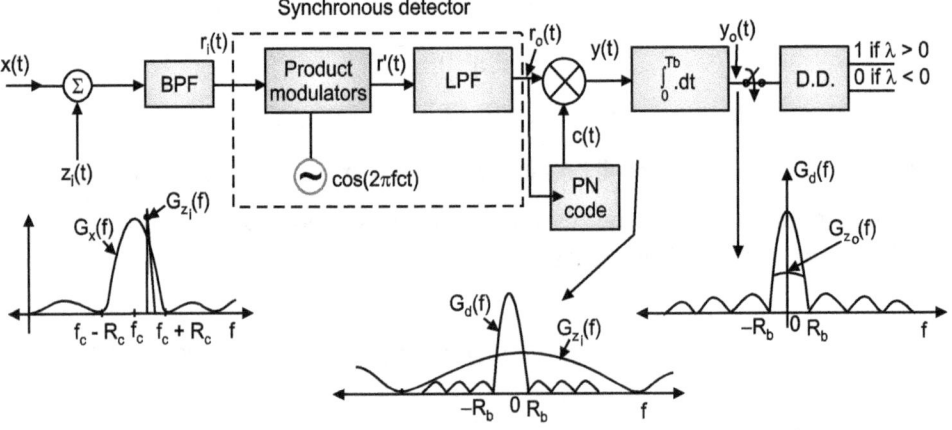

Fig. 10.7 : DSSS – BPSK Receiver

- We know that PSD of transmitted signal $x(t)$ is

$$G_x(f) = S_d\, G_c(f) \qquad\qquad\qquad\qquad ...(10.18)$$

Assuming unit amplitude carrier, average carrier power will be $\dfrac{A_c^2}{2} = \dfrac{1}{2}$, the received signal

will have average power $S_R = \dfrac{1}{2} S_d$

- The output signal power in $\quad y_o(t) = d(t) + z_o(t)$

$$S_d = 2S_R$$

Where S_R is received signal power with assumed carrier amplitude = 1

- To find average noise power, let $Z_i(t) = W(t)$ (AWGN) $r_o(t)$ consists low pass filtered AWGN. The PSD of low pass filtered AWGN is given as

$$G_{n_i}(f) = \frac{N_o}{2}; \ |f| \le B \qquad\qquad\qquad ...(10.19)$$

where $B_T > 2R_c$

- The auto correlation function of low pass filtered noise will be obtained by taking Inverse Fourier Transform of the PSD

$$\therefore \qquad\qquad R_{n_i}(\tau) = N_o B_T\, \text{Sinc}\, (B_T\, \tau) \qquad\qquad\qquad ...(10.20)$$

- This low pass noise is clipped by multiplying with PN code. The auto correction function of clipped noise will be $R_{ni}(\tau)$. But $R_c(\tau) \approx 1$ for $\tau << 1/R_c$. Hence clipped noise in $r_o(t)$ will have same auto correlation function as $R_{ni}(\tau)$. The PSD of noise in $r_o(t)$ will be obtained by taking Fourier transform of $R_{ni}(\tau)$

$$\therefore \qquad\qquad G_{n_o}(f) = N_o\, \text{rect}\left(\frac{f}{B_T}\right) \qquad\qquad\qquad ...(10.21)$$

- The noise in $r_o(t)$ will be filtered by the integrator. Hence output noise power will be

$$N_D = \int_{-R_b}^{R_b} N_o\, \text{rect}\left(\frac{f}{B_T}\right) df = 2\, N_o\, R_b. \qquad\qquad ...(10.22)$$

- An interference $Z_i(t)$ is added in the channel which can be AWGN signal or interference from other users or intentional jamming from intruders.

- A bandpass filler is used to eliminate noise outside the frequency band $-R_c$ to R_c. But note that the interference and noise inside this band is not eliminated.

- The bandpass filtered signal $r_i(t)$ will be

$$r_i(t) = s(t)\cos(2\pi f_c t) + Z_i(t) \qquad\qquad\qquad ...(10.23)$$

This signal gets multiplied the locally generated carrier $\cos(2\pi f_c t)$ to generate $r'(t)$ as

$$r'(t) = s(t) \cos^2(2\pi f_c t) + Z_i(t) \cos(2\pi f_c t) \qquad \ldots(10.24)$$

$$= s(t) \left(\frac{1+\cos 4\pi f_c t}{2}\right) + Z_i(t) \cos(2\pi f_c t)$$

- The low pass filtering of $r'(t)$ will give

$$r_o(t) = s(t) + Z_i'(t) \qquad \ldots(10.25)$$

- The output of synchronus detector is multiplied by PN code $c(t)$ to generate output $y(t)$

$$y(t) = [s(t) + Z_i'(t)] \, c(t) = s(t) \cdot c(t) + Z_i'(t) \cdot c(t) \ldots(10.26)$$

But $s(t) = d(t) \cdot c(t)$

$\therefore$ $y(t) = d(t) \cdot c^2(t) + Z_i'(t) \cdot c(t) \qquad \ldots(10.27)$

$$= d(t) + Z_i'(t) \cdot c(t) \qquad [\because c^2(t) = 1]$$

- Thus because of multiplication by PN code, the message signal gets despreaded and interference $Z_i'(t)$ gets spreaded in frequency.

- The output $y(t)$ is passed through an integrater which works as LPF to eliminate the spreaded interference to give $y_o(t)$

$$y_o(t) = d(t) + N \, Z_o(t) \qquad \ldots(10.28)$$

Where $Z_o(t)$ is filtered version of spreaded interference

- The spectral characteristics of each wave from are shown in Fig. 10.7
- Assuming $Z_i(t)$ to be AWGN signal we will find the SNR of DSSS-BPSK system.
- Hence signal-to-noise ratio in the output $y_o(t)$ will be

$$\left(\frac{S}{N}\right)_D = \frac{2S_R}{2N_o R_b} = \frac{S_R}{2N_o R_b} \qquad \ldots(10.29)$$

- When the message signal $d(t)$ is binary, $s_R = \dfrac{1}{2} s_d = \dfrac{E_b}{2T_b} = \dfrac{E_b R_b}{2}$. The object signal to noise ratio will be

$$\left(\frac{S}{N}\right)_D = \frac{E_b}{2N_o} \qquad \text{where } E_b \text{ is energy per bit duration.}$$

- The signal and noise is unaffected by the spreading and dispreading in the system. Hence the error probability of the system will be same as the BPSK system. Therefore the error probability of the DSSS-BPSK system when the interference is AWGN is given as.

$$P_e = Q\left(\sqrt{\frac{2E_b}{N_o}}\right) = \frac{1}{2} \text{erfc}\left(\sqrt{\frac{E_b}{N_o}}\right) \qquad \ldots(10.30)$$

10.4.1 Concept of Jamming and Processing Gain

- Now let us assume the interfering signal $Z_i(t)$ as jamming signal in Fig. 10.7. A jamming signal is a signal with very high power concentrated in a band of frequencies around carrier frequency.

- We assume the jamming signal to be a single tone means single carrier is used to generate the jamming signal.

- If average power of the jamming signal at frequency $f_c + f_z$ is J then the signal can be expressed as

$$Z_i(t) = \sqrt{2} \, J \cos \left[2\pi(f_c + f_z) t + \theta \right] \qquad \qquad ...(10.31)$$

where f_z is small deviation from carrier and θ is used for phase ambiguity between original signal and jamming signal.

- When the jamming signal is multiplied by carrier and low pass filtered in synchronous detector, the output will be inphase component.

$$Z_i'(t) = \sqrt{2} \, J \cos (2\pi f_z t + \theta) \qquad \qquad ...(10.32)$$

The PSD of this component will be,

$$G_{Z_i}(t) = \frac{J}{2} \left[\delta (f - f_z) + \delta (f + f_z) \right] \qquad \qquad ...(10.33)$$

- Multiplication of $Z_i'(t)$ with c(t) results into spreading of the spectrum over the frequency band $- R_c$ to R_c.

- The jamming power J gets spread uniformly over the entire bind. Therefore the PSD of clipped jamming signal will be,

$$G_{\overline{Z_i}}(f) = \frac{J}{2R_c} \qquad \qquad ...(10.34)$$

- This is passed through an integrator which is low pass filter with cut off equal to R_b. Therefore the output jamming power will be,

$$J_D = \frac{J}{2R_C} \times 2R_b = \frac{J}{R_C} \times R_b \qquad \qquad ...(10.35)$$

- The output signal to jamming power will be,

$$\left(\frac{S}{J} \right)_D = \frac{S_R}{\dfrac{J}{R_c} \times R_b} \qquad \qquad ...(10.36)$$

$$\left(\frac{S}{J} \right)_D = \frac{S_R \times R_c}{J \times R_b} = \frac{S_R/J}{(R_b/R_c)} \qquad \qquad ...(10.37)$$

where S_R is received message signal power.

- It can be observed that, the signal to jamming power depends on very important design parameters of the system $\dfrac{R_c}{R_b}$. R_c is clipping vale and R_b is bit rate. This ratio $\dfrac{R_c}{R_b}$ is called processing gain (PG).

$$\therefore \left(\text{Processing gain PG} = \frac{R_c}{R_b} = \frac{T_b}{T_c} = N \right)$$

$$\therefore \qquad \left(\frac{S}{J} \right)_D = \frac{S_R}{J} \times PG \qquad \qquad \dots(10.38)$$

- In order to find error probability, we can treat the jamming signal as source of noise. Hence, the error probability of DSSS-BPSK system with single tone jamming signal is given as,

$$p_e = Q\left(\sqrt{\frac{2E_b}{N_J}} \right) \qquad \qquad \dots(10.39)$$

where N_J PSD of output jamming signal.

$$\text{Now,} \qquad \qquad N_J = \frac{J}{R_c} \text{ and } E_b = \frac{S_R}{R_b} \qquad \qquad \dots(10.40)$$

$$\therefore \qquad \qquad p_e = Q\left(\sqrt{\frac{2 \times S_R/R_b}{(J/R_c)}} \right)$$

$$\therefore \qquad \qquad p_e = Q\left(\sqrt{\frac{2 \cdot R_c/R_b}{(J/S_R)}} \right) \qquad \qquad \dots(10.41)$$

$$\therefore \qquad \left(p_e = Q\left(\sqrt{\frac{2PG}{J/S_R}} \right) \right)$$

- J/S_R is the jamming power to signal power ratio.

$$\frac{J}{S_R} = \frac{N_J \cdot R_C}{E_b \times R_b} = \frac{R_c/R_b}{(E_b/N_j)} = \frac{PG}{(E_b/N_J)} \qquad \qquad \dots(10.42)$$

Converting the ratio J/S_R in dB,

$$10 \log \left(\frac{J}{S_R} \right) = 10 \log (PG) - 10 \log (E_b/N_J) \qquad \qquad \dots(10.43)$$

The term $10 \log (J/S_R)$ is called jamming margin.

- Jamming margin gives an idea about the system's ability to perform in presence of interference. If we have a small value of p_e and small value of E_b/N_j ratio but large value of processing gain then system will have margin against interference.

10.4.2 Signal Space Dimensionality

- For the purpose of analysis, let us interchange the two operations synchronous detector and spreading as shown in Fig. 10.8.

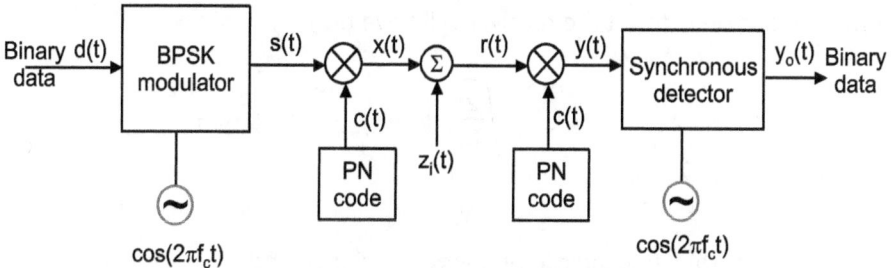

Fig. 10.8 : A model for DSSS-BPSK System

- The received signal r(t) is given as,

$$r(t) = x(t) + Z_i(t) \qquad \qquad ...(10.44)$$

$$\therefore \qquad r(t) = c(t) . s(t) + Z_i(t) \qquad \qquad ...(10.45)$$

- Output of synchronous detector will be,

$$y(t) = c(t) . r(t)$$

$$= c(t) . [c(t) s(t) + Z_i(t)]$$

$$= c^2(t) s(t) + c(t) . Z_i(t)$$

$$= s(t) + c(t) Z_i(t)$$

- Let us define the orthonormal basis functions as,

$$\phi_k(t) = \sqrt{\frac{2}{T_c}} \cos (2\pi f_c t) \qquad ; \quad kT_c \le t \le (k + 1) T_c$$

$$= 0 \qquad \qquad ; \quad \text{otherwise}$$

$$\overset{*}{\phi_k}(t) = \sqrt{\frac{2}{T_c}} \sin (2\pi f_c t); \qquad kT_c \le t \le (k + 1) T_c$$

$$= 0 \qquad \qquad ; \quad \text{otherwise}$$

- The transmitted signal in terms of basis functions will be written as below

$$x(t) = s(t) . c(t)$$

substituting,
$$s(t) = \pm \sqrt{\frac{2E_b}{T_b}}$$

$$c(t) = \sum_{k = 0}^{N - 1} c_k \text{ and } T_b = NT_c$$

We get,
$$x(t) = \pm \sqrt{\frac{E_b}{N}} \sum_{k=0}^{N-1} c_k \phi_k(t)$$

where,
$$c_k = [c_0, c_1, c_2 \ldots\ldots c_{N-1}] \text{ is PN sequence.}$$

- The synchronous detector at the receiver will have output,

$$v = \sqrt{\frac{2}{T_b}} \int_0^{T_b} y(t) . \cos (2\pi fct) \, dt$$

$$= v_s + v_{cz}$$

where v_s is due to despreading of message signal and v_c is due to spreading of interference $Z_i(t)$.

- The jammer cannot have knowledge of phase of the signal. The interfering jamming signal can be written as,

$$z_i(t) = \sum_{k=0}^{N-1} z_k \phi_k(t) = \sum_{k=0}^{N-1} z'_k \phi_k^*(t)$$

where,
$$z_k = \int_0^{T_b} z_i(t) \phi_1(t) \, dt$$

$$z'_k = \int_0^{T_b} z_i(t) \phi^*(t) \, dt$$

- Now the spreaded interference will be,

$$v_{cz} = \sqrt{\frac{2}{T_b}} \int_0^{T_b} c(t) z_i(t) \cos (2\pi f_c t) \, dt$$

$$= \sqrt{\frac{T_c}{T_b}} \sum_{k=0}^{N-1} c_k . \int_0^{T_b} z_i(t) \phi_k(t) \, dt$$

$$= \sqrt{\frac{T_c}{T_b}} \sum_{k=0}^{N-1} c_k z_k$$

- V_{cz} is dependent on z_k which is random quantity. Hence v_{cz} is a value of some random variable.

- V_{cz} we can characterize the random quantity by finding its mean and variance.

- Mean of V_{cz} will be,

$$E[c_k z_k/z_k] = 0$$

$$\therefore \qquad E[V_{cz}] = 0$$

- Variance of V_{cz} will be,

$$Var[V_{cz}/z_k] = \frac{1}{N}\sum_{k=0}^{N-1} z_k^2$$

But Jamming power

$$J = \frac{2}{T_b}\sum_{k=0}^{N-1} z_k^2$$

$$\therefore \qquad Var[V_{cz}/z_k] = \frac{1}{N} \times \frac{JT_b}{2} = \frac{JT_c}{2}$$

- Thus the output signal energy is E_b and output noise (jamming) energy is $JT_c/2$.
- The output signal to Jamming power for DSSS-BPSK will be,

$$(SNR)_D = \frac{E_b}{JT_c/2}$$

$$= \frac{2E_b}{JT_c}$$

- The input signal to Jamming power for the receiver is,

$$(SNR)_I = \frac{E_b/T_b}{J}$$

- Hence we can write,

$$(SNR)_D = \frac{2E_b}{JT_c}$$

$$= \frac{2E_b}{JT_b} \times N$$

$$= 2\left(\frac{E_b/T_b}{J}\right) \times N$$

$$= 2(SNR)_I \times \left(\frac{T_b}{T_c}\right)$$

$$= 2(SNR)_I \times PG$$

- Thus output SNR of DSSS-BPSK is improved due to despreading of signal and spreading of noise by a factor equal to processing gain of the system.

10.4.3 Advantages of DSSS

(i) Security of transmitted signal :

The DSSS signal can be decoded only with PN code used for generation of signal. So there are very small chances of intercepting the signal.

(ii) Resistance to Jamming or Intereference :

Because of spreading of signal over a larger band-width information signal is desentitised from intentional jamming or interference.

(iii) Ranging capability.

(iv) Combat multipath fading.

10.4.4 Disadvantages

(i) Bandwidth requirement is very high.

(ii) Performance degrades rapidly because of timing or synchronisation error.

(iii) Performance depends on processing gain which cannot be practically increased beyond certain limit.

Example 10.1 :

A BPSK-DSS system using coherent detection is used to transmit data at 250 bps and system has to work in the hostile jamming environment with minimum error performance of one error in 20000 bits. Determine the minimum chipping rate, if the jamming signal is 300 times stronger than the received signal. Assume Q (3.9) = 0.00005.   **[May 2004]**

Solution : From the given conditions,

Probability of error, $P_e = \dfrac{1}{20000} = 0.00005$

For a BPSK-DSS system, $P_e = Q\left(\sqrt{\dfrac{2PG}{J/S_R}}\right)$

Jamming signal $= 300 \times$ Received signal

∴ $J = 300\, S_R$

$$PG = \dfrac{T_b}{T_c} = \dfrac{R_c}{R_b} = \dfrac{W_c}{250}$$

∴ $P_e = 0.00005 = Q\left(\sqrt{\dfrac{2R_c}{250 \times 300}}\right)$

$Q(3.9) = 0.00005$

$$\therefore \qquad \sqrt{\frac{2R_c}{250 \times 300}} = 3.9$$

$$\therefore \qquad R_c = 570.375 \text{ kbps}$$

Thus, the minimum chipping rate required for the given system is 570.375 kbps.

Example 10.2 :

The information bit duration in a DS-BPSK spread spectrum communication system is 5 ms while the chipping rate is 1 MHz. Assuming an average error probability of 10^{-5} for proper detection of message signal, calculate the jamming margin.

Solution : Processing gain, $\qquad PG = \dfrac{T_b}{T_c} \times \dfrac{5 \times 10^{-3}}{1 \times 10^{-6}} = 5000$

For a coherent binary PSK receiver,

$$P_e = Q\left(\sqrt{\frac{2E_b}{N_0}}\right)$$

Thus, for $P_e \cong 10^{-5}$, $\dfrac{E_b}{N_0} = 10$

Jamming margin $\dfrac{J}{P} = \dfrac{PG}{E_b/N_0}$ or Jamming margin in dB.

$$= 10 \log_{10} PG - 10 \log_{10} \frac{E_b}{N_0}$$

$$= 10 \log_{10} 5000 - 10 \log_{10} 10$$

$$= 26.989 \text{ dB}$$

$$\approx 500$$

Hence, information bits at the receiver output can be detected even when the interference at the receiver input is upto 500 times the received signal power.

10.5 FREQUENCY-HOP SPREAD SPECTRUM (FHSS)

The ability of DS-SS system to combat jamming effects is determined by the processing gain of the system, which further depends on the PN sequence length. However, the practical limitations of PN sequence generation hardware imposes limitations on processing gain. To enable larger processing gains, the PN generator can drive a frequency synthesizer that produces a wideband sequence of frequencies that enables the data-modulated carrier to hop from one frequency to another. This process is called Frequency Hopping Spread Spectrum (FH-SS). Thus, we observe that the message is spread over numerous carrier frequencies and hence the jammer has to spread its power over a wide frequency range in order to be effective.

Frequency hopping does not cover the entire spread spectrum instantaneously and hence, we consider the rate at which hops occur. Normally, the message signal is M-ary FSK modulated to some carrier frequency f_c. This modulated message then mixes with the output of a frequency synthesizer which has 2^k values where 'k' equals the number of outputs from the PN generator.

We can identify two types of FH-SS systems :

(1) Slow hop SS : One or more symbols are transmitted on each frequency hop. ($R_S = h R_h$)

(2) Fast hop SS : Carrier frequency will change several times during the transmission of one symbol. ($R_h = h R_S$)

A typical block diagram of frequency-hopping system is shown in Fig. 10.9 (a). Binary data is fed into a modulator using some encoding scheme such as FSK or BPSK. The resulting signal is centred around some base frequency. A pseudonoise which drives a frequency synthesizer produces different carrier frequencies. At each successive internal (k PN bits) a new carrier is selected. This frequency is then modulated by the signal produced from BPSK/FSK modulator to produce a new signal with same shape but centred around the selected carrier frequency. This signal is the spreaded signal and transmitted over the channel.

At the receiver the received spreaded signal is demodulated using some PN sequence and then demodulated using BPSK/FSK demodulator to produce the output data.

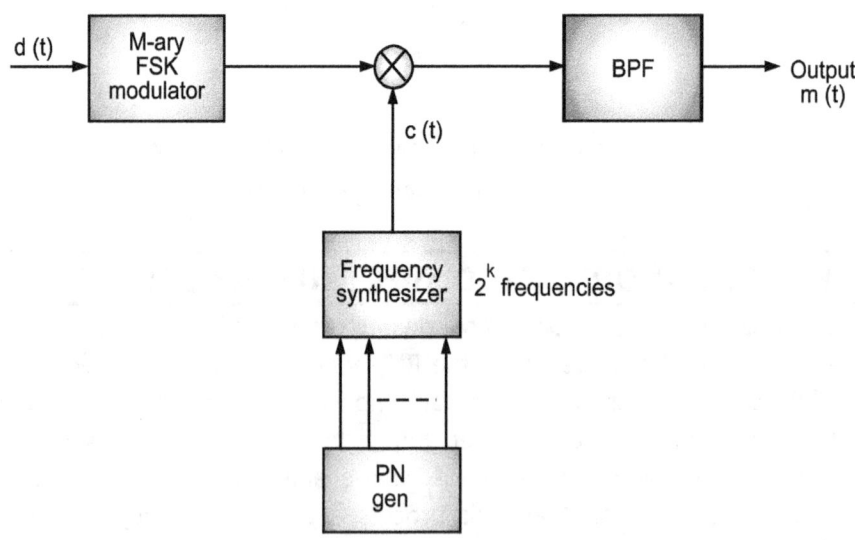

Fig. 10.9 : (a) Transmitter of FHSS

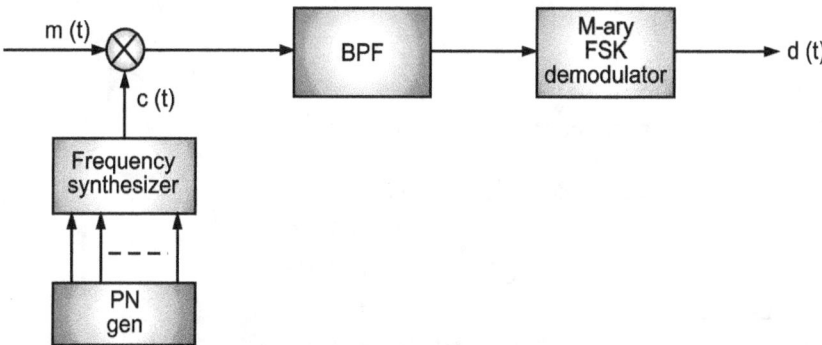

Fig. 10.9 : (b) Receiver of FHSS

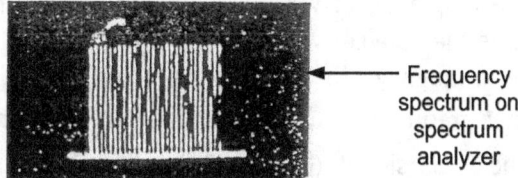

Frequency spectrum on spectrum analyzer

Fig. 10.9 : (c) Spectrum Analyzer Photo of a Frequency Hop (FH) Spread Spectrum Signal

Fig. 10.9 (c) indicates frequency hop spread spectrum as observed on a spectrum analyzer.

10.5.1 Advantages of FHSS

(i) Resistance to jamming and interference :
Because of randomly varying centre frequency, jammer will not be able to keep track of the centre frequency.

(ii) Interference avoidance :
We can avoid intereference by skipping the band of frequencies containing intereference.

(iii) Operation over larger band-width is possible through FHSS than DSSS.

10.5.2 Disadvantages

(i) Continuity of signal over multiple hops is difficult to maintain.

(ii) For better performance (low error probability) very high hopping rate is required.

A commonly used modulation technique with FHSS is M-ary FSK (MFSK). We have seen that MFSK uses $M = 2^n$ different frequencies to encode the digital input k-bits at a time. The transmitted signal is of the form.

$$S_i(t) = A \cos (2\pi f_i t) \; ; \; 1 \leq i \leq M$$

where,

$$f_i = f_c + (2i - 1 - M) f_d$$

f_c = Carrier frequency

f_d = Difference frequency

M = Number of signal elements = 2^k

K = Number of bits per signal elements

In FHSS, the MFSK signal assumes a new frequency every T_c seconds by modulating the MFSK signal with FHSS carrier signal having frequency f_c.

Let the data rate = $R_b = \dfrac{1}{T_b}$.

$\therefore$ Duration of signal element = $T_s = nT_b = \dfrac{1}{R_s}$.

Now, we can specify the two types of FHSS systems as below.

If $T_c \geq T_s$ it is slow-FHSS.

and if $T_c < T_s$ it is fast-FHSS.

They are described as below.

Slow FHSS :

Fig. 10.10 (a) shows an example of slow FHSS, using the MFSK. There are four different frequencies used to encode the data i.e. M = 4. It means two input bits are going to produce a signal of corresponding frequency. The total bandwidth of MFSK signal will be $W_d = Mf_d$; where, f_d is the difference frequency. Further, we use four different channels of each of width W_d to transmit the FHSS signal. (i.e. k = 2, hence $2^k = 4$). Thus, the total FHSS bandwidth = $W_s = 2^k W_d = 4W_d$. Each 2-bit PN sequence is used to select one of four channels. The channel remains same for two signal elements i.e. for 4-bits duration.

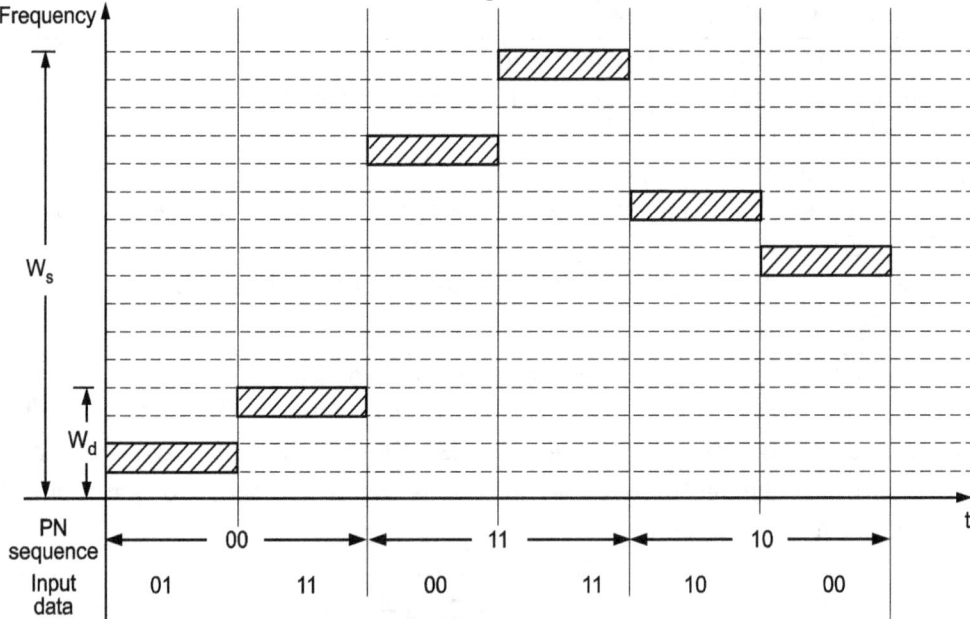

Fig. 10.10 : (a) Slow FHSS using MFSK (M = 4, k = 2)

$$W_d = Mf_d, \; W_s = 2^k W_d$$

Fast FHSS : Fig. 10.10 (b) shows an example of fast FHSS using same MFSK as described in previous example (M = 4, k = 2). Each signal element (2-bits) is represented using two frequency tones. Each 2-bits of PN sequence is used to select one of the four channels. The channel is held for a duration of half signal elements i.e. one bit i.e. there is fast change of frequency. Fast FHSS has better performance compared to slow FHSS. If three or more frequencies are used for each signal, the receiver can decide which signal element was sent based on majority of chips being correct.

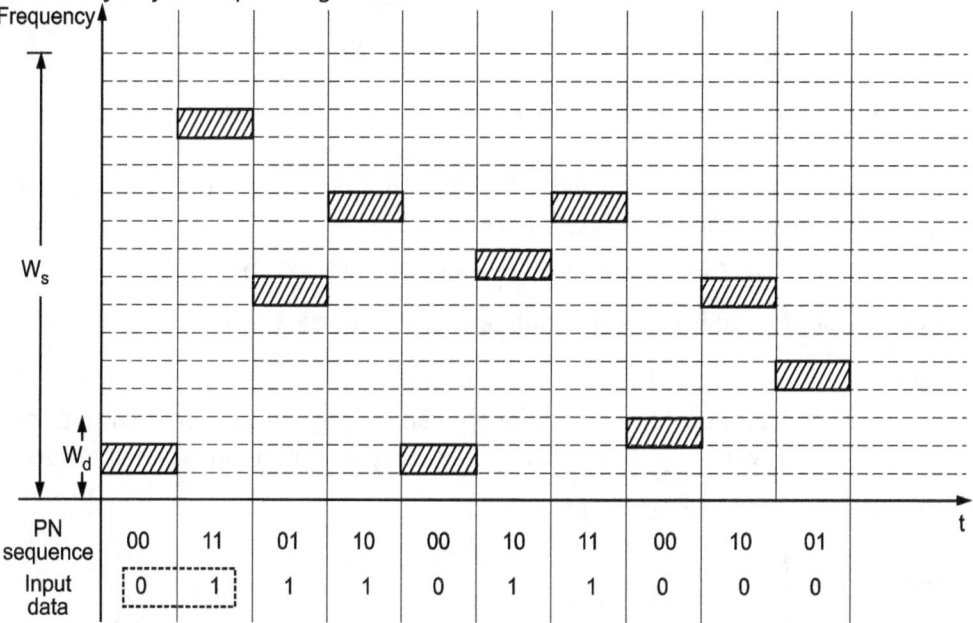

Fig. 10.7 : (b) Fast FHSS using MFSK (M = 4, k = 2) W_d = Mf_d, W_s = $2^k W_d$

Performance of FHSS :

In FHSS, typically a large number of frequencies are used in FHSS, so that W_s is much larger than W_d. One benefit of this is that a large value of k results in a system which is resistant to jamming. Consider an FHSS system with MFSK transmitter bandwidth = W_d and noise jammer of the same bandwidth and fixed power J on signal carrier frequency. Thus, we have the ratio $\dfrac{E_b}{N_0} = \dfrac{E_b W_d}{J}$.

If frequency hopping is used, jammer must jam all 2^k frequencies. With a fixed power this reduces jamming power in any one frequency by $J/2^k$. The gain in signal-to-noise ratio or processing gain is,

$$PG = 2^k = \frac{W_s}{W_d}$$

- The error probability of FHSS will be similar to non-coherent M-ary FSK. For white noise the error probability is,

$$p_e = \frac{1}{2} e^{-E_b/N_0}$$

- In case of jamming signal or intereference with power spectral density,

$$N_J = J/N_c \text{ then the error probability will be}$$

$$p_e = \frac{1}{2} e^{-E\phi\, (2(N_o + N_j))}$$

Example 10.3 :

For a slow hop SS with binary FSK and a PN generator with k = 3 outputs, the message transmitted is using the following PN sequence.

{010, 111, 011, 101, 001}. The message data stream is {10 11 00 01 10}.

Sketch a neat diagram showing the output frequency versus data input.

Solution :

With k = 3, system can hop to 2^3 = 8 different carrier frequencies. For each hop, output frequency is $f_{c_i} + f_d$, where f_{c_i} is the carrier frequency at hop 'i' and f_d is the frequency deviation from a particular carrier frequency.

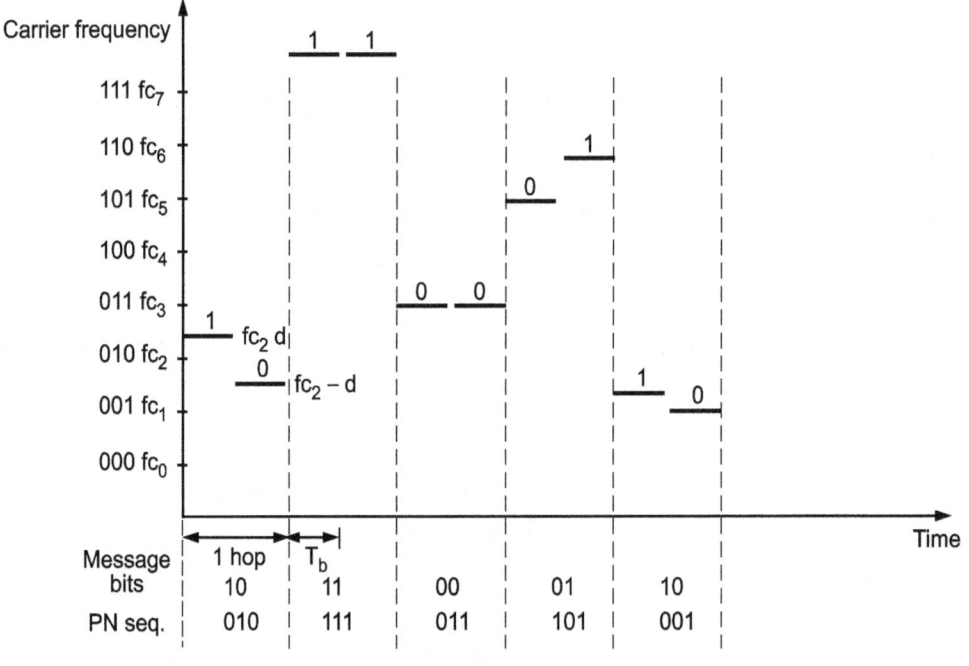

Fig. 10.11

10.6 PERSONAL COMMUNICATION SYSTEM

The evolution of radio and mobile core network technologies over last two decades has enabled development of personal communication system (PCS)

- PCS can provide the mobile user with voice data and multimedia services at any time, any place and in any format.

- Because of the recent government telecommunication deregulation 900 MHz abd 1.8 GHz (1.9 GHz in Europe) band is available for portable digital phones. They use either Time Division multiple access (TDMA) or Direct Sequence Spread Spectrum (DSSS) Code Division Multiple Access (CDMA).

From the technical perspective, PCS is the U.S Federal Communications Commission (FCC) term used to describe a set of digital cellular technologies deployed in the U.S. Also referred to as digital cellular, PCS works over CDMA (also called IS-95), GSM, and North American TDMA (also called IS-136) air interfaces. PCS still belongs to 2G mobile communications technology and includes enhanced personal communications services such as SMS text messaging or caller ID. However, PCS is not a totally yew 2G technology. Three of the most important features of PCS systems are: (1) completely digital; (2) operating at the 1900 MHz frequency range (unlike other cellular systems that operate in the 800MHz frequency range); (3) they can be used internationally.

To understand PCS, we first review the history of technological development in personal communications.

Mobile Radio : Mobile radio is the earliest system for personal communications. It was proprietary and costly. It could be used within a certain region. The first recorded mobile radio services that provided interconnection to the switched telephone network was in 1946 when the FCC allocated six radio channels for the first public correspondence system in Saint Louis. During the 1950's and 1960's the service evolved into manual Mobile Telephone Service (MTS) where mobile units called into operators who manually placed the calls. The modulation type was narrow-band FM and a single high-power base station provided coverage of some 20-30- mi (30-50 km) radius to several hundred mobiles per 20-30 KHz-wide radio channel. In 1964,a new service was introduced called Improved Mobile Telephone Service (IMTS). IMTS replaced MTS and allowed a mobile subscriber to directly dial a telephone number. In IMTS, on the order of 8 channels per major city were available with an automatic channel selection mechanism (Stuart, 1994).

Cellular Telephone : It was not until 1983 that today's analog cellular services were introduced to the U.S. on a commercial basis. However, it is the crucial step towards PCS. The first cellular systems were built in Chicago and Baltimore and within a few years were serving tens of thousands of subscribers. The cellular analog standard used in North America was called Advanced Mobile Phone Service (AMPS). AMPS represents the first-generation wireless communication networks. It allocates frequency ranges within the 800 and 900 MHz spectrum to cellular telephone. Each service provider can use half of the 824-849 MHz range for signal reception and half of the 869-894 MHz range for signal transmission. The bands are divided into 30 KHz sub-bands, called channels. The division of the spectrum into sub-band channels is achieved by using Frequency Division Multiple Access (FDMA). As a user moves out of a cell's area into an adjacent cell, the user begins to pick up the new cell's signals without any noticeable transition. The analog service of AMPS had been updated with digital cellular service by adding to FDMA a further subdivision of each channel using Time Division Multiple Access (TDMA). This service is known as digital AMPS (D-AMPS), which is a 2G technology.

Cordless Telephone : It is a telephone with a wireless handset which communicates with a base station connected to a fixed telephone landline via radio waves. It can only be operated close to (typically less than 100 metres of) its base station. Cordless telephone is an attempt on location-independent communication with limited useful range. With it, people can keep in touch out in the garden, up in the attic, and over at the next-door neighbour's. Modern cordless telephone standards, like Personal Handy-phone System (PHS) and Digital Enhanced Cordless Telecommunications (DECT), have blended the once clear-cut line between cordless and mobile telephones by supporting cell handover, various advanced features like data transfer and even, on a limited scale, international roaming.

Cellular Data : 2G is based on circuit-switched technology where each call requires its own cell channel, which makes transmission of data quite slow. The representative technology of 2G is GSM (Global System for Mobile communications). Voice is digitally encoded and transmitted through the GSM network as a digital stream. A variety of data services is offered and the most popular one is SMS (Short Message Service). GSM was initially deployed in Europe and soon became popular worldwide. GPRS (General Packet Radio Service) is a representative 2.5G network that supports low rate mobile data communications. It uses a packet-mode technique to transfer data and signaling in a cost-efficient manner over GSM radio networks and also optimizes the use of radio and network resources. 2.5G is a transitional technology between 2G and 3G. 3G mobile communication technology is also called IMT-2000 by International Telecommunication Union (ITU). 3G networks will provide voice communication quality on a par with telephone networks, with minimal interference and noise, and support diverse multimedia content. Using 3G terminals, users can access a wide range of telecommunication services supported by the fixed telecommunication networks (e.g., PSTN/ISDN/IP), and to other services which are specific to mobile users.

Satellite Communications : True personal communication must be ubiquitous, meaning that two-way voice and data should be available anywhere in the world, no matter how remote or underdeveloped that location. Such services have become possible with the aid of low earth-orbit (LEO) satellite network. These satellites move around the earth with orbits low enough to permit portable PCS telephones and data terminals to communicate through one or more satellites to a regional gateway earth station, which can provide a connection into the public switched telephone network.

PCN : Expansion from cellular to personal communications services occurred at a quickening pace worldwide. Personal communications networks (PCN's) provide mobile two-way and mass-market communication services, the most advanced offering of the PCS area. The terms PCN and PCS are often used interchangeably. PCS refers to a service which may not embody all of the PCN concepts, but is more personalized (i.e., lightweight terminal, better performance, more flexibility and user options, etc.) than cellular-radio. PCN refers to a concept where a person can use a single communicator anywhere in the world. The idea behind PCN is to make communications truly personal and ubiquitous, so that the users can call each other, no matter what the location of the user.

Internetwork : An Internetwork functions as a single large network, which is a collection of individual networks connected by intermediate networking devices. A local area network (LAN) enables multiple users in a relatively small geographical area to exchange files and messages, as well as access shared resources such as file servers and printers. Wide area networks (WANs) interconnect LANs with geographically dispersed users to create connectivity. Internet, the largest Internetwork, is a global WAN and interconnects various data communication networks. Internet is mainly designed and used for data communications. Now a days, with the advance in technologies, more and more people conduct voice communications through the Internet. Compared to the cellular networks, the Internet can provide cheap voice communications with competitive quality.

With these in place, the ever-quickening pace of technological advances has made available a wide variety of personal communication services, universally and ubiquitously.

10.6.1 Key Issues in PCS

Spectrum allocation

The 1992 World Administrative Radio Conference (WARC92) of the ITU resulted in a worldwide allocation for mobile services in the 1.7 to 2.69 GHz band. This brought all three regions of the world into conformity under the Future Public Land Mobile Telecommunications Systems (FPLMTS, now IMT2000), which are systems capable of providing a wide range of services including personal communications with regional or international roaming. The FPLMTS concept incorporates both terrestrial and satellite-delivered PCS services. The conference identified the sub-bands 1885 to 2025 MHz and 2110 to 2200 MHz for implementation of terrestrial PCS components on a worldwide basis. The conference also allocated spectrum for LEO satellite services that can provide PCS-type services to remote areas. For LEO systems operating below 1 GHz, a primary global allocation in the 149.9 to 150.05 MHz band was made and secondary allocations at 312 to 315 MHz and 387 to 390 MHz were made. For LEO systems above 1 GHz, primary allocation in the 1610 to 1625.5 MHz band (Earth to space) paired with the 2483.5 to 2520 MHz band (space to Earth) and a secondary allocation at 1613.8 to 1626.5 MHz were made.

The spectrum allocated to PCS is divided into three major categories: broadband, narrowband, and unlicensed. The FCC controlled the spectrum allocation for broadband PCS in the U.S., and defined rules for auctioning the spectrum to potential PCS service providers. The most challenging and controversial decision confronting the FCC was to determine a frequency allocation for PCS that takes into account the competing demands of existing licenses for scarce spectrum. Fortunately, these new rulings received a lot support and praise by the industry. Broadband PCS operates in the 1850-1910 MHz and 1930-1990 MHz bands.

Narrowband PCS operates in the 901-902 MHz, 930-931 MHz, and 940-941 MHz bands. For unlicensed PCS services, a 20 MHz spectrum in 1910-1930 MHz band was allocated.

Since the spectrum resource is not unlimited, one of the most fundamental issues concerns overcrowding on the radio frequency spectrum. Efficiently sharing the spectrum resource is of paramount importance in wireless communication systems, in particular in personal communications where large numbers of wireless subscribers need to be served. There is always a desire to promote increased flexibility, innovation, and efficient usage of the spectrum resource. The frequencies most favored are below 1. GHz because they diffract around objects better, but this limited bandwidth could not satisfy the demand without reusing the band many times. The simplest form of reuse is geographic separation. In addition, one of the most promising alternatives to spectrum reallocation is to use the current spectrum more efficiently. By using multiple access, digital technology has improved frequency efficiency and decreased costs to the point that personal communications appeal to people around the world. Multiple access refers to the simultaneous transmission by numerous users to or through a common receiving point. The three types of multiple access presently used with personal communications are code-division, frequency-division, and time-division multiple access, i.e., CDMA, FDMA, and TDMA.

Mobility

PCS supports the mobility of users both as they roam from system to system between phone calls, and supports handoffs between base stations within and between adjacent systems. The functions of mobility management include: handoff, location management, and registration for service while roaming. The functions control the location of PCS end users, the use of terminal equipment, and the availability of PCS anytime, anywhere. Three types of mobility have to be considered in PCS [1]: terminal mobility, personal mobility, and service mobility (also called service portability). According to the definition given by the T1P1 Committee of the American Telecommunications Standards Institute (ATSI), PCS must contain the following three functionalities:

1. *Terminal Mobility* – From the user's viewpoint, it is the ability of a mobile and wireless terminal to access communication services from different locations while in motion. From the service provider's viewpoint, it is the ability of the network to identify, locate, and track the mobile terminals.

2. *Personal Mobility* – Personal mobility also has two layers of meaning. From the user's viewpoint, it is the ability of a user to access communication services based on a personal identification code on any terminal irrespective of wireless or wireline connection. From the service provider's viewpoint, it is the ability of the network to locate the terminal associated with the user and provide those services according to the user's service profile. Once the terminal associated with one user is located, the network needs to do addressing, routing, and charging about the user's calls.

3. *Service Profile Management* – It refers to the ability of a user to access and manipulate the user's service profile. Service profile management may be realized by the database system, which controls the access to and handling of data. The consistency of information in the service profile can be guaranteed by the service profile management functions.

4. *Service Mobility* – It can be seen as a combination of terminal mobility and personal mobility, is related to service profile management. Service mobility refers to the network capability to provide subscribed services (e.g., a user's individual service profile at a user-designated terminal or location) and identify the user at any access location by supporting terminal and/or personal mobility.

Standardization efforts

PCS is based on digital architecture, generally using TDMA or CDMA protocols. A remarkable technical characteristic of PCS is its high capacity and spectral efficiency. International standards were developed to meet the global standardization demand for PCS equipments and systems. For specifying the functionalities and standards of PCS, the standardization organizations include ITU, ETSI (European Telecommunications Standards Institute), TIA (Telecommunications Industry Association, affiliated with the Electronic Industries Association), and the Committee T1. A joint technical committee between T1P1 and TR46 subcommittees has coordinated the joint work on the PCS standards between T1 and TIA. The joint technical committee has defined methodology and selection criteria in selecting appropriate radio interface technology.

In U.S., the T1P1.2 and T1P1.3 have defined high-level requirements for PCS standardization and documented these in technical reports. The T1P1.2 developed a reference model for PCS and identified six different configurations as potential ways of implementing the reference model. T1P1 also has played a significant role in defining personal mobility, also known as UPT (Universal Personal Telecommunications). TR-46 subcommittee of TIA specified a reference model from the perspective of a cellular service provider. Other organizations such as PCIA (Personal Communications Industry Association) also have specified PCS reference models and proposed implementation options. PCS data standards were investigated by the joint technical committee of Committee TI and the TIA, the ITU—T (ITU—Telecommunications standardization sector), and others.

SOLVED UNIVERSITY QUESTIONS

Dec. 2010

U.Q. 1 :   State and explain properties of PN sequence.   **(6)**

Solution :   Refer Section 10.2.

U.Q. 2 : The information bit duration in DS-BPSK spread spectrum communication system is 4 ms while the chipping rate is 1 MHz. Assuming an average error probability of 10^{-5} for proper defection of message signal, calculate the jamming margin. Interpret your result.

Given Q(4.25) = 10^{-5}. **(6)**

Solution : Given: Information bit duration, T_b = 4 ms

Chip rate = 1 MHz

$\therefore$ Chip duration, T_c = 1×10^{-6} s

Error probability, p_e = 10^{-5}

$\therefore$ Processing Gain PG = $\dfrac{T_b}{T_c}$ = $\dfrac{4 \times 10^{-3}}{1 \times 10^{-6}}$ = 4000

For BPSK

$$p_e = Q\left(\sqrt{\dfrac{2E_b}{N_0}}\right)$$

$\therefore$ $\sqrt{\dfrac{2E_b}{N_0}} \geq Q^{-1}(10^{-5})$

$\therefore$ $\left(\sqrt{\dfrac{2E_b}{N_0}}\right) \geq 4.25$

$\therefore$ $\dfrac{E_b}{N_0} \geq 9.03$

Jamming margin $\dfrac{J}{P} = \dfrac{PG}{E_b/N_0} = \dfrac{4000}{9.03}$

= 443

Jamming margin in dB = $10 \log_{10} 443$

= 26.46 dB

Information bits will be defected even when interference is 443 times more than received signal power.

U.Q. 3 : Explain Frequency Hop Spread Spectrum System (FHSS). How is FHSS advantageous over DSSS? **(6)**

Solution : Refer Section 10.5

$\boxed{\textbf{May 2011}}$

U.Q. 4 : State classification of spread spectrum and explain FHSS in detail. **(7)**

Solution : Refer Section 10.5.

U.Q. 5 : A pseudo-noise sequence is generated using a feedback shift register of length $m = 4$. The chip rate is 10^7 chips per second. Find the following parameters.

    (a) PN sequence length.

    (b) Chip duration of the PN sequence.

    (c) PN sequence period.   **(4)**

Solution : Given:
$$m = 4$$
$$\text{Chip rate, } r_c = 10^7 \text{ chips/sec.}$$
$$T_c = 1 \times 10^{-7} \text{ s}$$

  (a) PN sequence length $N = 2^m - 1 = 15$.

  (b) Chip duration, $T_c = 1 \times 10^{-7}$.

  (c) PN sequence period $= NT_c = 15 \times 10^{-7}$ s.

U.Q. 6 : The information bit duration is DS-BPSK spread spectrum communication system is 10 ms. while the chipping rate is 1 MHz. Assuming an average error probability is 10^{-6} for proper detection of message signal, calculate the Jamming margin.   **(6)**

Solution : Given : Information bit duration $T_b = 10 \text{ ms} = 10 \times 10^{-3}$

Chipping rate, $r_c = 1 \text{ MHz}, T_c = 1 \times 10^{-6}$

$$p_e = 10^{-6}$$

For BPSK

$$p_e = Q\left(\sqrt{\frac{2E_b}{N_0}}\right)$$

$\therefore$
$$\sqrt{\frac{2E_b}{N_0}} = Q^{-1}(10^{-6}) \times 4.7$$

$\therefore$
$$\frac{E_b}{N_0} = \frac{(4.7)^2}{2} = 11.05$$

$$PG = \frac{T_b}{T_c} = 10000$$

Jamming margin, $\dfrac{J}{P} = \dfrac{PG}{E_b/N_0} = \dfrac{10000}{11.05} = 905$

U.Q. 7 : Explain DSSS in detail and state the applications of the same.   **(6)**

Solution : Refer Section 10.4.

Dec. 2011

U.Q. 8 : Design a 4-bit PN sequence generator and verify the properties of maximum length sequence. Assume that initial state is 1000.   **(8)**

Solution : Refer Section 10.2.

U.Q. 9 : Consider a fast hop spread spectrum system with binary FSK, 2 hops/symbol and a PN sequence generator with outputs with a binary message 010010010000. The message is transmitted using following PN sequence {010, 110, 101, 100, 000, 101, 011, 001, 001, I 11, 011, 001, 110, 101, 101, 001, 110, 001, 011, 111, 100, 000, 110, 110}. Plot the output frequency for the input message. **(8)**

Solution :

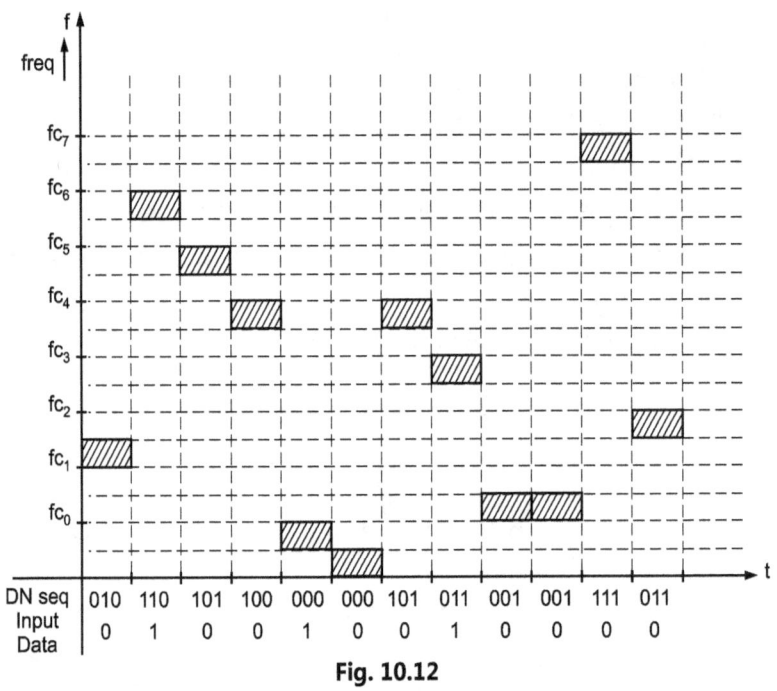

Fig. 10.12

May 2012

U.Q. 10 : Explain DS-SS BPSK transmitter and receiver with suitable block diagram and derive the power spectral density of the same. **(8)**

Solution : Refer Section 10.4.

U.Q. 11 : A DS-SS BPSK system has f_b = 3 kbps, $N_0 = 10^{-10}$ w/Hz and is receiving signals with $P_e \approx 10^{-7}$ in the presence of single tone jammer whose received power is ten times larger than original signal. Calculate the jamming margin and draw the antijam characteristics. **(10)**

Solution : Given: f_b = 3 kHz

$\therefore$ Bit duration, $T_b = \dfrac{1}{f_b}$ $= 0.33$ ms

$$p_e = 10^{-7}$$
$$N_0 = 10^{-10} \text{ watt/Hz}$$

Average signal power at receiver

$$\text{Input} = \frac{E_b}{T_c}$$

Original signal power $= \dfrac{E_b}{T_b}$

$\therefore$ $\dfrac{E_b}{T_c} = 10 \dfrac{E_b}{T_b}$

$\therefore$ $\dfrac{T_b}{T_c} = 10 \dfrac{E_b}{T_b}$

$\therefore$ $PG = \dfrac{T_b}{T_c} = 10$

For DSSS BPSK

$$p_e = Q\left(\sqrt{\frac{2E_b}{N_0}}\right) = 10^{-7}$$

$\therefore$ $\sqrt{\dfrac{2E_b}{N_0}} = 5.2$ $\therefore$ $Q(5.2) = 10^{-7}$

$$\frac{E_b}{N_0} = \frac{(5.2)^2}{2} = 13.52$$

Jamming margin

$$\frac{J}{P} = \frac{PG}{E_b/N_0} = 0.74$$

$\therefore$ $\dfrac{J}{P} = -1.31$ dB

Dec. 2012

U.Q. 12 : What is PN sequence? Verify the three properties of PN sequence with the help of 4 stage shift register.   **(8)**

Solution : Refer Section 10.2.

U.Q. 13 : The signal has the following parameters.

Number of bits per MFSK symbol K = 2

Number of MFSK tone $M = 2^K = 4$

Length of PN segment per hop K = 3

Total number frequency hops $2^K = 8$

Sketch the output transmitted frequency of fast FH/MFSK signal.   **(8)**

Solution : Refer Example 10.2.

U.Q. 14 : Derive the expression for signal to noise ratio of integrate and dump receiver. **(8)**

Solution : Refer Section 10.3.

May 2013

U.Q. 15 : For the shift register given in problem, demonstrate the balance property of PN sequence. Also calculate and plot auto-correlation function of the PN sequence produced by this shift register.   **(10)**

Solution : The PN sequence generated at the output will be as below.

Q_1	Q_2	Q_3	Q_4	Output
1	0	0	0	0
0	1	0	0	0
0	0	1	0	0
1	0	0	1	1
1	1	0	0	0
0	1	1	0	0
1	0	1	1	1
0	1	0	1	1
1	0	1	0	0
1	1	0	1	1
1	1	1	0	0
1	1	1	1	1
0	1	1	1	1
0	0	1	1	1
0	0	0	1	1
1	0	0	0	0

It can be observed in the output that the sequence repeats after 15 states. There are 8 ones and 7 zeros in the output sequence. Thus, the balance property is satisfied. The Autocorrelation will be as below.

Here,
$$T_c = \frac{T_b}{15}$$

$$R_c(\tau) = \left[\frac{16}{15}\Lambda\left(\frac{t}{T_c}\right) - \frac{1}{15}\Pi\left(\frac{t}{15T_c}\right)\right] \sum_{n=-\infty}^{\infty} (t - 15nT_c)$$

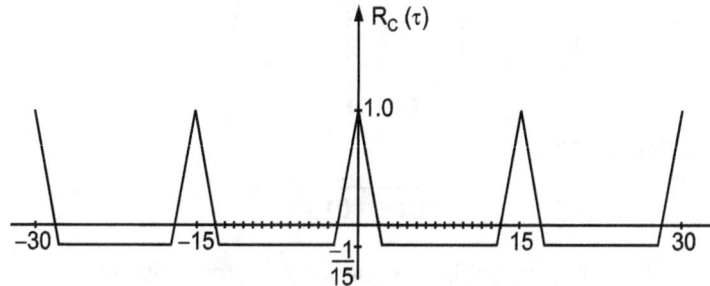

Fig. 10.13

$$S_c(f) = \frac{1}{225}\delta(f) + \frac{16}{225}\sum_{\substack{n=-\infty \\ n\neq 0}}^{\infty} \mathrm{sinc}^2\left(\frac{n}{15}\right)8\left(f - \frac{n}{15T_c}\right)$$

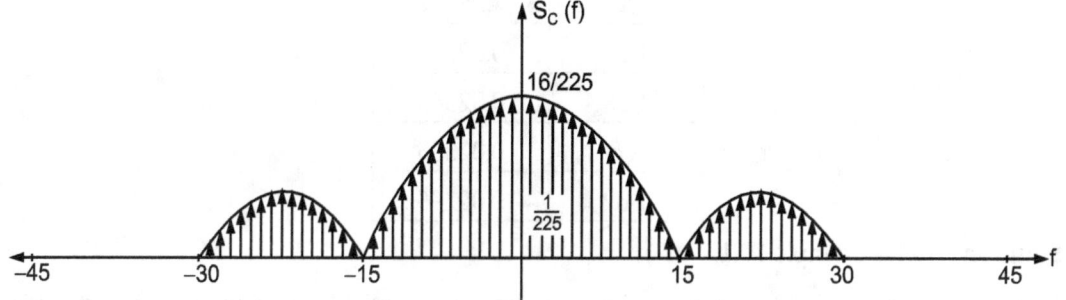

Fig. 10.14

U.Q. 16 : Consider a slow hop spread spectrum system with binary FSK, two symbols per frequency hop, and a PN sequence generator with outputs with the binary message of 0 1 1 0 1 1 0 1 1 0 0 0. The message is transmitted using the following PN sequence with

k = 3:{010,110,101,100,000,101,011,001,001,111,011,001}, plot the output frequencies for the input message.   **(8)**

Solution : Refer Example 10.3.

U.Q. 17 :   Derive the error probability of Matched Filter   **(8)**

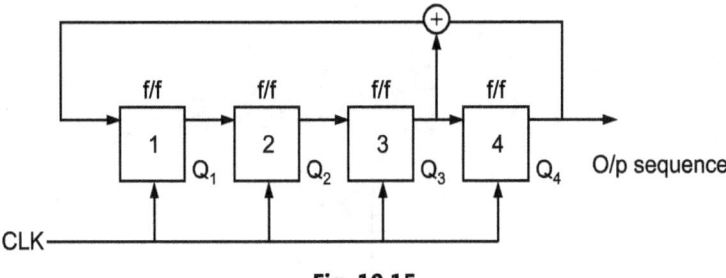

Fig. 10.15

Solution :   Refer Section 10.3.

Dec. 2013

U.Q. 18 :   Find the bit error probability for a BPSK system with bit rate of 1 Mbps. The received waveform $S1(t) = A \cos \omega c\, t$ and $S2\,(t) = -\,A \cos \omega c\, t$ are coherently detected with a matched filter. The value of A is 10mV. Assume that noise power special density $N_0/2 = 10^{-11}$ W/Hz and that signal power and energy per bit are normalized relative to 1Ω load.   **(8)**

Given:

X	erfc(x)
1.56	0.02737
1.58	0.02545
1.6	0.02365
1.62	0.02196

Solution : Refer Example 10.1.

U.Q. 19 :   In a DSSS-BPSK system, the feedback shift register used to generate the PN sequence of length 15. The system is required to have an average probability of symbol error as 10-5.   **(8)**

Calculate: (i) Processing gain   (ii) Antijam Margin

X	erfc(x)
3.01	0.00002074
3.02	0.00001947
3.03	0.00001827
3.04	0.00001714

Solution : Refer Example 10.2.

U.Q. 20 : Represent variation of the frequency of an fast hop spread spectrum system with binary FSK, having following parameters **(8)**

Number of bits per MFSK symbol K=2

Number of MFSK tones M=2^k=4

Length of PN segment per hop K= 3

Total number of frequency hops 2^k=8

For the binary message of 01111110001001111010

Generate the PN sequence for the message to be transmitted. The period of the PN sequence is $2^4 - 1$=15 with initial shift register content of 1100.

Solution :

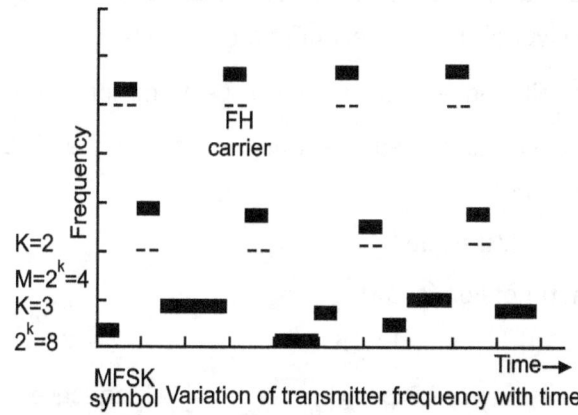

K=2

M=2^k=4

K=3

2^k=8

MFSK symbol   Variation of transmitter frequency with time

Input binary data 0 1 1 1 1 1 1 0 0 0 1 0 0 1 1 1 1 0 1 0

PN sequence 00111001100100100111001100100100111001100100100111001100100

(a)

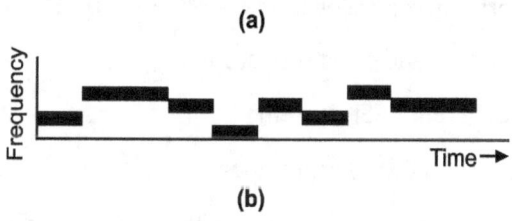

(b)

Fig. 10.16

U.Q. 21 : What is multi-user communication? Describe different multiple access techniques on the basis of channel sharing and applications. **(8)**

Solution : Refer Example 10.3.

May 2014

U.Q. 22 : State and explain properties of PN sequence **(6)**

Solution : Refer Example 10.1.

U.Q. 23 : Explain FHSS Tranmitter and receiver with suitable block diagram.   **(8)**

Solution : Refer Example 10.2.

U.Q. 24 : A DS – SS BPSK system has fb =3kbps $N_0 = 10^{-10}$W/Hz and in receiving signals with Pe =10^{-7} in the presence of single tone jammer whose received power is ten times larger than original signal. Calculate jamming margin and draw anti – jam characteristics.   **(10)**

Solution : Refer U. Q. 11.

EXERCISE

1. Explain the typical spread spectrum process briefly.

2. What is the difference between spread spectrum signal and normal signal ?

3. Explain the typical spread spectrum transmission and reception process in SS communication.

4. Classify the SS techniques.

5. Write a short note on following :   **(May 04, Dec. 2006)**

    (a) FHSS   (b) DSSS   (c) 802.11 standards

6. What is PN sequence ? Explain properties of PN sequence.

                                (May 2005, Dec. 2007, Dec. 2008, May 2009)

7. Write a short note on following :

    (a) Baseband spread-spectrum system

    (b) DSSS coherent BPSK system   **(May 2006, May 2007)**

    (c) Jamming and DSS performance

8. What is probability of error with BPSK modulation in spread spectrum communication ?

9. Write short notes on :

    (a) FHSS using MFSK   (b) Slow FHSS

    (c) Fast FHSS   (d) Performance of FHSS

10. Explain personal communication system.

APPENDIX A

The Power Spectral Density (PSD) is very useful in describing how signals and noise is affected by filters and other devices in communication systems. For defining PSD we first get the truncated version of power signal as,

$$g_T(t) = g(t) \qquad -\frac{T}{2} < t < \frac{T}{2} \qquad \text{... (A.1)}$$

$$= 0 \qquad \text{otherwise}$$

i.e.
$$g_T(t) = g(t) \times \text{rect}\left(\frac{t}{T}\right)$$

∴ Average normalise power of the signal is,

$$p = \lim_{T \to \infty} \frac{1}{T} \int_{-T/2}^{T/2} g^2(t)\, dt \text{ ... (A.2)}$$

$$= \lim_{T \to \infty} \frac{1}{T} \int_{-\infty}^{\infty} g_T^2(t)\, dt \qquad \text{... (A.3)}$$

If $G_T(f)$ is Fourier transforms of $G_T(t)$.

Using Parseval's theorem, we can write,

$$p = \lim_{T \to \infty} \frac{1}{T} \int_{-\infty}^{\infty} |G_T(f)|\, df \text{... (A.4)}$$

$$= \int_{-\infty}^{\infty} \left(\lim_{T \to \infty} \frac{|G_T(f)|^2}{T} \right) df \text{ ... (A.5)}$$

The quantity $\lim_{T \to \infty} \dfrac{|G_T(f)|^2}{T}$ is called Power spectral density denoted as $S_g(f)$.

∴
$$S_g(f) = \lim_{T \to \infty} \frac{|G_T(f)|^2}{T} \qquad \text{... (A.6)}$$

Now, consider a digital signal d (t) defined as,

$$d(t) = \sum_{n=-\infty}^{\infty} a_n \, g\,(t-nT_s) \qquad \text{... (A.7)}$$

where,

g(t) is symbol pulse shape.

T_s is duration of one symbol.

a_n is 1/0 depending on data stream.

To find PSD of above signal we have to truncate it as,

$$d_T\,(t) = \sum_{n=-N}^{+N} a_n \, g\,(t-nT_s) \qquad \text{... (A.8)}$$

where,
$$T = 2\left(N+\frac{1}{2}\right)T_s$$

∴
$$D_T\,(f) = F\,[d_T(t)]$$

$$= \sum_{n=-N}^{+N} a_n \, F\,[g\,(t-nT_s)] \qquad \text{... (A.9)}$$

∴
$$D_T\,(f) = \sum_{n=-N}^{+N} a_n \, G\,(f)\, e^{-j2\pi fTs} \qquad \text{... (A.10)}$$

where, G(f) is Fourier transform of g(t).

∴ The PSD of d(t) using equation (A.6) is,

∴
$$S_d\,(f) = \lim_{T\to\infty} \frac{\left|D_T\,(f)\right|^2}{T}$$

$$= \lim_{T\to\infty} \frac{1}{T}\left|G(f)\right|^2 \times \left|\sum_{n=-N}^{+N} \overline{a}_n \, e^{-j2\pi fTs}\right|^2 \qquad \text{... (A.11)}$$

Ensemble average indicated by overbar is due to data being random. We can rewrite equation (A.11) as,

$$S_d\,(f) = \left|G\,(f)\right|^2 \lim_{T\to\infty}\left(\frac{1}{T}\sum_{n=-N}^{+N}\sum_{m=-N}^{+N} \overline{a_n a_m}\; e^{j\,(n-m)\,2\pi fTs}\right)$$

Put m = n + k and

$$S_d\,(f) = \left|G\,(f)\right|^2 \lim_{T\to\infty}\left(\frac{1}{T}\sum_{n=-N}^{+N}\sum_{k=-N-n}^{k=N-n} \overline{a_n a_{n+k}}\; e^{jk2\pi fTs}\right)$$

$$\text{... (A.13)}$$

$\overline{a_n \cdot a_{n+k}}$ is autocorrelation of data.

Let : $R_k = \overline{a_n \, a_{n+k}}$

and substitute $T = (2N+1) \, T_s$ we get,

$$S_d(f) = |G(f)|^2 \lim_{T \to \infty}$$

$$\left[\frac{1}{(2N+1) \, T_s} \sum_{n=-N}^{+N} \sum_{k=-N-n}^{k=N-n} R_k \, e^{j2\pi f k T_s} \right] \qquad \text{... (A.14)}$$

Now, the autocorrelation function of data,

$$R_k = \overline{a_n \, a_{n+k}} = \sum_{i=1}^{M} (a_n \, a_{n+k})_i \, p_i \qquad \text{... (A.15)}$$

where, p_i is probability of getting $(a_n, \, a_{n+k})_i$ and there are M possible values of the product $a_n \, a_{n+k}$.

Interchanging outer and inner summation of equation (A.14) and noting that –

$$\sum_{n=-N}^{+N} = 2N+1.$$

We get,

$$S_d(f) = \frac{|G(f)|^2}{T_s} \lim_{T \to \infty} \frac{2N+1}{2N+1} \sum_{k=N-n}^{k=N-n} R_k \, e^{j2\pi f k T_s} \qquad \text{... (A.16)}$$

$$\therefore \qquad S_d(f) = \frac{|G(f)|^2}{T_s} \sum_{k=-\infty}^{\infty} R_k \, e^{j2\pi f k T_s} \qquad \text{... (A.17)}$$

❖ ❖ ❖

APPENDIX B

MATHEMATICAL IDENTITIES

I. **Trignometric Identities :**

1. $\sin x = \dfrac{e^{jx} - e^{-jx}}{2j}$

2. $\cos x = \dfrac{e^{jx} + e^{-jx}}{2}$

3. $\tan x = \dfrac{\sin x}{\cos x} = \dfrac{e^{jx} - e^{-jx}}{j(e^{jx} + e^{-jx})}$

4. $e^{\pm jx} = \cos \pm j \sin x$ (Euler's theorem)

5. $\cos(x \pm y) = \cos x \cos y \mp \sin x \sin y$

6. $\sin(x \pm y) = \sin x \cos y \pm \cos x \sin y$

7. $\cos\left(x \pm \dfrac{\pi}{2}\right) = \mp \sin x$

8. $\sin\left(x \pm \dfrac{\pi}{2}\right) = \pm \cos x$

9. $\cos 2x = \cos^2 x - \sin^2 x$

10. $\sin 2x = 2 \sin x \cos x$

11. $2 \cos x \cos y = \cos(x - y) + \cos(x + y)$

12. $2 \sin x \sin y = \cos(x - y) - \cos(x + y)$

13. $2 \sin x \cos y = \sin(x - y) + \sin(x + y)$

14. $2 \cos^2 x = 1 + \cos 2x$

15. $2 \sin^2 x = 1 - \cos 2x$

16. $4 \cos^3 x = 3 \cos x + \cos 3x$

17. $4 \sin^3 x = 3 \sin x - \sin 3x$

18. $8 \cos^4 x = 3 + 4 \cos 2x + \cos 4x$

19. $8 \sin^4 x = 3 - 4 \cos 2x + \cos 4x$

20. $A \cos x - B \sin x = R \cos(x + \theta)$

   where, $\quad R = \sqrt{A^2 + B^2}$

   $\quad\quad\quad \theta = \tan^{-1}(B|A)$

   $\quad\quad\quad A = R \cos \theta$

   $\quad\quad\quad B = R \sin \theta$

II. Important Integrals :

$$\int x \sin(ax)\, dx = \frac{1}{a^2}[\sin(ax) - ax\cos(ax)]$$

$$\int x \cos(ax)\, dx = \frac{1}{a^2}[\cos(ax) + ax\sin(ax)]$$

$$\int x \exp(ax)\, dx = \frac{1}{a^2}\exp(ax)(ax - 1)$$

$$\int x \exp(ax^2)\, dx = \frac{1}{3a}\exp(ax^2)$$

$$\int \exp(ax)\sin(bx)\, dx = \frac{1}{a^2 + b^2}\exp(ax)[a\sin(bx) - b\cos(bx)]$$

$$\int \exp(ax)\cos(bx)\, dx = \frac{1}{a^2 + b^2}\exp(ax)[a\cos(bx) + b\sin(bx)]$$

$$\int \frac{dx}{a^2 + b^2 x^2} = \frac{1}{ab}\tan^{-1}\left(\frac{bx}{a}\right)$$

$$\int \frac{x^2\, dx}{a^2 + b^2 x^2} = \frac{x}{b^2} - \frac{a}{b^3}\tan^{-1}\left(\frac{bx}{a}\right)$$

◈ ◈ ◈

APPENDIX C

THE COMPLEMENTARY ERROR FUNCTION Q(z)

$$Q(z) = \frac{1}{\sqrt{2\pi}} \int_z^X e^{-\lambda^2/2} \, d\lambda$$

$$Q(0) = \frac{1}{2} \quad Q(-z) = 1 - Q(z) \qquad z \geq 0$$

$$Q(z) = \frac{1}{2} - \text{erf}(z)$$

$$\text{erf}(z) = \frac{1}{\sqrt{2\pi}} \int_0^z e^{-\lambda^2/2} \, d\lambda$$

$$Q(z) \approx \frac{1}{\sqrt{2\pi}} e^{-z^2/2} \, d\lambda$$

(C.1)

Table : Complementary Error Function $Q(x) = \int_{u}^{\infty} (1/\sqrt{2\pi}) \exp(-u^2/2)du$

					Q(x)					
x	0.00	0.01	0.02	0.03	0.04	0.05	0.06	0.07	0.08	0.09
0.0	0.5000	0.4960	0.4920	0.4880	0.4840	0.4801	0.4761	0.4721	0.4681	0.4641
0.1	0.4602	0.4562	0.4522	0.4483	0.4443	0.4404	0.4364	0.4325	0.4286	0.4247
0.2	0.4207	0.4168	0.4129	0.4090	0.4052	0.4013	0.3974	0.3936	0.3897	0.3859
0.3	0.3821	0.3783	0.3745	0.3707	0.3669	0.3632	0.3594	0.3557	0.3520	0.3483
0.4	0.3446	0.3409	0.3372	0.3336	0.3300	0.3264	0.3228	0.3192	0.3156	0.3121
0.5	0.3085	0.3050	0.3015	0.2981	0.2946	0.2912	0.2877	0.2843	0.2810	0.2776
0.6	0.2743	0.2709	0.2676	0.2643	0.2611	0.2578	0.2546	0.2514	0.2483	0.2451
0.7	0.2420	0.2389	0.2358	0.2327	0.2296	0.2266	0.2236	0.2206	0.2168	0.2148
0.8	0.2169	0.2090	0.2061	0.2033	0.2005	0.1977	0.1949	0.1922	0.1894	0.1867
0.9	0.1841	0.1814	0.1788	0.1762	0.1736	0.1711	0.1685	0.1660	0.1635	0.1611
1.0	0.1587	0.1562	0.1539	0.1515	0.1492	0.1469	0.1446	0.1423	0.1401	0.1379
1.1	0.1357	0.1335	0.1314	0.1292	0.1271	0.1251	0.1230	0.1210	0.1190	0.1170
1.2	0.1151	0.1131	0.1112	0.1093	0.1075	0.1056	0.1038	0.1020	0.1003	0.0985
1.3	0.0968	0.0951	0.0934	0.0918	0.0901	0.0885	0.0869	0.0853	0.0838	0.0823
1.4	0.0808	0.0793	0.0778	0.0764	0.0749	0.0735	0.072i	0.0708	0.0694	0.0681
1.5	0.0668	0.0655	0.0643	0.0630	0.0618	0.0606	0.0594	0.0582	0.0571	0.0559
1.6	0.0548	0.0537	0.0526	0.0516	0.0505	0.0495	0.0485	0.0475	0.0465	0.0455
1.7	0.0446	0.0436	0.0427	0.0418	0.0409	0.0401	0.0392	0.0384	0.0375	0.0367
1.8	0.0359	0.0351	0.0344	0.0336	0.0329	0.0322	0.0314	0.0307	0.0301	0.0294
1.9	0.0287	0.0281	0.0274	0.0268	0.0262	0.0256	0.0250	0.0244	0.0239	0.0233
2.0	0.0228	0.0222	0.0217	0.0212	0.0207	0.0202	0.0197	0.0192	0.0188	0.0183
2.1	0.0179	0.0174	0.0170	0.0166	0.0162	0.0158	0.0154	0.0150	0.0146	0.0143
2.2	0.0139	0.0136	0.0132	0.0129	0.0125	0.0122	0.0119	0.0116	0.0113	0.0110
2.3	0.0107	0.0104	0.0102	0.0099	0.0096	0.0094	0.0091	0.0089	0.0087	0.0084
2.4	0.0082	0.0080	0.0078	0.0075	0.0073	0.0071	0.0069	0.0068	0.0066	0.0064
2.5	0.0062	0.0060	0.0059	0.0057	0.0055	0.0054	0.0052	0.0051	0.0049	0.0048
2.6	0.0047	0.0045	0.0044	0.0043	0.0041	0.0040	0.0039	0.0038	0.0037	0.0036
2.7	0.0035	0.0034	0.0033	0.0032	0.0031	0.0030	0.0029	0.0028	0.0027	0.0026
2.8	0.0026	0.0025	0.0024	0.0023	0.0023.	0.0022	0.0021	0.0021	0.0020	0.0019
2.9	0.0019	0.0018	0.0018	0.0017	0.0016	0.0016	0.0015	0.0015	0.0014	0.0014
3.0	0.0013	0.0013	0.0013	0.0012	0.0012	0.0011	0.0011	0.0011	0.0010	0.0010
3.1	0.0010	0.0009	0.0009	0.0009	0.0008	0.0008	0.0008	0.0008	0.0007	0.0007
3.2	0.0007	0.0007	0.0006	0.0006	0.0006	0.0006	0.0006	0.0005	0.0005	0.0005
3.3	0.0005	0.0005	0.0005	0.0004	0.0004	0.0004	0.0004	0.0004	0.0094	0.0003

3.4	0.0003	0.0003	0.0003	0.0003	0.0003	0.0003	0.0003	0.0003	0.0003	0.0002
4.00	0.0003									
4.25	10^{-5}									
4.75	10^{-6}									
5.20	10^{-7}									
4.60	10^{-8}									

APPENDIX D

B.1 Error Function

The error function erf (u) is defined as,

$$\text{erf (u)} = \frac{2}{\sqrt{\pi}} \int_{0}^{u} e^{-z^2} \, dz$$

Note that,

$$\text{erf (0)} = 0$$
$$\text{erf } (\infty) = 1$$
$$\text{erf } (-u) = -\text{erf (u)}$$

B.2 Complemenetary Error Function

It is defined as,

$$\text{erfc (u)} = \frac{2}{\sqrt{\pi}} \int_{u}^{\infty} e^{-z^2} \, dz$$

These two fnctions are related as,

$$\text{erfc (u)} = 1 - \text{erf (u)}$$

Table of Error Function

u	erf (u)
0.00	0.00000
0.05	0.05637
0.10	0.11246
0.15	0.16800
0.20	0.22270
0.25	0.27633
0.30	0.32863
0.35	0.37938
0.40	0.42839
0.45	0.47548
0.50	0.52050

(D.1)

0.55	0.56332
0.60	0.60386

u	erf (u)
0.65	0.64203
0.70	0.67780
0.75	0.71116
0.80	0.74210
0.85	0.77067
0.90	0.79691

0.95	0.82089
1.00	0.84270
1.05	0.86244
1.10	0.88021
1.15	0.89612
1.20	0.91031
1.25	0.92290
1.30	0.93401
1.35	0.94376
1.40	0.95229
1.45	0.95970
1.50	0.96611
1.55	0.97162
1.60	0.97635
1.65	0.98038
1.70	0.98379
1.75	0.98667
1.80	0.98909
1.85	0.99111
1.90	0.99279
1.95	0.99418
2.00	0.99532
2.50	0.99954
3.00	0.99998
3.50	0.999998

Model Question Paper In-semester Examination

T.E. (E & TC) (2014 Course)

DIGITAL COMMUNICATION

Time : 1 Hours   **Max. Marks : 30**

Instructions :
1. Answer Q. 1 or Q. 2, Q. 3 or Q. 4, Q. 5 or Q. 6.
2. Neat diagrams must be drawn wherever necessary.
3. Figures to the right indicate full marks.
4. Use of logarithmic tables slide rule, electronic pocket calculator and Q (z) function table is allowed.
5. Assume suitable data, if necessary.

Q 1 (a) State and prove the sampling theorem.   **(6)**

   (b) Draw the block diagram of PCM transmitter state role of each block   **(4)**

OR

Q 2 (a) An analog waveform with bandwidth 15 kHz is to be quantized with 200 levels and transmitted via. binary PCM signal. Find rate of transmission and bandwidth required. If 10 such signals are to be multiplexed find the bandwidth requirement.**(6)**

   (b) Compare DM and ADM systems.   **(4)**

Q 3 (a) Draw the line code formats for 1 0 110100.

   (i) RZ unipolar, (ii) NRZ polar, (iii) AMI, (iv) Manchester, (v) RZ polar, (vi) Polar Quaternary (NRZ).   **(6)**

   (b) Explain the need of scrambler.   **(4)**

OR

Q 4 (a) Draw and explain frame synchroniser.   **(4)**

   (b) Write the functions performed by a multiplexer. What are three main categories of multiplexers.   **(6)**

Q 5 (a) What are the conditions for a random process to be wide sense stationary. **(4)**

   (b) Consider a random processes X(t) given by X(t) = A cos ($\omega_c t + \theta$) where ω_c and θ are constants and A is a random variable. Determine whether X(t) is wide sense stationary processes.   **(4)**

OR

Q 6 (a) What is Ergodic process?. Explain in brief   **(4)**

   (b) Show that if a wide sense stationary process X(t) is passed through a LTI filter with impulse response h (t) then its output has constant mean square value.   **(6)**

Notes

Notes

www.ingramcontent.com/pod-product-compliance
Lightning Source LLC
Chambersburg PA
CBHW081353090726
47908CB00011B/2663